Scales and Honor:
The Dragon's Paladin

Justin Lee
Edited by Aryn Storm

Map by Lane Hudson
Editing done by Aryn Storm
Cover art done by Vanessa Hughes
Symbols done by Anastasiya Petrova

https://twitter.com/UNSCforces

Dedicated to my father. Whose spirit is soaring high with dragons.

VEIEDAR'S LAIR
DEET
WOOD ELF TERRITORY
DRAGON NECK MOUNTAINS
RUBY MOUNTAIN
FOREST OF DESPAIR
NEARON
ROTHDELL
THE SILVER
ZARCANA
THE WOLF DESERT
MIRE FIELD
MARSHLANDS
COYOTES RESPITE

MESA
RRITORY)
THE DRAGON'S CROWN COAST
HAICAN
WHITEDELL
LUMARA
THE VOICELESS MOUNTAINS
RG
ROYAL MARSH
OST
PLAIN OF THE SWORD
DRENEDAR
STRURPORT
DS
WALLOWDALE MOUNTAINS
WALLOWDALE PASS
TREGARON
THE FOGGY MOUNTAINS (DWARF TERRITORY)
RRITORY)

Table of Contents

Prologue

Skywing flapped his broad wings against the cold night air that drifted all around him. The snow colored, black striped gryphon angled his wings as his keen amber eyes caught sight of the goal he had to accomplish during this pitch-black evening. Among the darkened trees of the forest was the collection of lights that signaled to the party of mortals that someone was watching out for them. They were like spotlights among the darkness that seemed to get worse with every moment they remained within the Forest of Despair. A terrible name for a terrible place, to be sure. A location where no soul could thread, unless they were given permission by the forest's mysterious ruler. Skywing had heard the rumors, of course. All the gryphons in his flock had, only he never thought his wings would take him to this dreadful place. Not before this night.

For when the king himself asked you to protect him, no matter the rank, no matter the pride, no matter the wealth...you had no other option but to obey.

The gryphon tilted his wings downwards, following the currents that moved beneath his feathers until he was gliding towards the ground that stretched below his limbs. Onyx claws protruded from the tips, sharpened for deadly purpose. Skywing might have not been a dragon, blessed with an armored hide or a fierce breath weapon, but he was more than capable of fending for himself.

The gryphon glanced to his left and right, more as a reminder to himself that his flight mates were still around. To his left flew a female gryphon going by the name of Cetaz. Her feathers were an earthen brown, tipped with bright reds that were very pleasing to the eye. Her stern gaze was one of determination, as she spoke not a word the entire time they had been keeping watch. Skywing figured that was her way of keeping her calm. To his right was another snowy white gryphon. Although Skywing's fur and feathers had the stripes of a tiger on them, this other gryphon had spots very much like a cheetah. His radiant blue eyes kept scanning the ground below, following each of the mortal soldiers that walked the earth. His name was Petat, and since he was always worried and watchful, he made the perfect spotter. Skywing looked to his own fur, where leathers covered up the vital areas like his chest. Painted in gold, there was the great rampant gryphon of Lumara, its inspiring presence potent enough to spread a smirk over the gryphon's black beak.

Skywing back-winged as he led his flight through an opening in the twisted dark branches of the ominous forest. He tried to not pay the gnarled wood any mind as he landed softly among a collection of ten mortal knights, all of different races, clad in full plate armor. They had shields with golden gryphons slung around their backs, swords stowed in scabbards of worn leather made from cured hide, and crossbows that were adorned with runes and metal vents. From each one of these weapons came a dull resonating hum that always caused the gryphon's ears to splay and twitch. Skywing grumbled under his breath as humans, elves, and dwarves eagerly told him how they could not hear the noise that plagued him so. He strode past a few of the knights, who seemed to pay him no mind as a lone wind rustled their earth-brown tabards. Those too bore the familiar golden gryphon present in every banner, shield, or armor made in Lumara.

Skywing tucked his wings to his sides as he proudly puffed out his chest and scanned the tree line for any movement. His ears perked up when he heard the twin sounds of his flight mates taking position around him.

"Keep your eyes peeled." He said calmly to his fellow gryphons. With a swish of his tiger tail, he strode over to the man that led this expedition, for this entire operation relied on protecting the most valuable person in all of Lumara. They were here to protect its king, Cornelius. With a slight chirp, the white gryphon dropped to a bow before the onyx haired man, who was clad in dark red leathers that had pictures of golden gryphons stitched into the edges. His warm eyes looked to the gryphon with fondness, and in a few moments a smile came to his face.

"Your majesty. The skies are clear. It appears as though the seer had not sent anything in the way of ambushers to surprise us."

"I am grateful for your service, Skywing. Your loyalty to the crown shall not go unnoticed." Cornelius spoke softly. "You may rise now, friend. This forest cares not about our rank. Under its dark canopy, we are all of the same flock."

The king paused for a moment, closing his eyes. "Listen to the murmur of the trees. Breathe from this chilly air. Do you feel it? The hint of darkness that plagues this place? It's almost like a shroud, wrapping its tendrils tighter around us the more we linger here." Cornelius shivered slightly. "Let us meet with the Emerald Lady and be done with this mission before the shadows claim us all."

Skywing rose up to all fours and offered the king a nod of acknowledgment. He had remembered the conversation earlier as they spoke of this plan. This...entity they were here to see called itself the Emerald Lady. Of course, nobody really knew what she was. Some said an immortal sorceress. Others whispered of something a lot more grotesque.

Skywing merely knew her as the ruler of this forest, a position she held for many, many years, going further back than the current king or his great, great, great, grandfather. She had apparently helped the crown in the past by offering whispers of the future or knowledge of power.

Such knowledge made the gryphon uneasy, filling his paws with doubt at what could be waiting for them. He hardly knew of creatures that could live this long. All of the ideas that came to mind were growing more devilish by the minute, with the worst of them taking the form of a great dragon, or a horrible blood sucking Vampire. It was she that had requested the king come to her forest by night, with only two guards at his side.

The same idea that made Skywing scoff in the face of such ridiculous request. He thought back to earlier that day, when he shared a piece of his mind with Cornelius.

"Two guards?" he had said with a few squawks and a click of his beak. "Does she think you struck by madness? If I may speak plainly, sire, she insults you by spewing such a ridiculous request. Deny her your visit."

The king had just held his tongue and listened to the gryphon's words with a series of quick nods. "You are right, my loyal gryphon. It is a most.... unusual request, that I should only bring two of my guards in a place of such peril...However, I have no need to remind you who stands to gain most from this audience."

"Surely you will bring more guards then!" Skywing had squawked out in surprise. The thought of this seer somehow disposing of his beloved king made his heart turn cold. "Promise me you will bring a greater-"

The king had held up his hand and silenced him. "I shall. Of course I will. I am growing old, not stupid. I want you to accompany me to the forest of despair...Bring your other wing-mates. They will be most valuable at spotting any danger from afar."

"I don't see anything." Petat said nervously. His voice pulled Skywing's attention back to the present, and away from the ever-watchful king.

He padded carefully over to the rest of the group as they continued to their intended destination at a snail's pace. Normally, he would have complained about the inadequate speed. Skywing was always one to get a job done quickly and efficiently. To have to wait now sent an itch through his bones that made him twitch in irritation. "Take heart, Petat." He said with a courageous voice, walking past the other gryphon with a graceful stride. He noticed that some of the knights had even removed their helmets to lend him their ears. "We are here only for a simple conversation with the ruler of this forest. I am sure we will be fine as long as things remain peaceful between us."

He watched the others start to relax. The steel-like grip on their weapons loosened for a moment before they returned to sweep the dark trees with their lights attached to their crossbows. With a sigh, Skywing strode next to his wing-mates, and joined the others in their watch.

They continued along the path that carved its way through the cluster of sinister looking trees. The way the bark curled and twisted made it look like there were hundreds of eyes watching them as they slowly made their deeper into the tenebrous forest. Skywing looked to the ground, scratching the dirt with one of his talons. This dirt thing made him feel uneasy. He could not shake the feeling of nervousness about this path that dwelled within this untamed area of the forest. It just seemed too convenient.

"Well, well, well." A deep, loud, amused voice seemed to radiate from every direction of the woods.

All the soldiers suddenly stopped with the sound of clinking metal, raising their weapons to point them nervously at different sections of the forest. Several of the men whispered questions as to where the voice was coming from, who it was, and how to defend against malevolent charms if this was indeed a sorceress.

Skywing tensed his own body up, kneading the ground with his claws. He readied his wings for flight in case he needed to jump out of the way of anything that came his way, his eyes looking to the canopy above. How he wished to be in the sky right now, instead of a captive on the ground. It made him feel so trapped, especially in this moment where disembodied voices rang around him.

"I believe I only allowed you TWO guards, little human." The voice continued, ending with a chuckle. There was suddenly a rustling from a nearby bush that drew the fire of several crossbows.

They lit the area with great red pulses of magical energy, impacting the small poor bush that was incinerated in moments from the combined fire, until the king held up his hands and shouted at them.

"Cease your firing, you silly monkeys! Have we become so paranoid that we attack bushes now? We risk setting this whole forest ablaze. Weapons down. All of you!"

"Wise words. You are all so unnecessarily nervous around these trees. What can they do to you? Uproot and crush your feeble forms under their roots?" The voice chuckled again. **"Now, human king, riddle me this. Why did you bring more guards than I gave you permission to?"** The voice started to sound aggressive, as it punctuated its words with a growl. **"You requested this meeting, and now dare to insult me? This lack of manners might prove more damaging than you believe."**

"No!" Cornelius replied, turning his head from side to side. It seemed he was unsure where to direct his voice. "I do not seek to insult you, but to protect myself. You wanted to meet me in the dark woods with only two guards?" The king crossed his arms and wrinkled his brow. "What if I was ambushed by thugs or bloodthirsty creatures? I am a wanted man by those who seek vengeance against my kingdom. There are millions of things that could have denied this meeting."

"Accidents are not likely to happen in MY forest, human. I think you are all in need of a lesson on what happens when you disrespect your betters."

Skywing felt his blood run cold. He backed into a circle formation with his wing-mates. The soldiers around them started to do the same thing, the hum of their nervous chatter only adding to the rising anxiety.

"Do you see anything?" asked a female knight, her crossbow held tight.

"Nothing yet. Keep ya eyes peeled." replied a shorter armored clad warrior that sounded like a dwarf.

"There!" Another person yelled out, firing their crossbow repeatedly. Their red shots illuminated the dark trees around their intended target, which appeared to be a slithering pile of green snakes.

The collected knights let out cries as they suddenly fired into the tree line. Those green snakes were revealed to be vines of all sizes that shot from the forest like arrows. They slithered along the ground, avoiding most of the energy bolts before finding two of the knights. The vines suddenly wrapped around their legs, quickly binding them together as the two let out cries of terror.

"Save them!" Skywing bounded towards the two knights as the others were too busy trying to hold off more of the vines that attacked them from all directions. Skywing dove after the knights that were being dragged along the ground by the green slithering vines. He lashed out with one of his claws and managed to separate one knight from their attacker. The other one was not so lucky. They were dragged into the depths of the forest, screaming for dear life, and in a few moments, dark, chilling silence.

"Bless ya, gryphon!" The female knight replied swiftly, her voice full of gratitude. She pushed herself up, and pulled out her sword. "Looks like this might be the better option in here."

Skywing nodded, looking around to see if anyone else needed his help. His eyes widened as it appeared anyone meant everybody. He bound from knight to knight with the learned agility he nurtured over many years of sprints and grueling exercises. Always pushing himself to the limit. Always striving to be better, to do more. His talons tasted many vines, freeing knight after knight from the grasping vines intent on dragging them to their doom.

"Take that!" He cheered out, slashing another vine in two.

"Hail Skywing!" A knight shouted. "The very gods blessed ya feathers when dey gave you yer wings! I owe ye a drink, mate!'

"Maybe more than that!" Skywing screeched, ripping another vine in two. It looked like with the help from the gryphon squad, the vines had stopped their advance on the collection of mortal knights. In the confusion, only three of the knights had been dragged off into the woods. Thankfully, the king was still within the center of their formation. He had pulled out a small version of the energy crossbow, one that could be held with only one hand so he could pour some of his own shots into the clusters of vines.

"You continue to struggle against the inevitable, little rabbits. You have entered MY forest without my permission. What is the punishment for such insolent trespassing, I wonder?"

Suddenly, the ground opened up beneath Petat like a vast, grotesque mouth. The gryphon and the two knights he was protecting fell into the pit with a collected groan of pain.

"Petat!" Skywing screeched, turning to his wing-mate. He bound to them with a push of his mighty hinds. However, the ground closed almost instantly, silencing the terrified screams and screeches of the victims. "PETAT!" Skywing shrieked out, his claws digging into the ground, as if all he had to do was remove the top, and they would still be there. Scared of course, but still there. However, it soon became apparent there was still tons of gravel in the way and absolutely no sign of his fellow soldiers.

"Wh-what in the blazes happened? The ground can open up now?" Screamed one of the knights, crossing his sword with a vine.

"Anton, watch out!" screamed another female, moments before a large vine sprouted from the ground, wrapped around her armored body, and with a violent yank, pulled the knight into the tenebrous depths of the menacing dark forest.

Skywing ripped several more vines in two, even slicing one that had wrapped itself around his hind leg before it could tug on him.

"Your highness, we have to leave!" The gryphon screeched out, bounding over towards the king who had a look of horror on his usually cheerful face. Skywing did not wait for his words, simply wrapping his scaly forelimbs around the king. "Sorry about this, your majesty." He opened up his wings and readied himself to fly, trying to push back the wailing cries of the other knights that were being picked off one by one. He knew the battle was lost. All that mattered now was getting the king to safety. All of their lives -even his own- were less important compared to the great and wise king of Lumara.

Skywing jumped into the air, feeling a dagger plunge into his heart as he heard the screech of Cetaz erupt into his sensitive ears. It was full of pain, fury, even a bit of fear.

He looked down to see that the female had attempted to leap after him. She had even grabbed two knights with her talons to save them from the encroaching vines. However, the brave gryphon had only managed to get several feet into the air before vines grabbed hold of her hinds.

"No. No! Skraaaawk!" The female gryphon desperately pounded her wings against the air to no avail as the vines slowly pulled her closer and closer to the ground. "NO! Rawwkaaaaak!" She screamed out, before eventually being pulled into the forest with another screech of fear.

Skywing looked away again. "Don't worry, sire. I got you. At least we'll get out of this mess...together." He beat his wings against the air, carrying them to the canopy when, much to his horror, he felt the same wicked vines latch around his hinds, tighten around his limbs, and yank him down violently. *NO!* He pounded his wings against the air, unable to slash at the vines while he clutched the king within his grasp. *NO!* He internally screamed once more, as with each flap, he was pulled closer and closer to the forest below. His mind dreaded to think of what awaited him past the tree line, but it appeared as though he was going to find out soon enough.

"We surrender!" Cornelius shouted out. Skywing crashed into the ground, pain flaring up in his side. "We surrender!" the king screamed again. Skywing was dragged against the ground by clusters of vines.

"An expected result, tiny human." The voice chuckled. The vines released Skywing much to the gryphon's relief.

Skywing groaned, letting the king fall from his grasp as he pushed himself to all fours. His eyes glanced around to the empty clearing, where moments ago, a whole squad of guards had stood vigilant. He narrowed his eyes as he felt his blood begin to boil, and his breathing quicken. If he ever got a chance to tear into the source of that voice, he would gladly introduce them to his claws. With a flick of his tail, the gryphon refolded his wings behind his back and turned his attention back to the present.

"Now bow before your better.... brave king. Cement your defeat with something stronger than words. Show me how much you want to preserve your life, at that of your gryphon." The voice said that last part in a laugh, almost like the very word was laughable.

Skywing looked over to his king. Surely Cornelius would ignore this voice. He would stand tall and defy their wishes. However, to his amazement, the king immediately went down onto one knee with his head held low.

"Submit. It is...the only way," Cornelius looked over to the gryphon, his eyes hollow, his voice, defeated.

The gryphon lowered himself to the ground and pressed his beak against the same earth that stole so many of his squad...companions...even friends.

"Very good." the voice said. Skywing noticed a large green scaled limb step into the clearing. **"Keep your eyes down, gryphon."** the voice focused on him, and he felt his blood run cold. **"You would not want me**

to consider this an act of defiance so shortly after you cast down your pride at my feet.”

Skywing lowered his eyes as the owner of the voice walked past them. They were large, at least three times the size of Skywing himself. He could make out the emerald green scales strewn over the creature's hide, and the large winding tail that swished behind the imposing body. His eyes widened as he realized he was looking at the long form of none other than a dragon.

“It pleases me to see reason finally dawn upon your primitive mind. Tell me, wise king, why you wished this meeting with me. For now, you have my undivided attention.”

The dragon flicked their tail so that the webbed spines slid across Skywing's beak. He could have snapped at it, offered one last bit of resistance against this towering beast. However, he found his body unable to respond, as if his mind, his instincts, the very core of his being surrendered completely to this dragon.

“We came to find the red dragon you spoke of in prophecy.” Cornelius blurted out. “We have searched high and low within the borders of our nation, yet managed to grasp no sign of them. I fear that, without your help, this herald you speak of will come, and we will find ourselves pinned under the weight of this threat before we even get the chance to retaliate.”

“Oh, you speak of that.” The dragon chuckled, settling down onto their haunches, as if they wanted to make sure the black onyx talons on their hinds were pressed right up against Skywing's beak.

Such a humiliating thing to endure. Skywing kept his eyes closed, if only to numb part of the shame that coursed beneath his feathers.

“Oh, my sweet, little gryphon…do you not like the curves of my claws settled so close to your beak?” The dragon lowered their head so that Skywing could see their lighter green frills twitch in anticipation at his response. Their glowing purple eyes made his feathers stand out in terror, and the dragon opened their maw in a tooth filled smile of glistening white fangs. **“I could make you *lick* my talons right now if I wanted to.”**

Skywing offered no response, causing the dragon to chuckle deep in their throat. He just lowered his eyes and let them gloat; let them win this already failed battle in order to fight another day.

“That's right, little gryphon.” The dragon snapped their snout to Cornelius once again. **“You will need the red orb of dragon kind.”** It spoke clearly, and Skywing thought the voice sounded feminine for a moment.

“And where is this red orb you speak of?” Cornelius asked. “More importantly, will it help us find this herald that threatens the future of my people?"

"The red orb will help you locate the dragon, human, but it will not remove the threat on its own. Use your wits for once. Despite you being a lesser being, I know you possess some measure of wisdom, otherwise your armored form would not be gracing the throne of your kingdom." The dragon looked up to the trees, almost like it was looking at something they could not see. **"As for the orb...it will soon be found by a wizard called Vargus, located to the west in Lumarian lands, past the dragon neck mountains. There will be a temple close to his house that resides near the hovel you call Gladenhill."**

"That...that is excellent news!" the king's eyes brightened. "I shall send a group of knights to retrieve it at once!"

"NO!" The dragon snapped their maw inches from the king's head, causing the man to let out a small whimper. **"You will send a group of knights two weeks from now to find it, and I shall make a request of you, wise, powerful king."**

"Why two weeks? And what is this request you speak of?" Cornelius asked, not raising his head for an instance as he continued to shiver.

Skywing heard the dragoness give a loud, drawn out sigh as she tapped her tail on the earth softly. **"You will mind my words, or the retrieval of this item will be at risk of failure. My request is that you place the human dragon hunter Arcturus Lund at the head of your squad."**

"Arcturus Lund?" The king's voice filled with surprise. "He is an excellent knight on the field of battle, to be sure. But why send him?"

"Because this is the best way for the plan to succeed, puny human. Now rise, take your gryphon before his spine starts to bend from all this kneeling, and leave my forest before I decide to amuse myself further. Now BEGONE!" The dragon roared into the night, shaking the very trees and making Skywing's limbs shiver.

Despite his fear, he found himself able to rise to all fours. "What...what about the other guards?"

"They are mine now, gryphon." The dragon whirled around, placing their snout close to his head. **"Consider them payment for breaking our initial agreement. And if your friends refuse to be mine, I will use them as stone statues around *my* forest to deter anyone else from making the same mistake."** The dragon bared its teeth at him with a growl, making the gryphon feel ever the smaller. **"Now begone from my presence. I will only tolerate your insolence for so long."**

Skywing gulped, nodded, and turned back to the king, who was waving him over silently. He turned back to the grinning dragon and cursed himself. To think that lone beast had disposed of his squad so easily...

The gryphon flicked his tail and padded his way over to the king, where he wrapped a wing around the human's shivering form.

"Come on, Skywing. The night's getting colder. Take me away from this place before my boots stick to the ground." Cornelius said softly.

"Right away, your majesty." The gryphon touched the ground with his belly to allow the king to settle upon his back.

With a spreading of his wings, the gryphon bounded into the sky, not even looking back towards the smug looking dragon that watched their departure. He hoped that, one day, he would get a chance to strike back at this monster. To avenge the sacrifice of his fellow soldiers, and if they survived, rescue them from this forest's accursed grasp.

Chapter 1: Dread Flame

Our story begins in the kingdom of Lumara, a rather large nation located on the continent of Sethera. Lumara was well known for its cold winters, said to chill a person to the very bone, even while hugging their fire for warmth. It also bore some of the wettest summers where rain soaked the countryside for months. Some outsiders that lived in such climate spoke of Lumara as the worst place for anyone to live. However, in spite of the ill rumors, Lumara was not without its bounty. Several races inhabited these lands, and even though the majority of them were human, the other species were not treated any lesser.

To the other kingdoms of Man, Elf, and Dwarf. Lumara appeared a violent nation, never satisfied with its borders. Many years ago, the forefathers of present day Lumara found ruins that contained knowledge of mana crystals, and -most important of them all- their creation. These crystals had been used eons ago by the Dragons -one of the oldest races of the world- to fuel vast magics in their empire, and keep the mortal races tethered under their claws. By making use of the knowledge they uncovered, Lumara entered a new age of prosperity where evolution knew a pace unlike any other race discovered before. They were able to build marvels like flying ships, castles that could fly amongst the clouds. They were even able to project beams of concentrated magical energy. With the help of these deadly devices, Lumara took upon itself to spread this newfound prosperity to the rest of Sethera.

Now, far away from Lumara's capital city of Entis, far away from even its ruling king, past the Dragon Neck mountains to the west, even further than the forest of dreams, there was a village called Garricksville. An old wizard lived there, and Vargus was his name. Vargus had recently returned from an expedition into one of the ruins of the dragon empire where he was able to walk away with a treasure unseen before by his kin. He had found a red orb, perfect in shape, weighting almost nothing, and if one stared at it long enough the night sky appeared in the orb's bosom.

Vargus had put many of his years into studying the ruins of old. He now resided in the study of his large house, personally crafted to suit the wizard's needs by the best masons in the land.

In the confines of his trusted home, Vargus, wielder of the orb, found himself blissfully unaware of the knights sent to retrieve the treasure from him, by any means necessary.

* * * * * * * * *

An airship sailed across the dark night sky, hardly making a noise louder than the creaking of the wooden boards upon its deck. In the space where a mast would stand, there was a large balloon-like structure that was tethered to the hull of the grand ship. Two large propellers -powered of course by mana crystals hiding deep in the hull of the ship- stood in place of a rudder to guide the ship through the darkened sky. It was made of a dark brown wood with scratches and signs of wear acquired over the years of her service. On her balloon was painted the symbol of Lumara, a gold roaring gryphon painted over a brown shield. At her front of the ship stood a wooden carved woman with her arms outstretched, as if welcoming the sky's embrace. Painted below this statue was the name of the vessel "RLA Destiny" which stood for Royal Lumara Airship, a vessel commissioned only at the orders of the king of this great nation.

On the Destiny's deck, her crew preformed last checks on the three beam cannons. These formidable weapons stood large enough for a person to sit in, and although bulky in form, they could turn on a dime if situation demanded. Other crewmen checked the heat oozing from the engines below, and navigators calculated the distance to their destination. Standing out from the rest of the crew was a group of knights clad in gray and silver armor, ten in total, all of various heights and genders. Each one, however, bore features filled with experience, grim determination plastered over their faces to denote the urgency of the task at hand.

One man walked around, inspecting the troops to ensure that tabards were in order, longswords stowed, shields strapped to their backs, and energy crossbows slung in proper place. This man was their leader, and his name was Arcturus Lund. He was a man of twenty three years and had already achieved the rank of Paladin in Lumara's military. Arcturus stopped at another knight whose crossbow was slung around the wrong shoulder. His green eyes narrowed at the man whose gear was out of order.

"Harrison!" he barked to the man, "tend to your weapon or see danger bite you in the ass."

"S-sir?"

"Other shoulder, soldier." Arcturus said firmly.

The man called Harrison quickly switched the position of his weapon. The large crossbow looked like a normal one at first glance, but a critical eye could notice exhausts to vent the heat from the mana crystal used to power up the weapon.

Arcturus swept his short brown hair as he looked to the remaining nine knights. Experienced, they may have been, but worry still managed to creep its tendrils across their faces.

"Steady your hearts, my warriors!" Arcturus spoke loudly, "I have seen you all perform on the battlefield with honor and skill unmatched by any other knight. Today will be no different. Focus, and we shall see this mission to its end."

He turned to walk the other way as he continued his inspiring words. "Though our foe might be a wizard of experience, with men like you at my side, I know we will emerge victorious."

He held up his gauntlet clad hand. "Look to your fellow knights, keep your shields up, and don't give the spell slinger an opportunity to conjure anything."

Arcturus smiled. He saw the worry drain from their faces, replaced with courage. Satisfied with himself, he dismissed the men for preparation as he looked to his own gear one last time.

At his right hip was a smaller version of the energy crossbow, designed to be used in only one hand. He felt for the grip, thinking back to the day when he received the weapon at his promotion. On its side, he had marked with ink all the lives the crossbow had taken. Around his waist, to the left, was his trusty longsword, still in use since he joined the ranks of the Lumarian army when he was but a boy, at the frail age of fifteen. The blacksmith kept on telling him to replace the weathered sword, but Arcturus never listened, always reforging the same blade over and over again. He laughed inside as he remembered teaching his son Geoffery on how to hold his training sword, and how the first swing's momentum had the boy tumble to the ground. Arcturus then thought to his wife, Selina. Of how her brown eyes shined with anger that day. The paladin reached into one of his pouches to check if they were still tied properly, then pulled out a handkerchief, light blue in color, given to him by Selina before he boarded this ship on the king's orders. Arcturus gripped it tightly. Some people thought him superstitious, yet in spite of what they believed, he always prayed to the gods in a whisper for the safe return back to the arms of his beloved wife.

The Paladin smirked and pocketed his precious family treasure. Tonight was not going to be an exception. He flipped the visor of his helmet down as the ship started to descend. He fastened the helmet's leather strap, noticing how the other Knights followed his example.

Ahead of them rose a dark castle illuminated by moonlight, nestled between rolling hills. The structure had many towers, but in spite of its impressive arsenal, the stone crumbled in places, giving the castle a disheveled appearance. Its windows were dark, the light of the moon still too weak to pierce through their veil of shadows.

"No one mentioned a castle." Arcturus heard a knight whisper.

"Well, it's fitting, don't you think?" he said. "The wizard we seek is just as old. It makes sense he'd inhabit a place that matches the man. Perhaps he's trying to give us a message. What kind of knights would we be, to strike down an old man in his crumbling home? Best turn around, eh?"

The others chuckled nervously in the night air.

Arcturus scanned the castle's battlements. No weapons of any kind could be seen upon its ramparts. However, wizards always had a trick up their sleeves, or a few fireballs to throw your way when not paying attention.

Although, the Paladin told himself, *at least I'm not facing a dragon in there.* A beast of that magnitude would be a different challenge altogether. Despite being trained to fight them, even Arcturus wasn't sure if his knights would be up to the task if a dragon showed up.

"Do not fall back into the clutch of despair," Arcturus patted the wooden railing of the ship. "Even if fate turns against us, we have the Destiny here for support. Between our crossbows and the beam canons, the only way our friend is getting away is on the back of a dragon."

"Like there's a man in this world crazy enough to ride a dragon!" one of the men said, and laughter quickly followed.

Perhaps this wizard is just that kind of crazy, Arcturus thought. *Guess we're going to find what hides in the depths of his castle in a bit.*

Arcturus watched intently as the Destiny descended towards one of the makeshift walls. He spied small cracks in the wall, a sign of arcane crafting. Was it possible that the wizard knew of their arrival? His fingers brushed over the slung hand-crossbow at his side. If that were true, they might have been in for a nasty surprise when they pierced the wizard's domain. He signaled to the others to move out as the ship's plank touched down. As his boots hit the stone, his knights drew their weapons, filling the night air with a small hum. Arcturus felt a gust of wind from behind, a sign that the Destiny had left just as the last one of them made it off the ship. Arcturus pressed a small rune on the side of his helm, allowing him to send a message to the ship.

"Retrieve us if I send out a flare."

"As you command, Paladin," came a reply from the captain, his voice sounding as if the man were inches from Arcturus' ear.

With his escape secured, the troops mobilized. Arcturus followed the knights through the courtyard. What looked like a normal castle from far away turned into a much stranger show on the inside. The walls were jutting out at odd angles, and carried growths of stone on them, looking like some sort of warts. It was obvious whoever participated in the crafting of this castle held time in much higher regard than aesthetics.

"I don't like the looks of this." A knight had spoken.

"Like your face looks any better." Another replied, chuckling. "Keep focused." Arcturus approached the two men. "We don't fully know what secrets hide between these walls, marred as they may look." The group kept on walking until they arrived in front of a sizable house, an odd thing to see in the middle of this collection of arcane-bound stone. The structure seemed to be attached to a large stone tower growing out of the building's side, stone fusing with the wood to form a grotesque whole. Its front door was distorted by magic, making it much bigger than any door crafted by men. Arcturus guessed it would have to be at least thirty feet tall, and just as wide, and like the walls, the door too carried the small cracks characteristic to arcane tampering.

Arcturus signaled with a hand to the others to open the door, a heavy thing that took five of the knights to crack open. In silence, the men flowed inside, weapons drawn. Arcturus' view was filled with a bizarre hallway, so long it hardly matched the size of the house he saw from the outside. The hallway's walls were lined with what appeared to be knickknacks and odd pieces of what Arcturus might call metal garbage that didn't seem to have any rhyme or reason. Among the refuse were torches powered by magic to light the way.

It really looks like he's been expecting somebody. Perhaps this wizard has company in the depths of his crazy mind...

"Alright men spread out!" he told to the knights as their boots sullied the orange rug lining the floor. His eyes found themselves drawn to several paintings of an old man. Possibly Vargus himself. His hazel eyes almost seemed to follow Arcturus at every step as he walked down the hallway. Arcturus shrugged and kept going. In this strange place, even the rug beneath his feet could twist at moment's notice.

"You lot. With me!" Came a woman's voice, a knight garbed in armor scratched by swords and dented by hundreds of powerful blows. Arcturus walked past the half orc knight who had proven herself over the years to be his most trusted follower. Half of the others followed her through a door they came across, including Harrison. She busted it down with a single shove and a loud cheer. "Knock Knock! Your delivery has just arrived!"

Several shots from her crossbow bathed the knights in flashes of red light.

"Room's clear boys." she casually walked out, a puff of exhaust coming from her crossbow's vents. "Seems our prey is hiding in another room." "Or another castle." Someone laughed.

The knights continued down the hallway, keeping a close look on their surroundings. Though they tried to keep a positive attitude, the ominous nature of this place put even the most seasoned men on guard. Arcturus scanned every cobwebbed stone, every, crevice, every creepy self-painting in search of any hidden traps.

Fortunately, the wizard had none in store for them thus far, and the knights stopped at a cross intersection of doors, each one a different shade of brown with a handle that failed to match its color. These colors were gold, silver, and bronze. Arcturus pulled out his hand-sized crossbow and flipped the activation rune, the rising hum of its power music to his ears.

"Form squads. Two men." He signaled the knights to enter in pairs. He turned towards the bronze door, the one he planned to go through with the knight Erin. Erin was relatively new to the squad, selected for her expertise in lock picking and trap disarmament.

"Are you sure about this, sir? Shouldn't you have someone more skilled at your side?" she spoke on a soft, worried voice.

"You happen to be a fine shot, Erin. Put mind to purpose. If I didn't think you could handle yourself, you would have remained on the deck of the ship, far removed from any sort of danger."

He pushed open the door after she gave him a thumbs-up to find the inside safe to walk in. The room was made of stone, with a singular pedestal containing a small palm sized red orb resting on a purple cushion. The dim light cast dark shadows that crept up like beasts along the walls, sending a sense of dread up the paladin's spine.

"Looks like the perfect den of horrors in here." He turned to back towards the others. "What did you find?"

Spit froze in his throat when, instead of his knights, stood a wall of stone. Arcturus found himself alone with no sign of the others or the door he came through. He raised his crossbow at a moment's notice, then scanned the dim light for any sign of movement, any hint at what had just happened. His steps were slow and placed with care, as if he was treading on very thin ice. Slowly, Arcturus made his way to the opposite side of the room, finding no exit, as expected.

"Damn it. There has to be a-"

He spun around when a faint noise buried itself in his ear. It sounded like a great roar, coming from behind him and very far away. His finger hugged the trigger of the crossbow almost instantly. The once dim room shone with brilliant red light and the wall hissed with three energy impacts on the stone surface. Arcturus stood in silence, listening to his own thumping heartbeat, trying to focus on the source of the strange roar. His eyes hovered over to the orb that sat there, the most single mysterious object in this entire chamber.

An itch prodded him in the back of his mind, drawing him to the orb. Slowly, the paladin stretched his hand towards the object, sheathing his crossbow. The orb was what drew him to this forsaken place, right? That was his task. To retrieve the orb and return it to the king.

Arcturus took one more step. Then another. He was but a hand away from the orb now, trapped in the agonizing moment when his mind all but screamed for the danger that lurked ahead.

However, despite his rising anxiety, Arcturus grabbed the orb and gritted his teeth.

But no spell came out. No trap. The orb was perfectly safe in his hand, cold to the touch like any other metal.

"Well, that was easy," Arcturus let out a long sigh, then smiled. "Guess I'm going home after all."

"Don't judge a book by its cover!" a voice suddenly said, as if from every wall.

"Blast it," Arcturus looked around as Vargus seemed to emerge from one of the many walls around him. Arcturus' first instinct was to grab hold of his crossbow, yet he found himself unable to move a single muscle.

"I don't know what shallow twist of fate allowed you to bypass my defenses and get into this room."

Vargus made his way over to Arcturus until he stood several feet in front of the paladin, his hand stretching towards the orb. "Regardless, I would have you return the orb to its rightful place."

"You...forgot to...say please..." Arcturus strained as he felt his body compelled against his will to walk towards Vargus.

"Would it make any difference? The orb is mine either way. You but have to place it in my palm."

"Nghhhh." Arcturus grunted. Every step felt like pulling against thousands of thorn-vines, a fight against himself. "What's this red pebble to a man who can build a castle out of nothing anyway?"

"The feeble mind of an iron-clad brute could not possibly comprehend my intentions," Vargus said.

"Try me." Arcturus hissed. He knew the wizard was a proud sort from the way he expected the orb to be handed to him. While the bastard filled the air with his boasting voice, Arcturus moved his trembling hand towards his crossbow, almost touching the activation rune.

"Rah!" With a sneer of the wizard's mouth and a twitch of his wrist, the crossbow flew from the knight's grasp.

"That was a clever trick, but useless still." Vargus chuckled. "When a wizard speaks to you, you would do well to listen. But ah. I am afraid we are getting ahead of ourselves. We have yet to be introduced! Now what should I call you, knight of Lumara? Enforcer of our Dictator's will?"

"My name is Arcturus...and I am no mere knight!" he said, pride resonating in his voice "I am a Paladin. I suggest you don't forget my name, nor the title attached to it...when you contemplate the choices you've made in chains."

"Paladin, you say? Now that is a title forged by skill, and prestige. Perhaps fate planned to bring us together this night," Vargus said, amused. He placed a hand on his chin, then walked around Arcturus, no words filling the void chamber until the mage stopped but a few steps away from the Paladin's face.

"But alas, I stand unimpressed. Paladins used to wield so much more than steel in the past. I speak of magic, a power that might rival my very own!" Vargus sighed. "Ah...it is a pity the glory days have faded. There was one time where your order used to stand for something more than a crumpled piece of history. Now, you are but a flea straddling the fur of a beast beyond your understanding."

"I am sorry to disappoint you, wizard." Arcturus said. "I shall pass your wisdom to our king, after I see you bound in chains."

"Oh, but I don't think you shall have that opportunity, paladin." Vargus chuckled again. "You see, I have you in chains now. Your whole body is at my command, and soon enough your mind shall eagerly follow."

Arcturus disregarded the wizard's poisonous words. Instead, he focused on the faint pounding sound starting behind the wizard. The voices...they had to be those of Thraka and the knights.

"Throw your backs into it, or the paladin will have you clean latrines for a week!"

Vargus immediately spun towards the source of the voices. The door bust down to reveal all the knights and Thraka holding her crossbow at the ready. A blue shimmering energy shield appeared before the wizard as shots slammed against his magic barrier, only to rebound and hit harmlessly on the stone walls. The other knights filed in adding their own shots as Vargus backed up, blocking each shot with his energy shield but having little opportunity to do much else.

"Enough of this nonsense!" Vargus cried out.

A wave of magic spread out towards the knights, causing their weapons to suddenly smoke and fall from their grasp. However, Erin managed to pull a knife out just as Vargus casted his spell and threw it at the wizard.

"Grrraaaaaahhh!" Vargus screamed as the knife sunk into his shoulder. Arcturus felt control return to his body. He ducked as Vargus threw several rays of fire around the room in retribution. Harrison groaned as the knight hit the ground. Arcturus had no time to even look at the damage. he grabbed his crossbow from the ground and quickly hit a second switch on the crossbow. He raised it and fired. Instead of a red energy blast, a blue projectile fired at Vargus, taking the wizard squarely in the back while he was distracted by the other knights.

"Damn the...luck." The man mumbled before he hit the ground like a sack of potatoes.

The thump announced an end to the crazed wizard's threat. Arcturus lifted his helmet's visor to wipe the sweat from his brow. The other knights rushed towards him, bombarding him with questions, all background noise to him as he gazed into the orb held within his hand. It seemed to call to him. A whisper, far different than the spell Vargus used on him.

A pat to the shoulder shook him out of his trance.

"Are you alright, Arcturus?" Thraka said, her tusks slightly to the left, a sign of worry as Arcturus came to know from the time they spent together on various missions.

He straightened up and laughed "I'm great! This is what we came for, after all." He held up the orb for the others to see.

"That small thing?"

"What's that do?"

"It's what the King wanted. We couldn't let this stay in the hands of this rebel filth." Arcturus gestured to Vargus. "The fact that he was also a talkative bastard takes second place."

"Uh sir, we only fought summons, not rebels." Harrison added.

"Yeah I thought that was odd. This mage must not have trusted his compatriots enough to guard his treasured ball."

"Well, what should we do with the spell slinger?" Thraka lightly shoved the unconscious Vargus with her boot.

"Carry him back to the ship, shackle his hands, cover his mouth, and throw him in a cell. I'm sure the interrogators will love to break some words out of his mouth."

The others chuckled, picking up the drooling wizard and dragging him back towards the entrance. Arcturus holstered his crossbow and followed the others out.

The knights gathered outside in the quiet courtyard as Arcturus reached for a thin piece of wood on his belt. He gripped the worn wood engraved with various runes, then raised it above his head. Three yellow lights burst into the skies. A few moments after, the flare gave away the position of the troops, the airship appeared, landing a few feet from them. The knights boarded with a collective sigh of relief, dragging Vargus up the plank. Arcturus stopped midway to look back to the castle, his ears still troubled by the faint roar in the distance. He remembered the stories he told Geoffery about a dark shadow beast that stalked the night in search of little boys to devour.

"Are you coming sir?" one of the deck hands asked from above.

"Yes. I just...it's really good to be out of that place." Arcturus turned back to the ship and walked on its deck, his mouth devoid of any other words past what was customary after a mission. He felt the engines roar to life, and a slight lurch as the ship ascended back into the dark skies.

When they gained cruising altitude, Arcturus strode across the deck towards his quarters. His mind could definitely use rest from Vargus' incessant blabber. If he spent more time with the wizard, Arcturus feared he would've collapsed under the mage's unending spree.

Why did you need that orb, Vargus? It must be of importance to seclude yourself in the castle, more so when you came to punish me yourself. Arcturus thought for a few minutes on how easily they breached the castle. Could it be that the mage wanted them to find the orb?

Possibly. Then again, many seers claimed to have untangled the strings of the future.

Arcturus purged his mind of the wizard. The mission was done. For now, that was all that mattered when they had hours left before they reached the capital and his men were more than capable of watching the subdued wizard. He nodded to another crew member as he opened the oak door to his quarters.

His quarters were nothing too extravagant. A bed with tan sheets sprawled over to the left, big enough for a single man to rest in. There was a stand for his armaments a few feet away, followed by a desk and a sizable storage chest for his clothes. Arcturus detached his armor, letting the plates softly hit the bed., each piece removed accompanied by a sigh. He then fell onto the bed, his eyes closing softly at the comforting warmth of the cushion. With such a long night under his belt, sleep came to him before he even knew what hit him.

* * * * * * * * * *

Arcturus opened his eyes to find himself on the cobbled path of a street. He looked up into the dark sky to see clouds gathering overhead. They were moving around as if thousands of insects crawled beneath their surface.

A drop fell from the sky. Then another, and another. Arcturus soon felt the rain starting to soak his dark gray clothes. A streak of lightning arced across the night sky, followed by thunder soon after. Arcturus turned his head, looking for anything in this black void, not seeing the ship, his knights, or his family.

Another lightning bolt flashed in the sky, the booming thunder forcing Arcturus to cover his ears as he collapsed in pain.

From all directions echoed a mighty roar of no earthly origins. Arcturus jumped on his feet, immediately falling into a combat position.

"What are you?" he shouted into the storm above. The clouds parted before him, pierced by a great scaled head that descended like a great meteor. Following suit, its mighty platinum wings opened up as the great dragon circled the lone knight briefly before landing on its claws. The great beast's eyes stared at him, fluid, as if filled with liquid mercury. The Paladin stood his ground as he looked up at the dragon that easily towered over him several times over. He noted the smooth scaled head with less pronounced horns belonged to a female, a boon owed to years of studying these majestic beasts. The dragoness opened her maw, each inch lined with sharp teeth gleaming even in the muted light. She raised her head, and let loose another thunderous roar that shook Arcturus to the very core of his being.

"GAH!" Arcturus woke with a start only to find himself in the bed of his quarters. He grasped the sheets tightly in his hands, sweat starting to drip from his forehead.

"Just a dream," he muttered, sighing in relief. "It was just a blasted dream not even half as crazy as that blabbering mage."

A strong knock rattled his door.

"Yes! I'm well awake."

"Sir, the prisoner wishes to speak with you." Harrison's voice echoed through the door.

"I'll be there in a moment." Arcturus grumbled. He got out of the bed, hastily donning his belt and longsword. He opened the door to find Harrison, his face pale. Arcturus ignored this as Harrison started leading him through the ship.

"He just started talking... different."

"Different?" Acrturus frowned. "What do you mean, different?"

"In another language or-or something akin to organized gibberish, so we tightened his bindings to prevent him from weaving one of his spells. Then a moment ago he asked for you, and put up quite a stir."

Arcturus was brought to the lower parts of the ship, where iron bars were bolted into the wooden floor. Besides that, there was a small enclosure with a tiny porthole, barred by a door. Vargus sat on the lone bench, still tied up with ropes. His face was stern, mouth straight, head un-moving, and his eyes staring straight at Arcturus, following him as he walked, similarly to how the paintings on the castle's walls reacted to the men that trespassed within its walls.

One of Arcturus' knights sat next to the cell, reading a book with the title 'A Bard's tale' written by some halfling that Arcturus had no knowledge of.

"Vargus," Arcturus said coldly. "I hope you realize that causing a stir will just make your stay with us all the more difficult."

"You just had a dream. Did you not?" He smiled as recognition appeared on the paladin's face. "It was of a dragon descending from the heavens."

Arcturus did not say a word as he stepped closer to the bars and whispered, "how did you know that?"

Vargus smirked, "You touched the orb, paladin. Only one other man managed such a feat, and he is standing right before you."

"Cut the nonsense! You can peer into my head now? How's that possible?"

"It's not me who does the peering."

Arcturus gritted his jaws. "Don't play with me, Vargus. You will find my mood sharp and cold, just like the edge of a blade. Now tell me straight. How did you know what I dreamed of?"

The mage seemed to ponder for a bit. "Send your peons away and we can discuss this matter further." Vargus gestured to the knights. "They make poor company for men such as us."

"You are no elven ray of light yourself, old man." Harrison snapped back.

Arcturus put out his hand, signaling to the others to be silent. "Leave us."

"S-sir, is that wise? Bound or not he's still a-"

"I said leave us," Arcturus hissed. "I wish to find out what he knows. Stay close though. If you hear any sort of commotion, come to my aid at once."

"You heard the paladin!" said the book reading knight. "Leave them alone lads!" He stood up and left the room along with Harrison. As silence filled the air, Arcturus pulled up a chair, dragging it across the floor with a loud scrape. He sat down and stared at the wizard.

"I have done as you asked, old man. Now explain yourself."

"Why, it's magic of course!" Vargus laughed. "Honestly, my good iron-clad jailer, you should know better than to trust the words of a wizard." Vargus' voice grew deeper.

"Impossible. We have you tied up right now!" Arcturus shot back.

"There are some magics that require no hand gestures, or words of power." Vargus sighed. "But what can really be expected of a whelp like you?"

Arcturus scowled at Vargus. "Call me that again, and you shall find out how sharp this whelp's fangs can pierce when provoked."

Vargus smiled. "Stroke a chord, have I? The mighty paladin's ears find themselves sensitive to anything lesser than praise."

"You know nothing of duty, of honor!" Arcturus said. "You'd use your powers to achieve selfish goals, a man who believes in nothing but himself."

"As should you." Vargus said. "We come in this world alone. Why should the rest be any different?"

Arcturus grew tired of his babbling. "Straighten your tongue, mage. I asked you a question and demand an answer."

Vargus let out a long sigh. "Veeery well. What you felt was only the residual energy of the orb playing tricks on your mind. Remember the voices? No?

The roar, perhaps?"

"Residual," Arcturus put his hand on his chin, "Where has the rest of the magic gone, then?"

Vargus straightened his back, smiling as if he just achieved some great goal. "You understand speech! That is good, my dear paladin. Keen mind. Sharp as your sword!" Vargus then chuckled in his throat. "Could it be that I have already harnessed the orb's power, perhaps? Or that, when you stand before your beloved king, all you'll have is a broken trinket to show for your valiant efforts?"

"For your sake wizard, I hope you have not done what you've just said." Arcturus spat out. He was starting to tire of Vargus. The man's laughter was like a thorn on his side. His words, spikes driven into his chest. Even the wizard's face started to become more offending the longer Arcturus stared at it.

"Of course, there's the matter of ever arriving to your king's court. I haven't forgotten to mention that, have I?" Vargus' eyes narrowed.

"What does that imply, exactly?" Arcturus replied sternly.

Vargus raised his eyes, adopting the same cocky grin that made his face a hard thing to look at.

"I am only trapped in this stinky cell because I allow it, and you, paladin... you are only alive because you entertain me more than the other fools that came after me. To believe you'd be the only one to actually manage to touch my orb...well, that is a reason in itself to prolong your existence."

Arcturus balled his hands into fists. "If you try anything even resembling a spell, you will find yourself executed quicker than you can blink. If memory fails you, dear wizard, recall how you fell on the ground when my stunning bolt struck you in the back. You drooled on the ground as the rest of my men carried you into this stinking cell, as you so fondly named it." Arcturus boasted, his own grin finding its way to his face.

"Ah, here it comes. The cockiness of youth. You know, I've been wondering how long you'd resist the temptation to show off. Knights are so predictable. Haven't you wondered why your journey through my castle went so smooth? How Vargus, the greatest mage in Lumara, perhaps in the whole world, fell at the hands of a ragtag band of idiots? It is because I allowed it!" Vargus rasped. "I wanted to be trapped here with you so I could share these very words right now!" Vargus' voice kept getting deeper with every word he uttered. Arcturus had to admit the situation started to get strange really fast.

"Have you lost your wits, old man?"

Vargus opened his mouth to form a toothy smile. His bright white teeth seemed to be sharpened to points. His eyes had also changed from hazel to orange and his round pupils replaced with reptilian slits. Arcturus tried to stand up, but found himself unable to, the dull noises of the ship fading away, leaving nothing but Vargus chanting in his deep creepy voice. Arcturus did not know what the words were, but the way they hissed upon the mage's breath couldn't be good.

Arcturus watched in utter bewilderment as the room slowly began to melt slowly. Its droplets collected beneath him, vanishing as if getting sucked down a drain. Arcturus' eyes never strayed from Vargus as he was plunged into darkness. The wizard's ropes seemed to uncoil from around his limbs, then faded into nothingness.

"No, paladin. You did not face me when you captured my pitiful vessel!" Vargus approached, outstretching his hand. The flesh on it seemed to slowly peel off out of its own accord, managing to touch Arcturus on the chin. Arcturus could see four black talons ripping their way slowly from Vargus' flesh. If the wizard was in pain, he did not show it at all.

"Now let's see what kind of man you truly are!" Vargus sneered. The blackness around them slowly became a fuzzy vision of Arcturus' house in the capital of Entis. Despite the darkness looming all around him, he could still recognize his wife cooking stew on the fireplace. As the vision cleared, he could see her straight brown hair, draped behind her and adorned with beads. She wasn't cooking now, her brown eyes filled with worry over her frozen face.

"Ah, so you left your mate and child alone to heed the command of your king. Hunt Vargus down, as you would a stag!" the wizard paused to tilt his head as he inspected the frozen woman. "You chose me over her...in spite of your wife's protests."

Arcturus struggled to move even a single finger. Whatever magic Vargus had over him was much stronger than it had been inside the orb's chamber. He made the mistake of looking into Selina's eyes. He didn't abandon her...did he? He just heeded his duty, as would any other man in his place. Despite the wave of guilt washing over him, Arcturus swore to the gods that he would make it back to her.

"S-Selina?" Vargus said. "The name barely wants to part with the tongue." He stopped again and raised an eyebrow "Selina and...Geoffery!" The wizard wrinkled his brow. "It pains you to have me gain knowledge of their names, does it not?"

A grunt was all Arcturus could muster.

"There is no point in struggling, whelp! My magic has you bound tighter than my vessel had ever been on the deck of your filthy ship! But alas, we must not let ourselves get carried away," Vargus spun around once again to face Arcturus. "There's more I would know about the great iron-clad man that captured me. Arcturus, the shining paladin." Vargus waved his hand, the flesh dropping away in large meaty chunks that slapped wetly onto the floor. All that remained was a red blood covered claw covered in scales.

Arcturus' house melted away, leaving nothing but utter darkness. With another wave of Vargus' claw, Arcturus found himself in a field outside of Entis, where his father used to train him.

"Oh, this is intriguing. You are a Lund, after all!" Vargus shouted as his slitted eyes widened. "A Lund!" He jumped for a moment, moving close to Arcturus' face. "Dragon slayers, are you not? Men with tradition!" Vargus laughed deeply as cracks appeared on his face. "Such misery your family has brought upon dragon kind, and such good fortune that we have met together at this point in time. It's like fate wished to pit us against each other!"

Arcturus renewed his struggle and got rewarded for his efforts. The scene before him faded away. He once again found himself back in the cell of the ship. He had his sword in hand with Vargus in the other. The man's eyes had not returned to normal. He shook his head once and quickly noticed that Harrison and the other guard were currently tugging on his sword arm, causing him to fall backwards onto the floor. Vargus just cackled as he collapsed onto the bench once more.

Arcturus rubbed his head in circular motions. "What happened?" he muttered, turning to the others. "The bastard must've casted a spell on me. I'd never...raise sword against a defenseless man like that..."

"Don't know, sir," stammered Harrison. "You just entered the cell, weapon drawn. That's all I know."

"But...we shared words. I ordered you out, and-" Arcturus stopped when the confusion only grew on Harrison's face.

"Mages and their kin, ugh!" Arcturus rose from the ground, shooting daggers with his eyes at the wizard. He grabbed a piece of cloth and tied it roughly around Vargus' mouth once more.

"There will be no more trickery coming out of your mouth tonight, wizard. My blood but warms at the thought of handing you over to the king himself. You'll meet true justice in the dungeons of our glorious capital." Arcturus turned and slammed the door to the cell shut.

* * * * * * * * *

Hours seem to shuffle past on the deck of the Destiny, never seeming to end. Arcturus watched soldiers shuffle by, performing the needed checks with looks of worry present on their faces. He was amazed to see the story of his private time with Vargus in the cell spread so quickly throughout the crew. All their eyes were filled with worry, uncertainty, and even fear. He didn't blame the men for their reaction. You didn't see many powerful wizards just roaming the streets or halls of Lumara. Only the High Wizard seemed to have that quality. However, if you really wanted to see powerful mages, you had to go west, to the nation of Rothdell. The wizards there ruled over the populous in a council made up of three elders wise beyond their years. Each territory was divided to a different wizard, much similar to how Lumara did it with lords. Arcturus stopped in the middle of his thoughts to look over balcony of the Destiny, onto the endless horizon. He could already see familiar mountains growing in the moonlight. He knew the landmarks well. In spite of everything that happened tonight, he was close to his home, soon to be in the loving arms of his wife and child.

A smile graced his face at the thoughts of his family. Geoffery was most likely asleep, holding fast to a stuffed gryphon Arcturus made for him last year. He pictured his face buried snugly in the cushy body of the toy without a worry to trouble his sleep. He imagined Selina waiting, looking up into the night sky for any sign of his airship, her eyes longing to gaze upon him once more. He felt the ship start to descend slowly, yet another sign they were close to home.

Arcturus made his way to the bow of the ship to see the city of Entis, his home, truly a sight to behold for those who have not yet set eyes upon such a marvel. Spread way below the bulk of the airship flickered lights from the city lamps, illuminating every alley, bearing the semblance of little fireflies from this distance. Closer, stone and wooden houses awaited with fine roofs routinely inspected by the city for damage. Banners of every color hung off street corners and windows for various noble houses, guilds, or announcements. Yet despite such striking sights, Arcturus looked to the two wonders that towered above all others.

Floating above the city were two large fortresses. Stone guardians held aloft by large mana crystals. The brown banners of Lumara hung atop them, billowing down to the base. Behind them was the castle, standing high above the city with many gargoyles and towers. Arcturus remembered that, even when he was much younger, he realized how long these structures endured, before elves graced the kingdom with their presence. It was even rumored that dragons would have attacked its walls, fended off by heroic knights of old. He remembered passing the gates to the castle as a child, seeing large claw marks across the surface of the stone walls. His father had pointed them out, reminding him that his great, great, great ancestor had slew the beast in his final moments. He remembered smiling at the story, imagining himself as the great, great, great ancestor, a man garbed in glorious plate armor fending off the great wrym that threatened his marvelous city with a giant, two handed sword held in his burly hands.

Arcturus pulled himself out of the memory and made his way back to his quarters. He was going to be home soon, and he wouldn't even dare to greet his wife without the proper gear. He donned his armor carefully over his gambeson. With each strap. he remembered how the armor had saved his life from countless blades over the years. He stopped, grabbing the helm with his gloved hands. He ran his hand over a scratch down the center, over the vision slit, when, suddenly the ship lurched. The helmet dropped from his hands and clattered to the floor, the sound drowned out by thunderous explosions that raged within the bowels of the ship.

Arcturus sheathed his weapons and swung the shield around his back. Armed this way, the metal-clad paladin walked out of his chamber. As he walked along the hall, his thoughts turned to the prisoner in the hold, and another explosion rocked the ship. Screams came from ahead, piercing through the splintering wood to fill Arcturus' heart with dread at the sound of his crewman being shredded into nothingness. He feared the worst when he passed a knight in the hall, his armor torn to ribbons and blood leaking from each deep gash on his body. Arcturus tried to look away but found himself unable. The knight was an elf named Croecear, he could tell by the elven rune on his blood covered gauntlet. He hadn't been the most talkative of the group, but he didn't deserve such gruesome end.

"Paladin!" a voice gurgled out. A quick scan of the hallway revealed two things. Smoke was beginning to billow down the hallway, and Harrison, lying on the floor several feet ahead. His limbs seemed to have been bent at odd angles, his mouth saturated with blood, and his eyes tearing up from the excruciating pain that undoubtedly coursed through the man's broken body. Arcturus noted the rising and falling of his chest; Harrison was alive, if just for the moment.

"Harrison," Arcturus knelt beside his broken comrade, his face grim. He had lost soldiers before, but even after years of fighting, he hardly got used to it.

"Hang on, soldier." Arcturus grasped Harrison's' hand. "I need you to hold on for just a moment longer. Tell me what happened."

"B-Big," Harrison spat.

Arcturus grimaced at the droplets of blood that painted his chest plate in a sickly layer of crimson. "The wizard, h-h-he turned into some sort of b-b-beast. B-big. With....wh...with..." Harrison clenched his teeth, gasping in pain.

Arcturus looked left and right for maybe a cleric that could help, but not even the gods themselves could have saved the fallen knight even if they poured down from the heavens.

"Crocecear. Harrison." Arcturus said, rising up from the fallen knight. "I will be sure to honor your fall once we deal with this blasted wizard."

That said, Arcturus broke into a run down the hallway, following the trail of blood and corpses that made the Destiny look like a flying cemetery. Each door he passed was cracked or destroyed outright, the splinters of them thrown across the floor. Bodies of those who manned the ship could be hardly recognized from the pieces that remained, but with each fallen comrade, Arcturus was filled with a greater determination to put an end to Vargus' machinations. It didn't matter that he was wanted alive by the king. The man was clearly too dangerous for any other course of action, and if the king disagreed with his methods, Arcturus would find a way to enter his good graces once more.

Arcturus burst through the shambles that used to be the engine room door to find several more of his knights, all dead. Thraka, his trusted orc commander, was suspended in the air by three black talons impaled in her chest.

"N-no," Arcturus's throat tightened at the sight. "Not you too..."

His eyes looked past the fallen orc. Through the smoke curtain of smoke that was coming from the engine emerged a great beast that towered over Arcturus, its ominous eyes glowing like fire in the dark. It was adorned with worn red scales all over its long body, tail poised around, with great wings spread to cover the great hole in the ceiling. The beast's head was equipped with two long black horns and gleaming sharpened teeth that dripped long strands of bright crimson gore.

"The esteemed paladin comes at last. For a moment I thought you perished in the bowels of your pathetic little ship." said the dragon in a loud booming voice, gesturing to the dead knights. "Please excuse the dreary company. I would've kept some of your knights alive...if only to watch you suffer as I tore the hearts from their chests. Your feeble kin thought their lesser minds could rival my genius! That their steel sticks and mismatched crafts could match the power of a dragon. Oh, I enjoyed seeing them crumble around me as I tore their ship asunder. I assume you have the same delusion, to stand before me when the only place a human has before a dragon is on his knees."

The engine started to sputter and howl, its screeching groans more painful than the dreaded dragon's roar. Arcturus was no expert in engineering, but clearly the ship's heart could hardly endure more than a few moments. He looked back to the menacing red dragon and swelled up his chest.

"I am a man...and I am still standing, beast! You put on a charade this entire time, but you will not catch me unprepared like you did with the others." His hand brushed his crossbow as he stared into the piercing eyes of the dragon. "Whatever fancy polymorph potion you ingested will not-"

"I AM NOT THE WRETCH YOU SPEAK OF!!" the dragon roared, smoke flaring from its twitching nostrils. "Do NOT compare me to that pitiful excuse of a creature." The dragon thrashed its tail against the ground with a loud thwack. Arcturus' hand touched the crossbow in his holster.

"If you're not Vargus...then how should I call you, you mean scaled beast?" Arcturus smiled with the corner of his mouth as he started to back away from the dragon who had taken a step towards him on four limbs. Arcturus had to admit he had never felt so small before.

"Grah!" The dragon growled. "You prolong your pitiful existence with a few more minutes, but I shall entertain you for amusing me thus far, even if I doubt your stupid mouth could even form the words." The dragon sneered. "Dread Flame. Does this name satisfy your curiosity?"

Arcturus carefully watched the dragon's eyes move to the crossbow as Arcturus hit the activation rune. "Fondling your little toy so soon? I'm surprised to see you throw yourself into the jaws of death so eagerly, but alas, everything that has a beginning bears an end." The dragon snarled, smashing his tail into a piece of machinery and crushing it to pieces.

"I hope you'll put up a more valiant effort than the pile of dented steel and broken bones you call knights!"

Arcturus saw the dragon's nostrils flare, already starting to kindle the flame that was sure to be unleashed. He dove to the side, pulling out the crossbow in midair and firing three times in rapid succession. His bolts bit into the dragon's neck, just below the head. The destroyed room flared to life in a shower of blue light that emerged from his crossbow. At the same time, Dread Flame opened his maw to unleash his own devastating attack.

But what greeted Arcturus was not the sea of flames one would expect. Dread flame shook his head in irritation as only a small plume of black smoke sprung forth from his maw.

"How do you like that, beast? Not so powerful now, are we?" Arcturus stood up as Dread Flame gasped in surprise.

"Oh, you clever little whelp." Dread flame chuckled. "So, you know where my fire glands reside! I commend your efforts, although they do little to protect you against my CLAWS!" Dread Flame pounced towards the paladin, black talons poised to rip him to shreds.

Arcturus had only a split second to react. On the dragon's upper portion was a scorch mark, most likely from his comrades attempts of bringing Dread Flame down. Arcturus took aim and fired quickly into the exposed spot, then tried to roll out of the dragon's way. His shots hit home, causing Dread Flame to roar out in pain, but a claw still found its mark, slicing into Arcturus in a haze of sharp, seething agony.

"Nrraaaahhh!" The paladin hit the floor, wincing in pain as the dragon skidded past him. His crossbow was pulled from his grasp and shattered onto the wooden floor with a golden flash.

"That was a fine shot, paladin." The dragon hissed. "You do live up to that family name of yours. I am impressed you managed to wound me." Dread flame spun around, claws ready to deliver a second blow, but Arcturus pulled off his shield and slammed it hard against the slashing talons. His shield screeched as the dragon's humongous claws scraped against the steep incline of his metal barrier briefly before Arcturus was thrown back several feet.

"See how you crumple before me?" Dread Flame advanced slowly, with an audible deep growl rumbling within the depths of his maw. "You're lucky I am holding my rage back, paladin, or that metal scale of yours would not have saved you."

"One of the last mistakes you'll ever make." Arcturus gritted his teeth as he got up, unsheathing his sword with a sharp hiss. His crossbow was all but mangled scraps, yet there was another way to strike back at the beast. Arcturus blocked another slash from Dread Flames' claws, then nimbly avoided the dripping teeth that lurched forth to claim his life. The dragon snapped at the air where his head would've been. Arcturus felt his adrenaline pumping as shield met teeth, sword parried claws, until Arcturus saw an opening in the dragon's attack. Pouring all his strength into a single counterattack, Arcturus struck an unarmored portion of the dragon, his blade shoving deep into the creature's flesh to taste warm, dripping blood.

"Hrraaaaaahhhh!" Dread Flame backed away from him. "This is preposterous! How can a wretch like you muster such strength?" The dragon's eyes looked to his own blood as it dripped and splattered onto the floor. Dread Flame snarled and backed towards the sputtering engine. "I have underestimated you, paladin. Perhaps you are worthy to soar above the mediocrity displayed by the knights I've killed, but your life will still end at the tips of my claws. It is a rule, you see. Like the sun that rises in the sky, or the ivory moon that takes its place at night. Humans are made to kneel before their betters. It simply boils down to our superiority as a species, and in the end, you too will bend the knee."

Arcturus shook a few drops of viscous blood from his sword. "False words that mask true intent. You don't seem so superior, retreating from a mere human. If you make a god bleed, people will stop believing in him, and you, dear dragon, bleed all over the floor of my ship." Arcturus advanced towards the dragon, arms at the ready.

"You would think that, despite the answer that's staring you blatantly in the face. All this ingrained cockiness clouded your eyes to the obvious," snarled Dread Flame. The dragon grabbed the engine tight with both of his claws and spread his wings. "I can FLY, and you CAN NOT!" Dread flame gave a mighty flap of his wings and with a great rip, he tore the engine from its resting place and flew out the hole in the ship.

The broken ship shuddered one last time before it started to plunge towards the ground below.

Arcturus had only time to sheathe his sword as his hands desperately grasped for anything to hold onto. He found his salvation in a chain that dangled from one of the walls. His arms strained from his own weight as the chain pulled taut. The whistling winds screeched at his ears from the sizable hole where the engine should've been, the night sky getting further and further away by the second. Arcturus took a deep breath, then scanned his surroundings for a way out of this deathtrap.

The escape boats! his mind screamed at him, as he remembered the emergency boats that came along with every ship. These miniatures flying crafts fit six to eight people. He found one such craft on the wall along with a lever to release it away from the Destiny. The only snag in this plan was that the emergency boat was located a fair distance away from him. It would require a great swing from the chain he was holding onto, and if he missed the jump...

Arcturus shook his head. He had to try, otherwise he was going to perish with the rest of the ship anyway.

He started to swing on the chain to get momentum before he flung himself at the lifeboat. The armored paladin landed with a thud and scrambled to find a good hold as he started to slip. His arms felt like they were on fire as he pulled himself to grasp the activation lever.

Please work...by all the gods above...please get me back to my family...but not before I kill this blasted dragon.

Arcturus closed his eyes and pushed the lever with all the strength he could muster. It slammed into place with a loud clunk as the gears and mechanical parts sprung to life. With a small explosion, the lifeboat shot itself out of the doomed ship and gently sailed into the night air, its propellers unfolded to keep the little craft aloft. Arcturus breathed a sigh of relief as the life boat came to a hovering stop in midair. He watched the Destiny collide with the cobblestone streets of Entis with a thunderous crash. Wood beams split at the contact, machinery ripped and flew in all directions from the Destiny's crumbling carcass, and windows shattered in the wake of the shockwave created by the rough impact.

"Nice trick!" boomed the dragon's familiar voice.

Arcturus had no desire to quarrel verbally with the deranged beast. He quickly grabbed the controls of his little ship and descended along with the lifeboat. He had to at least give the dragon a moving target, not one that simply waited to be killed. He turned the lifeboat around to see Dread Flame following him with a wicked smile of delight on his snout, which quickly opened to release a great cone of orange fire that spread in the darkness of the night. Arcturus swerved the boat hastily to barely avoid the brunt of the flames, the heat still licking at his neck.

"You cannot flee from my wrath, little wretch!" roared the dragon with another flap of its mighty wings. "We share a bond of pain, you and I, and I shall wound you deeper than you've ever wounded me!"

Arcturus hated to admit it, but the dragon was right in both regards. He would not rest until he saw the beast dead for the massacre on the ship. However, Arcturus was well aware he could not fulfill his task if he perished prematurely. With every passing moment, the dragon was gaining on him thanks to his mighty wings.

Arcturus needed advantage, and fast. He brought the boat around 180 degrees, then reached for an unstrapped spear that clattered to the floor of the boat. With the lifeboat facing Dread Flame, he pulled the spear up and held it pointed at the beast, controls veered to maximum speed.

If the dragon was concerned, Arcturus could not tell, for Dread Flame just flew straight towards him, looking as malevolent as ever. At the last moment the dragon tilted his wings, as to avoid the spear meant for his chest, but Arcturus used the controls to change direction. With a thunderous crack the spear's head found purchase in the upper right of the dragon's chest. Carried by unearthly momentum, its iron head pierced through the beast's mighty crimson scales. Arcturus was flung forward towards the dragon as Dread Flame roared out in agony. The paladin crashed hard onto the dragon's chest even as his own was filled with a dull pain. He started to fall, but quickly grabbed his knife and stabbed it as well into the dragon, hard and fast, until the blade found purchase into an unarmored spot. Arcturus plunged the dagger deeper, then twisted it hard.

Dread Flame screeched out into the night as he struggled to remain in the air. The dragon's sharp claws immediately came in the defense of their owner, trying to tear the pesky human off, but the paladin clung onto the dragon with all he had. He thanked the gods for his armor as the otherwise deadly claws scrapped against the hardened steel instead of his own flesh. The dragon shuttered below him as they impacted a chimney, scattering the brick everywhere before the debris littered the street below. With a loud thud and a groan from the dragon, the two crashed into the street.

* * * * * * * * *

Arcturus lay on the ground, his body aching all over from the tough impact. He could feel the cold wind licking through the cracked parts of his armor. With a breath that felt like a thousand little needles pressed firmly into his lungs, he propped himself up. Several feet away from his position, Dread Flame slowly picked himself up with the same difficulty. With a tight grip of his claws, the dragon ripped the spear out from his chest. Dread Flame's eyes narrowed as the blood covered spear clattered to the street, but not for long, a smile replacing irritation when the orange eyes noticed the blood starting to drip from his approaching enemy.

"You are a tenacious little wretch...I give you that. But your heroics are about to come to an end." Dread Flame growled mockingly as the two of them slowly approached each other.

Arcturus groaned in pain. He had to keep moving, or the dragon would surely kill him. Dread Flame realized this as well, pouncing to Arcturus with his claws outstretched. With a herculean effort Arcturus rolled away from the deadly dragon, its claws striking the stone hard enough to send sparks along the cobbles of the street. With adrenaline filling his body, Arcturus stood back up, grabbing his sword and shield, trying hard to keep his trembling arms still, and his weakened legs from collapsing under his own weight.

"How intimidating." Dread Flame growled. "No words left to mock me, paladin? I've killed your squad, destroyed your ship, landed straight in the heart of your city...yet you say nothing! I bet you used the last of your energy to stand up and draw those pitiful weapons of yours." Dread Flame started to limp around him. "So, how's this going to go from now? Will you strike me again? Or finally accept your place before your betters?"

"I think you are trying to hide your wounds through talk." said Arcturus through gritted teeth, trying to ignore the pain coursing through his veins.

"Rrraahh." The dragon shook his head as his lips curled with obvious pain. "It comes hard for a dragon to admit its flaws, but I believe compliments are in order. As inferior as you humans are, you...Arcturus Lund... wounded me far greater than anyone had ever managed before." Dread Flame sneered.

"However..." The dragon stopped in his tracks. "Your quest for retribution comes to an end. I will not be giving you the satisfaction to finish me off in the same way your ancestors killed my kin!" Dread Flame turned to spread his wings, and Arcturus willed himself to sprint at him, so focused on the sinking feeling rising from his gut that he didn't notice the threat in time. With a sharp whip of the dragon's tail slammed into his side, Arcturus tumbled to the ground with a pained grunt.

"Your family stole more lives from dragon kind than you can ever comprehend, so it is only fair of me to return the favor."

"Straighten tongue, you blasted dragon!" Arcturus roared. "Tell me your plans before you die!"

"You already know, paladin, for nothing was hidden in your mind when I peered into it."

Arcturus' heart skipped a beat. His blood turned to ice as his thoughts quickly turned to his family.

"N-no. No, you can't!"

"Can't I?" the dragon sneered. "I still have enough life in me to pay them a visit."

"NOOOO!" Arcturus shouted. "Stand and face me you vile wyrm! My family has done nothing! I've pierced the gates of your castle. I captured you. I wounded you! Your quarrels are with me, not with them!

"Do you mistake me for a fool, human?" The dragon spoke. "Another bout with you might very well claim my life," said Dread Flame, a devilish grin spreading on his snout. "But I will hurt you, in a way that my claws and fangs never can. Stand there. Writhe in agony. Cry in despair as your retribution crumbles into dust!"

Dread Flame flapped his great wings, leaving Arcturus to slice empty air with his sword.

"Selina! Geoffery!" he screamed at the top of his lungs. Arcturus looked around in a panic, but what could he do against such a beast? The ship was in tatters. His lifeboat, gone. He had no horse, and to top things off his own body barely allowed him to take a few steps without a burst of crackling pain shooting through his muscles.

I must...protect them. Must...defend...my family. Arcturus looked to all the houses, finding he recognized them. Through sheer adrenaline he started to sprint towards his home. He was only a few blocks away from his family. With each footstep, he feared that he would be too late.

"No," the paladin shook his head and prayed to the gods the dragon would take time to gloat, buying him enough time to catch up.

Arcturus dashed down the street as parts of his armor started to fall off. The leather straps snapped one by one from the strain. His limbs arched, his lungs struggled to draw breath, but he still pushed his body to his limits in order to protect his most beloved of treasures: his family.

He heard screams from nearby houses. Possibly from the fire that stared to spread after his ship fell from the sky. Or more likely because of the dragon. His steps fell back into pattern with the bells ringing from the roof tops, signaling an attack on the city. Arcturus rounded the last corner of the street, to find his house enveloped in flames. Its front seemed to have been crushed in with a mighty strike of a claw, or even a tail. Definitely Dread Flame's work.

Arcturus' eyes focused on the red beast. The dragon lay collapsed on the street, blood oozing out from the numerous wounds inflicted by the fall, as well as the paladin's frenzied attempts to end his life. On its pebbly snout rested the same grin that became characteristic to this dreadful beast. Arcturus could see that the dragon still drew breath as he approached. He noticed there was another spear piercing its chest, close to where Arcturus had stabbed. Dread Flame chuckled as Arcturus tried to run by to his house. When he tripped in his haste, the dragon had reached out and grabbed his leg. He landed with a painful thud, and a hoarse laugh from Dread Flame.

"Not so fast, human..." growled the dragon.

Arcturus struggled to pull himself free. His eyes found the dead form of a man clad in chain mail, obviously one of the guards. It looked like the dragon had sliced through his armor, inscribed in the red lines of blood that marred the man's broken chest. Arcturus pulled again on his leg but no matter how hard he pulled, Dread Flame had no desire to let go.

"Linger a while. I don't want you to be alone when your family gives their last breath. We shall watch them die together." Dread Flame taunted.

"Not today...you vile monster!" Arcturus unsheathed his sword in reply and whirled around. "I owe you pain!" he gritted his teeth, then rammed his blade with both hands through the dragon's skull, right through his eye and into his brain, silencing his taunting forever.

Arcturus gave another pull of his leg. Even in death the dragon held firm. He tugged again, then again, and finally the reptile's dead limb gave way. Arcturus scrambled to stand, stumbling through the first attempt, then rushed to the burning frame of his home.

Pieces of debris started to collapse among the flames, nearly hitting Arcturus as he searched in desperation for a way through the debris. Like an enraged bull, he pushed through fire and smoke, passing rooms filled with memories, now engulfed in the flames that threatened to consume them forever. The paladin valiantly pushed aside debris and burning wood. He shouted his wife's, then his son's name.

Coughing from the thick smoke, he quickly covered his mouth with part of his ragged clothes and kept on searching, straining his ears, hoping for anything other than the sound of burning wood, collapsing house, and the pounding of his heart. He started to feel the shimmer of hope in him starting to die when a sudden cry made his eyes bulge out.

"Daddy!"

Filled by a second wind, Arcturus rushed towards the voice of his son. Arcturus found him among the wrecked items of the house. Geoffery was covered in cuts and bruises, gasping for air. Arcturus quickly picked up his son with care. He tried not think about the dried blood on his son's face, how or why it was so pale. When the little boy smiled up at him even through all that pain, Arcturus all but felt his heart break. He looked around for Selina, only spotting her burned body under a collapsed beam that trapped her forever.

"N-no," Arcturus stammered. "Gods, why...why did you...?"

"Daddy...pl-please..."

"It's alright," Arcturus caressed through the hair of his boy. "You'll be alright, Geoffery."

With a heavy heart, he turned away from his once-beautiful wife. He couldn't mourn her fate. Right now, he had to get his son out of there. He clutched Geoffery tightly to his chest and pushed his way through the debris. It was all a blur as he struggled to get out of the burning wreckage of his home, but somehow, he made it.

Arcturus found himself in the panic filled streets of his city. He passed the dragon's corpse in haste, as even in death Dread Flame had that wicked smile about his snout, taunting him from the grave.

"Cleric!" he cried out with tears forming on the edge of his eyes. His steps were now filled with stabs of pain, and they collapsed from under him a second later. "Hold on Geoffery. I got you, son. I got you..."

"D-dad, I saw a dragon." Geoffery said, his voice barely a whisper. Arcturus watched in horror as the last color on his son's face drained away.

"N-no! No no no no no!" Arcturus clutched Geoffery tighter than ever. "Just stay with me, son. You have to be strong for me, Geoffery. Fight through this, the same way I fought for you. Cleric!" he cried out. "My boy. My boy is...CLEEERIIIIIC!"

A soft tug on his chin pushed Arcturus' head down to his son.

"She was- she was so pretty, dad... all silver...with eyes like...mer-mercu...mmmercury..."

Geoffery sighed for a final time, his tarnished body going limp in Arcturus' arms. His hands went to his son's face, smacking him softly.

"Son. Please don't...please don't do this to me. Fight through this, son. Don't let that monster take you too!"

But Geoffery had no fight left in him. After a few failed attempts at resuscitating his son, Arcturus collapsed his head into Geoffery's chest as he sobbed and screamed into the night.

Chapter 2: A Dragon's Day

Two years had passed over Lumara, although those who did not inhabit a city or found themselves breaching Lumara's lands during times of strife would not have noticed the time pass by. The country kept expanding, and slowly, its enemies had no option but to fall back further into their territory. Our story takes us to the north-western border of Lumara, into a wild mountainous area where a dragon soared freely through the skies.

Veledar spread his wings, gliding upon the gentle currents of the wind, basking in the warmth of the sun falling upon his crimson scales. Few things felt as exhilarating for a dragon as flying. The dragon tilted his tan wing membranes and did a spin, closing his eyes in happiness. He loved every little thing about flying. The foreign smells carried by the breeze, the gusts brushing against his wings, even the way his tail swung back and forth. With another flap and a slight tilt of his wings, the red dragon descended toward the tree covered mountain top below. His blue eyes narrowed on a stream he usually visited during warm days. He landed as softly as a dragon of decent size could, but even so, the animals took notice of his presence, which produced a low rumble within the dragon's throat. He didn't mind the reception. Such reaction was warranted when you happened to be an apex predator. Veledar walked towards the river, then opened his maw and slurped in the water with his dark pink tongue, sighing in relief as the coolness of the water washed over his weary body. His front claws twitched slightly to anchor him in the rock bed of the river, and Veledar paused for a quick moment to gaze upon his own magnificent reflection.

The dragon considered himself in better shape than the scrawny body presented upon the water's surface. He stood at roughly 28 hands high, and 22 feet long from nose to tail, a presence that already intimidated every animal around.

Probably not humans though. Veledar snorted. He wasn't exactly small by even dragon standards, but there was no drawback for a larger size, especially with dragons. The larger wyrms controlled vast territories, with wisdom to match their legendary deeds. Veledar had a mind to become a legend himself one day. It was amusing, to think of humans reciting tales of his deeds to their children.

The dragon immersed himself into thoughts of self-grandeur until an ungainly rumbling from his stomach drew his attention back to the present.

How annoying! Veledar hissed as he brushed his belly with a wet front paw. He had no mood to chase his prey through thick trees and trip on their gnarled roots, but alas, even dragons had to submit to the basic needs of every living being. Veledar sniffed the air, looking for a trail that he could follow for an easy meal. He moved his snout from side to side until his eyes sprang open. He recognized the smell of deer, one of his favorite prey to feast upon. The dragon took flight from the river's shore and chased his prey from the air until he isolated a single doe. The frills lining his snout twitched in anticipation as she made him work for it, so in return, Veledar planned to give her an honorable death. The dragon crashed back on the ground and chased with great speed after the creature. With a great pounce and slice of his claws the doe crumbled to the ground, giving her life to prolong Veledar's own.

The dragon burned whatever remained of the doe to honor the female's sacrifice, then returned to the stream to clean the blood from his claws and teeth. Although he liked the intimidating image of himself all covered in viscous blood, he rather disliked being dirty.

"Why not do something about this?" The dragon growled happily before he jumped into the stream with a great splash. He swam around for a bit, then hopped out onto the shore to shake the water off his dripping scales. How he hated the cold water! The stuff poked through his scales like daggers, although a hot bath every now and again lessened that hatred. Veledar relaxed on the river's shore for a bit to soak in more sun. He spread out his tail frill, twitching it slightly, then looked at the sky to notice that the white clouds sailed away from the blue sky while he was feasting. Time passed quicker than he had expected.

The dragon rose on his fours, then unfurled his wings to take to the skies when a faint cry reached his ears. Veledar turned his head towards the sound and quickly found the source behind a small bush. The culprit was small, perhaps not even the size of a little house cat.

Curious as he was to check on the source of the disturbance, Veledar remember his mother scolding him once for trying to peek on the elves near his old home. He scrunched his snout up at the ridiculous notion he was forced to swallow that day. It had something to do with privacy or some man-made nonsense like that. The red dragon pushed it from his mind and moved the bush with his front claw, yet the thing was persistent. Hard to gaze through. Veledar ripped it from the earth rather harshly, scattering dirt all over.

"Yaaaaawwwwhhh!" The fairy screamed and darted out of his reach. She was a small humanoid in appearance, with wings sprouting from her back. She began to flutter in front of him roughly at the same height of his head, pointing and cursing his lack of decency. "Have you no respect for a fairy's privacy, you big, lumbering scale-head?!"

"Scale what?" Veledar's snout curled with irritation. "You don't get to call me names, little thing!"

"Fairy. I am a fairy in case you are not familiar with my kin, which your lack of manners clearly suggests!"

Veledar found himself quite amused by the creature's courage. She wore a green dress to go with her short brown hair. Her blue eyes dripped with half cried tears not from the brief exchange they had, but for some other reason that Veledar could not understand. The fairy looked at him, unsure of what to do.

"Sorry about the outburst. I might've gotten a bit ahead of myself, but just so you know, it's rather rude to rip up a girl's hiding place from her!" she shouted at him.

"Outburst, again." Veledar growled slightly. He often hated when a lesser creature addressed him with such a lack of respect, but the fairy was right in one regard. He did intrude upon her.

"You're not making it easy, you crimson-scaled brute."

"Brute now, am I? Well, excuse my lack of patience, gentle creature, but I had to find where that annoying noise was coming from. From what I know you could've been in danger!" He shot back, sounding perhaps more aggressive than he meant to.

"No, you!" The fairy slapped him on the snout with her tiny hand. "You are the danger, sticking this oversized snout into somebody else's business!" The fairy flew back several feet to avoid Veledar's pokes. "First those nasty humans, and now a dragon? What else can possibly go wrong today? I feel like the world is playing a joke on me, after...after....yaaah I can't even say it!" she cried out in frustration.

"Lady, you need to calm down," Veledar said calmly.

"I'll calm down when you give me back my bush!" The fairy sounded even more irritated now.

Veledar sighed and pieced back the bush as well as he could with his ungainly claws. "There. Your shrub is back. Feeling more protected from the crimson scaled, big nosed brute now?"

"Slightly." The fairy rubbed the last remaining tears from her eyes. "But...

it doesn't fix the damage that's already been done."

Veledar strained not to growl at her. Her persistence to seek justice was unwavering, but he remembered his mother's advice regarding the lesser creatures. She had said that, in situations like the one Veledar found himself in right now, there was a far greater reward than coin or gems to be earned with little effort.

"Fine," Veledar rolled his eyes and sat down on his belly, paws crossed. "Nasty humans you say?" he cocked his head. "How did they grieve a small- no, a gentle creature such as you?"

The fairy seemed irritated at first, but then she crossed her arms, as if considering her reply. "Why should you care about my problems, dragon? Don't you have a village to burn, or a maiden to capture for ransom? I heard what your kind is capable of."

Veledar fought the instinct to bare his teeth, and simply smiled instead. "Oh, you are mistaken, my good fairy. I do try to lend my skills, my wings, and my paws to lesser creatures whenever I find myself...available." He emphasized lesser louder than the rest. "For the right price, I might be able to do something about this...situation you find yourself in," he finished.

"I don't have any coin or shiny gems that can ever match the size of your ego," the fairy grumbled. "But the humans I speak of are even nastier than you, dragon. They trampled over my grove with no regards for my flowers, which they plucked one by one until there was nothing left. Even my favorite fell prey to their fat, greedy fingers!"

"What kind of flower are you speaking about, fair fairy?"

"I don't reaaaaaally remember what name it bears in human or dragon tongue... but we call it the sun's tears on account of its orange color."

"Of course," Veledar rolled his eyes. "When in doubt, go with the obvious. Now, where did the humans run off to? Perhaps you can illuminate me on their whereabouts."

"Illuminate you?" the fairy looked at him as if he suddenly spoke a different language. "You want me to turn your scales white?"

"No!" Veledar jumped on his feet. "I mean...graaarrr, I mean...."

"I can show you then!" The fairy zipped around his head. "I promise not to use any spells on you...unless you ask for it!" she started to fly away, then turned back towards him, "I'm curious about your name though!"

"I did not give it. I request you give yours instead." Veledar started swelling his chest as he usually did when he would proclaim his title.

"Trixie," the fairy said, a smiling forming on her face. "It rolls like a river on the tongue, does it not?"

Veledar wasn't really going to provide his real name to a lesser creature, be they fairies or otherwise. Titles were what dragons used for such encounters, and even though she proved herself somewhat reliable, Trixie wasn't that special yet.

"You may call me..." Veledar paused and grinned, "Crimson Sky. Easy to pronounce and obvious on the eye."

"Well, Crimson Sky, can you follow me please?" Trixie turned to fly off, going upstream with the dragon following close behind.

Trixie led him to a clearing not too far from the spot she had been crying in. The bushes and local flora were sliced into pieces, with orange petals scattered all over the ground. Trixie immediately burst into tears.

"Nyyyaaaaaaaaaah! I can't bear to look upon this...devious devastation! See what they have done? See?" she zipped erratically around the dragon's snout before she pointed in horror to a particularly large growth of leaves and bisected vines. "Most humans come here in peace, but those smelly, two legged, pelt-wearing bastards took all my flowers!"

Though the tragedy hardly had the same impact on him, Veledar felt a sliver of remorse for the fairy. He paced back and forth, disappointed by the carnage that had been wrought through this once-peaceful grove.

"Why did they harvest your flowers, Trixie? Have they said anything to you before...well, before this happened?"

"They didn't give a reason," Trixie sniffled. "They just... stomped around in their stupid boots and ripped my flowers with their fat, sausage fingers!"

If you were as sharp with your spells as you are with your tongue, perhaps they wouldn't have had the chance, Veledar thought, but even a proud dragon like him realized that was the wrong thing to say in this situation. Instead, he looked around and searched for tracks with Trixie sobbing behind him. She would occasionally point out more damage the humans had caused, until at last he found boot prints leaving the clearing.

"Worry not, Trixie friend. I, Crimson Sky, will return your flowers back where they belong, and as a bonus for your unique form of hospitality, I will also make sure these humans never set foot near your grove again." Veledar dipped his head to her with pride.

"Thank you! Oh, thank you so much. You are a good dragon, Crimson Sky. Very good dragon!" Trixie hugged a scale on his snout with her little arms.

When she retreated, Veledar moved quickly after the trail of boots. He raced through the underbrush, following a combination of boot prints and smells of what he remembered to be human in origin. He barely avoided a head-on encounter with a tree as his mind planned for what he was going to say when those two oafs gazed upon his magnificence. Perhaps he would make a threat or two or open the short-lived dialogue with a great roar. He would knock them around a bit to put them in their place, then take back the flowers. He grinned, already celebrating his victory in his mind when he was pulled out of his pleasant daydreams by the sound of two voices talking.

"Quiet, Jenn! I think I heard something nearby." A male voice said, bristling with concern.

"I was quiet until you opened your mouth again! I would be concerned if this was not the twelfth blasted time you warned me of nonexistent threats!" an angry woman's voice yelled back.

Veledar stalked around the two. One was a rather large man dressed in furs of various kinds with a large pack hoisted upon on his back. Beside him was a woman with long brown hair, resting on her studded leather armor covered in tribal markings. She held a bow at the ready, scanning the foliage with her brown eyes.

"Listen here," she began, "you can't be jumping at every sound while we make our way back to town. That's not what a man does! That fairy we met will not be coming to retrieve her lifeless plants. Besides, think of the children. We need these herbs to brew healing teas and cure their ailments."

The man sighed. "I know, I know...I just...I find myself wishing to have a tenth of your bravery, lass." Morca replied, and Jenn smirked. Then Veledar made his move and pounced in.

He collided with Jenn, knocking the girl off her feet. She slammed into the hard ground with a thud, the bow falling from her grasp. Morca went to pull out his quarter staff tied to his back, but quickly found his legs dislodged from the ground by a quick swipe of Veledar's tail which sent Morca in the ground's embrace in the same way as his woman.

"Why hello there, humans!" Veledar swept the bow from the ground, snapping it in pieces between his jaws. "Now that weapons are taken care of, we can share words in peace. What brings you out to this dangerous part of the forest? After the encounter with that fairy, you never know what kind of beast you could run into. It might've been a bear that got you, but today, you have the luck to stand in the presence of a bigger, and much better-looking predator."

"You forgot to mention your pride," Jenn managed to squirm her way out of his grasp, jumping back to stand beside Morca. Veledar's eyes locked on them as he began to circle the terrified man and his much more confident woman.

"T-that's a D-Dragon!" Morca exclaimed, clutching Jenn tightly. "How can you address his Brightness in such a crude way? What in the blazes we gonna do if he feels insulted?"

"Well, it seems your mate here is a master of stating the obvious." Veledar chuckled. "My fairy friend would like him...if he put his mouth to use instead of his hands! She likes to hear tales, that is, when she is not screaming at you."

"Cut to the point, dragon. What is it you want from us? Money? Steel? We carry nothing of worth on our bodies or bags," Jenn said sternly.

"Is that so?" Veledar puffed his chest. "I believe you happened to steal some rather unique flowers from an acquaintance of mine. Small of size, carried upon the air by gentle wings. Oh, and you might've heard her rant at me if you happened to be in the vicinity."

"See? See?! I told you that fairy would find a blasted way to get her revenge on us!" Morca cried out, color all but draining from his face. "We are dead, woman! We are dead dead DEAD!"

"Shut your cryin' mouth for scale's sake!" Jenn hissed, her defiant eyes fixing on Veledar. "We did take those flowers, but not to make coin from them. The children in our village are ill. They need tea brewed from these flowers. I promised the wee lads that I'll return to them with hope in my bags, an' you're not getting in me way."

"Fascinating," Veledar said. "You say that with such bravery. Or as some others would say, foolishness." he grinned, "You are aware of the repercussions that can fall upon you if you fall on the wrong side of a dragon?"

"I focken do, red scales, but these plants are worth the risk! Didn' ye hear a word I said? Our young 'uns are sick in their beds."

"Can you provide proof of that?"

The woman shrugged.

"Hard for me to trust the words of a thief. Produce proof, or-"

Her sword poured from its sheath with a hiss, so Veledar offered a threat of his own, fangs barred.

"You are about to make a huge mistake, human. You can swing that feeble spike at me, curse my name, or punch my scales until you scrape your knuckles bare, but that is not going to change anything. Place the flowers on the ground and leave, or you will find out how deep a dragon's retribution can cut." Veledar growled, flexing his claws into the dirt.

Jenn's eyes darted to Morca, huddled over with fear. "I will not get any help from my man, nor justice from the pain you've just caused, you heartless thing," she exclaimed. She reached into her pack to throw a group of flowers onto the ground. "Take your plants back, but know that retribution will find you one day. You mark my words, beast."

Veledar laughed. "A thief telling me I'm in the wrong! That's beyond precious," he thrashed his tail and roared. Jenn and Morca sprinted for their lives away from him. Veledar grinned to himself and looked to the small flowers. They were far too fragile for his paws, too gentle to be carried in his mouth. He sighed and performed a quick gesture with his claws, muttering a quick phrase in draconic. A small disk just large enough to fit the flowers appeared underneath the bundle of plants and lifted them three feet into the air. Veledar turned and made his way back towards Trixie's grove.

"Cry no more, gentle Trixie, for I, Crimson Sky, have returned with your flowers." he boasted with his chest swelling with pride.

Trixie flew over, barely able to stop her cries of joy as she hugged the dragon's snout in whatever ways she could.

"Hey, I gave you no permission to get all teary-eyed again!"

"I'm sorry, Crimson Sky." The fairy wiped her eyes. "I am just so relieved to have my flowers returned, damaged as they may be." She floated over to the disk to retrieve the flowers, then reattached the cut stems to the flowers, making her garden whole again before Veledar's own eyes.

"See how beautiful they look? Tell me, tell me!"

"Yes, they are positively radiant!" Veledar tried to keep a straight face.

"All because of you!" The fairy added. "There has been no braver dragon strolling through my forest until you happened along."

Veledar pushed out his chest again. "What can I say, Trixie? I really am the best!"

"Owwwh, you really are," the fairy hugged him again. "I would offer you something else in return apart from words and hugs, Crimson Sky. You see, my grove is connected to my sister's, far, far away."

"What do you mean by that?" he asked, cocking his head to the side.

"With the right words, a passage forms, which allows the user to be transported there!" she beamed. "Whenever you are in need, come here and I will allow you to use its power."

Veledar sighed. A reward was a reward, after all. Certainly, better than nothing.

"Very well, Trixie. I will contact you if the urge to experience the wonders of fairy magic strikes me one day." Veledar turned towards a mountain that overlooked the forest and pointed with a claw. " And if you ever need my help again, my lair can be found up there near the top of that mountain."

The fairy smiled warmly. "Thank you again, Crimson Sky, for your valiant victory. You truly are the bravest dragon around!"

Veledar smirked at the honest praise. He always loved the sound of praise no matter where it came from. With a flap of his mighty wings he left the forest far below and returned to the sky.

Veledar flew towards the mountain that had been his home for the last two years. On his way there, he admired the forest rolling below him, the river that snaked its way down the slant, and the vast mountainside that encompassed his domain. His territory was truly a gift; one that Veledar would protect with his very life if it ever came to that.

The dragon dove down swiftly, startling a flock of birds as he passed by them. The cave that was his home was nestled near the top of the mountain at the perfect altitude for a dragon to look over his territory. It was hard to get to without wings, and deep enough to shelter a sizable amount of treasure. The dragon landed at the mouth of the cave, inspecting the slashes carved into the top center. This crude symbol would tell any dragon that this cave was claimed. With a smile, Veledar strode past the entrance, lighting the torches lining the walls with his breath, his flame funneled into a small strip that would not damage the frail things.

The rear of his cave was filled with piles of gold pieces and various gems. As he approached the pile, the dragon let out a satisfied sigh. His hoard was large enough for him to sleep on, but paled in comparison to his mother's mountains of treasure. Though Veledar was somewhat happy with his possessions, he still longed for more riches, just like any respecting dragon would.

In time, he would get there, but for now the red male strode over to his collection of soft furs and laid in them. How could he multiply his fortune? Through deceit and destruction like other members of his kind? The prospect of something so distasteful turned his stomach. His mother had raised him to respect the lesser creatures, not frighten or hurt them beyond the necessary amount, like he did with the two humans that messed up Trixie's garden. They deserved a scare, not to lose their lives over some healing tea flowers.

Veledar wondered if another dragon would've showed the same mercy. He picked up one of his golden goblets and tossed it across the stone floor, watching it until it collided with a tower of books and other objects.

On top of the tower lay his favorite item, a collection of stories depicting the dragons that inhabited the various places of the world. He walked over to the pile of books and picked up the top book. The cover was orange with the title *Knights and Knaves* scribbled in the middle. He quickly tossed it aside to grab onto the next book from the pile. This wasn't the right book either! The dragon stifled his frustration and pulled book after book harshly from the stack, tossing them from the rapidly shrinking pile. When he had gone through all his books he started to remove gold and search beneath that as well. He was certain the item he searched for was there in the morning, right before he went on his hunt.

His hunt. Humans! Veledar took a deep breath, growling as he noticed a scent that evaded him when he entered the cave. It smelled like fear, sweat, and horse. His green eyes widened at the realization.

"You little thieves!" he shouted aloud. He searched around, and soon enough found a faint trail of boot prints.

"How dare you come into MY HOME, and STEAL my POSSESSIONS?" he roared. Oh, he would do a lot more than scare them this time around. Blood burning hot, Veledar followed the tracks outside, but their lead came to a premature end. Veledar sniffed around. There was another smell along the human stench. Something he hadn't smelled in over two years. It was the smell of a gryphon, heading eastward, towards a village bearing a name he had long forgotten.

Veledar paced around, claws clicking on the stone of the cave's ledge, his tight jaws trying to hold control of the anger that now boiled in his blood. He tried to breath in and out to calm himself but all he could see as he closed his eyes was a human male holding his book and laughing with glee. A wretch without manners, just like the flower thieves.

"I will teach you what befalls those who steal from a dragon!" Veledar took off into the sky with haste, ignoring the words of his mother as they rang in his ears. *Rage must be tempered. Instincts too can lead you astray. The quickest decision is rarely the wisest.*

Veledar ignored every word of his mother's wisdom, following the trail of that vile scent all the way to the village, to a humble house on the outskirts. The small house was made of wood, with a golden gryphon painted on its door. Shadows covered the building from some nearby trees, giving it a false sense of protection.

The dragon landed softly and slowly crept to the building, making sure there were no others around. He made sure that with each paw placed on the ground he made as little noise as he could. The smell he followed led right inside.

Veledar flared his nostrils and slammed his bulk into the door, causing the thing to splinter and collapse inward. His momentum carried him over a wooden table that broke itself upon his body as well. Veledar flared his wings and roared out for all to hear.

"Little thieves! How DARE you sneak into my lair and--" he began, only to be cut off by the scream of a little girl dressed in a simple brown dress. A man stood in front of her, cold fear in his eyes as he held a broken chair. Veledar paused to see the kitchen he had destroyed with small pots tossed over, their contents leaking onto the floor.

"W-what do you want from us, monster?" the man stuttered as the child clung on to him, with tears rolling down her terrified cheeks.

Veledar held his maw agape for a second before cocking his head to the side. Was this really what he wanted? To unleash his vengeance upon a defenseless girl? "I..." his eyes narrowed. No. He couldn't appear weak. Humans were known to be adept liars. "You have stolen something of importance from me, human! Did you not think I'd notice your stench laying around my cave? That my vengeance would not find you, no matter how far you ran?" he asked aggressively.

"I-I am a simple carpenter, dragon! I swear I have not left this house since morn!" The man's hands started to tremble along with the broken chair he held. "Ppp-please...my daughter...let me take her to a safe place, an-and then we'll talk, alright? We'll talk about this."

"Hraarrrr..." Veledar hissed. "The culprit is here. I know it for a fact. Unless you are suggesting your whelp grew wings, entered my lair, and snatched away my possession, I will hold you accountable." Veledar said, strutting in the cramped house still eyeing the family. "Where is your mate? I would have words with her as well."

"My w-wife works for the king, dragon. If you are to kill me, please... spare my daughter, for she is young and innocent. Truly the purest soul you can find. My-my greatest treasure of all! Spare her. Please, forgive us!" the man cried, dropping to his knees before Veledar to grab and kiss at his toes.

Veledar was almost insulted to have his paw touched by the human's trembling fingers. He took a step back, holding his paw aloft. "I wouldn't kill your whelp, human, nor I appreciate you throwing your life at my feet." said Veledar, gently guiding the man around to a chair that was still standing. "Take a seat and tell me where your mate is."

"Wife." the man replied, a bit calmer now that his trembling body found purchase on the chair. "She'll be here at sundown."

To wait almost an entire day on this man's promise? Veledar did not feel fully convinced. "Where can I find her? I said it before. The item in question holds significant value to me, and the more I wait, the higher the chances are that your wife will pass it into another pair of hands."

"Oh...do you...are you referring to the book me mum had?" the little girl asked softly.

Veledar turned his head towards the little whelp, who was currently wiping tears from her eyes.

"I've...seen it. Had pretty pictures of dragons in it. You would be pretty too, if you weren't so angry."

Veledar approached her, his neck and head low. His eyes were locked on her, and as he neared, the father raised from his seat.

"What do you intend to do, dragon? She but complimented your-"

Veledar hissed at him, but the man already grabbed his makeshift weapon and swung, though the hit missed its mark. Veledar tripped him with his tail, causing the man to collapse lightly onto the floor with a groan.

"Gah, you and your infuriatingly long tails. Don't lay a claw on her, dragon, or I swear by the Gods above that..."

Veledar ignored the man's empty threats and focused on the girl. "Let us make a deal, little one. You tell me where your mother took my book, and I will allow you to touch any scale of mine you like."

"She didn't say..." the girl looked down. "I'm sorry. I really wish to help you, dragon. I really do."

Veledar rumbled softly. "Can you tell me where she is then?"

The girl nodded a few times. "But only if you promise not to hurt her."

"I promise." Veledar said.

"You swear?"

Veledar held up a paw to his chest, "I vow upon the very scales of my body."

"That's good enough for me," the girl smiled, extending a hand towards his snout. "So red...so pretty! Can I...touch?"

Veledar closed his eyes, bowed his head, then waited for that petite hand to make contact with his snout.

"Don't trust him!"

The girl drew back, Veledar opened his eyes to the shout that came from the outside.

"Vern!" the voice was the first among the chatter of at least twelve other voices. "What manner of misfortune befell your house? You alright in there?"

"I got a focken dragon in here." The girl's father rasped. "Raise weapons. Sound the alarm. He's just about to eat my little daughter!"

"I'm so sorry about this," Veledar whispered. He had all the intentions to smile when he watched that girl's eyes widen as his snout made contact with her curious hand, but unfortunately, he had no time to fulfill that bargain anymore, thanks to loud mouthed Vern. Veledar knocked him down again with his tail, then bounded out of the house into the twelve men wearing chain mail, carrying a combination of long spears and crossbows.

"By the gods above. Vern spoke the truth!" one of the men gasped aloud.

"Dragon! Focken dragon!"

"It's red like fire. He gonna burn us!"

"Can we even fight something so big? We'll all die!"

Veledar had no time to deal with this nonsense. He spread his wings and charged them, tossing the men aside like pebbles. Two bolts glanced harmlessly off his scales, but by the time the men gathered their bearings, Veledar already pierced through their ranks, his wings taking him into a realm where they could not hope to follow.

He looked back to see most of the guards back on their feet, firing uselessly as the distance between them grew larger with each wing beat.

That could've gone so much better if I didn't barge in like a tempest. The dragon shook his head and scolded himself at how reckless and stupid that was. His sister would've made the humans comfortable with her presence. Maybe even bring them gifts to pave her way through to their hearts, while Veledar brought with him only rants and destruction. The red dragon flew through a curtain of rain clouds to cool off his blood, then landed outside his lair once more, looking to the far-away dot that was the village. It had already started to disappear as the sun sank beneath the mountains. He would probably spend the night looking into the stars. Veledar laid down in his usual spot, a patch of earth that had left an imprint of his form. He looked up as the stars started to reclaim the sky and sighed. Tomorrow would give him another chance to right today's wrongs.

<u>Chapter 3: Back to Duty</u>

A pounding knock rattled the simple wooden door of a seemingly empty house. The only furniture inside the home was made up of a small table with the plates and utensils of previous meals scattered about, and an aging bookcase covered in dust with tomes of various sizes and colors. Atop of that bookcase stood two painted frames, one of Selina Lund, and the other of Geoffrey Lund.

Knock! The sound rumbled again from the door, startling a nearby alley cat who let out a rather loud yelp. However, despite the ruckus, the simple house's black curtains remained drawn. In one room of the house rested a suit of plate mail, all dented, scarred, and a sword held aloft next to a damaged shield engraved with the symbol of a gryphon. The knock came again, this time accompanied by a shout. "Rise up already! The ninth bell had just rang, which just about marks you as the laziest bastard in this town!"

Arcturus slowly opened his eyes, instantly shutting them from the radiant light streaking in from one of the missing blinds. "I'm up. I'm up!" he shouted, his voice coarse as he tried to stifle a morbid cough that had been with him for the past days.

"You alright in there, sir? Your voice threatens to descend into a dragon's growl if you keep that up." came the voice.

"Oh, leave me bloody alone, Gus." Arcturus yelled, his voice already sounding better. "It's just a minor annoyance. Happens every morning."

Arcturus rose from the small bed, scattering the sheets all over the place. He quickly threw on his customary brown uniform, then released a drawn-out sigh as he looked into the body-length mirror on his wall to find a grizzled looking man with pain filled eyes staring back at him. He admired the tan cloak he tossed over his shoulders, and placed a golden broach of an eagle on it. The symbol that belonged to the captain of the guards. Arcturus had been honored with this position shortly after the incident with the dragon. He scowled whenever he thought of the grisly details he endured through that day, yet more so at the implications of it. This position was supposed to be much easier. Alas, fate had a way of twisting up every now and again. Arcturus almost imagined himself home that night, in the loving embrace of his wife. And then...

Arcturus snatched up his leather belt and stowed his long sword. No time to think about that now.

"Any disturbances to report?" he asked Gus.

"We had a small theft from Petunia's, but nothing else that's worth mentioning. The king told us to retrieve you."

"Retrieve me? What, am I unable to find my way to him now?"

"You know that's not what he meant, mate."

"Yeah...I know." Arcturus shoved on his black boots, then grabbed a piece of stale bread off of his table before opening his front door. "So the king wants to see me, you say? What would he have of me this time?"

The man standing in front of him was a portly looking guard, with chain mail one size too small. Though Arcturus kept his tongue reigned, he always felt that the man's girth threatened to burst out of the armor at any moment.

"You look deceptively better than you sound, sir. Though I can still tell you had a rough night. Are the nightmares getting any easier?"

Arcturus' frown was answer enough.

"Never mind that. We should turn our attention to more pressing matters. No time like the present, eh?"

"Quite so." Arcturus grabbed a bite from the tough hunk of bread he carried. "Did the king say what he wanted?"

Gus scratched his beard. "He didn't mention that much, with your ears so far removed from his mouth. But he did make it sound urgent. Figured he must have something grand in mind for the slayer of Dread Flame."

"You know better than to utter that creature's name." Arcturus grumbled, and that put an end to the discussion for now. To distract himself from the dark thoughts that prodded at his mind, Arcturus started to look to the streets, bustling with people of different races. They were all conversing or haggling with merchants in the street. The air smelled of cooking meat roasting in a menagerie of spices. Arcturus' stomach tightened as a horse-drawn carriage strode past them. It was driven by a stern-faced human in a well-kept purple suit. On the carriage was painted a black raven symbolizing the house of Raverst. Odd. They usually kept away from public roads.

Arcturus and Gus rounded a few corners, passing a number of armored guards. Each one of them pulled off a quick and crisp salute as they walked past them, to which Arcturus either bowed his head or saluted in response. He had to admit. The guard force was more efficient than ever before. Over the last two years he had the mayor retrain the guards, see them better equipped with both armor and weapons, and he even hired a couple of elven rangers to tutor the lookouts and archers on the weak spots of many beasts that could pose a threat to the town, dragons most of all. The first two weeks of that training had been amusing, as the ranger he knew whipped the soft men into shape. Arcturus' mind focused on her stern discipline until he was pulled out of thought by a familiar voice.

"Hey Arcturus! Care for a few rounds with a friend?" shouted a man clad in dark half-plate, only lightened by the scars the armor bore. He was leaning against a stone wall adjacent to a training ring full of fledgling swordsmen. The figure appeared to be in his late twenties, with shaggy black hair that reached to his shoulders, lightened up somewhat by bright blue eyes. The man was also tall, standing at about two meters.

"Garroth!" Arcturus shouted, a small smile growing on his face. He extended his hand for a shake. "I did not think to see you here so soon. Is the whole band with you?"

Garroth grasped his hand firmly. "Hah! The tombs were not as harrowing as those lost mines."

"The ones plagued by ghasts?"

"The very same." Garroth beamed.

"What in God's sweet name is a ghast?" Gus asked, scratching his head. "Some sort of ghost made of poisonous gas?"

"A fearsome undead creature that can paralyze people with but a single touch." Arcturus quickly replied.

"I always admire men who know their craft!" Garroth pointed at Arcturus. "Stay a while. I would share many tales of adventures with a man I'm proud to call friend!"

"Ah, I am afraid pressing matters must keep my legs moving." Arcturus frowned. "Wish I could linger, but the king is requesting my presence. We will catch up another time."

"Hmmph." Garroth laughed, putting his hands on his waist. "Don't want to get in your way then, lordship!" He laughed. "Hopefully you have time later to get your accomplishments bested by an experienced adventurer."

"Bested? When did that ever happen?"

"Hush." Garroth whispered. "I don't want the others to know I'm beaten by a bloody captain of the guards every time. I've got a reputation to uphold, after all!"

"Well, if whatever the king wants is not too time consuming, I would definitely be up to hearing about your latest adventure."

Both men wished each other the best and went off in different directions. Arcturus made his way with Gus toward the castle, while Garroth remained behind with his band of adventurers.

"Sir, who was that man?" Gus asked the moment they were out of earshot.

"Garroth? He is an adventurer that stops in from time to time. He and his lot tend to live between towns, fulfilling all sorts of quests, collecting bounties, adventuring, most of all. I spar with him every time they return to Entis." Arcturus chuckled. "You should have seen our last contest. Garroth stumbled backwards into a Siigonis woman, I have never seen a man battered so thoroughly by one of those lizardfolk!"

Minutes passed in silence as they passed several more streets with wares and goods. Out of the corner of Arcturus' eye, he spotted a sign in the shape of a large gear. It was a shop run by a gnome woman named Matilda, who always loved to tinker with things. She was one of the best crafters ever to create swords, armor, basically everything a guard, knight, or adventurer would ever need. Gus filled the time talking about the weather, then politics with nobles, and even corraled Arcturus to the right side of the road, for in the center of this street was a stuffed head of Dread Flame thrust on a spike for all to see. Arcturus scowled at the grisly memento. He remembered the King and various others trying to convince him the dead dragon was a symbol of hope; of a brave man's victory against unfathomable odds.

But all Arcturus saw was the constant reminder of his empty house. Thankfully, they walked rather quickly away from this dull red eyesore, heading into the docks.

The docks were located close to the floating fortresses that watched over the city. It was busy this time of day, with several vessels docked and crews unloading cargo, most likely from the eastern coast. Arcturus waved to the men he passed by, knowing many of the ship's crews. It wasn't until they passed the aviary that they stopped once again.

Gus had just started a conversation about his favorite airship to enter port. No surprise it was the RLA Destiny B, reported as the fastest ship of them all. Arcturus spotted a trio of gryphons gliding gracefully overhead with their golden wings outstretched. Entis had teams of them patrolling the city to aid the guard. Today they were being led by a woman named Elizabeth. Arcturus saw her wave a hand as the team circled back around one more time to offer him a warm and vocal greeting. The gryphons landed on their paws softly on the stone streets. Elizabeth was in the center of the others with a large smile on her face, her blonde hair tucked neatly in a bun.

"How goes the patrol, Elizabeth? I trust Swift Wing there hasn't been up to his usual mischief," Arcturus said, gesturing to the gryphon.

"Your wounds hurt me such, human," protested the gryphon, his voice a tad high pitched.

"Oh, don't furrow your feathers over his words, Swifty." Elizabeth said, petting the gryphon on his head. "The captain's jokes are known to miss their mark more than they find it." Elizabeth returned her green eyes to Arcturus who couldn't help but smile at the jape. "New ship came in this morning, quite a big thing. What was the name again George?" she turned to a strong built human guard atop an earthy brown furred gryphon that had teal tipped wings. The man raised a brown leather gauntlet to his chin in thought.

"There's none bigger and stronger than the Indomitous!" he said with a grin. "Lots of soldiers on board of that hulking beast. If I didn't know any better, I'd say someone is gearing up for an important task."

"Maybe Rothdell finally got the guts to push us back?" asked the third guard, who was easily smaller than George and had the face of a young recruit.

"I don't think those silk-wearing, finger twiddling spell-weavers will make any meaningful progress while we are around." laughed Elizabeth. "Our ships are powerful enough on their own, and the gryphons only reinforce our strength. We are blessed to have such stalwart allies at our side." she added as Swift Wing looked to start a fuss. "Well Arcturus, as nice as it is speaking to you, it's time we returned to the sky. Fare you well." The group gave a quick salute before their gryphons spread their wings and swiftly returned to the busy   air   above. "They're quite something when you see them take to formations." Arcturus observed.

"Did you ever consider joining the air patrol, sir?" Gus asked as the two men resumed their walk towards the castle. "It might do you good to have a partner by your side. Or under you. When you're in the air, that is. Because the saddle- gods I'm just getting deeper in my own pit, aren't I?"

"Tends to happen when the tongue gets ahead of the head." Arcturus laughed.

"I would be in your debt if you don't mention this to Garroth. That man looks perilous."

Arcturus laid a hand on Gus' shoulder. "Worry not, my friend. What we talk remains between us. As for riding a gryphon...the appeal is lost to me when I have so many years of experience leading troops. I am used to having land under my feet, not bare, empty air. If you are interested, I can put in a good word for you. Get you trained by the best, only that you have to loosen a bit of that girth you don't want your gryphon to fall out of the sky."

"That would be fantastic!" Gus exclaimed. "I'll do anything you ask of me, sir. Train harder. Move more. And...try to take it easier with the meals. Graaaah! The hardest mission of all, eh? With so many quality inns around I'm surprised the king himself isn't a tad portlier."

Arcturus smiled. "You have an exciting future ahead of you, Gus. Though I am afraid you won't be so grateful when the time comes to get acquainted with your gryphon. They are as picky as they look, and quite needy if my memory serves.”

“I don't care what it takes to bond with a gryphon. I just want to soar upon the winds, free like a bird.” Gus closed his eyes. “Would be the experience of a life time sir. And-and of course my appreciation will extend to the gryphon. I don’t just want to borrow its wings, you know. A partner. That’s all I ever wanted. To have someone to share my happiness with. I was always a bit jealous of your squads, sir. The men look up to you. Respect you. Obey you without question, while I’m...I’m just a simple guardsman...”

“Not for much longer.” Arcturus draped his arm over the man’s neck. “I might’ve not been able to help everybody, but I will see you ascend to the skies, Gus. You have my word.”

The man could barely keep his eyes from tearing up, so he kept on discussing gryphons as they walked past many stores, inns, bars, and brothels, until they finally stood outside the great stone gates of the castle. The walls had been carved by the most skilled dwarves ages ago. They also engraved runes every few feet as a mark of their craftsmanship, along with scratches. Arcturus recalled the stories that spoke of dragons that laid waste to the city. In its darkest hour, the city summoned its bravest heroes, who stood up against the tide of darkness and protected these very walls with their lives. Between the walls was a very large wooden gate painted with a mural of a mountainside, where a large snowy gryphon spread its broad wings. On the gate's top, Arcturus could make out six guards standing at attention, ready to give alarm if anything out of the ordinary threatened the city.

“Hail, paladin!” shouted one of the guards clad in polished half plate mail. The man wore a barbute helmet adorned with gold that marked him as part of the king’s royal guard.

Arcturus had only been to the castle a few times in his lifetime. Once when he was still a child, during his knighthood, when he obtained the position of a knight, when he ascended to the paladin rank, then finally after he had slain Dread Flame, the biggest menace known to the city at that point. Each time, he remembered the small dose of pride he carried within his soul, although the same exhilarating feeling eluded him on the fateful days after the dragon’s fall. Arcturus had nothing pleasant to think about. Even now he struggled to keep the dragon’s smirk out of his mind, the dead bodies, his son’s whispers as he gave out his very last breath.

Arcturus shook his head and focused on the guards as a smaller door in the gate cracked open, right below the painted gryphon.

“Come on, you blasted thing!” came a struggled shout from behind the door. “Put your backs into it, men, and haul this bastard up before the paladin has words with you!”

With a struggled grunt, the door swung open and two guards fell through, onto the ground.

"There we go, paladin," said one of the humans, dusting himself off. "That damn thing gets stuck from time to time. Apologies you had to see us like this."

"A thing of no consequence." Arcturus replied quickly. He remembered that each time he had visited the castle, the door always posed a problem or two. If there was ever a symbol for the things royalty did not care about, this was clearly below their notice.

From the opened door emerged an old man clad in orange robes adorned with runes. The robes easily draped over his body to cover his feet, and dragged behind him on the stone. Upon the man's waist circled a brown leather belt with many bottles held by straps, spaced carefully so they did not rattle together as he walked. His hair was grey and cut thin to hide his receding hairline. He smiled with bright white teeth in the middle of a grey beard that seemed to devour his face, though even amongst all that hair his eyes remained clear and full of kindness.

"Arcturus!" said the man. "I can see you took your sweet time coming here. Luckily, the king has been very busy this morning and barely noticed your tardiness."

"Fortune finally hears my prayers, Father Devlin." Arcturus sighed in relief, in spite of the joke. The last thing he needed was an angry royal, especially the king.

Arcturus had many dealings with father Devlin during his time as the leader of the order of knights and paladins that served Lumara. He also acted as one of the king's advisors in spiritual matters.

"Come, come. We must see Cornelius at once. You are of course well aware that the matters we have to discuss are of great importance.

However...ummmm." He gestured to Gus. "Guard.....ummmm.."

"You sent me to find him." Gus said, "By the light, has my name eluded you again?"

Devlin put up his hand to silence Gus. "Hmm, don't give up on this enlightened mind just yet. Mhhhmmm...something with a K, right?"

Gus shook his head, then Devlin's eyes lit up. "Ken...Kenvar...no, Peter!!" he exclaimed. "Ah yes. Peter! Well, the maters at hand are only for our ears only, so you will have to excuse us."

"Very well, although my name is not Peter." Gus insisted.

"Wh-what?" Devlin stroke his beard, as if lost in thought. "I could've sworn I knew your name better than I know my own beard. Hmm, how curious. It just slipped away from my mind. Might you refresh my memory, please?" asked Devlin, crossing his arms.

"It's Gus!"

"Well that is a terrible name!" the old man said. "No wonder I forgot it. Now, if your parents had named you something simple, like Peter, I'd have remembered it, of course."

"Yeah...I bet." Gus just sighed and rolled his eyes. With a quick goodbye Gus, walked off back to the town.

"Alright now, where were we?" Devlin turned to Arcturus, placing his two palms together. "Oh yes, I was telling Griff there that king Cornelius wanted to talk to you about a little town on our North Western border."

Arcturus sighed. He was led from the main gate to the castle's inner halls. Father Devlin kept getting lost in his own conversation, often forgetting who had told him what and half remembering tales. Arcturus feigned attention as they made their way through the well decorated halls. They had been adorned with rugs of various colors, artwork from different ages and kings, and antique armor and weapons. The halls were much cooler inside, much different than the last time he had been here. Noticing the paladin's expression, Devlin mentioned a cooling spell took effect ever since the king complained about the heat. Arcturus sniffed the air and found a very pleasing aroma laying about. The air smelled of roasted ham, probably being prepared for the upcoming meal. His stomach rumbled as he remembered the exquisite meal he had at his paladin promotion. His mouth began to water as it had been the best meal of his life. It had a bed of vegetables that put any other dish to shame, coupled with wines from all over the continent. Arcturus tried to keep a stern face even as his stomach rumbled like a dragon's throat. He didn't want Devlin to think him unshackled, acting upon instincts like those beasts.

"Hungry, are we?" laughed Devlin, "I'll suggest the cook to whip you up something before you go. We can't have our mighty paladin fall prey to starvation, can we?"

"Much appreciated." Arcturus nodded quickly. He found the walk to the king's audience chamber much shorter than it had ever been. He was brought through a well-made sturdy oak door that looked like it never gathered a speck of dust on it. Past the door stretched a long hall with two large windows that allowed the viewer to look down upon the city. Various other doors that led to different wings of the castle spread like a spider's web along the hall. Two thrones sat in the center of the hall, raised up on a section of stone steps. Behind the thrones was a large brown flag with the symbol of Lumara on it. King Cornelius sat on the right throne, a small crown with jewels atop his raven black hair that reached his shoulders. He was currently wearing navy blue silk clothes, and stared with his emerald eyes towards a kneeling soldier in plate mail. Cornelius picked up a sword and placed it on each of the soldier's shoulders, one slowly after the other. There was a collection of onlookers that looked at the ceremony with pride on their faces.

"Now recite the paladin's oath." The king said to the woman before him.

"As a paladin, I am sworn to valor. My heart will know only virtue, my blade will defend the helpless, my might will uphold the weak, my word will speak only truth, and my wrath will undo the wicked." the woman said a smile growing on her face.

"Then rise, lady Elwin, and take your place alongside Lumara's paladins." said Cornelius as he sheathed his gleaming sword.

Elwin stood proudly with the smile that occupied most of her face. Arctutus got to shake her hand as the other group of guests bombarded her with praises and cheers. Arcturus was reminded of his own ceremony, of Selina running over to him, hugging him deeply as tears of happiness cascaded down her perfect cheeks. Now he felt all alone, staring emptily ahead as the guests drained out of the room.

Cornelius made his way over to Arcturus. "If it isn't my favorite paladin!" he clapped a hand on Arcturus' shoulder. "My heart soars to see you again, Arcturus. Tales of your valor are not enough to explain what you've done for our city. The way you've plunged your blade through that monster's eye...tell me again how it felt to end the beast's life."

"Good."

The king shrugged at the lifeless reply he got. "Good? That's all? Hardly inspires the same courage I hear in the taverns!"

Arcturus had nothing to say. Even the king noticed his brooding mood, so he looked past Arcturus to the departing guests. "You know what I love most about these celebrations? Each one is a chance to get another one like you! Now imagine what we can achieve if I have a full squad of heroes like you; men who fell from the sky, who overcame crippling injuries, who ended dragons ten times bigger than them!"

Noticing Arcturus' silence, the king quickly shifted his feet and led Arcturus over to the window overlooking Entis. "Alas, mere talk of better times is not why you are here." Cornelius turned toward Arcturus as his face grew stern. "We received word of a dragon that's flying loose around one of our villages." Cornelius sighed. "The beast has destroyed a house, kidnapped a little girl, and burned our valiant guards to cinders." he waved his hand. "The beast's foul deeds are all written in the report if you want to glance over it."

Arcturus felt his hands tighten up. "Why me, sire? Surely you can find another slayer who can go after the beast."

"Ah, but that's the problem. Arcturus is but one man."

"A man who's had his fill of dragons!" Arcturus immediately lowered his voice. "Apologies. I have overstepped."

The king's eyes filled with pity. Arcturus remembered those eyes from the night Dread Flame attacked. "I am aware of what that monster took from you Arcturus. I would not wish this fate to befall anyone. It is a cruel, cruel thing to watch your own family wither before your eyes..." The king looked back to the city. "But for this task I would have no other man. Your legacy lives in you! Your family is the best at hunting down the vile monsters that darken our world and steal the smiles off our children's faces. I shudder to think of what else we can lose if another dragon happens upon the city."

The king turned back towards Arcturus. "Please. Before you make your decision, think of the families that live in that village, robbed off their guards, crippled by fear. Would they deserve a second-rate hunter to deliver them from the terror of the monster that haunts their nights?" The king tilted his head to the side, causing Arcturus to shake his head. "If our man fails to accomplish his task, everyone in that village will die. Dragons are not merciful like we are, and when provoked...well, you've seen first hand the gruesome things they are capable of."

Despite knowing the king as a friend, Arcturus admired how well Cornelius understood him. He was a man that saw the spirit, not the armor and flesh that made a man who he was.

"What kind of dragon are we talking about? I would have more than vague mentions." Arcturus said.

"The beast is said to have scales of fire, with piercing eyes of sapphire."

"A fire-breathing dragon, then?" Arcturus said coolly. "This cannot be a mere coincidence."

"Exactly what I'm afraid of. This whelp can belong to DreadFlame's clutch, seeking vengeance in the name of his father."

Arcturus gritted his jaws so hard they hurt, focusing to try and wipe his mind of the image of Dread Flame looming menacingly over him. "That is a risk we cannot take. What resources will I have to bring the beast down?"

"I want you to assemble a team of apt men." Cornelius waved a hand. "Do not even think about the price, I want only the best to accompany you in this task. We will be assigning a vessel to you as well. The Indomitous carries a dozen men and has enough firepower to slay dozens of these beasts. I shall have it placed in your command, to do as you see fit."

Arcturus nodded. The ship would definitely come in handy, especially with its beam cannons. "As for the men, I will need a team of shieldguards, or a party of adventurers who know at least the basics of dragon slaying, fire resistant armors and ropes, energy crossbows, and traps."

Cornelius clapped his hands together. "Done! Although there is something else I would ask of you. Something that might make your task a bit more difficult."

"What?" Arcturus asked.

"I want the beast brought back alive."

"Alive?!" Arcturus exclaimed in shock, a little angrier than he intended. "It was hard enough to slay Dread Flame, and now you want me to bring his offspring all the way here?"

Cornelius raised a hand. "I merely wish for my citizens to see that even a dragon cannot stand up to the might of our army. They have lived in fear of dragons long enough for superstitions to run rampant through the taverns. We need to quench the rumors that dragons are stronger than us, Arcturus."

"Didn't they get a taste of a dragon's pain when I slew Dread Flame two years ago?"

"Ah yes, of course they did," Cornelis spoke quickly. "But between you and I." the king placed a hand over his mouth and spoke in a whisper, "Morale has been wavering lately, and we need to reinforce the belief that our city stands strong no matter what creature smashes itself against our walls. I believe this vile beast's capture, and eventual humiliation, will provide us exactly what we need, not to mention we will make it answer for the hundreds of crimes it and its vile kin committed against our people. We shall hold trial, then perhaps...a public gathering to witness the beast's helplessness first hand. I would look into its teary eyes as it squirms for freedom, and deny it, over and over again, until every flicker of fight leaves its body."

"Your word, my hands." Arcturus nodded sternly.

"Excellent!" The king cheered. "I will pick the best men for the job. I suggest you pack with haste, for you will leave immediately. Now let Delvin and I discuss your supplies."

"As you wish, sire."

"Hunt well, Arcturus. We'll shake hands when the beast stands on our soil!"

Arcturus began to leave, but was stopped by a firm hand from father Devlin, who thrust a scroll into his hands.

"All of the information you will need, Arcturus." He smiled. "I know you won't let us down."

Arcturus nodded, and wished the two farewell as he made his way out of the castle and back to the city below. As he walked, he unwrapped the manila colored scroll, avoiding the other people, careful to side step around the numerous obstructions that arose in his path. His eyes were drawn to the name of the village in question, Deet. Arcturus stopped and tried to remember why the village sounded so familiar to him. He thought for a moment before it came to him. A while ago, he had swayed the village leaders at the time to join Lumara rather than stand in their way. Arcturus frowned as he remembered the clang of steel and the smell of death that the conflict with Rothdell had brought. He placed the grisly war back into his mind as he continued to read the scroll in his hands. He noticed that the report revealed the testimonies of the present guards and the rough description of the red dragon. The image of a great dragon with sharp teeth, razor like claws, and terrible fire filled his mind. He looked up to get that image out of his head, barely avoiding a sign that was shaped like a gear. Arcturus quickly rolled up the parchment and opened the bronze covered door of the building.

Immediately, his nose was assaulted with the smell of oil, burning fumes, and something he did not recognize but of an equally gruesome tint. The room was filled with knickknacks and devices whose purposes were lost on a man like him; a mere warrior who wore the armor crafted by wiser hands. Some were small in all various shapes roughly the size of his palm, while some dangled from the ceiling with multiple limbs that looked more like a giant spider than any metal thing he had ever seen. With his first step into the cluttered place, a bell chimed rather loudly, even louder than the sound of gears that filled the room.

"I'll be with you in a moment!" came a high-pitched voice that definitely belonged to a female, which he instantly recognized as Matilda's.

With a small explosion from the back room, a burst of smoke, and toppling of what was most likely a stool, a small woman entered covered in soot, cursing silently under her breath. She was a gnome, goggles strapped to her onyx hair. Her face was not too old, but had lines of late nights and signs of experience. What started as a neutral expression on her face turned into a warm smile at the sight of the man that entered her shop.

"Arcturus my dear! You should have said it was you!" she exclaimed, "I mistook you for dear ole Fergus that came to remind me to fix his darn glasses." She turned to a cylinder-like device on the wall, and pulled its brass handle. "Care for some tea?" she said, grabbing two cups. There were small wisps of steam rolling up from the surface of the liquid.

"Some other time, perhaps. I came to check on the armor you were making for me. The mission I am embarking upon requires your exquisite craft."

Matilda had a frown flash across her face for a second before placing the tea cups back and clapping her hands together with a smile. "You know... I totally forgot to send word about that. Can't tell you how many things I tend to forget these days." She laughed, grabbing his hand and starting to pull him towards the back room. "Come oooon! You've got to see it! The armor is all finished and in pristine condition. Come, come!"

Arcturus followed Matilda as she tugged him into the next room. He was always surprised by the strength she always showed, much greater than her size led to believe. She led him down a hallway, down some wooden steps, into a well-lit basement. Arcturus had to look twice to the torches that lit the place to observe that, instead of fire, stood small mana crystals. Matilda stopped before the suit of armor, a white sheet draped over it. She let go of his hands and clasped the sheet with her small fingers. "Presenting, one of a kind, Matilda's Marvelous Mechanical Production!" she then pulled free the sheet, letting it fall to the ground to reveal her marvelous creation.

It was a set of full plate bearing no marks of a particular house or even a crafter. It was metallic silver that perfectly reflected the room around them, with a barbute helm that had its visor down.

"Well, what do you think?" Matilda asked, her voice shuddering with pride. "Is she not the most beautiful suit of armor your eyes have ever seen?"

"It looks...outstanding! But doesn't it look exactly like my suit of armor back at home? The similarities are quite...how to put it? Rather...striking, one would say."

"NO! No, they're neither this or that!" Matilda shouted, her brow scrunching up in anger. "That's an insult if I ever heard one so vile. Armor is not like a dress, to judge with eyes alone! Pick up a piece and feel it before you start babbling about!" She crossed her arms and began to mutter to herself.

Arcturus took the armguards off the suit and felt them in his hand. They were smooth to the touch, slightly cold, and missing buckles for the black leather straps. He noticed a small gear engraving near the elbow. "Why didn't you include any buckles? How could it possibly fit me? And what makes it so light?"

"The paladin finally realizes the armor's intricate beauty." Matilda said, the smile returning to her face. "Infused the metal with mithril. Makes it light as a feather but harder than steel. As for your straps problem," she laughed, "try pressing the gear and see what happens."

Arcturus did what Matilda said, and found the leather straps hanging loose. He looked to Matilda who held up a hand and waved for him to continue. His fingers grazed the engraving to find blue runes light up all over the armor as it started to segment and shape itself to his arm. The leather straps receded until they fit firm, but not too tight to feel uncomfortable. The hand portion conformed to the exact fit of his hand, with segmented plates forming over his fingers much like the scales of a dragon. Arcturus clenched his hand into a fist, amazed that he could hardly feel the armor at all. "This is amazing!" he said, turning to his friend. "How could you achieve something like this?"

"Just a special order from a friend. Who wouldn't want a self-fitting armor that hardly weighs a thing? Plus, it's also resistant to fire, which makes it the most desired item against dragons and what not." Matilda blurted out so fast

Arcturus barely understood what she said.

"Whoa...this must have cost way more than I paid." he said softly.

"Think nothing of it. Or better, consider it a gift from a friend." said Matilda.

"Thank you." he smiled. "I...don't know what else to say other than how amazing you are when you put your tools to the right purpose."

"I knooooow!" Matilda giggled. "But I'm curious about one thing. What will you be using it for?" she asked, raising an eyebrow. "It's dragons, right? Actually, I really hope it's something else, but y'know, fire breathing and all..."

Arcturus' smile vanished from his face. "The king wants me to hunt down a dragon that might or might not be one of Dread Flame's offspring."

Matilda let out a small gasp.

"Alive."

She gasped again.

"Yeah...I had the same reaction, minus the gasping. Cornelius wants to make an example out of the beast. To remind the city that we are more than scared rats waiting for a dragon to swoop down upon us."

"He isn't wrong. Many people still talk about the night when...you know...anyway, where is this vile creature?" she asked. "Have any whereabouts of its location?"

Arcturus sighed. "A small village to the north-western border. It's a red, just like...you know. Probably male, though I don't know for certain until I find it."

"What if it's not?"

"What, male?"

"Mhm!" Matilda nodded her head. "Females are worse at fighting, right? Easier to catch."

"Hardly," Arcturus found himself chuckle. "Male or female, it will be a struggle to subdue it without making full use of our arsenal. Our king would not have the beast expire before he has the chance to parade it through the city as a symbol of human endurance in the face of their greatest enemy, so we have to be gentle in how we capture it."

"That's twisted." Matilda scrunched her face.

"I know, but in a weird way, I believe Cornelius is right," Arcturus said. "These beasts prey on fear and deceit. If we show the people of this city that we can stand up to them, maybe...we can win this war."

"Maybe."

Arcturus had to admit, for a person that was shocked to learn about another dragon attack, Matilda recovered rather quickly. The witty gnome put her hands on her hips and started bossing him around. For several minutes, she showed him how to put each piece of his armor on until she soon found herself smacking his armored back plate out the door.

"Be careful now! You best not let that dragon scratch you too much, or kill you!" she shouted to him. "I have a reputation to keep!"

"Don't worry, I don't intend to do any dying anytime soon!" He laughed back to her, placing the helmet on his head.

Arcturus returned to his house to gather his belongings. He figured the king would supply what he requested, so Arcturus picked up his leather pack, a black belt with a small pack of marbles, a brown cloak with the symbol of a paladin stitched into it -an eagle holding a sword in one claw and a book in the other, then his scabbard. He latched that one to his belt before gathering up his trusty sword. Arcturus gave it a few practice swings, feeling the familiar grip and warmth spread to his fingertips.

I can't believe I'm doing this again, he thought, then grabbed his energy crossbow, placing it in a holster strapped to his right side.

With that done, Arcturus walked over to his cabinet. He looked quickly through the cupboards to find two vials of semi-clear red liquid inside of them. He closed his eyes and thought to Selina and Geoffrey. How he wished he had one of these when he had returned home. He gave a small sigh before he placed the potions carefully in a pouch on his belt labeled with a small red caduceus. The last thing he grabbed before shoving a hundred feet of rope into his pack was his sacred shield, swinging the thing over his shoulder by the leather strap before buckling it.

With his gear in place, Arcturus prepared to head out, then stopped when he saw a picture of Selina, looking as if to wish him farewell, like she had always done in the past.

"Oh, my dear, beloved wife...what has the world come to?" He sighed, picking up the picture carefully. He could feel his heart begin to ache painfully, so he gently set the memento down and looked away,

"Why do I keep these things when they only serve to torment me?" He said to himself aloud. "The past is already written. There's nothing I can do to change it...except look towards the future." A stern frown took hold of the paladin's face. "Don't worry, my heart," he said softly as he turned walk out of his home, "I will hunt that dragon down and make sure he gets exactly what he deserves for his heinous crimes."

Arcturus grabbed the knob of his door, finding that it felt a tad different than what he got used to. He felt a small tingle start at the base of his feet, slowly working its way up his leg, along his spine, and finally to his head. He turned his head back to look at the place he called home, wondering if this would be the last time he would ever set eyes upon it.

"Farewell." Arcturus said, then took upon the road with brisk steps.

His walk to the docks was anything but slow. Though a few people called his name or saluted him, nobody got in his way. Arcturus looked to the sky. The sun started to fall over the western mountains, casting a long shadow over anything it touched. Orange and red clouds stretched across the sky. Arcturus remembered his mother had told him that these were a sign of tough roads ahead. He had argued with her so fiercely. After all, how could something so beautiful bring trouble and strife? She just chuckled and picked his brain further. Arcturus had replied without missing a beat that it meant good luck, fortune, and anything your heart longed for.

How quickly those times had passed. It almost felt like yesterday, when he ate a warm meal together with his wife, when he heard the joyous laughter of his child...

Arcturus was brought out of his memory when the clamor intensified around him. He was already at the docks, and the ship laying in front of his eyes was one of the largest vessels that he had ever seen. She stretched out at least twice as large as the first Destiny had been, with large propellers hanging off her, unmoving slabs of metal standing vigilant until they were called to spring her aloft into the sky.

The Indomitous was painted brown like all vessels of Lumara, with a mural of a gryphon at the front of her port and starboard sides. Atop her deck stood at least twelve shining energy cannons with numerous crew members shuffling about in dark brown uniforms. The ship had a ramp stretching down from her midsection to the dock below. From the ramp came a group of humans clad in dark red leathers, swords strapped to their belts, crossbows at the hip, and shields around their backs.

After a quick introduction, the soldiers picked up their collective things and boarded the vessel in silence. Arcturus was the last one to climb the ramp, knowing the worry he spotted on their faces. No matter the supplies, no matter the experience a soldier had, few things could prepare you for the encounter with a dragon. Arcturus had been lucky in that regard. He grew up learning about dragons, even if most of those teachings focused on the various ways to end a dragon's life. When it came his turn to face a beast like that, Arcturus was far from afraid. He thought to the long grueling days of training filled with many aches, cuts, and bruises, a journey that led him to this day, when he would put another dent in Dread Flame's legacy.

"Excuse me."

Arcturus turned to an aged man with a scant amount of hair on his head. To him, it looked as if the hair had simply migrated to the man's mustache. The man twirled the bushy thing that seemed to take up the majority of his face.

The man held out his rough hand, easily dwarfing Arcturus' hand. "It is truly an honor to be in your presence, sir. And to work with you, of course."

"Likewise...Captain," Arcturus looked for the man's rank on his collar.

"Fredrick Ruthgar." The man said, his barrel of a chest swelling with pride. "Captain of the Indomitous, with over a dozen victories over Rothdell at the helm."

A silence filled the air, as he expected Arcturus to be clapping or cheering. He soon coughed into his fist.

"Anyway, let me show you to your quarters, paladin. We have quite the journey ahead of us, eh?"

"It's not the first time I'm sent to hunt down a dragon."

"And probably not the last," Frederick added. "Rest. I would have your mind sharp for when the time comes to face the beast."

Arcturus allowed the captain to lead him below the deck, his mind as silent as his lips. The engines of the ship started purring. A strange sense of serenity washed over him. With Frederick in charge of an experienced crew, Arcturus felt liberated of the burden of choice. As he lay in his bed, his mind ventured not to the beast, but to the vast skies his ship threaded upon, a realm far removed from the torment he suffered in the city that became smaller with each passing moment.

Chapter 4: Draconic Heroics

Veledar's wings carried him swiftly through the air. He pierced the fluffy clouds that stuck to him in the form of watery beads, startling any bird that dared to get too close to him. Ahead of him stretched the small human village he visited before, during his quest to recover his lost book. It had taken him a few days to work up the strength to return to the place where he made a fool of himself, but to Veledar, the book was far more important than his pride, even if he'd never admit that to anybody.

Veledar felt his muscles tighten when he replayed the events in his mind. He could've slain all the guards and wrecked the entire village, an option that remained available even now, but Veledar knew better than to give in to such basic impulses. He had to resist the urge to smash buildings for just a simple theft. He thought back to the days he spent around his lair, hunting, swimming, and even flying, while his mind focused on that human woman that had dared steal from him. It had taken several attempts of looking into his mirror to strike up a pose that, he figured, would not inspire fear in the humans. Veledar found such a simple task deceptively difficult, especially for such a great dragon like himself. Why, every feature on his body looked like a potential weapon: the spikes on his back, his broad tail that ended with a leaf-shaped tip, even his horns could impale somebody! Veledar had no mind for killing though. No. He deserved something far better. He imagined a gathering of humans, with their soft, fat faces praising him for being so polite, sympathizing for the loss of his beloved book. He thought that, perhaps, they would even bring that woman to justice. This line of thought brought a smirk to the red dragon's face, although he reminded himself not get too deep into his own fantasies. More often than not, reality turned out to be completely different.

The dragon tilted his wings to make a slight turn down towards the village. The small buildings grew larger with each wing flap. Small houses made of wood, of various shapes and rough sizes, made the village look like a collection of half cut stumps to Veledar. The amalgamation of human dens was spread out in random directions and only connected by a dirt road that was beaten down with the passing of too many hooves. He started to correct his flight as the center of this mess came into view. The dragon stretched his hind legs first, then landed with a spray of dirt and rocks, quickly followed by the most annoying sound a creature could conjure:human screams.

"Dragon! There's a focken dragon!"

"It's the red bastard again! He's back-back to finish what he started!"

Veledar's snout scrunched as more men joined in to point fingers at him and shout derogatory terms. This was definitely not the sort of reception he expected. Not when he landed so properly in their midst.

So Veledar drew his head back and unleashed a deafening roar to silence the unruly crowd. What a mistake, to think the humans had more than rocks in their hollow heads. As he looked around, his disappointment only grew further as the cowards sprinted to hide behind piles of hay, water troughs, wooden poles, and just about anything that would fit. The brave ones stood their ground, loud and red with fury.

"Leave us, Gods be damned!"

"We don't wan' ya here!"

"Aye! Don't need your kind causing any more problems, ye wretched scaled beast!"

"Wait. Hold on. I-" Veledar covered himself with a wing as the mob dwarfed his voice. "I don't mean you any harm, you rowdy simpletons!" he growled again, then sat upright on his haunches. "I actually came here to-" one of his horns caught a banner hanging overhead as he turned his head.

"Grarrrr," Veledar tugged the blue banner in frustration, breaking off the frail thing from the building it was attached to.

And it still remained locked around his horn.

"Let go, accursed piece of inanimate cloth!" Veledar sucked up his hiss of frustration as he flailed his head around.

But the banner was stubborn, stronger than he realized. The dragon couldn't stop himself this time. He hissed loudly in frustration as he bowed down his head and scraped the blasted thing off with a forepaw. The banner crumpled under his claws into the pile of crap it deserved to be. Veledar breathed in and out as he looked with satisfaction to the shredded remains of the banner before he stomped them into oblivion.

"As I was saying, I don't mean any harm, humans. I simply think we got off on the wrong claw the other day-"

"Oy! Red scales!" A new voice joined the mumbling crowd. "That was me mum's banner you just trashed! What she ever do to you, to disrespect her work like that?"

Veledar narrowed his eyes at the peasant, a simple farmer dressed in a brown tunic and frayed leather leggings. "That banner attacked me first! You've seen it. You've all seen how viciously it refused to let go even when I asked!"

The mumbling picked up. Some humans looked at him like he lost his mind, while others smiled and chuckled to themselves.

"As I was saying, before the banner got in the way of things, I came here to discuss the theft that happened at my lair a few days ago."

"Did you hear that? The dragon says he hates Gerald's mum!" shouted a woman hiding behind a wooden post.

"Heard'im too, spouting hatred and callin' it honey!" another man answered.

"Oh, shut it Voskren. I never really liked the crone, always naggin' about me debts! I'd rather hug the focken dragon than work with that old hag again!" replied another man.

"Aye! I can attest to that too! She never gave anyone fair prices. Y'know, mayhap this be a sign from the gods, to bring dragon here an' rid us of the crone's greedy fingers!"

"Are you hit in the head? This beast isn't here to help us. He's here to pillage and destroy until there's nothing left but dust!"

"Focus and listen, you chatty monkeys!" Veledar hissed in irritation. "I'm not here to fulfill your weird prophecies, and I am even less qualified to act like a mediator for whatever menial issues you have between yourselves. I wanted to talk about the theft that happened in my cave a few days ago! That's all."

"How warm you speak," an old woman walked slowly towards him, aiming her cane at his head. "You destroyed a house for no reason. Attacked a girl in her home. Harmed her father while she watched. Oh, if you would see her crying...her cheeks still wet from all the tears she shed even after you left."

"Attacked? I did no such thing, you ill-speaking fossil!" Veledar turned to lock eyes with the old woman, his nostrils flaring with irritation. "The wall simply got in the way. Maybe you should make your homes bigger, so that a polite dragon doesn't have face such problems again."

"Aye? An' who pays for all the work? You?"

"I don't mind, as long as you rename the village in my name." A toothy smile spread along Veledar's snout. "And maybe build a gate engraved with my likeness. Or should it be a statue? I think a statue fits me much better. Right here in the center, where everybody can marvel at the fine looks of Crimson Sky, slayer of poverty, beloved of the people!"

The crowd burst into the loudest, longest fit of laughter Veledar had the misfortune of hearing. He didn't stop them this time. Instead, he looked around at the growing crowd of people that was starting to get far too close for his liking.

"I do love a cult, but you're all starting to get a bit too close for my liking."

"Only to see ya betta!"

Cheers accompanied the brave fool's words.

Veledar didn't buy that. "Aren't you afraid of what damage I can inflict to your feeble little bodies if you anger me?"

"Na we're not!"

"Because," a man clad in a guard's uniform continued. "We all heard the tales of how this Crimson whatever you call yourself turned tail and ran from our mighty guard force."

Veledar closed his eyes as yet another collection of laughter filtered through the crowd.

"Crimson Sky! Hah, more like the fearful strawberry!"

"Shiverin' Raspberry sounds betta cause the scales look like a-"

Veledar had enough of this barbaric nonsense. He flared his wings, then bounded towards the guard who instigated this feast of insults.

"Listen here, you pink little worm. I restrained myself from turning your valiant defense into armored steaks, but my patience wears thin, and your lack of respect slowly makes me reconsider the wisdom of my choices."

"Oh G-god," The man started sobbing. "Pppp-please, don't kill me, oh mighty dragon. I'll-I'll clean your scales. Polish your claws! Just please don't kill meeeeeee!"

"I might hold onto your promises," Veledar got off the man, then helped him onto his feet. "See?" he turned towards the townsfolk as the man dusted himself off with a blessed smile on his face. "I can be reasonable to those who behave themselves."

"He's bloody right!" The guard stammered. "This dragon is good!"

"Bull's piss!"

"I don' believe tha'!"

"Don't listen to them." The guard hugged one of Veledar's forepaws. "Talk to me. Anything you need, anything you want, I'm the man for the job."

An obedient pet was not what he had in mind, so Veledar gently pushed the man away. "I'm searching for the vile woman that stole my book! She's the mother of the girl I allegedly attacked, though I swear by my fine scales I did no such thing."

"The woman whose house you destroyed?" a man shouted.

"Damaged!" Veledar growled, "That thieving, manner-less female stole a possession of mine and I demand it returned at once."

No suitable answers came until an older man joined the fray. "You there!

Why are you tormenting my guards like that?"

Veledar turned his snout to see a man walk towards him in a suit of clanky, shining metal armor. He carried a sword and shield, and he was flanked by at least a dozen more guards with spears and crossbows. "I say again, dragon whatever your name is, what manner of ill curses have you inflicted upon my guard there?"

Veledar hissed with amusement. "I was telling your minion here that my property was stolen by a woman that lives here, in your village."

"Which woman is that?" the man asked, raising one of his large grey eyebrows.

"The one that lives near the edge of town, in the house I...allegedly damaged, though it was nothing more than a slight dent. Barely noticeable."

"You mean Jizrah?" The captain scratched through his beard. "She has been gone long before her house got smashed to pieces. Left poor Vern here 'lone with his daughter. You accuse her of thievery?"

"I do," Veledar groaned. "I assure you that human woman is a mischievous, selfish thief that got on the wrong side of a dragon. Now, would you kindly point me in the direction she went? I would like to talk to her privately."

"I won't obey your instructions, dragon. You come here to our peaceful town in a rampage, destroying houses, wrecking banners, threatening guards! Makes me believe you have nothing but ill intentions hidin' beneath your those shiny scales of yours!"

Veledar strolled towards the man. People parted before him like water, muttering praise and insults alike. He had been polite, and though some smarter individuals appreciated his arrival, most of the mob still saw him like pestilence incarnated. How thick were they? Haven't they understood he could burn them all to cinders?

"Now you listen here, white beard." Veledar stuck his snout into the valiant captain's face. "I have been nothing but polite and infinitely patient with your angry mob, while your people have responded with only with rudeness and intolerance. That aggravates me, but no more than safeguarding a thief who stole from me!"

Veledar snorted angrily as the captain stood his ground. "Do you forget that a dragon stands before you? That I can, with but a simple yawn, unleash true devastation upon this village?" His eyes narrowed on the man who gulped emptily, his blue eyes filling with genuine worries. Veledar knew he overstepped again by using fear to persuade these people, but there was simply no other way to get past their inferior intellect.

"Now humans, all I seek is a thief. Provide me with her whereabouts and I shall take my leave in peace, just like I did when I first arrived here." he shouted, flaring wings and thrashing his tail, smashing a water trough in two.

"She went s-south, towards the capital! Please stop destroying my mum's store!" shouted the mumbling man others referred to as Gerald.

Veledar turned towards the man. "Where can I find this capital? How far is it from here?"

"I dunno, I dunno!" the man gulped, "Best I figure it's about two weeks travel by horse. Just follow the road south! You can't miss it!"

"Ya! Has floating castles and such!" shouted another person from the crowd. "Hard to miss for a dragon."

"See? Was this any harder than throwing petty insults at me?" With a flap of his wings, Veledar once more found himself back into the tranquil realm of the high skies, thankful to be away from that boisterous group of miscreants. He was also grateful for the amount of self-control he exhibited under duress. A few days ago, he would've surely unleashed his wrath upon the village.

While he flew, Veledar wondered how big this capital was. He had never ventured deep into human controlled lands, but he figured anything man-made couldn't be much bigger than that village. Still, the floating castles posed a few problems.

If they are even real, Veledar shook his snout and laughed at that simple joke, for not even dragons had floating castles, and he was certain one of his kind would've built such a thing.

It wasn't long before his eyes spotted the rough dirt path the man had spoken about. It stretched as far as his eyes could see, winding the earth like a serpent. Veledar felt bad for the humans that had to take the long and slow path, but he quickly shrugged it off with another beat of his wings.

Minutes later he found himself miles along the path stretched out before him. His eyes fell to a rather large green hill covered in a sea of flowers. However, what stood apart from the multicolored flora drew his attention. From the tree line came a figure running for its life. Arrows zipped past her, barely missing the flowing brown cloak that flew behind her back. The figure made it several hundred feet before at least two dozen other humanoids came in fast pursuit. They were hooting and cheering as they bounded through fields after their prey. They soon had the brown cloaked person surrounded with weapons drawn. Veledar could see that they were talking, but he knew not of what. He circled overhead as the cloaked figure removed their hood to reveal a brown-haired female.

The woman found herself beset on by all sides as the crowd closed in with sharp blades and even sharper grins on their faces. The woman seemed to be holding her own with a series of flips and kicks to the jaw that caused some thug to collapse to the ground a bloody mess. She pulled out a rapier to cross blades with the few that would have struck her, then laughed loudly as her rapier found its mark, to hide the fear that Veledar could smell. He honestly was surprised that nobody spotted him.

However, the woman's victory streak seemed to be coming to a close as a blade nicked her shoulder. A solid fist collided with her gut, knocking the wind out of her with a gasp, then another took her on the side of the head. She collapsed to the ground as the men closed in to mock her in their usual sneering voices.

"Awwww, what's the matter, Lyndis? Where is that smart mouth now? Bleeding all over the place?" one of the men laughed, spraying his spittle all over the ground.

"You're the ones who'll bleed!" The woman grunted. Lyndis sprung up to stab the man through the chest with her rapier. She flipped over his dumbstruck face, but when her feet hit the ground now stood four of her copies. They all moved hair from their faces to reveal small pointed ears.

"Fock's sake! Nobody told me the bloody half elf was a mage!" another man shouted as they rushed the four standing half elves. Veledar chuckled to himself as the warrioress sprung from man to man. Her attackers seemed unable to spot the real half elf amongst the copies, but Veledar of course had spotted the real one right off the bat. It was all a matter of close examination, for the copies of the half elf could not land a blow, lest it caused them to vanish, so Lyndis was having them duck, dodge, and jump around the frustrated thugs. Through all the chaos, she would get in a good stab, and a man would collapse to the ground in a pile of screams and blood.

"I got her!" came a cry from a thug as his sword struck her shoulder. Lyndis gasped aloud as her illusions vanished under her lack of concentration. The man followed with a punch to her face, causing her to fall to the ground.

"You're a feisty bitch, lass, but your games end now," the man breathed heavily at the bleeding Lyndis. He turned his head to the side to spit out some blood.

"Well, ye can go get yerself bent," Lyndis groaned back. "Only took twenty four of ya to get me, ya bloody small cocked bastards-"

The man slapped her in the face to silence her vile tongue.

"You know, before we be getting this one to the boss, I figure we should have a little bit of fun." One person hissed, to which the others chuckled and nodded in agreement.

"Don't worry, princess," the man said, putting a rough hand to her chin. "We won't go too hard on ya. Gotta preserve whatever prettiness we can for the boss."

Veledar had enough. Fighting to the death was fine as long as the person deserved it. However, to violate the other person was simply crossing a line. With a flare of his nostrils and a swell of heroic pride, he swooped in and landed behind the man. Veledar smiled as the collected survivors of Lyndis backed away in terror as he spread his wings and unleashed a loud, angry roar. They stood before him like cowering rats, their faces draining of color, their hands tightening over their weapons, and dread filling their eyes.

"Well boys, seems your moment of fun has come to an end. Maybe if you wouldn't have laughed like snorting pigs, my partner wouldn't have heard your squeals." Lyndis laughed in a series of coughs, then, with the other men distracted, she twisted free of her captive's grasp and in one fluid motion she pulled a hidden dagger and sunk it deep into the leader's skull. With a dull thud, and a quick gasp of pain, the man collapsed dead onto the ground.

Veledar watched as the men barely cared for their leader's fall. Instead of running, like common humans, they charged him. They carried their weapons high as they bellowed in false bravery. With a flick of his red tail, Veledar let loose a deep breath of orange and red flame that enveloped six of the charging men in its fury. They collapsed in screams as the fires consumed their burning bodies. Veledar bounded from the rest, brushing them aside with his scales.

"Retreat!" one of the men cried. Veledar had to admit. This might have been the smartest thing one of them said so far. The man looked around to find that he was the last one there, as his compatriots had left him the moment Veledar had incinerated the stupid six. "Wait for me, you focking cunts!" The man shouted as he sprinted for the trees. Veledar considered chasing the man down and ending him, but in a way, it was better to let him spread word of his greatness. He turned back towards Lyndis, for despite this show of force, she was still standing before him.

She did not move as her messy hair waved with the wind and her eyes of amber locked onto his movements. "Nice work. Wha'd you want?" She asked.

"A simple thank you would be enough," he said, striking a rather regal pose. "I did rescue you from a real bind, have I not?"

"I think I dispatched more of them than you, dragon." She smirked, limping over to one of the dead men and rifling through his pouches. "Name's Lyndis Kuxion. What should I call my valiant rescuer?"

"Crimson Sky, terror of thugs and slayer of unwashed men." Veledar beamed with his great white teeth.

"Very well." Lyndis spoke curtly.

Veledar moved closer to her. "Hey, would you be able to satisfy a curiosity of mine? Why were those thugs after you?"

"Well..." she started to say, cutting a pouch from another man. "Beat this group's boss to a job, took his share of the treasure when I learned what exact kind of man he was, then kinda pissed on his name. You can imagine he wasn't very happy to have his reputation smeared through filth. He's lucky to get latrine duties now."

"And what kind of job would this be? You don't see many mages doing back flips like you showed back there."

"Nope. Maybe not," Lyndis said. "I like to think of myself as an adventurer, thrill seeker, sometimes a sword for hire. If you need something gotten, I can also do that."

Veledar noted the swell of pride in her voice.

"You sound like a thief!" he snorted.

"I am very well not." Lyndis laughed. "Where were you off to anyway, oh brave and beautiful Crimson Sky? We don't see many dragons around these parts."

"I'm-" Veledar stumbled over his words for a moment. "Yeah, I'm off to retrieve a thief that has stolen something of great importance to me."

"Do you know where they headed? Maybe I can help you find them. For a price of course." Lyndis moved over to loot another dead scoundrel.

"They say she went to the capital of this land, located somewhere in the south." said Veledar as he shifted a paw through the flowers. For all the bravery and majesty he inspired in Lyndis, exposing such a blatant lack of knowledge made him feel exposed. Lesser, somewhat.

"Entis?" the woman's eyes widened briefly before they narrowed down to the same confident look. "You can count me focking out then, dragon. Unless you want to live the rest of your life in chains or get your head parted from your body, I would suggest you count whatever was stolen gone." Lyndis wiped her blade clean of blood, then sheathed it back at her hip.

"And let them get away with stealing from me? Do you realize how that sounds? To a dragon?" he said as he moved his tail, ready to thrash the ground. "Might as well tell me to cut off my own wings."

"Aye. I imagine how bitter defeat sounds on that big boastful tongue. However, I am talking about real danger here, not whatever distorted scenarios you created in your mind. This is not a quest that ends in victory, but then again I guess you haven't even heard what happened to the last dragon that went against Lumara." Lyndis said, pulling out a brush and running it through her hair.

"Lumara? Where is this thing you speak of?" Veledar asked, puzzled.

Lyndis rolled her eyes at the dragon's ignorance. "This land is called Lumara, and the last dragon was killed by some veteran going by the name of Arcturus Lund. Word on the street says he's quite the dragon slayer."

"One mortal doesn't scare me." Veledar snorted in dismissal.

Lyndis gritted her jaws. "This one should. Didn't you just hear what I said?

Dragon slayer."

"Can you see me trembling?" Veledar snorted again.

"Fine. What about millions of trained humans? And flying machines? And gryphons that can hunt you down no matter where you flee? I suggest you return home and count yourself lucky the king didn't put a bounty on your head." She looked towards the forest. "We've spoken enough about this matter. If you're as smart as you look, you will consider my words before you do anything foolish." she stated. "It was pleasant to meet you, Crimson Sky. I honestly hope you will quit this silly crusade. It would be a shame to lose a dragon so quick to jump to a lady's rescue," she smirked, "even if she doesn't really need it."

Veledar watched the lady leave as he settled comfortably on his belly to contemplate his next move. Flying castles? Dragon slayers? Gryphons? Flying Machines? This place was sounding worse every time he learned something new about it. Worst of all, it was starting to sound like this place actually existed, and was not just a simple story from a peasant told to mislead him.

Veledar closed his eyes and tried to imagine what his mother would say at a time like this. She had always been the best at dealing with the lesser races, although she always interacted more with elves than with humanity, or this place called Lumara. The dragon frowned. He knew exactly what she would have said to him. His thoughts turned instead to the dragon slayer. This Lund character sounded familiar. Not the person, of course, but the name. He was certain he had heard it before, maybe in a story or two when he was but a hatchling.

The dragon shook his head. The sun moved a bit in the sky, and Lyndis was nowhere to be seen. Realizing he spent too long on this hill surrounded by corpses, Veledar spread his wings and returned home, the only environment where he felt confident to make the right decision.

Chapter 5: To Capture a Dragon

Arcturus stood on the deck of the Indomitous, watching the men assigned by the king -his men now- train for the upcoming task. He had demanded their best to ensure that minimum mistakes were made. He drilled them in a dragon's weak spots, reminded them how to disable the beast's fearsome breath, as well as how to best spread out if the dragon had the chance to unleash its fiery fury. This rigorous training made the sixty-hour journey pass in a blur for him. By the end of the fifty fifth hour, Arcturus was sure they would at least hold up against the dragon. He had instructed the men specifically on using the stun setting on the crossbow to avoid hurting the beast more than necessary. The bolas they brought, the weighted fire proof nets, flash bombs, and the other various gear he requested also had its part to play. Even so, the soldiers seemed to keep to themselves, away from the paladin, as if he bore some curse that could rub off on them. Arcturus didn't mind the extra distance. If anything, it allowed him to mentally prepare for the encounter with the dragon. He pictured the beast's movements, the lunges it was bound to make, preemptively plotting out his tumbles and dodges to best avoid the creature's inferno of a breath.

Dread Flame...it's been two years since I've stained my name and my blade with your unworthy life. Why do I feel your claws squeeze me ever tighter. Will I ever be rid of you? Am I even deserving of peace, when I failed my family?

Arcturus stared into the cloudy sky, the drifting clouds, the perfect picture of serenity. Thankfully, there had been no sign of storms on the way to the village, even if his mind felt like one. No matter where he ran, what he did, the memory of Dread Flame latched onto him at every turn. From time to time, he would hear what he would describe as the faint roar of a dragon in the distance, Arcturus knew it was not real. Each time he would shake his head, to convince himself the sound was a product of his tired mind, for no one else made any mention of it. Arcturus tossed it up to his nerves and went through various sword stances on the ship's deck. He stepped to each movement in tune with his heartbeat, letting his arms flow gracefully with each swing.

"Town in view!" a crew member shouted out, interrupting his rhythm. "Keep an eye out for the beast, men! Prepare for the fight of your lives!"

"This is what we've been training for!" Arcturus sheathed his sword into his scabbard and strode over to the wooden railing at the ship's front.

"Aye aye, sir."

"We'll show this dragon what happens when they mess with us!"

Arcturus put a faint smile on his face as he made his way through the soldiers that gathered by the railing. He patted their shoulders, shook hands, emboldened them with a few words to calm their undoubtedly racing hearts. Some of these men had never seen a village from above before, their honest fascination and glee reminding Arcturus of what it meant to live. To truly live.

The town was small from the air, relatively tiny compared to Entis, a sea of masterfully crafted buildings that seemed to stretch on for miles. The small roofs could already be seen like tiny pebbles on a clear floor of green. He only lingered on the sight for a moment before looking to the surrounding skyline, almost expecting to see the dragon descend upon the ship with its teeth bared.

"Ready up, men! The dragon doesn't care who inhabits this ship. In its eyes, we're all kindling for its flames. Prey to sink its deadly teeth into, So quit your staring, pack up your gear, and be ready to disembark at a moment's notice!"

Arcturus smiled as the men gave him a sharp salute before scrambling for their gear. He descended below deck with them to fetch a clipboard that had a list of questions he had prepared for the townsfolk who saw the dragon. He wondered how terrible of a beast this one would be, only to see Selina looking at him in his mind. Her eyes stared at him with the same familiarity Arcturus got used to whenever he his left home. He remembered how she had made him recite the paladin's oath before he left each time. It must have brought her comfort, he thought, to hear himself center his mind, his actions, and his beliefs.

So, as he picked up the pieces of his armor that Matilda had made for him, Arcturus began to recite his oath once more like he had always done for Selina.

"As a paladin, I am sworn to valor." He placed his leg armor one at a time, left, and then right.

"My heart will know only virtue." Next, he set the greaves, then tassets.

"My blade will defend the helpless." He placed on his chest-plate and back-plate.

"My might will uphold the weak." He attached the pauldrons next, hearing them click into place.

"My words will speak only truth." His armguards completed him, his form already turned into a metal soldier. "And my wrath shall undo the wicked."

Arcturus held up his helmet in his gloved hands before donning it softly, letting the straps tighten around his chin to perfection. Through the visor, he gathered his longsword and crossbow, before returning to the ship's deck. Along the way, several soldiers joined him some wearing smiles on their faces, others worry. Arcturus knew the feeling well, and offered them some words of encouragement. He spoke of their training too, praising the men for their unmatched skill. The soldiers thanked him with large smiles, almost forgetting that mere hours separated them from a clash with a potentially deadly dragon.

The Indomitous drifted into the small town, settling in a clearing not too far from the center of the town. From her plank filed out the soldiers clad in heavy armor, each carrying a different weapon, all equipped with packs of gear upon their backs and spirits of determination on their faces. Arcturus gave each an assignment, from rounding up the witnesses, to questioning the other townsfolk about the dragon. They all scrambled off, ready to please the paladin. He had not ventured far into the town before he was approached by the guard captain, with a retinue of four other guards. Arcturus remembered the bald man from the reports, but could not place the name just yet. He knew it started with a B though, for whatever it was worth.

"Welcome, Paladin Arcturus. Tis truly an honor to have you and your men aid us in the hunt for the wicked beast." the blue-eyed captain said. "Your presence already put our fair town at ease." he gestured to the buildings around them. "If we can be of any assistance whatsoever, please don't hesitate to ask."

"Yes, thank you, captain Borbaneous--" nodded Arcturus.

"It's Sirius." The captain interrupted, making Arcturus mentally kick himself.

"Apologies. My mind is focused on the dragon. Captain Sirius, you should be commended for your unrelenting bravery. You and your men survived an encounter with a dragon! That is no small feat, considering the list of things the beast has done to your cozy town." Arcturus gestured to the town center, which, despite the missing banner, looked rather pristine.

"Well, we had the best carpenters on the job to fix up all the damage caused by that rampaging monster. If you would've arrived after the cowardly beast fled, you would've gazed upon one of Devastation's many faces." said the captain as he smiled nervously. "Anyway, for the value of the damages, you would have to ask the councilman Troy Gestaurin. He handles all the book keeping affairs. Will the king send us money to cover the extensive repairs? My men worked day and night to-"

"I have every reason to think he will," said Arcturus, eyeing Sirius with suspicion. It was not unheard of for towns to exaggerate threats so they would receive compensation for supposed damage. While they had been talking, a crowd began to gather, each person trying to thank Arcturus for arriving to finally free them from the dragon's tyranny. Arcturus held his clipboard at the ready, asking anyone who had a story for details, and strangely enough, everyone had their own version of things.

"See, the big scaly bastard came down, spoutin' fire, and when he popped his jaws open, I saw teeth so many I lost count! He tore through my mum's poor banner, he did!" a man sobbed, holding up pieces of a thoroughly shredded banner. "But thanks to the brave guards, the beast fled before he had the chance to gobble me in revenge. Should he return, I fear for my safety, good sir. You need to catch it before he destroys anything else!"

"He?" Arcturus raised an eyebrow. "So the dragon's male?"

The man scrunched his face. "I dunno!" he spouted. "Not like I had the chance to glance 'tween his legs when he rampaged aroun' our town, sir!"

"Alright, I'll just take that as a vague no." Arcturus rolled his eyes, doubting a dragon would take the time to shred a banner, less likely in any villainous form. Thankfully, his soldiers had brought him other people to question, more importantly, townsfolk who had seen the dragon firsthand.

Arcturus settled comfortably at a table brought over by one of the many inns. The wood was rather thin, and covered in signs of wear. Across from him sat the little girl and her father that had seen the dragon during its first arrival.

"So, this dragon burst through your door, just like that? Had he no reason to target your house specifically?" Arcturus asked, looking up from the testimonial he had from the man.

"Not out of random, papa!" came the little girl's voice. "He was after something like...something like a book of sorts!" the girl's eyes lit up with realization. "Yes, he was searching for a book stolen by-"

"Hush now, Abigail. The paladin was talking to me." The father quickly grabbed his child and bounced her on his leg. "Sorry to confuse you, my lord. The girl, she's just shocked by this dreadful act of vandalism. Truly, she means nothing by it. The book, that's just something she conjured to cope up with all the confusion and fear our town has been put through."

"I understand," Arcturus said. "However, there is a reason why you both stand here. I heard your version. Now I want to hear hers," the paladin smiled back at the girl. "Abigail, you said the dragon was after a book? Why would you imagine a big, angry lizard like that would be after something so...ordinary?"

Abigail's lips threatened to cover her face with the size of the smile that had sprung forth. She took a deep breath before answering.

"T'wasn't a normal book! He was looking for this one, with pretty pictures of dragons in it! Told me so himself!"

"Oh, oh, h-hold on!" Arcturus chuckled as he struggled to keep up with the little girl. "You have to slow down there. I simply cannot write that fast."

Abigail blushed and apologized before repeating herself at a slower pace.

"Me mum came home with a pretty book, full of pictures. It looked like a fairy tale, and...I love these kind of books, sir. They make me happy!" she said, putting her hands together.

"What kind of pictures did it have in it?" Arcturus asked as he wrote the description on his paper.

"Of dragons! All different colors! They were so pretty, sir paladin. I want a dragon of my own!"

Arcturus chuckled. "Well, Abbi, if I find an abandoned egg, I'll know exactly what to do with it. Now, did the book say anything that can help our investigation? Who the dragon is? Perhaps why he was after this particular item?"

"Me mum dunno. It had strange scratch marks that could be letters, I suppose. Then, after she left, the dragon came into me home with a big boom like thunder!" Abigail held up her hands and mimed the wall crashing down.

"Were you not afraid of the dragon, Abigail? You tell the story with such excitement." Arcturus chuckled. "Why' you're almost leading me to believe this dragon and you are best friends!"

"Well..." the little girl cocked her head back a bit. "I was a bit afraid, you know, when he barged in like the storm. The dragon was very angry."

"Why was the dragon angry?" Arcturus raised an eyebrow.

"He said mum stole his book, and he wanted it back." She started to lean back in her chair. "Are you going to kill the dragon, sir paladin?" she asked.

Arcturus stopped writing to look into her eyes, which started to fill with tears.

"You can't kill 'im. Please! He promised not to hurt me mum!" her little hand grabbed onto one of Arcturus' fingers.

The paladin's gaze softened. "Oh, sweet child. The dragon probably meant that he would kill her painlessly. You cannot trust the words of a such a deceitful creature."

"Nuh-uh! I don't believe you!" said Abigail, placing her hands on her hips. "You weren't there to see him! He's not evil, just pissed because his book got lost, but he only wants it back, I swear. He never hurt anybody!"

"How can you be so sure of that, dear?" Arcturus frowned. "Dragons mastered the art of weaving lies. That's why they live so long. They lounge in their caves, plotting from the top of their treasure hoards. No matter what this one told you, dragons can be very deceptive at times."

"Abbi," said the father. "Trust the paladin. He is more experienced in dealing with dragons." he placed his hand on Abigail's shoulder. "She's just a child, sir. You know how creative young'uns are. I've been there to look into the eyes of real terror. Believe me, this beast is nowhere half as accommodating as she makes it sound."

"But I saw it in his eyes!" Abigail continued, turning her head to her father. "Papa, he wasn't a killer! Please, please, please, don't make him the bad guy!"

For a moment, Arcturus believed what she said. The devotion she held onto the dragon's sincerity was remarkable.

Then Dread Flame roared in his mind, reminding Arcturus of all that he lost at the claws of a dragon.

"You were fooled, my dear." He released a long, drawn out sigh. "Listen to your father this time. I believe this dragon would have harmed your mother grievously for stealing his item. I suggest you count yourself lucky he didn't want to extract his revenge on you or your father."

"But that's not-"

Arcturus heard enough by that point. He thanked the two for their time and had a guard escort the family out of the room.

The next person to enter was a guard who had been with captain Sirius on that day, in the man's words own words "the dragon attacked the village." Arcturus endured through a tale of heroics that the man listed off as performed by many of his fellow guardsman, This valiant defender had just finished telling how he had struck the dragon with an arrow, when a half-elven woman strode into the room with her face full of anger.

"That's a load of goblin spittle you's bein' fed!" the woman pointed a finger at the paladin, brushing her brown hair out of her face.

"Excuse me?" One of the guards said.

She crossed her arms over her studded leather armor, worn from use by scrapes and patches.

"Let her speak!" Arcturus said to the two men that moved to restrain the woman.

"I met the dragon all these liars claim to have attacked the town, and he just doesn't seem the type to do something so nonsensical."

"Lady, forgive me for being blunt, but who are you to throw such claims?" Arcturus narrowed his eyes.

The woman must've been an adventurer, judging by all the gear she was carrying. She had a bedroll strapped to her back, torches, rope, and a backpack. Arcturus was ready to bet his week's salary she was definitely one of those traveler types, or a mercenary.

"Name's Lyndis Kuxion." she said, "and that dragon you're all ready take revenge on saved my life from a band of fockin' bandits."

"Is that so?" Arcturus replied, his voice thick with skepticism. "Please, expand. No. Enlighten us on how this supposedly benevolent dragon saved your life."

"Glady, you Lumarian brute." Lyndis said. She dragged her own chair over to the table, quickly turning it around so the backing was facing the table. She sat down, then started to tell her version of the story.

Arcturus listened to her tale of events. It all started on a nearby hill along the road. He figured she was exaggerating her abilities. What else was new with the adventurer types? They all slayed dragons single handedly, stood against dozens of enemies, and somehow always found a priceless artifact, all on the virtue of their own singular skill.

One thing stuck out, though. Arcturus considered himself generally good at picking up when someone was lying, but when the woman spoke of the dragon saving her, she certainly sounded like this was the truth. When her mouth ceased forming words, she just looked to him with a great big smile on her face.

"How does that sound? More believable than...murdering dragon descends upon a town to destroy buildings from the thrill of it, aye? They're strong and full of themselves sometime, but dragons ain't stupid. You should know that better than these cryin' oafs."

Arcturus frowned as he moved his fingers over to the report. He had two accounts of the dragon now that did not paint him in the same light as the rest of the town had shone on him. Most importantly, it certainly didn't match the official report the king had given him to study.

"Well, you can believe it if you want, paladin. I've no reason whatsoever to lie to you. Buuuuuut if you'd prefer to hunt monsters and blindly swing your sword at things, be my guest, of course." She shrugged, stood up and brushed past a guard on her way out. "Best not waste your time with the others. They'll just trickle the same squirt of urine and call it wine!" she yelled back to him.

Arcturus rubbed his forehead. This day seemed to drag on forever. "Alright, who's next?"

Next to enter the room was captain Sirius with his usual guards around him. In his hands rested a brown cloth, clutched tightly, as if this bag was of the utmost importance. Arcturus noted that the guards were giving the captain a wider birth than they had previously.

"My lord," the captain bowed as much as his back allowed, "I have returned with an item that may prove fruitful in your endeavor to capture the beast."

He held up the cloth bag and undid the string that held the thing together. When the mouth of the bag parted, a single crimson scale was revealed, clearly belonging to the dragon Arcturus was sent to hunt.

"When the dragon burst into the house the first time, he must have scratched himself on a beam. Left this crucial piece of evidence behind without checking, like the proud fool he is."

Arcturus reached out to grasp the scale in his left hand. It was smooth to the touch, like he figured it would be. He looked up to the captain with a slight smile of relief on his tired face.

"This will actually be of great help, captain. You have my gratitude for your contributions." He gestured to a soldier that had just walked in, then handed the scale to the man, gently. The last thing he wanted was to damage the scale too much. "Make your way back to the ship and tell the captain to get ready for lift-off. Once that's done, head to the gryphon keeper. I believe we have a way to find the beast's lair."

It had only taken an hour to round up all the soldiers and take off in the indomitous. The ship rose into the sky gracefully, being led as if on an invisible wire by the tawny gryphon leading it towards the mountains. Arcturus stood on the deck, eyes scanning the forest below, occasionally drifting to the sunflower-colored wings of the gryphon. He held up the scale, then smiled to the bird, still amazed at their tracking ability.

This is good. We'll wrap this unpleasant story, and in a few hours, and after that, I guess I'll go back to my usual life. What remains of it, at least.

Arcturus turned back towards the group of men that gathered on the deck. The squad fidgeted with the same anticipation that stirred within Arcturus' breast. Despite being a force of destruction, he had to admit to himself. Seeing a dragon in flesh was a special feeling.

They flew for quite some time before the gryphon screeched back towards the ship as they reached the top of the largest mountain. The gryphon circled as Arcturus ordered the men to the lifeboats. Arcturus took the lead with his lifeboat as the four other boats followed him down towards the cave. He noted it was a tad small, for someone he considered the offspring of Dread Flame.

Arcturus jumped over the side of the boat as they touched down gently. He gave hand signals to the men to follow as he slowly advanced into the cave's mouth. He saw some of his soldiers hovering their fingers over the trigger of their weapons, or gripping the grip tight.

"Set up the traps," he whispered to the others. They grabbed and set up several launchers for the nets, just in case the dragon decided to fly away from his lair. "You stay outside with the launchers," he pointed out towards the sharpshooters. "Get ready to stun him if he tries anything funny."

Arcturus turned back to his hunting party. "As for the rest of you, keep your weapons up and your eyes peeled. We don't know what manner of beast we're dealing with here."

"What if he's friendly?" A man suddenly asked.

"Are you ready to take that risk?" Arcturus hissed.

The stern look in the paladin's eyes allowed for no comebacks. Once his men nodded, he made his way into the cave, the steps of their boots akin to the click clack of a centipede. The air smelled of stale cooked meat, and something specific to the scent of a dragon. Arcturus crouched along the cave wall, the others right behind him. They hugged it as if the wall could very well be the thing that would save them from what lay ahead.

The torch-lit hall led deeper into the cave, wide enough to fit at least two dragons. He found himself eyeing the tracks on the floor, along with scratch marks from what were no doubt horns on the ceiling.

"Why's the dragon havin' a focken-?"

Arcturus held up a finger to silence the man, cursing to himself. Although the man had a point, dragons could very well see in the dark. However, maybe this one just liked the illumination of the pleasant torchlight. He moved the thought away from his mind as he peeked around the corner ahead of him, barely stifling a gasp.

Forty feet away the dragon was lying on makeshift blankets and mattresses next to a pile of gold and books. His eyes were closed shut, and his chest was moving up and down with the deep breaths characteristic to deep sleep. Between the dragon's front limbs was some kind of toy, that, upon careful inspection, revealed itself to be a stuffed dragon of some kind.

The Gods are with me today, Arcturus' heart quickened as he grabbed hold of his crossbow. *Let us see if you are indeed the-*

"You know, it's somewhat rude to sneak up on a dragon at the height of his laziness." The red beast yawned, opening one eye lazily. He stood up on his four limbs and stretched very much how a cat might. "To what do I owe the displeasure of being roused from-"

"Aim at his throat!" Arcturus shouted, interrupting the dragon mid speech. Bolts of energy sailed past his gleaming armor as he fired his own crossbow at the dragon. Veledar yelped in surprise and tried to leap out of the way, but the barrage was much too thick to avoid every missile.

"Fan out! Trap him in the corner!"

"You insolent slugs!" Veledar growled as he inhaled a deep breath, only to have small sparks of useless fire escape through his jaws.

"Hah! Missing something?" Arcturus pointed a finger at the dragon. "Guess you'll have to stretch your limbs after all! Men, advance!"

"How dare you?" Veledar hissed as he bounded past several men. With a whip of his tail he slammed them against the cave wall.

"FIRE!" the paladin's voice washed over the scrapes of steel and claws.

Arcturus' men fired another volley, then he quickly tossed a flashbang towards the dragon. It exploded with a brilliant light that forced the dragon to leap behind his pile of treasure.

"Trap him!"

The men took positions around the cave, weapons at the ready, hearts thundering in their chests.

"Sir, we have him cornered. Shouldn't we bring the nets?"

"Not yet!"

Veledar then burst out from behind the gold, wings spread wide. He swooped around the men as they fired, before suddenly turning towards the exit. The soldiers followed him with their energy shots, one man even tossing a bola. However, none of the attacks seemed to have an effect on the dragon, who spread his wings to fly out of the cave unmolested.

"What in the blazes happened?"

Arcturus took aim with his own crossbow at the departing dragon. He spied a slight glitter in the dragon's form, followed by more bolts from his men impacting the scales.

"It's an illusion!" he cried out to his men in shock. He turned back towards the gold, but it was too late. Veledar had already pounced out onto several soldiers, flailing his limbs and tail, carving his way through the wall of steel-clad men that stood between him and freedom. The dislodged men landed on the ground with hard thuds, not rising when the dragon moved onto their comrades. The remaining soldiers and Arcturus fired volley after volley into Veledar's wings and torso, causing the dragon to recoil in pain.

"Rraaaah, what an annoying itch!" he roared out, smashing two soldiers together with his paws.

"You come to my home!" He smashed another soldier into the ground. "And attack me!" He toppled over soldier after soldier, the bolts of energy only a slight inconvenience to the red beast. He deflected nets that were tossed at his wings, bolas that would've rendered his legs useless, and even hitting back a flashbang thrown his way. He stopped only when the other soldiers were all scattered on the ground before him, with only Arcturus and a handful of soldiers left to stare him down.

"Take your leave, you ill-mannered monkeys, before I push you out myself!" Veledar hissed through ragged breaths.

"I don't think so," Arcturus raised his crossbow and shot another bolt into the dragon's torso, followed by more from his soldiers.

"Nrrr...nraaaawarrhhh..."

Arcturus smirked as Veledar's limbs splayed uselessly around his collapsing form. On his way to greet the floor, he still flailed his tail at several soldiers foolish enough to get close. They flew through the air with little grace, hitting the floor hard. Arcturus watched Veledar try to stand, the dragon's limbs unresponsive, dragged down by invisible weight. Although he managed to keep his head up as his shaking limbs collapsed beneath him, the dragon stared at Arcturus' visor with his blue eyes full of spite.

"You filthy cowards! Not even daring to face me in a fair fight!" he gasped out in pain. "I guess...that steel dress suits you well...woman."

"Fair?" Arcturus chuckled. "Take a look at yourself, beastie. You tower over me, weight more than all of us combined, bear scales that put even my own armor to shame, and to top that off, you can take wing whenever you please. I can hardly imagine how a fight would play out fairly between us, so please, illuminate me with your esteemed wisdom. You are, after all, much better than us, right? Isn't that how your kind sees us? Playthings to combat boredom? Perhaps even prey to fill their bellies with?"

"If only you fought the same way you talk... You're putting me to sleep just by talking," the dragon snorted tiredly.

"Aye. But I'm the one who stands, while you're the one to greet the ground. Sleep well, beastie."

Arcturus didn't even restrain himself this time. He just laughed in the dragon's face, then ordered his remaining men to bring shackles.

He took off his helmet and set it down close to Veledar, who collapsed his head on the ground, his breath becoming increasingly steadier. The beast looked deceptively pleasing to the eye when incapacitated. A small itch even flared the words spoken by the two girls, Abigail and Lyndis. What did they see, when they looked upon this beast? A monster? Perhaps something else?

Arcturus almost felt pity for the creature. His hand twitched above his sword, not to grab the weapon, but to stop the men from carrying his orders. Perhaps it was wise, to have a few moments alone with the dragon. Just to consider his options.

Then Dread Flame roared inside the depths of his mind. Arcturus saw the ship going down. His desperate escape which led him to the very streets of his home, where the beast locked his claws around his leg to prevent him from giving aid to his terrified family.

The fear, the pain, the anguish...it all reflected off the scales of what Abigail and Lyndis branded as a friend and savior.

Arcturus rested his hand on the pommel of his sword, then approached the beast's fallen head. The dragon's moist breath stained his armor, but Arcturus felt anything but warm. His cold eyes bore straight into the beast's blue gaze, hard as the steel he wore. "I am Arcturus Lund, dragon. Remember my name well, along with the day when you fell at my feet."

"Y-You did not best me," Veledar hissed, his voice growing quieter. "You brought an army into my home...ambushed me just as I fell asleep... and worse of all, you think your actions are justified."

"Gah. I cannot waste anymore time with this nonsense." He waved to his men. "I've had enough of this unpleasant tongue. Shackle him."

The soldiers clasped large iron shackles onto the dragon, pinning his rear and front limbs together.

"Steel suits you, beast." Arcturus said, feeling a strange, almost cruel manner of satisfaction from besting his second dragon since Dread Flame.

"Like false justice suits you." The dragon shot back. "Why are you doing this? I only damaged a house and crumpled a stupid cloth on a stick called banner."

"Oh, is that what you truly believe?" Arcturus pressed.

"It's...the truth. Ask anyone around." The dragon answered.

"Sir, is it wise to-"

Arcturus raised a hand. "I've already interrogated the town you terrorized. I am not doing this because I like it, dragon. I do it because it's just. For crimes against our land, our king, and our citizens, you are going to be brought to our capital and made an example of." Arcturus finished that off by picking his helmet.

"A trial for a wooden wall and a cheap banner...that doesn't...sound right..." The beast managed to say before fatigue overwhelmed his senses.

Arcturus walked away from the dragon in silence. He was certainly a tad smaller than Dread Flame had been, but that made sense in a way, for the offspring to always be smaller than the father. Arcturus waved to the survivors to start moving the dragon out of the cave. They tied up some ropes around him and dragged the dragon down the hallway and out to the ship. Arcturus stayed behind with a group to recover the soldiers the dragon had attacked. He noticed something while they came to the first body. The man was still alive. He quickly gave a look to the others brought down by Veledar to notice with utter surprise that all of them were alive as well. It looked like the dragon had simply knocked them out instead of killing them. He called over a soldier with healing herbs and potions, praising the Gods for their intervention.

"Pah! The Gods. Are you asking for their aid, or mine?" The healer shook off his belt of vials.

"I'm asking both. Do what you can for my men please. We must depart immediately."

"Hah. Bruises and simple scrapes are all the afflictions I can count. Either your dragon doesn't know how to fight." laughed the man, "or he didn't attack with the intention to kill anybody."

Arcturus walked outside to where the dragon now laid unconscious. Veledar was held tight by the ropes that now bound his wings together. Arcturus certainly didn't expect the dragon to spare anyone. Perhaps he really was as lazy as he described himself before the attack began.

"Collect his treasure before we leave." he called out to some of the men. "It will be good to rid this beast from his ill-gotten gains."

"What shall we do with it, sir?"

"Give back to those he stole from." Arcturus said confidently, even if the same creeping feeling of doubt resurfaced beneath his confident smile. He dropped down between the dragon's legs to rest his back against the beast's scaly belly, warm, in spite of the hard scales that protected it.

Who am I really dealing with here? The paladin wondered as he looked upon the dragon's sleeping form. *Am I making the right choice, to condemn this creature based on shady evidence? To take his hoard without justification? What if...*

Arcturus grabbed one of the dragon's talons, a sharp, wicked thing he knew too well from his encounters with Dread Flame. He couldn't allow himself to be pinned a second time. To be helpless. To stand idly and watch others suffer at the claws of a dragon.

With a grim look about his face, Arcturus stood up, took one last look at the dragon, then ordered him hauled onto the ship.

Chapter 6: Restrained Questions

The morning sun slowly pierced through the overwhelming amount of gray clouds cluttering the distant sky. Its warm rays descended from the heavens briefly, illuminating the green treetops that swayed every so often in the cool spring breeze. These verdant giants were alive this morning, during the first day of spring. Birds with vibrant plumage flew quickly through the curtain of leaves, darting from branch to branch like little thrill seekers determined to test their mettle. They seemed exhilarated, to bask in the embrace of blessed warmth, now that winter relinquished the frigid grasp it had over the land. Mammals of all species and sizes also seemed to spring from their dens like little flowers, helping turn the forest that had been crippled by the winter's frozen blanket into a verdant realm that was bursting with life.

On this particular morning, a young doe grazed in a nearby field, her brown and white fur cast in the shadow of the nearby trees. Though her ears flicked this way and that, she was blissfully unaware of the crimson scaled hatchling that stared at her from the tall grass.

The little dragon prowled on all fours, trying to keep his red body from showing through the foliage. His haunches stood tense, ready to spring, like the limbs of a cat on the verge of pouncing its prey, with his tail swaying from one side to the other. His front claws fidgeted for a moment, digging into the soft earth with excitement from the prey yet uncaught. Though he felt the urge to pounce, his wings remained close to his body, biding their time to flare.

The hatchling opened and closed his snout, displaying rows of sharp teeth. Oh, how much he would've loved to terrify his prey. Show it what a powerful dragon he was!

Unfortunately, such approach would surely lead to failure, so the dragon shook his head and closed his blue eyes, trying to focus on the current hunt, not the taste of what was to come. As he advanced towards his prey, he breathed carefully, not smelling the usual stench of fear erupting from an animal on the brink of death. He grinned to himself, proud that he had snuck this close to her undetected. He was almost poised to strike when he heard a crack from what sounded like a nearby tree branch, causing the doe to lift her head. She sniffed and bolted into the trees, its legs almost slipping in haste.

The wrymling pounced from his hiding spot to find his claws grasping at thin air instead of the succulent flesh he imagined in his mind.

"Manticore's bottom!" The wrymling snarled angrily, smacking his tail on the ground with a dull thump. "I was this close to catching it!"

While his claws tore through the earth in frustration, his mind raced with what could have gone wrong. By all accounts, he made sure to be downwind, kept hidden from sight, and remained as silent as a dragon could be. His eyes squinted as he thought to the twig snapping. The dragon's nostrils shuddered as he drew in a deep breath. A familiar smell he knew far too well was the source of all his pains.

"Veledar!" A feminine voice shouted. A silver wrymling pounced from the grass, tackling the red one.

They rolled around, smacking and clawing playfully at each other, following up with a bite to the shoulder.

"Get off, pest! Get off I said!" Veledar protested, pushing the annoyingly clingy silver wrymling off him. "That wasn't funny, Adalina. You ruined my hunt is what you did."

"You hunt?" Adalina laughed, rising up onto all four paws and smirking with a wide grin. "What hunt is that? I don't see any prey laying around."

"That's because you soured it with your clumsy paws and your...your stench! Your stench is what drove my prey away!" Veledar stuck his tongue out at her.

"Why did you even go out?" Adalina brushed the insults off without a care in the world, her amber eyes filled with curiosity instead of anger. "You know momma doesn't like it when you wander off on your own."

"Grah! She's silly, to think I'm helpless as a squirrel. I was going to show her what a great hunter I am." He strode over to her. "I'm ahead of any dragon my age. Probably the best that ever lived!"

"That's not true." Adalina stuck her tongue out in mockery of him. "Momma is a way better hunter than you. She kept us fed. What did you do? Scare a deer like a clumsy little hatchling."

"Shut up."

"Not until you admit you're still a hatchling instead of this great dragon overlord."

"Well, obviously." Veledar rolled his eyes and stomped his paws. "But that's not fair. Momma is all grown up! When I'll be her age, I will have a gigantic cave filled with treasure and-and humans to do my bidding! I'll be their new king!"

"Somehow, I doubt they will listen to any word you say. Besides, they love their current king." Adalina remarked. She darted away into the grass and crouched into a similar stance that Veledar had. "Besides, while you will be proclaiming yourself the king of humans, I will be busy ruling the whole world. You have such simple views, Veledar. Still a hatchling in both body and mind."

"Am not!" He shot back, sniffing the ground where the doe had been.

He could probably track the damn prey to wherever she had gotten off to. Prove to his sister he was the better offspring, and make his mother radiate pure pride in the process.

"Hey, Adalina...Hey!" He shouted as, once again, his sister tackled him to the ground. After another round of play biting and scratches, Veledar had his sister pinned to the ground, smugly looking down on her.

"Stop these stupid games! I need to hunt." He let her go as she sighed.

"When will you be back from this extremely important task?" she asked. "It's been boring without you around. Momma's been making her usual trips. That leaves the cave silent. And cold..." Her head dipped slightly.

Veledar almost felt bad for mistreating his sister. With his head bowed in shame, he moved closer and nuzzled her scaly neck. "Once I catch this doe, we can have the rest of the day for ourselves. What do you say?"

"Deal!" Adalina smiled back. "You know...it's male dragons who usually provide for their mates. Bring me something good!"

Veledar blushed slightly as her warm tongue rolled over his cheek. What did she mean by that? He shook his head off the strange butterflies that caught hold of his scales, but Adalina was already gone, off toward the mountain top they called home.

Left alone, Veledar quickly dashed after his missing doe, quietly as a young dragon could be, careful not to crush a twig under his paws or tangle his horns in a bush. The doe was easy to follow for a hunter with keen senses. His mother had told him once how elves hunted without relying so much on their instinct of smell, which made him wonder how they caught any sort of prey. The doe's path took Veledar up the river that ran down his mother's mountain, snaking its way up patches of loose rocks that looked like they could dislodge themselves at only the slightest of nudges.

The dragon stopped when he caught sight of the doe once again. She was standing in a ring of trees, oblivious to the threat hiding in the shadows.

Veledar crouched low into his hunting stance, his tail once again twitching in anticipation, He wriggled his haunches, and when the doe went down for another bite of succulent grass, he pushed the ground with all he had and latched himself onto his prey. His claws found new purchase into the doe's hide, and his teeth quickly followed. Veledar fell along with his prey, blood spraying everywhere around him. In a moment, the anticipation, the thrill, the concentration, all of it dispelled once he picked up his prey by its dead, clammy neck.

Veledar would've celebrated his victory if his eyes didn't catch two fawns staring back at him from the river's bank. They were brown in color, naturally smaller than their dead mother. They scampered off into the underbrush, still watching with dread-filled eyes from the new hiding spot.

"I...I'm sorry," Veledar muttered to himself. He was well aware of the fact that simple animals could not comprehend his words, but still, he felt like he had a duty towards the two orphans. "I will honor her. She did not die in vain."

That said, he grabbed the doe by the scruff of the neck and started to drag the corpse back home, to share it with his sister. Every once in a while, he'd throw a look back to the blood-stained spot where he ended the promising life of a mother. How could he tell Adalina something like this?

The answer was simple. He wouldn't. Instead, he was going to spin this into a tale of bravery that would surely make his sister proud -and perhaps even envious- of his skill.

* * * * * * * * *

"Wake up!"

Veledar didn't really want to, despite the voice's desires. It was a distinctive male one, quiet at first, as if the sound was muffled through a piece of cloth. Veledar tried to ignore it, but the voice returned with renewed fury. The scenery around Veledar started to blur and fade away. His limbs seemed to lock up with the ground, and with a growl of panic, Veledar merged with the earth, darkness filling up his eyes in an instant.

Veledar opened an eye and tried to move his limbs, only to find that he could not. He was currently strapped to the floor of a wooden room, with leather straps that felt slightly too tight. The room was lit by a single lantern hanging by a large dark red door, and somehow, the dragon realized could open his mouth. Veledar did the first thing that came to mind. He took a deep breath, letting his glands flare open to let out the molten fire brewing within them. He was going to show those foolish humans how stupid it was to keep him contained in an environment predominantly made of wood. Veledar growled. Hissed. Spat. Yet no matter how much he struggled, fire refused to spring forth, and he was only left with an unpleasant burning sensation in the back of his throat. It was then that he noticed another belt, tight around his neck, right where his fire glands were, its purpose to keep them tight enough to render him unable to breathe out his blazing fury.

93

"Wicked pink-skinned rats!" Veledar unleashed a hiss of frustration. He tried to thrash around in hopes to loosen up the bindings. There had to be a weakness somewhere. Had to.

"Try as hard as you like, dragon. All this growly effort of yours serves to make you tired," laughed a man's voice.

Veledar's eyes squinted. "Why don't you come closer, and see what else I can do?" He hissed. "I would be surprised if you managed to keep your breeches clean more than a few seconds."

"Ah, as much as I'd enjoy proving you wrong, I find myself quite content to observe you from here. Besides, the paladin wanted to have words with you. Preserve whatever strength you have. Why, it's your only chance to explain yourself."

The paladin? Was that the man in the fancy metal suit? Veledar wasn't completely certain. He had the eyes of a hunter though, unafraid as Veledar leaped to his men and knocked them out one by one.

"By all means, bring this paladin thing in here," the dragon said. "I would like to talk to the coward that sneaks into the lairs of innocent dragons to ambush them in their sleep with his little army of metal-clad ants."

The man laughed again. "Mighty words robbed of their meaning considering your current position. You still believe you're innocent?"

"I know I am! Bring your leader here so I can tell it to his face. What was his name, by the way? The one with the fierce eyes and silver armor."

"Forgot already?"

"Human names are like the birds that relieve themselves on the roofs of your homes. Only you care about the stench they leave behind. Me? I'm hardly ever hit by their..." the dragon smirked. "Is it considered rude if I make an ungainly comparison between their droppings and the fur you wear on top of your head?"

"My. He was right, after all. You've got a way with words, beastie. They pour out of your mouth like a waterfall. Haven't you accused the paladin of talking better than he fights?" the human chuckled. "It's...it's just amusing, with you all tied up and everything."

"Yes," Veledar narrowed his eyes. "It definitely looks like the droppings of a-"

"Oh, come on, don't go there," the human brushed Veledar off. "His name's Arcturus Lund, dragon slayer and Paladin of Lumara. You ought to feel lucky he didn't drive his sword through your eye as you lay broken at his feet. Heard that's what he did with the last red that got on his angry side. Heh. For all your size and scales, you die just as easily as the birds you prattle about."

"Delude yourself all you want, human. I was hardly broken by your foul trickery." Veledar jerked in his restraints a little. "Do I seem weak to you? Helpless? You would not have done such a thorough job with these restraints if you thought me broken. Now go. Fetch that paladin of yours, I dry my throat uselessly by talking with one so filled with fear that he will not even show his face to me."

Silence filled the next few seconds before Veledar heard the man leave the chamber. A soft sigh left his maw. It was obvious they did not want him dead, otherwise he would have had his guts opened up in his lair by that annoying, loud-mouthed, self righteous paladin.

"I'll show him when he gets here." The dragon strained against the leather once more. "He's just a human, after all."

One that managed to capture him. What would Adalina think of him? He, the mighty Veledar, captured by humans for who knew what reason. Veledar truly had no idea why Arcturus ambushed him like that. Could be an order from a deluded higher-up, or maybe he acted as the hand of vengeance for the flower thieves that stole from Trixie's garden. What if that fierce healer-woman spoke the truth? An entire village of children might've perished because he decided to brush off the pleadings of a desperate woman.

No. That can't be it. Her mate almost pissed his pants. He would've fought if the stakes were that high.

Nevertheless, Veledar emptied his mind of theories as his eyes shifted to stare at the door, waiting for the sound of the guard's steps. There was no need to think so hard when answers were going to grace his ears soon.

He did not have to wait long, as only a couple minutes passed before he heard steps heavier than the man that had left. What he would say to the paladin crossed his mind. Would he start with an insult? Or perhaps a boast? That was a bit too crude. Maybe the best course of action was to taunt him again and find out what the humans truly wanted with him.

Veledar was still in thought when a soft click and turn of the knob opened the door in front of him. Standing there was the accursed man that captured him -Arcturus- still wearing the same shiny armor, only this time his helmet was off and he carried no weapons Veledar could see.

"You know... coming in here to lay eyes on a trapped dragon with no weapons to protect yourself with is not exactly a sound decision." Veledar couldn't help himself even if his mind rebelled at the unwise choice to start off this dialogue.

Even Arcturus agreed it was stupid through a soft, disappointed sigh. "I see old habits die hard with you dragons." The human's eyes quickly scanned the straps before stepping closer towards his captive.

"You can leave us now." Arcturus said to the guard behind him.

"As you wish, sir." The man said as he shut the door softly. "Be careful with the...beast."

"Yes, leave us so you don't die of boredom when I walk your precious paladin in endless loops of dialogue." Veledar said drily, his blue eyes moving onto the main event. "How do you feel, Arcturus? Knowing that you only came here to have your time wasted? You can bark orders to your minions, eat something fancy, perhaps even rest. And out of all these more enticing options, your first choice is to come here, to me." Veledar smiled as a wicked thought crossed his mind. "Maybe the reason you've come here is to admire my radiant scales. Who knows? Given the way you look at me now, you've probably watched me through all the hours I slept, crippled by a late sense of guilt. After all, how could you, a man with a sense of morality, with honor, restrain such a noble dragon? You feel bad. Admit it."

Veledar had hoped to get a reaction out of the paladin, but there was barely any to speak of. This man stood like a mountain, straight, confident, and completely emotionless.

"This is going to turn into a very drab affair if you keep looking at me like that. I have been known to kill humans with boredom before." Veledar grinned.

Arcturus said nothing. Instead, he pulled out a scroll from his pouch and rolled it out until it was held tight in his hands.

"What you say bears no significance to me, unless spoken with purpose. I will be asking you a series of questions, and if you truly care about your future, you better do your best to answer truthfully, dragon."

Veledar was taken back for a moment. The human said the last word with such disdain, such anger. He guessed it was no surprise coming from a man who literally earned his living by claiming the lives of dragons.

"Engage in whatever fruitless endeavor you see fit, paladin. Though I must warn you. This crusade of yours is nothing like the stories of old."

"Why do you believe such?" Arcturus asked, poking his head out from the scroll. "Loosen tongue and see the veil behind your words lifted."

"Why am I not dead, for one? The heroes of your stories believe only in blind justice. They do not give dragons like me second chances. All they care about is returning home with a dragon's head in their cart, to be cheered and admired by the gloating crowd of simpletons. The king, mayor or whatever grants them land, title, then our hero finds a woman, falls in love, mates, lives happily ever after off the blood spilled. You find such tales heroic. I find them disgusting to the last."

"Amusing, but far removed from the truth." The paladin said. "My king wanted you alive so you can face justice for your crimes against our kingdom."

"Crimes? What crimes?" Veledar hissed. "You keep babbling about these crimes as if you found me bathed in blood amidst hundreds of corpses!"

Veledar's claws scraped against the floor in anger. "You're no better than the rest of your guild, fattening your pouches with gold bought with the lives of innocent dragons."

"That word again. Innocent. Why should I believe a word you say?"

"Because...because of the facts!" Veledar snarled again. "How did you find me? Tell me! Say the truth for once instead of demonizing me!"

Veledar noticed a tense in the human's jaws before he spoke. "Asleep."

"Asleep how?" Veledar pressed on. "Did I hold a captive in my paws? A dying knight? The pitiful remains of my last meal?"

"No, You had a...something akin to what we give to our children."

The words felt heavy on the man's tongue, and Veledar extracted much joy from his clever ploy. As embarrassing as it was to admit, a mighty predator like him slept with an inanimate gryphon. Veledar was slowly, but surely, cutting his way into the human's frail heart.

"A toy. Out of all the things I listed, all the dreadful weapons those simpletons are afraid of, it had to be a toy. Tell me, paladin. Was my gryphon so threatening that you had to wrestle him away from me along with the entirety of my hoard? You said you want to judge me for my actions, but I would like to hear again of the charges brought against me. I admit to damaging a man's house and one woman's banner, but this hardly matches the crimes you've committed against me!" Veledar snarled.

"Is that so?" Arcturus brought the scroll up again. "Let's see if a wall and a banner are what is listed here."

The paladin listed what Veledar already knew, but the similarities ended after his first couple of words. What followed after was a cacophony of nonsense, including murder, kidnapping of children, and stealing from merchants on the king's roads.

Veledar's maw went agape with disgust. He heard nonsense before, but this amalgamation of filth felt like hedgehogs burying into his ears. How vile was this human king? To fabricate such lies in order to get an innocent dragon captured?

"That..." Veledar let his fierce growl sink into a depressed sigh. He had to play his part, even if that meant striking a blow to his pride. "That cannot be what you truly believe, is it? You are a dragon slayer, yes, but I have to hope the paladin in you is stronger than that. My mother...she told me tales of resplendent men that carried the light of the sun upon their armor. Men who are sworn to valor. Men who are just." His eyes slowly rose from the ground to look at Arcturus. "Are you one of these men, Arcturus?"

The paladin's gaze faltered, but only for a moment. "I...there have been some who see things differently. I trust word of mouth to a degree, but the written word holds much more power." Arcturus answered, to which Veledar snorted in disgust.

"Fine. Trust that pile of stinking horse crap if it makes you feel any better." He turned his eyes as much as he could away from this joke of a paladin. "All I know is that your people stole from my treasure and accuse me of things that make even my stomach revolt at the thought of d-doing such things!" He strained against the leather, making Arcturus back away from him for a moment. Veledar slumped to the ground when the straps refuse to budge, pleased to see the human breathe a sigh of relief as he stepped back to his previous spot.

"I admire your fighting spirit, dragon. Perhaps you even hide some chaffed scales beneath those bindings. Do you truly believe that all these charges are simply lies fabricated to implicate you?" he said, his hand moving to stroke his chin. "That does not make any sense no matter from which angle you look at it."

"Just like your title, paladin." Veledar spat that word, eyes narrowing at the distasteful human.

"What?" Arcturus eyes widened for a brief moment. "How dare you accuse me like he did?"

"He? You've gone and captured another dragon, have you?" Veledar pressed on, driven by an innate urge to see this human implode on himself. "Are you reading him the same lies? How many are there in the bowels of the ship besides me? I'm just curious, to know how many lives are enough to sate your thirst for innocent blood, dragon slayer."

"No!" Arcturus stomped the ground. "I haven't captured more. You are my only mission."

"I don't believe you," Veledar said, making the human clench his fists.

"Stop it. If you're trying to use my anger to your advantage, know that I am trained well against the poison that courses through your tongue with every word you speak."

Veledar had to give at least a brief smile. He might not have managed to persuade the human of his innocence, yet seeing him simmer felt just as satisfying. "Stings, does it not? To be accused of falsehoods. If not me, who else were you speaking about?"

Arcturus sighed. Arms crossed, he paced around the room, lost in thought for a bit. "It was another dragon, bearing crimson scales not very different from yours, and no, it isn't my desire to expand that topic further. Instead, I'd like to hear why you tarnished my title."

"You know why, human." Veledar said. "In the tales I've been told, paladins had a sense of honor and virtue. They could wield impressive magic, inspired bravery in their allies, and fought against the agents of evil across all world. Whatever you are is nothing like that. What you wield is an empty name, a mockery of what my mother's tales spoke of."

Veledar noticed the human stop and study his response. Good. He had gotten under his skin at least. "Tell me, slayer. How many dragons have found their end at the tip of your blade? Rumors say you come from a family with a particularly vicious taste for dragon blood. That you have this urge, this drive to kill that only ceases when you take a dragon's life."

A dark frown creased Arcturus' face. Within two long strides he was upon the cage, armored hands wrapping themselves tight against the bars. Veledar could choose to maim the human, but the pain inflicted by his words felt more satisfying than any physical wound.

"What you heard is no truer than the claims you deny!" Arcturus spoke. "I've only ended one dragon, and I can assure you, it was quite an effort to put him down. I also did not murder him in his sleep or anything ridiculous of that sort. Merely brought the light of justice down upon that...that monster."

"Is that how you live with yourself?" He mocked the human by poking his fingers with the top of his snout. Arcturus pulled back immediately from the dragon's moist breath. "Admit you are a dragon murderer. Say something true just this once."

Arcturus put his right hand to his nose and squeezed gently at its length with his eyes shut briefly.

Veledar accepted the gesture for the time being.

"In exchange, I also wanted to know why you did not kill any of the soldiers I sent into your cave," he said, reopening his eyes and looking into the dragon's eyes. "That was something I did not expect to see."

"You already know that answer. I am not the monster you or all of the oafs in that village paint me out to be. Are we not talking without raking at each other's hides right now? Imagine how fruitful our encounter would have been if you would have talked with me instead of charging me like a dumb orc."

"I couldn't take any chances," Arcturus said flatly.

"Spare me the lecture. Just because another red dragon fractured your heart, that doesn't make me guilty of the same sins. Now, if you don't mind, I would like to know what your plans with me are. My limbs are starting to feel really stiff." Veledar would have thrashed his tail, but the leather strap on it stopped that, of course.

"We are several days away from the capital. Unfortunately, that means we'll be holding you tied up until the time comes to face justice for all that's written in this scroll." Arcturus replied, placing his quill at the top of his clipboard. "May the Gods forgive me if I'm wrong. Like I said before, I cannot take the risk."

Veledar's snout crashed back on the ground. This human paladin was disappointing him further and further. "Not that pile of dung again. For the sake of the paladins of old, can you at least pretend I'm speaking the truth? Does this sound like justice to you? A trial based on lies and your people's hatred for dragons?" Veledar replied harshly. He noticed Arcturus would not meet his gaze, clearly the human was conflicted about this issue.

"It does not." he admitted as he looked into Veledar's eyes. "But it is my king's will you defy. The words of dozens of villagers that claimed to have seen you perform these very crimes. I..." the human faltered. "Tell me again you did not do those things. Slowly."

What the human was up to, Veledar did not know, but without hesitating, the red dragon picked his head up, his unwavering gaze staring straight into the human's eyes.

"I swear by my integrity as a dragon that I have not done any of those things. I only damaged the house accidentally in pursuit of my...well that's private, but again, I did not harm anyone physically. Might have called them pink-skinned rats a few times, but that's just a truth your species has to live with. You have a myriad of jokes about us too, right? Tell me one. Go on. Amuse me. I know I will not get any justice here, so might as well try to have a bit of fun, before..."

Veledar let his words wither. Arcturus sat in silence, looking at nothing in particular, as if contemplating Veledar's reply. He waited for the human to say something about deceit. Honestly, he had no idea why he even put up with this ridiculous charade. One way or the other, he was going to end up roasted in the capital city of Entis, surrounded by the biggest, meanest group of pink-skinned rats a dragon could ever see.

"I believe you." Arcturus said, much to Veledar's amazement. "Now tell me what happened, in your words, and leave nothing to assumption." Arcturus settled down near Veledar's head and put the quill to the paper. "Also, for the purpose of this note, I will need a name to refer you by. I can simply write dragon if you don't want to tell me."

"Write Crimson Sky on your paper, human. I want your king to know the dragon he has wronged this day. Although mark my words, I do not believe he will listen to anything I have to say."

Arcturus started writing down the moment Veledar started speaking. Crimson Sky spoke about the theft, the little girl's house, his trip to town, and finally the fight with the bandits. The dragon of course spoke with much flattery about his actions. Although he insisted that someone threw the banner he had ripped at him. Crimson Sky mentioned how he heroically swooped in to save the half-elf Lyndis and how the half-elf woman had been in awe of his greatness.

Arcturus doubted, of course, that the strong, spirited half-elf had really bowed before the dragon's greatness, but he humored the dragon anyway. Veledar snorted when he finished, causing Arcturus to flinch slightly.

"Is that satisfying for you, dragon slayer?" he asked, raising a scaly eyebrow.

"I prefer you not call me that."

"It is what you are though."

"As you are a dragon. I will say again that I did not murder the other red wyrm out of cold blood. He was a monster that had done plenty of killing before he tried to end my life. Then...just before he faded into the depths of death, he took something very precious from me. Some things can't be replaced, Crimson Sky...no matter how much we struggle." Arcturus replied. Veledar noticed he reached into the pouch on his belt and seemed to be feeling for something within when he said that last part.

"So he took back a gem, coin, or possibly a piece of art as a memento of your confrontation. I imagine you deserved whatever happened. Your people seem very skilled at twisting stories according to their needs." He hissed.

He watched the human's response for the moment. Arcturus sighed and seemed to grip whatever was in his pocket tighter, then wrote more on the paper, but the human now looked drained. Veledar guessed whatever he said had hurt the human deeper than intended.

"Perhaps you are telling the truth as well, and I am wrong to assume vile things of you." Veledar said, causing Arcturus to look at him once again. "However, I am curious as to what is going to happen to me now. What is Crimson Sky's fate? Will he be sentenced to death? Perhaps tortured?"

He saw what could be described as confusion in the paladin's eyes, so he pressed the point harder. Perhaps he would even be able to manipulate the man now that he gained a small measure of lenience.

"Would that be the just or noble thing for a knight to do?" he said, watching Arcturus return the gaze.

"I will make sure the king hears your side of the story," the man stood up, putting his clipboard to his side, much to Veledar's disappointment. "Do you require anything? I can have food brought to you if you want. It's not the best we have, but should keep you satisfied until...well, you know." Arcturus said.

"I wish to be set free, not feast on whatever scraps you find on your tables. Now send me my armored jailer back. I have a few words to share with him."

"Will do. Fare you well, Crimson Sky," Arcturus said before walking out of the room, letting the guard from before slip into his shadowy corner.

"Well if it isn't the mysterious armored monk, coming to marvel at my ferocious beauty. What's the matter? Are my scales so dazzling they tangled your tongue?"

"Aye. You are a sight to behold, tied up like a juicy ham eager for the fire's licks," the guard chuckled. "Reminds me of this roasted lizard I ate once. Kinda looked like you, minus the wings."

"I weep for your faulty sight, human." Veledar snorted, blowing some dust over the floor. How dare this guard insult him by calling him a common lizard.

"You a winged lizard then. No, a serpent, like the trickster from my mother's tales. D'you happen to hear the story of Lenrogor the Muffin Thief?"

"I might tell you if you call me by my name, title, or species, you pink skinned brute."

"Lizard wants to play games now?"

"Grah but you're thick! I am a dragon you metal-clad, urine drenched urchin! Is the king so drowned in debts that he snatches illiterate orphans from the streets to serve as his knights now?" He grinned at the last bit, thinking he had the human backed to the wall.

"Oh, hahaha! Good one, good one! Can't have a discussion with a dragon without resorting to petty, thoughtless insults. Just you wait until the rest of Lumara gets a piece of the great comedian. Then we'll see who's laughing, serpent."

Veledar stuck his tongue out at the man before tugging on his leathers one last time, then slumped to the ground defeated. He closed his eyelids and tried to think back to the dream he was having before he was so rudely awakened by the brute's shouts inconvenient shouts.

* * * * * * * * * *

Arcturus swiftly ran back to his quarters with the manuscript from the dragon rolled up under his arm. He was currently holding his hand to the ridge of his nose. He had just received a message from one of the king's wizards consisting of an unexpected change in his orders. Instead of bringing the dragon back to the capital, he was charged with killing him while he was still firmly bound in the hold of the ship. The news struck him particularly hard after the unpleasant discussion he had with the dragon.

What if Crimson Sky is right? That nagging voice in the back of his mind kept whispering thoughts Arcturus would have considered treasonous under normal circumstances. However, the more he pondered, the more he realized how rotten this course of action was. In serving his king, he could very well send an innocent creature to a premature death. Arcturus didn't know if he could read dragons as well as he did people. He tried not to think about what Crimson Sky had said about justice, honor, and doing what was right. Clearly the dragon had a silver tongue. With its life at stake, he'd not leave any stone unturned, no matter what terrors lurked underneath. As he closed his eyes for a faltering moment, the image of his burning house sprung to his mind.

Selena...Geoffrey... Dread Flame's talons locked around his useless leg, forcing Arcturus to watch as his family withered before his very eyes...

The paladin placed a hand on the sturdy door that led to his quarters. He took a moment to regain his bearings, then opened the door and collapsed onto the cot with a thump. Despite everything his gut was telling him, a big part of him still believed the dragon. There had been some stretching of the truth involved, but he could still not shake the truthfulness in the creature's cerulean eyes. They had not wavered, nor were they filled with malice when he spoke. He imagined how it would have looked if the dragon was any other species. Would there even be a debate on this matter?

"Selina..." He whispered, pulling a small locket from his pouch. He flipped open the silver case to reveal a picture of his wife and son, side by side. "If only you were here to soothe my troubled mind. What would you do, hmm? Is a dragon's life worth going against my kingdom? Betraying a king that trusted me to..."

Arcturus' words faltered. He came here to capture the dragon, not end his life based on an order sent through a mage.

"Gods be good, what am I getting into?" He sat up with his hands on his face. He knew what Selena would have said. She would have reminded him about his oath, strengthen his wavering beliefs with her sweet, calming voice. She would have also pointed out that none of those words referred only to humans. Was not every life precious in its own, intricate way?

Arcturus sighed. He imagined her face all scrunched up, annoyed that she had to renew his faith yet again, but in her eyes hid love too, not just concern.

He stood up, stashing the locket back into his pocket. If he was to kill the dragon like his king commanded him to, an innocent life would be lost forever, and that, he could not allow. Not as a paladin.

Arcturus grabbed his pack from his table and started packing his belongings.

"If any of you are watching, now would be a good time to grant me your favor," he whispered to the skies as he slung his shield around his back. He did not yet know how he would go about this task, but one thing was certain. Today, Arcturus, paladin of Lumara, was going to save a dragon from the clutches of impending death.

Chapter 7: Next Time Let's Just Fly

Arcturus returned to Crimson Sky's cell after the crew had their dinner. With a casual order from his lips, the guard was relieved of his duty, and no one would be the wiser. He turned the knob to the room and opened the door slowly. The plan was simple. Let the dragon escape and take the full blame for the mishap. Of course, it sounded easy when you put it like that. The lies that followed after said deed put Arcturus on edge. He didn't want to stick to his oath by betraying his people, so he tried to focus on the immediate future for now. More precisely, on how to convince his men -and even the king- that he had no involvement in the dragon's escape.

Arcturus imagined himself standing before the foot of Cornelius' throne, with a grave look about his face. *I've seen the cage give way before the dragon's might with my own eyes, m'lord. We got lucky to escape unscathed. Yes, the dragon's gone, but what matters here is that we're all alive. The beast didn't kill anyone.*

He kicked himself at how stupid that sounded. A full squad of the king's best men, outsmarted by a captive dragon? It was a hard sell, but Arcturus still remained determined. Whatever justice the king would bestow upon him was better than the regret of having an innocent creature killed. Man or dragon, red or black, male or female. It was a living, sentient creature that deserved better than to be put down like a sick dog.

Arcturus shut the door behind him with a soft click, then turned to the dragon. Crimson Sky had not moved, and his eyelids were closed. Was that snoring he heard? He internally laughed at the thought.

"My favorite inquisitor just can't get enough of me." The dragon yawned, his tongue curling like a feline's before it returned back inside its toothy cage. "What brings you back here, paladin? Surely it's not only my charming looks or irresistible humor."

Arcturus chuckled. This dragon had quite the mouth on him.

"That brooding look again? Does this mean I will be subjected to another round of questions?" Crimson Sky crossed his paws, one on top of the other, a curious look in his cerulean eyes. "Or is it that reason finally dawned upon that furred head of yours?"

The dragon tried to bite at his straps in vain, "Despite how stylish these bonds are, they start to feel really uncomfortable, especially around my hind legs, and I'm not even speaking about what's tucked between them. Did it ever occur to you, at any point in this journey, that your captive might need to unburden himself?"

"Shut your nonsense, dragon." Arcturus whispered. "I've got a set of explanations in my head, but there's no way I can tell my guards the dragon crapped himself with a straight face."

"As if I ever would." The dragon snorted. "So why are you-"

Arcturus hissed again. He approached the dragon slowly and carefully, a hand extended ahead to test the beast's reflexes.

"You were not really sleeping, were you?" he whispered.

"As if I ever could." The dragon snorted. "How can you lot even sleep in this contraption is beyond me. Entertain me for a second."

"No. I'm not talking about dragon-sized outhouses when I'm about to-"

The dragon probably sensed something was amiss. "About to what?" he tilted his head. "You're thinking of something good, aren't you?"

Arcturus rolled his eyes at how chatty the dragon was today. He fought evil beasts, lazy beasts, but he rarely had the misfortune to face off against chatty ones. The paladin made his way to the strap at the dragon's neck, then hesitated. What he was about to do next was going to set a whole lot of weird events into motion. Was it really worth it? A dragon's life for-

The human shook his head. He couldn't think such thoughts. Not when the dragon looked at him with such peaceful eyes.

"I've noticed that twitch, you know. You are thinking of setting me free, after all." said Crimson Sky with a grin. "Oh, you can't tell me you got cold feet now when you've already come all the way here. Approach. I might even offer you my wet appreciation in return."

"Ugh, I'm better off without dragon drool on my clothes." Arcturus said. He kneeled and looked Crimson Sky in the eye, "I'll set you free, but in exchange, I need your word that no one else is to be harmed."

"Of course, of course. When did I ever lie to you anyway?" replied Crimson Sky, his eyes not straying in the slightest. "Besides, even if I had this silver tongue you seem so wary of, I'm not stupid to attack a warship. You have my word on that."

That was the final push Arcturus needed. After brief pause to gather himself mentally, he loosened that strap around Crimson Sky's neck, and immediately, the dragon pushed his head up, letting out a long sigh of relief.

"Much better."

Arcturus tensed for a brief moment, but there was no deep breath, no intense flame coming out of the dragon's mouth.

"You're looking at me as if I grew another pair of horns."

"Nah, it's just- no, no, don't even think of-"The dragon's snout descended upon him, and if that sea of scales wasn't bad enough, his slimy eel of a tongue poked out, along with the dragon's less-than-likable breath. Arcturus' fears came true. Crimson Sky was definitely going to slobber and drift his tongue all over his fine clothes.

"Gods..." he grimaced as he flung off ropes of translucent goo from his vestments while the dragon stared at him with a very pleased look on his face. "You know what? I'm not even going to bother talking."

"Good. Because I will." Crimson Sky went into a pompous lecture about his features, starting with his silky wings, then following up with his tough scales, even talking about the perfect curves of his claws. For a brief moment, his words made Arcturus feel as if he was actually releasing a deity from hundreds of years of imprisonment. That's how convincing the dragon's words were. After he finished with the front half, he moved to the dragon's bottom to unstrap his legs one at a time. The creature's swishing tail tip reminded Arcturus of the slap he got back in the cave, and if the circumstances were better, he would've gotten his revenge right here and now.

But this was not the right time. "Alright. You're done."

Crimson Sky threw a quick look behind, then propped himself up on his fours to stretch his limbs.

"Grrrraaaaatitude," he said as he turned around to face Arcturus. "I owe you more than a few licks, human."

"Consider us even."

"Oh. Even you say? Even?" the dragon paced closer, clearly trying to intimidate him with his size. Then, in a flash, that bothersome tail whirled around, sending Arcturus slamming against the wall, hard enough to hurt. He collapsed on the ground with a cough, then groaned as the dragon trapped him underneath a clawed forepaw.

"B-bastard," he grabbed onto his scaly fingers to pry them apart, only to find them strong and sturdy.

"Do you feel even now, human? Imagine how I feel." The dragon snarled. "First, you roused me from my sleep, then attacked me with your mob of angry peasants, stole my treasure, brought me here, forced me to sit for hours with the most annoying sound buzzing in my ears, and to you, we are even?" he growled. "Don't think I will forget what you've put me through."

Arcturus felt his pulse quicken. Out of all the scenarios he conjured in his mind, finding himself pinned and helpless was not on the list. He cursed himself for letting his guard down. This bastard was probably just like the other red he faced. A lying, manipulative sod who-

The prison of toes receded, and with a deep breath Arcturus' fears went away.

"Still, you have freed me. This has to count for something, right? Now show me the way out of this place before I really lose my temper."

"That's rich," Arcturus picked himself up. "You should see how it feels to be rammed to the wall when you put your trust in a blabbering Red."

"I hope you're not speaking about me."

"Yeah. I'm not." Arcturus lied to avoid another word warfare with the dragon. "Follow me, and heed my instructions if you want to leave this place on your own paws. All I have to do is pull a lever to open the hatch and you can fly away." Arcturus replied as he turned and opened the large door for the dragon. "Yes, it's that easy, unless my guards get suspicious."

Hopefully, that was not the case. Together with the dragon, Arcturus made his way into the empty hanger just as he planned. Crimson Sky was quickly behind him, squeezing his way through the hallways. Luckily, the staff was on a lunch break, so the two of them had a clear way through.

"What convinced you to let me go? Was it my greatness? Or was I able to masterfully manipulate you into doing my bidding?" Crimson Sky whispered from behind.

"Believe it or not, that loud maw of yours told me things I didn't expect. I... decided to put my trust in someone." Arcturus sighed. His thoughts went to Selina.

"So, what you're saying is I was able to manipulate you." the dragon grinned, causing Arcturus to sigh a second time.

Arcturus walked to a metallic console with different buttons and levers, clearly labeled for their uses. He grasped the one that opened the hangar, then looked back at Crimson Sky.

"Once I open this, you fly away. No questions asked, no farewells given," he said. "Make sure you get far away to a place where my king cannot find you. I will sort out this nonsense with the false charges on my own." He turned to Crimson Sky who had narrowed eyes. "Ready?"

"I cannot do that." Crimson Sky shook his horned head. "Your king demanded my capture, you grieved me in more than one way, and you expect me to just leave?" Crimson Sky cocked his head to the side. "I am going to find your king and make him give back everything he's taken from me over a pleasant chat about how he thinks it is within his right to steal from a perfectly peaceful citizen of his realm."

Arcturus could not believe the dragon's bravery, or ignorance. "Gods. You...this is the biggest nonsense I heard yet. Do you realize how many soldiers we have? How many airships, how many men, and teams of gryphons? You couldn't possibly get anywhere near our king without a cage to house you or fetters to bind your limbs." He said calmly, gripping the lever tighter in his hand. "Now, I did my part and freed your scaly bottom, so how about you do yours?"

"You had contact with your king?" Crimson Sky asked as he raised an eyebrow.

"Yes, I have met with him on occasions." said Arcturus as he peeked to make sure no one was coming. The hangar was still empty. All that remained for him to do was convince this stubborn dragon to leave.

"And you know the layout of the castle?" continued Crimson Sky, and Arcturus noticed the growing grin on his snout. Crimson Sky pounced on him before he could respond. The dragon had him wrapped tight under a scaled limb, then his other paw reached for the lever. The floor of the ship opened up to reveal the ground far below.

"What are you doing?" Arcturus struggled against the dragon's grip, but the red beast was too strong, and he was pulled firm against the dragon's chest. He slammed his fists against the dragon's scales, his efforts as useless as everything he previously tried.

"Put me down, you deluded beast!" Arcturus shouted over the howling wind.

"That's not a smart thing to say." The dragon chuckled.

Over on the other side of the hangar, the door opened with one of the guards holding a wooden tankard.

"Hey Arcturus, the lads upstairs are having this- by the gods he's got you!" he dropped the tankard to the floor with a thud, ale spilling over the wooden boards. "The dragon has escaped!" he cried to the hallway. "Beast's loose! He has the Paladin! To arms, men, to arms! Beast's loose!" The man sprinted back the way he came to most likely grab a weapon.

"Alright. Alright." Arcturus spoke quickly. "You had your fun now, but they're never going to let you leave, so put me aaaaaaaaahhhhhhhh!!!!!"

He felt his stomach lurch as the dragon dove headfirst out the hatch with the paladin tightly held in his claws. Arcturus felt the other forepaw grip him tightly as they descended rapidly from the shrinking ship. Despite not really wanting to be kidnapped in this embarrassing sort of way, Arcturus held onto the dragon as tight as he possibly could. His mind went numb with fright, and his throat never stopped vocalizing said panic.

"What's the matter, Arcturus? I thought a man that travels in flying machines wouldn't be afraid of heights!" Crimson Sky laughed deeply. "Or is it just for dragons that you scream like a banshee?"

"Do you know what you've done?!" Arcturus shouted, his nerves starting to ease as the dragon steadied his flight.

"I have escaped your flying machine, captured a valuable resource that will help me, oh, and I get to hear you sing." Crimson Sky said, his voice oozing with narcissism.

"All you've accomplished is getting us neck-deep into stupid, scaly dragon crap! They'll hunt us down to the end of the earth for this. Gods be damned, I was giving you a chance, you arsehole of a dragon, and you've messed everything!" Arcturus shouted as he still gripped his captor. "Put me down, already. PUT ME DOWN!"

"Not a very good choice of words for a wingless human." Arcturus felt the dragon's grip tighten on him. "Would be a very long drop for you."

"Where are you taking me?" He asked. Surely the dragon wasn't going back to his lair. That would have to be the most stupid plan, and hopefully even this blabber-mouth was smarter than that.

"I have a plan, and I have my ways."

"Yeah. Your devious, careless ways. Excuse me if I'm not feeling overly optimistic about your plan."

"All you need to know is that we are going somewhere safe." Crimson Sky replied.

The rest of the flight went in silence as Arcturus tried to not focus on the ground, so very far removed from his feet. It made his stomach queasy, and his head ache, to even look at the wobbling skies. He instead focused on the scales that adorned the dragon's chest and forepaws. They were smooth and segmented as to allow fine movements, but possibly even stronger than the armor that Arcturus was wearing. He felt Crimson Sky's wing beats with every flap, and inhaled the dragon's scent with every breath. Arcturus had to admit, he smelled dogs a lot more displeasing than this dragon. If it were not for the fear of falling, the flight might have even been relaxing.

"Hold tight. We're going down."

Arcturus wrapped his fingers around the dragon's limbs and felt his stomach churn one last time as Crimson Sky started his decent towards the ground.

He landed with a thud, the cracking of wood following shortly after. From the darkness, Arcturus spotted the form of his crossbow splintered in pieces across the dark ground. He stood up and pulled out his sword, holding the gleaming metal between Crimson Sky and himself.

"I get it, you vile, overly loud beast! You lie to me, kidnap me, take me to a secluded spot and eat me." He looked for an opening, but with Crimson Sky now standing in front of him, he did not see a way out. He most likely could not out-fight the dragon like this, with hardly any equipment. So Arcturus reached into his pouch to pull out a small yellow stone, that, with a simple touch, illuminated the area like a torch.

"Come. Fight me. I assure you, I won't go down that easily," he said sternly, gripping his sword tightly. The dragon became all the more intimidating in the stone's light that reflected off his scales.

"Really?" The dragon just stared at him for a moment before he rolled his cerulean eyes. "Are we going to do this now?"

"What else is left?" Arcturus hissed.

"Oh please. If I wanted to kill you, I would have just dropped you the moment I dove out of your machine."

Arcturus hated to admit as much, but Crimson Sky had a point. He hesitated a moment before stowing his sword. "So where does this put me? I am your captive? Or maybe...a friend?"

A small smirk appeared on Crimson Sky's snout. "That can be arranged if you help me recover all what I've lost. You owe me a lot of things, friend," the dragon empathized that last word with a hiss.

Crimson Sky started to circle him slowly, with each paw hardly making a noise on the ground.

"Now that's rich. Why should I be helping you? You kidnapped me!" He shouted, but despite this, Crimson Sky just grinned with his pointed teeth. He settled onto his haunches with his tail flicking back and forth.

"That's all? I expected a better rant from the mighty Arcturus Lund, paladin of Lumara, vanquisher of scaly evildoers."

"And I expected an honest dragon!"

"Well, I did save your life, so there's that."

Arcturus narrowed his eyes. "This is even better. Out of all the possible things you could say, this is the worst. Please, enlighten me. How in the world did you come to such rational conclusion?"

"It's easy. By freeing me, you turned your back against your king's orders. Oh. You probably thought he's going to fall prey to your simple lies, is that it? This might be hard to hear, but you are not a good liar at all, paladin. The king would've seen right through you, then what? Torture? What punishment do you humans have for freeing a dragon?"

The dragon had a point. Curses, it had to come to this, stranded in the middle of nowhere with the same dragon he was supposed to deliver back to Lumara.

"Why are you still thinking? Just admit the truth. Right now, I am the best chance you have."

"Thank you...Crimson Sky," Arcturus replied, much to the dragon's surprise. He even looked another way to avoid showing too many emotions.

"That...that came a bit faster than I expected from a pompous paladin."

Arcturus let the snide remark go for now. "I have to admit, you don't sound half as stupid as I imagined. Lay out the rest of your plans for me."

"No. You share first." The dragon said.

Arcturus sighed. "I thought that's obvious." Arcturus looked back at the sky. "I figure they already came up with the obvious course of action. There will be several gryphons coming after you that will track us both down and attempt to recapture you."

"Hmmmphhh, well, luckily, we won't be here for long," grumbled Crimson Sky as he was yet to look away from the trees. "I have an acquaintance in this forest that owes me a favor, and I'm sure she would be glad to see that debt paid."

"Another dragon? How far are they?"

The dragon snorted. "Never mentioned the species to keep you guessing. Besides, I quite enjoyed the clattering feel of your armor rattling over that shivering body of yours. Leaves quite the impression of a brave knight." Crimson Sky snickered as he stretched his wings wide before turning his snout to a collection of bushes.

"What do you think of our brave knight, Trixie? Quite a sight to behold, isn't he?"

"Oh yes I did! How loud did he cry?" came the sound of a small female voice. Arcturus turned to see a little fairy emerging from the bushes with a small flash of blue light.

"Oh, you should have been there. He screeched like a proper banshee. Almost hurt me to see him squeal like that," said Crimson Sky as he stood up and stretched like a cat.

"You're speaking vile things, dragon." Arcturus said. "And as the sole being without wings here, I think it is fairly reasonable to be scared of falling to my death when a certain dragon kidnaps me out of nowhere." He crossed his arms defensibly, a gesture that made the fairy and dragon laugh even harder.

"Crimson Sky, have you returned to collect your favor?"

Crimson Sky nodded at the fairy. "This human and I need to use your portal. He claims that his companions will dispatch gryphons and capture me again. I, of course, intend to lose them before they make any progress."

"Of course you may use the portal, Crimson Sky, but be wary. Fairy magic has a way of messing around with non-fairies."

Truthfully, Arcturus had never studied or heard too much about fairy magic. "Could you tell us more please?" He walked closer to the fairy with an eyebrow raised.

"There's not much to say. You need to have a clear head during the process of gate-hopping, otherwise you may be pulled to whoever knows where." Trixie said while flying around Arcturus' head.

"Where would that be?" asked Crimson Sky as he tilted his head to the side.

"No one knows!" she cried. "That's what I just said!"

Crimson Sky laughed at her little outburst.

"I wouldn't laugh if I were you. The other realm affects dragons in the same way it enfeebles other mortals. Even if said dragon is full of hot air." Trixie scolded the dragon by waving her tiny little index finger.

"Watch your little tongue, Trixie. Friend or not, I do not take kindly to anyone besmirching my name." Crimson Sky growled, "Let's just get this over with so I don't have to listen to more of this *be careful it's so dangerous nonsense*. I can handle myself just fine."

Despite trying to hold it in, Arcturus let out a small laugh. He tried to stop as Crimson Sky turned to him with unblinking eyes.

"You have something to say, paladin?" Crimson Sky asked. He approached slowly, his tail curling around him. "Something you found funny, perhaps?"

"It's nothing. Just that...I've got firsthand experience with this hot air she speaks of." He burst out, causing Crimson Sky to turn to the fairy.

"See what you've done? Now my human is snickering at me!"

"I'm not YOUR human, dragon!" Arcturus pointed out, to which the dragon let out a gust of hot air.

"Didn't seem so when you held on to me for dear life."

"Maybe I wouldn't have if you didn't kidnap me!"

"Ok, ok ok ok!" Trixie held up her small arms to split the two arguing males apart. "You guys are making my head spin. If you are serious about using the gate, you need to be a lot closer. Much safer to travel with a buddy if you're a non-fairy." She gestured towards them to get closer. Arcturus moved slightly towards Crimson Sky, who did the same.

"Closer. Has to be much closer than that." she put her arms on her hips.

"Ah, blast it. A few steps closer and you'll ask me to kiss him!" Arcturus scoffed.

Crimson Sky puffed out his chest. "Oh, Arcturus, I know I look good, but you don't have to-"

"Shut it, you gnarly lizard."

Crimson Sky stuck his tongue out at him much to Trixie's disappointment, who zapped them both with a touch of fairy magic.

"If you two keep arguing, I'll leave you here to sort this conflict out with your chasers."

The two males shared an angry glance before they nodded at her.

How did I get here? Arcturus inched closer little by little towards Crimson Sky. *I had a good thing going on that ship. I had my squad, my honor, all traded for a gorram blabber-mouth with an ego the size of Lumara.*

Arcturus was still pondering his misfortune until Trixie pushed him into

Crimson Sky, who dragged the paladin against his chest with a scaly forepaw.

"There, there. Wasn't that hard, was it? My little human pet..."

Arcturus didn't even bother speaking with this... distasteful dragon.

"Now, Crimson Sky, put your claws on his shoulders. You have to have physical contact with your buddy."

"What, this hug isn't good enough?"

"It's better the way I say it. Just do it."

Arcturus figured the fairy's advice wasn't completely selfless. The dragon probably did too, only he enjoyed extracting amusement from this unfortunate situation. Arcturus felt the dragon's fingers give way. The beast looked down on him not with malice, but with amusement, and maybe...something else. He certainly was much gentler than Arcturus imagined, his sharp, curved claws barely making a sound as they fell onto the metal shoulderpads.

"Is this good enough for you Trixie?" he glanced over the fairy to obtain a quick nod from her. "Praise the Gods. Any closer and we'd be smacking our lips together."

Arcturus rolled his eyes, still as a statue. The dragon probably noticed the discomfort showing on his face, for he broke the silence shortly after with a simple question. "What happens now?"

"You will feel a small numbing sensation, then feel as if the ground wants to swallow you whole. A faint path will appear in front of you. One you must follow no matter what happens." Trixie explained as she clapped her hands together. Then Arcturus and Crimson Sky nodded in unison.

"Now stay still. Both of you. We'll part ways in just a moment. Try to have fun, alright?" Trixie gleefully cried as she started to circle them, chanting in a language Arcturus did not understand. It sounded soft and easy on the ears, with numerous oooo sounds. As she spoke, the surrounding trees started to blur, as if he was falling to sleep. The night sky started to darken, as if the moon and stars just vanished into nothingness. Even the bright crystal Arcturus held in his hand started to fade away, until the only thing he could see was the dragon clasping his shoulders. The last thing to fade away were Trixie's words as they started to drift away until they became mute, uncomfortable silence.

Arcturus turned his head away from Crimson Sky. He saw a blurred forest around him, in dull colors of blue and purple. The once pleasant murmur of the forest was replaced by a soft humming every few minutes, but not loud enough to be annoying.

"Should we let go now?"

Arcturus slowly nodded to the dragon. He let go of Crimson Sky to feel the ground. Soft just like the forest they had left behind. He breathed in deeply, yet strangely enough, only Crimson Sky's scent lingered upon the air.

"Eerie place we've gotten ourselves into," said Crimson Sky as he tested the ground with one of his claws. "Do you suppose this ugly earth will swallow us if we stray off the path? I don't like things that try to eat me."

Arcturus couldn't help but chuckle at the irony of that. "Indeed. Not like you have a perfectly fine pair of wings to wrestle yourself out of trouble." Arcturus started to inspect his surroundings. "This forest feels the same, but something is amiss. There's no sound, no smells..." he trailed off to look around.

"There it is." The dragon started walking towards what looked like a small worn path through the blurry trees. That must have been the trail that Trixie spoke of.

As they approached the path, Arcturus noticed that the trees seemed to bend away from them. The corridor was large enough for Crimson Sky and himself to walk alongside each other, without either one feeling cramped. Arcturus reached out to touch a purple leaf, only to have the plant recoil its branch before his hand even made contact. Startled, he pulled his hand back.

"What an odd place," he gasped, turning towards Crimson Sky. The dragon apparently had been watching what he was doing intently.

"I agree. Most bizarre. I have not seen anything like it before. I suggest we follow the path like Trixie suggested. She can be a bit of a joker sometimes, but that piece of advice didn't strike me as random." Crimson Sky gestured to the path with his neck. "At the front, paladin. Pretend you're leading your valiant dragon-slaying knights into battle, only this time you seek to please the dragon, not slay him." Crimson Sky grinned.

"The more time I spend around you, the more I start to realize what an odd creature you are."

"Oh, there it is. A compliment after a downpour of ill-intentioned japes."

"You're not supposed to take it that way."

"Nevertheless, I will, because I am painfully aware of how striking I am."

Arcturus eyed the dragon's teeth with a slight hint of worry, then quickly realized he had better chances to drown on his mead than get harmed by this joker of a dragon.

"So? Who leads if I refuse to please the dragon, as you put it?"

The dragon's claws tapped Arcturus' backside.

"Oh, fine then...I suppose if Crimson Sky is scared, a paladin will of course have to lead the way until the fearsome dragon's bravery returns." He smirked at the dragon.

"You're so full of yourself."

"Hah! Get a good look at who's talking, your strikingness." Arcturus took the lead and they both started walking on the strange path laid before them.

They walked for hours, the path never seeming to change direction or turn. Several times they stopped at the sound of a slight roar. Crimson Sky confirmed that it was indeed the sound of a dragon. A quick discussion was held about the possibility of lost dragons in the woods, followed quickly by arguments against such nonsense. Arcturus stopped for a moment as his feet had begun to ache, at which Crimson Sky causally bumped into him.

"Why did you stop?" the dragon asked, sitting down on his haunches.

Arcturus had to sit. It felt like they had been walking for days. When his rear touched the soft ground, an utter wave of exhaustion washed over him. Like days upon days of exercise had suddenly caught up with his weary body. All his limbs felt as though they were weighted down by armor five times heavier. He slumped down backwards as his eyelids threatened to close. They shut only for a few seconds before he opened them again. He saw Crimson Sky was fighting to stay awake as well, as the dragon's head was slowly descending towards the ground. It rested softly beside him with a small groan.

"I rrrrreally need to rest for a bit..." The dragon mumbled as his words slowly descended into snoring.

Arcturus felt his eyelids once again insist on closing. He found them even heavier than before, and this time he did not think he had the strength to keep on fighting. He remembered slumping over and laying down beside the dragon before his dreams took him.

Hours later, Arcturus awoke with a deep yawn, sitting upright and feeling completely refreshed. Beside him still lay the sleeping Crimson Sky. His wings were draped over him like a veiny, semi-transparent blanket. Arcturus looked around. The once dull colors of the night had been replaced with very vibrant greens and browns lit by a very bright blue sky. However, as he looked around, he could still make out a slight blurriness, a sign that they were still in the faerie's realm. He quickly checked his gear, finding everything was where he left it, except the crossbow that got smashed by the dragon.

He felt his stomach grumble, so he started digging through his pockets. After minutes of pulling out every gadget he had, Arcturus held a small brown bag in his hand, containing a stash of trail rations. He greedily grasped the dried fruit and nuts, stuffing them into his mouth. While he was chewing, in the back of his mind, he realized he was way hungrier than he thought he would be. It felt as though he had not eaten in days. He pulled the water skin from his pack and took a swig from it. The water was cool to his tongue as he gulped it down. He gasped before wiping his mouth. When he was done he turned back towards Crimson Sky, who, by the sign of his deep breaths, was still very much asleep.

He rolled his eyes as he sighed. Out of all the possible dragons he could get paired with...

He moved over and placed his hands on the dragon's head, ready to shove him awake. He stopped of course, to think about what Crimson Sky would do if he was -again- rudely awoken.

"Now, Arcturus," he said aloud to himself, "this is either the worst decision of your career, or just one of many. Eh. What's an extra boulder on top of a mountain?"

Arcturus dragged his voice, then moved his hands down the dragon's scaly neck. He knew just what this lazy lizard needed.

"Wake up!!" he slapped the dragon's tan belly. "We can't be resting the day away!"

"Well maybe YOU can't do that, but I certainly intend to." Crimson Sky yawned lazily before opening one of his eyes. "Hold on. Are we still in Trixie's realm?"

"Take a look around, your highness." Arcturus waved sarcastically.

"You're a crap servant."

"Why thank you, my liege." Arcturus gave a mocking bow. "Please, pardon me for not cleaning your claws or polishing your scales during your rest."

"That's an idea." The dragon stood up and stretched his spine, following with his wings, and then slamming his tail onto the earth.

"How long have we been asleep?" Crimson Sky asked as he flung off patches of dirt from his belly with the help of his claws.

"Just slept the night. Gods, I have never been so tired before. I didn't think we were walking for THAT long." Arcturus said.

"I noticed that as well." Crimson Sky started to scowl, "I imagine that in this place, time moves at a different pace." Suddenly, Crimson Sky grabbed his stomach as it gave a loud growl, which was a very terrifying noise to Arcturus.

Arcturus met Crimson Sky's eyes briefly. "Oh, don't be frightened," laughed the dragon. "I am not so hungry as to eat you. Although...." The dragon looked into the blurred woods. "I fear I must go hungry, for I have not seen a speck of wildlife, and even I'm not stupid enough to venture off the path just to sate my hunger."

"How about some nuts?" Arcturus stretched out whatever remained of his rations.

"No." The dragon said sternly. "The quicker we're out of this place, the better. Move your armored ass now," said Crimson Sky as he pushed Arcturus along with his snout.

They started on the path again, with Arcturus still in the front and Crimson Sky very close behind him. They would both stop to stare at the myriad of different bizarre plant life they encountered, some with many branches that ended with eyeballs, or flowers they spotted that gave off a purr like a cat. As they walked, the path seemed to be less and less verdant. They even saw what possibly could have been birds overhead, but Crimson Sky cited Trixie and decided to not take a closer look. They stopped at the next clearing for a rest, Arcturus looked up to find no sun, so he was unsure of what time it was supposed to be.

Crimson Sky laid down onto the grass and sprawled out as he stretched. "You know, I realized something."

"Oh my. I stand in awe before your intellect. Please. Amaze me."

"I hate all this walking." Crimson Sky said as he sat up and stretched his neck into an S shape.

"Yeah. I can see that on your snout as you look to the sky throughout the day, praying for it to end. Still," Arcturus groaned as he stretched out his arms, "you'll find no disagreement from me here."

"Never felt this way since I was a hatchling. Suddenly find myself unable to take to the skies, that is." The dragon paused. "Grarr, how annoying. Imagine how quick this journey would've been if your dwarfish legs didn't slow us down."

Arcturus let out a dry laugh. "Try harder, Crimson Sky. I'm sure you can do better."

"I don't want to!" the dragon complained. "Thinking takes energy, and time. I just want to fly."

Well, that was something he did not learn from his studying of dragons. "You can't fly as a hatchling? I thought dragons came out chirping and darting every which way through the air." He mimed his arms to be like wings, to which Crimson Sky frowned.

"No, our wings are not strong enough to carry us at that age. It falls to our parents to carry us around." Crimson Sky said as he closed his eyes, "I almost pity you for not experiencing that blissful safety of soaring over the world in the claws of a loving parent."

Arcturus figured the dragon was picturing himself flying once more in the sky.

"Hmm...I imagine it is more enjoyable when you are not plucked suddenly from the ground against your will."

Crimson Sky just grinned, "That scream you gave was pretty hilarious. Maybe we should do it again when I need a laugh."

"Don't even try." Arcturus said, pointing a finger at the dragon. "Or I will make sure you are missing one of your claws next time you wake up." He brandished his sword around.

Crimson sky just replied with a smug look. Then a moment of silence. "I don't think you are capable of harming me."

"Why would you think that?" he asked. "I was trained to kill dragons, you know."

"Yes, but you have a different heart than the men I speak of. You are...frail. In a good way. Gentle is the word I seek, yes."

Arcturus smiled. "Crimson Sky just gave me a compliment!"

The dragon snarled, but couldn't find anything to say in his defense, so he just draped that annoyingly slimy eel of a tongue over Arcturus' hands as the human struggled to protect his face.

"Stop that!"

The dragon pulled his snout back. "What? I'm expressing my affection!"

"Express it somewhere else," Arcturus grumbled. "You know how I feel about dragon drool."

"Get over yourself." Crimson Sky playfully shoved the human back. "Speaking of which, now that we have the time. I wanted to know why you freed me."

Arcturus put the licking behind him. Silly or not, the dragon had enough mockery for now. "I believed your words, dragon. Everything you said about me as a man and a paladin... it made me realize I could not put an innocent life to death."

Crimson sky laughed, "Innocent, am I now?" he rolled in the grass, "Yes yes yes! An innocent hatchling free of any sins!"

"Well innocent of those crimes." Arcturus chuckled at the dragon's playfulness. "My king changed his mind and ordered me to kill you."

Veledar rolled back onto his belly. "And the person you mentioned that you put your trust in, what was that about?"

Arcturus paused when Crimson Sky asked about Selina. "Let's just say the person would have given you a chance. I reminded myself that my oaths were not to just humanoids, and could extend to any living creature, including dragons."

This just made Crimson Sky grin again. "This person sounds very wise."

"She was." Arcturus went to feel the locket in his pouch.

"What's there? More little nuts?" Crimson Sky approached with his head tilted to the side. "I saw you reach in there when we were talking on the ship."

Arcturus pulled out the locket, opened it, and showed it to the dragon. "These were my son and wife. They were the ones taken from me by the...other red dragon I mentioned."

The dragon stared at the pictures of the paladin's dead family for a moment in silence. "I did not know. That is certainly more valuable than a coin, gem, or piece of art."

"Yes." Arcturus placed the locked back into the pocket. "Yes it is."

"I cannot claim to know the dragon you've killed, but to rob the lives of your family…it takes a monster to do that, you know?”

“Indeed. Thank you for…you know.” Arcturus mumbled, stroking the dragon over his snout more as a reflex. Crimson Sky gave no signs of discomfort. Quite the opposite. He started purring like a cat, only in a much deeper way.

“You don’t mind this?”

“Nraarrr.” The dragon growled in a rather cute way. “Not many humans touched me like this. Believe it or not, you are the first human to not be a complete arse to me, in spite of the incident at my cave.” He finished speaking with a growl.

“I'm sorry about that. Truly.” Arcturus grabbed both sides of the dragon’s jaws. “I will make sure every coin is returned and that your name is cleared of any false accusations.”

“And my books? What about those?” the dragon mumbled.

“New ones if I can get them.”

“New ones?” Crimson Sky said, getting his snout closer to Arcturus' face. “I want old books, not fresh ones.”

Arcturus nodded, “Of course. Old ones it is. Valuable at that.”

This seemed to please Crimson Sky as he sat back down next to him. His attention was drawn to what appeared to be a silver wrymling running out towards the clearing. The wyrmling was female. Arcturus could tell by the less pronounced horns and spines. She stood as half as tall as Crimson Sky and eyed him with a look of playfulness. She opened her mouth and seemed to speak in a language of hisses and growls.

Crimson Sky turned his head in an instant, his face frozen in terror. The little wrymling darted away from them into the forest away from the path.

“Who was that?” Arcturus placed his hand over the shocked dragon’s leg.

“T-that,” Crimson Sky began, “That can't be her. She is much older than that!”

Crimson Sky stood up to pace in front of Arcturus, “It has to be an illusion.” He started to ramble nonsense in the same growls and hisses the silver dragon had talked in.

“Crimson, who was that?” exclaimed Arcturus. This seemed to snap Crimson Sky out of it as he turned towards him. “I think what I witnessed - what we both saw in fact- was an illusion of my younger sister, and when did you start calling me Crimson?”

“Just now. I decided it was easier than Crimson Sky all the time, and somewhat better than dragon.”

“I don't like how it feels, bare and insignificant.” Crimson Sky replied as his muzzle scrunched up. “Use the full title. Don’t be lazy.”

“Fine, Crimson Sky.” said Arcturus in a monotone voice.

"That's much better!" Crimson Sky beamed.

"I shouldn't be surprised you have a family, but in a way, I find myself...mystified." Arcturus said. Although now that he thought of it, it seemed natural for dragons to have families. It was just something he never thought of.

"Go on. I'll tell you in a moment."

They started walking once again, although Crimson Sky was walking more slowly than he did.

"I had a sister. That was her, back when she was still a hatchling. We both had a mother as well, in case you're wondering."

"Well I figured that, unless you dragons just sprout out from the ground..." he stopped as Crimson Sky turned to him with his teeth barred.

"Bad joke. Sorry," he said quickly, then decided to ask him another question. "So, what were their names?" He quickened his pace to now match the dragon that was leading.

"I see what you are trying to do." chuckled Crimson Sky. "But you will not get their names from me. You will have to earn their names from them. You can of course have their titles. My sister was known as the Radiant Gem of the East, and my mother's favorite title was the Indomitable Aegis. She was quite fond of that one. Said an elven caravan gave it to her when she fought off a large group of bandits that had beset them."

"She had the best stories." Crimson Sky sighed, "Not like your human stories at all, where dragons capture maidens, pick on humans, or wreck devastation on the countryside."

"You are kind of picking on me." Arcturus pet the dragon's side to keep him from growling. "And I am sure we have a good dragon in one of the stories. Definitely. We know you're not all that bad," he protested, but with a quick stare and the dare, "prove it" he was wracking his brain for one. After a moment of thinking, he sighed and admitted defeat to the dragon that thrilled at having bested him.

"I can't think of one right now, but I will let you know when my memory returns."

"Sure. Something tells me I will be waiting till your death bed until you remember one." Crimson Sky chuckled.

The two of them suddenly stopped. The road they were walking on had been bright and colorful, while the road ahead looked dark, dreary, and covered with clouds. Arcturus looked to the path that was littered with worn stones and gnarled roots. A crack of thunder later, and the downpour started. It was a strange sight to see, as if an invisible wall separated the bright trail from its much darker counterpart.

"I am starting to hate this fairy magic." Arcturus said with a stern face.

"A sentiment well shared." The dragon agreed.

They both took a step onto the dark path, finding it was not a trap, but it did make them wet. As they walked, the sound of the rain hitting Arcturus' metal armor suddenly came to a stop after a few hundred feet. Looking up, he saw what had happened. There was a tan membrane of a wing overhead, sheltering him from the rain like an umbrella.

"Much obliged, dragon," he said with a smile, pointing to the wing.

"I only did it to stop that annoying sound your scales make when the rain hits them," grumbled Crimson Sky. He then turned his snout to the path ahead, as if to ignore Arcturus. Although Arcturus swore he saw a smirk on the dragon's snout.

"Sure dragon, sure." He poked the dragon's chin, then continued walking down the path in the company of the only worthy dragon he knew. Perhaps in a few years, there would be a story of a good dragon out there. The tale of Crimson Sky the Bold. Arcturus merely had to witness such heroic acts...and hope both of them lived to see the tales spread throughout the taverns of the world.

Chapter 8: Escaping Sorrows

Veledar closely followed Arcturus down the wet path of earth. His wings still covered the human to at least keep him dry from the rain that pattered upon his tan membrane. He breathed in deep into the smell of fresh rain, then opened his maw to catch a few droplets of water onto his tongue. The liquid certainly tasted like normal rain. There was nothing odd about it. The dragon stared at the dark clouds that filled the sky, where he would see the occasional flash of lighting spear through the heavy curtain. However, every time that happened, there was no bang. Veledar was sure he never heard the deafening roar of thunder ever since he entered Trixie's realm.

The two of them kept on walking, paws and boots splashing through the mud. His joints would occasionally ache during the drip, a dull pain that he could manage, but he still let out a loud groan to startle the human. This amused the dragon as Arcturus would then apologize for capturing the dragon and throwing him in the bowels of the Lumarian airship.

They had come to a gnarled tree in the middle of their path, easily dwarfing Veledar in size. He stared up at the trunk that had two large knots at a split that looked suspiciously like eyes.

"Well, nothing wrong with a bit of creepiness as long as I can sit on it." The human found a dry bit of earth and sat against the tree, letting out a sigh of relaxation.

"Aren't you feeling watched?"

Arcturus waved dismissively at the eyes, comparing them to a weird type of fairy flower.

"Grrr, fine." Veledar sat beside him. He started poking and licking at his wing joints to ease the tension while he flexed his limbs slowly to keep the blood from pouring through his weary muscles. They sat there in silence for a while. Veledar noted that the rain had not exactly stopped, but simply did not fall beneath this tree or its branches. He tilted his neck in curiosity, as the tree had no leaves at all to protect them from the water droplets.

"How long do you think we have been walking?" Arcturus rested his back more comfortably against one of the roots.

"Can't tell in a place where there's no sun or moon to speak of..." Veledar replied as he dashed his tongue over a hind paw. He could already feel the ache in his joints starting to go away, in spite of the human's silly comments about the taste of dirt and what not. He called this practice barbaric. As if he knew anything about being a dragon.

"Fine. Lick them all away. I don't know why we're arguing about grooming habits when you yawn like a cat, stretch like a cat, eat like a cat and probably even mate like one."

Veledar had a few answers prepared, but the grooming felt far too relaxing. Besides, he didn't want to give the human the satisfaction of another silly debate.

When Veledar finished with his paws, he continued with his tail. Arcturus mumbled something about continuing the journey. Veledar, however, loved his tail too much to leave it cold and damp.

"I am more interested in why the rain does not fall beneath this tree, adding that to the list of other things we have seen." He answered to one of the human's many concerns.

"Maybe you're right. Perhaps we shouldn't look a dragon in the mouth." Arcturus chuckled.

"Horse. It's horse. I have heard this human saying before, so please don't compare me with those things."

"I've seen plenty of horses in my life, and at the risk of inflating your immense ego, I do have to admit you look much better than a horse."

Veledar stopped mid-lick. "Thank you." He quickly continued to distract himself from the hot blood rushing into his cheeks. It wasn't the first time he heard a compliment from this human's mouth. Why was his heart beating so quick? The dragon nibbled onto his scales, figuring it must've been some weird fairy magic that made him feel awkward.

"Stretch your wing in my direction. I can use a bit of warmth over here."

Veledar did. He stifled a weird growl when the human started caressing along his sensitive membrane.

"Strange, how soft your wings are when your entire body is made for battle." Arcturus traced his finger along a thick blood vessel. "When we get to a village, I'll speak with one of the blacksmiths to fashion you something for the wings. It only takes a single claw to rob you off the ability to fly."

"I won't get hit." Veledar said. He tried to pull his wing back, only to find himself unable as the human held onto two of his phalanges.

"It's mine now. You offered it, remember?"

The dragon mumbled something about rudeness, then continued with his grooming.

Thankfully Arcturus was too tired to poke fun at him. The human put his hands beneath his head and reclined onto the ground. "Figure it would a good time to rest for a while." the human opened one eye to look at the dragon. "Unless you have something else to lick, Crimson Sky."

Veledar groaned. Even with all the licking, his muscles still felt fatigued. He snorted before he coiled around himself, resting his head on top of a hind paw. He hated how bare, cold and hard the ground felt. If only he had materials to build himself a proper nest...

"I only disagree because this place lacks any soft beds for us to sleep on. Since SOMEONE decided to take mine." He looked to Arcturus to see a wave of regret wash over the human's face before he apologized yet again. Veledar smiled and closed his eyes.

"How old are you anyway? I figure you're in the hundreds. Somewhere close to that figure anyway."

"That's an odd, sudden question. Do you really want to know?"

The human mumbled a quick yes.

Veledar remained silent for a moment. Age was something he never really thought about when he simply existed without any worries about the changing seasons or the passing of time.

"Alright. If I had to say, I would guess five hundred and twenty seasons?" Veledar cocked his head, seemingly unsure of himself. "Wait. That's not right. Or is it? Human years are so odd!" Veledar frowned slightly, knowing he wasn't as old as other dragons, but he hoped Arcturus would not notice that.

"Five hundred and twenty seasons?" Arcturus said, sitting up and opening his eyes. It took him a moment before he replied. "Oh, that means a hundred thirty something. Still, rather young for an adult dragon. You've got so many more years to go, my scaly friend. Good health to you."

Veledar sighed. He felt rather embarrassed by the human's deductive skills. It made sense for the paladin to know that. He had studied dragons, after all.

"So, dragons measure their ages in seasons. That's something books never mention, probably because how redundant that is. Much easier to count years than seasons."

"Well honestly, it is only a rough guess, I honestly don't care about my age too much."

Arcturus looked to him as if he might have something to say before shutting his mouth quickly. Well, since the human had asked him, Veledar figured he might as well return the favor.

"What about you, paladin?"

"Twenty-five. That's a hundred seasons in dragon age."

"Is that old for humans?"

Arcturus chuckled.

Veledar had to admit to himself, he was not too sure about the life span of humans. He had heard they were not long as long lived as the elves or even their trusty gryphons. He sighed in pity for their race. Almost a drop of water in the bucket that was Veledar's life span.

"Humans can live for eighty or up to one hundred with the right spells. Past that...I'm not even sure it's worth living."

"Only one hundred? Then the tales I have heard are true!" Veledar replied, "You have such a short time in this world. How can you manage to achieve anything of worth?"

"Simple. We strive to do the most with the time we are given." Arcturus beamed, "Live for the day. Absorb as much knowledge as we can from our surroundings. We are kind of forced to do it faster than the other races. Trust me, you're not the only one to ask me this question. You should hear some of the stories of elves in our city. Sometimes, they can be cold, heartless bastards." Arcturus then paused for a moment as Veledar just looked at him during the silence.

"How about your stories, dragon? Is this the first time you have a meaningful interaction with a human?"

"I met two scavengers when I encountered Trixie, then made acquaintance with hundreds when I blundered into that man's house. Before that, I had only heard of you in stories from the wood elves."

"You knew wood elves?"

"But of course," The dragon said. "Hard not to when you live next to their great forest."

"That must have been hard, you know, being a fire breathing dragon in a forest full of flammable elves." the human smirked.

Veledar just chuckled. "Yes, that would be a very big problem for an irresponsible hatchling, but mother kept us away from them for the most part. They gave her plenty of leeway in raising us."

"Did you have any other siblings besides the one you mentioned before?"

Veledar frowned. He usually enjoyed his talks about the past. However, that was a topic he never enjoyed. "Yes, I had a brother who was older than I," he said slowly and more quietly than he usually talked.

"Have you stayed in contact with him? I have heard dragons live very much in solitude."

"That is not a hard rule. We generally like to live alone, but we enjoy companionship as much as any other living being."

He thought to the day that he and Adalina had decided to leave the nest and fly away from his mother. She had been relieved they were heading out, but he had always remembered how she looked a little sad.

"Although we are separated, we do keep tabs on where the other ones keep their lairs." He thought to his sister's lair that resided over the sea in another country.

"Well, how long ago did you separate from your family?"

"Twenty-five years ago, in human time." he let out a mighty sigh. Sometimes, it felt as though it were just yesterday that they were all one big happy clutch. He frowned again as he thought back to his brother, imagining how he would have looked now, all grown and strong. Veledar turned his head as they both heard the snapping of a twig behind them. What he saw made his blood run cold, and a shiver of dread tingle up his spine. In the span of that lone moment, Veledar found himself completely helpless.

Standing about one hundred feet from the tree was a silver hatchling on the verge of adulthood. He stood half as tall as Veledar on all four limbs, with armored scales bearing the color of silver. He had two white horns, with one of them severed around the middle. The hatchling had frills along his back all the way from head to his tail, and even under his chin. His gray wings were drooped, dragging against the earth as he moved around.

Veledar shot up when he noticed a sickly red streak slashed around the hatchling's hind leg. When the hatchling turned, more gashes came into view; nauseating things that dripped with crimson goo.

"No. No, not again. Rrraaaaaaaahhhh!" Veledar found himself bounding over to the wrymling as the form of his dying brother collapsed onto the ground. He heard Arcturus shout something to him, but he ignored the human as he desperately reached for his brother. He collapsed as he caressed the dragon's snout. There was no air coming out of his nostrils, no warmth in his cold body. Veledar placed his head on the dead dragon's back, already feeling the tears that plagued him during the moments of depression that followed his brother's death many years ago.

"How can this be?" He cried out. "You were dead for so many ages! Why must you return to torment me so?" he asked as he softly ran his claws over the cuts in his brother's scales.

"If I had......" he trailed off as the tears began to fall down his cheeks now, translucent trickles that splashed onto the ground below. "If only I had been stronger to...to protect you..."

"Dragon. Dragon..." A faint voice called to him. "Crimson Sky!"

Confused, Veledar turned his head around as something warm touched his shoulder.

"Your brother?" The human asked, his voice but a whisper.

"Yes." Veledar's breath shuddered. The dragon closed his teary eyes. He thought back to when his brother began to fall from the sky, spiraling down towards the ground. He shook his snout to clear the memory from his mind.

"How did he perish?"

"That." Veledar sniffed, "That will be a tale for another time." He then wiped his eyes, then opened them to find that his brother's corpse had vanished. He felt his anger grow at the realization this was all an illusion brought on about by this accursed place.

"Graaaaarrr! I hate you!" Veledar smashed his tail into the ground. "This mud that sticks to my feet, the cold air, the oppressive clouds that never stop weeping. I hate everything!" Veledar roared out at the blurred forest, using all his four feet to rake gashes into the ground while his tail left gape after gape until he found his rampage blocked by the human's defiant form.

"Get out of my way."

"No!" Arcturus stretched a hand towards his snout. "This place...it pulses with our memories, unveiling deepest secrets. The more we linger here, the harder it will be to leave. We should get some rest, then get out as quick as we can, especially after... that." Arcturus said.

Veledar threw his snout into the human's arms. He didn't care how ungainly it was, but right now, he needed something warm to banish the cold dread pulsing within his veins. After he got a healthy dose of scratches and a tight sympathy hug from the human, Veledar was ready to leave. He thanked Arcturus for his support, then returned back to the tree, where he acted as a makeshift bed for the tired human.

It must've been a while since they dozed off. Veledar had been having such a wonderful dream. He remembered dragons, and Arcturus too, although anything beyond that out of his grasp. He looked around while his jaws parted in a healthy yawn to find Arcturus missing from his resting place.

"Arcturus?" The dragon lifted each wing at a time to make sure he wasn't missing anything.

There was a trail of boot prints leading towards the blurry forest.

"Arcturus!" he shouted, practically jumping to all fours. *Damn that human*! Veledar cursed to himself. He should have tied him to his tail to stop this from happening, or maybe sleep on top of him. Nevertheless, there was nothing to be done now. Veledar quickly followed the tracks to the trail's edge. He inspected the boot prints, still fresh. That was at least some good news, if the human had not left long ago, he could not have possibly gotten that far. Veledar hesitated before placing a paw into the woods off the beaten path. He remembered Trixie's words, but leaving Arcturus alone in this world of lost memories was just not the right thing to do. Veledar thought back on his own experience, when he tore the ground in grief over his brother's demise. It was Arcturus that calmed his rage. Arcturus that offered him comfort when the coldness of the skies closed down on him.

After a moment of mental preparation, Veledar bounded into the forest. Creepy trees surrounded him from all sides, their gnarled branches almost reaching out to him. Veledar kept away from any roots, avoiding every form of vegetation until he found Arcturus not that far from the path. Arcturus was crouched over what appeared to be two burned corpses. One was the size of an adult, and the other was the size of a small child. The human was holding one in each arm, sobbing quietly into their seared flesh.

Veledar had an idea about who those humans could be. He approached the human, poking him hard in the back.

"Leave me, you vile beast!" Arcturus shouted with animalistic fury, almost catching Veledar on the snout with his sword. "Can't you see that they need me?!" He pointed the sharp tip at Veledar's eyes. "I need to tend to their wounds, and you are not getting in my way!"

"They're not real, Arcturus. What you are seeing now is a lie."

"Wh-what?" The human shook his head. "No. No, they're here. Can't you see them?"

"Only the roots of the trees. You're staring at roots, Arcturus."

The human dropped on his knees to grab onto the other two figures. "No, they're here. I can smell their seared flesh. Touch their...their... "

Veledar grabbed onto Arcturus. "It's all in your mind, human. The forest is feeding on you. Let go. Let go now!"

He could almost feel the forest's grip tighten around their forms. Urging them to remain here. Give themselves to the phantasms of the past.

"I know you're in pain. I know they need you. But so do I!" Veledar snarled as he began to drag Arcturus away from the two corpses.

"Nooooo! Don't do this! Please don't take them away from me again!"

Veledar ignored Arcturus as the human punched and kicked like a wild, caged beast.

"Let go. Le'go!" The human wailed, grabbing onto a branch and holding firm. "Noooooo!"

With a final tug, the human's grip slipped, and Veledar pulled him all the way back to the tree. He plopped Arcturus down, who now seemed to be calm, with no fight left in him. The human just slouched, hugged his knees, and continued sobbing silently to himself.

"I lied."

Arcturus looked at the dragon, so much pain welling in his eyes. It almost hurt Veledar, to see the once stern paladin so...broken.

"I saw the burned corpses...what remained of your family. But I couldn't leave you there alone, because I need you here, with me."

"Why did you do that, dragon?" Arcturus whispered, drool coming out of his mouth to join the streams of tears that fell down the sides of his pained face. "They needed me...without me by their side, they'll be lost again." Arcturus said softly. "I can't do this...I cannot abandon them again."

"That was not your family. Only an illusion meant to lure you off the path. Just...just like my brother." Veledar stated calmly, although he felt a pang of pity for the deceased dragon. He sat quietly as Arcturus continued to sob silently to himself.

"What were their names?" Veledar asked as he slowly eased the human against his scaly chest.

Arcturus sniffed and wiped a hand across his face to clear his tears. "My wife's name was Selina, and my son was named Geoffery. Two years ago, a red dragon going by the name Dread Flame killed them in revenge after I bloodied his scales. For that deed, and all the suffering he caused, I plunged my sword so deep into his eye that his hot blood washed over my knuckles. Dread Flame...if there ever was a beast more deserving of my blade. My only regret is that I hadn't killed him slower." Arcturus hissed. "He should've suffered just as much as my family did!"

Having vented out his inner demons, Arcturus slowly regained his calmer state.

"I held my son in my arms when he gave his final breath. I screamed for a cleric until my voice gave out but...it was too late. I failed them. I failed my squad, my king...I failed everyone." Arcturus looked up at the dragon, "You're the only left, Crimson. The only one I managed to save."

"I know," Veledar placed his head in the human's lap, ignoring the fact Arcturus had referred to him simply as "Crimson" twice now. "We cannot think about the past now. Let us get some rest before our bodies collapse."

He grabbed the human and pulled him tightly against his scaled chest. He was surprised to find him so soft. In many ways, he reminded Veledar of the stuffed animal he used to hug every night in the comfort of his lair.

"I will be holding you close to me so you don't wander off again...if that's alright with you."

Arcturus nodded and replied with a simple "Good."

"Rest now. When we both rise, we shall see this path to completion." Veledar yawned, curling his head and draping his wings over them both. He closed his eyes as he felt the human fall asleep, hoping that tomorrow he would greet the real world once more.

Veledar awoke the next morning when he felt Arcturus' trying to wiggle free from his grasp. He opened his eyes and yawned a healthy ten seconds tongue-curling yawn before smirking at the human's futile struggles.

"Did you sleep well?" he said coyly.

"How could I not, when your big scaly bum kept me warm as a baby?"

"Bum? Do you really want to see how it feels to sleep at my other end?"

"No! Gods no! Fair, mighty, crimson dragon, I beseech you, never try something so wicked with me."

"Grawr, fine." Veledar relaxed his front limbs. Though he wanted to have a bit more fun with the human, he couldn't antagonize him when he spoke such honest, beautiful words.

Veledar slowly stood up. He sprawled his wings on either side, his joints trembling as they stretched to their limits. The dragon flapped them lightly a few times to wear off the stiffness, then continued with the usual stretching motions of his other pairs of limbs.

"Do you have to moan like that when you stretch?"

Veledar was well aware of the rumbles coming out of his throat. Of course, an inferior creature like the human could not possibly understand how good it felt to stretch after a long night of resting.

"I don't know. Can you stop scratching your face-fur?"

"It's called a beard," Arcturus felt around the brown bush that started to cover his whole jaw. "And if your scales itch for an answer, know that I plan to get rid of it as soon as we return to civilization."

"Why's that?" Veledar lifted a forepaw to poke at his obviously sharp claws. "I have everything I need right here."

Arcturus unsheathed his sword. "This is a lot sharper."

"Then use it."

"Yeah," he pointed towards the dragon's tail. "Kind of like you use your claws to scratch your ass, eh?"

The little mink was getting the hang of this game of teasing, a revelation for which Veledar hadn't planned ahead. For a dragon, losing at anything felt like a dull throbbing headache that persisted for days.

"That was a joke, in case you couldn't tell." The dragon waved a paw around, his voice dripping with sarcasm. "I'm not as cruel as to sit on your tiny, crumbly body when we rest. Besides, you barely even stirred."

"Indeed. I just love being held like a babe when I sleep. Why, I should've married a dragon instead of a woman!" Arcturus rolled his eyes. "You are good at many things, dragon, but even you have your limits."

"So what you are saying is that you would rather sleep out in the cold?"

Arcturus nodded. "Why did you even do that? I would have been fine without getting the special treatment. Knights are trained to endure much worse than a bit of cold, and I am a-"

"Paladin." It was the dragon's time to growl. "Heard that enough times already."

He was a bit annoyed that Arcturus did not realize he had done him a great service. "Excuse me for trying too hard. All I did was make sure you did not wander off in the middle of the night again. I found you holding the forms of your dead wife and child in case that memory eludes you."

Arcturus froze in place and looked to Veledar as if the dragon suddenly sprouted additional heads. "I did what?" He asked in disbelief.

Veledar tilted his head. Was it possible, that the human did not remember the night before? Just in case, he explained everything that had happened, especially enjoying the part when he told Arcturus about how he had bravely rescued the paladin from wandering the forest for all eternity. He ended with the tale with how Arcturus crawled into his embrace all by himself after a heart-touching moment shared prior to that.

"Whoa. Well...I almost feel like a different person did all that, but I'm here, you're there, it happened, so thanks." Arcturus shook his head. "Are you absolutely sure it wasn't a dream?"

"You are now both testing my patience and insulting my acuity, dear human." Veledar smiled, "I am a dragon. Doubt is like the wind that comes out of my other end when-"

"Alright, I heard enough. Thanks again for warming me like a campfire. You're a lot warmer and comfortable than I initially believed, alright? Is your scaly ego satisfied now?"

Veledar beamed at the human's words, then looked quickly around and noticed something was off. They were not in the same place they had fallen asleep in. Instead, they were in the middle of a field of bright green grass. There was a tree where the previous one had been, but instead of a creepy leafless monster, leaves of all different colors sprouted from this one's branches. The trunk too looked to be vibrant and full of life.

"Uh, do you suppose we wandered off some more?" Arcturus asked, scratching his head in confusion.

If they had, Veledar did not know, but he spied the path again, parting the grass and leading off deeper into the forest.

"Crimson Sky!" Arcturus shouted.

Veledar turned to Arcturus, who was busy scooping what looked like berries out of his pack. His belt pouches were similarly loaded, and the paladin quickly formed small piles of fruits on the ground.

"Looks like someone filled my pouches and pack with berries while we slept. I don't know whether to be terrified something snuck in on us or thank them."

"Who cares?" Veledar shrugged and speared one of the purple berries with his claw. He inspected its soft surface and the juice that slowly dripped down his claw, then quickly popped it into his maw, much to the disapproval of his human companion.

"Wait! We don't even know where those came from."

"Mrawrm, who cares??" Veledar mumbled as he took another. He felt the hunger that had been growing over their journey fade away almost instantly. He remembered that druids shared some of these berries when he was a hatchling, so he was well aware of what happened.

"Are they safe?" Arcturus asked, placing one next to his eye.

"Not for humans." Veledar lied. "Quickly, give me yours." He laughed.

Arcturus quickly snatched up three or four of the berries, eyeing them with suspicion. "You greedy bastard! They're perfectly safe, aren't they?"

Veledar rolled his eyes in amusement. "Yes, Arcturus. Trixie's friends won't suddenly poison us just to see what kind of faces we make before we die. Actually, I'm pretty sure every last one of her friends has heard of my heroic exploits, which explains these berries, obviously a tribute to my greatness."

"Oh, shut that prideful mouth before it infects me." Arcturus laughed. Both of them ate about half of the berries. Arcturus put the rest back into his pouch and patted his belly.

"Well, that really hit the spot. What are these things again? Dragon berries, dragon balls, dragon-"

"I'll show you balls." Veledar bared his teeth, then suddenly burped loudly. "Night's essence or something of that sort. One of them can sustain a human for an entire day."

He expected some sort of praise from the human for knowing such a fact, but Arcturus kept staring at him. "Do I have some juice on my snout or something?"

"You burped!" Arcturus said in disbelief.

"So?" Veledar shrugged.

"I didn't think dragons to be capable of that!" Arcturus started to laugh.

"Of course we burp!" Veledar cried, "What did you think we did, blow flames out of our nostrils?"

"Ah, it's just something that never occurred to me." Arcturus mumbled as his face turned red. "Wonder what else you dragons can do."

Veledar stood up and started walking towards the path. "I can show you how I blow gas from my other end, but we should go before you annoy me to the point where I'll really do that."

He didn't have to look back to hear Arcturus swiftly trying to catch up to him.

"What's with the rush, Crimson Sky? This path just seems to keep going and going."

Veledar could feel a sensation running through his bones, a hunch some might call it, or a premonition.

"I feel as though this path nears its end, and we shall soon find ourselves returning to our world. "He said, slowing his pace slightly so that Arcturus caught up next to him.

"Good. Fairy world has its fair share of surprises, but honestly I think we've both seen enough." Arcturus replied.

"Is it the place, or the company?" Veledar asked, raising an eyebrow.

"The place, you silly dragon. The company hasn't been too unpleasant. Although there is this really annoying dragon who keeps making fart jokes." Arcturus laughed.

"Annoying?" Veledar asked. "That's the best you could come up with? Not dreadful, honorable, handsome, or wise?"

"Nope, just annoying."

Veledar playfully smacked Arcturus with a paw. "Be careful, human, I am much bigger than you."

"Well that just means you have a bigger ego to bruise when you are swiftly outsmarted."

Usually, Veledar would get annoyed with the playful insults, but he instead found himself arguing with the human playfully as they walked until they had made their way out of the forest, out towards another green field. It seemed to stretch as far as Veledar could see in all directions. He and Arcturus were currently talking about magic and who was better at casting it. They stopped only when they looked to what seemed to be a clearing in the middle of the field.

Within the clearing of grass was a symbol in the shape of a tree made out of small, worn gray stones. The symbol was ten feet in size, with many branches, kind of like a portal to another world.

"Well, it looks like we are finally at the end of this journey." Veledar smiled, "We can talk about how dragons are better at magic in every other way than humans later."

"And I'll pretend to listen. Now, wise dragon, maybe you can divine us a method of using this portal." Arcturus said while kneeling beside one of the stones, running his hand along it. Veleder decided to do the same with another stone and found them very smooth to the touch. He felt a small aura oozing out of the stone, something that happened with every magic-imbued object."

"Well, the stones are magical," Veledar said aloud, "but I have no idea on how to activate them."

"Great! We're stuck."

"Not yet." Veledar scratched at the stone surface slowly, careful not to leave any lasting marks. It was a shame they had to leave this place. Dark things it did have, but the other things were rather fascinating. Veledar decided he would have to question Trixie about this fascinating realm when this was all said and done. After he was done yelling at her, that is.

They spent the next hour prodding, scratching, and Veledar tried some can-trip spells. Despite this, nothing happened. Nott even a single rock moved out of place. Veledar roared loudly in frustration, smashing his tail into the rock strong enough to recoil in pain.

"Raaarrhhhh, This stone taunts me!" Veledar hissed. He turned towards Arcturus, who was busy drawing the symbol on a pad of parchment. He walked over slowly, trying to take a peek at the drawing.

"Why are you drawing that?" Veledar snarled, placing his snout inches from the parchment. From the looks of it, Arcturus had done a fairly decent job of duplicating the symbol on the ground.

"Figured an actual representation of our conundrum here would help me think of a different way to solve this thing, instead of thrashing my tail, baring my teeth and snarling like a beast." Arcturus replied with a smirk.

"You don't have any- hey, that's part of a dragon's thinking process!" Veledar put his snout up high, "If something doesn't require a baring of teeth and a good tail smack, then it clearly wasn't worth our time." He opened one eye to peer down at the human, who was looking at him with an amused grin.

"Why are you making that face? You're not supposed to be amused! Besides, it's better than that smudge you barfed on your crumpled little piece of-"

Something suddenly moved in the corner of Veledar's eye, causing him to stop talking mid-sentence. He spun around to see something mightily peculiar. Eight figures seemed to have sprouted out of the earth like trees. They stood at roughly eight feet tall and seemed to be made completely of shadows. Where humans would have had hands, they instead seemed to have large claws, and instead of a face all they had was a blank space with no features. Veledar flared his wings as his tail flicked back and forth behind him. He heard the metallic hiss of Arcturus' unsheathing sword, and a quick glance revealed four more had appeared around Arcturus. The figures in front of Veledar started to move, seemingly gliding along the ground.

Veledar fought the urge to take flight and let his fire breath burn the lot of them. He lashed out with his claws instead as the silhouettes moved in to strike at his scales. He bit at one with his teeth only to have it dissipate inside his jaws. He felt some claws dig into his flesh, his blood smearing against his scales. The dragon growled in pain and lashed out at the shadows as he cursed his inability to leave the human behind. As a dragon, Veledar was not used to protecting someone during a fight. To Veledar's shock, each time his claws sliced through one of the shadows, it would burst into two other copies instead.

Despite his success at ripping and biting them asunder, the dragon soon found himself surrounded on all sides. However, his scales could not protect him forever as he roared out in pain when a beast struck his hind leg.

Veledar swiped the human close to him with his tail, took a deep breath, then unleashed a jet of fire that washed over the shadows like the river pouring through rocks. The shadows melted like wax, giving way to nothingness without any sort of sound.

"That does it." The dragon stood proud, breathing heavy and aching as he looked over where his foes once were.

The sounds of grunts and shouts reminded him of the human, who had a sizable amount of shadows around him as well. Veledar quickly dove over the human and crashed the bulk of his body into the shadows before him. However, as he turned his snout to look around, he found the ones he had melted with his fire reforming before his eyes. He pushed the shadows back and started to draw a circle on the ground around himself and Arcturus. "Protection!" he yelled out.

The circle shone bright white before forming a wall of light between them and the shadows. Veledar winced from the pain in his side. It was a minor wound by dragon standards, but it still hurt. He stared at the shadows as they raked the shimmering wall with their claws like a pack of rabid wolves. He knew the shield would not last for very long if they kept striking it.

"We need to find a way out of here!" The dragon hissed.

"Did you notice the symbol on their backs?" Arcturus asked, his breath just as labored.

"No, I was too busy destroying them." Veledar hissed. "Why do you even care what is on their backs?"

"It is the same symbol as the stones on the ground. They must be a puzzle on how to escape. It must be one last test of endurance for you to leave."

"How do you mean?" Veledar cocked his head to the side.

"Trixie said to focus, and that's why she sent both of us. I think we need to ignore the shadows and focus on leaving."

"Are you sure?" Veledar growled when a dark claw started to pierce through the wall.

"No, course not, but what in god's name are we supposed to do?!"

"Well, aren't you just a great fountain of inspiration, my dear paladin?"

"Crimson Sky, do what I tell you just this once!"

"Graawwrh." Veledar turned towards Arcturus, "Fine. But if we die here, I will haunt you throughout the entirety of afterlife with the worst jokes I can think of."

"Deal! Now do it!"

Veledar closed his eyes and tried to picture his escape from this place. He imagined himself once again in the sky, flying alongside other dragons. He smiled, thinking about the morning dew between his toes and finding a decent meal. He felt the barrier collapse, but he pushed the grim reality of the present situation far from his mind. He imagined a large ornate door made of mahogany, engraved with grand dragon carvings. He turned to his right to see Arcturus smiling back at him.

"This is incredible, Veledar." He said, and the dragon didn't even notice he used his name. They both turned to a faint roar from the other side of the door. "Ready, my friend?" the human said, drawing his sword. Veledar nodded as he felt something shake him.

"Wake up, you lazy son of a lizard!"

Veledar's eyes opened, followed by a deep yawn. Had he been sleeping? He thought he had closed his eyes to avoid the shadows. He looked around at the clearing they were in. It looked like the one they had been in when Trixie performed the ritual. Although, when Veledar looked around, he realized there was no mountain. The sun was high above in the sky, hinting at noon. He stretched out on the grass, letting his claws dig into the earth. He peered down at Arcturus, who was on his feet, checking his pockets.

"I am not familiar with your lands. Do you know where we ended up?" Veledar asked.

"Don't know yet." Arcturus replied. "We first need to see what's out of this clearing." The human crossed his arms when he seemed satisfied his gear was in order. "Ready for another journey?"

"I was thinking the same thing." Veledar grinned as mischief sprung to his mind.

"So which direction should we inspect first? I think north makes the most seeeeeenssss. Gods, not agaaaaaaaaaain!" Arcturus cried as Veledar snatched him up into the vastness of the skies.

The dragon shot into the air like an arrow loosed from a mighty bow. Veledar felt the sun cascade upon his scales. The rushing air traveling all around his wings in the form of favorable currents. Everything was so perfect.

"Oh, cheer up already. You know I won't drop you." He looked down at the less than thrilled human as he began to beat his wings to steady his flight path.

"You bastard!!" Arcturus shouted as he pounded against the dragon's scales.

"Sorry, I forgot how much you enjoy flying," he replied, stifling down a laugh. "Besides, I need to look around. Figure out our position."

He heard Arcturus gulp as he gazed out to the rolling hills that were covered in patches of green, yellow, and brown. Every so often, there seemed to be buildings that had sprouted from the ground, dotting the hills with the obvious sign of human habitation.

"She sent us far south!" Arcturus shouted in disbelief. "We are close to

Drenedar! I recognize these hills from the time when I was still a wee boy!"

"Hits me right in the heart. So where do we go next?" Veledar asked. He had never ventured so far into these lands before. "Grawwr," the dragon complained over the vocal rumble of his belly. "I think we may want to find something to eat. Are you as hungry as I am?" Veledar chuckled.

"Hungry like a wyrm! Haven't you heard my stomach rumble almost at the same time?" Arcturus laughed. "There is a village not far from here where we can find a much better meal than the unsalted, stringy deer you're thinking of right now."

"You make a fair point, human. Would they mind a dragon suddenly showing up in their midst?"

"I am sure they have seen stranger things in that village. Put me down first. There is no way I am being carried like a package to the village."

"Well, I don't think you have a choice in the matter," laughed Veledar as he decided to dive, only to stop after a couple of seconds.

"What is the name of this village that treats dragons with the respect they deserve?" He asked to a pale faced Arcturus.

"T-T-T-T-T—rost" Arcturus stammered, "Please, do NOT do that again."

"As you say, captain of knights, paladin of whatever," Veledar grinned, letting the currents carry them eastward.

Chapter 9: Town of Trost

Arcturus had never been as grateful as he was in that blissful moment when the dragon placed him softly on the grass hill overlooking the village of Trost.

"Thanks...for the ghloooaaaaahk, " he immediately fell to his knees and vomited all over the ground over the dragon's throaty chuckle.

"I really hope you can avoid doing that while I am carrying you."

"Didn't it strike you that this happens exactly because your inability to ask before swooping me up? Stop picking me up without warning!" Arcturus coughed, spat a few more times, then ripped a fistful of grass to wipe himself off the disgusting sludge. He stood up with a groan and joined the dragon, looking down to the village. It looked just like it had when he was just a boy. In a way, it seemed the passage of time hardly had an effect on the place. There were about three dozen wooden cottages huddled together on the rolling hills, bathed in the light of the afternoon sun. Arcturus could make out the tiny specks of people from the distance, hurrying to deliver all sorts of goods back to their homes.

"Are you sure these people will be more accepting of a dragon? This village looks pretty much like every human settlement I've seen."

"And how far does that number reach, wise, centered Crimson Sky?"

"One?" Veledar tilted his head, scrunching up his snout. "Or is it...two?"

"Yeah," the human chuckled. "Two out of hundreds. You see, Trost is amiable to dragons beca-"

Arcturus was interrupted by a loud screech and a sudden blur of feathers. Three gold and white gryphons landed in a triangle pattern around them. They wore specially crafted, brown leather armor to cover their vulnerable joints, and each had a small tabard hanging around their necks by golden chains. Crimson Sky immediately bared his teeth and flared his wings. Arcturus only rolled his eyes at that. The dragon moved closer to no doubt protect him, even if he would most likely not admit such a thing.

Arcturus calmly stood his ground as the gryphons stared at them with unmoving brown eyes.

"A scaly? I've never had the pleasure to gaze upon a dragon around these parts." said the gryphon closest to Arcturus. Arcturus could see the gryphon's chest getting bigger, obviously in an attempt to appear more threatening.

Arcturus sighed, closed his eyes, then spoke calmly. "Because they have the most gryphons compared to any other village in Lumara," Arcturus finished saying to Crimson Sky.

The gryphons gave a collection of confused looks to this. "That wasn't an answer to my..." one of the other gryphons started to say.

"Sorry 'bout that." Arcturus intervened. "Please, allow me to explain myself. I was just telling Crimson Sky here that Trost is defended by more gryphons than any other town in Lumara." Arcturus gestured to Crimson Sky, who still was showing his teeth.

"Oh, of course you were," the gryphon said. Arcturus noticed he started to strut. Crimson Sky closed his maw and rolled his eyes.

"I speak the truth. This dragon happens to be my official escort, erm, sorry. That doesn't sound right." Arcturus calmly rephrased. "He's both a guard and a method of transportation. You see, we are conducting official business in the name of the king. Information I sadly cannot disclose to a patrol. I'm sure you understand the nature of these tasks." Arcturus said calmly to the gryphon that was now strutting around him. It appeared none of them noticed how Crimson Sky rolled his eyes in irritation.

"Official business?" the strutting gryphon asked. "Never heard of official business with a dragon involved. Your story smells worse than that one's wings." The gryphon pointed a claw at Veledar's scrunched snout.

"Oh please, you should take a whiff from that broom you call fur before-"

Arcturus slapped the dragon's neck and placed himself between the gryphon and the dragon. "This is starting to get bothersome. I am Arcturus Lund, dragon slayer and paladin of Lumara. If you haven't heard my name, then you probably hatched from rocks." Arcturus said, trying to not sound a little smug.

The gryphon ruffled his feathers as he clacked his beak a few times. "Perhaps we did. What value does a name bring to our town?" The gryphon's eyes looked away, just like Crimson Sky did when he was trying to hide his curiosity.

"I have orders to bring him to the king." Arcturus slapped Veledar's foreleg a few more times. "Got some big plans involving this big scale bum here."

"If you call me that again, I swear you won't have a hand to-"

The air rang with the screech of gryphons, who flared their wings in an instant.

"Stand down!" Arcturus barked. "Dragon's of no value to me or the king if you three start a fight over bad jokes. My scaly friend here...he's special, you know." Arcturus smiled, patting Crimson Sky on his scales again. He felt the dragon's hide tense for a moment before it relaxed. He was a tad taken back as the strutting gryphon suddenly moved in close and put his beak very close to his face. Although, after he found himself face to face with a dragon not very long ago, moments like these had very little effect on Arcturus. The gryphon breathed in deep as he stared at him square in the eyes, as if searching for the slightest flinch.

"Will you let us proceed?" Arcturus asked.

The gryphon whirled with a satisfied squawk and let his lion tail smack Arcturus on his leg armor.

"Checks out. The name's Mek, and my companions are DuskTalon and Miraka." Mek gestured to the other gryphons one at a time. "As much as I would like to continue our conversation, we have a patrol to finish. I advise you both to stay out of trouble while you are in our village. Paladin, dragon, or whatever you are matters little to us as long as you behave properly."

"Of course we will, you pampered bird." Crimson Sky said, putting a paw to his chest. "I will be an example of harmony. Who knows, your town might love me so much that next time we come around we'll see dragons flying around instead of gryphons."

"Dream on, scale-wings." Mek said curtly before spreading his golden wings wide. With a puff of dirt from their wings, all three gryphons launched themselves high into the skies.

"Well that was certainly a delightful experience." Crimson Sky said sarcastically as the human led him down the hill. "Walking feels good. The earth's soft under my paws and the grass tickles my feet in lovely ways. However, I cannot help but observe we are making the wrong choice here. Why burden our legs when we can fly?"

"You want to fly after that delightful talk we just had?" Arcturus narrowed his eyes. "You insulted Mek in front of his squad. Do you realize how deep this sting goes?"

Veledar snorted dismissively. "My scales suffered worse."

"Good for you. Now keep on walking. We'll be there in just a bit."

"Graaarrr! I so wish I could fly. Imagine how fast we'd get there. Ten wing beats and we are done."

"No." Arcturus said.

"Choice is an illusion. You know I can pick you up any time I want."

"And I thought I might ride on your back for a change!" The human shot back, much to the dragon's surprise. "Yeah. I'm not afraid of heights or flying. It's your...method of transportation that brought out the banshee in me."

Arcturus cringed at the growly laughter that came out of the dragon's throat. He waited for him to calm down, then continued. "I can handle straight flying. It's only diving that gets me. Same goes for the ascension, so if you can smoothen those for me, we can be flying partners."

"Really?" The dragon cocked his head, blinking a couple of times. "You're serious?"

"Why not? Flying can be quite refreshing, and certainly feels much better than being caged in the wailing bowels of a flying machine."

"I think I might just feel insulted by your request." Crimson Sky replied, Arcturus was not sure if the dragon was being serious or not. "You wish to ride upon my back like I'm some common animal. Method of transportation, am I? Or one of those horse things you rest your arses on whenever you feel too lazy to move on your own legs?"

"Ah, but you'd be a noble and dignified steed. A dragon worthy of a paladin!" Arcturus laughed.

"A fancy title to obscure the nasty weight of your armored ass." The dragon snorted, then paused for a bit before speaking. "Let me think about it, Arcturus. It might be easier to swallow my pride than to watch you retch every time we land."

"Ah, so you dragons are able to choose reason over pride. I'm thrilled. This way, everybody wins!"

"You're an awful paladin, know that?" Crimson Sky replied, squinting his eyes. "There would be one more thing to say though. I never got the chance to say your idea of escaping the fairy realm had a spark of draconic brilliance in it. Sounds almost like something I'd think of!"

Arcturus smiled at the dragon's words. "My dear dragon, I do believe you're trying to leech my merits, because I haven't heard you come up with this exact plan before me."

Crimson Sky scrunched up his snout in slight disgust. "I was trying to pay you a compliment, you thick armored buffoon! You could do better than poke at my shortcomings. If I didn't erect that magic shield, there would be no brave paladin to save us from those shadows, so I win!"

"Oh, come now, Crimson Sky, I said that in jest. I had no idea a strong dragon like you could be so easily wounded." Arcturus said, playfully shoving the dragon in the shoulder even if Crimson Sky showed no signs of feeling the nudge. Moments later, while they were walking towards the village, Crimson Sky returned the favor and shoved Arcturus onto the grass with one scaly paw.

"Down your armored ass goes! Now you can consider us even." Crimson sky growled with glee.

Arcturus spit out some grass that had gotten into his mouth and dusted himself off. The dragon was nothing but amused, even pleased with his juvenile way of thinking.

"My fault! It's my fault?" The paladin pointed a finger at the silly dragon. "I severely overestimated your intellect. Beneath these fancy scales and big, pompous words, you're nothing but a child!"

"Hatchling." The dragon swished his tail playfully. "Go on. I am intrigued by what comes next."

Arcturus chuckled. "Hah. I take it we are starting to be friends now?"

The dragon settled onto his haunches to look at the human with what could be described as an amused look. "You are indeed growing on me, paladin Arcturus." He then looked away with the same silly smile, "Like damp, stinky cave mold that clings onto everything it touches."

"Ugh. Where did you get that from?"

"I can always make another joke about my backside."

"No, Gods no! We can be friends without sharing these types of jokes, can't we?"

"I don't know, human. Dragons don't have friends besides other dragons."

"Really? What about Trixie? She certainly thought of you as a friend," he said, but felt instantly guilty as he saw a look of remorse grow on Crimson Sky's snout.

"I knew a female dragon once, so full of life, always up to mischief, but her light had dimmed. She's...gone."

Well, that was certainly something he did not plan on doing to the dragon. "Apologies. It was not my intention to remind you of your loss."

"I did not say she was dead, Arcturus. She went east to explore a continent far away. Unfortunately for the both of us, I decided to stay here, and a precious bond we forged over the years crumbled to dust. Do not pity me. It is the way of the dragon, to live a life of solitude."

"Yeah, but...I can't help but feel bad about it."

The dragon said nothing. Instead, he allowed the human to touch him, and Arcturus walked with a hand on Crimson Sky's side in silence until they reached the village at the base of the hill.

Arcturus made his way onto the bustling streets, avoiding the gawking faces made by the various people. The red dragon seemed to bask in the attention he received. Paper cutouts of gryphons hung between each wooden building that dotted the small village. Despite the stares, gryphons were passing over frequently to get a good look at the dragon. Arcturus noted that things were going well so far. No one was rushing over to instigate a conflict on purpose. If anything, they were curious about this unlikely pair. Arcturus had to send the insistent birds away despite Crimson Sky's protests, whose only desire was to stop and tell anyone that would listen about his magnificence. After the third such instance, Arcturus had no option but to grab the dragon by his pompous snout.

"Listen here, you pampered mink! We are supposed to avoid drawing too much attention to ourselves. A dragon is already big news without you stopping to make idle chit chat with every passing person!"

Crimson sky just smirked with his teeth and growled quietly. "Mrawr, awwr, Arcturus. I was simply making these townsfolk feel more confident about my benevolence. I imagined would be proud of what I am trying to achieve here; cooperation between our two **very** different races."

Arcturus bit his lip. The dragon did have a point. The last time Crimson Sky landed in a human village, he not only angered the people, but messed up their village, albeit in much minor ways than another dragon would.

"Alright, alright!" Arcturus said. "You're doing much better than last time, but that doesn't change the fact that you are going against the very thing we try to achieve here." He sighed, "I thought you'd be satisfied with a full stomach and a soft place to rest."

Crimson Sky quickly nodded. "Honestly, I would have made more of a fuss if not for the curiosity of these people. Why can't the rest of your race act like normal people, instead of petty little things with corn up their arses?"

"I won't even try to debate that." The paladin said. Crimson Sky started following Arcturus, who had started leading him to a rather large wooden building that seemed to be built with purpose in mind. Everything about the inn was twice the size of anything else in the village, from its clear glass windows to its great wooden door. The sign outside was pristine and hardly looked a day old. In gold lettering, it read *The Gallant Gryphon*, and beneath the letters was a mural of a golden gryphon standing proudly in front of pair of rolling hills.

"So why this place and not the inn we passed five minutes ago?" Crimson Sky asked. His snout sneaked inches from Arcturus' head, making him jump in surprise. Arcturus caught his breath and narrowed his eyes at the chuckling dragon.

"Do I startle you so easily, Arcturus?"

Arcturus ignored him, "This place is more suited for a creature of your stature." He gestured with his arms to Crimson Sky's body. "You might have felt a tad cramped in the other places I had in mind."

He watched Crimson Sky turn back towards the previous inns they passed, and Arcturus thought he saw a hint of disappointment on his snout when his words were proven true.

"You're right. They're smaller than my...you know, what I have between my legs."

"That's your tail." Arcturus said quickly. "Come now, before somebody else hears you."

Crimson Sky turned back towards *The Gallant Gryphon*, quickly barging through the front door with a smirk. Arcturus quickly heard a crash and the cracking of wood from inside.

"Don't worry, good people! My human friend will pay for all the damages I cause." he heard Crimson Sky say loudly.

Arcturus opened the door to find Crimson Sky sitting in the middle of a cracked table with a group of laughing gryphons and humans.

"There he is. The finest in all the land. Quite a looker too, am I right?" Crimson Sky said, pointing at Arcturus.

Arcturus made his way past the patrons. On his way to the bar, he heard Crimson Sky already ordering what sounded like a banquet of food. Behind the bar stood a bald man cleaning an iron mug with a frown plastered over his hard, pockmarked face.

"Damages for the table will be fifty silver pieces," he said in a gruff voice.

"My word is my bond," Arcturus sighed, reaching into his pouch to find the coins for the man. "Need two rooms as well."

"Only got one. Tis' a busy day to be wantin' a room, friend," the barkeep stated.

"Fine, we will take the one room you have. Hope it's big enough to house a dragon." Arcturus sighed. He turned back to the sound of a waitress in a blue uniform holding what looked like a stack of food rather than an order.

"That dragon ordered everything on the menu!" she exclaimed in surprise. "Not even the gryphons ever order this much! I hope you're all hungry!"

The barkeep just eyed Arcturus with a grin as he forked over more coin to the man. "Very well," Arcturus placed a small bag of twenty gold pieces. "That should cover everything my scaly friend has ordered."

After he paid, Arcturus took a seat next to the dragon, who was sitting at an over-sized table, talking with a group of three gryphons. They seemed to be one upping each other in tales of courage and skill.

"Then I pounced on the shadow creatures, claws ripping at their throat, flames coating everything! I could have flown away, of course. Incinerate them all from above, but that would have meant abandoning a helpless human to a most gruesome fate, and I, Crimson Sky, defender of the realm, vowed to protect those who cannot defend themselves." Crimson Sky said, swelling his chest in pride.

"How did you save him?" a gryphon asked.

"Well, it started like this." Veledar narrated the incident, only this time he made himself the hero who came up with the brilliant idea to leave the fairy's realm.

The gryphons gave a collected gasp at the story, with one turning towards

Arcturus, "Is this true, human? Did Crimson Sky here really save you from thirty shadow creatures?"

The others looked to him with eagerness while Crimson Sky's snout seemed to say, "tell them".

He smirked. This wasn't a bad place to craft a little telltale in Crimson Sky's name.

"Ah, but my scaly friend here is too humble to recount the true danger of our predicament. I reckon it must've been at least fifty shades, one more wicked looking than the other." Arcturus said. "Those dreadful creatures had us surrounded. Our weary bodies were covered in wounds, our magic, fading. I had no hope of victory. And if not for my brave dragon savior, I would surely not be here telling you this tale."

He folded his arms while the gryphons turned back to Crimson Sky and bombarded the dragon with questions and praises. Arcturus was glad for the steaming food as several of the cook's assistants brought it over in the middle of another tale of unmatched bravery from Crimson Sky. Arcturus dug into a roasted goose. Its taste was sweeter than anything he ate recently. He washed it down with a mug of bitter, but not bad tasting ale.

It was when a song started up from the others that Arcturus joined in the revelry. He looked to Crimson Sky, who had a large smile and was singing along with the rest, looking utterly ridiculous.

"What's the matter, Arcturus?" Crimson Sky slurred, his tongue hanging from his mouth, eyes cloudy from the amount of ale he ingested.

"Crimson Sky, you're...Gods, this is better than any tale I've heard today. You...you're drunker than guard on his free day!" Arcturus exclaimed in surprised.

"Nonsense!" The dragon growled, almost losing his balance as he wobbled around the inn much to the fright of the staff that scampered out of his way. "I am a m-mighty dragon, and it takes a lot...a lot more than that to get me properly drunk!" Crimson Sky shouted, his voice filling the inn.

Arcturus gestured to the two empty kegs at the dragon's side. "Like those?"

Crimson Sky stuck his nose into them. "They're empty!" he snarled angrily. "Servants! More drink!"

"No no no," Arcturus ran over to the unsteady dragon. "You've had more than enough, my friend. Let's get you out of here before you wreck the whole inn."

Arcturus helped the dragon to a door labeled *room seven*. It matched the key the barkeep had given him while he had enjoyed his meal. Inside, the room was lit by a single mana crystal that bathed the walls in a pleasant shade of orange that could be mistaken for candle light. There was a simple dresser for their clothes, as well as a bed large enough for a gryphon in the shape of

a nest. Crimson Sky collapsed onto the bed as Arcturus removed his suit of
armor piece by piece, sighing in relief.

"Are you going to bed me?" Crimson Sky hiccuped from behind.

"W-what?" the paladin's eyes constricted with panic.

"Are you going to come to bed with me?" the dragon repeated in an eerily
calm voice.

"No! I have my own bed, right...here." Arcturus whirled on his feet.
"Alright, nowhere." The human sighed after he checked the room twice. "A
single bed for two people? Who does that?"

"It is not uncommon for friends to share." The dragon spread his wings
invitingly. "Come now. Don't pretend there's a choice involved."

"You're bloody annoying even when you're drunk." Arcturus grumbled as
he walked over to the dragon.

"You afraid someone might get some ideas between the two of us?" the
dragon continued with a sly grin. "I've seen the way you look at me."

"You stay on your bloody side, and try to keep that babbling maw shut."
The human replied, pushing the bulk of the dragon to the other side of the
nest bed. He was soon drifting to sleep, even with the dragon poking about
his naked body, chuckling in that growly, drunky way of his.

* * * *

Arcturus found himself in the sky. More accurately, on top of Crimson
Sky's back, with his arse rested upon a saddle. Arcturus was holding tight
onto the makeshift thing as the dragon's wings carried them both through the
blue expanse. Every wing beat from the dragon filled him with excitement as
he looked to the horizon, finding he liked the feeling of wind flowing through
his hair. Strangely enough, the paladin felt a smile come to his face as he
realized he was much calmer than usual. Somehow, he knew there was no
danger involved. More than that.

He knew this was a dream. Surely in the waking world the dragon would
detest this to the end of time, but within his mind, Arcturus enjoyed the dive,
the turns, and somewhat scary barrel rolls. Despite being this high up in the
sky, Arcturus felt warm, the heat radiating from the dragon ensuring he
suffered no grievance from the biting gusts of the shifting winds.

In a few moments the sky warped around them, changing until Arcturus
found himself free-falling without the dragon. He screamed out as fear found
its way into him. He held his eyes shut, telling himself it was just a dream,
until he fell hard not onto a grassy field, but a cold, stone floor.

He opened his eyes to find himself in his father's old study. The chamber
was adorned with dragon bones of all sizes hanging ominously by thin wires.
Books lined the walls, filled with techniques studying these beasts, various
ways to subdue and kill them. Arcturus stood up, finding his joints all ached

with a dull pain that made him wince. He turned towards a fireplace, already lit and bathing the room with a flickering light. In front of the fire place rested a couple of pale, green chairs. One of them turned to face him, revealing no one else than his father, a stern look upon his aged, bearded face. His short hair was lined with gray hairs, and his piercing blue eyes stared at Arcturus as if they could pierce the man's very flesh.

"My son..." the man said with a voice full of disappointment.

Arcturus soon heard whispers around him. Words such as tricked, traitor, dishonor, each one of these words making Arcturus slowly fall to his knees. Part of him wanted nothing more than to drop to his hands and beg forgiveness before he heard a faint roar that made him pull his attention away from his father to find Crimson Sky towering over him, looking ferocious. His teeth were bared, and his eyes focused solely on him, with his tail twitching from side to side.

Arcturus reacted by trying to reach for his sword. Instead, his hands found cold, empty air. Somewhere in the darkness, he heard his father's ominous laughter.

"This is what you get for bargaining with monsters instead of killing them."

Arcturus ducked as Crimson Sky tried to snap his jaws on him, so close that he could feel a spray of saliva coat his neck. He fell backwards as Crimson Sky shoved and pinned him underneath a sharp claw. Arcturus grasped the paw that was holding him down, trying to force it off him. He gasped in pain as Crimson Sky let his claws dig into his chest, drawing blood.

He sensed pity from his father as Crimson Sky bared down at him, and he opened his maw wide. Arcturus watched a glow start in the back of the dragon's pink throat before the flame exploded outwards. Although, instead of intense heat, he felt a warming sensation. He felt the dragon's weight lift off him, and he sprang to his feet. Arcturus darted towards the door of his home. He had to get out of here and end this nightmare. He grasped the handle of the large door that was covered in dragons of every color. Their little gem eyes stared at him as he pressed down on the metal handle. The eyes seemed to follow him as he sprinted down an endless hallway. He could hear his father's voice calling for him, urging him back to his home, but Arcturus pushed it from his mind.

He gasped when a silver dragon sprung from one of the walls, wrapping itself around him as he struggled in its tight scaled grip. Arcturus cried out as he fell onto the floor with the dragon. His heartbeat quickened as his struggles continued against the thing. When his foot sank into the floor, he went to cry out, but found he was unable to voice anything.

Wrapped in complete silence, Arcturus sank entirely into the floor, his eyes filling up with nothing but darkness. He could still, however, feel the tight grip of the dragon holding him in this abyss. He tried to speak, but like before, he found his words lost to the air, making no noise.

From within, he felt sorrow on a level he could not have imagined before. It filled him quickly, and he felt tears well up in his eyes. Like hundreds of pieces of him had been scattered all around, and he was holding onto this world by a thread. The feeling passed as quickly as it had entered, and Arcturus once again felt warmness return to his body. He felt his chest grow tight, almost too hard to breath. He could feel what felt like breathing on his neck and sighed in relief rather than fear. That was the sound of the Crimson Sky he knew. His friend.

His eyes bolted awake instantly.

He was being held by Crimson Sky, who was clearly still asleep. The dragon must have snatched him in his sleep and held him close against his frame like a child might do to a stuffed animal. Arcturus was angry at first, but sighed as he relaxed in the dragon's warm embrace. He admitted that, with a source of warmth draped over him, it was much nicer to sleep than in the embrace of the usual cold air that was common in Trost. He felt the dragon kick his left leg, causing Arcturus to wonder what the dragon could possibly be dreaming about. Could it be drinking? Flying? Female dragons? A conquest? Or simply winning an argument? Arcturus squirmed his way slowly out of the dragon's grip. He came free several minutes later, and instantly regretted his choice as he felt the chill of the air wrap its tendrils around him. As he looked back to the slumbering Crimson Sky, he fought the urge to crawl back into the dragon's embrace and fall asleep once more.

Maybe later, Arcturus shook his head and dismissed the idea. His stomach rumbled a most enticing counter offer.

He made his way to the bathing room and washed himself thoroughly in a comfortable iron tub. He found the warmth of the crystal-heated water appetizing, just like the smell of eggs and bacon that filled the room. He chuckled at the thought of gryphons eating eggs, but his thoughts changed when he rounded the corner and found a whole party of gryphons digging into a heaping pile of scrambled eggs. Arcturus sat down and asked for a cup of coffee from one of the elven waitresses, who looked to him with amusement in her green eyes.

"I know you. Paladin, right? You have that red dragon following you around, am I right?" she asked, while scrambling some more eggs.

"That's me," Arcturus gave her a quick nod as he took a sip from the coffee mug placed in front of him. He sighed as the liquid warmed and did its intended effect of waking him up.

"Quite an odd pair you two make. That says a lot when we get a bunch of feathers like them." She gestured to the gryphons. Two of the birds squawked at her, she waved them back, then shifted her eyes back to Arcturus. "Didn't know dragons still fly around these parts. I only ever heard stories 'bout them, including the one in Entis," she said before sighing, "do you two ever go on grand adventurers, or is your position keeping you tied behind the walls of your city?"

Arcturus chuckled as she looked to him with those curious eyes. She must have been at least one hundred years old, although she was looking at him as if she were a kid.

"I'm on a journey right now, as fate would have it, filled with a tad too much excitement for me to stomach," he said, taking another sip from his mug. "Though your coffee surely helps. Listen. Do you have anything to help with the nausea when he takes me up there?"

The waitress smiled. "We've got plenty of herbs for airsick lowlanders. Want me to bring you some?"

Airsick? Lowlander? Somehow, feeling nauseous suddenly became the smallest concern when pitted against an eternity of teasing.

"Nah. Only way to stay sharp is to fight that which you fear."

"Or fly." The woman pointed out.

"Yes. Exactly that." Arcturus took another sip from his mug.

The waitress excused herself back to the kitchen. Arcturus sat in a few moments of silence before he found another person sitting beside him, a familiar looking half elf wearing a grin.

"So, if it isn't the stubborn, metal-clad jester who wasted his time prosecuting an innocent dragon," she said, picking up a mug of coffee handed to by a kind, smiling waitress. "Didn't think I'd see you again, your highness."

"Same. And you don't have to call me that. Arcturus will do fine."

She grabbed a fork and knife as a plate of food was placed in front of her. "I don't really care about it, although now it's more intriguing why an officer of your prestige ran away from his duties." She watched him closely with her eyes full of questions. "What ever did happen with that dragon anyway? Last I heard he swept you off your feet and carried you away. Could be to eat you, could be he took a fancy to you. Or possibly...mayhap it's you who took a fancy to him!"

Arcturus clenched his jaws at the annoying waterfall of prattling sounds that poured from her mouth. "Maybe it's not your business to know why I'm here."

Suddenly, revelation ran through his mind. What wind brought the half-elf here? Trost was very far from the village of Deet. "Actually, do entertain me for a moment. Say my memory's a bit fuzzy. How many days passed since our last encounter, and how did you find me here? You must've moved on quick feet to-"

"Quick?" she asked in surprise. "You really must've hit your head or something. I took nearly a month to get here. Been side tracking as I made my way back home."

"A month?!" Arcturus shot up from his chair, making several patrons gasp. "But I saw you merely four days ago!"

His mind raced with the possibilities of the Fairy's magic. Was it possible he had been walking with Crimson Sky for thirty days they had not noticed because of the realm's weirdness?

"You might want to lower the tone of your voice a little. The gryphs are starting to get queasy."

Arcturus sat down, holding his head. He thought to all of his friends, who probably believed him to be a pile of bones abandoned somewhere. "A whole month?" he scratched through his beard again. "Oh, blasted...."

"What happened that you lost a month of time, my friend?" She laughed. "Partnered up with your cup a bit too long last night, haven't you? I heard that dragon has a lovely singing voice."

Arcturus put his hands down and told her everything that had happened up until that point. Not sure why felt the need, to be honest, but as he went along with the story, somehow the words started to pour naturally from his lips, while the half-elf seemed to grow more curious with every passing moment.

"That's all I have to say." Arcturus finished up his recounting of the events. "We're now trying to find our way to Entis so that my drunk, singing dragon can get his special book back from whoever had the brilliant idea to snatch it from his lair."

Lyndis just held a sly grin as she finished sipping the last remainders of her coffee. "I'm in."

"In where?"

"In this adventure, madness, nonsensical quest or whatever you two are up to!"

Arcturus frowned. "Listen, lady. We're not exactly a team, you and I. We barely know each other's names!"

She held a hand up to cut him off. "Perhaps you should listen to me, metal-clad. Your lack of subtlety is legendary, and you will need someone who can get you into Entis without drawing much attention to yourselves." She gestured to the broken table. "Does that look like the work of a master of shadows to you?"

At that point Arcturus had to admit the truth. The woman was right. He could not think of a way to get Crimson Sky into the city, least of all the castle without being incarcerated by the city guard.

"Alright. Say I am considering this mad proposal. How exactly will you be able to help, miss Lyndis?"

"Well...." She pulled out a knife to stab it into the table. "I'm not only good with illusion magic, but I also have skills in stealth and adventuring. I know this land almost as well as I know my own clothes." she smiled.

"Fine. You can come with us, although we will need to get horses. Crimson Sky is not exactly the type of dragon who would eagerly offer you a ride out of the kindness of his heart" he laughed, imagining the dragon ranting at the two adventurers that demanded a place upon his back.

"No problem. I'll go pick two of the best mounts while you tell the big guy the news." Lyndis dropped a small bag of coins for the inn, thanked the innkeeper for her meal, and left quickly. Arcturus finished his own scrambled eggs in much needed silence. He needed to think of the proper way to approach his proud partner.

"You mean we have another person with us?" Crimson Sky shouted, "And why haven't I been made aware of this before you took this ridiculous, stupid, careless decision?"

"She practically ambushed me." Arcturus defended himself.

"That may be, but you could've stalled her until I woke up. I'm the leader here! Me. Crimson Sky the Brave, savior of humans, beloved of the gryphons, singer of tales and proud owner of Lumara's finest paladin."

Arcturus scratched his head. "Yeah, that...that's not going to do so early in the morning. I heard the word paladin, but the rest is gone."

"Gone?" the dragon growled. "Oh, human, you insult me so."

That made Arcturus raise an eyebrow. "Maybe I wouldn't, if we were proper partners for one! What made you think you were the leader?"

"Why, I am a dragon, of course! How can I be anything less than the leader? This is my quest, my rules." Crimson sky paused and did the thing where he looked away but still had his eyes on him. "Who did you find anyway that could possibly be of help to me?"

So, the dragon did not entirely hate the idea after all. "A half-elf that is good with illusions. Goes by the name of Lyndis. You should know her from the-"

Crimson Sky seemed to perk up at the name. "Lyndis!" He shouted. "Lyndis, as in the half elf I saved from certain death?!"

"Well, her version of the story is a little different."

Veledar beamed at that. "Kind, selfless Lyndis. She must've increased the number of bandits tenfold."

"Actually, she claimed you just helped."

"Mrrrrrffff," Crimson Sky snorted, "We both know that's not how it happened, metal ass! But still," he grinned, "It will be nice to talk to someone who can actually use magic."

"Magic? Even peasants know what that is." Arcturus laughed.

"Yes, but I'm not speaking about theoretical magic. You know what it is, but as far as I know, you cannot even create a spark without rubbing two stones together like a primitive." Crimson Sky wagged a talon at him with a coy grin.

Arcturus missed his energy crossbow. If he had it right now, he would've stunned this joker's prattling tongue.

"Now that you have been once again made aware of the superior nature of my species, I must leave to attend more pressing matters." Crimson Sky shoved him aside and worked his way to the dining room.

Yeah. Go and feast, you loud, rude beast. Arcturus thought as he went over to his armor, reciting his oath with each piece he strapped upon himself. When he stowed his sword and slung his shield around his back, the human grinned at the image presented in the mirror; that of a young man ready to take on the whole world.

"Today is going to be a good day." He looked around the room with nostalgic fondness before he left the room, and the memories he formed in this place, forever behind.

Chapter 10: Dragon's Trust

Horses smelled horrible to Veledar. That earthy smell of fur, manure, and whatever else stuck to their mangy coats made the dragon sick to his stomach. Veledar even started hacking when Lyndis brought a bay horse within close distance of his sensitive nose.

"Please, take...take that horrible thing away." He addressed the lady in the most polite way he could given the situation.

"Tis just a horse. Can't tell me you're getting a queasy stomach from a mere animal. You've no problem slashing your way through bandits, or dropping in the middle of a village unannounced. I'm not even talking about heading to Entis to recover a silly book, a journey that, by the way, can get us all imprisoned, or worse, killed." Lyndis frowned as she pulled the horse's reins to lead the animal away from the nauseous dragon.

"Grahhhr," Veledar rubbed his nose with his paw. "I know why you must get these beasts, but why something so ugly and stinky like horses? Surely you'd be better off traveling upon the back of two gryphons." He said, thankful that the half elf put more distance between of them. He had another one to deal with; a beast just as vile as its brethren. If it wasn't for the man astride the horse, Veledar would've flown off long ago.

"You agree with me, right?" Veledar shot a quick look in the paladin's direction, only to have Arcturus shake his head with a meek smile. "Why? How can this wingless creature suit a man of your stature better than a gryphon? Even your banner has them. Why not us?"

"Because then, my dear, valiant dragon, we would not see the pretty look you've got on your face right now." Lyndis continued to laugh from afar, clutching her sides as she tried to stay in her saddle.

He squinted his eyes at her, "I should knock you off your saddle for that." he hissed, "now that would be a funny sight to see." Veledar moved his tail, getting ready to strike the half elf off, but stopped when Arcturus moved along his other side.

"You'd better behave properly around a lady, Crimson Sky, or you will answer to me." the human said with a smirk.

Oh, so he thought himself funny as well? Veledar walked right next to Arcturus. "Don't think I won't knock your armored ass into the dirt, paladin. Why, the combination of metal and horse smells even worse than our half breed over there does." Veledar moved his tail, gesturing to Arcturus now. The human watched it carefully as he brought his horse past the dragon.

"You still haven't answered my question," he hissed.

"Do I have to? I thought the answer is obvious." Arcturus said.

"It would be best if we avoid taking to the skies, least we attract unnecessary attention to ourselves."

"And why is that, elf lady?" The dragon's throat rumbled with irritation. Few things annoyed him more than a two-legs spouting their inferior wisdom at him.

"Just trust me." Lyndis waved him to keep up.

Veledar groaned loudly. He hated the walking part, more so after their recent, month-long journey through the fairy realm. Part of him still couldn't believe it had been that long; he certainly hadn't believed it when Arcturus told him at breakfast. Veledar guessed they lost track of time, when the realm itself did not follow the same rules as the real world. However, Veledar was thankful when Lyndis suggest casting a spell to disguise him. *Pass without trace*, she had called it. Said it would make him blend in the clouds overhead if he prevented himself from roaring with glee like a fool.

"Tell me again why this fancy spell doesn't work on all of us." Veledar hissed with obvious annoyance.

"Two words. Gryphon Riders."

Veledar cocked his head, which in turn coaxed a sigh out of the half-elf. "And here I thought dragons were all-knowledgeable. Fine. Let me put this in bare terms. Between Entis and us stand hundreds of lookouts. Mages who are just as proficient as I in the use of spells, and most important, the detection of said spells are going to have an easy time with you. Believe me. We wouldn't be the only ones who'd try to sneak into the capital with a simple invisibility trick. So how about, instead of getting caught on account of your pride, we take the safe option? Wouldn't you agree this is the better plan?"

"No. I do not agree. We should analyze our options and come up with an even better plan!" Veledar growled.

It was Arcturus' turn to sigh now. "There is none we haven't already went over a dozen times. What Lyndis is saying is that a lone camouflaged dragon can wriggle himself out of a bind. A dragon with a human deserter and a half-elf on his back?" the human shook his head. "No way of getting out of that one."

Veledar preferred to win in any kind of contest, be it an argument, flying, or fighting, but this time, his companions had the upper hand. He straightened up as Lyndis placed a hand on his right side, slowly speaking the words *Pass without trace* in elven. The magic felt like cool drops of water rolling over his spine as the spell slowly took effect. Veledar looked down to find his scales blend in almost perfectly with the grass beneath his feet. He disliked the idea that his scales were no longer red, as he very much loved their fiery radiance when the sun's light reflected off them. The dragon sighed in understanding. He would be able to fly in the sky, at least. Unfurling his wings, the dragon gave one last big grin before he launched himself into the skies, away from the two puny, wingless humans and their stinky horses.

"I wonder what ill names he's cooking for us." Arcturus looked over to Lyndis, who smiled back at him. "What? You too?"

"I'm not about to get beaten by a dragon."

Veledar flew higher and higher, leaving his two traveling companions far behind on the ground. He turned, did some barrel rolls, and dove a few times before he once again rejoined the group. The dragon spread his wings wide and started to glide carefully behind them, gazing out onto the path ahead. A path that led them to the capital city of Entis. He thought of another town that he had seen on the map shown to him before they had left. It lay between here and the capital, a settlement going by the name of Drakenburg. Veledar remembered the name from his youth, particularly how much he despised it. His mother had made frequent trips to that place after his brother perished, probably to distract herself from the same pain that kept Veledar crippled for years. He glided for a moment as he shook his head, clearing the dark thoughts of his brother's demise from his head. There was no sense in ruining a perfectly good day by remembering such a sad moment.

The three of them traveled for the course of several days, stopping to rest and eat along the way. They slept by firelight, as Lyndis had cast an illusion to hide their campfire. Veledar found himself talking to Arcturus more and more each night. Each time they spoke, it usually involved the stories of old, especially dragons.

"I think our adventure will make for a great story to tell your fellow humans about." Veledar smirked. "Filled with adventure, excitement, and danger, as our brave dragon leads a team of adventurers to retrieve a precious heirloom taken unjustly from his lair." He said, very much liking the idea of people cheering for him and offering him numerous praises.

Arcturus just reclined on a rock and laughed quietly for a bit. "Should I leave in the parts about how you wobbled around like a slithering snake after you had one too many barrels to drink? Or perhaps I should tell the tale of Veledar the woodbreaker, who bravely vanquished the tavern's table? Now that is a feat to remember!"

Veledar held up his snout, but not so much as to lose the human from sight "You know how to wound me, paladin." The dragon let his head fall to the ground softly, closing his eyes. "You have killed me with your words...you murderer." he said with a quick display of his many teeth.

Noticing the half-elf was being silent, Veledar decided to turn his attention to her. "So. Lady Lyndis. I find myself curious as to what manner of winds or tangled circumstances brought you further south of Drenedar." he said, placing his head between his paws. "Still running from those folks you mentioned last time?"

"Oh, gods no." the woman flicked her hand dismissively. "I thought I would be heading home till I ran into you two. My dad used to say..." she held up a hand and dropped her voice, "never turn down a chance at adventure, daughter of mine. You only have one life to accomplish everything you wish." she said, growing quiet for a moment after spouting that.

Veledar watched how she just stared into the fire intently, letting the light dance across her face before she started up again. "Besides, how could I say no to you blundering fools? I bet you couldn't stay secretive even if your lives depended on it."

"How rude! I certainly possess the means to conceal myself!" Veledar growled. "Why, I have proven myself a great hunter to my sister over a hundred times!"

"That may be true, but I heard how you two got drunk and started singing along with some gryphons back there in Trost. That sort of thing can't happen in Entis. There are too many prying eyes, hidden agendas, and ears just desperate for any information worth selling." She said, pulling a stick to stoke the fire. "Imagine the challenge! If I can get you two into the city to pull this book stealing thing off, I will become one of the legendary travelers you hear about in taverns! I'll be a fockin' hero!"

Lyndis held out her hands, as if holding a sign in between them. "And I will be known as Lyndis, the best illusionist in the land."

Veledar admired the fire she spoke with, determined and fierce, not very different from how a dragoness would speak.

"Besides, any chance to get back at this evil bloated kingdom is worth taking." she spat out, voice teeming with hatred.

"Hey!" Arcturus chimed in. "Since when is our kingdom so vile that you have to spit in the fire?"

"Hah." Lyndis shrugged. "My tongue itches to unburden itself, but I'll just say this one thing. Since when does a good and just kingdom want an innocent dragon killed, hmm?"

"Yeah!" Veledar intervened. "What's that about?"

"You have already turned against your king by letting Crimson Sky here loose. How far will you go to prove your point then?" Lyndis asked, her eyes never leaving Arcturus.

"Now hold on a moment! I just decided to help the dragon get his book back, which is no good reason to squabble over!" the paladin snapped back.

So he said, although in the human's eyes, Veledar saw fury, and in his voice, heard confusion. It might just have been possible that the human was hanging onto the idea that what he heard must have been some sort of mistake.

"Well, you best not waver in your conviction to help Crimson Sky once we are closer to Entis. In spite of what I said, if the focken dragon trusts your resolve, I see no reason why I shouldn't." Lyndis finished with a slight frown.

There was a pregnant pause between them as they just stared into the fire. Of course, Veledar couldn't have that. He absolutely had to break the silence. "Why do you hate the people of this land, Lyndis? I have plenty of reasons to dislike dragon murderers and thieves, present company excluded of course, but what manner of grievance brings out such passion in your voice? Lumara must've done something terrible, to get under your skin like that."

Lyndis took a long, hard swig from her water skin. Her eyes turned to Arcturus, cold as ice. Although the smell on her breath suggested that her water container was being used to hold wine, she began to talk with a voice full of hatred.

"His people came to our towns, our villages." She spat out, then took another swig, "they dropped from their flying machines like conquerors, armed to the teeth. They washed over us like a plague of locusts, erasing everything in their path, until they forced our people to surrender."

Lyndis took a deep breath. "Sure. They had fair reasons and all. Every human spouted nonsense about spreading their prosperity, but all they gave our people is slavery and death!" she shouted out before capping her water skin and putting it away. "Every time I close my eyes, I can still see the *light* your people bring."

"Watch your tongue, woman. You might aid us in our quest, but that does not give you the right to insult my kingdom!" Arcturus shot back, his voice raised ever so slightly. "What you speak of are lies spread by impostors! I personally helped set up academies, barracks, places where your people can sharpen their skills. I brought in food and supplies so that the transition to your new lives was as easy as possible. I don't know what you heard or believed up until now, but I...I've made people's lives better, Lyndis!"

If the words moved Lyndis, she did now show it on her face. She continued her stare down of the human in her cold, emotionless way. Veledar was reminded of how his sister looked when hunting down some prey. She would focus just as intently as the half elf was doing now.

"Hmpf. I suppose that's to be expected from a paladin whose leash is yanked by the brutal hands of his mighty king. Have you ever gone back to those villages after your first arrival? Do you have the faintest idea of how they look now?"

Veledar watched the color drain from Arcturus' face. He could see the realization dawn on his face in the wake of a possibility the human had never considered.

"I will show you some of the villages close to Rothdell. Perhaps even around Drenedar. Together, we'll inspect this light your people have brought, and see for ourselves if it shines as bright as they say." Lyndis crossed her arms, "What say you, Paladin? Care to accompany me on this journey of discovery?"

"I...I'm...I..." Arcturus stammered. His own tongue betrayed him, and his face grew incredibly red as he quickly walked away from the campfire.

"Good. At least some of my words got through his tick skull, otherwise I would have cause of concern." Lyndis yawned as she dove into her bedroll. "Have an enjoyable night, Crimson Sky. Don't let the paladin stab you in the back while you're sleeping. I heard he has the tendency to ambush sleeping dragons in their own lairs."

"Sleep well," he replied shortly before he rose on all fours. The dragon looked longingly at Lyndis, wishing he had his soft things to sleep on throughout the night, just like the woman. Snuggle back into his nest and just forget about all the sorrows and the problems of the day.

He looked to Arcturus. The paladin had taken a seat on the grass about fifty feet away from the camp, on top of the hill. Although it felt mightily uncomfortable, Veledar decided to stride over to the human, his tail swaying lazily behind with every step.

Veledar took a seat beside the human. Arcturus was staring down at the lake overlooked by the hill, its calm waters seeming to twinkle in the moonlit sky. After the brief moment of silence, he turned his attention to the human. The paladin's face, usually full of purpose, was now filled with worry, doubt, and confusion. Arcturus' eyes were not only staring at the lake, but also at the forest beyond, and he slouched over instead of standing up straight like he usually did. The human picked up a stone and threw it hard over the hill.

"She wasn't exactly gracious, but it's just words, Arcturus. How deep can they pierce?" the dragon asked, moving a bit closer to so that he could sit a few feet away from the armored human.

"It's not her opinion that wounds me, dragon, but the implications that make my stomach tighten with the same pain I felt when my family..."

Arcturus sighed. "I have striven to do what was right for my family, my nation, for my life. If what Lyndis says is true, then I went against my oath. I've been helping evil flourish instead of plucking it from its roots. To go against the codes I stand for...that's..." He turned to Veledar, his eyes heavy, and his eyebrows furrowed not with anger, but with pain, All in all, he had the look of a defeated man on his face, very different than the paladin Veledar got used to.

"I am not worthy to even bear the title of Paladin. Selina would be ashamed if she saw me right now, and my son...how can I ever explain this to him? That his father, the great hero, brought so much suffering?"

"You are being too hard on yourself, human. Everyone makes mistakes. You are not a bad person. You say you have gone against your oaths, but need I remind you that when faced with my demise, you chose to free me instead of carrying out the king's orders?" Veledar yawned and stretched out his wings so that his membrane dwarfed the human. "I figure the decision you made that day, on that ship, took a whole lot of courage. It would have been easier to live in ignorance. Easier to lie to yourself than to your king, your squad, your country." The dragon snorted. "I am glad you decided to put your faith in me. For better or worse, we are together in this."

The dragon took a shuddering breath. "If what Lyndis says is true, what will you do?"

Arcturus sat in silence for a moment as he mulled the question over. He then sighed, " the right thing, as I have always done."

"Even if that means taking arms against the king you serve?"

"I see no other way." Arcturus said, a spark of the man Veledar came to know returning to those green eyes.

Veledar did not know how to go about comforting the human. He rarely mingled in the affairs of other races, and now here he was, close to a human he started to take a liking to. In his mind, he practiced it several times, not really deciding on how to do it. Should he get close? Look into the human's eyes and say it? Or perhaps, spread his wings, swell his chest and loudly proclaim his piece of mind? Both options seemed fitting for a dragon. Veledar was in the middle of thinking of another great choice when Arcturus interrupted his thoughts. He guessed he had been quiet too long for his own good.

"What are you thinking about, Crimson Sky? You seem ready to tell me something interesting, if not important," the human said with a smile.

Veledar's wings twitched for a moment. The human got the better of him. He, a dragon, figured out so easily? Preposterous!

"You are starting to know me well Arcturus. Why, you've read me faster than I care to admit," the dragon's claws sunk into the earth for a little bit.

This feeling of vulnerability did not crawl very often along his scales. Still, it was too late to back down now, so, with a silent growl of affection rumbling in his throat, the dragon crawled closer to the human until he settled down on his belly, eyes looking up at the surprised paladin.

"Making yourself comfortable, are you?"

Veledar used his tail to drag the pile of armor against his belly. "Whoa, hold on a moment!"

"Grrrrrr..."

"I don't like the sound of that," Arcturus said, even as his hands stroke along the dragon's snout. "What in the blazes got you so thirsty for this...petting?"

Veledar closed his eyes. The human's touch felt so...calming. If only he could enjoy it in silence for a bit longer...

"It's that thing, right? The important one."

"I..." the dragon sighed, then the human pressed his face closer.

"You know, it is a bit odd to see the mighty dragon so confused," Arcturus said on a calm voice.

"I'm not!" Veledar hissed. "It's just...I wanted to...awwr, this is deceptively difficult compared to what I had in my head."

Arcturus crossed his arms when the dragon pulled his snout away. "I haven't known a single thing that brought you down so far, Crimson Sky. We've escaped from the bowels of the Indomitous together. We've traveled through a fairy's world, almost got captured by gryphons. Then I heard you sing more beautifully than most minstrels in my city, and... gods! We even slept together! So straighten your tongue and say what you have to say, because you can't honestly tell me that a few words are harder than what we've already lived through!"

The dragon smiled, closed his eyes, then opened his maw. "Veledar. That is my name. My real name. You can still call me dragon or whatever, but since we're alone, I figured you should know," he said, slowly and carefully, although he made sure to speak his name louder than usual. No sense in having the human take him by surprise a second time.

Arcturus went to speak, although he did not get two words out before he did a double take. "Whoa...that's...you've held on to such a simple thing for ages. Your name. You told me your name!" he said loudly, his voice full of excitement.

"Correct. But I advise against blabbering out in the open. I don't want my name to sink into the wrong pair of ears." hissed Veledar. The dragon picked his head up, but made sure to keep his eyes on the human's reaction. He had at least shown joy at learning his name, and that made Veledar feel warmer inside than he usually did in the presence of a puny human.

"Well, Vel-Velar-Veledar" Arcturus said, struggling at first, but managing to say the name correctly in the end, "I thank you sharing this gift with me. I will cherish it well." he stood up and hugged Veledar's left fore-paw. "I'm also grateful for you keeping me distracted. You're a good... friend, to have around."

Veledar playfully rolled his eyes, "Don't get all sappy on me, or Lyndis will think we are betrothed." he then pushed the human away with a smirk, "although you are welcome to sleep with me any time you wish."

Veledar gestured back towards the campfire with the half-elf neatly wrapped in her sleeping bag.

"We best get back before she notices our absence, although I suspect she may be a tad passed out to notice that." He turned tail and started walking back towards the camp. He coiled around himself, as usual, then draped a wing over the human that snuggled against his belly.

"This feels almost like a proper bed," Arcturus mumbled as he stroked along the warm membrane of the dragon's wing. "Good night...Veledar."

"I'm sure it will be, now that we get to do this embarrassing, seemingly improper thing a second time."

A chuckle came from beneath his wing, putting a warm smile on the dragon's face. Veledar stared at the stars for a couple more moments, then joined his companion in the realm of dreams.

Veledar awoke the next morning refreshed and rested. He stretched his spine and limbs, as he usually did after a good night's sleep, yawned, then flew into the sky for a few minutes. The exercise breathed life into his wings, and the dragon pushed himself through a few acrobatics before he dived back for the first meal of the day. He looked around to see Lyndis sitting on a blue cloth, meditating in front of a crumpled piece of parchment scribbled with elven runes. He could hear her muttering under-breath. Incantations in elvish. No doubt she was preparing her spells for later use in the day, like she typically did each morning.

Veledar was thankful that dragons did not have to waste time on such archaic methods of focusing magic. As magical creatures, all dragons could simply will up magic whenever it suit them. He felt pity for the half-elf, thinking it sad that not everyone could hold the grasp of magic that dragons did. Although Veledar had heard of great sorcerers, bards, and warlocks being able to cast spells on demand, just like he did.

Veledar strode around the camp twice, noting the absence of a certain human. Since Lyndis was busy preparing her spells, he decided to follow the human's scent instead. He chuckled at the idea that he was now hunting the hunter. The scent was easy to follow. It led down the verdant hill, in a small glade where the human practiced in his own way. Arcturus had his sword out, performing what looked like strikes against the air. His sword would occasionally look as though a strand of the sun would pass by, each strike swung with purpose.

"You know, the air makes for a very poor opponent," Veledar chuckled as he strode over to the human.

"Well, it certainly doesn't talk back as loud as you do." Arcturus replied with a grin, "It's a practice technique. Figured I would keep my body in shape while Lyndis was preparing spells and you were off doing whatever dragons do."

Veledar noticed that, as Arcturus was striking the air, he would follow a pattern that would repeat every ten strikes. Each one would be a different side or height in relation to his body.

Arcturus must have sensed his growing curiosity since he began to explain it. Had he become able to predict all his thoughts now? Veledar thought last night had been an isolated incident. Perhaps it was his eyes, or his snout, or possibly the way he was currently holding his head to the side with an eyebrow raised that tipped the paladin off.

"You see," Arcturus slowed down his swings. "Each movement represents the flow of energy from my mind to my hand, which then follows up along my blade. Each step is to help focus my body and mind so that they act as one for the day ahead. Usually, while doing this, I would recite my oaths, to remind myself of what is expected of me, and where my loyalties truly stand."

This form of combat meditation had intrigued Veledar. It was at least a tad more interesting than watching the elf ponder in silence, and he was always up for learning something new.

"May I join you?"

The human nodded his head.

Veledar took a spot next to Arcturus, still watching the human. He knew Arcturus to be redeemable over his other, dragon slayer kind, but this reminded him of his mother's self-reflection each day, and the scale she held as to remind herself of who she was.

"Sure, although I don't know how this will relate to you, Veledar, since you have no sword to swing around."

"Who needs such pitiful craft? I have teeth, a tail, and claws!" he held them each up as he mentioned them to Arcturus, "my whole body is a weapon far greater than one mere sword."

Arcturus took a moment before replying with a, "so you do" he chuckled. "Very well. Start here, with your head held high."

Veledar followed his directions, and held his head high as instructed so he could still see the movements made by the paladin.

"I suppose you should shift to the right and lash out with your right limb."

Arcturus mimed the action with his sword instead of claws. Veledar mimicked him with a savage slash in the air.

"Very good! Now shift to the left and use your right paw, or whatever you prefer to call it!"

Once again, Veledar followed the paladin's instructions. He felt sort of silly as he slashed the air for a second time, but felt a cool sensation go down his spine.

"Now close your eyes and breathe deeply through your nostrils, then exhale through your mouth. Do it slowly."

Veledar did as he was told, closing his eyes carefully and letting a big breath of air fill his lungs. He let it hang in there for a moment, feeling his chest grow warm, then exhaled, letting a thin stream of fire escape his scaled lips. He opened his eyes in shock at that, as he clearly did not mean to do that.

"Sorry. Force of habit." He looked to Arcturus, imagining the paladin would be wearing naught but irritation on his face. Instead, he found the human amused by the mishap. Satisfied, Veledar repeated his actions and closed his eyes. He went to breathe in, but felt the ground rumble beneath him. It started out as small tremor, something Veledar was sure only he could feel beneath his paws. He looked around through a cracked eye for the source of the commotion, but he did not say anything. He didn't want Arcturus to panic if it was simply nothing.

There! He spotted among the grass what looked like a shark fin. Veledar had never been to the ocean to see such creatures, but he had read about them before. Although, in a way, it would be a bit strange for a shark to swim through the dirt.

The dragon pounced on Arcturus and rolled with him, tightly pressing the human's body against his. A large beast leapt from the earth as if it were water. It stood on four legs, and was roughly the size of a horse, armed with large, sharp claws, and a fat head very much like a whale. Where its mouth parted, there were rows upon rows of very sharp teeth.

The earth-brown creature eyed them with large, black reptilian eyes filled with murderous intent.

"What did you do that for?" Arcturus said, raising an eyebrow. He stopped and dropped into a combat stance he readied his armaments. "Wh-what is that thing?" he asked as Veledar spread his wings and hissed. If the creature cared for his display of power, it did not show any concern in the slightest, advancing slowly towards them.

"That's a bulette," Veledar said, watching the creature. "Some call it the land shark. It often travels in packs to hunt its prey." Veledar stopped as his eyes widened. That's why it was being patient! It was hunting them with a partner that was moving into position! Veledar went to turn and take off with

Arcturus, but it was too late. From the ground burst two more of the creatures. Veledar easily spun out of the way and sliced into the creature's leathery hide with a claw. Arcturus though had not been so lucky. The bulette on his side barreled into him, holding him pinned to the ground underneath its bulk. The paladin currently struggled against the creature's weight, and despite his sword cutting into its leg, the beast failed to relent.

Veleder gave out a battle roar, causing the buelette on Arcturus to raise its head and take notice of him.

Distracted, the beast became easy prey for Veledar, who crashed into the bulette and ripped it from Arcturus as he sunk his teeth deep into its hide. It tasted like dirt and he gagged slightly, but nevertheless, sliced viciously into the bulette's soft underbelly as he wrestled with the creature. It squirmed, kicked, and clawed against his crimson scales to no avail. Veledar continued his attack with pride now that his beautiful scales were holding the bulette's frenzy at bay.

He heard Arcturus shout out his own battle cry. The human had stabbed his sword through his bulette's head, causing the creature to collapse dead on the ground. However, even in death, it managed to pull the sword from Arcturus' hands and stick it out of its wounded body.

Veledar's attention was pulled back to the one he was fighting as its jaws found home around his neck. The dragon grabbed onto it with both forepaws, then ripped it open. The beast let go of the him with a roar of pain. Veledar managed to throw the creature ten feet away and stood back up to all fours. He watched the buelette eye him as dirt was fell off both of their bodies. Veledar could feel the bite of the creature throb through his muscles. It wasn't deep by dragon standards, but still packed quite the sting. Veledar smirked as the creature breathed in deep, obviously exhausted. Veledar admired its determination as it went to dive underground for an attack, but Veledar was faster. In a flash, the bulette was cut, bit, then roasted alive in a bath of blazing flames until the dragon let the creature's charred remains fall from his grasp.

He felt a tad bit of regret for eating early. Even though the creature's hide had a mediocre taste at best, its succulent insides were far better. Maybe he could convince the paladin to slice off a piece and preserve it.

The Paladin!

He turned quickly to find Arcturus beneath another one of the beasts. Arcturus was shoving the creature with his hands, trying to lift the bulk of the beast off him. However, as Veledar neared the two, it became clear that the creature was already dead from the two rapiers stuck in its back. Lyndis popped up from the other side, her face all red.

"So heavy! What do these things focking eat?" Lyndis shouted through grunts of effort.

"Probably a ton of rocks!" gasped Arcturus, before sighing in defeat. "Vele-Crimson Sky, could you perhaps lend me your strength?"

Veledar was pleased to see that the human had remembered the promise to keep his name secret. He smirked as he placed two paws on the corpse. With a great shove, a grunt, and thanks from his companions, Veledar pushed the creature off Arcturus, quite surprised that the little man held his own without him.

"So now that you two are done nearly getting killed by what is clearly bulette territory." Lyndis pointed towards a patch of dirt out in the field that looked upturned, most likely from the previous beasts. "We should be off to Entis."

Veledar agreed. He decided to watch as his two companions picked up their things. When they were ready, they mounted their horses, and Veledar shot into the air like an arrow. "I feel sorry for you two, having to tolerate such smelly creatures!" he shouted down at them.

"Well, it is a nice change of pace from your scaly arse!" Lyndis shouted back, making Veledar pout. That had been an excellent comeback, although he would NEVER tell her that.

"I shall name Arcturus' beast Smelly, and yours is going to bear the fit name of Stinky!" he replied loudly, watching the two laugh on their newly named horses. Both Arcturus and Lyndis seemed to be petting the horses, as if to comfort them on the nature of their new names.

Veledar pushed his wings higher and higher, until his companions looked like tiny ants below him. He flew into a cloud, letting the vapors condense on his snout before passing through with his next flap of wings. The dragon looked down far to the edge of his vision, past the rolling hills and the small mountains, past the forests sprinkled around the land. He saw a village, for that is all what those tiny specks could be. He thought about flying ahead, greeting his mother far before his companions could get there. He imagined his mother nuzzling him as she always did, grateful that he had stopped by. The dragon ultimately decided against it as he swooped down around to circle the two horse riders. No. It was better to stick together with them. Especially if he had to protect them from more monsters. He soared over their heads as they gave a quick wave to the cheerful dragon.

Veledar kept himself busy as the two riders made their way to the village as fast as Stinky and Smelly could carry them. Across the winding paths, it took them days compared to what Veledar could fly in a fraction of that time. Every night, he would watch them as if he were a mother protecting her hatchlings. He would keep the fire going and position himself to block the cold night wind. Veledar made a mental note to remind them how much he sacrificed himself for their comfort throughout this journey. That would surely add up to a suitable reward worthy of a dragon. The dragon did his duty every night, chuckling in silence as the bill kept rising and rising in his satisfied head.

When he was not busy, the dragon would watch the serene stars, with only the sound of the crackling fire to keep him company. On the fourth night of this leg of the journey, Veledar was once again stargazing, watching what dragons called Bahamut's tears.

"I've watched you these past few nights. What are you searching for, up there?" came the voice of Arcturus. The human walked over to him with a kind smile on his face. The pleasant sound of his voice did not startle Veledar, only surprised him. The dragon pointed a claw towards another one of Bahamut's tears.

"I always loved looking into the stars and seeing the souls of dragons shine down on us. I especially like the Bahamut's tears that go across the sky." he said slowly.

"You mean a shooting star. Some of the wizards say the stars up there are small portals to the realm of fire." the human said, sitting down beside him.

Veledar simply snorted at that idea. "That is a really mundane theory, I like mine better."

"I suppose yours is perfectly crafted for your views." Arcturus paused for several seconds. "Why do you call them Bahamut's tears? Must be an important figure, to name stars after."

Veledar's toothy smile completely dominated his snout. He LOVED telling that story, but not in a way that would scare the human off. With his smile shrinking to a more manageable size, the dragon got closer to Arcturus and curled his tail around him. The human looked to him with big eyes. They were so inviting, so curious, he simply could not resist.

"Long ago, there was a great dragon called Bahamut. She would travel across all realms, bringing life to the dragons of old. She was one of the first dragons, who taught her hatchlings that life was important, and specifically insisted on how much it should be cherished. It is said that she left this plane of existence when her children took to enslaving the other races and destroyed the life she held dear." said Veledar as he hung his head for dramatic effect, then continued slowly on a calm, silent voice.

"It was in those days of strife when she changed from a life giver into a creature of justice, good, and protection. Those tears in the sky represent her sorrow; the burden of having to take the lives of her misguided children, and the state of dragons today."

He watched the human sit in silence, contemplating the story. "I've never heard of her before today. I guess we humans know next to nothing of the dragons of old," Arcturus said with a shrug. Then his eyes lit up at having realized something. "Veledar, what was the color of her scales?"

That was a good question. Not surprising, considering what kind of man Arcturus was. "Her scales were a great silver in color, and her eyes were fluid, like liquid mercury. It is said she waits in the great beyond to help dragons reach their place in the heavens."

"My son mentioned a silver dragon right before he died, despite neither of us having any knowledge of this Bahamut." Arcturus said again after a moment of silence. His voice was once again filled with the pain of that memory.

"It is most peculiar, that she would appear to him instead of another dragon." Veledar replied, cocking his head to the side as he usually did. He had never known the goddess to appear to anyone, especially a human.

The two of them pondered in silence for some time before Veledar interrupted serenity of the night. "There is a town called Drakenburg nearby. I am going to go there." He turned to Arcturus, "and I am not asking for permission."

"I could tell." Arcturus coughed, "But still, a question is the right thing to do in a group. It's not like we would have said no to you. Why do you want to visit there anyway? You typically know next to nothing of my nation or its people."

Veledar thought back to the day his mother left, never to return. She had simply asked them to be strong before she went to the town of Drakenburg to fulfill a promise. Veledar frowned, remembering the reason for that promise...his brother.

"My mother resides there. She made a deal with the people of that town."

"Veledar, I have been across all of our villages and towns in Lumara. The town you speak of may have the symbol of a dragon stitched onto every building, but we have never seen a dragon around those parts for years." Arcturus said, his eyes filled with pity.

"Well, she was always good with magic. Perhaps she simply did not want to be found by your people." Veleder shot back with a grin.

"Perhaps...." Arcturus replied, putting a hand to his chin. "I will tell Lyndis of your plan in the morning then. I envy you, Veledar. You're going to soon have a touching reunion with your mother."

"Indeed," Veledar said, scratching his head with a wingtip talon. "You should get some rest before the sun rises. We need you in fresh shape to ride your trusty steed, the valiant horse called Smelly."

Arcturus nodded and returned to his bedroll, leaving Veledar alone once more. Veledar sighed. Arcturus and Lyndis were better company than he gave them credit for. Maybe, when this was all said and done, he could convince them to visit him every once and awhile.

As the dragon settled to sleep, he closed his eyes for a second, imagining the tales they would tell him during such exciting occasions.

Chapter 11: Drakenburg

The town of Drakenburg lay a few miles down the cobblestone road. The sun was starting to rise above the mountains in such a magnificent way that a single ray of light seemed to pierce through the permeating darkness, touching the sun with its radiance. You could say it was a busy town from the amount of foot traffic it received, both by carriage, and the occasional airship flying overhead.

Not that our travelers minded the crowd. Arcturus looked back to his two companions to see Lyndis busy creating a disguise for Veledar.

"Alright, enough prattling. My head is starting to ache worse than it did when this steel-head ambushed me in my lair." The dragon pointed at the human who feigned ignorance by scratching through his hair. "Just so we're clear, I will become small just to stop your nagging. Dragons are perfect the way they are. None should be forced to endure such humiliation, even for a good cause," Veledar hissed, than stuck his tongue out at Lyndis. "What are you smiling at? I just said-"

"Do you want to be focken spotted?" Lyndis whispered back. Arcturus just shook his head. The two had been fighting way before they arrived at this point.

"Well, be my guest then. Let the sun bathe your glorious scales. I'm curious how long till the guards have you in irons and shipped off to their grand, merciful king. Maybe he'll even prepare a feast in your honor!"

"Mrrrr, well, for your information, lady Lyndis, that's the same king that wants me dead. Secondly, I doubt the effectiveness of their entrapment team without their prized paladin there to inspire them. I give these fools about a month to find me, if they even manage that," Veledar chuckled, then jumped back as he avoided a playful smack by Lyndis.

"Just do your focken thing and spare us the rest of this lecture. Haven't joined your merry squad to listen to your babbling. We have a task to accomplish, and we shouldn't waver on account of something as silly as pride.”

“I think you just insulted our dragon, Lyndis.”

The half-elf scoffed, Arcturus chuckled, and Veledar just rolled his eyes at them both. The dragon moved his claws in a triangle fashion before ending it with what looked like a slap at the air with his claw. He then started to shrink, bit by bit, until he was no bigger than the average horse.

“Do I look pleasing now, your highness?” Veledar bowed his head mockingly before the frowning half-elf.

“Could be better. Oh, and pack your wings. One glance is enough to give away your secret.”

Veledar frowned as he pushed his wings close. He made another incantation, then the two beautiful appendages melded into his scales before disappearing altogether.

“I’m hideous,” Veledar slumped to the ground, snout in his paws.

“Oh, don't look so miserable, Crimson Sky. You’re still a dragon, wings or no wings,” Arcturus said, trying to cheer the dragon up.

“Easy for you to say.” The dragon said. “You didn't just become smaller than your two companions and lost the ability to fly on top of that. How do I look?” Veledar turned this way and that. “I want an honest answer. Better. A thorough one. Is my tail fine? What about my hinds?” he lifted one paw after the other, curling and spreading his toes to make sure there were no strange deformities.

“Everything’s as beautiful as ever.”

The dragon picked himself up. “Another lie to sweeten the bitter truth.”

“That's true, but it is the best I can provide for the time being. We’d better hurry up or we will lose the day.” Arcturus replied as he led Smelly down the road. Lyndis followed shortly behind with Stinky, and a grumbling Veledar.

They reached Drakenburg within the course of the hour, passing several merchants bound southward on the way. They seemed curious about Veledar, about what he was and where he came from. Arcturus threw them off the trail by suggesting he was from Rothdell, used to hunt dragons. To his amusement, Veledar stared at him with irritated eyes as the merchants had been amazed, even offered to purchase him. When they were out of ear shot, Veledar had started up a string of insults so long Arcturus lost count as the dragon shifted the blame to him for exposing his pride to such indignities. He watched the dragon's attitude change the moment they reached the town, for hanging from every building was a blue banner with a silver dragon stitched into the cloth.

“Look!” Veledar exclaimed with a grin, “they have dragon banners, just like you said!”

Arcturus and Lyndis tied up Stinky and Smelly outside a tavern painted in gray scales. It bore a great wooden shield with a silver dragon in flight.

"Loves dragons, this town does." Lyndis remarked as a peasant walked passed, gawking at Veledar.

"This place is wonderful!" Veledar whispered, as the dragon's head practically did not stop moving around, finding some new dragon decoration to look at. He quickly bounded to a cart littered with dragon shaped trinkets. "No wonder mother wanted to come here. These people adore her!"

"Ah, your little drake seems to like the banners." A wrinkled woman emerged from the cart's other side. She wore a dark green dress that seemed conspicuously clean. The woman ran an old hand through her gray hair as she looked to them with her amber eyes. Arcturus felt the hairs on his neck stand on end for some reason.

"Oh yes, the drakes from Rothdell are quite intelligent." Lyndis smiled through her teeth, "they can even recognize the picture of the creature they hunt."

Arcturus saw Veledar frown at her words before darting past her legs and nipping her hand. Though she mainly kept her composure, the half-elf did give a slight twitch as she shooed the dragon away.

"Is that what brought you here? Are you in search of a dragon as benevolent travelers, or after its tail as hunters? the old lady said with a grin, her hand moving to clasp a silver dragon amulet hanging around her neck. "Such a dangerous job, dragon hunting. Pointless. Unneeded. The dragoness has been our protector for years. What reason have you to take arms against her?"

Arcturus noticed several peasants stop to gawk at them, dirty looks being thrown especially at him and Lyndis.

"We are not hunters. Tell me. When was the last time you saw this guardian of yours?" He said, taking his eyes off the peasants and fixing them back on the woman.

"We have not seen her in five years, but that does not mean she isn't around. Dragons perceive time differently than you or I. However, dragon slayer-" The woman's eyes narrowed, "you will find not a single soul in this town that will help you find and slay our protector."

"I told you, we're not here to-"

Arcturus suddenly stopped when several guards dressed in chain mail walked over with spears in hand, their brown tabards a stark contrast to the blue banners that hung from virtually every building in the town.

"What do you need, dearies? Came here to hear a story of the great protector?" the old lady asked sweetly to the guards. She held out a hand to them with a silver brooch in the shape of a dragon. The gruff looking guard she held it out to swiftly smacked the lady's hand away.

"Listen here, you crumpled hag. You villagers talk about this dragon left and right, but none of me focken men or even the captain ever seen a glimpse of it. You should cease telling such lies to travelers and stop trying to get us to wear those things!"

The guards returned to their routine as they laughed to themselves as they left, like they pulled some great prank. The old woman sighed and picked up the brooch.

"My name is Lida, and I apologize for my harsh words. I forget sometimes that our true enemies walk among us." She gestured to Arcturus' ragged tabard that was torn almost to rags at this point. "Despite your allegiance to the kingdom of Lumara, I have judged you like our guards. Tell me, truly now, what do you intend to do when you find our protector?"

"We have a friend that would want to meet her and have a long talk." Lyndis said.

"Would this friend of yours be a dragon, dearies?" said Lida, gesturing to Veledar, who was busy eyeing a cart full of cooked lamb.

"How did you-"

"Old, I might be, but I can spot a spell, especially a crude craft such as this." The hag chuckled. "It's most fortunate the guards here don't seem able to spot such things. You best continue on your journey, but be warned. To find this town's protector will only bring about hardship and misery."

"Why is that?" Arcturus said, turning back to find that both the cart and Lida had vanished. He looked to Lyndis, who was staring as if struck by lightning, just like he was.

Veledar on the other hand was all growls and clicking claws. "Well, that just happened. Nothing to be done about an old lady and her vanishing cart now when my stomach rumbles like a war drum. I need to eat, now!" the dragon grabbed his belly with both paws. Arcturus just shook his head in disbelief. How could a ragged woman with no visible magic crystals vanish out of nowhere? The cost of that spell must have been-

"Thinking about an inn?" Veledar's poking snout drew the paladin's attention back to the present.

"Yeah, alright, alright! Just give me a moment." He nodded to the red dragon. That woman was an illusion the entire time? Or was she a spell caster like Lyndis?

"What do you think?" he moved towards Lyndis and watched the half-elf think hard for a moment as they walked back towards the inn. "I know illusions, and if that's the case, it must be some pretty focken good one. She was breathing an' talking as if she really was alive!"

Arcturus and Lyndis had to eat their lunch outside, as the innkeeper was insistent about the establishment's regulations. No quadrupeds were allowed. Not even intelligent ones. And especially...

"No pets!" the elven man had shouted with a vein popping out on his forehead. The meal wasn't too satisfying either. Just some meat that Arcturus could barely chew on, cheap fountain water, and a purple vegetable that was crunchy and in the shape of the letter L. Veledar seemed hateful of his meal too, but he ate with minimal complaints as they discussed their plan. They decided to split up and ask around about the lady, and more importantly, the protector's lair.

The party split up not a moment after lunch, with Veledar heading with Arcturus. Lyndis insisted they needed each other if they got into trouble. However, when asked about what sort of trouble, she just laughed, and said with a big grin that she was a people person. Over the first few hours, they only got repeated versions of the information they already knew. Arcturus was glad that no one recognized him. Even if they did, nobody connected him to the disappearing dragon incident. It confirmed one thing to him though. That his disappearance was not as wide spread as he originally thought.

The last two hours proved more productive than the previous. They got valuable information from a child all eager to tell them where the protector's lair was. The child said it was deep in the north western mountains, guarded by a raging snowstorm that kept everything away. Veledar rewarded the young child with a story about a brave dragon that naturally saved a maiden from a group of evil knights, and Arcturus watched with amazement. The child was not even phased that Veledar could talk. She just scampered back to her house with a great smile on her face.

They started to make their way back to the inn when the sun descended beneath the horizon. Veledar suddenly stopped. Arcturus watched him tense up, his head looking around quickly.

"What's the matter?" He asked, looking around as well. He did not see anything that looked out of the ordinary in the practically empty streets.

Then, they came. Men poured from the alleys, one after the other, all clad in a mixture of leathers and chain armor. They had short hairs, all clearly human, with eyes full of mischievous intent.

"Why hello there," he found himself saying. "Pleasant night for a stroll, eh?"

The gathered men sneered at his politeness. His gut told already had an idea on how this was going to end. Yet as a man of virtue, Arcturus had to give them a chance to prove their intentions.

"Fancy drake, that." One man pointed to Veledar with a club he was holding. "Figure he'd feel right at home in our group. What do you say, lads?"

The rest of the men grumbled, nodded, and chuckled when the one who spoke pulled out a net from his pack with his massively muscled arms.

One of the other men, taller than the rest, carried a bag that was tossed at Arcturus' feet. "Fifty plat says you walk away and we get that drake. Choose otherwise, and ma boys here will put a beat down on ya!"

"Wait wait wait. I have a better idea!" Veledar laughed, much to the surprise of the party, "We take the money you have given us, and you get to leave with your lives. How's that?"

Arcturus drew his sword as the dragon bared his teeth at the men. "Deal's more than fair. I'd listen to the drake, people. After all, we don't want to stain the streets of this fine town on our first visit."

Arcturus watched the group of thugs nervously grip their weapons as they looked to him, then to Veledar, who had started hissing at them.

"Anyone here can choose to flee, but if you decide to cross blades with us, consider this is your only warning." Arcturus continued. He took his shield off his back and held it firmly in front of him.

"Aye. We hear ya, lad. But you be missin' one thing." the bag tosser flicked his fingers to the men that poured from the alleys behind Arcturus. "We've got the numbers to topple ye over. Get 'em, lads!"

Arcturus whirled on his feet to indeed spy five more men with short swords and leather rags that seemed to be stitched together into a grotesque whole. He smirked as the men charged at them in disorganized fashion, with their weapons ready to bludgeon the two of them to death. Arcturus blocked the first club and shoved the man backwards as his sword tasted another one's flesh. The arc slash painted the cobblestone a dark crimson substance. The man collapsed on his knees to hold onto the ooze that kept pouring from his slashed throat.

Two more came at him. Arcturus ducked under a swing, then his blade sneaked under the opponent's and, with a brutal slash, the paladin took that man's hand as payment for his crimes.

"Hraaaaah!" the now hand-less man fell on his back with a mighty groan, trying hopelessly to stop the blood that gushed out of his stump.

Arcturus heard Veledar give a screech, a tiny roar that was more adorable than threatening. He would of course never tell the dragon such things in this moment, as he figured he would roar even louder just to prove something. The dragon sunk his teeth into a thug's arm, ripping a solid chunk of flesh along with whatever else clung to the limb. The paladin scrunched his face in disgust and charged at another man. He shoved his enemy to the ground with such force he thought he heard something crack. His triumph was short lived though. In less than a second, he felt a blade nick his side.

"Khh-" he whirled around for a counter-attack, only to see a club smash into his side.

"See? He isn't such a hard-ass!" the bag-man kicked Arcturus' plated chest.

"Wrong words!" the paladin rose with an upper swing that sliced the bag-man from balls to chin. The man gurgled and collapsed to the ground, clutching desperately at his escaping insides.

Arcturus turned to the others. He looked to the once confident thugs, who now had sweat dripping down their brows and eyes filled with doubt. He saw another shudder and fall, an arrow with green feathers sticking out of his back.

"Fock this!"

"I'm not dying tonight."

The four remaining men backed away as Arcturus advanced on them with his bloodied sword.

"Screw this! Let the bastard keep the drake! No amount of money is worth being gutted for!" one shouted as the sound of his boots disappeared into the night. The others soon followed suit, leaving Veledar and Arcturus standing among the fallen, looking rather proud of themselves.

"Well, at least some of them had the sense to do the right thing." Veledar grinned as he cut one of the man's purses to see what was inside. "I mean, they attacked us, so they were not entirely thinking straight, but mraawr, look! Ten gold pieces!"

Adorable, Arcturus smiled at Veledar, then went to each of the fallen men to retrieve whatever useful belongings they had. The entire time his eyes kept being drawn to the arrow sticking out of that thug's back. Arcturus walked over to it and pulled it out with a sickening noise.

"Veledar. Take a look at this." He stuck out the arrow to the dragon, who quickly scampered over. "I think someone saw the ruckus. Decided to lend a helping hand," he said, his eyes scanning the dark windows, empty alleyways, and wooden boxes around the street. "Although it looks like our mysterious friend prefers to remain hidden for now."

"Who cares? More loot for us," Veledar growled. "Hold it straight. I still want to find out who this person is." Veledar took in a deep breath near the arrow head. "I don't recognize the smell of who actually shot this thing, but there's an earthy tinge about it, very different from how you humans smell."

"Earthy?" Arcturus was impressed by the dragon's nose. For a moment, he wondered who was better at tracking. The gryphons of his kingdom, or the dragon before him?

"We'd better be careful on our way back to the inn. Maybe Lyndis has better information for us."

"Don't worry, Arcturus. If anything remotely dangerous crosses our path, I will be more than a match for it." The little dragon swelled up his chest and took a regal pose.

"You are such a cute thing tonight."

Veledar's happy snout scrunched when the paladin rubbed his gloved hand along his head. "You are aware that my cute claws and these adorable teeth can still pierce through your armor, right?"

"Normal steel, maybe. This one though had been crafted by the most skilled pair of hands I know. Even a sword would have a hard time piercing it." The paladin slapped his plate, then kneeled to Veledar's eye level. "But we both know you like me too much to even think such barbaric thoughts."

"I like you?" The dragon hissed. "You have it all wrong, paladin who crawls to my belly every night to whisper words of comfort to my ears. If anything, you're in love with me!"

"And what if I am?"

Veledar snorted, bits of mucus splashing on the human's face.

"Seems this joke has two sides, after all." Arcturus chuckled, wiping the distasteful goo off his face. "I'd ask you to lick it, but-"

"Don't even think about it."

Arcturus cleaned himself with a thug's rag, then walked side by side with the dragon, feeling Veledar's scales shift under his gloved hand with every step the dragon took.

"See, if you acted like that all the time, we would get along much better!" Veledar turned to head his way down the street. "Words for a dragon are ephemeral. True affection lays in the touch, although your personality is an improvement over most humans."

"I can see how, "Arcturus picked up his hand. "You really are enjoying this as much as I think?"

Veledar scowled for a moment before shaking his snout, "Oh yes, extremely. Now put that hand back to work."

They continued down the dark streets of Drakenburg. Arcturus watched as Veledar's snout would move from side to side to check every rooftop and alley. Each time he did so, Arcturus could see his muscles tense underneath his scaled body. No doubt his teeth were eager to bare themselves at the slightest hint of danger. Arcturus wondered if the dragon had taken the ambush as a failure on his part to detect it. Maybe a night of good drink, food, and entertainment would have the dragon back to his relaxed self. However, Veledar wasn't the only thing he noticed. They never encountered one guard, not a single torch bearing man on patrol, and no posts. The streets were completely empty of people. Arcturus kicked a loose stone in irritation. If he would be in charge of the city, he would have the guards of this town whipped into shape in no time. A sigh left his mouth at the thought of Gus and Elizabeth. Arcturus kept wondering if they had stepped up in his absence. Surely Elizabeth would take on the extra responsibility of a captain. It was in her nature, to always strive for excellence.

He was interrupted as Veledar bounded through the doors of the inn.

"You again? Get that beast outta my sight!" Came the shout of the elven man from earlier. "How deaf must you be? I said no pets near the tables!"

Arcturus entered to see the man picking up a tankard from the ground, while Veledar slunk away, trying to avoid the watchful eyes of the other patrons. The busy inn -despite that little hiccup- went back to their hot meals as the half-ling band started playing their melodious tune once again. Their music filled the inn with a happy, toe tapping tune that Arcturus wished to have heard at a better time of the day. It would have made a better impression than the rude guards from earlier, or the vanishing crone.

Arcturus made his way to the bar where Lyndis was sitting, holding a mug in one hand and a spoon full of soup in the other. Just as he sat down, he heard Veledar pounce onto a chair next to him, two scaled paws thumping onto the bar. The elven barkeep quickly made his way over, forehead vein still very apparent on his cherry-colored face.

"Oy! What's he doin' here? Oy! Armor! I'm talkin' to ya!" the innkeeper pointed an angry finger at Arcturus. "This is your damned pet, innit?"

"Happens that he is." The paladin spoke calmly.

"Then what did I say earlier, eh? You got dropped on your head as a kid or what? Take pet out or see yourselves gone from my establishment!" the unruly man jabbed a finger in Veledar's direction.

Arcturus was about to speak and apologize for Veledar, but the dragon's errant tongue beat him to it.

"Listen here, you barking dog of an elf. I am not a pet to anyone, especially to this armored, good mannered human. He and I are traveling companions." Veledar turned his snout towards Arcturus, "and if you kick me out, you kick him -and his heavy pouch- back into the streets! Do you want us to find a better inn? Fine! We're going."

Arcturus' mind screamed internally as Veledar looked to him with a grin that seemed to say *I got this*. He watched the elf, his mouth hung open in disbelief at the talking drake. Arcturus sighed at Veledar's complete inability to lay low, then the elf too sighed before setting his eyes on Arcturus, perhaps too proud to speak to Veledar as an equal.

"Sorry 'bout earlier. My mouth tends to...you know." The elf brushed off the sweat from his concerned face. "If that thing breaks anything, you will be paying for it. Understand? I'll bring your meals now. 'pologies again for losing my temper. Beasts tend to bring the worst in me."

Arcturus nodded to the man. "No problem."

"He's just being polite with an innkeeper that has serious anger issues." Veledar added.

"Fine," the elf snapped to Veledar, "just place an order with the waitress." He raised a bony finger to Veledar's snout, "don't make a mess, ya hear?"

Veledar's eyes narrowed at the elf, Arcturus thought he might snap at the man's finger, but to his surprise, Veledar simply nodded instead.

"Good. If you behave accordingly, there will be no trouble between us." the man laughed, to which Arcturus nervously joined him in laughter.

Arcturus returned his attention to Lyndis as the barkeep walked away. "So now that your little shout duel is done with, did you find anything useful?"

"There's a path used to travel up to the mountains. They don't share it with outsiders or guards because they want to protect the dragon, just as she protects them." Lyndis replied, pulling an old looking map from her pack. "The way is usually safe, but they admitted no one went up there in years. Five, to be exact, just like the crone said, although what focken dragon keeps count? Five years is nothing for them, so I don't know if that means anything."

"My mother probably has better things to do than cater to a village full of rude guards and loud barkeeps." Veledar mumbled.

"What do you think we will find up there?" Arcturus asked over the steps of a waitress that brought over a bowl of soup for him.

"Normal stuff, if you can call goblins normal, maybe a troll or two. However, the biggest obstacle is a storm that appears to protect the mountain. Drives unwanted visitors away if you're being optimistic, or kills them, if you want to think that way. Best we leave first thing in the morning. I have this symbol used by the townsfolk to approach the storm safely, and its previous owner would very well like it back."

"Really?"

Lyndis pulled out a small silver metal brooch in the shape of a dragon.

"You stole it?" Arcturus gasped.

"Nah, I only borrowed it, and trust me, the person it belongs to was anything but deserving of such token." Lyndis smirked, pocketing the brooch.

"Suppose I agree with you. Who did you take it from?

"Don't know him by name, but he runs the thugs here in Drakenburg. He is known around the streets as Knives. As you imagine, this charming fellow is the reason why guards don't roam the streets at night."

The waitress returned to pour a bluish liquid into Lyndis' tankard. It looked like partially frozen mush, with a sweet air about it. While Arcturus was staring at the liquid, Lyndis pointed to it, then took a sip. "It's elvish frost wine. Great stuff for long nights."

They went on to discuss the ambushes, which only coaxed a sigh from Lyndis' mouth, along with a single word. Typical.

Veledar ordered large plates of food that surprised Arcturus only in price, not in gesture. Like last time, he shelled out the coin to feed the dragon's humongous appetite. They eventually retired for the evening as the music died down, drinks ran dry, and people started to leave. Lyndis strolled down to her door, shutting it quickly to leave Arcturus and Veledar in their own room again.

The two fought over where to sleep for a brief while before Veledar just stole a side of the bed with a grin. Arcturus got onto the other side as he took off his gear and laid it on the floor.

"You know, you could have talked to the elf some more about the rooms. I could have gotten a proper bed to slumber upon." Veledar grumbled into his paws.

"No pets!" Arcturus mimicked the bartender. "Can't have a pet destroy my fine rooms." Arcturus laughed as Veledar suddenly placed his snout close to his face.

"Oh, very funny. Maybe I'll keep reminding you of your lack of tail, or wings, or maybe this useless hide that does nothing to protect your feeble body."

"Take it easy, Veledar, It's just a joke."

"You know what else is a joke?"

"What?"

Arcturus was suddenly shoved off the bed by a scaly leg. He fell onto the floor with a thump, the hissing laughter of the dragon hurting more than the fall. "Whimsy paladin! Now that's a more proper source of amusement!"

Arcturus started to grumble to himself as he got back onto the bed and collapsed into the pillow. He closed his eyes until he felt a snout rest beside his head. He could practically feel Veledar's grin, "Not very funny when it's your turn, is it?"

"I'm sorry for calling you my pet." he grumbled, eyes still closed. "But just so you know, I find you adorable in this form."

"Why thank you, human. Maybe next time I can think of something nice to tell you."

"Not tonight?"

"Not tonight." Veledar yawned as he curled up, hugging his own tail in the absence of his beloved wings.

Chapter 12: Crashing Hopes

There was a sudden knocking at Arcturus' door, quick and hard, almost like it happened inside his skull.

There better be a good reason for this, the paladin begrudgingly pulled himself from the sleepy dragon to look groggily out the window. Morning had not yet arrived. The stars still hung high in the sky twinkling every so often. Veledar snored as the bed strained against his weight. It appeared the dragon had returned to his normal size during sleep, and right now, that big body of his was taking up most of the room. Arcturus removed the dragon's forepaw from his middle, then took a few steps towards the door, shivering in the cold blanket of air that enveloped his body. From the door came the sound of the rapid knocking once more.

"Arcturus, open the fock up!" came Lyndis' harsh voice. Arcturus pulled open the door. The woman quickly bolted in and slammed the door shut. She was fully dressed in her armor, weapons, and gear. Her face was full of determination, but her eyes had a tint of worry in them as she turned to look around the chamber.

"Well aren't you a rude lady, waking a dragon from sweetest slumber," Veledar mumbled sleepily.

"Shut it, dragon. Now is not the time for whatever humor passes through that sleepy head." Lyndis snapped back, then lowered her voice. "Arcturus, get your gear on. We are going to have company in just a few moments.

"That doesn't sound bad." Veledar yawned and stretched out to take up the entire bed. "I wager the angry elf feels bad for last night, and to make up for his harsh words and complete lack of respect, he had his servants bring us food!"

"Unbelievable..." Lyndis sighed.

Arcturus figured whatever she spoke of was serious. "Lyndis, who exactly are you expecting?" he asked while he put on his plate armor piece by piece. During this time, Lyndis stayed at the door, cracking it open every now and again to see if anybody approached.

"Why the sagged face? Maybe these people heard of my exploits last night.

I know! They want to pay their respects to the dragon that kept their streets clean of thugs!" Veledar growled excitedly, slithering out of his bed on four tired paws.

"Wrong again. Honestly, dragon, you must be the worst guessing partner I've ever had. Here's the situation. The folks that had that brooch I took found out sooner than I would have liked, alright? We best head for your mother's den quickly, before they come to get what is rightfully theirs."

"Hmmph, hardly a challenge." The dragon snorted. "I can handle whatever company you have, dear Lyndis, for I am a dragon after all."

"Well, I remember getting the better of you on quite a few occasions, *dear dragon*." Arcturus pointed out, only for Veledar's snout to scrunch up,

"Well that doesn't count when I'm not talking to you." he hissed.

"Why not? Because you're a mighty dragon and I'm a puny little human?" Arcturus smirked. A loud crash of shattering glass came from Lyndis' room. Whoever broke into the room made a mess, throwing things around like a storm, undoubtedly searching for the brooch.

"The half-bitch isn't here!" a thug just said.

"Well then, check the whole damn inn, you lazy fuck! Knives wants her brought to him in one piece." yelled another voice.

"Oy, why does it have to be in one piece?"

"Cause boss says so. Now do as I say, or I'll carve myself a trophy from your own flesh."

Arcturus pulled his sword as the door from Lyndis' room slammed open. He heard the window open in his own room and realized Lyndis was no longer next to him. He turned around to find that she was already one foot out the window.

"The fock you're lookin' at? Thought we'll leave the normal way?" she hissed through clenched teeth.

"We can take them." Veledar whispered, hunching over and baring his teeth.

"No, you overgrown lizard. If you fight here, the entire inn will be destroyed."

"Fine!" Veledar groaned, "but let it be known I chose to let these fools live a while longer." He moved his claws and shrank down to his waist high size.

"If only you fought as well as you talk..." Arcturus sighed as he clumsily climbed out the window and onto the street below.

"Next time you say something like that, I'm going to bite your shiny metal ass."

Arcturus gritted his teeth when his metal boots clanked on the cobblestone street. He looked up to see Veledar flying out the window.

"Stupid dragon."

"Shh!" Lyndis whispered from a nearby alley. She was crouched over, gesturing to Arcturus to come over to her. She then pointed to a large group of men and women of different races gathered at the front of the inn. They were adorned in leathers, chainmails, and a select few even afforded the safety of plate mail. They had crossbows, spears, and all other sorts of weapons. From afar, it looked like a small army had gathered to bring the mean innkeeper to justice, with grim frowns and determined looks upon their faces.

Arcturus watched Lyndis sneak carefully from shadow to shadow, until she was well beyond the mercenaries' view. He rose to follow her when a yell pulled his attention; a shout of pain from the elven bartender.

"I told you, I don't know where your "princess" went! She was supposed to be in her room!" The elven man said before getting tossed through the door. He landed hard on the street, like no man deserved. Even from where he was hiding, Arcturus could see the large red stain on the man's brown tunic.

"NO! He already told you everything!" From the inn ran another elf wearing white undergarments. She quickly picked the wounded bartender up, pointing around the gathering of men. "You bastards. Why don't you believe us? We're a common inn! What would a princess do here?"

Arcturus figured the woman must've been the elf's wife. Then, when the situation already looked grim, two ogres smashed their way out of the inn, busily munching on whatever they could steal from the kitchen. These two brutes stood at nine feet tall, covered in taters of hide. Their faces were rough, with a large underbite of yellow teeth.

"Half ogres." Arcturus whispered quietly to himself

"Come on!" he heard Lyndis say in a harsh whisper. "We have to get out of here."

His attention turned back towards the man as one of the half-ogre's fist collided with the barkeep's face.

"P-please, he doesn't know anything else!" Cried the barkeep's wife as she desperately tried to hold back one of the ogres. The beastly creature simply tossed her aside like a ragdoll.

Arcturus looked to Lyndis. She had already began to leave the man to his fate. He looked again to the man and his wife. Could he really leave these two innocent souls into the hands of these rogues? Arcturus felt the familiar tug in the back of his mind.

His oaths, compelling him to stand against injustice.

Without another thought, he drew his sword, undid his shield, and marched out towards the group of mercenaries.

"Hey! Let them go!" The paladin bellowed confidently, holding his sword high and pointing to the elf with an armored finger.

The collected group looked dumbfounded for a moment before bursting out laughing, as if Arcturus was a mere squire brandishing a sword.

"And why should we do that?" one of the men sneered as he spit onto the street, "because you want to play hero? Don't you know who we are, boy?"

"No, and frankly I don't care. You let those people go, or this street is going to get messy." Arcturus said.

The group started laughing again as another man stepped forth from the collected group. He was dressed in fancy clothes, bright purple with gold runes stitched into them. He was a tough looking Half-elf, with a scar across his face, long braided hair, and blue eyes.

"Listen here, boy. Listen well, cause this'll be the only time I speak to a runt like you. Name's Knives. It would be best for ya to just put that sword away and walk the other direction. Pretend you didn't see a thing, eh? Make this easy for the both of us."

"So you're Knives, huh? Pretty stupid way to get your hands dirty."

"Not really," Knives chuckled. "I own this town." he held his arms out wide, "I own the food, the merchants, the very people in it! No guard would dare to stand against me or my army. I can murder you in the middle of the street and nobody would look twice at your mangled corpse, because they respect Knives more than a random lowlife who stole his daddy's armor."

"Interesting theory, Knives. But I have a different one." Arcturus smirked, throwing glances at Knives' minions, who continued to brandish their weapons threateningly. Arcturus counted thirteen people, not including Knives. This would be difficult, but with Lyndis and Veledar. it would be doable.

"How about you face justice for your crimes, here and now? The city will breathe a sigh of relief once I clear off the kraken that chokes it."

"Kraken...right. Someone kill this fool before he further embarrasses himself," laughed Knives.

Arcturus could feel Lyndis' eyes on him, scolding him for his actions. He closed his eyes and imagined another pair of familiar eyes. "Selina," he said softly to himself as the two half ogres bounded towards him. In one motion, he sliced deep into the half ogre that reached him first. The swing severed the limb in one clean slice, followed by a sickly smack. The ogre naturally collapsed near his missing limb with a groan of anger and pain.

The thugs were on him in an instant, with shouts of rage and bursting anger. Arcturus had to adopt a stance of total defense as they attacked him from all sides. Within the storm of swords, spears, and bludgeons, he had to constantly keep moving to stop the group from flanking him, and despite all the blocks ,parries, and glancing blows, he felt some of the weapons hit him square on.

He silently thanked Matilda for his armor. Without it, he'd be dead several times over.

"Grah!" A heavy blow knocked him to the ground before the sea of thugs. He recovered quickly however, punishing the fool that had done this by slicing off his fingers. Arcturus parried another strike before the remaining ogre grabbed his shield and ripped it from his grasp. Their next attack had him disarmed, and finally encircled by the thugs. They looked to him with sneers and grins of victory. He raised his gauntlet clad hands as if to fight them with his fists.

"Haven't you learned your lesson, boy? This is what you get for playing the hero." Knives chuckled from behind the wall of muscle. "Any last words? Perhaps telling me where that princess of mine is?"

"Yeah. I think I may know where she is."

Knives slowly revealed his broken -and in some places missing- teeth. Arcturus grinned as he saw the elven man and woman make it to safety. He looked up to the sky, where the sound of wings was quickly followed by a fireball detonating behind the thugs. Several men were incinerated close to the blast, while others fell in the wake of the blazing explosion.

"There's a-" one man started to shout before a rapier was plunged into his chest. The man fell to reveal Lyndis.

"Heard you were searching for me," she smirked, crossing swords with another thug.

"Lyndis! Bless your timing. I almost thought-"

"Now's not the time!" the half-elf hissed over the paladin's words.

Arcturus fought his way through the ranks of men and snatched his weapons in the confusion that followed. With several well-placed strikes, he felled three thugs easily. On the fourth strike of his sword, the thug he was aiming for collapsed with an arrow sticking out of him. Arcturus almost froze at the realization. It looked like their mysterious helper was back.

Throughout all the fighting, Lyndis was flipping, stabbing, and weaving her way through the remaining thugs. Knives was backing away from the whole fight as the situation was spiraling out of his control. Lyndis managed to jump her way over to him, holding up her rapier to his nose. "What's the matter, Knives? You think you can just muscle your way through everything?"

"Yeah, about that...just realized it's best for both sides if you can just keep the brooch, princess. You won't hear from me or my people. Just...just get out of here, will ya?" Knives said as a drop of sweat dripped down his head.

"Well you see, normally I would let you go, buuuuuutt. You see my friend over there? The one in the silver armor, currently cutting down the last of your thugs? Well, he isn't too keen on letting filth like you propagate further, so I am going to have to refuse your generous offer."

"Bad business, princess. Bad business when knives have to come out!" Knives said, pulling a hidden dagger from inside his shirt. He twirled it around in his hand before pointing it at Lyndis, "I am going to cut that smile off your face."

Arcturus cut down the last thug with a wide slash of his sword, then turned to face Lyndis as she faced off with Knives. The man threw him a quick glance before he focused back on his opponent, his eyes wide with fear. Who wouldn't be? A man in full plate striding over to you, covered in the blood of your minions?

If Knives was a good fighter, Arcturus would never know, as an arrow pierced him right through the shoulder. The rogue leader gasped in pain as Lyndis leaped in to take advantage of the distraction. In one swift motion, she had him pierced on her rapier, straight through the heart.

"You should have just let this whole business go, Knives," she said, kicking him off her rapier. Knives fell, clutching his chest, hitting the ground with a loud thump.

"Good to see that bastard come to deserved end. Why did he call you princess?" Arcturus asked, cleaning his sword with a rag he pulled from one of the dead thugs.

"It's a long story," Lyndis sighed, "Too complicated for me to go into right now, but at least this bastard is dead." She kicked Knives' corpse hard with her boot.

"Nrraaaaah! Get off my bear, ya big basterd!" Came a shout further down the street.

Without a thought, Arcturus moved swiftly towards the source of the voice. Perhaps it belonged to the person that had been helping them from the shadows. He did not have to go far, as -after he rounded a corner- he found seven more thugs attacking a large brown bear and a dwarven woman with braided red hair. In each of her hands rested a well-crafted hand axe, smeared in dried blood. At her feet was a bow, possibly what she had been using before the thugs had closed in on her, to protect herself against close-quarters danger. The dwarf was wearing dark grey studded leather with small golden dwarven runes around the edges. Her white furred leggings were almost in blur as she avoided several weapon strikes with a smirk on her face.

And by the looks of it, she knew how to fight. Arcturus quickly realized that when the woman ducked from a sword swing that nearly cut her hair clean off, then returned the strike by crashing her axe into the man's gut.

"Almost got me right in the 'ead! Ye got guts, ya do!" She laughed, pulling her axe out, causing the man's insides to spill out onto the street.

Arcturus joined her by smashing one man's head in with his shield, then he pulled out his sword and plunged it through the neck of another.

"Thank ye laddie! Pretty good for a human!" The dwarf lady cried as the large bear tackled a man and mauled his face. The man flailed with his sword, slicing into the bears muzzle and drawing blood before his neck got torn to shreds. The remaining thugs were cut down in a matter of moments from a combination of rapier, axe, bear, and sword. Once again Arcturus cleaned his sword and sheathed it in his scabbard, while Lyndis started to loot the dead bodies.

One of these days I have to do something about that habit of hers, Arcturus shook his head, then walked to the dwarf, who was tending to the bear's snout with a rag.

"Quit yer fussin' ya big baby. I've had bigger cuts to deal with in da past." She said, rubbing the rag deep into the cut. The bear let out a pained moan. "Oh, you'll be alrigh' in a few moments. Human," she turned her head to Arcturus. "Thank ye for helpin me outta that bind back dere. Although it be about time you returned the favor. Ya seem to draw a lotta bad attention." She said with a laugh.

"A most unfortunate consequence spurred from the desire to do good," Arcturus chuckled. "What do you go by? I can't simply call you our hidden friend, now that we've met."

"Ye can call me Merlia Gallowglar! Explorer at heart an' smasher of skulls when needs be. Dis moaning pup here is Ulga."

"Charmed. I'm Lyndis Kuxion," Lynidis slid over with a smile, handing Arcturus a bag of gold. "Your share of the loot, for now," she added quickly before resuming her business.

"I'm Arcturus Lund," he said, sticking out a hand to the dwarf who shook it with a big smile.

"Arcturus, eh? I saw you an' yer lizard friend walkin' around, gettin attacked like righ now. What are ya lot up to that seems to draw so much attention?"

"This one is on you," Lyndis placed a hand on his shoulder. "I am going to do a second pass and see if I missed anything worth taking." Lyndis patted his shoulder before returning to the field of corpses.

"I don't want to involve you in our affairs, even if you are as stout as you look. Merlia."

The dwarf didn't seem to take his words lightly. Frowning, she crossed her hands, then unleashed a piece of her mind. "Ya listen here, ya clankin collection of pots and pans! It sounds like ya three are on an adventure, I like me some adventures. Makes da best stories, an' I can handle trouble just as good as any man, don' you worry about that, laddie."

Arcturus sighed, "You have helped us quite a bit, so it wouldn't be fair to deny you a chance at adventure, as risky as it might get. We are heading to the capital to retrieve a book for a friend.”

“A book? What’s it made from, gold? Cause when ya put it like dat, it don't sound that excitin’.” She laughed.

“That’s only part of it. I also want to get some answers from my king. Especially why he wished me to end the life of an innocent dragon.”

“So ya sayin’ that little red scamp of yours is a dragon? Do I look like a fool, laddie? I tink he is a wee bit too small for a dragon.” She said, her eyes full of skepticism.

“Oh believe me, that one’s more trouble than you can handle, especially if he just heard you,” Arcturus whispered, then smiled as the dwarf squinted her eyes at him. “He just changed his size and hid his wings.”

There was a sudden scrape of talons on stone that made Arcturus hold up his arms and gesture to the form of Veledar. “He probably heard me say the word dragon and could not resist swooping down on us.”

“Now now, Arcturus, I think you are starting to know me a tad too well.” Veledar chuckled before strutting over. Arcturus could see he was clearing puffing his chest out. The dragon stopped several feet in front of Merlia before spreading his wings wide.

“I am Crimson Sky, easy to say and obvious to the eye...Merlia, was it?”

Arcturus watched the dwarf’s face. If she was concerned or scared of the dragon's presence, she did not show it in that big, gleeful stare.

“Well, best keep yer big wings hidden in dis town. Knives there probably has more idiots waitin’ in the alleys. Best we head to me camp. It's a couple miles north of here. Once we get dere, ye can tell me wha’ else ya lot up ta.”

“I find myself confused by your request, Merlia. Do you invite us to your camp out of kindness, to question us, or perhaps join in on our adventure?” Veledar asked, strutting around her.

“Why else would ye three be askin’ bout da silver dragon? Rumor says lives on dat dere mountain?” she pointed to the towering mountains overlooking the town. “I’m comin’ with ya, and there’s nothin’ ye can do ta stop me.”

Arcturus had a quick discussion about traveling to Merlia's camp. Veledar moaned that there was yet another person wanting to travel with them on HIS adventure. Lyndis brought up the point that the more work force they had, the better chances to succeed at getting the dragon's book back. Veledar complained, but gave in to the half-elf's compelling arguments.

“Fine, Merlia. We shall follow you to your camp. However, if this is a trick, I will do things to you that will make you swear in every dwarvish word known to your kind,” Veledar squinted his eyes with a resounding snarl.

“Ya don have ta worry bout me stabbin ya in the back. Who do ya think I am, a sneaky goblin? Cause I gotta tell ya, dragon, dose be fighten’ words!”

“Just lead us to your camp.” Veledar sighed, looking towards the sky.

"Good, now da lot of ya get ya horses and follow Ulga and me."

The group quickly left the town on horseback, with Merlia leading the way atop Ulga. Veledar flew overhead, following them closely. They spoke little as the night wind battered them from all sides. Arcturus saw even Veledar struggle against the gale, although he doubted the dragon would ever admit to having such trouble. They arrived at Merlia's camp within the hour. It was made up of a simple tent and a dead campfire tied down to resist the harsh winds. It was next to a tree where, it looked like Merlia had hung several pelts to keep the place dry. Arcturus led Smelly over to the tree and tied him up. He turned around as he heard Veledar land behind him.

"Gods, can we get a fire going? My focken hands are freezing," Lyndis rubbed her hands together."

"Ah, forgot ya elves couldna stand da cold," chuckled Merlia, pulling out flint and steel from a pack on the ground. After several failed attempts to light the humid wood, Veledar let out an annoyed groan.

"That little thing is going to do nothing to this wood. Here. Let me show you how it's done, dear Merlia," the dragon snorted, then unleashed a jet of flame from his mouth to light the wood in an instant. Arcturus took a seat beside Veledar, who had settled down by the fire. The others gathered around as the red dragon started telling Merlia of their journey thus far. Although he started the whole tale with the "Great injustice done to him by Lumara's treacherous paladin." He spoke of the trip through the fairy realm, the fight with the bulettes, and smiled fondly of their time in Drakenburg, up until Knives ruined everything.

"Dats all well an' good, Crimson Sky, but what's yer business with da silver dragon?" Her eyes went wide, then a coy grin grew on the dwarves face, "Oh, I get ya! Yer lookin for a she dragon to keep ya big bum warm at night!"

"Gods no!" Veledar replied, scrunching up his snout and sticking out his tongue in disgust. He stopped only to make gagging noises as he turned away from Merlia. After a few more moments, he was able to respond with, "Nothing of that sort, you perverted dwarf. That dragon is my mother. Is it so strange that I only wish to pay her a visit? It's been years since I last had any contact with her!"

As Merlia and Veledar talked back and forth, Arcturus took note that Veledar did not mention the lady Lida. He must not have heard what the old woman said, that the journey to his mother's mountain would only bring hardship and pain upon them.

He perked up as Veledar started telling a story about how his mother had put on a play with magic for his sister, brother, and himself. When he mentioned his brother, Veledar frowned, but continued with the story. Once it was finished, he was going to ask Merlia what wind brought her around

Drakenburg, but Lyndis beat him to the question.

The cheerful dwarf frowned during a sigh. She looked hurt, somehow. "I'm on an adventure, of course!" she said, her face perking up. "Little Ulga an' I get inta heaps of trouble while we explore da unknown."

"Lumara is the unknown?" It was Arcturus' turn to frown. Far as he knew, Lumara encompassed most of the continent.

"Well ta me anyway. I'm from da south of course. Straight past that other place." She paused for a moment in thought, scrunching up her brow, "Drenedar!" she exclaimed, "Da one with all da trees and pegasi. Alhough, tha place wasn't a great fit for a dwarf. Everytin' was so tall, bright and clean!" She laughed, "Can ye believe I watched a group scrub down da streets ta have dem perfect? Ridiculous!"

She leaned up against Ulga and pulled out a knife from her side, then slowly started to carve a piece of wood she found nearby. "If ya ask me, things need ta get a little dirty, rough, take a few scraps, den ye can tell da difference between what's cheap an' what's important."

She paused again for a moment to cut off a large section of the wooden stick. "Anyways, I'm from a small village beneath da mountain o stonehammer. Da village has me whole clan. It be called da village of stone in case yer wonderin'."

"A tad bit ironic, is it?" Veledar smirked, "It's granite this, steel that, perhaps another village called pebble?"

"Well ya scaley git, dere is a town called pebble." she replied, locking eyes with the dragon. They stared each other down with unblinking eyes before they both burst out laughing. "Back to me story den! I had a yearnin' to see da world outside me village, so I set out for da surface. So far, I find humans da best....no offense lass." she said, looking to Lyndis. "I have found da elf folk are a tad slow moving for me tastes."

Lyndis silently mimed half-elf to herself as she pointed to her ears.

"Humans though, they always be striving ta move forward, dey always seek ta learn, always eager ta explore. Determination is sometin ta admire in dem."

"I agree as well, even if said determination seems to get them in trouble more than it's worth it." Veledar said. Arcturus felt the dragon put a claw on his shoulder. "Isn't that right, Arcturus?"

"Are you talking about yourself again, dragon? Because I sure didn't dive myself out of an airship before I met you!" Arcturus laughed.

"Your words wound me, human. I thought we are kind of simpatico." Veledar grinned, placing a paw to his chest.

The group laughed and spent the last bit of the night talking until they all fell asleep around the fire.

Arcturus woke in the morning to the sound of Veledar's rustling. He breathed in the cold morning air before stretching his arms. The morning sun had already peeked through the clouds high in the sky.

"Arcturus, I am not a convenient table to rest your arm upon." Veledar said, bumping into him, nearly causing Arcturus to fall.

"Maybe if you weren't so darn good at it!" he said, turning towards the dragon to catch him sticking his long tongue out at him. The dragon took off after his stomach gave a loud rumble, leaving Arcturus in a spray of light snow. He tended to Stinky and Smelly, noticing that the two females -Merlia and Lyndis- were meditating around the fire with a spellbook in front of Lyndis and a scroll in front of the dwarf. He took a spot at least ten feet away and began his own ritual of combat meditation. He swung at the air, slashed and thrust for half an hour before taking out his rations and stuffing the nuts and dried fruit into his mouth. He downed them with a swig of water from his water skin, longing for a hot meal served from an equally warm bowl.

Arcturus' mind went from one tasty meal to another until he thought to a steak he had a couple of months ago back in Entis, and his mouth watered as he remembered the succulent flavors that washed over his tongue. He mentally shook his head to rid the image of that delicious treat from his mind, but the following roar was a much better distraction.

Veledar landed in front of him in a spray of snow, after which he shook off the white powder from his scales. Arcturus noticed the look of worry on Veledar's snout, something he had never seen before on the dragon's face.

"Let me guess. You stepped on someone's toes and now they're coming back here to demand payment for yet another one of your misdeeds."

Arcturus was almost ready to grab onto his gold pouch when the dragon growled. "I saw a bunch of gryphons, and on top of them, I'm pretty sure we have riders."

"How many?" Arcturus immediately frowned.

"A dozen. Maybe more. I didn't exactly stay there to count them."

Arcturus gulped, feeling his heart skip a beat. He had a pretty good idea what was coming for them. "Ah, blasted. You got us in real trouble this time. Why in the world have you gone out there, on a whim, without even thinking of using a protection spell? That's stupid, even by dragon standards."

The dragon snarled, but dared not to say anything. Even someone as proud and mighty as Veledar knew better then to make a fuss in this sort of situation.

"So what's the plan? Are you going to stand there and dazzle them with your scales?" Arcturus clenched his jaws.

"Shut up." The dragon hissed as the human paced around, muttering angry things beneath his breath.

"It don't fockin' matter who messed what. It's done now. Get your things and MOVE. Go! MOVE!"

Arcturus knew gryphons were fast fliers, possibly faster than even Veledar. "How far away are they?"

"Far enough to give us advantage." The dragon said.

Arcturus nodded and quickly donned his armor. He reminded himself to thank Matilda again for crafting such a wonderful thing. Within the span of five breaths, he was already suited up.

Arcturus threw his stuff into his pack and quickly mounted Stinky. He held the reins tight as the others gathered around him, all their things packed into bundles, although by the look on their faces, the females didn't have enough time to fully prepare all their spells. Lyndis pulled out the same map she read at the inn and held it inches from her face.

"If we follow this path, we will reach the passage point, and with the brooch we have in our possession, we should be able to pass unhindered. Hopefully the gryphon group will lose us in the snowstorm." Lyndis said, pointing to a drawing of a mountain pass on the map.

"It is a good plan. May the Gods show us favor." Arcturus said, quickly taking the lead with Lyndis, Merlia, and Veledar flying overhead.

They rode over the snowy land, not even taking a moment to hide their tracks. Arcturus patted Stinky's head and pushed the horse to keep running past his normal limits. He did not want to see those gryphon knights right now. More than that, he dreaded the thought of claiming responsibility for his actions until he had everything squared away. If these two sides got into a fight, it was going to be difficult pull his swings against people that were just doing their jobs. People that he could have met, talked, and dined with during his years of service.

Arcturus' heart quickened when the skies rang with the distant screech of a gryphon. The hunting party was closing in now, and even with all his armor, the paladin felt the hair on the back of his neck straighten, and his blood warm up with anxious anticipation.

"Lyndis!" he shouted back to her, eyes scanning the skies for their winged friend. "How much farther until we reach the pass?"

"Not far!" She cried back, "Perhaps a mile to go before we get to the spot on the-"

She was interrupted by the sound of Veledar's roar, and Arcturus knew that type of roar well. It was the sound of a dragon in pain. Splinters and leaves burst from the forest as Veledar descended towards the ground. He fell in the snow alongside the two gryphons that tried to hold him down.

"You trespass in the king's lands, dragon!" One of them screeched with all his might, "Stand down, or we'll have to subdue you by force!"

"Isn't that...what you're already doing, you stinky pair of squawkers?"

"Crimson Sky!" Arcturus called out to him.

The dragon didn't hear his shout; not with his roar deafening any other sound. Arcturus cursed under his breath as he pulled his horse towards the squabble of scales and feathers.

Please, Gods. Be merciful. Don't let this turn into another bloodbath.

The paladin quickly ran over his oaths over the beat of Stinky's hooves. "Crimson Sky! Crimson Sky, stop!" Arcturus shouted in vain as the dragon shoved his smaller captors away. His tail smacked one of the gryphons unconscious into the snow, while his forepaw managed to get around the other's neck.

Arcturus pushed the horse as hard as he could, shouting from atop his lungs. "Crimson Sky! Do NOT kill that gryphon!"

The dragon seemed to have heard something, turning his angry, spiteful gaze to the rider that dismounted a close distance away.

"This little wretch would have me delivered back to his king in chains! Isn't that right, birdy?" Veledar tightened his grip until the gryphon's defiant screech slowly turned into a softer, helpless squawk.

"Don't." Arcturus ran up to the dragon. "Please....I know how it feels to hold someone's life in your hands, but this is not the way."

"Could you pick a worse moment to lecture me? There is no choice here, paladin. It is either us, or them!" the dragon smashed his tail into the ground. "If we do not stand our ground here, they will never stop chasing us. Their king wants me dead, remember? And these gryphons blindly obey him without a shred of remorse. I would have their lives before they chain me again!"

Arcturus approached the angry dragon unarmed. "I know how it feels to be powerless. I too had my choices stripped away when Dread Flame wrapped his vile claws around me, holding my tattered, exhausted body while my family died in front of my eyes. You are not him, Crimson Sky. You are not a monster, but if you strike this gryphon down now, your claws will forever be stained with the blood of the innocent."

"Listen...to him..." the gryphon croaked.

Veledar brought his bared teeth closer to the creature's beak. "Say another word. I dare you."

"Crimson Sky. Crimson Sky! This power you feel...it is not justice, dragon. Please, I beg of you...think what you're about to do..."

The dragon's body shivered with pent-up tension. Arcturus noticed a few minor wounds along his sides, undoubtedly inflicted by the two gryphons. This wasn't the Veledar he knew from before, so instead of wasting his time on words, Arcturus quickly checked the unconscious bird. His heart still pumped, even in the slow rhythm of deep rest. Arcturus muttered a silent gratitude to the gods, then looked at Veledar from his knees.

"You're lucky this human has more mercy than your king, gryphon." The dragon let his captive fall on the ground, then leapt over to Lyndis, who quickly put the gryphon to sleep with a quick charm.

Arcturus let out a sigh of relief. "Great job, everyone. Lyndis, try to do what you can to shield us from their eyes. Merlia, shoot them down if they get too close. Aim for the wings. We want them off our tracks, not dead."

"Got a soft heart in ye, laddie. Think they'll show us da same mercy?"
"Only the Gods know for certain. We are not Knives, to use fear and intimidation as our weapons, just as we're not cutthroats, to slay our way through those who stand against us. We're better than that!"

"I'll remind you these words when you'll be tied up in the bowels of an airship." Veledar growled.

Arcturus got back on his horse, and the party got moving again, leaving the two gryphon scouts behind. Arcturus knew the hunting party wouldn't go easy on them. That's not how he trained his men.

The same men who now inched ever closer to his position.

Arcturus felt an arrow wiz by his head to strike another gryphon that appeared overhead.

"We've got a whole flock coming down!" Lyndis cried out.

Arcturus quickly put his party into combat formation, with Merlia and Lyndis striking from afar while Ulga and Veledar held the line on the ground.

Several gryphon landed around them, one more surprised than the other.

"Paladin! You're alive!" a gryphon said, quickly silenced by a white one with black tiger stripes encased in silver armor.

"Snap it shut, DuskWind! We have orders to capture the target at all costs!"

"Doesn't have to be that way, SkyWing," Arcturus approached the flock leader. "Order your flock to stand down. I will talk to whoever is in charge of this operation."

"The time for words passed the moment you allowed your prisoner to escape. ATTACK!"

The gryphons charged or leaped at them from a spearhead formation. Arcturus knew his chances of success would be minimal at best. After all, he fought alongside gryphons like these for years. They were the best Lumara had to offer, specifically requested by him when he believed the king to be a selfless, honorable man.

Arcturus threw one last look at Veledar. "We're better than them," he spoke softly, only for the dragon to hear, before he drew his sword and charged forward.

He aimed to injure the head of the snake, but a screech was all he heard as he was lifted out of his saddle by another gyphon. He felt claws press hard around his torso, and within two heartbeat, Arcturus was dropped hard onto the ground. The gryphon was on top of him in an instant, tearing at the joints of his armor without saying a word.

"Stop this madness!" Arcturus hissed before droplets of saliva pelted his face alongside a deafening screech.

Arcturus didn't strike back with his voice. He hit with his fist, right on the side of the gryphon's beak, stunning the white gryphon long enough for him to free his sheathed sword and slam it on the back of the creature's head hard enough to put the creature to sleep.

"Nghhh, heavy bastard." With a great shove, the paladin pushed the unconscious gryphon off him. He stood up slowly to see that Stinky had been cut deep into his neck and now lay bleeding in the snow. He did a look around to find that Merlia and Lyndis were nowhere in sight. They must have been separated by another flock. Another screech pulled his mind from his friends, and Arcturus quickly ran to Veledar's side to help him. Three birds lay incapacitated on the ground, leaving four to deal with. The dragon kept them at bay with tail swipes and short bursts of fire, but Arcturus knew the flock would adapt to the situation. He was halfway there before a gryphon got close enough to leap onto his back.

Veledar roared, thrashing about as the others latched on different parts of his body to drag him down.

*Hang on…just a moment longer…*Arcturus unstrapped the shield from his back, the cacophony of growls, hisses and screeches getting louder the closer he got to the heart of the combat.

When he finally reached Veledar, Arcturus smashed his shield into the side of the first gryphon he found, a purple male that fell prey to Veledar's tail. The gryphon crumpled to the ground under the heavy smack, never to rise again. With him out of the way, Arcturus pulled onto the tail of another, not to hurt, but annoy the creature, for once it looked back, Veledar shook himself free.

"BlackPaws, SunWing!" the flock leader inspected his fallen kin.

"They yet live." Arcturus brushed off the gryphon's concern.

"Thanks to our mercy," Veledar accompanied Arcturus with a tired huff. "I have to say, you gryphons don't fight half as bad as you look…"

"Then you'll find my beak more than a match, scaled one!"

Arcturus cursed as the two of them were forced back on the defense. Gryphon after gryphon came down from the sky to reinforce their leader, and soon enough, Arcturus found himself in total defense as the sea of feathers struck at him with beak and claw.

"Enough!" A familiar voice called out from above. The gryphons backed away from Veledar and Arcturus, their keen eyes locked on their quarry.

One gryphon landed in the snow in front of Veledar, carrying a man in familiar black plate upon its back. It was Garroth, standing before them with a tabard of Lumara draped over his pristine armor. He held a crossbow that pulsed with the familiar hum that Arcturus had gotten used to during his long years in the service of the king's knights. He looked above to find ten more gryphons hovering, with men wielding more of the same crossbows that Garroth held in his hand. They all had them pointed at Veledar.

"You won't escape our grasp this time, dragon. Tell me what you've done to Arcturus, and I might find a spacious chamber for you to spend the rest of your miserable days in." Garroth said, his voice full of hatred. "You are going to pay for all the grievances you've caused to the Crown."

"Grievances?" Veledar scoffed. "The only grievance I'm guilty of is existing in your land! Your dragon slayers came into *my* home, stole *my* treasure, accused *me* of unspeakable deeds, and now you're here, blabbering about imprisonment, when the man you seek is right in front of you!"

"Arcturus?!" Garroth pushed his visor up. "By the Gods...I thought someone stole your armor. Lift your visor up. Let me get a quick look at you."

"Garroth," Arcturus dipped his head, took off his helmet, then looked back at the man. "This isn't how I imagined we'd meet."

"Same here, lad. You can imagine my surprise. I thought you'd been kidnapped; held for ransom by this band of thieves you're traveling with."

Arcturus got in front of the dragon when Veledar started to snarl.

"I'm on an important quest that allows no delays. Garroth, if my name still means something in Lumara, you will allow me to depart."

The man grumbled before he let out a long sigh. "It is true we have history together, but the king requested your return, along with the quick delivery of the red beast."

Arcturus knew things were about to blow. He saw it in Garroth's eyes when he moved his hand over to his crossbow. Felt it in Veledar's quickening breath.

"Garroth-" he began to speak, but was cut off as Veledar suddenly bounded towards him, grabbed Arcturus, and bolted into the sky.

"Arcturus! Incapacitate the red beast! Shoot it down from the sky!" he heard Garroth shout orders as Veledar carried him higher into the sky.

"What...the fock was that?"

"They're going to imprison you, right after they throw me into that spacious jail!"

He felt his stomach lurch, but thankfully, his mind was still too focused on Garroth to pay attention to the nausea. Storm clouds had suddenly appeared in the sky, making Veledar's flight more unsteady with every passing moment. They must have been close to the point Lyndis had talked about. Arcturus looked back down to the tiny forms of Garroth, his men, and the gryphons now chasing after them.

Veledar carried him further and higher into the sky. "Nice friends you've made during your time in Lumara." The dragon said between deep breaths, "Why, my mind bristles with all sorts of exciting scenarios, like my first meal in prison, or my first crap. Do you figure they have crapholes dug into the earth, or they'll slowly let me fill up my own bed with-"

"Shut up. Please...stop talking. We're still not safe enough for prattling..."

"As if their feeble wings can keep up!" Veledar roared joyfully. "I got you out, human! I have you, they don't! You know what this means, right? You owe me!"

"Stupid...bumbling fool... They have gryphons! They can still catch you!"

"Nonsense!" Veledar said, "Those creatures could not hold a candle to me. They are basically oversized kittens!" the dragon chuckled weakly. Arcturus could feel the dragon's wing beats; they were different than the last time he was carried into the sky. These were slower, and the dragon seemed to be straining. Despite him not saying anything, he was clearly hurt.

"Besides," Veledar said, flapping his wings again. The snow started to whip by Arcturus' face, causing him to shield his eyes with one of his hands. "They would be foolish to follow us into my mother's snowstorm."

"The same storm that will smash us into a mountain! Lyndis and Merlia have the brooch. We will be lost without it!"

Veledar did not reply for a few moments, clearly weighing his options on what to do next. "Well you see-" Veledar was cut off as the battle screech of a gryphon sounded from behind, followed by at least twelve others.

"Graaarh, they have the most impeccable timing!" Veledar said, his voice clearly masking worry. "You know, I really don't want to be captured by this bunch of feathers. I don't think they will be as rational as you were."

"Arcturus! We're coming for you! Hold fast, paladin! Lumara's light outshines every darkness!" he heard the voice of Garroth bellow into the sky.

Arcturus looked back down to see the form of three gryphons closing in on the red dragon's tail. Their eyes locked onto him, then shifted back to the dragon. "Don't worry, Paladin!" one of them squawked. "We'll get you!" The gryphon that spoke swerved out of the way as a stream of fire shot towards him.

"The only thing you need to get is away from this dragon, you fools!" Arcturus shouted back as he clutched Veledar's forelimbs tighter. He felt Veledar pull him closer as the gryphons inched ever closer.

One of them flew towards the dragon's wings. Veledar let out a roar of pain, as the gryphon undoubtedly attacked his scale-less membranes. A second one flew towards the dragon's left, and let out a loud screech. This one seemed to dance in the air as Veledar tried to snap at him with his maw, his teeth only clamping onto thin air. The last one flew below the dragon, his eyes locked onto Arcturus. The golden gryphon angled his wings slightly and maneuvered into position below the dragon.

Veledar suddenly thrashed his body as he did a swift turn. The dragon pounded his wings against the air and the gryphons were suddenly left behind. They recovered quickly however, and in another heartbeat, they were right on top of the dragon all over again. Veledar let out another roar, as claws no doubt ripped into his flesh a second time.

"Fly away, you damned fools!" Arcturus shouted to the gryphons again, "I don't need to be rescued! You're going to get us all killed!"

The gryphon below moved closer as the one to his left suddenly grabbed onto Veledar's limb with his talons, ripping into the scales with ferocity.

"You are not safe with him! We'll get you back, sire, no matter the cost." The gryphon slashed again quickly, drawing more blood from the dragon.

"Ngrraaaaawrrrr. You want to play rough?" Veledar hissed.

"Crimson Sky!" Arcturus screamed from the top of his lungs, then the gryphon screeched right over him.

"He's almost through, sire. Just a few more moments and-"

Arcturus felt his body lurch as Veledar slammed his wings against the air. However, the gryphon holding his limbs made headway, and Veledar's paws found themselves spread apart by the gryphon's stronger talons. Arcturus felt himself drop, with the gryphon below extending his paws, ready to snatch him from the air.

"Got you sire!" The gryphon exclaimed.

But Arcturus felt no talons grab onto him. In his possessive fury, Veledar returned for him, slapping and fighting his way through the gryphons just like the birds said: by any means necessary.

Arcturus looked up as the wind howled past his ears. Terror clutched at his heart as he dropped into the void below

This is how I die. In the cold, storming, with nobody to hear my screams, he thought as Veledar was currently lashing out at the three gryphons that surrounded him. The dragon bellowed something, and lightning seemed to arc from the sky to his claws. In a flash of bright blinding light, Arcturus saw lightning bolts fly out in all directions around the dragon. They sprung from him to the gryphons, who erected their own spheres of light just in time to deflect the deadly surge of electricity. The magic must've costed them all a heavy price. The gryphons glided down towards the ground, almost numb, while Veledar too seemed to struggle to remain conscious.

Arcturus dared not look down at the ground that rushed to meet him. He closed his eyes and waited for the sudden stop, hoping the dragon had the sense to at least save himself.

Don't come for me, you pile of thoughtless scales. For once in your life, do the selfish thing. Save yourself instead of dying with me...

* * * * * *

Veledar was not like Dread Flame, interested in only protecting his own hide. He dove through the sky, his pain forgotten as his wings pounded at the angry air. It was replaced by the sickening fear as he watched Arcturus grow further away from him. The worst thing was Arcturus' silence as he fell. He had joked around with the human about his screech when he picked him up first, but that armored lump of meat had always been safe in his paws. Well, except now of course, when Veledar watched the human tumble through the air, his front cape flowing through upwards against the wind. He knew why the human was silent. It was the absolute dread of inevitability.

Veledar willed himself to go faster as he saw the human clench his eyes shut, probably to pray in his last seconds; make peace with himself and the rest of the world.

In turn, Veledar tried to avoid thinking about his dying brother...the look of fear the silver dragon had on his own snout when he had plummeted to the ground, never to rise again.

"Arcturus!" Veledar gave an ear-splitting roar, the loudest his wounded throat could muster. The human HAD to know he was coming.

I will not let you die. Not in my story! Veledar grit his teeth as he willed himself to go on. He was going to give this damned kingdom the story of a hero. A dragon who saved his human instead of monsters who kidnapped innocent maidens. His name would be spoken across the taverns of every human settlement. Veledar the protector, savior of paladins, conqueror of fiercest storms.

Veledar streaked through the air, silence only broken by the sound of the whistling wind whipping by his snout. Arcturus was falling, and falling, and falling faster, still very much out of his reach.

He tucked his wings, then his limbs, trying desperately to increase his speed. The air became a stinging menace, and the pain increased tenfold. Veledar tried to focus on Arcturus, and not the ground rushing towards his outstretched talons. Nothing else mattered now.

Nothing but Arcturus.

Pull up now, or you are going to die, instinct screamed inside his skull.

But he was so close now. He almost had Arcturus. There was no way he could pull a selfish move now. If he was going to die at this moment, he was going to at least save the human. Let himself be the hero he knew he was. Let his tale be something people remembered in song. Veledar the heroic red dragon. He narrowed his eyes as he closed in on the human. They were going to live together, or die the same.

"Arcturus!" he roared again with the same ear-splitting ferocity.

Arcturus opened his eyes as Veledar closed in on him. The dragon reached out with one of his paws, and in that terror-filled second, he realized if that if he just grabbed him and opened his wings, the air would break the human's back due to the shift in weight. Possibly even tear his wing membranes to pieces. There was no room for error in this, not with the ground coming so close now. Veledar continued to reach out with a paw as Arcturus rose his arm in return to grab at his talons. He felt the human wrap his gloved hand around a cold, scaled finger, then Veledar pulled him close and clutched him against his chest.

They fell together.

Veledar slowly opened his wings a nerve wracking fraction at a time. He felt the wind slice through him like thousands of daggers, and though his membrane was being ripped apart, the descent started to slow, but he knew it was not going to be enough. He spread his wings wider, feeling the bones in his joints crackle with mind-numbing pain. He could see the snow dunes approach, the grey stones littering the place, the trees in the distance.

The world was always so beautiful seconds before death.

Veledar angled his wings down and aimed himself at a possible landing. "Arcturus. Remember this part of the story." He shouted as he tilted his wings and flipped his body, placing himself between the ground and the human he clutched tightly in his limbs.

"N-no! VELEDAR!"

Veledar felt his body crash into the snow. Pain shot through his entire body like a flood of electricity. It made his teeth rattle, his spine quake, and his bones shift inside his body. He felt his wings break into thousands of painful fragments, and he gasped out, the air driven from his lungs through a horrendous growl. He clutched Arcturus tighter as they skidded through the soft snow, leaving behind splotches and streaks of red.

NO! I...I must... Veledar internally screamed as his own body started to wither. He could not move. Not with so many broken things inside his crumpled body. His next gasping breath brought in the taste of blood, and the dragon spat the substance onto the ground, unable to take in the air he sorely needed. Stars danced around his vision as he flopped his head back into the snow, letting out choking breaths as the skies above them grew darker. After a few heartbeats, even the pain died down. Veledar felt nothing.

Nothing apart from the darkness that wrapped him in its tenebrous cloak.

Chapter 13: Paladin of Bahamut

Arcturus' entire body trembled with pain. He slowly opened his eyes to the swirling snow that spread around him. He sat up, his head still spinning from the shock of the impact he experienced mere moments ago.

"Aghh...I don't remember the fall being this bad when that bastard Dread Flame brought me down from the sky." Arcturus touched his forehead with his hand and grunted in pain. Even something as simple as massaging his throbbing head made him feel sore. He shook his head slowly, and soon enough, the blurry image he saw before his eyes slowly came back into focus. He was in a wild, uninhabited area by the looks of it, and the compressed snow he had tumbled on when he hit the ground made his eyes widen with grim realization.

He held me...right before- Arcturus' eyes frantically scanned the area around him, desperation lodged in his chest like a nail hammered in too deep. That's when he saw the dragon, and he wished he had not. Lying not that far away in the snow, was the grim spectacle of blood, torn scales and wounds that made up the broken version of a dragon he once knew in a very different form.

"Oh...oh Gods, don't let this be." Arcturus tried to stand. He immediately gasped as a sharp pain stabbed his chest. He struggled. Groaned. Cursed as he forced his weakened limbs to obey.

Gods... it feels like my limbs... are weighed down by boulders. Arcturus scrunched his face with effort. With another pained murmur, the paladin succeeded to get on his feet.

"Least my legs aren't broken," He quickly looked over his own body. Thankfully, nothing appeared to be broken. Arcturus took a deep breath, sending another wave of painful flames up his chest.

"Nghhh, aaaaah, that's...fock me, that rib's twisted like a dragon's tail, but I'll live." Arcturus muttered. "That's not important right now. Veledar. I need to..." His eyes focused back on the bloodied dragon that had yet to move from the dented snow he rested in.

"Please...Don't be dead..." Arcturus gathered all the strength he had in his aching body. "Veledar!" he shouted out as he painfully limped towards his friend. "Please..." He nearly stumbled and fell as his next footstep made him gasp in agony. He caught himself, his eyes never leaving the dragon's broken body. The snow around Veledar was painted in dark crimson streaks, a grim reminder of the gryphons that forced him upon this course of action. Arcturus closed the distance painfully slow. He was now within arm distance of the dragon, and there was yet a movement to notice from his fallen friend.

"Gra...rrrrraaaahhhh,"

Arcturus' heart but leaped inside his tight chest as he saw the dragon's chest rise.

He was alive. The Gods had mercy on them both. Even with their blessing, Arcturus tried to not get his hopes up. He knew too well he was in no position to mend a dragon's wounds, not to mention he was a wanted man by the king's chasers.

We're not safe yet, but at least he's alive. Tears of gratitude fell along the paladin's scratched cheeks as he looked upon his dragon friend. Veledar's wings, once so proud and big when they flapped up there in the skies, were now twisted at odd angles. Slash marks covered the tan scales of his underside, oozing small rivulets of blood. Small pools were already forming in the snow from various places on Veledar's broken body, but he was alive, even if the heart-wrenching breath that oozed out of his throat dared otherwise.

"Veledar," Arcturus dropped beside the dragon's proud head to cup his chin in his cold, trembling hands hands. "Veledar, look at me. Up here. Look into my eyes."

"I'm...ghlouarugh," Veledar coughed suddenly, painting Arcturus' chest with a splash of warm, viscous sludge as red as his scales.

"N-no. Don't! Breathe, Veledar. Breathe!" Arcturus tried to warn in vain.

"I'm fff-fine." Proud as ever, the dragon slowly stirred and tried to stand onto all fours. His legs wobbled for a moment, as Arcturus was certain he was going to collapse.

"Stop. Stop!" Arcturus tried in vain to keep the dragon down. "If not for the Gods themselves, do it for me, you stubborn dragon!"

"W-w-we can't... stay here. The gryphons...they'll smell our blood, then..." Veledar's eyes scrunched in pain, followed by the rasping sound of his voice. Arcturus tore his eyes away from him to look for a place to hide in this snowy area.

"Nothing...There is nothing!" He cupped his hand and placed it next to his eyes to protect himself against from the sun's glare.

"Come on, you bastards! Are you coming for us or not?"

He heard the screeching of gryphons from behind, closing in to their position. His eyes strained to see anything within the swirling winds, but all he could make out was the sky above and the sea of white snow beneath, dotted with red blood.

Arcturus narrowed his eyes. Kept looking. Then, as if by a miracle, large cave not too far away appeared before him.

"Veledar, look! A shelter. We have a shelter. It's not far. We just have to make it there." Arcturus said. Then in his mind, he figured out the next step.

If Veledar could set an illusion over the cave's entrance. we might stand a chance at remaining undiscovered. He turned back to his broken friend, trying to not show too much worry on his wounded, aching face. When he reached him, he wrapped his arm around the dragon's neck. "Come on, Veledar. You can do this, you big scaly bastard. I know how stubborn you are when you put your mind to something, so show me. Show me how strong a dragon really is."

Arcturus had no idea how Veledar mustered the power to stand on his fours, but together, they limped forward, the snow crunching beneath their steps. "That cave...it's not an illusion, is it? Your eyes can see it too. Maybe if you set up an illusion of your own, we can hide from the search party."

"N-Not like we have any choices, human." The dragon growled in pain. "Tell you what...it w-w-would be better than bleeding out in the snow." Veledar gasped weakly as he moved one limb after the other. The dragon seemed to strain himself with each step, his eyes scrunching practically with each crunch of the snow beneath his paws. Arcturus shuddered when he heard the dragon take a deep breath, followed by an even larger groan of pain. Veledar coughed deeper than before, spraying the snow with a rain of blood.

"Almost there, Veledar. Just a few more steps." Arcturus said calmly even as he fought the urge to try and rush him. He could hear the gryphons getting closer.

"Come on you big scaly bastard! You're not going to die in this frozen place, do you hear me? If I can ride in your claws, you can take a few more steps!"

"Look at these streaks. The beast bled all over the place. Spread around. I want him found within the minute, d'you hear me? Go, go!" Arcturus heard a man shout from behind.

Arcturus slightly turned his head to see only the rush of snowflakes carried by the bitter wind. The snow that whipped his body with relentless lashes was a blessing in disguise, starting to restrict vision to several feet in front of them.

Good. If I'm blind, they're blind.

Arcturus had never thought several feet of travel could seem so long. He knew the whole ordeal probably only lasted a few minutes, but with his friend's ragged breath, painful gasps, and crunching wings drilling into his ears, the journey to the cave seemed to last forever.

When he finally reached the rock wall, Arcturus finally breathed a sigh of relief and followed Veledar inside.

We did it! Praise the Gods and their infinite mercy. I have to remember to extend my gratitude to them when we're safe.

Arcturus forgot about his broken ribs, the cuts on his face, his weighted limbs. He forgot about everything in the rush of relief that washed over him. He was about to lay a hand on his dragon and offer his heartfelt praise for the titanic effort, but his hand found nothing. Veledar collapsed onto the floor with a pained grunt, his wing drooping over the ground, splattered with yet another dose of blood.

"I- I can't...make it any further." Veledar gasped in pain, his claws tensing on the cavern's floor.

"No. You're not dying on me here. I will not allow it!" Arcturus pulled off his pack, emptying its contents onto the cold floor. He swiped his hands through the mess and grabbed a small box with a red caduceus on it. He fumbled with it as he tried to rush, managing to spring it open with a small click. Inside the box was bandages, materials for stitches, and two healing potions.

"Just...keep your eyes open. Focus on my voice and try to stay awake. You're going to be fine, Veledar. You're going to be just fine." He said confidently, trying to hide the worried crack in his voice. He felt an icy grip tighten around his heart as he looked to his friend, unable to shake the feeling of dread that sprung forth whenever he gazed over Veledar's wounds in detail.

Arcturus suddenly drew his sword as he heard yet another gryphon screech, too close for comfort.

"Plan to stab them...with that feeble iron stick?"

Arcturus reluctantly dropped the medical supplies with a soft clatter of wood on stone. The dragon was right. If it came to a fight, there was no way he could defend himself and help Veledar. He held the sword in front of him at the ready as he assumed a battle stance.

"I will not let these bastards take you."

"Y-you were a good human. Best I know, actually...but you're being foolish." Veledar muttered as if in a daze, his voice trailing off as he thumped his tail weakly.

Arcturus stared at the cave's entrance to see several shapes start to emerge from the storm, with Garroth at the head. His friend wore a worried expression on his brow, clearly following the tracks left behind in Veledar's wake. He was flanked by several others in red leathers that held energy crossbows slung at the ready. He could see their eyes, desperately trying to see where they had gone.

"I told you to hold your fire!" Garroth shouted, turning to one of the men. "That blasted dragon had Arcturus. You could have killed them both!" Garroth turned away from the man, placing two hands around his mouth, "Arcturus!" he shouted desperately. "Where are you?"

The man's voice cracked with genuine concern. Garroth stood for a few minutes in silence as if waiting for Arcturus to reply. Part of the paladin wanted to call out to his friend and give away their position. Garroth had more than a few gryphons. Maybe even an airship fitted with enough healers to restore the dragon. Arcturus fought with himself as his friend paced around, staring at the blood on several occasions. Garroth held a hand to his chin, and slowly trailed to a stop.

"The tracks of blood end here. Clearly the beast survived the fall, but for how long? Where could it possibly go?" Garroth thrust a finger towards the paw prints in the snow. "Here you can see the boots. Arcturus survived as well." Garroth smiled, tracing the path Arcturus had made with a sweep of his arm. "Arcturus!" The armored warrior shouted, and once more waited for a response.

"Were did they go next, Garroth?" One of the men asked as Garroth looked around. His eyes were narrowed as if he were desperately searching for something. It then dawned on Arcturus. Garroth and his men could not see the cave right in front of their faces.

"Veledar. Veledar, when in the blazes did you have the time to cast an illusion?" Arcturus whispered as he turned his head back towards the dragon. Veledar had not moved from where he fell, and his eyes were closed.

"Oh no...no no no, don't do that!" Arcturus whispered, scrambling to his medical supplies. He grabbed the two health potions firmly and bounded to his friend's broken body. He grabbed Veledar by the snout and with a forceful thrust upwards, he parted the beast's fearsome jaws. He uncorked the bottles, tossing the cork aside as he dumped them down the dragon's throat.

"Swallow. C'mon, do it, you sleepy beast." Arcturus shut the dragon's maw and rubbed his neck to stimulate his swallowing reflex. Veledar stirred and coughed multiple times, forcing Arcturus to clamp his maw shut, least Garroth heard them. With each cough though, Arcturus watched the dragon's body shiver, shake, and twitch.

"T-tastes terrible, I would rather have wine." Veledar grumbled as he held his head back.

"You can have wine when you make it through this. We will get the best, and in large quantities to befit a dragon of your stature."

Arcturus pulled out the materials for stitches after he took off his gauntlets. Next, he got his hands on the mana crystal that gave light and activated it with a hasty touch. He would need the illumination for what followed, although part of him wished his eyes remained in the dark, for in the warm glow of the crystal, he could see his friend's wounds even clearer. The cuts were deep. Part of the dragon's scales were actually torn open to reveal the muscle and sinews that hid beneath. Arcturus stifled a terror induced gasp as he grabbed the cool needle and metal wire. He paused and looked to the dragon, brow wrinkled with pained concern. "This is going to hurt a fair bit. Try to keep as silent as you can, unless you want our friends to come after your tail again."

"M-more than falling out of the sky? That's-" Veledar coughed up more blood and gasped with ragged breaths for air.

Arcturus moved to the largest wound that was on the dragon's chest, closest to one of his ribs. He moved several smaller scales out of the way to get a better view of the wounded flesh. "So tell me, wise, powerful dragon. Where are your wings going to carry me once we leave this adventure behind?"

"I-I think I'll find a mate... and mount them till I am Ra-" Veledar started, then muffled his growl within the depths of his jaws as the cold metal needle pierced his flesh.

"I thought you said falling from the sky was worse?" Arcturus chuckled. He went up the dragon's hide with the needle, each additional pierce followed by another wince and gasp of pain from his scaled friend.

"I take it back. Th-that stings worse than a gryphon's claws! I-If I wasn't so hurt, I'd smack you silly!" Veledar replied with a groan. Arcturus felt the dragon's tail move slightly in support of his words. "I take it that it must look pretty bad if you're fussing over me like this."

Arcturus focused on sealing the wounds and stayed quiet.

"Silence? That only works for peasants, Arcturus. Act like a paladin for once."

"That I can, but I'm not sure you're gonna like a stern touch given your condition."

Arcturus finished with the current wound he was working on. The tightened, tattered flesh did not look pretty being pressed together and was slowly oozing blood. He felt one of Veledar's paws move to his side and caressing him gently for a few moments before Arcturus pushed it aside. He let the dragon know of the seriousness of this task, and after Veledar muttered an agreement, the paladin started sealing up the next closest wound located on the dragon's shoulder.

"So why did that butt-head commander, captain of gryphons whatever, consider you his friend? I have to admit, for all his efforts in trying to capture me, he may have done a better job than you at trying to kill me." Veledar laughed weakly, which prompted another one of those raspy coughs.

"Oh, Garroth? He's a darn fine adventurer. His tools of the trade are vast, just like the methods he employs to get the job done. In this case, he took the very gryphons I handpicked to capture you." Arcturus kept his calm, for he knew that, in spite of Veledar's wounds, Garroth held only part of the blame. "Even though he is an adventurer at heart, Garroth is still a man of honor. A good soldier that follows his king loyally. I wish I had time to introduce you properly. Who knows, even the gryphons might've been persuaded to like you."

"Find that hard to believe… after what they've done to my scales."

"T'wasn't personal, believe me. The gryphons, including Garroth, were just following the king's orders. Blazes, dragon. The whole of Lumara thinks you killed me that day in the airship." Arcturus replied.

"What do you know about me?" Veledar cocked his head to the side.

"That you're a pompous dragon full of hot air for start, but… Your heart's in the right place. I wouldn't be dipping my fingers in your blood to save your stubborn arse if I felt otherwise."

"What if I were lying to you this entire time? Your fondness for me can very well be an elaborate charm I placed on you from the first moment we met."

Even with the dragon's hot blood on his fingers, Arcturus couldn't help but chuckle. "Why am I using these barbaric tools when his winged highness can amaze me with a display of magic?" Arcturus said with a mischievous smile. "What's wrong? Surely a simple charm like mending flesh is not beyond the abilities of Veledar the Amazing."

"Are you mocking me, human?"

"A bit," Arcturus admitted as he put his needle back to work. "Sometimes, you need a slap over the bum, like any other child."

"I can slap back."

"After you're better, sure." Arcturus laughed again. "It doesn't take magic to know someone's heart. I can tell if you lie just by looking into your eyes."

"Sure. Try not to fall in love with me please. I have enough sycophants already without adding a disgraced paladin to their ranks," Veledar laughed weakly, "Damn, but you know how to lift a dragon's spirits."

Arcturus smiled sincerely when the dragon looked down at him as he worked, probably curious to see if his human really did his best. "By the time you will be done brandishing that needle around, I will look like one of your quilt things, very ill fitting for a hero of my stature."

"Hero, are we?" Arcturus replied, moving to another wound as he felt Veledar twitch. "How do you see yourself earning such esteemed rank, dear dragon? Planning on diving on your butt a second time?”

“O-of course not, you bumbling sack of rocks. Let’s see. Saving his knight from capture, snatching him from certain death, keeping him from fainting while he stitches his first dragon... This will make a great story, of course."

“Only if you don't scare or annoy your sycophants away." Arcturus grinned.

"You and Lyndis seem very fond of me."

“Aye. We do. However, I think we are different than most people. As you might’ve noticed from our travels, not many humans are ready to drop and worship at your feet."

“Not yet, but we’ll teach them, " Veledar said in a whisper. “The valiant dragon and his selfless paladin...This will be a tale for the ages...” The dragon smiled as his eye lids closed softly.

“Veledar?" Arcturus looked over to the dragon. His head was on the ground, eyes closed, seemingly asleep...But the cold dread that rushed along his spine spoke of much graver things.

“Do I bore ye to the point of sleeping on me? Come on. Wake up.”

No reply came from the dragon.

“Veledar?!" He knelt beside the dragon’s head, his voice cracking. He rushed to place his hand on the drake, feeling around for his pulse. He felt a dull thump against the warm dragon’s hide.

“No, come on! I almost healed you. You’re fine. You have to be fine.” His face darkened as he felt the dragon’s heartbeat weaken.

Arcturus slowly got onto his feet. He paced around like a caged animal. The stench of Veledar’s blood filled his nostrils with every breath. He had no idea what else to do in the wake of such horrid fear. To have the dragon die on him now, after everything they’ve been through...

“No!” Arcturus moved to the dragon's snout and gave it a serious smack. “Wake up, dragon. This isn’t how a hero’s quest is supposed to end!” He slapped his hard scales again and again, each time getting the same silent void in his stomach.”

“You got to stay awake, Veledar! You can't go on leaving me or this world just yet. You have adventures to embark upon, humans to amaze, mates to mount in whatever weird ways you dragons do it!”

In spite of the humorous approach, Arcturus could feel the pit in his stomach growing, turning into a twisting, painful knot.

“Don’t die...Please don’t die on me. I’m begging you, Veledar. I’m begging you...come back to me...”

When the dragon failed to give his answer, Arcturus went back to check the pulse. This time, he scrambled to get there to find that -to his horror- instead of a faint pulsing, there was no tremor at all. No heartbeat.

Nothing.

"Come on, you cheeky bastard!" Arcturus shouted, placing his arms together and slamming down on the dragon's rib cage with all his might. "YOU!" Smack! "CAN'T" Smack! "DIE!"

After several desperate thumps, Arcturus took in a deep, chest-aching breath as the dragon's heart came back to life. He let out an enormous sigh of relief and collapsed against his friend's scaled chest, resting only for a moment before he grabbed some spare torches from his pack and arranged in the form of a campfire. Arcturus pulled out his flint and steel and quickly started a fire. Hopefully, the warmth of the flames would at least warm the wounded dragon. He looked to Veledar. The dragon was still breathing shallow breaths. Arcturus felt the dread once again creep over him. He padded over to the dragon's side, looking over the rest of the cave, dimly illuminated by the crystal and torchlight. The cave was larger than he initially noticed, and it seemed to have carvings on the walls. The carvings' writing looked like it was drawn with harsh lines, possibly with a claw. Arcturus made out a picture of a large dragon cradling another one in its paws. It was painted a metallic silver, and the human somehow remembered it was a picture of Bahamut, the goddess of dragons. He was drawn from the image by another one of Veledar's ragged breaths, just like when his heart had stopped. Arcturus collapsed on top of his friend and grabbed one of his scaly paws. He rolled his fingers over the dragon's cold fingers, and placed another hand on top of his paw.

"You can't die. Not after I brought you back a second time." Arcturus sniffled, for he felt the same helplessness now as he did when he held his fading son within his arms. He looked to his broken and dying friend, fighting back a sob. Tears started to well in his eyes as he clutched the dragon's paw even   tighter.
"I've...I've tried all I can, Veledar...But I am running out of ways to save you." He said weakly. "The potions barely healed your gashes, and that's only what my eyes can perceive. I've got a broken rib, but you..." The human squeezed his eyes shut, remembering the overwhelming shock that spread throughout his body when the dragon crashed into the snow. "No. I can't think of internal bleeding, broken bones and what not. I can't mend that. All I can do is stitch flesh and sit and watch how you fade... just like my son did."

Arcturus felt the tears start to drip down his face now. "I...Gods. Why does it have to end like this? Why...? You're... the first friend I have made in a long time. Have I ever told you that? You can't just go and die now...Not when I still have so many unspoken words to share," He said, gripping his friend's paw   tighter.
"Veledar...I speak of the Gods often, but truth is...I am not a pious man.

Before Dread Flame, I believed in the power of my will and the strength of my arm, and after the monster robbed me of my family, there was nothing left. No faith, no hope. Nothing. "Arcturus looked to the carvings and the pictures of Bahamut scribbled on the wall. "But I am going to pray now for you, cause it's the last thing I can think of to save your proud, stubborn arse." Arcturus placed his sobbing head onto Veledar's chest and closed his eyes. "Please...please hear me now," his voice trembled in the same manner as his body as a torrent of emotions boiled inside him.

"If you're really up there...if you can see this broken dragon and hear my whispered pleas, do something." Arcturus gritted his teeth, "DO SOMETHING!" He screamed, thinking of the dragon goddess Bahamut. If anyone would try to answer his prayer, it had to be her. He knew it sounded selfish, even arrogant, to think a God would suddenly care about an insignificant mortal, but he still had to try.

Arcturus focused on his friend, on his pain, his wounds, and the absolute need to see him healed. He sat in that uncomfortable position until his neck went stiff and his joints ached, sobbing softly onto Veledar's scales until he started to feel odd. Just like he did when he had been transported into the realm of the fairies.

Arcturus opened his eyes, still puffy and red from all that crying. He wiped the moisture that clouded his vision with a hand to see what lay before him. Where the cave had been mere moments ago now stood a large swirling vortex of dark grey clouds. Suddenly, a bolt of lightning shot across the sky, illuminating the entire swirling storm for an instant. Arcturus looked down to find that he was floating mid-air, and panic soon raced through his mind at the prospect of being swallowed by the angry clouds that surrounded him on all sides.

It's a dream. Just a representation of my grief. It's not real...or at least not as real as it seems. Arcturus thought to himself as he sought to calm the primitive signals of panic that shot all across his body -that which Veledar often referred to as instincts. He breathed slowly, in and out, and relief slowly replaced dread as he realized he was not going anyway, least of all plummeting to his death.

"Hello?" He shouted out to the clouds, "Is anyone there?"

No answer came.

"I must be here for a reason. Please, if anyone hears my pleas, help me! My friend is leaning closer to death as we speak. There has to be something I can do to save him. Has to! I won't allow him to just...to-" Arcturus broke down into sobs for a few emotional seconds. The only reply he got was a large bolt of lightning streaking across the sky. He thought he was alone, abandoned by the Gods themselves.

Then he saw it. In that brief flash of light, he noticed something emerging from the dark clouds. It was enormous, easily dwarfing the puny human that stared with shocked eyes. The creature, if it could be called such, was covered in platinum scales that shone with bright light, wings that seemed to stretch on forever, and eyes like liquid mercury. Then he knew it, deep into the marrow of his bones. Hovering before him stood none other than the massive form of the dragon goddess, Bahamut.

The dragon glided closer to him, twisting around his form, as if to measure the creature that entered her realm. Her eyes never took a moment away from him. If he did not know better, he would assume they had the intent of murder behind them.

"I-I know you !"

"Do you, mortal?"

Arcturus slowly dipped his head in reverence. "Veledar told me about you. I've seen...pictures on the cave's walls. Pictures of you. You are the goddess of dragons. As for me, I am nothing but a mere human, here to beseech you for your aid." Arcturus gulped nervously, almost convinced that no God, dragon or not, would pay any heed to the soft, broken words of a desperate man.

"Please..." Arcturus bowed before the enormous dragon. "My friend, Veledar, a dragon with the most beautiful red scales I've laid eyes upon, is marred and broken, d-dying as we speak. He is beyond my help, but maybe...maybe you have the power to alter his fate. Perhaps...you can do what I could not and save him!"

Bahamut stopped and looked slightly away, as if to relay the response, "Why should I care about this Veledar, mortal? All creatures perish, even dragons. It is the way of the world."

Arcturus felt something akin to hope when he saw her mercury-like eyes peek a glance back at him.

"I know what you mean, wise, powerful Bahamut, but I am not here, standing before you, to fight against the way of the world. All I need is one chance for one dragon. That's all."

"One, a hundred, perhaps even a thousand. All is the same to me. Intervening into the affairs of the mortal world is impossible."

"That's not what he told me!" Arcturus shouted out in a flash of anger. "Nothing is impossible. Not to you!"

Arcs of lightning traveled through the clouds, the light so bright it brought Arcturus to tears. "You dare defy me, in my own sanctum?" Bahamut's voice crackled in the dark vortex that once again surrounded Arcturus' diminishing form.

"I dare to plead mercy for a dragon that-a dragon who's..." Arcturus choked as the image of Veledar coughing his last words appeared into his mind. In pain, coughing his last, and he still cut through the gloom with jokes not to brighten his own fading spirit, but to keep the embers of hope alive for the paladin that mended his wounds.

The man that failed him. The man that even now, within the domain of a Goddess, felt just as powerless. Arcturus closed his eyes shut, then tried his best to get onto his knees even as a thin stream of hot tears ran down his contorted face.

"Speak." Bahamut beckoned. "Release the burden trapped within you, human. Who is this dragon you speak so fondly of?"

"An insufferable bastard that I can proudly call friend!" Arcturus rasped, his chest tight, breath shallow. "He's the only dragon I ever befriended...the one who filled my void with hope years after I've lost my family to another red. I ask of you...nay. I beseech you for a way to save Veledar's life, just as he saved mine."

"He...saved you?" The platinum dragoness spoke with a softer voice, and Arcturus nodded several times as flashes of the past rushed through his mind.

"I was falling fast, so fast that I even made peace with my inevitable demise. Then... he grabbed me." Arcturus winced. "I felt his paws wrap around me, holding me steady while I shivered like the useless burden that I am. When the ground rushed to meet us, he took the brunt of the fall. He..."Arcturus sobbed. "Veledar broke his body to preserve me, and even crippled, wounded, bleedin' from more places than I could count, his only concern remained with me, and my safety."

Arcturus wiped his tears and looked at the dragoness, searching for any traces of emotion, hoping to see a small result of his words.

"You spin a memorable tale, but a tale on its own will not persuade me to break one of the most ancient rules of this world."

"But this is no mere tale! This happened. Veledar is truly dying, right now, while we waste our time talking of rules and what cannot be done." Arcturus bowed his head as he realized emotions started to cloud his judgment.

"I mean no offense, great Bahamut. Just please...hear me out. Listen, instead of allowing my voice to simply fly past your ears. This Veledar, my friend...He is the worthiest dragon you'd meet if you but only give him a second chance. Please...he sacrificed himself because of me. I'm the reason he's inching closer to death, so let me bear whatever punishment you see fit. I will do anything it takes to save his life, great, wise Bahamut!"

Bahamut considered his words, then Arcturus shuddered when the female brought her humongous snout inches away from his face. He had seen the look she was giving him on Veledar's snout before. It was a smirk. A clear sign of mischievous satisfaction.

"That is an intriguing proposal you are laying at my paws, mortal. *Anything*, you say?"

Arcturus dipped his head. The dragoness stared straight at him, her eyes seeming to pierce the veil of flesh in search of the color of his very soul. Though Arcturus felt bare before such imposing presence, he stared right back, eyes focused, unblinking, as if this were the most important thing in the entire world right now. He knew it, in the back of his mind, that this was a dangerous game he was playing. After all, this was how things went sour in the stories told to children by their mothers, or the ones written in the scrolls of adventurers. Making deals with entities outside the material realm rarely attracted anything good, but as he stood on his knees, with his eyes focused on scales, Arcturus' mind traveled back to Veledar. He pictured his friend laying on that cavern floor, the blood oozing out of his impromptu stitches, his throat convulsing with painful spasms, giving out his last pained breaths. That was all the encouragement he needed. With utter conviction in his voice, Arcturus voiced his decision.

"I would go to the void and beyond if that's what it takes to save Veledar's life, so yes," Arcturus stood up with a stern look about his face. "I'll do anything you ask of me."

Bahamut flew around him, flapping her enormous wings before returning with a great gust of wind. In spite of the tempests created in the aftermath of her wingbeats, Arcturus hardly moved from where he was hovering. With her claws, the dragoness formed a pedestal that hovered right in front of him, a thing made of stone as bright as her scales. On the pedestal lay a sword forged of bright gold, encrusted with many gems, and armed with a blade that gave off a faint blue radiance. Bahamut hovered, once again her eyes focusing on the human before her.

Arcturus breathed in, and somehow, willed himself to glide towards the pedestal. The entire time he did so, the hairs on the back of his neck stood on end. He came to a stop, and with his right hand, the paladin reached out towards the sword. Each inch that brought him closer towards his prize increased the power radiating towards his hand. The power to conquer the whole world, the power to bring the mightiest evil down to its knees. Arcturus pictured himself returning to his king with this word in hand, ready to deliver holy wrath upon Lumara's enemies.

Then the image of him kneeling before the king flickered, and Arcturus stood upon the throne instead, with an entire squad of paladins offering their swords to him, a good, benevolent king that had the power to-

"No..." Arcturus shook his head. "That's not...*this* is not what I seek!" He pulled his hand away from the blade as if bitten and threw Bahamut an angry glance. She was still looking at him, but her eyes seemed to be filled with curiosity. If he had to guess her expression, it would be one of "Well?"

"This is a test for you?" Arcturus hovered away from the pedestal, not even looking at the accursed blade that stole his eyes for too long already. "I lay out my heart and my thoughts before you, and this is how you repay me? With games and tests while my friend is-"

"We are unbound by time, unshackled by any of the laws you know. Believe me. Your dragon friend is not suffering more than he already had."

Arcturus thought of a way out of this stupid test. *If I don't want the power presented before me, what will I do? All I want is to save my friend, to heal him, to not have yet another soul I care about die in my arms.* His thoughts briefly shifted to Geoffery, particularly to the moment when his son gave his last breath. Arcturus shook his head and wiped his eyes.

He tried to speak and reason with the Goddess. Perhaps it was time for another approach. Something more befit for a dragon. Arcturus willed himself to fly up to Bahamut's snout. He reached out with a hand and placed his palm softly on her snout tip. It was cool to the touch, but not uncomfortably so.

"You think a mere touch will strengthen your arguments?"

Arcturus said nothing. Instead, he pictured a healed Veledar in his mind, protecting innocents against perils. Then, he thought of his vows, Selena, and his son. "I know you can feel this. This is the choice I make. I wish not the power for myself, but to heal and protect others." he said aloud.

The dragoness seemed to chuckle, deep in her throat. She then swirled around him in a blur of silver. Her form seemed to shift and change shape until, in a quick motion, the small silver blur flew straight into Arcturus' chest, where his heart was. He clutched at it with his hands as he felt like his chest had caught aflame. He collapsed in pain, white hot, and blinding. His eyes exploded in stars and his ears rang with a deafening roar, just like the one he had heard faintly the entire time.

Human Arcturus." A soft voice spoke. However, he could feel the ancient power that it carried, as it seemed to come from within his very mind. "The honesty displayed by your words and deeds have moved me...deeply. You shall go back to your world and be my paladin, like I had always intended for you. Go now, human, and bestow my light upon your wounded friend, along with anything else that follows."

Around him, the clouds gave way to reveal the stars above, with the shapes of thousands of dragons nestled within their light. They were all swirling around, snouts pointed towards him. He could see the twinkle in their eyes as he felt his chest glow warm once again. He could not help himself as his mouth fell open, at the sheer beauty of the spectacle presented before him.

Then another flash of light came, and everything went dark.

Arcturus' vision cleared like the dark clouds in Bahamut's timeless realm, only now, instead of cold platinum scales, he found himself still holding Veledar's crimson snout. It was warm...but so were his hands, giving off a faint radiance similar to the azure blade of Bahamut's sword. It felt strange, like he was pouring his very being into the dragon, though the sensation felt anything but uncomfortable. Like hot water, it was warm and soothing, the soft glow rippling against the dragon's scales like beams of sunlight. Arcturus watched the stitches burst apart as the wounds healed themselves before his shocked eyes. The gashes that had filled him with worry vanished along with the blood oozing out of them

And then, Veledar opened his eyes once more.

Arcturus lost himself in the tide of happiness that washed over him and hugged the dragon as tightly as he could.

"Veledar, thank the Gods!" He mashed the side of his face against the dragon's scaly chest.

"What madness got into you?"

"The madness of joy, you stupid scale-head!" Arcturus sobbed loudly in happiness as he squeezed the base of the dragon's chest tighter. Veledar pressed his paw against his back, offering back his own form of awkward hugging, and Arcturus could not help himself. Hot tears formed once again in his eyes to stream down his grateful face.

"Well, I obviously missed the hidden stash of wine you gulped down...or whatever paladin magic you worked on me, because clearly, that needle of yours accomplished just about as much as my arse sitting on this stone." Veledar said with a grin, pushing the paladin slightly back to nuzzle away the tears that fell down his cheeks.

"Oh, come on, you silly dragon, you know you don't have to lick me."

But he did, and Arcturus enjoyed every smothering stroke of that silky tongue across his flushed face. "Alright, that's enough," he patted the dragon's silly snout. "I'm fine with rubs, but no more licking please."

"You loved it! Admit it, or I will rid you of your clothes and give you a proper bath."

"Come on now, you scaly oaf. Nuff about that, unless you want your brave paladin to break down in tears again."

"It's not that bad," the dragon flicked his tongue out a few times. "Apart from the slight bits of grime and the salty taste, crying shows me that you genuinely care about me. I am touched. I may not show my emotion as openly, being a dragon and all, but here. Feel for my heart. See how quickly it   beats."

Arcturus put up with the dragon's request. "Blazes!" he chuckled happily. "Don't tell me a bit of stitching and two potions are all it takes for a mighty dragon to fall in love with a puny human!"

"You're not THAT puny. Besides, there's plenty of tales where love begins just in moments like this."

"Really?" Arcturus arched an eyebrow. "Quite the reader of stories, are you?"

"I do enjoy a good romance once in a while. You humans are...interesting, to say the least." Veledar admitted before he quickly looked away, probably too embarrassed to admit his feelings.

"Tis fine, you crafty dragon. I won't tell anyone, as long as you don't fly from village to village, spoutin' tales of the weepin' paladin. I have a reputation to maintain."

"Excellent idea!" The dragon straightened his head, chest puffed out. "I shall leave no details out on how this proud paladin -the elite of Lumara's army- all but succumbed to my greatness. Imagine the songs about me. The tales! It's glorious!"

"Aye. Glorious indeed." Arcturus patted the dragon's paw. "If we leave out the part where you crapped yourself during the landing."

"I did not!" the dragon bared his teeth.

"Same way I didn't fall for your charms? That's what you're saying."

"Not yet," the dragon grumbled.

He was back to his old self, and Arcturus couldn't be happier. He sniffled one last time, as he could not remove the smile that was still spread wide on his face.

Praise the blessed light that brought him back from the grip of death. I'll never forget the kindness you've done me this day, Bahamut. I shall be your champion and carry out your light into the world, just like I promised.

"Silence, mrrrm? Looks like you're pondering on something." The dragon lowered his snout to Arcturus' level, then flashed a quick smile. "That look in your eyes, that smile...it's happening isn't it? You're falling for me!"

Arcturus slapped the dragon's snout with a quick smack of his palm, but Veledar offered another type of retaliation. He moved in and hugged the paladin just as tightly as he had before.

"Gaaaah, you're squeezin' the breath out of my lungs!" Arcturus scrunched his face in theatrical fashion. "No wonder you need to practice hugs on stuffed animals."

"Quit your sissy fussing, human." Arcturus felt Veledar' wrap his neck around him. "This isn't the first time I held you in my paws."

"Yeah..." Arcturus smiled as the dragon's wings draped over their heads. "You have this thing of sleeping with your toys like a big-nosed, winged, tail-carrying child."

"You're quite heavier and much better looking than a human whelp." The dragon mumbled.

You too, Veledar, Arcturus thought in his mind, allowing the dragon's soothing warmth and gentle breath to lull him to sleep.

Chapter 14: Draconic Bonding

Veledar sat relatively quiet as Arcturus told him, in his own words, all of the events that transpired after the crash. He honestly did not remember much through the thick haze of pain inflicted by his wounded condition. Memories were still just a blur to him, so Veledar nodded at the right parts and gave little gasps at others. He would occasionally twitch his tail, lick his healed wounds or scratch the top of his head with one of the talons on his wings whenever Arcturus spoke about thick storm clouds and magic swords imbued with the power to change the whole world. Arcturus ended his story with his return to the waking world, then took a deep, shaky breath. By the sound of it, he needed a bit of time to recover from the tempest of emotions he braved through.

"Bahamut...I knew our Goddess does more than gawk at her subjects. She listened to you, a human! You know what that means, right? Our Goddess is far better than these silly gods you blabber about when you find yourself in distress." His lips lifted to reveal a tooth filled grin across his snout, "I am astonished she decide to save my life through you. I mean, I've always known I am destined for great things, but to be snatched back from death's grip by a puny human is something that surpasses my wildest expectations!"

"Puny, huh? That's how you address your savior, you scaled brute?"

"Why, your return from Bahamut's mystical realm certainly hasn't made you any bigger! You might have glowing hands now, but I have mighty wings and a tail that can smack some righteous sense into any human that would cross words with me!" Veledar tilted his snout up to look as regal as a dragon could, letting his wings spread out magnificently at the sides.

"Oh. Excuse me, your scaly brightness," Arcturus bowed in front of the dragon, then returned with an amused grin. "It's just difficult for me to believe that the vision gracing my eyes is the same whelp that moaned his heart out when my tiny needle pierced through his bleeding flesh."

"It was just a quick hiss." The dragon stuck his tongue at Arcturus, who just chuckled heartily.

"Aye. A hiss that threatens to eclipse the screams of our women!"

Veledar pushed his head under a wing to lick one of his healed wounds again.

"No need to hide, dragon," Arcturus patted his chest. "I'm well aware of how you came to acquire those injuries, and I certainly hope my mirth doesn't bring up enmity. That's one type of pain I cannot easily heal."

"I might be proud...but I'm not thick," Veledar surprised Arcturus with a fond nuzzle along his chest. "I know I owe you a debt that cannot be repaid even if you were to return my stolen belongings to me."

"You mean those rags you slept on?" Arcturus arched an eyebrow. "The gryphon...you're thinking of that silly toy you cuddled when we found you!"

"Along with my nest, my books, my pots, and the rest of my treasure. I'm curious if your glowing hands have the power to materialize those!" the dragon snorted, pelting Arcturus with bits of gooey mucus.

Even so, he had no room in his heart for ire, as he probably understood his dismissal of his healing of him was a joke. Or at least he hoped he understood that. Sometimes, it was hard to tell what thoughts roamed through the human's head, considering he lacked a proper muzzle to read at times.

"I'll see what I can do about that when the time comes." Arcturus said. "Now, is there something significant going to come out of that maw, apart from self-inflicted praise?"

"Do allow me to indulge in a bit of self-appreciation, my dear human. I have been touched by Bahamut herself, after all." The dragon gestured to Arcturus by waving a paw at him, "With a little help from you, of course. But make no mistake. You are but a vessel to a much higher power."

"Oh, thank you for finally admitting my importance. You are most humble, Veledar. Maybe, just maybe I will remember how utterly skilled you are next time you lay bleeding. I might just avoid interfering altogether so that I can study how a greater species e deals with crippling, life-threatening injuries."

"Well... let's not get too carried away now." Veledar replied, scrunching up his snout at the mere thought of being abandoned. "However, I think we should figure out how we are going to find our half-breed friend and that dwarf we encountered in Drakenburg." Veledar tried to stand on all fours, but his limbs shivered with weaknesses.

"Don't you dare!" He kept the human away with a sharp hiss. "I can...do this on my own just fine."

After a few attempts, he finally collapsed onto the ground with an annoyed growl, causing the human to shoot up in worry.

"But not now." Veledar groaned, "I'm fine, doe-eyes." He brushed Arcturus away with a paw. "You do not have to worry about me like I am some wee, helpless hatchling." Veledar once again tried to stand, his paws shaking during the entire attempt. He tried to avoid the look of dread painted on the paladin's face. After several minutes without falling, he let out a small cackle of glee.

"See? I knew I could do it!"

He turned towards Arcturus. Veledar figured that the human would be impressed by how fast he had recovered some of his mobility. However, his glee quickly festered into disappointment. His friend, the man that moments ago had his hands all over his scales, was busy inspecting the carvings on the cavern's walls.

I did this. I sent him away, Veledar wanted to roar in anger at his stupidity. Once again, pride got the better of him. However, he could not appear weak in front of the human, so Veledar licked his snout, relaxed his lips, then walked over to Arcturus.

"Fascinating, is it not?"

"Aye...This is quite the work." The human had the same look of curiosity about his eyes as he did when he asked about Bahamut beneath the star-lit sky. Veledar imagined it must have been a shock for a dragon slayer -even one out of commission like Arcturus- to discover this side of dragons. In fact, it was a lot for Veledar himself to take in.

"I'm curious about one thing." Veledar stuck his snout next to Arcturus.

"Haven't found any hint of a gender, if that's what you're wondering." The paladin worked his fingers carefully over the dragons scratched on the walls.

"Females? You think my mind's on-"

"I know there's all sorts of weirdness locked in this scaly ball of yours."

Veledar hated how easily the human brushed his hand over his head, like he was some sort of big, scaly dog.

"I actually meant to ask a proper question."

"Then ask. Don't expect me to read your mind."

Veledar waited for the paladin to move over to another set of drawings, to avoid disturbing him at the wrong time. "How does it feel to be an actual paladin, instead of a mere pretender?" He said with a grin.

"Really? That's your burning question?" Arcturus shook his head. "Thought it might have something to do with these drakes scratched on the walls." The human traced the outline of a dragon that lounged on the ground, its head pointed towards the stars. "It feels like... having a fever, only without the headache or the illness."

"A fever?" the dragon cocked his head. "That's the best Bahamut's chosen can come up with?"

"It's not exactly easy to describe for a so-called pretender!" Arcturus sighed. "It feels warm and weird, hard to describe in a way we could both understand."

Veledar shook his head. "That isn't descriptive at all. I was expecting something more significant, after the swirling vortex of lightning-spewing clouds and the thousands of star-dragons that noticed you."

"Well, then I must humbly apologize for shattering your sky-high expectations." Arcturus turned to inspect another set of drawings, though Veledar was sure he did it only to avoid looking at him. "I have just found out I can cast something most soldiers dream of. All my life I've relied on objects to do that for me. Here, let me try again." He placed both hands on the cold stone. "It feels like that tingling you get when your limb has gone to sleep. First, it's cold, but then you move it, and coldness gives way to warmth. Now imagine the same feeling is all over your body, extending around you like a curtain, going as far as your fingertips, or claws in your case."

The dragon dipped his head in acknowledgment. "Must be odd for you, to lack something your entire life. I imagine it must feel like seeing for the first time."

"Or maybe like spreading your wings in the wind for the first time. Dragons aren't born fliers, from what you told me."

The dragon once again dipped his head. "It is just a small step on the road of learning. Even I don't know everything I can do, Arcturus, and I am about four times older than you." The dragon smiled in that toothy way of his, then walked over to the makeshift fire that Arcturus had slapped together. It wasn't what Veledar would have liked, but it had to do for now. After he settled himself comfortably on the warm ground, Veledar dragged a claw over his chest, clenching his snout with discomfort. He could almost feel the gape that split his scales apart before Arcturus healed him.

I do owe him more than I ever owed anybody, save for the mother that birthed me and the one that raised me. Veledar pondered. Sure, he was glad the human had been by his side during the most trying moment of his arguably short life, but never in a hundred years had Veledar imagined Arcturus -the same man that stormed into his cave and imprisoned him atop the deck of his ship- would hold his life in his hands. For a long time, he only thought of the human as a toy with benefits. A companion who only recently acquired the noteworthy rank of a friend. Veledar had given him his name out of trust rather than complete fondness, but to have Arcturus submitting himself soul and mind to the sole purpose of healing him? That was something no mere toy or friend could provide.

"What are you plotting in that horned head of yours?" Arcturus settled by Veledar's side, with his back against his shoulder and the pack between his legs. The human barely waited before he started to rifle through his pack in search of something.

"Nothing worth talking about."

"Really? During all the time we've spent together, am I to believe that your thoughts had never strayed to a female of your own?"

Veledar didn't like the smirk that started to take shape on the human's face. A devious thing, no doubt. "What reasons have you to believe I cannot control such basic urges?"

"Oh, I don't know," the human scratched his beard in jest. "I might remember the word mounting escaping your lips."

"When pain clouded my senses!" The dragon hissed. "What dirty mind you have, to think I'm a mere beast that ruts whenever the season's right. Preposterous!" the dragon gave a long, growly sigh. "I can see I won't be rid of your eyes unless I lay my thoughts bare, so have at it. I was just thinking about the journey thus far and the people I have met." He said, scratching another phantom wound to distract himself from the flush of embarrassment coursing through his body. "I did not think friendship could grow so fast as it did, and...I also believe you are starting to corrupt me."

"Yes, Veledar. You best be careful. Before you know it, your fondness for me will turn you into a proper human." Arcturus said, holding up a hand and twiddling his fingers.

"Dreadful thought, to be sure. I have heard transformations like that cause the sort of pain I recently endured," He gasped, imagining the cracking bones of werewolves. He looked to Arcturus and only found the human giving him a look of *Oh really?*

"Regarding your newfound magical abilities, we do have the rest of the day to explore them, so why not do something more interesting?" Veledar extended a wing over Arcturus. "My mother used to have an ancient book from a long-since-dead paladin. She said it was his tome of divine blessings or some human nonsense like that. Perhaps it could contain what you are seeking, or tell us how to get started, at the very least."

"Well, that's awfully convenient. Why would your mother keep one of those tomes?" Arcturus asked, pulling out a small bag of trail rations to eat.

"She always had a knack for storing items, dreaming about the days when she needed them most." he said, his stomach rumbling rather loudly. *Oh right*, his eyes squinted. *I never had the chance to feast with those gryphons interrupting my morning hunt.*

Arcturus extended a hand full of rations towards Veledar's snout. "Care for something to take the edge off?"

Veledar shook his head slowly, "No, I will endure this. The amount of gold and belongings that you owe me will sustain my body and mind for generations to come.

"Owe you?" Arcturus asked, raising his eyebrow in surprise. "If I remember correctly, you were the one that conscripted me in this heroic quest of yours. How is it I possibly owe you any money at all? When I indulged you at every tavern you snuck your hungry head into?"

Veledar gave the human a predatory smile. Oh, he was going to enjoy this. He wiggled his tail in excitement, gave his wings a stretch, then took a deep breath. He could see Arcturus was already regretting his question.

"Well you see, despite me hiring you to assist me in my quest to get that book back, we have suffered some complications that you need to be billed for."

"Yeah?" The paladin scratched his beard with a playful smile. "Would you be so kind as to illuminate me on these...complications?"

"Let's see," the dragon imitated Arcturus by scratching his jaw with his one of his claws. "Putting up with horses is the biggest annoyance. Dragons have very sensitive noses, as you probably guessed. Then there is that suggestion you made about riding me like a beast, the way you joke around with me as if I was not a fire breathing dragon, how you shove me about when you have a point to prove, and lastly, risking my hide to protect you and the others at every turn due to your humongous inability to avoid attracting trouble." He finished, watching Arcturus' reaction as he got closer to the human's face with a grin.

"That's going to be one heavy bag of coin, isn't it?" Arcturus asked, giving a playful fake gulp.

Veledar made sure to give Arcturus an eyeful of his numerous rows of very sharp teeth. "It will be a fortune. Doubt I can even carry such hefty amount," He chuckled, "Now, since a dragon decided to hear your plea and make you her paladin, I imagine it is only fair that a dragon teaches you how to work this magic."

"And what possibly could you teach me?" Arcturus smirked, "You're only just a normal dragon compared to Bahamut."

"Arcturus!" Veledar gave a pained gasp as he held a paw to his chest. "Such blatant disregard for my abilities pierces me far deeper than any gryphon's claw! I know everything you need to know for the time being. I am a magical creature, after all, while you're still a man who wears a steel dress and glows like a fairy."

"Yea that may be true, but how much will this tutoring cost me once everything's said and done?" Arcturus asked, standing up and brushing himself off. "Tis not a bargain, to save your life and put up with whatever you'll throw at me in this cave, only to become destitute."

"I assure you, my fees are more than reasonable." Veledar closed his eyes

and tried to focus on his first lessons in magic. "Alright. First, I want you to focus on that feeling you described. Now imagine yourself grabbing that feeling within your claws. Grrr, hands. A term I can never get behind. Now imagine forming the energy into something."

"Like your flame breath?"

That's ambitions." Veledar growled with amusement. "I was thinking of something crafted for your abilities. Let us start with a small bolt of fire. Imagine a small orb of red and orange held aloft in your paw....grarrr, hand." Veledar opened his eyes to see what he had described being held in his left paw. He tried to not be proud of it, he really did, but it was no use. He gave a big grin at how his innate skill managed to produce a most beautiful flame.

Then he looked over to Arcturus, who did not have a red and orange orb within his outstretched right hand. His hand instead held a glowing, soft white light.

"That doesn't look like any flame sphere I know. You obviously did something wrong." he said flatly. "Typical of such short-lived race, although what could I expect from a puny human?" He gave Arcturus a smirk, letting him know he was not being serious. He tapped the human with his tail softly for good measure.

"Oh, cheer up, that is certainly good for your first try. I honestly expected you to produce smoke, or light. Something very different from fire, like I did on my first tries." He turned towards one of the cavern walls, gesturing Arcturus to do the same. "Now picture yourself throwing it at the wall." Veledar moved his paw in a striking motion, and the fire bolt flew from the dragon and exploded on the stone. He turned to Arcturus to see his pupil give it a try.

"That's child's play." With a look of determination, Arcturus punched his hand out, and not one, but three separate white bolts flew from his hand and exploded on the wall. "I did it!" Arcturus cried with a big grin on his face, "It wasn't fire, but who cares? I can use magic!"

Veledar just watched the human laugh and just be plain excited at something he had mastered long ago. He imagined his mother had the same look when he had cast his fire bolt for the first time.

"So, when did you learn to cast your spells, master?" Arcturus said, once again turning towards him with those eyes of curiosity that Veledar could not resist.

"About ninety-five of your years ago." He groaned while he stretched his wings, limbs, and finally his tail. "Although I ended up setting several of my mother's books on fire. My excitement knew no bounds, and years did so very little to change that," he continued with a yawn.

Arcturus took this in and grew silent, as if he was thinking about something.

"Something on your mind, Arcturus?" Veledar asked, cocking his head to the side.

"Nay. I mean...aye. Was just thinking about how I came to earn these powers."

"Move on. You've been given a great gift this day. One that will help you just as much as you helped me in my time of need." Veledar groaned, "but continue, I will try to indulge you for now. However, if I ask you to stop.... please obey my request."

"Of course. I just wanted to know if you were afraid up there, with all those gryphons coming at you."

"Of course I wasn't!" The dragon hissed, "What coursed through my bones was excitement, for I knew I was going to make it through everything those little birdies put me through. Dragons are strong, after all." He said, turning to the statue of Bahamut.

He tried to avoid thinking of how the ground had been rushing to embrace him, or how the winds tore at his wings. Veledar shook his head as he remembered slamming into the ground. The pain that shot through his body like forked lightning. Truthfully, he was terrified of meeting his end in such a brutal way, but he couldn't tell Arcturus that. He had to keep up the appearance of the strong, independent dragon that he was. Although, judging by the look Arcturus was giving him, Veledar had the sneaking suspicion the human had seen through his little lie.

"It lifts my heart to hear such bravery, Crimson Sky. Although you didn't seem so convinced while you were bleeding on the very stone we stand on."

"Graaah, the incoherent ramblings of a pain-addled dragon." Veledar scoffed. "Think nothing of them. At least I know I wouldn't take anything I said for a silver." He waved a paw dismissively at Arcturus, "Let's try to discuss something else before you compare me to a frightened kitten." He returned his gaze to the man who had taken a stance with his arms stretched wide, like he did when he practiced in the morning. Veledar sat amused as he watched Arcturus go through his combat meditation. He wondered how often others defaulted to something familiar in the process of learning a new skill.

Veledar suddenly smelled something as his attention drifted from the smooth movements of his friend. He sniffed again. Strangely enough, the smell was faint and familiar. He followed the scent with his snout, finding it was coming from the entrance. He looked out to see the raging blizzard outside, but found that the snow seemed unable to enter the cave. It was no doubt a spell, he thought to himself.

"That friend of yours was unable to see the entrance to the cave, you said? Are you sure that he has good eyesight? For all I know, he could be having one of the many ailments attracted by your kind." Veledar chuckled, picturing the dark armored warrior walking straight into a tree.

"I've never known Garroth to have any difficulties locating his friends -or enemies- from a fair distance. There is an illusion at work at the cave's entrance. I'm sure of it."

"Yet you did not go outside to test your theory?" Veledar asked, as he moved to the cave entrance and extended a claw tip towards it, as if to tap an invisible wall.

"Apologies. Found myself far too busy saving your life, but the thought occurred to me. Although...if this is indeed a temporary sanctuary granted to us by the benevolent Bahamut, is it not wiser to remain here while you completely recover? I would rather rest and wait for Garroth to move on. For all we know, he can have his sentries posted around the cave, waiting for us to fall into his clutch."

"You're far too paranoid." Veledar went to tap the wall, but his claw did not strike anything. It simply moved through the empty space. Veledar wrinkled his snout in disappointment.

"Bah." he growled in irritation, smacking where the wall should have been. He sniffed again trying to analyze the smell.

"Dare I ask what prompted such deep sniffing?"

"If you must know, this place smells familiar. I know the scent, but I can't seem to place it."

"Growing senile already? I thought dragons lived for a lot longer than a few hundred feeble years." Arcturus chuckled.

"Grarr! Mraawr. Go ahead. Keep laughing at the forgetful dragon, for all the good it will do." Veledar smacked his tail as he sat on his haunches. "You know as well as I do who is the leader of this party, and if you want to pay your debt while you live, you'd better avoid stepping on my toes."

"Hah! As if my boots can do any damage to your chicken feet!"

Veledar was about to unleash another one of his growls, but the honest smile on Arcturus' face seemed too much of a decent trade-off to pass. He liked seeing the human in such bright spirits, for he could only imagine what the paladin went through a couple of moments ago. Veledar tried for a moment to think of the reverse situation, then snarled, too afraid to delve too deep into such a gruesome scenario.

"So... your friend in the black armor. This Garroth you spoke of. What should I be worried about?" he turned towards Arcturus. "Does he have any more friends he can reach to? How about one of those flying contraptions? Should we worry about them on our great quest?" Veledar mentally patted himself on the back. He liked the sound of that. *Veledar the heroic dragon,* he grinned wide to himself. *That has a nice ring to it. One that many more humans should appreciate.*

"Garroth, eh?" Arcturus put on his story-telling face. "I met him on a tour in Rothdell. He and his band helped us secure one of the villages there. Rothdell managed to summon a great earth elemental that gave us a fair amount of trouble."

"You...banged your heads against mud? Really?"

"T'wasn't mud we faced. The elemental was almost twice as tall as you. Made out of hardened stone that makes even your scales seem like leather pitted against steel."

Veledar licked his snout as he pictured the creature lumbering around, smacking Garroth and some other people around. He liked the image of that...then he wrinkled his nose when Arcturus popped in his mind flying across the battlefield, battered and hurt.

"T'was a tough fight, but we managed to subdue it with minimal casualties. After Rothdell, Garroth and I became friends. He would spar with me every time he visited Entis. He always had a story to tell, as legs always kept him on the road."

"How come you never went to have adventures of your own? Is that not what you humans do?" Veledar replied, tilting his head to the side. "You obviously have some skill with the sword, and you know your way around numerous enemies. Even your personality is agreeable, most of the time at least." he smirked.

"Gratitude, Veledar. You can be a valuable friend too, when your pride doesn't choke the goodness in you." Arcturus smiled, then his lips puckered, and his eyes fell to the ground.

"What's wrong?"

"It just occurred to me that Selina and Geoffery were still at home back then, when I last sparred with Garroth."

Veledar's eyes went wide. Flames! He had completely forgotten about those two.

"I...I'm..." He mentally whipped himself with his tail. "Envious of this Garroth now. Wish I had the chance to match my claws against your metal stick. Any more friends I should know about?" the dragon casually asked, trying to divert the conversation from such a sad turn. This seemed to work as Arcturus resumed his stances, his sword now expertly held in his hands. Veledar wiped his head with his wing in relief.

"I've got Elizabeth and Gus back in Entis, two of my fellow guards. Then there is that bird brain of a gryphon, Elizabeth's Swiftwing. We all play cards every Fireday night, although Swiftwing has a mind for drink rather than cards."

Veledar grinned, "That reminds me of two gryphons I met years ago, traveling west. They stopped by and paid me tribute in respect for my greatness." He momentarily paused as Arcturus gave him a concerned look. "I did not bully them into doing it if that's what you're afraid of," the dragon said, holding his snout high. "It was a few barrels of wine that turned the night into a merry revelry. Their names were Rundak and Vik." Veledar made his way closer to Arcturus and put his snout into his paws.

"Speaking of friends...how is that other dragon that went to explore the east? What was she like?"

"Looking to replace me already?" Veledar raised his head to stick his tongue out at the human. "Because I have bad news for you, sire. This red dragon is here to stay."

"Yes, I know it takes a lot more than a few words to be rid of your pestering snout," Arcturus sighed playfully, "I am still curious as to her whereabouts."

"Well if you must know, then who am I to keep you bursting with curiosity?" Veledar replied, the mental image of his friend coming to the forefront of his mind. "Her scales had the color of the sky at early sunrise, a pleasant shade of dark purple, her eyes were molten amber. Her breath was of red lighting. She had a little chip on her scales, but she always had fun with me. We would fly everywhere together and got into so much trouble you wouldn't believe! She called herself the Pale Lightning." concluded Veledar, although he thought to her real name, Zyadel.

Veledar remembered when they had played a game similar to what mortals referred to as king of the hill. They would use their breaths to disqualify the others. His siblings, her, and himself would play to see who had the most skill. He remembered diving down, spinning to avoid her lighting breath and the look of shock on her snout as he tackled and pinned her to the ground. He unfortunately remembered getting thrown off and getting his wings tickled. He looked to his wing membranes as he began to flex them slightly. He hated to admit it, but years did little to harden them against such mischievous attacks.

"Aha! Would you look at that!" Arcturus exclaimed, much to Veledar's annoyance. He liked remembering annoying little details.

He looked to his friend, who fortunately had his attention focused on something else other than his wings. Arcturus had his sword in both hands, swinging it around. However, the blade was glowing a soft blue. "Look here, Veledar! I have applied some sort of enhancement to the blade!" The human swung his sword a few more times at the air, a big smile on his face.

"I am not blind," Veledar squinted his eyes, "Clever trick, though not very useful when trying to stay hidden."

"You don't always need stealth, my perceptive friend. The thugs in Drakenburg certainly couldn't be taken by surprise. Remember how we disposed of those?”

“Yeah…I’d have more of a challenge smacking my head against the walls.” Veledar yawned as he felt his limbs grow tired. His eyelids started to grow heavy. “I think…I will rest for a moment. Keep practicing magic, or do… whatever you humans do.” He waved his paw before curling up on the cavern floor.

“Veledar, wait! I have a question that has been bouncing around my head for ages. Why do you pull me in when you sleep?” Arcturus’ voice was calm, yet excited. Even without looking Veledar, Veledar could feel the smile on his face.

“Ever have a stuffed animal you used to sleep with before a marauding band of armor-clad pillagers removed it from your embrace?” Veledar snorted, “It's pretty much like that.”

“So, in this idea of yours, I am the stuffed animal?”

“Well, you and your minions stole mine. I figured it’s only fair you replace it until I get it back.” He waved a paw for Arcturus to come over, “If you feel tired, feel free to come close and assume the position, unless you prefer the company of cold and dampness.”

“A generous offer,” he heard Arcturus mumble before the swish of his sword started to cut through the human’s steady breathing. Veledar sighed, breathed in deep, and let the tiredness claim him in its embrace.

*

He was flying high into the peaceful sky. Veledar flapped his wings as he gracefully danced above the white blanket of clouds. With a slight tilt of his wing membranes, he started circling upon the gentle gusts, then, when the wind grew fiercer, Veledar unleashed a roar of happiness. He went below the clouds to peer over his domain of green hills, dotted patches of brown earth and grey stone mountain tops. He could just barely make out the tops of little houses where humans had no clue of the mighty creature that flew overhead. At this altitude, even the larger dragons could easily be mistaken for birds, or at least gryphons.

“Veledar!” A familiar voice rang out from nearby, making the dragon hover in midair. With each beat of his wings, Veledar turned, looking for the source of the voice. It had sounded like Arcturus, of course, but Veledar was certain that humans lacked the ability to fly. However, now that he thought about it, he wasn't too sure where he had seen him last. He thought hard as he looked to the moving clouds. He remembered a cave, and shivered at the creeping cold he suffered in that place. He roared out to the paladin, hoping for an answer.

But nothing happened.

Veledar waited in silence for a few minutes before he began flying once again. Perhaps it had been nothing more than his imagination. He had certainly been through a lot lately, like being chased by gryphons, falling towards the ground at blinding speeds, and surviving a close encounter with death. He recalled the howling winds that passed his ears as the ground rushed up to greet him. Suddenly, the peaceful sky around him crackled and thundered, turning cloudy and grey. Veledar blinked in bewilderment at the sudden change in scenery.

"What is this?" He said cried out in confusion. It couldn't be *Bahamut*...could it?

Veledar began to fall.

He tried beating his wings, but found them of no use against the fierce wind that blasted him from above. The dragon roared in terror at the rapidly approaching earth.

"Veledar!" Arcturus' voice came louder this time, practically a scream.

Veledar forgot about his predicament for a moment, looking around as he fell to see the clouds swirling and changing shape and color before his very eyes. He noticed that he could no longer feel or hear the wind anymore. Around him, the swirling clouds started to form into fuzzy shapes, and when they came into focus, the dragon found himself in a very large room.

Veledar looked down first. He was standing on all fours on what felt like a stone floor. Even though he could make out his legs and claws, the area around him was still fuzzy, and appeared to be covered by a thick fog that constantly shifted about. A humanoid shape suddenly approached him from the eerie mist. Veledar squinted his blue eyes to make out the shape of a sword held at the ready. The red dragon swiftly turned and snapped at the figure. He was not going to give it a chance to catch him unaware. The figure ducked as Veledar tried to slice it with his claws, then tried a swipe from his tail next as a surprise. However, the figure raised what looked like a shield to block it. The tail met the shield with a crackling slam, causing the dragon pain, but also pushing the figure on the opposite side.

Veledar roared his victory and leaped onto the figure. His bulk pinned the figure to the ground, but it still struggled beneath him. Veledar tried to snap at him. Put a swift end to this pitiful conflict. His maw opened, moving for the kill, but suddenly, the figure's arms wiggled free and caught his snout between them. Veledar tried to bite down, but somehow, he found himself unable. Either he was growing weaker, or this small figure had more strength than a dragon!

"Die! Why...won't you...just...fall beneath me?" He struggled, snapped, and hissed in the figure's grasp as saliva coated its bare, muscular arms.

"Veledar, s-stop!" Arcturus' voice rang out again, only this time, it came from the figure itself.

Veledar's struggles ceased as the room suddenly cleared. He was in some kind of throne room, adorned with high marble walls, torches, and paintings. Great pillars lined the room every ten feet or so. He focused on the figure, where his friend was struggling beneath him. The human's face was red, covered in sweat, and scrunched up in pain. His arms were holding Veledar's jaws from closing on him. Veledar obviously tried to lift his snout to prevent himself from eating his best human friend, but just like before, when the skies themselves cast him down, the dragon found himself unable to act on his own volition.

"I...can't...rraaaauuurrghhh!" Veledar roared. His body thrashed on its own and panic set in as he found himself taking on the role of an observer; a passenger inside his own body. He tried to focus hard on stopping this madness, but his maw kept getting closer to closing to the one human he really cared about.

Fight back, he screamed to himself, *do something, or you are going to end the life of the man that saved you!*

Veledar couldn't even shake his head from how ludicrous this situation became. How did he get here? He was in the cave, cuddled up against Arcturus...

It is a dream. Has to be.

For a dream, it certainly felt frighteningly real. The hard stone beneath his claws, his struggling friend, sweaty and covered in bulging veins that pumped with terrified blood, the dim light of the torches on the walls... and the feeling of his fire glands starting to open up to unleash devastation upon the pathetic prey that struggled in his grasp.

"Fight it, damn you! I didn't save your life just to die at the tips of your claws!" Arcturus shouted as Veledar's snout descended another inch, despite his struggling defense. Veledar felt his throat get hotter, another sign of the impending inferno that was going to roast his friend in front of his very eyes. If was going to save Arcturus, it had to be now, for he knew it deep within the marrow of his bones that he would not get another chance. The dragon focused with all his might to move his maw just a little bit, just enough so the flames would miss the human. He strained internally, roared in his mind as loud as he could, and he would have even thrashed his tail if he was able.

"No, Veledar, don't!" Arcturus screamed in terror at the rising flames.

Then came the fire, pouring out like a geyser of red and orange. It flowed out into the air, striking a wall to leave a large scorch mark of blackened stone.

"By the Gods...you did it," Arcturus sighed in relief. "For a moment, I almost thought you'd..."

Veledar tried to smile as he felt control return to his body, but before he could speak and comfort his friend, the floor vanished again, and he was falling once more into the swirling clouds.

"NO! I was victorious!" Veledar shouted out to the angry clouds that surrounded him from every side.

Why was this happening? Was it some sort of test? A punishment? Veledar blinked as the air was rushing passed his snout once more. The dark clouds had vanished once again to be replaced with the blue sky and the white fluffy clouds from the beginning of his dream. He was once again diving in the sky, looking down at what the sun had illuminated on this fine, beautiful day. That's when a small silver streak flew past him, causing him to turn around with a stifled gasp. Flying right beside him was his brother, his silver snout open in joy as he unleashed a playful growl.

Veledar continued to dive as his brother circled him quickly, poking his underside with one of his white claws. Veledar looked to him with sorrow. He had forgotten how nimble of a flier he was.

"That tail is mine!" His brother sped out of his reach as Veledar tried to catch his cute tail.

"Only if you catch me! Your lazy wings can never match my speed!" His brother smiled back, sticking his tongue out at the red dragon. Then the young dragon started to do a loop in the air.

Veledar closed his eyes and covered them with his paws. "I don't want to relive this dreadful moment," He breathed to himself, trying to think of the cave he knew he was sleeping in. He tried to imagine Arcturus doing his little movements. Pictured the human held in his grasp, which became the norm for a while now.

But none of those warm memories protected him against the dreadful sound that pierced his ears. The roar of pain broke through his feeble concentration like a flaming blast, and he knew what it was. Veledar felt the familiar sting of panic as terror welled up inside his body just as it did all those years ago. The feeling of hopelessness paralyzing his wings as his brother tumbled to the earth. The terror that opened his eyes wide to a most dreadful image. His brother, an agile flier mere moments ago, turned into a choking, moaning pile of misery with a huge bolt protruding through his chest. Veledar shook his snout, trying to not picture the dragon's shocked expression as his body tumbled lifelessly to the ground.

"Nooooo!" Veledar found himself roaring, tears welling up in his blue eyes. He shut them tightly, trying to focus on anything else. But that was hard. Too hard, even when that place was one of relief. "Please..." he said weakly to himself as he imagined the relief on the paladin's face right after Arcturus returned with Bahamut's light in his hands. "Please...take me back...take me back to him..."

Veledar opened his eyes, finding himself in a cave, but not the same one where he fell asleep in. Another silver dragon lay next to him, but instead of his deceased brother now stood his sister, Adalina. He could hear her sniffling as she struggled to stay quiet, and Veledar slowly wiped his own tears from his eyes. He looked up at a large silver dragoness that slunk into this portion of the cave to curl around the two wrymlings. She had frills lining her spine, bone white claws, and large, grey membraned wings. Her scales were smooth and covered her entire body from head to tail. The dragoness carried them with a grace Veledar always had seen her display. Her horns were less pronounced than those of male dragons, and her white claws were smeared in thick, half-dried blood.

Veledar whimpered as she began to stroke him with the upmost care, her paws gliding over him and bringing such gleeful warmth to his shivering form.

"It will pass. In time, even the gravest of wounds heal," she said softly in a calm, soothing voice.

Veledar admired the strength she had always shown around them, but even he could see the heavy pain carried in her green eyes when she looked to him.

"Time will only make my vengeance burn hotter. I hate them!" Veledar hissed to her, tears welling up once again in his eyes. "It isn't fair! We were just flying in the sky like we always-" he found himself unable to finish the sentence as he collapsed onto his mother's chest, sobbing out his misery.

"I know it's hard to find mercy in your heart now, little one, but you have to remember to not judge a race based on the actions of a few. Humans too lose wives, husbands, children..." She rested her head on Veledar and curled her tail around Adalina.

"Besides, the ones responsible for this atrocity have been taken care of. There's nothing left to worry about now, my little Veledar." His mother squinted her eyes, a grim look on her snout. Judging from the blood on her claws, the small dragon knew what she had meant. His mother licked Veledar across his head affectionately as he continued to cry.

"I...I miss him so much. Are you sure.... there isn't a way to bring him back?"

"I treasured him just as much as you do, little one," She whispered, "But sadly, there is no way to bring a dragon back once death has claimed them. It is the way of the world, unfair as you may now think. Try to find comfort in knowing that your brother is in a better place...Where there is no pain. No suffering. Not even hunger."

"He doesn't have to hunt?"

"No, my little one. Bahamut will see him provided with everything he needs." She laid down her head, and Veledar finally saw large tears roll down her snout.

"Then why are you crying, mother?"

"Because..." The female's voice cracked for a moment. "Because I wished to feel his presence under my wing for a few more seasons before...before he-"

The young Veledar nuzzled her neck and cuddled close to his mother to shiver and weep together.

*

Veledar awoke with a start. The smell he had sniffed before. He knew what it was!

"Up! Up! Move your heavy, glowing arse, sir paladin!"

"What is that noise?" Arcturus mumbled. "Shush your snout for just a while longer. Isn't even morn yet."

Veledar had none of that. He tried to get up from his resting spot, ignoring the complete darkness that surrounded him for a moment, a good hint at how long he's been asleep. Still, even in pitch black darkness, he figured that his wing was being held down by the paladin, who had wormed his way between his paws.

"Comfortable, are we?" Veledar teased the human with a few strokes along his curled body. He was hugging a forepaw, head rested on a hind one.

"Aye. Very. Wing's warmer than a stove. So very...soft and pleasant."

Veledar quite enjoyed seeing Arcturus make some sort of love to his wing, but unfortunately, he found himself pressed by more important concerns.

"Arcturus! You have to move now, or I'll get up. Believe me, you won't like it if I do that." Veledar chuckled, poking the human with one of his claws.

"Just give me a few more moments." The human mumbled, griping his wing tighter like a blanket. "What got you in such rush anyway? There's nothing to do here apart from sleeping."

"That's what a sleepy head would say." Veledar rolled his eyes as he poked Arcturus a tad harder this time. This left him more frustrated as the human vehemently refused to stir. Veledar grinned to himself as a mischievous idea came to mind. He opened his maw wide, looked in Arcturus' direction, then unleashed his loudest and messiest of roars. Arcturus' eyes bolted suddenly open, and Veledar held him tight as the human tried to bolt up.

"You didn't have to blast my ears and pelt me with saliva, dragon." Arcturus grumbled, "I would have gotten up if you just gave me a couple more moments like I bargained for!" Arcturus lifted the dragon's paws off himself. "So what's so important you decided to wake me up with a near deafening roar?"

"I've identified the smell that evaded me before." Veledar smiled, showing

233

off his white teeth. "You're going to like this."

"What, is it a female in heat? Cause they're problem for all species, not just dragons." Arcturus replied sarcastically.

"It's my mother's scent, you clanking bucket of pebbles-for-brains! I am a tad disappointed that I did not recognize it before, I must have been distracted by all the excitement that poured over me once I saw what your glowing hands can do. Imagine if I would've been the one graced to stand in Bahamut's presence. Do you think she would've made me more resplendent than I already am?" The dragon quickly looked over his features. "Or maybe she could have fashioned me an iron suit like yours to mraaauuurrghh," He was interrupted by his stomach rumbling loud like a lion's roar. Veledar clutched his chest as it felt like a wolf was tearing at his insides.

"You know, for most people, waking up to that roar, being held tight by a dragon, and hearing his stomach rumbling in hunger would be a nightmare. Me, however? That's just a normal day." Arcturus grinned.

Veledar growly chuckled as the human fumbled around in the dark, trying to find his pack. He figured dark vision was something humans did not have.

"But you're the lucky lad. Chosen of dragons, and champion of Bahamut as it now stands. You get more than the bare privilege of spending time with me. Aren't you grateful you let me out of that cage? Imagine how boring your life would be if you followed your bloated king's plans."

"Yeah. Lucky me," Arcturus said, then paused for a moment. "Correct me if I'm wrong, but if that's your mother's scent, does this mean we are now occupying her cave?

"I don't know," The dragon paced around, the sound of his claws clicking on the stone accompanying his steady breaths. "She has at least been here long enough to impregnate the cave with her scent. Trust me, her home is much bigger and far better looking." Veledar yawned, stood up, and stretched from wings to his tail. He ignored yet another growl from his stomach. "I can tell you're up to something. What are you looking for?" He asked, moving next to the human.

"Maybe a torch that I did not burn earlier." Arcturus replied. He stopped his hand within his pack and frowned. "Well, I guess that lake is all dried up. Oh, the things I'd do for something to eat right now..."

"I can produce some feeble flames if sight is an issue."

"I guess that could work if we needed it. What would you eat, Veledar, if given the chance?"

The dragon cocked his head. "Are we talking about the kind of prey I hunt or cooked food?"

"Gah, is that even a question? I am talking about prepared food of course. I really don't want to picture you ripping through an innocent animal's belly after all the wounds I had to stitch."

"Fine. If you insist, I shall delight you with my desires. Right now...in this present moment... I would want one of those sheep animals that humans breed in their fenced meadows." Veledar licked his snout. "A good sheep roast with some thick spicy sauce to bring out the flavor. My mouth waters at the thought." He laid his head down and folded up his wings. He pictured the food on a silver platter, swallowing often to keep the strands of saliva from fleeing down his jaw.

There was a sudden clatter sound close by. The dragon stood up, looking around in the dark cave to discover that on the floor suddenly rested a large silver platter with what looked like a roasted sheep coated in the same mesmerizing spicy sauce he thought of earlier.

"Is there a new smell in this cave, or am I starting to hallucinate?" Arcturus put a hand on Veledar's flank.

"Not unless I am too. By an oddity of fate, or perhaps a striking twist of magic, there appears to be a plate of roasted sheep waiting for me right after I pictured it in my mind."

Veledar approached the meat slowly. He had no idea his mother had this sort of enchantment in her cave. He knew there were spells that could summon food, but this was more than he had heard it could do. Throwing caution to the wind, the dragon sunk his teeth into the meat, letting the juices sit in his mouth. He savored their flavor, smoky, with a hint of lime.

"I take it you're stuffing your snout then?"

"Wiser words have never been spoken!" Veledar meant to say, but all that came out was a jumble of sounds and sheep meat.

"Can you try to picture other things? Perhaps you can summon a fire for us?"

Veledar stopped his feasting. He had not thought about such insignificant things for the moment. He gulped down his last chunk of food and reluctantly left his meal to grab Arcturus and pull him against his chest.

"Hey, get your clawed paws off me! I don't want to smell like roasted sheep." The paladin ranted, struggling lightly in his grip.

"You may want to be close for what I picture next." Veledar smiled, closing his eyes.

He pictured a banquet table several feet long, adorned with food fit for kings. He pictured various meats, breads, fruit, and cheese. He focused lastly on a chair.

Only one though? No, he needed three. Had to have one for Merlia and Lyndis whenever the women stumbled upon this cave. He pictured them adorned with red cushions, and a place at the table for himself. Afterwards, he imagined torches lining the cave walls, complete with a roaring fire in the center to provide an aura of much needed heat.

I'd be surprised if the human doesn't bow before my ingenuity now, the dragon thought proudly. He opened his eyes to gaze upon the magnificence of his mind, given form.

"It's...perfect." His tongue rolled out as he let go of the shocked human.

"Bloody blazes! I-it came right out of thin air!" Arcturus exclaimed in shock.

"Best grab some food before I devour it all, you loud mouthed slug!" Veledar bounded over to a roasted turkey.

"I think you may have forgotten something," he heard Arcturus say from behind.

"And what could that possibly be?" He chuckled, turning to the human who had sat down to start grabbing his own favorite food.

"The drinks, you silly red snout. What kind of feast would this be without a wide selection of beverages?"

"Of course!" Veledar exclaimed, his eyes growing wide. "Of course. How in the world could I miss those?" He closed his eyes and thought of several bottles of wine adorning the table. He grinned to himself as he also imagined several barrels of the same liquid next to him.

"That's more like it!" Arcturus said, grabbing a bottle swiftly, uncorking it, and taking a deep, hungry sip straight from the bottle.

"Don't you dare get started without me!" Veledar hissed loudly as he ripped the lid off one of the many barrels beside him. He dunk his head practically in the wine to take a large gulp of the red liquid. He swished it around in his maw, savoring the bitter flavor before swallowing it and returned to stuffing his snout with meat. Arcturus asked something, but Veledar found himself too lost in the cycle of meat and drink that kept repeating inside his maw. It was on the tenth cycle of feasting when he finally heard the human clearly.

"If this is your mother's place, where is she hiding?"

Veledar paused from his eating duties, some of the wine still dripping down onto the cavern floor. That was a great question. Of course, she could always just be out. Flying, hunting, tinkering with spells. Any number of these things sprang to his mind.

"Probably dragon stuff," Veledar replied quickly, grabbing what looked like a roasted hog from the table.

"Well yeah. What else could a dragon do? Sew clothes and dress up like a human?" Arcturus replied, and by his tone he was no doubt rolling his eyes. "But what's your plan with her anyway?" Arcturus paused for a moment, "Don't tell me. It's wait here until she gets back, isn't it?" The human took another sip from a bottle of wine, "I mean how long could that take? Days?

Weeks? Months, perhaps? From what you've told me, dragons aren't holding time in the same regard we humans do."

"My mother's not a dumb hatchling to get lost in her own territory. She will be here in a day or two." Veledar lied, hoping that would at least sooth the human's worry. "I figure we enjoy this feast, delight in the lovely drink..." Veledar took another gulp of red wine, emptying the barrel, "Drink again and bask in each other's good company while we wait for Lyndis, Merlia, and my dear mother to show her face."

Veledar watched the human mull it over for a moment. "Solid plan, that. I suppose they do have the brooch, and it will most likely lead them here. It does not sound like too terrible of an idea, considering what happened today." Arcturus said, then a smirk sprang onto the human's face, "Although I shudder to imagine what your mother will think when she finds her proud Veledar passed out drunk in her cave."

"Hey! You stuff those back in your little maw, sir paladin. I fell out of the sky, nearly died for it, and bled over the snow when I dragged my wounded body over to this cave! I think a dragon who gets saved from the brink of death deserves to get as drunk as he wishes!" Veledar exclaimed, opening another barrel of wine. He finished his words by sticking his wine-dripping tongue out at Arcturus.

"Do you know what I think she will do?" Arcturus continued.

"What, oh, dearest and wisest of humans? What will my mother that you know so fabulously well will do to me?"

Arcturus cleared his throat suddenly, "GET YOUR SCALY ASS OFF MY CAVERN FLOOR, VELEDAR! YOU'RE EMBARESSING YOURSELF IN FRONT OF THE MORTALS!" The human raised his hands and smacked them together as if slapping his hand, "YOU BROUGHT THIS UPON YOURSELF, YOUNG DRAGON."

Veledar narrowed his eyes at Arcturus, causing the human to stop and laugh.

"Is that so? And do tell me, Arcturus... you find such outburst... funny?" He asked slowly, trying to let his voice come off threatening as he advanced onto the human. He let his chest swell up too, in good measure.

"Aye! I think I do!" laughed Arcturus, crossing his arms, "What are you going to do about it? Get me drunk too?"

Veledar grinned at the human's final words, He had asked for it, after all. With a playful shove Arcturus found himself sprawled onto the floor, his voice nothing but laughter.

"So what do you, oh great dragon, possibly do for fun before we came along?" Arcturus asked, getting back into his chair. "I've only seen you hunt, complain, fly, and do your little jokes." Arcturus lifted a finger up for each one.

"Hmmmm," Veledar started to say, pondering for far too long. The thought popped into his head that the drink was getting to him and he drowned that thought with another gulp of wine. He then continued with his "hmm".

Arcturus watched him in disbelief before returning to his laughter. He took another sip from his own bottle. "Perhaps you had enough for now, my scaly friend. I don't think I will survive the wait on your hmmmms."

"They certainly do not last forever. You're just being impatient, like you were this morning when I woke you up." Veledar swung his head up to look more regal, of course. "We like to hunt each other, which of course ends in wrestling, telling riddles or stories, dancing, one upping each other in magic, and of course, mating."

Arcturus spit out his drink. "What was that last one again?"

"Dancing?" Veledar said with a grin.

"Oh, you very well know which one it was, you perverted dragon. If not before, I certainly think you have had a bit too much wine now." The human laughed, taking another sip of wine.

Veledar just had a hissing fit of amusement. The paladin turned several shades of red, and Veledar did not know whether the color came from the wine, or the embarrassment of imagining how dragons mated. He certainly would have to press this further. How could he miss such grand opportunity?

"Dear skies, you look like a ripe cherry that's about to burst. Should I assume you don't mate on a regular basis just for the pleasure of it?" He tilted his head to the side and raised a scaly eyebrow.

"What a human does is between them and their friends, families, acquaintances and what not. Not that I would discuss to you, dragon, or anyone in casual conversation about such uncivilized things."

"Your loss, Arcturus. Just remember you could have learned a few things that no book ever mentions. Besides...I had the opportunity to see many things during my life." Veledar replied, taking another gulp of wine. He now could feel the fuzziness around his head, a pleasant warmth that pulsated with a dull throb.

"Ah, fine. Just so you don't go into describing the particulars of your matings, what is dancing to dragons?"

"Do you not have dancing in your culture?" Veledar laughed," Well I guess not, considering the lack of wings and all."

"Since when does dancing require wings?" Arcturus asked. "I think the drink has blurred your thinking, my scaly friend."

"Nonsense! Dancing is when two dragons hold one another by the paws and fly high into the sky. They then do maneuvers in the air with one another, which is obviously why you don't have it in human culture."

"Oh, another form then. Our dances don't require wings, and there is typically music attached to the timing of the steps."

"How strange," Veledar wrinkled his snout, "But how do you do aerial maneuvers without wings? Well I suppose you could just strike poses on the ground, but where is the fun in that?"

"We don't do maneuvers, you deaf dragon. There is usually a sequence of movements, but nothing too elaborate."

"I shall have to observe what you call dancing after our quest is done. It certainly sounds like something you lot stole from dragons." Veledar pouted before finishing off his second barrel of wine with a loud audible burp.

"And since I have answered all of your pestering inquires, human, I of course have some...*burp*...of my own." said Veledar, looking over to the third barrel of wine briefly before turning his attention back Arcturus. "So, enlighten me. What did you do for fun before I fell into your care? I imagine your life was all tidy before you found yourself stuck with me. How does Arcturus, *paladin* of Lumara, *champion* of Bahamut, entertain himself when he's not too busy warming up to a dragon?"

Arcturus gave him one of those amused human faces before taking a swig of wine.

"When I am not practicing, meditating, or studying dragon anatomy, I fancy painting."

"Dragon anatomy?" Veledar laughed loudly. He parted his legs, thrust a claw between them, then gestured very close to the slit he had near the base of his tail. "All dragon anatomy?"

"Not that kind of anatomy, you drunk fool! I'm speaking of the fire glands, the wings, weak spots, things of that nature. What good is knowing whether you have a cock or not 'tween your legs when you're trying to kill me?"

"So, in all your books, there was never anything about that?" Veledar grinned, still trying to make the paladin turn red.

"Alright, fine, yes! There was a book or two that covered that topic. However, it failed to grab my interest, so I only leafed through it." Arcturus sighed, "You happy now?"

"But of course. The mental image alone of you staring and learning about our weakest of spots is priceless. Funny, how nobody ever thinks of striking us there, where even an arrow is enough to provoke serious injuries," Veledar chuckled, "Now, about your painting, did you go about painting 'that' as well?"

"Of course not! I painted buildings, landscapes, plants, trees, dragons who've got better things to do than flaunt their scaly crack." Arcturus coughed at the last one, clearly trying to hide his embarrassment.

"So, despite training to kill our kind....and looking up our anatomy, you painted us as well?" he nudged the human playfully.

"Yes, I see the irony, but there was something about painting dragons..." Arcturus gestured to all of Veledar with his hands, "Something is worth painting. At least in my eyes. I cannot speak for the thousands of other humans that prefer to stick to their own kin."

"Ah, how amusing. I suppose I will have to pose for you sometimes. Get a painting or two of my glorious self to adorn the walls of my lair." replied Veledar as he pictured himself sprawled out on his cavern floor, with Arcturus painting away with a stern, focused look on his face.

"Why not just get a mirror if seeing yourself is all you're interested in?" the human laughed. "You clearly don't have to force a poor painter to get every last bit of you right."

"Because then, dearest Arcturus, I would have to stand in front of it all the time. Have you any idea of the kind of aches you get from sprawling on solid stone? Course not. You're a human, wearing silly boots and clothes because your body is not good enough for this cold, rugged world," he stuck his tongue out once more. "So, you mentioned you studied a dragon's weak spots. Amaze me with your knowledge. Show me what you know."

"Well, for starters, generally your joints don't have as much scales on them, if any. Your eyes are another prime spot for an arrow or a blade to pass through. Certain parts of the underbelly are also soft to either sword or spear. You have to look for how the scales go. Then there's the wings of course."

"What about my big, beautiful wings?" Veledar spread them to his side, as if to admire himself.

"I'm surprised you're asking. They are one of your weakest features, letting even pebbles through if swung with a modest amount of force. Like I mentioned earlier, the joints are hardly armored at all, attracting both archers and gryphons." Arcturus stood up and walked over, grabbing one of Veledar's wings. He paid this no mind as he opened the third barrel of wine.

"All this talk of wounds makes my head ache. How are you feeling?" he massaged along the hot membrane.

"Quite good, if not a bit too warm, and don't get me wrong, it's not because you're standing right next to me."

"Too ugly for your scaly brightness?"

"All humans are. Perhaps that's why you favor dragons in your paintings. Your eyes simply rebel at the thought of splattering the face of a fat, gassy merchant onto the canvas."

"You're being a rude dragon now."

"I'm being truthful!" The dragon groaned and rolled his eyes. "You know...if you keep rubbing me like that, you might just get a peek at what makes me a male."

"So you're enjoying this?" The human smiled.

"Of course. You said it yourself. Wings are sensitive to harm, touch...anything, really."

"Good, because I know another weakness of the wings. They are usually very ticklish!"

Suddenly, Arcturus started tickling his wings like his sister and friends used to. Veledar collapsed to the floor in a bout of laughter, thrashing with his claws and tail, and even amidst that storm of claws and flapping wings, Arcturus kept going. He started to really get aggressive, tickling the dragon around the whole wing, not slowing down for even a moment.

"That's for shoving me around like your toy!" the human laughed in drunken cheer. "Not fair now when the little human gets the better of you, eh dragon?"

"Pause. Raaaaarr, please stop!"

The human thankfully put a momentary reprieve on his frenzy so that Veledar could regain some of his senses and dignity. He was breathing deeply, staring at the human. Arcturus was still laughing. Oh, how he thought himself so clever. Veledar would certainly have to remind him that he was still very much a scaly, fire-breathing dragon.

"You might've gotten the upper hand by ambushing me with your fingers...but if you think you can out-wrestle me, you are more mad than I ever gave you credit for."

"Really?" Arcturus smiled. "Why don't you give me a try? I am, after all, the chosen champion of your Goddess."

"Not against the GREAT AND POWERFUL VELEDAR!" The dragon puffed out his chest. "Why else would you start your assault with the customary wing tickles? Trickery and deceit to mask your human weakness!" He hissed as he grabbed the human with his claws.

"I think I can manage something when said dragon is quite inebriated!" The human laughed. "Come now. Show me if you fight as well as you talk, great and powerful wyrm!"

Veledar quickly did a triangle pattern with his paws, then slapped the air. A slight tingle moved through his body. The spell he had just used would make himself lighter. That way, he would avoid crushing the human when the glee of contest washed over him. Of course, it also gave him an excuse if the human somehow managed to best his four agile paws, tail, and wings.

"That thing you did with your paws...was it magic?"

"I'm not cheating, if that's what you're implying."

"That's exactly what I believe, dragon. Admit it. You're afraid of me."

"Never!" Veledar growled. He grabbed Arcturus by his side and went to flip the human onto his back, then pin him down, just like he had always done with his sister. However, the human was prepared for this. He used the momentum to roll over, together with the dragon. Veledar felt his tail knock over a chair that crashed onto the floor with a loud thump.

"Well, this may be more interesting than I thought!" He snorted as both combatants tried to pin the other beneath them. Veledar felt his blood quicken as they tumbled. He could not resist nipping the human with his teeth every now and again.

"You bastard! I knew you'd be cheatin'!" Arcturus shouted as he struggled to get a better hold on the situation. "Got your scaly arse now, dragon!" Arcturus exclaimed, almost pinning the dragon beneath him. Veledar struggled to break free. He was not going to lose. Not to a human, be he the king of the world himself! He was of course the mighty and powerful Veledar, after all.

He's not half bad at this game, he frowned as his mind quickly analyzed the human's practiced techniques. He guessed he would have to take it a tad more serious than he originally intended. With a loud growl, the red dragon turned the tables quickly as Arcturus let out a surprised yelp. Veledar managed to finally pin the human with his claws, and this time, it was Arcturus that struggled in his grip. With his blood burning hot, he let out a roar close to the human's face, signifying his victory over him.

"You know, I did not intend to go deaf in this cave. What would your mother say for stealing the gift of hearing from the man that saved you, right here in her cave?" Arcturus laughed weakly.

"Perhaps you should have given up when you had the upper hand!" replied Veledar before moving his snout mere centimeters away from the human's face. "It's not wise to challenge a dragon, after all. I admire your courage, but the result is as expected. I am the victor."

"Bahamut's bright arse! It does indeed look like I have been vanquished!" Arcturus closed his eyes, dropped his head onto the cold stone, then let out one last loud sigh.

Veledar's heart skipped a beat. Arcturus laying dead at his feet...it felt too close to that horrible dream he had. "Arcturus," he nudged the human's head. "Hey. Steel-head. I don't appreciate my prey going dead on me. Get up. Come on. We have plenty of other games to try."

But Arcturus said nothing. Upon closer inspection, Veledar realized he didn't even breathe. In a fit of instinctual desperation, he pushed his snout against the human's face, opened his mouth to breathe his air into the human's lungs, then suddenly froze as a familiar voice came from the cavern's entrance.

"Are we missing anything good?"

Veledar pushed his head back as if struck. "I-no, I was just checking if he's indeed as drunk as he admitted." He turned towards the voice to see Lyndis standing there with Merlia. It looked like they had been in a few scuffles on the way here, as their armor was covered in slash marks. The half elf had brought out a bag of trail rations and was currently munching on a handful. She was holding out the bag for Merlia to take some.

"You usually have to pay to watch this sort of thing. Please, proceed. We will just...sit here and let nature take its course." She said with a mischievous grin.

"Right you speak, lass! Big scaly bum was practically makin' out with Arcturus!" Merlia exclaimed as she walked over the table, "Does dis sort of ting happen all da time wit you boys?" she asked, grabbing a bottle of wine and taking a swig of it.

"What are you talking about?" Veledar asked, kneading his claws gently into the trapped human beneath him, "I have vanquished this paladin here, and then I took a closer look at him to see if he's..."

"Hot fer yer tail?"

"...Passed out drunk." Veledar finished with a hiss. "Go check the barrels if you don't believe me."

"I think they believe you alright," Arcturus picked himself up with a groan. "Dragon, let me go before Lyndis over there springs a leak or something."

A geyser of red wine accompanied the next loud laugh from Merlia, spraying all over the floor. "Dats funny lass, he is talkin' about your bits!"

"Don't think I won't!" Lyndis shot back toward Arcturus with laughter. The half elf strolled over the table to join the dwarf in feasting on the collected food.

Veledar guessed Arcturus had enough, being pinned like common prey and being teased by the girls. He released the human, who sighed and patted the dragon's scales.

"Thank you for the contest, but next time I won't go so easy on you," he said with a grin.

"You tell yourself whatever you need to mask the bitter truth," replied Veledar with a hiss, "I look forward to besting you once again."

The two of them walked over to join Lyndis and Merlia at the table, who were busy shoving food into their respective mouths.

"So how did you get here, you two?" Veledar tilted his head to the side. His eyes strayed to the third barrel of wine.

Lyndis held up her pointer finger as she finished swallowing. "It's an interesting story to tell." she started, holding her hands up. "And this particular adventure started when we got separated in the woods..."

Chapter 15: Royal Pain

Lyndis was savagely thrown to the ground, crashing with a flash of pain in the cold snow. It had happened so fast; fast enough that she could not even have gotten a shout out. She went to stand, her trained eyes looking for the gryphon that had ripped her out of Stinky's saddle. She remembered the horse's pained cry as the gryphon's talons ripped through its tender hide, silencing it forever.

Feathery bastards. I'll show them what happens when you mess with an angry half-elf, she pulled out a rapier and held it aloft in front of her as she twitched one of her sensitive ears. She could feel her heartbeat quicken as her grip on the hilt tightened. Within seconds, she heard the flap of wings, and Lyndis bid her time, waiting for the gryphon to swoop down on her before she rolled out of the avian's outstretched claws. The gryphon landed on the snow with an angry screech. He wasn't an ugly specimen by any means, with golden fur, white pristine feathers, and black, sharp claws.

Lyndis felt a slight measure of regret for what she was about to do, but such was the way of war. You either hunted, or you became the prey. She didn't intend to be a hapless doe this day. Her eyes locked to the creature's powerful body, its sharp claws, and more importantly, the keen eyes that fixed her down with a predatory stare. She gave one of her own right back. Being a rogue, she had been naturally trained to look for weak points on any opponent. A usual human needed thrice, even five times more time to find an opening in the opponent's defense, while Lyndis needed a mere moment to capitalize on an opponent's mistake.

"Your move, little elf." The gryphon started circling around her, waiting for her to make a mistake no doubt. She could hear the sounds of Crimson Sky's roar. Clearly the dragon was struggling with several more of this gryphon's flock. This little duel with the gryphon could wait, as right now, getting to her friends was way more important.

"See, you probably think you have gotten lucky in your little hunt." She smiled to the proud bird, "That you got the elf all for yourself. Under normal circumstances, I wouldn't mind sharing a few words over a drink, maybe even gawk at your plumage."

"Really?" The gryphon cocked his head. "Because to me, it seems we're very much enemies."

"Temporary adversaries has a better ring to it." Lyndis put on a smug smile.

"Fancy words. Let's see how you speak when I squeeze your frail body under my talons!" The gryphon parted his beak to unleash a loud, savage squawk.

Lyndis shielded her face against the droplets of saliva, then revealed her squinted eyes along with a mischievous smile. "I have to tell ya, gryphon boy, that could not be furthest from the truth."

She flicked her wrist and whispered *Mirror Image*. Three copies of herself sprung from her body to stand next to her, matching exactly what she was doing. The gryphon gave a screech as it charged at her, talons ready to slash her to ribbons. She sighed as she dodged out of the way. The gryphon had gone for her over the illusions. She chocked it up to a lucky guess as she stabbed down into the gryphon's side, drawing blood before leaping away from the wounded creature.

"Skraaaa. You quick little mink!"

"The more you move, the faster you bleed. Stand down. My quarrel is not with you."

"Wrong..." The gryphon shook off his wounded hindpaw, drops of blood pelting the pristine snow like water trickling from a pierced waterskin. "You defy our king and expect to go unpunished? You'd better finish me off, half-breed, because I will never stop hunting you!"

"It's your choice," Lyndis readied for a second assault. She saw the gryphon twitch as blood was starting to drip in rivulets down his muscular flank. Good. She had hit one of the main blood vessels, and though it knotted her stomach to see the gryphon's leg spasm with painful jolts, Lyndis drew strength from the rule of any battle. Any advantage you had over your opponent made things a lot easier, for she did not have the brute strength of the dragon, nor the heavy plate of the paladin. All she had was her wit, her rapier, and of course, the ability to weave spells. The gryphon tried to pounce again, this time choosing the wrong copy of her. Its beak snapped at thin air as the bird screeched in anger. She rewarded him with another hit and run, as her rapier struck the other side right under the wing, then she flipped away again to observe the gruesome result of her actions.

"Raawkraaaakkk," The gryphon fell to the ground. "You're...the fastest prey I encountered. Seems to me...I am destined to die at the end of your blade." The gryphon reached towards her with a talon. "I expect nothing of an honor-less rogue, but...at least grant me the mercy of a quick death."

Lyndis gritted her teeth. She owed nothing to this bird, yet something kept her from plunging her blade through its feathery neck.

"You're not dying today, runt." Lyndis rummaged through her pack for a quick healing potion and lunged towards the creature's drooping head. "C'mon, open this up. You had no problems snapping and tearing at me a few moments ago"

The bird gasped for breath as even more blood dripped onto the ground. "No...what are you..." it struggled in her grasp, still trying to get away...to survive for a few more painful minutes before death took him.

"Something your *merciful* king never did for my people," Lyndis managed to crack the bird's beak open and poured the liquid into the gryphon's gullet. He started choking, trying to spit the substance out, but Lyndis clamped his beak shut with both hands, watching the bird's throat attentively. When he swallowed, she let him crash in the snow to quickly patch him up with the little strips of bandage she had in her field kit. She kept a close eye on his limbs and wing, as she very well knew the gryphon could strike back at any moment.

Fortunately, he was smarter than that.

"There," Lyndis slapped the creature's back once she stopped the brunt of the bleeding. "Live to fight another day, crow, and when you find yourself in a warm, cozy bed aboard an airship or whatever, let your commander know who spared your life."

She expected a screech of defiance, as gryphons were proud, loyal creatures, yet close encounters with death had a way to change one's perception. The golden gryphon dipped his head, a few soft chirps escaping through his beak instead of the violent screech of a warning call.

"I cannot promise they'll listen, but I promise to never forget this kindness. Run now, matron of mercy. They're...coming for you."

As if on cue, she heard several more shrieks, followed by the roar of a dragon. Lyndis waved the gryphon a quick farewell and broke into a run in that direction.

Curses. Why couldn't I just plunge my blade through his eye and be done with it? They prey upon my kin, destroy our villages, treat us like animals! She curled up her fists at that. She could help Crimson Sky and Arcturus, and instead, she wasted precious time to heal the enemy. Heal him! What would the dragon or any of her people say of such thoughtless deed? Would they consider her weak? A traitor to her own kin, perhaps?

It didn't really matter. Not now, when half of her mind raced as she tried to formulate a plan. Step one, regroup with the rest of the party. Step two, flee into the forest while they all use magic to aid in their escape. She did not know what spells Merlia knew as a ranger, but clearly they would be of use.

She found Arcturus and Crimson Sky relatively quickly, arriving just as the dragon snatched up the human and flew into the sky.

"Follow them closely, and avoid attacking at all costs. I need Arcturus alive, hear me? I want him alive!" Shouted a man clad in black armor that quickly mounted a gryphon and took off. His face was one of surprise and desperation. She knew the expression all too well, as she too was no doubt wearing the exact same one.

Lyndis ducked behind a tree, pulling out the map from her field satchel. She just had to remain calm for now. The dragon was clearly trying to lead the gryphons away from the rest of the group, to a place where he'd snatch an advantage. Most likely he was scared as well, for she had never seen him fly away from a fight.

Lyndis licked her lips and quickly pulled up the map that they had been following before the gryphons had attacked. Her eyes scanned around the various landmarks. She was very close to the location indicated on the map. All she had to do was make it there and pray the magical defenses would help shield her from the gryphons and their armored allies. She could fight off one gryphon by herself, sure, but the whole flock? That was something she did not think she could pull off if they came at her with murder in their minds.

Lyndis hugged a tree once more as she heard the flapping wings. Two gryphons landed nearby, with riders dismounting onto the snow. They wore dark red leathers with gold stitching on the edges. They were both human, towering above the average individual, with muscled, well trained bodies. Their eyes were both brown and squinted as they were turning their heads back and forth, looking for something.

They're after me, she thought as she traced her thumb along the hilt of her rapier. That damn gryphon she saved must've betrayed her at the first opportunity.

"Come on out, half-elf!" One of the men called out in a deep voice, "The boss only wants to talk to you. The dragon is the only one he wants captured."

Lyndis silently clasped her hands together as if to break an egg. She then placed them on her head and let go as she muttered, "Vonuzez."

It felt like the yolk of a large egg landed on her head. The lukewarm sludge started to drip down her hair. The feeling worked its way down her head, into her chest, and all the way down to her feet in a matter of moments. She knew that the spell had worked when a cold tinge ran up her spine. She was invisible now. With a grin to herself, she sprinted away from the collected four, towards her destination on the map.

The spell only lasted for a minute. She knew this when she felt a warming sensation flow through her body. It happened just like the previous one, starting from her head then finishing in her feet. She made sure to hug a tree when the enchantment wore off. Lyndis held a hand to her elven ears, listening for anything that could be the sound of gryphons, or worse, mercs. The half-elf waited for several minutes before moving from her spot, thankful for the blessed silence of the forest. It might have meant her companions were having all the trouble while she sneaked away exactly like a selfish rogue, but in war, this was an advantage she had to exploit.

Gather your wits, Lyndis. You're not the bad gal here. Fock sake, you wasted bandage and potions on one of the king's winged killers! She frowned at the thought of that same bird inflicting misery upon her people months later, all thanks to her mercy. *No!* Lyndis scrunched her eyes shut. *Focus. I need to focus on what I hear, what I see, what I smell...*

Slowly, her eyes opened up. That's when she noticed a pair of boot prints heading off in the direction she was currently aiming at. She might have dismissed them as anyone's at first, but there were clearly large paw prints next to them. She did not know what kind of animal had such a large foot, but she was pretty sure a bear was the most likely outcome. *Good.* That meant Merlia had made it as well. Lyndis shrugged herself. She figured the ranger had not been as slowed down as she was, and if there was any chance to reunite with her party, this was it.

Lyndis broke into a quickened pace. She followed the path left by Merlia, thinking back to a friend of hers in Drenedar. He would have followed these tracks better than anyone. She scowled as he would wear a smug look on his human face and laugh with those blue eyes of his. How his messy blonde hair would jiggle while he enjoyed his moment of fun. She would punch him in the shoulder for good measure at his teasing, and they would move on. His name was Gerald Wind-chaser, a Pegasus knight of the realm. Oh, how she wished she had his skills right now. It would have saved the whole party the trouble of traveling to Entis, after all.

As she jumped over a log, Lyndis remembered the day she left Drenedar, fed up with how everything had gone in her home. She simply got tired of constantly chasing her parents' expectations and decided to pursue a life of adventure instead of looking pretty and dancing and wasting her time on art. More than anything, Lyndis craved to go out there and see the world she had only read about in stories. Besides, why should she not? Her parents had gotten the best teachers of the realm, taught her how to fight, how to defend herself, how to weave magic. Wasn't it a pity, to know such skills, and never put them to proper use?

Lyndis ducked behind another tree, remembering Gerald's sad, lovingly stupid face as he asked her not to go. Deep down, she figured the man had a crush on her, but he had never admitted it. Instead, he provided her with a sending stone that helped them stay in touch; that way, she could tell him if she ever had gotten herself into trouble. She had laughed at the time, "Trouble, Gerald? That's what I am looking, for you silly, silly man."

Lyndis stopped to listen once more. If she had the chance, she would have told her younger self to practice running for the day when her legs would have to outrun a gryphon's wings. She scowled, realizing she knew what her reply would have been, "That sounds fantastic!"

The tracks were getting fresher. Or so it seemed. Although Lyndis wasn't entirely sure, she felt she was making progress. However, something odd had happened with the shapes in the snow. It seemed like Ulga and Merlia had split up. She crouched low for a moment or two, trying to figure out which pair of tracks she should follow. Ulga's tracks seemed to head deeper and deeper into the woods, while Merlia's seemed to have gone towards a clearing.

"Merlia, what in the world were you up to?" Lyndis said to herself softly as she started following Merlia's tracks to the clearing.

When she got closer, she heard the dwarf suddenly shout out.

"O, come now, is that the best ye got in yer gut? I 'ave endured harder hits from me mum!"

Lyndis broke into a run towards the duo. Not to dismiss Merlia's fighting ability, but she figured the dwarf would be happy for some type of help. She made it to the clearing, but stuck to the side, remaining concealed in the shadows of the forest, biding her time to strike. She saw two things before her. One was the motionless gryphon lying in the clearing with an axe beside its body, while the other rested under the creature's talons, probably snatched from Merlia's grasp after a bout of close combat. The second thing she saw was the black armored man, his gloved hand dug into Merlia's neck.

"Oh, come on now, ya can at least put me outta me misery. Tha' breath o'yers could kill a dragon, it can!" Merlia gasped with a chuckle.

"Nobody has to die today, dwarf. All I want to know is the red beast's location. Where did it fly off? Tell me!" The man shouted in anger.

"What's he to ye?" Merlia rasped.

"A thief who stole my best friend, you boulder-headed creature!" The human's face flushed red with anger. "Tell me now, or I'll send my chasers all over the forest with an order to capture the enemy no matter the cost. Do you want to get your dragon back in tatters? Hmm?"

"Awww, did dey get away from ye, y'said? And all yer doing is sit here an' pout? You's a grown man, lad. Slap dat gryphon o'er the head a few times an' find the dragon instead of pickin' on women!" Merlia taunted as the man clearly tightened his grip on her throat.

"I'm interrogating you, lass." The human brought his angry face closer to Merlia's scrunched features. "That means I ask, and you answer."

"Now you're un BEARable," Merlia gasped out, her voice barely audible. "I said you're un BEARable!" She cried out in a weak voice.

"That some kind of code?" The armored man asked as he looked around. "What's that? TELL ME!"

"Gods damn't Ulga, I said the focken word!" Merlia cried, struggling in the man's grasp.

It appeared she was going to succumb to the man's brute strength before Ulga emerged from the other side of the clearing to charge right towards the man in armor. The man dropped the dwarf in surprise as he drew an energy crossbow to blast the bear, but she proved too quick for him. In an instant, the crossbow was torn from his grasp, forcing him to back from the angry bear with his sword drawn.

"That how you wanna do it, lass?" he grunted. "Think well before you strike. My blade never misses its mark."

"Oh, I think today's just not your day, metal-ass." Lyndis took this moment to walk out as well. With a rapier held out in the left hand, she lifted her right hand up as if to curl a ball. She pictured an orb of fire resting in her hands, then let it fly towards the man. From her hand, she threw a fire bolt that collided into the man's back. He was pushed towards the bear in surprise, as Ulga swatted him to the ground with one of her paws.

"See, dats dey way, Ulga!" Merlia cried with a hoarse throat as she grabbed her axes. "Nice of ye ta join da fight, lass!" She raised an axe, pointing to the man in armor. "Help me axe him a few tings." With a dwarven cry, Merlia charged the man.

But he had managed to roll away from Ulga, who was still trying to maul him. Lyndis decided to help as she closed in on the rolling man.

The armored warrior finally stood up. He swung at her first. Lyndis ducked below the blade as she went to stab for his armpit. The man moved quickly to deflect her blow, and instead of his armpit she nicked his forearm. She felt a boot collide with her hard before she could get away like she usually did. Lyndis was shoved to the ground, landing on her backside. The man moved aside as Ulga went to attack him. He side-stepped the bear, then used the momentum to slice deep into Ulga's neck. His sword severed the brave bear's head from the rest of her body in one clean strike.

"Ye wee, clankin' basterd! Do ya know how long it'll take Ulga ta get better from this?" Merlia snarled as she started swinging wildly at the man with her two axes.

"There's no coming back from a severed head, dwarf," The man grunted as he parried Merlia's frenzied attacks.

"It'll take all afta noon, ya stupid egg suckin, full plate wearin git!"

Lyndis shot up as the two fought. Taking advantage of the situation, she moved in to flank the warrior, who was doing a fine job of holding off the dwarf on his own. In fact, his fighting style sort of reminded her of how Arcturus handled his sword. He was maneuvering well enough that she could never get right behind him.

"You're going down, lass!"

"Not before ye!" Merlia rasped.

The man cried out in pain as an axe struck his armor at his left shoulder.

"Ha! Guess ya can't handle all of dis dwarven fury!" Merlia shouted in laughter, but it was short lived as he moved his right hand and punched the dwarf square in her face. Merlia fell back dazed onto the ground. Her eyes were closed, but she was still breathing; merely unconscious from the man's thundering punch.

The man turned towards Lyndis, his face red with irritation.

"It brought me no pleasure to do that, but you're giving me little choice in the matter."

"Yeah?" Lyndis raised an eyebrow. "Looked to me like you enjoy cutting things."

"Only when they attack me first!" The man shouted. "I come to you with questions and orders from my king, and instead of talking, you take off and strike my party back like a bunch of thugs!"

Lyndis scowled at the man. "That tends to happen when you announce your approach with screeches."

"Gah. I would've gotten what I want from the dwarf, but since you're the only one I have, guess you'll have to do, half-elf." He suddenly stopped mid question to stare at her.

"Wait. Have we met before?" He casually asked, holding his great sword out in front of himself.

Lyndis tried to place the face to anyone she had known in her life, back in Drenedar, even when she was exploring. They paced in front of one another for a moment or two. *No.* She had never seen this man before. Why would he even say something like that in the middle of a fight? To distract her? Throw her focus off-balance?

"What's it to you?"

"I like to know who I am fighting, miss. And that dwarf over there would not stop yelling at me. "He said, just as his eyes then went wide. "Aye. My memory didn't falter. I know you!"

*

Lyndis suddenly stopped telling her tale to the dragon and human who listened with utmost interest. Or at least, she thought they were. Crimson Sky kept on taking gulps of wine every few minutes before returning his inebriated stare to her, which only happened after he wiped his snout. He was gasping at all the times she mentioned the fights.

"Did he really know you?" Arcturus asked suddenly. "How is that possible? He never told me anything about a quest in Drenedar."

Lyndis thought for a moment, letting the paladin's question sink into her mind. Would she tell them at this moment? Or would it ruin the image as to why she was really helping them get into Entis? She figured it could wait for later.

"He knew me from your reports on Crimson Sky. Aye. He read them before coming to get us, the literate bastard. Not often I meet a man with a sword who reads out of his own volition," She lied, putting on a fake smile and hoping the paladin was drunk enough to fall for it. Perhaps it was because of the wine, but he just nodded.

"What happened next?" Crimson Sky asked, cocking his head to the side, "Did you die? Or wait, that would mean I'm talking to your spirit or worse, an impostor." The dragon laughed with little hisses before taking yet again another gulp of wine. "Carry on, carry on. Do not mind a drunky dragon's silly comments!"

So, with a slight laugh, and another swig of wine, Lyndis continued her tale, conveniently skipping over to the good part.

*

There was a growing pit in Lyndis' stomach when she stared into the man's eyes. Some silly part of her still hoped he was wrong, and that he only made this up to gain an edge over her, but she had seen those eyes before.

"I never put much faith in Gods, but they certainly have a sense of humor. You're the princess of Drenedar, are you not?" The man said with a grin, "Well princess, my name is Garroth."

"Well then, my kind, confused Garroth, I think you may have me confused with someone else." She said, trying to act indifferent, although she could from his stern face that the man was not buying her lie.

"Nope. I might not trust the Gods to whisper truths in my ears, but my instincts never betrayed me so far. I saw you eight years back, when my crew visited Drenedar."

"Alright," Lyndis shuddered. "Let's say I go with this wild tale you spin, and I am indeed the princess you speak of. What was a brute like you doing in my kingdom?"

"We are adventurers, dear princess. We go where the stream of coin leads us. Long story short, we were paid quite handsomely for a job." Garroth, grinned at his boast. "My, the Gods do seem to piss their favor out of the heavens. I came out here to capture a dragon, but you can imagine my surprise at how the day has unfolded. I have found not only the dragon, but the knowledge that my friend is, thank the gods, alive. To top it off, I also find the princess that conveniently seemed to have plopped right into my lap! Is this your plan, dear? To get revenge for your kingdom by consorting with that red scaled bastard?"

"What do you mean by that, brute? Elaborate!" She spat out, her face full of hate.

"Oh my. Have you not heard, princess? Your kingdom signed a non-aggression pact with us. The war between our kingdoms is finally over!"

"You mean... my family just gave up the fight? After everything your marauding soldiers put us through!?" She shouted, remembering stories of villages being raided and looted by the Lumarian soldiers.

"Yea, I heard from the king himself that your family decided to *see the light of reason,* as it were." The human rested his hands on his hips. "War...such an ugly business. I've not a lot of love for either side, but frankly, this pact frees our armies to focus on the real threat, Rothdell."

Lyndis could not believe the words that came out of that armored bastard's mouth. He was clearly trying to mess with her head. She never had been interested in politics before, hence why she had left to explore in the first place. However, to hear about a pact of peace with Lumara was more than troubling. Clearly her parents were not in the right state of mind, to get into the same bed with the same vile humans that defiled their lands and spat upon their people. They had always advocated standing up to evil, and Lyndis had no reason whatsoever to believe they would give all that up without a fight.

"My words take roots, do they not? Let me explain myself further. At the beginning of this month, we had to stop a band of Pegasus knights. The bastards were doing hit and runs within our borders. They gave us quite a chase, but the result is the same it's always been. We stand, they fall."

"The gods spit on you, vile creature. Answer me one thing before I have your head. Was there a man named Gerald leading them?" She suddenly found herself asking.

"Tall man, blue eyes?" Garroth stroke his chin before a smile crept up his chaffed lips, "Yea, I believe it was him. Last I heard, he and his crew came up north, looking for ya. Had to drop him off to some inquisitors, whose payment is...how should I put it? Enough to turn the other cheek at the distasteful outcome of our mission."

"You fockin' bastard!" Lyndis shouted. With rapier in hand, she charged at the black armored monster, striking towards Garroth with the speed and efficiency of a viper.

The human grinned at her mistake and dodged out of the way. He sliced down with his great sword in a flash. She tried to dodge, but her reckless attack had extended her stance too far. The sword managed to cut through her leather and into her side. Thankfully, her attempt at a dodge had stopped it from slicing clean through her. She fell to the snow, her rapier falling from her grasp.

"That was a bad move, princess. I actually don't reaaaally want to hurt you more than I wound my enemies, but if you force me to fight, a fight you'll get." Garroth said sternly as he approached her prone form.

"B-bastard," Lyndis rasped. She crawled towards her weapon, trying to grab her rapier as her other arm held the blood from gushing out of her sliced flesh. Little spikes of pain made her cry out as she inched herself towards the sword.

"No no no." Her attempts were cut short. Garroth placed a boot firmly on the hilt of the rapier, denying her the weapon. "Come now, princess. You know you can't win against an armored opponent. Just come with me and we can set everything right. I promise it'll be easy. You only have to answer some questions about the dragon, and past that, I am sure we can send you home without too much trouble...or the pain you sought by challenging me. Bold move, that, but what can I say? I've fought too many battles to be taken by surprise." Garroth smiled smugly.

If Lyndis could kill him with her stare, she would do it several times over. How she hated that bastard right now. Once she got out of this binding, she would have to check up on everything she learned from his poisonous mouth. It just did not make any sense, for the world to spin in Garroth's direction. First, the deal with her parents, then Gerald coming to find her with a company of knights? She sat in silence, staring daggers at him.

"This is getting tiresome. Admit defeat. Stop being a sore loser. I am being nice to you right now, which my contract doesn't necessarily require. I could black you out with a punch, tie you up, then haul you over my shoulder If I wish, but instead here we are, talking like two civilized people, so let's make this work, shall we?"

"Yeah..." Lyndis whispered. "Let's work something out."

Garroth smiled. With her eyes locked onto the human, she grabbed his outstretched hand as she pressed down with her boot firmly against the snow. Hopefully, there was not enough that it would stop it from hitting the ground. What luck! She felt the small click of the four-inch dagger popping out from the front of her boot. Lyndis didn't think. She suddenly kicked up, the dagger plunging into Garroth's stomach right below the breastplate with a schlick noise.

"Grraaaah!" His eyes went wide as he felt the blade move inside him, then shortly stumbled back, clutching at the now bleeding wound.

"You thrice-damned bitch! Wha'd you do that for?" He screamed out in pain as he wrenched that monstrous sword out of its sheath, holding it high above his head. "I'm going to slice that pretty body of yours in half!"

"Ye know, perhaps you shoulda bought him dinner lass. It's not good ta slip inta someone without doin dat." Merlia's sudden voice paralyzed the armored warrior.

"Wh-what?!" Garroth's eyes went wide.

Lyndis turned her head to see Merlia holding her bow tight, with an arrow at the ready. "I suggest ya put that sword down, boyo, or I'll send dis arrow here straight inta ya skull."

"You think you scare me with your little bow, dwarf? I dispatched you easily." Garroth spat on the ground. "A single punch was all it took to bring you down, and if you challenge me now, I will make sure the snow turns red with your blood!"

"Tis' true ya got da better of me, but ya been fightin both of us now. Armor or not, yer growin tired, just like any otha' man. Also, now ya got a new hole in ya. Me? I am used ta getting pounded in da face, if you tink ya can get ta me before I loose this arrow, then take yer best shot. However, ya best be thinking what dere lass will do with that rapier. I'd be worried meself, is much larger den da dagger she has you squirmin over."

Garroth looked to the dwarf with fury lit in his eyes, then to Lyndis, who had reclaimed her rapier. She stood up, wincing as her side ached with burning pain.

"I will not be dropping this sword, dwarf. You can pry it from my cold dead fingers before I let it go."

"Suit yerself," Merlia loosed the arrow straight into Garroth's knee. The man howled in pain as the arrowhead went straight through the metal plate covering his kneecap.

"How do ya like dat adamantite arrow, ya clankin bucket o'curses?" Merlia chuckled, "Stings, don't it?"

Garroth still stood his ground with a twisted look of pain on his face. Lyndis slowly advanced on him as Merlia readied another arrow. Garroth suddenly pulled a horn from his pouch, pressed it to his lips, then blew as loud and hard as his lungs allowed. The horn gave out a deep vibrating noise that echoed all around them. Lyndis heard the cries of gryphons returning the horn's call.

Merlia let loose another arrow, but this time the wounded human managed to deflect it with the sword before falling over, grimacing in pain.

Lyndis limped over to Merlia as the dwarf gave Garroth a sour look. "Let's see how ya can be an adventurer now, ya blasted git!"

"Here lass, dis will help wit da pain" Merlia held a hand to where Lyndis had been struck with the greatsword. She tried not to think about the area now stained dark red with her blood. It would not take too long to solve, thanks to the spell prestidigitation, but it was still irritating.

"Vakraas aruune," Merlia uttered, her hand starting to glow green. Lyndis gasped as her side started to feel warm. Within moments, the wound started to seal itself. Lyndis stood up once the spell ended, with a smile of relief on her face.

"There. Nothin' like a cure wounds spell ta set ya straight." Merlia chuckled.

"What about Ulga?" Lyndis started making their way towards the point labeled on the map at a brisk pace.

"Don' worry about Ulga. She's fine," Merlia pulled out a small white orb of light from her pouch. "Ulga be a spirit dat takes on da form of an animal. So don worry yer head about 'er."

Lyndis sighed in relief, "Well that's handy. Where did you end up finding her?"

"Dat be a story for anoder time, lass. Let's just say it be in a, southernmost of Drenedar."

"I look forward to hearing about it." Lyndis grinned.

*

"What forest in Drenedar?" Crimson Sky interrupted, his words shortly followed by another burp from the great beast's throat. "I want to hear that story, lassie!"

"I am in the middle of a story right now, you drunken dragon. Mind your manners, and maybe I'll satisfy your curiosity," Lyndis shot back.

"I for one would like to hear both stories," Hiccupped Arcturus, who was leaning on the dragon for support.

"See? Arcturus here gets it. We demand two stories! Two! Not one, not three, not five. Two's a perfect match. Like us," Crimson Sky dragged the human against his chest with a big grin.

"Let da lass finish da first story before ye get naughty with each other, ye dolts," Melia said, "Den we can focus on tellin my story, if I want ta."

"Do you want to?" Crimson Sky turned his head to the dwarf. His tail was starting to twitch.

"Not righ now dragon!"

"Grrawwww!" Crimson Sky groaned as he looked back to Lyndis.

"Come now, Veled...Crimson Sky. You just have to be patient. Good things come to those who wait. Didn' your mother teach you that?" Arcturus patted the dragon on his scaled back.

"Nice catch paladin. You almost blabbed it out to everyone here!" Crimson Sky hissed.

"I am drunk!" Arcturus cried, throwing his hands up in the air.

"Maybe I should tell them what you paint in your spare time!" Crimson

Sky started to chuckle.

"Buildings and landscapes, of course." Arcturus defended himself. "Wha' d' you expect? Naked ladies? I am a paladin of Lumara for light's sake, claiming no responsibility for whatever comes out of this dragon's maw. It's not my fault your mind goes to the gutter, you red pervert!"

"LADS, LISTEN TO DA ELF'S STORY OR GODS HELP ME I WILL BATTER YA INTA NEXT WEEK!" Merlia shouted so loud that Lyndis thought she might be part dragon. There was a pregnant pause as Crimson Sky and Arcturus looked to Merlia, then to Lyndis. It seemed their squabble was done for now.

"Can I finish the tale then?" Lyndis asked with a coy smile.

"Yes, Lyndis lass. I am most excited to hear how your tale of unmatched bravery ends," Crimson Sky said, his eyes casually looking to Merlia before he scrunched up his muzzle.

"You may continue," Arcturus added at practically the same time.

"Good! Glad you two drunks can still see the same road. So, there we were, once again making our way towards the point on the map..."

*

Lyndis and Merlia had been making their way towards their destination for roughly ten minutes before they had come to a rough landscape littered with rocks, where even the trees had started to recede. Thankfully, they had not heard the screech of gryphons, nor felt their wing beats for a while. Lyndis figured even if they did, Garroth would not be able to keep pace with them, considering the arrow he carried in his knee. Merlia was still chuckling about that incident.

"Imagine what he is gonna say when somebody comes ta him with a contract," She laughed, "I used ta be an adventurer till I took an arrow to da knee!"

"He is most likely going to find a cleric and get it healed. Beasts like him are used to such wounds. They'll just stand up, again and again, until you put them down for good" Lyndis sighed. "Although it will of course buy us some time. Good shooting, lass."

"Ya spoil it, lass. Ya can't let me enjoy his sufferin', can ye?"

"Oh, by all means, keep making the joke, I enjoyed watching him brought down a peg." Lyndis became serious. "So Merlia, how much did you hear back there with Garroth? I forgot to ask after all the action."

"Oh, about how yer actually a princess? I swear on me life I didna hear a word." The dwarf smirked

"And that doesn't bug you in the slightest?"

"Why would dat bug me lass? I be travelin with a god damn fire breathin scaly hatchie an' a paladin outta all the humans in Lumara! Why would ya bein a princess affect me in da slightest?

"I...don't know. I guess I like staying in the shadows." Lyndis sighed in relief. Even if she felt uncomfortable to have someone know her real identity, at least that was a load off her mind. When people had seen her as a princess, they were always trying to impress her, show off. They always acted like they were walking on egg shells around her, and that had always annoyed the eggs out of her. It was different now. As an adventurer, she could be who she wanted; travel unburdened by the needs or opinions of others.

"I still have a favor to ask. Can you not tell Arcturus or Crimson Sky? I am not ready for them to know the truth just yet."

"Why are ya hidin' it? I figure da best way ta have a friendship is ta get everytin on the table. Hidin things only brings pain down da road."

"I don't want them to treat me like a princess, and knowing Crimson Sky..."

"Aye, dragons and princess. Say no more on dat one, but what about the paladin? Seems like a good lad ta me."

"Princess of Drenedar? The land his people were fighting with?" Lyndis raised her shoulders. "Benevolent or not, I think he won't trust me to stay my blade when I get close to that rotten king of his."

"Well, are ya goin to cut da stem off dat rotten apple when we get dere?"

Lyndis thought this over for a moment, thinking about Garroth's words and how her kingdom had given up. She then thought to Gerald. Hopefully, he would be alive, but regretfully, in the hands of inquisitors, who would no doubt try to torture him for any sliver of information.

"If I had the chance, I think I would." Lyndis sighed, "Although I doubt we will get that chance. I need information first. Like the location of a friend of mine, and the details about my parent's surrender. I'd have better luck divining the future in a dragon's dung than trusting the word of that armored git."

"A boyfriend?" Merlia asked with a coy grin.

"Just a friend." Lyndis hissed. "Not that it's any of your business."

"Such a shame. Thought I was gonna hear some juicy details for a moment dere." Merlia chuckled before holding up her pointer finger at Lyndis, "Well dont ya worry ya pretty head about it, I won't say a word about ya bein a princess, even if I tink ya should tell em yerself." The dwarf crossed her arms, "Tho' if you ask me, I'd tell dem soon, before tings get outta hand."

"Thank you Merlia. I'm in your debt."

"Fo dis? Dan't worry 'bout it lass. Tis no problem keepin yer secret."

"Ah, well, I still appreciate it," Replied Lyndis with a shocked smile. She had almost expected the dwarf to go blabbing to Arcturus and Crimson Sky the moment they were reunited. "I will think about telling them soon, like you said. Get everything out on the table. Just not right after I've been chased by gryphons and slashed apart by lying mercs."

The two slowed down to a snail's pace as they approached one of the rocks pictured on the map. Lyndis had brought it out once again, holding it tight as cold winds swept over them. Despite the generously thick clothes, the wind still managed to cut into her flesh like a knife, making her shiver in its embrace.

"How much farther we got?" Merlia asked, "Is it dat rock, I wonder?"

"Not much, and I figure it sort of looks like that rock." Replied Lyndis as they walked over to the prominent landmark. They sat there for a moment in silence as nothing happened.

"Do we gotta say a magic word or somethin?" Merlia asked, "Ah lemme try. Open up, will ya?" she grinned. When nothing happened, her cheerful smile turned to a frown, "Well, it was worth a shot."

Lyndis pulled out the brooch she had stolen from the gang leader, Knives. She rolled it over in her gloved hand, feeling how smooth it was, then walked over to the rock and looked around for a small indentation or something to fit in the brooch. It could be that it activated a hidden door or something. After all, she had seen plenty of hidden doors throughout her many tomb raiding adventures.

"What ya lookin for? I tink it may jus' be a rock."

"Wondering if there's a space I can fit this brooch into..." Lyndis sighed in irritation. "This is a lot harder than it looks like."

"Well I will try it da way passed down onta me by me venerable ancestors." Merlia said, "Stand back lass, yer goin ta see ta legendary dwarvin technique of figurin stuff out."

"If it's so legendary, how comes I never heard of it?" Lyndis crossed her arms with an amused smile.

"It's because it was passed down from dwarf ta dwarf. So, stan' back. A half elf such as yerself could not be doin dis." Merlia's face grew serious as she suddenly gave the rock a good, hard kick.

"That was the technique? To just hit something?" Lyndis shook her head and closed her eyes.

"Aye, but a wee reminder, lass. I kicked it extra hard."

"Greetings, mortals," Came a monotonous voice from the rock that made Lyndis' eyes open wide. She could not believe it; the dwarf's sudden kick must have truly done something, for standing...well, floating before them, was a spectral dragon made of mists. It stood next to them, a transparent blue color that made it hard to make out among the snow, and it looked roughly like Crimson Sky. It had spikes that lined its spectral back, but no wings. Where Crimson Sky had slitted eyes, the spectral dragon had mere holes. The dragon looked to Merlia, then to Lyndis.

"Told ya it'd work!" Merlia cried in laughter, "I could tell by ya face ya didn belie'e me!"

"You may call me Auron." The dragon said, "I am the master's magical guide for mortals that wish to visit her lair. What do you call yourselves, and what is your purpose for coming this far up the mountain?"

"My name is Lyndis Kuxion," Lyndis held out a hand to shake by instinct. Auron just looked at her hand before looking to Merlia. Lyndis put her hand to her side, smiling awkwardly.

"And you are?" asked Auron, once again in that monotone voice of its.

"My name is Merlia Gallowglar, explorer extraordinaire! Merlia shouted out.

"That is quite a long name to bear, Merlia Gallowglar Explorer Extraordinaire." Auron replied.

"No, ya stupid ting. My name is only the first part." Merlia said.

"That is a weird name, Only the first part. Perhaps you have spoken mistakenly?" Auron tilted its spectral head to the side, like Crimson Sky usually did when faced with a conundrum.

"LISTEN CLOSLY YA STUPID, SPOOKY, MONOTONE SPEAKIN, FLOATIN, GHOSTY GIT! MA NAME IS MERLIA GALLOWGLAR!" Merlia shouted, her face turning all red.

Lyndis burst out laughing as Auron just floated in silence for a moment, while the dwarf breathed heavily.

"You did not have to shout so loud, I am not deaf!"

"That's it!" Merlia shouted, holding up her hands as if to strangle the dragon, but Lyndis held up a hand to hold her back.

"Kind Auron, we are here to meet the silver dragon that resides on this mountain. We were with her son, but our party got separated."

"I care not for such details, but since you have a brooch, I will bring you to the master's lair." The ghostly dragon turned and started to float further along the path. "I suggest you follow me closely. The snow has been known to play tricks on the eyes."

"Well, it's not like we have any oder choice, ye spectral basterd," Merlia shrugged, "Guess we gotta follow your bloated butt an' hope ye don' lead us astray."

"Cheer up, Merlia. Perhaps there will be wine there when we arrive. This bloated butt, as you so eloquently put it, is most definitely a valet to a respectable host. When we tell the ruler of these mountains how valiantly we fought to defend her son, she'll see us to a most deserving, most proper reward." Lyndis laughed.

"I can only hope we don' get da short end o' da stick, lass. Most dragons I learnt 'bout weren't the friendly sort."

Lyndis and Merlia followed Auron as he led them around the girth of the mountain, though the ghostly dragon did not speak about his master much unless they asked a direct question. He simply gave out simple answers, that she had lived there for quite some time, and was there to protect the mortals. When asked about her current location, the dragon would not answer. He said something along the lines that his master did not like to give out her location to strangers. Lyndis accepted that much. It made sense, after all. In the back of her mind she hoped her companions were safe and sound, although she had no idea how they would find their way back to the rock. She asked Auron about this, but the dragon instead pointed to a cave that they could see in the distance.

"They are inside already," The dragon said. "You can find the master's lair in there. I suggest you enjoy your stay until the master can be with you." Right after he spoke his piece, Auron suddenly vanished out of thin air with crackling noise akin to thunder.

Lyndis and Merlia made their way to the cave with smiles on their faces. It would be nice to see those two again, especially after the hectic time with Garroth and his gryphon riders.

"Dere!"

Lyndis looked in the direction where Merlia pointed at, and her face filled with dread as she saw the large area of blood in the snow, and the tracks leading to the cave.

"Come on!" Lyndis cried, breaking into a run towards the cave. It could not have been that bad, as judging by the tracks, both of them had walked away from whatever happened. Although, with the amount of blood she saw, she did not know how one of them wasn't dead already. A grim image of Veledar appeared in her mind, as only he would have that much blood to smear along the snow on his way to the cave.

Lyndis was most relieved when she walked up to the cave to find that the two were playfully rolling around the cavern floor. She did not even take notice of the table, the torches, or the food. She was just happy to see her party members alive and in good health.

Chapter 16: Treasure of the Aegis

Lyndis finished the rest of her tale with Arcturus leaning against Veledar's scales. The red had listened well enough, to the point where the dragon didn't even interrupt the story after Merlia scolded them.

"Wonder what's with all the decorations for this fancy cave of yours. You two could not possibly have gotten all of this in here by yourselves," Lyndis raised an eyebrow as she put more food onto her plate.

"Maybe we did. Not like you were here to keep an eye on me." Veledar snorted.

"Or learn the secrets of dragon magic," Arcturus whispered.

"Or that!" the dragon brought his head down and nuzzled through the paladin's hair. "Quick thinking there, partner." He said in return before picking his head up, then flashing a toothy smile at Lyndis. "Oh, it must be inspiring to live with someone as talented as me. Right, half-elf?"

"I've seen better," Lyndis bit onto a chicken leg and chewed a couple of times before the words sunk in deep enough to make her eyebrows furrow. "Wot did you call me? I'm a fockin' adventurer, ya whelp! Been travelin' the land while you practiced the art of sleeping like the lazy wyrm you are!"

"You caught me, Lyndis," Veledar put a paw to his chest. "It burns to have the truth splattered all over my scales. In fact, we dragons don't even need sleep. Laying down with our eyes closed is merely an enjoyable activity we use to trick the other mortals into believing we're similar." Veledar took a quick breath. "While I'm at it, we also don't require such base necessities like food or drink, and our eggs sprout from the ground after we bathe it in flames!"

Lyndis placed her chicken back in the bowl. Eyes narrowed, with a scowl about her face, she pointed the goblet she grabbed at the dragon's snout. "You takin' the piss with me, dragon?"

"No, of course not. Why would I do that?" Veledar cocked his head to look not only confused, but also harmed by the half-elf's words. "Eons ago, our mother Bahamut cursed us to speak only the truth. It's very similar to the words he babbles when he trains," Veledar nudged Arcturus again, who just shoved the snout back with both hands.

"That's not something to make fun of, you little monk. What code do you live by, eh?" The human lunged to grab onto one of the dragon's wings. "The code of eating? Or is it TICKLING?"

"Rawwraaahh!" Veledar swiped his paw around, trying to get the human away from his sensitive membranes...only that Arcturus dodged around and vaulted over his limbs with the agility of a fairy. "Stop. Cease that!" Veledar snarled. "Blasted tickling mink! Your dragon overlord orders you to-"

"I'm sorry. Can't hear you over all the growling!" Arcturus' maneuvers took him behind the dragon, where he straddled the dragon's tail in order to tickle both of his wings at the same time.

Veledar found it infuriating, thrashing about like an untamed beast, while Lyndis and Merlia were laughing their hearts out, going as far as placing bets on who'd win. However, in spite of Arcturus' nimbleness, Veledar had to get lucky only once to dislodge the paladin from his back and restrain him underfoot.

"Not so funny now, is it?" the dragon approached his snout to the human's flushed face. In spite of his tiredness -and drunkiness- Arcturus still kept a serious face on. "Maybe I should get you out of these clothes and repay you in kind."

"Oh noes! I denna think I'm drunk enough ta see dat kind 'o ticklin," Merlia drained her mug with a long swig to cover her eyes with it. "Dere. Ye can hug an' kiss an' do wateva' long as ye keep me ears outta it."

"Yeah, please keep your passions in check until you're secluded in your little private chamber. Feasting isn't all that glamorous when I have a dragon and his human smack their drooly lips together." Lyndis added.

"Hey, nobody said we-"

"No way!" Arcturus cut through the dragon's words, pushing him off. "Get this thing off me, you big, gnarly lizard?"

Veledar did, though he wrinkled his snout at the paladin's *compliment.* "Arcturus saved my life, but I don't like him THAT much. Especially when he besmirches my beauty with his ill-intentioned comments."

"Aye, you insufferable scale-head," Arcturus exchanged a quick eye contact with the dragon before he started to dust himself off. "We're just friends. Not even best friends. Just good ones."

"Who, through a series of unfortunate circumstances, ended up in this cave, alone."

"With him bleeding all over the ground," Arcturus pointed over at the dragon, who nodded his head and agreed with everything that came out of the human's mouth. At the end of that awkward amount of explanation, they resumed their seats at the table, and, in Veledar's case, his original string of thought.

"So you see, my dear master of evasive charms and shadows, we dragons have a secret compartment were we stash food and furniture, among other important items of course." He said, holding his snout up. There was a pregnant pause as Arcturus and the others just sat in silence.

"Does that include presents for your lover?" Lyndis raised an eyebrow. "Cause even after that mile-long explanation, I still notice the way you look at him."

"Hmph, I guess you don't get sarcastic humor, or the fact that I'm heavily in his debt after what he did to me after I passed out," He closed his eyes. Everyone burst out chuckling and laughing.

"No. No. No! I didn't mean- That wasn't the joke!" Veledar shoved the human forward. "Arcturus, explain to these two harpies that they are laughing at the wrong part of my joke for all the wrong reason!"

"Wha' just came outta yer mouth?" Merlia shouted as Lyndis and Arcturus continued laughing. "C'mon, say it again. What did ya call me, ye scaly rug?"

Veledar moved behind Arcturus. "Well you see, I referred to you as a harpy. You know, one of those screechy ladies with feathery wings." He stuck his tongue out at her playfully. Merlia waved a turkey leg at the dragon and gave him the stink eye.

"Someday, that mouth o'yers is gonna get ya in trouble!"

"Never did so far," Veledar turned towards Lyndis. "As for you, dear Lyndis, I believe the cave has a spell cast upon it that creates whatever I want, as long as I visualize the particular object in my mind." Veledar stepped around Arcturus. "Dragon magic is such a marvel, isn't it?"

"That is a neat little trick to have. Wonder why it is you that can create things. I honestly wish the places we visited had the charm of this cave." Lyndis smiled, then took a bite from her meal.

"Probably a leftover spell left behind by Mother to accommodate in case her son visited. Or maybe it applies to all dragons. No way to know for sure unless I make you all sprout scales, right?" Veledar cocked his head to the side like he did whenever he was feeling smart or guilty.

"Like that's ever going to happen," Lyndis said. "So, you know what happened to us, but what about your romantic story of blood, death, and revival? Last I heard, you were being chased by gryphons. Then there was all the blood splattered outside. I was afraid one of you was going to be stiff as the stone. Which reminds me," The rogue stood up to walk over and placed a finger on Arcturus. With a quick flash of purple light, all the blood stains on his clothes were gone. "Little prestidigitation. Cleans up clothes faster than his tongue." She made a quick funny gesture at Veledar.

"Gratitude," Arcturus mumbled. He guessed he did not even notice the messy state of his clothes with everything that followed the discovery of this cave.

Arcturus looked over to the dragon, who was busy slurping more wine from a barrel. Lyndis' words made him think back to how his friend had laid so broken before him. Past all the jokes and food. there was real pain to talk about; so Arcturus told Lyndis and Merlia the story of Veledar's flight through the sky. Garroth's pursuit, and the dreaded crash that had almost claimed the dragon's life. He watched Lyndis' eyes light up with worry as he described the extent of the dragon's wounds. Luckily, her concerned gaze quickly shifted to one of curiosity.

"He doesn't look too worse for wear now. I wonder how his wounds healed so well. Did you kiss him on the snout like that prince charming you humans love to write about?"

"I am naturally a fast healer." Veledar said, puffing out his chest, "And that's just one of my many amazing abilities as a dragon."

"Even so." Lyndis said, voice full of skepticism." It sounds like you should be dead, oh, amazing one."

"Well that is a different story, I-" began Arcturus.

Veledar then extended a wing to block off Arcturus from Lyndis, "Pleaded for my life to the dragon goddess Bahamut, who was kind enough to heal my wounds." Veledar interrupted.

"Really?" he heard Lyndis reply, "I don't picture you pleading for anything. Some little spark in me tells me that you might be lying, your greatness."

Arcturus grabbed the dragon's wing and forcibly folded it to once again see the half elf.

"It was sort of like that, except Bahamut made me her paladin to save this one's life."

Arcturus held up a hand and thought back to earlier, on how he had healed Veledar's wounds. His focus was rewarded with the white glow he became familiar with.

"And you doubted me like a bunch of silly harpies," Veledar hissed.

"You did not tell the whole story!" she shot back.

Lyndis then leaped towards Arcturus, grabbed his hand, and held it close to her amber eyes. She bombarded him with questions like how this new power felt, if it made any changes to his body or carried any obvious side effects. He answered each one in turn, watching as each answer simply added to her curiosity.

"Okay, okay. This story sounds reasonable after you explained everything that happened." She took another swig of wine. "So I figure Crimson Sky's plan is to simply get drunk and wait for his mother to return?"

Arcturus began to nod as Veledar let everyone know his thoughts on the matter. "Yes, dear Lyndis, that is indeed my master plan...won't mother be surprised after she sees all these barrels?"

"I bet she will." Lyndis chuckled. "Course, I think we all need such moments after the days we had. And since you are such a good host, can you think of some more delicious food and wine to dull the mind and raise the spirits? Try to picture up some better wine than what we had so far. Not that it isn't good, but I'm sure a splendorous male like yourself can do better."

Arcturus watched the dragon sit perfectly still as he was no doubt picturing what Lyndis had asked of him. On the table, instead of empty mugs, breadcrumbs and chewed bones, suddenly appeared another feast. The wine bottles were refilled, and of course Veledar's barrels soared along with them.

"Are you satisfied with my incredible abilities now?" He grinned, opening his eyes with a tap of his tail.

Lyndis grabbed a bottle, some more food, then replied with a cheerful, "I could kiss your scaly tail right now!"

Arcturus grabbed some more food for his plate, mashed potatoes, and some peas. "Tell me, Crimson Sky, what is in this book of yours? I know you explained why it was so important to you, but what's really in it?"

"The book that was stolen from me? It has writings in it, of course." The dragon turned away, obviously trying to avoid the subject.

"You didn't answer the question, O', scaly one." He said, pushing the dragon a bit.

"Ah....well..." Veledar turned to each one of them before sighing and closing his eyes. "It is a hatchling book. Filled with stories of valiant dragons.

"You mean ta tell me, yer willin ta go bring yerself ta near death ova a children story?" Merlia burst out.

"And let them get away with stealing it? No way that's going to happen. Besides it being a strong memory of my mother and brother, I cannot let him, even if he is a king, to get away with that." Veledar growled.

"Besides, with all of your help, once we get inside and have the king where we want him, I'm sure he will tell us where this precious item of mine is."

"Why would he go about telling us such a silly piece of information?" Lyndis asked.

"Oh, dearest Lyndis, you know that I am a dragon. So, by extension, you know I can be quite persuasive when the need strikes." Veledar snorted, letting a small plume of black smoke escape his nostrils.

"Now I'm curious about one thing. What accounts as children stories to a dragon." Arcturus asked.

"Still nagging me? After I have spilled my heart out to you?"

Arcturus stared at the dragon without even blinking. He just took another sip of wine, then downed it in one single gulp.

"Curse you!" Veledar cried, throwing his head back in a hiss of laughter.

"It is the story of an evil dragon that had enslaved the whole world in his claws. Then, a heroic dragon rises against him, and being beset upon by all sides by the evil dragon's minions, he emerges victorious through cunning and courage. He takes the villain's magic items and such, locking them away in a place where evil can never use them again," Veledar waved his paw dismissively at the last part. "Are you satisfied?"

"I most am now, kind dragon. Thank you for sharing." Arcturus replied

"Why lock the magic items away instead of destroying them? Seems to me they would simply fall into the wrong hands later." Lyndis reclined in her chair with a creaking of the wood.

"Lyndis...isn't your throat starting to sting after all these questions you ask? It is because dragons don't destroy beautifully created items. Even if they were weapons." Veledar turned to her, speaking as if to a child.

Lyndis seemed to catch onto this as she narrowed her eyes and shot daggers with them at the dragon. Merlia just let out a loud laugh, followed by a loud burp.

"Reminds me of home, da bickerin, da drinken, ah, tis good."

"Really? A dragon, human, and half-elf remind you of home?" Veledar tilted his head to the side.

"Well... close is a betta word fer it. Bein da middle child of eighteen brothers an sisters, ya see a lot o dis." She then held up a hand, "Before ye can say anytin, yes, me mum and dad got busy a lot. No dat is not usual for dwarves." She took another swig of wine, letting out a satisfied gasp.

"See, Crimson Sky here reminds me of me brother, Ustis, always full of himself and quick to act. Lyndis dere is like me sister Rita, who always likes ta push buttons and see what she can git away wit."

"And whom does Arcturus remind you of?" Veledar grinned, "An uptight uncle? Or a nervous runt of the family?"

Everyone let out a chuckle as Arcturus simply stared at the dragon.

"Oh, come now, Arcturus, it was just a jest." Veledar said, strolling over and wrapping a wing around the human, then turned back to the others and said in a hushed voice, "He's a bit sensitive on the ears."

"I heard that," He replied, trying to shove the dragon away, but the wing held tight.

"Oh, I know you did, my bipedal, skinny little hatchling," Veledar leaned in with his snout, then suddenly stopped. He sniffed in deeply, then grinned. "Did you know you smell good?"

"Excuse me?" Arcturus asked, taken aback by the strange nature of the question. He was not sure how to respond to that as Veledar moved in, and despite his squirming, started sniffing his hair.

"You don't smell like you did before. You smell more like a dragon."

Veledar explained, each word accompanied with a sniff.

"Yea, because I have a dragon that won't stop grabbing at every part of me!" Arcturus said, still trying to shove the persistent dragon away from him. He turned to the girls, "Ladies, can you help me get this ornery bastard off?"

Lyndis stifled a laugh, and Merlia just burst out once again. "I tink you will do a fine job gittin da dragon off."

With a final shove, he was finally able to get the dragon away from him.

"What was that about?" he asked. Veledar sat down on his haunches, still looking at him.

"You just smell different! Why is that so difficult to believe? By Bahamut's light. You would think you'd take that as a well-meant compliment. Figures it's beyond a human to take a compliment from a dragon." Veledar replied, but Arcturus noticed he was fidgeting. It looked, by the way his muscles tensed, that he was bracing himself for something. Was he trying to goad him into tackling games? He watched Veledar get up and start to stroll right past him, the dragon's eyes on him the entire time. Arcturus feigned a pounce at the dragon for Veledar to suddenly leap away.

"Aha! You were trying to start another grapple!" He shouted as Veledar started hissing in laughter.

"Well played, Arcturus. You have picked apart the veil of my expertly crafted plans." Veledar said, giving a slight bow. The dragon returned to the table and started feasting once again, although he almost knocked Lyndis out of her chair.

"Watch where you're fockin going!" the princess barely caught herself from falling.

The night continued with revelry as the group tried darts from Merlia's pack. The dwarf, of course, was the best at it, nearly getting bull's eyes the entire time. Veledar on the other hand complained about the dart's size for ages. After another round of drinks and a round of giggling laughter, Veledar tried once again to sniff Arcturus, however, this time, the human thankfully remained out of the dragon's grasp.

When they were all starting to tire from the revelry, Veledar summoned up some beds for them to sleep on, while the tables, food, and drink vanished into thin air. Arcturus climbed in the bed meant for him, which was very similar to the one he had at home. However, despite how much it looked like it, the bed hardly felt or smelled the same. He looked over to Veledar. The dragon had curled up on a bed of cushions and blankets. He looked peaceful as he clutched the small form of a stuffed purple dragon he had conjured up.

Although Arcturus sighed in relief that the dragon finally had a stuffed animal to use, he felt a hint of disappointment in the back of his mind. He missed the warmth of the dragon, along with the soothing sound of his heartbeat. Arcturus shook his head and settled his head into his pillow. There would be time to talk about that tomorrow, so he closed his eyes and let sleep take him.

*

The next morning, Arcturus awoke soundly, stifling a loud yawn as he stretched out within the sheets. He looked around the dimly lit cave. It looked like Lyndis was still asleep in a bed covered in blue and gold; Drenedar's colors. Arcturus sat up, noticing that Merlia could not be found within the cave. He scanned several times with his eyes to confirm this, then pushed the worry from his mind as he figured she was simply out hunting for breakfast or doing her usual dwarf things. Lastly, Arcturus looked over to the sleeping form of Veledar, who was still curled up on his cushions. With each breath, the dragon had bits of smoke escape from his nostrils. Arcturus figured the dragon would have a hangover. The amount of drink he had the night before was a tale in itself.

Arcturus rummaged through his pack to find a roll of toilet tissue along with a small shovel. He did not relish the idea of heading out into the snow to do this task, but nevertheless, it needed to be done. With a sigh, he left the cavern to be greeted by the sun just starting to rise over the mountains. Arcturus breathed in deep, his breath letting him know just how cold it was, almost making the moist air that rushed out look like a dragon's smoke. If only he could warm up the air around him with a spell...With a sigh, Arcturus went as quickly as he could about his business, then returned to the toasty comfort of the cave.

He placed his things back into the pack, noting that Veledar had rolled over so that his belly was facing towards the ceiling. Arcturus grinned at such wondrous sight. He would have to remember this undignified way his friend was sleeping in. It would probably annoy the dragon that his regal attitude would be a tad tarnished, although this was one of the many things Arcturus cooked up on his list of mischief. He snickered, starting his morning stretches with a smile on his face.

With his eyes closed, the paladin focused on his movements, just like he had done every morning. This time, he also tried to focus on his new powers. Maybe he would gain some insight into the strange power that cured wounds no man ever heard of. He had gotten halfway through his routine when he felt a pair of eyes on him. He opened his own to find Veledar within arm's reach, mimicking his movements. Arcturus did not know how the dragon had been so quiet as to avoid detection. Perhaps he had been too deep in thought to notice.

"How's the head?" Arcturus gestured towards a mug of ale. "Must have been quite a night for your stomach to make sense of all that alcohol."

"Not as bad as you might think. Dragons have a stomach for such things." Veledar replied, puffing his chest out, making Arcturus roll his eyes.

"Will you ever admit your shortcomings? Just a little one, at least? Nobody's perfect, you know."

"Perhaps..." The dragon lowered his head so that the two of them stared into each other's eyes, "but that doesn't stop me from trying."

Arcturus returned to his last set of movements, arms stertched, palms open. If you had told him months ago that he would be in a cave, doing his morning ritual with a dragon right beside him, shadowing every movement, he would not have believed one word of it.

"Did you see Merlia leave?" Veledar asked, copying Arcturus perfectly. "I noticed that she is not to be found within the cave."

"I figured she is out hunting or something, although I can't imagine why, when we can simply summon all the food we need here."

"Take it from a predator of no equal. Nothing beats the thrill of the hunt, or taking pride in your success after a difficult chase." Veledar replied with a grin. The dragon's stomach gave a loud grumble, causing him to grab at it and look down. "Although I think this morning I will go with the conjured food. We don't need your old, crazy, sword-for-hire friend spot me in the sky a second time." The last part must've been quite distasteful as Veledar wrinkled his snout.

"Garroth's gone to explain his failures and honor new contracts. He won't be bothering us unless we're stupid. And we're not stupid, right?"

The dragon gave a quick nod of his head. He closed his eyes once again and thought on the morning menu. The tables and chairs from last night reappeared in an instant, although now they had breakfast food upon them, with steaming hot coffee replacing the wine. Arcturus felt his mouth water from the smells of the eggs, toast, waffles, bacon, and other assortments of incredible foods.

"Well, I figure I can eat as well now that my concentration has been blown to pieces. You do know how to distract me, Veledar."

"Oh, I can distract you?" The dragon replied, showing off his teeth with a coy grin.

"Aye." Arcturus chuckled, taking a seat beside the dragon, who had settled onto his haunches at the table. Arcturus emulated his example by sitting on a chair. He picked up a fork and dug it into a stack of toast, pulling it over to his plate and taking a bite. He only stopped his eating to sip from his coffee. That's when Lyndis came over and sat into her chair without a word.

"Have a good night Lyn..." Veledar went to say, moving his snout lower towards her. She held up a hand and silenced the dragon by placing her hand on his snout.

"After my coffee, Crimson Sky." She grumbled, not even turning her head towards him.

"Fine, fine." Veledar pouted. "But mark my words. I will have my revenge."

"Yea, whatever you say, wise lord." She grabbed a cup of coffee with two hands and took the smell of it with a satisfied sigh.

They ate in silence after that. Arcturus kept eyeing Veledar, and the dragon kept looking to him and Lyndis as if planning his next move. He was about to ask what it was about when Merlia strolled in from the entrance.

"Well good ta see ya sleepy heads up! Thought ye were goin to sleep da day away!"

The dwarf strolled over to the table and clasped her hands together loudly.

"Looks like ya got quite da spread dere." She said, "Don' mind if I do," she continued, taking a bit of everything onto a plate of her own. "Ya know, you humans haf ta be given credit fer coffee. It's da best ting ta have in the mornin."

"That's not true. The best thing in the morning is the morning hunt, closely followed by the first breath of fire." Veledar announced loudly and proudly.

"Oh really? Well, some of us arn't fire breathin' scaly birds, are we?" she laughed, taking a bite of bacon.

"I am not a bird. Clearly, I am a dragon, and if you are dense like the stone beneath your..." Veledar said as he started to trail off. "But of course, you already know who I am, what I am. You're trying to provoke me, Merlia, and that is not a wise decision when I speak from an empty stomach." He squinted his eyes as everyone held back a laugh. "Fine, I guess I will go about finding the REAL entrance to my mother's cave while you eat." Veledar stood up and strolled over to the far cavern wall, with his snout held high, and his tail swaying as he walked.

Arcturus turned to the others as they continued to eat as if nothing happened. "I best go see what that silly winged lizard is doing before he brings down the cave or something worse on our heads."

The girls just nodded through mouths full of food as Arcturus stood up. He turned around and made his way swiftly to the dragon who had started pacing along the wall. Veledar had his left paw on it, touching and scraping in locations. The red dragon seemed to ignore him as he stood there, but he did see the dragon's eyes find him once or twice for a moment before he continued with his inspection of the wall.

At some point in his search, Veledar sat on his haunches and touched a claw to his snout, as if in deep thought.

"Your mother...she do this kind of stuff before?" Arcturus finally asked the silent dragon.

"Of course she did. She would move her entrance around on us when we were but a bunch of underdeveloped scales and tiny, flappy wings."

"Wait. You mean to tell me that…" the human gave a shake of his head. "Gods, this sounds just as ridiculous as the infinite food spell, but did she move the entrance to her cave…in another place?" Arcturus asked. "Surely she did not hire people to move her treasure afterwards."

"You're thinking just like a human, Arcturus. Mundane. My mother connected her cave to another plane of existence, all for the purpose of hiding her treasure. Think of it like one of those magical bags of holding." Veledar gestured to one of Arcturus' coin purses. "Just think of it like that, on a much, much larger scale."

"Bag of holding?" Arcturus asked. He figured it was a magical item of sorts, obviously meant to hold things.

"Yes, they are much bigger on the inside. I had heard stories that adventurers simply love those spacious things. Mother's treasure trove was sort of like that. Too big for any other place to hold it," Veledar explained. Suddenly, he stopped as his claw touched the wall. "Aha!" he cried out.

Arcturus looked to the dragon's sharp claw tip. It simply looked like a normal spot to him. Veledar then traced a line with the claw towards the cavern floor before walking over a few paces and tracing the same line up. Arcturus could see that, as the dragon worked. a large grin spread over his snout, his chest swollen with bursting pride. Veledar finished his work by letting out a harsh growl, but Arcturus figured he had just said something in draconic.

Veledar looked back for a moment as a red glowing light emerged from the place where the dragon had drawn the line with his claw. It looked like the outline of a door, fifteen feet roughly high, and twenty feet wide. Arcturus felt his jaw open and stay agape as the wall then parted into two sections that slowly gave way to a tunnel. The tunnel seemed to go off towards the left, and its floor was made of rough, uneven stone.

"May want to close your ugly human snout," Veledar said with an amused snort. "Save your awe for when you see my mother's enormous hoard."

Arcturus looked back towards the girls, who were still eating. They seemed to be unfazed by the fact that a large door had just appeared and opened.

"Come. Let's go see it for a moment. I am sure they won't mind in the slightest."

Arcturus thought about the dragon's offer for a moment, then his thoughts began to race at what they were going to see. Surely it could not be that much. He pictured a large room, perhaps filled to the ceiling with coins and gems…

"Arcturus?" Veledar snapped Arcturus out of his day dream.

Veledar had moved ahead twenty feet and was gesturing for Arcturus to follow.

"Going to scout ahead, lasses!" Arcturus cried out back to his companions.

"Don't get yourself killed by falling rocks or smothered by that lizard's snout!" Lyndis replied through a new mouthful of food.

Arcturus shrugged off that joke, took a deep breath, and followed his friend into the tunnel. On his way, he picked up a torch that was lining the walls. It was a relief, not to have to walk in the dark and rely on Veledar's eyes the entire time. He planned to ask how far they had to go when he accidentally bumped into Veledar when the dragon suddenly stopped still. Arcturus made his way to his friend's side and gasped at what he saw. What lay before him was something no man could imagine. Not even in his wildest dreams could he picture a hoard like this. Mountains of gold coins as far as his eyes could see. Every so often, there was a small bowl of fire that would illuminate the metallic coins around them with a warm glow. Among the sea of gold, he spied specks of every color, no doubt gems stashed away within the hoard. He could not tear his eyes away from the shiny metals, for the longer he stared, the more and more he could see scattered within the treasure trove.

He saw bookcases with rows upon rows of books, weapons, art of all sorts, and even suits of armor on stands. Within the vast sea of treasure there was path, a division within the gold, obviously meant to be walked upon. It was roughly fifteen feet wide and seemed to be made of silver coins. From the edge of his vision he saw Veledar's snout get close to his face. So close that he could touch it by simply reaching out.

"I told you." The dragon nuzzled his cheek. "Behold my mother's hoard! No doubt the greatest treasure trove in the entire land, if not the entire world!"

Arcturus heard Veledar boast before, but this sounded a bit different. Was that jealousy that he heard in his voice? He grinned as he crossed his arms. "Gods above...you're jealous!"

"I am not jealous of my mother, you silly human. That would be RIDICULOUS!" Veledar replied. However, Arcturus noticed that the dragon would not look at him when he said that.

"Yet here we are, dragon-jealous-of-his-own-mother's-treasure-trove."

Veledar only held up his head for a moment before letting out a large groan. "Fine. Yes, as a hatchling, and even when I was younger, I yearned to have all of this." Veledar held out his paws and gestured to all of the treasure. "I mean, what dragon wouldn't dream of something so vast? However, I grew up, realigned my priorities, realized life's not only a quest for treasure."

Arcturus' grin grew larger as Veledar still kept his head away as he spoke.

"That has to be the worst singular lie I've heard from you. I can practically see that jealousy as you look out at all that bounty of jewels and gold. Admit it, dearest Veledar."

"No." Veledar replied, sticking his tongue out.

"Yes."

"No."

"Yes."

"Fine!" Veledar hissed, then groaned loudly. "I am incredibly jealous of my mother's ability to amass such riches. She almost never left us alone for more than a couple of days. How in the world did she get her paws on...on this glimmering mountain of pure beauty?!"

"So why not fly ahead and greet her? I'll get the others and follow the path to catch up." Arcturus said, patting Veledar's side.

"I can't do that. Would be rude to abandon my guests."

"Can't a grown dragon go about seeing his mother when he pleases?"

"It's a tad more complicated than that." Veledar fidgeted, then turned his snout as if to look for his mother. "I brought you three to her lair, I need to lead you to her. To let you three wander would be rude and foolish," Veledar grinned, showing off his teeth. "Besides, you get the benefit of my company!"

"Come on. We both know there's more to that. You don't want to let her know something is wrong. Or that you might be desperate for help." Arcturus added, to which Veledar simply answered with a silent growl, although the dragon did look to him out of the corner of his eye. Arcturus figured he had hit it right on the head.

"What ever gave you the idea that I was desperate?"

"The incident with the gryphons is pretty obvious. I figure you might take your time explaining the situation to her. Then ask her for help without actually asking for it."

"Bahamut's platinum scales...you might understand dragons better than I thought." Veledar tapped the tip of a claw to a coin on the ground. Then the dragon turned around, his tail passing inches over Arcturus' head. He followed the dragon back through the tunnel. It did not take long to get back to the main cave. Lyndis had packed her things and was meditating on a small rug that she had laid out. The rug was of course blue and gold. Merlia had both hands cupping the little orb of light that was Ulga. She appeared to be whispering to it, if her closeness was any indication.

Arcturus made his way to his armor and started to strap the pieces one by one. He paused as he looked to the tabard that had been practically shredded to pieces, now back to a pristine condition. He shifted his gaze up to find Lyndis looking at him.

"Figured I'd fix it with another prestidigitation. Can't have you running around with a ruined tabard." The half-elf smiled.

Arcturus offered her a quick thanks and continued putting on his gambeson and armor. He would have to thank Matilda a thousand times every time the armor attached itself at the mere press of a rune. Not only did it save him plenty of time donning the entire suit of his armor, but it allowed him to do it himself. He stopped as it occurred to him he was being watched. He turned to find Veledar sitting on his haunches, staring at him intently.

"You know, if I had killed you, I would have taken your armor and hung it in my lair." The dragon said.

"Touching, to think you would've held on to a piece of me long past my death." He replied, giving Veledar a glare.

Realizing his error, Veledar soon continued further, "I mean to say that anything magical in nature should be treasured. I was trying to pay your fancy steel suit, and thus you, a compliment."

If Arcturus knew better, he believed he just saw a look of embarrassment on the dragon's snout.

"Now, continuing about the armor, who made it for you?" Veledar inched closer and grabbed Arcturus' right arm, his grasp firm, but not to the point of hurting the man inside. Veledar held fast as Arcturus tried to pull his arm away. The dragon held out a claw and traced it over one of the small runes on the vambraces.

"All of these pieces have fine craftsmanship. It's obvious you didn't make it."

"How did you know that?" He replied, slightly offended that Veledar simply could not fathom a paladin making anything as grand as a suit of self-attaching plate.

"I have observed your talents, and trust me I, don't think you would spend your time donning the role of a blacksmith, unless you're hiding that part of yourself from me."

"Well I did mention I like to paint, so I do create when the possibility arises."

"I remember that." Veledar smirked, no doubt remembering the night before. "However, painting is not the same as creating magical armor."

"Fine, you inquisitive beast. A gnome made it for me. One going by the name of Matilda. She was one of my remaining friends back in Entis. You should actually meet her, now that I think about it."

"And just why should I grant this gnome my esteemed presence?" Veledar replied, letting go and starting to circle him closely. It was obvious he was still inspecting the armor.

"Why have you not done this before? We have been traveling for a quite some time now." Arcturus tried to push Veledar away lightly, but the dragon did not yield and continued his inspection.

"I figured I was doing more important things. Now back to your gnome friend, and the clever way you avoided my question."

"Thought it's obvious by now. She loves magical things, items, armor, weapons, and even creatures. I think it is kind of a fancy of hers to meet a dragon in person. Well, one not like Dread Flame. You get my meaning."

"I will have to think about it, granted, if she shows the interest you speak of."

"So let me get this right. You only want to meet her if she fawns over you?" Arcturus smirked as he grabbed his vambraces and attached them. He clenched his gloved hand, testing the feel. Thankfully, he found everything snug. Next up, he swung his pack around his back, stowed his longsword, and picked up his shield. He looked up to see that Merlia and Lyndis had strolled on over. They had all their gear ready as well. Lyndis was the first to talk and asked the same question about Veledar going on ahead to meet his mother. Veledar just sighed and gave her the same answer that he had given him. Arcturus noted the slight hint of confusion on her face.

"Should we expect trouble then?" Lyndis asked, looking past the dragon, into the depths of the tunnel.

Veledar seemed slightly taken aback. "Of course not. My mother would never harm me or my guests. Now, if you were not invited, you might be in trouble because she might think you were thieves." With that final word, Veledar turned his eyes to some other place.

"Well, how big is it?" Lyndis asked, her eyes seeming to grow in size.

"It is rather hard to do it justice with mere words, but it's probably the most amount of coin and treasure I have ever seen." Arcturus blurted out, causing Veledar to turn his snout to him.

Lyndis dismissively waved at Arcturus. "I'll be the judge of that. I have certainly seen a lot of coin in my time."

"That so?" Merlia replied with a sly grin.

Arcturus was about to ask Merlia why Ulga had not reformed yet, yet instead, he had to rush after Lyndis, who started sprinting down the tunnel. He followed the half-elf down the route Veledar had brought him until he was once again standing before the great hoard of treasure. Lyndis stood unmoving and speechless, Merlia joined them and added, "By Thor's beard..."

"This has to be a trick! No way this is real!" Shouted Lyndis, spinning around and pointing her finger at Veledar.

"There isn't even this much treasure in all of Drenedar's vaults. This has got to be an illusion. No dragon can ever gather this amount on its own. What, are you going to tell me your mother can will gold and jewels into existence? It certainly worked with our meal back there."

Veledar held a paw up to his chest, "My dear Lyndis, I assure you, everything your eyes see is real." His lips stretched into a toothy smile, "But

I'm glad my mother's hoard got that reaction out of you. It's funny when an experienced adventurer makes that kind of face."

"Alright then, red butt. Why are you so proud of it all of a sudden? It isn't your treasure yet. I figure that a proud dragon like you, who has to state how amazing he is every few minutes you, would be jealous before proud of something greater than his."

Arcturus held back a laughter filled snort. Somehow, Lyndis had hit the nail right on the head.

"Not a word unless you want to replace my toy tonight," Veledar growled quietly at him.

"I wouldn't mind that." Arcturus chuckled.

"Really?"

The dragon's eyes widened a little. With hope or excitement, Arcturus did not know.

Veledar then started leading them along the silver coin-laden path.

"You see, Lyndis, all of this -as in every coin, sword, book, gear, shield, and scale polishing tool you can find- will be mine in due time."

That surprised Arcturus. He always considered dragons hid everything from their families. Or was it simply possible that Veledar's family was something of an exception in that regard? He had assumed that even in death, a dragon would refuse to part ways with their hard-earned hoard.

"Why would she do that? Arcturus, is this normal for dragons?" Lyndis asked.

"Why would you ask the human about what is normal for a dragon?" Veledar snorted.

"I would not know," Arcturus replied. "I have actually heard the opposite is common." He then looked up to Veledar. "Although I find with each passing day that Veledar here is something of a conundrum in many ways. He's...special."

Veledar grinned at being called special and returned his gaze to Lyndis, "If you must know," he started inspecting a grandfather clock that was half buried in coins, still ticking away. "My family left behind the tradition of being buried along with one's treasure. We instead passed it to the next of kin. That way, the hoard would grow and grow, reaching the amazing size you can see right now, before your very eyes."

"Speakin of which." Merlia suddenly said, "I been meanin ta ask ya that, Crimson Sky." The dwarf lifted an eyebrow and moved her hands to her hips. "How is it yer mum is silver and ya happen to be red? Do dragons just turn any color they want?"

"Merlia, you wee dwarven lass," Veledar replied, continuing down the silver path, occasionally brushing coins back into their piles with his tail. "I was adopted by the owner of this fine cave. She said she found me in the wilderness, hunting for myself, tougher than most hatchlings she had seen."

Arcturus saw the look of pride grow on the dragon's crimson snout once again. It seemed that, even when talking about himself as a mere child, it was something the red male took pride in. They moved around something that looked like a royal stage coach. It had banners along its white frame, blue and gold, clearly from Drenadar. Arcturus only gave it a momentary glance before walking past it, only stopping when Lyndis shouted out the obvious.

"What is your mother doing with a royal carriage!?"

Arcturus turned around to see a look of confusion and rage on her cherry red face.

"Does she go about stealing my people's things?"

Before Arcturus could speak, Veledar sped right past him, his tail brushing against his side before the dragon was right next to Lyndis.

"Again, you jump to the wrong set of conclusions. I can assure you, from one friend to another, that everything in this hoard was either gift from a benevolent patron, or taken from people of ill repute. My mother was a paragon of goodness and an example to all dragon kind, not just me." Veledar said in a soothing voice. "I saved you all numerous times. We ate together, drank together, adventured together. My mother's better than I. Try to imagine how that looks."

The comparison seemed to calm Lyndis down as she touched the wooden carriage with the palm of her left hand.

"Alright, I believe you, Crimson Sky. Sorry for the outburst back there. I'm just...adventuring always has you assume the worst, you know? That's how you stay alive."

"Thought ya might have some dwarf blood in ya!" Merlia laughed, clasping a hand on the half-elf's shoulder.

"Think nothing of it," Veledar replied, turning his attention back towards the path.

"If you think that is something, you should see the boat of erisaid. It used to belong to a noble or another in some kingdom to the west. Sadly, the name eludes even my great memory."

"Do you mean Rothdell?" Arcturus asked.

"Of course, that's the one, yes indeed," Veledar pointed to Arcturus, "Supposedly, my mother flew overhead, scaring off a group of pirates that had boarded the noble's vessel. After everything was said and done, the man was so grateful to my mother's timely act that he gave her the entire vessel, to which...it is slightly embarrassing to say this, but my mother took that literally." Veledar chuckled, "I figured he meant that he was offering his services or something of that nature. After all, no sane human would part with something so valuable. Right, Arcturus?"

The paladin brushed off his armor teasingly in front of Veledar. "Not for sale." He patted the grumpy dragon on his chin.

They passed through what appeared to be a forest of banners and tapestries hanging overhead by flagpoles. Each flag was either in pristine condition or a tattered mess, depending on their origin.

"Neva ast this, despite bein' in me mind fer a while. How old is yer mother?" Merlia asked.

"That's something you can ask her yourself. I won't be coerced into revealing the secrets of another dragon to a mortal, even if she happens to be a friend of mine," said Veledar, scratching his head with one of his wing talons.

Merlia just crossed her arms and gave a quick "Hmmph. Stella' dragon thinkin' dere. Mayhap I shouldna' argue with ya."

"That is a wise decision. There aren't many times when I emerged victorious out of that one," the paladin said. "Have you decided on what form is Ulga going to take once he is restored?" Arcturus then asked as he let Merlia catch up to him. Lyndis passed ahead to chit chat with Veledar about something.

"Hav'na figured it yet. I'm thinkin' it best be somethin with wings on account of da dragon." She then cupped her hands around her mouth, "If he evah decides to fly us dere!"

"And sully myself with you riffraff? I'd rather eat this hoard than let that happen!" Veledar responded by sticking his tongue out at them.

Arcturus was about to bring up the promise Veledar had made about flying him, when he felt his foot shift. The coins below started to slide all at once, sending the paladin on a ride down a large hill of rolling metal. He tried to grab onto something on his way down, but found nothing for purchase apart from tricky, slippery metal coins. His friends yelled out something as he tumbled down, barely avoiding a rack of armor. He tried his best to avoid all the valuables on the way down. No matter how nice Veledar claimed his mother was, Arcturus did not want to upset the dragoness. Luckily, he managed to grab hold of what looked like a purple looking bar. It was hard to make out in the low light, but with a firm grasp of his metal-clad hand and a tug, he managed to stop his decent down the hill of clattering coins.

What in Bahamut's name happened? Arcturus looked around as the coins slowly started to settle. He looked back up to his friends that were now just small specks on the hill of coins.

"Arcturus! Are you alright there, partner? Must be that armor, dragging your weighty ass down like a boulder. Maybe you should consider borrowing me a few pieces to lighten yourself up." Veledar roared out.

"Yea, I'm fine!" He shouted back, "Caught myself on some sort of purple bar! Don't worry about my armor just yet!"

He tried to move his hand, grabbing the bar, but found it stuck to the surface of it. He gave one large tug and managed to free himself. The paladin then fell backward into the coins with a thump.

"Just was stuck is all! Managed to break free!" he shouted to keep his friends informed of what was happening.

He stood up, reminding himself to not grab the purple rod, just in case he got stuck again. His eyes strained to make out what it was even attached to. He then noticed that it seemed to be part of a larger network of things that resembled a huge spiderweb.

"Oh crap..." he muttered under his breath. Surely Veledar's mother kept away any large spiders from her lair...

"Hey, just to be sure, your mother didn't have a spider problem, did she?" He shouted as his hand went for his sword out of instinct. He scanned the area for the smallest amount of movement.

"What are you even mumbling about? We're on a different plane of existence! There is no way a spider could even get in here!" Veledar replied, Arcturus pictured that he had tilted his head to the side like he usually did in this sort of situation.

"It's kind of weird that I'm faced with something that looks exactly like a web! How do you explain that?"

There was a rustling of coin that caught his attention. Arcturus forgot all about the party upstairs and spun towards the noise, drawing his sword and shield to find...nothing. Another rustling of coins drew his attention. This time the hairs on his back stood on end as he whirled around. Once again, nothing.

Then, he heard it. A slight clicking sound; the same two mandibles might make. He had a second to react as a large bulk collided with him. Sharp mandibles met his shield. Despite the blow being successfully blocked by his shield, he was tossed back into the pile coins by the sheer momentum of the blow.

"Gah, what in the world-" Arcturus looked up to see a spider that stood just as tall as he did. "Oh, figures. Spiders...why does it always have to be spiders?"

The creature had a bluish white carapace and eight blood red eyes that stared menacingly at the human. It went in for another attack as Arcturus lashed out with his sword, his attack managing to slice off two of the creature's legs with a flash of white magic that seemed to burst when his sword met the spider's legs. The spider recoiled in pain, skittering away from him.

"That's convenient," The human smiled and prepared for another assault.

The spider soon recovered and curled its body on itself. For a moment, Arcturus was fazed by such bizarre behavior, then a flash of memories made him remember hearing about how some of the larger spiders could toss webbing at their enemies. His eyes widened in realization as he remembered the purple web from before. He ducked behind a multicolored rack of clothes as the spider loosened its webbing everywhere.

"Gah!" Arcturus gasped. Thankfully, he was protected quite effectively behind the bulwark of clothing, as no bits of webbing latched onto him. He breathed a sigh of relief right before he heard the sound of a large crack. He stood up, sword in hand, to see that the spider was nowhere to be found. His eyes looked in desperation at all the scattered treasure, the mounds certainly large enough to hide the spider. The grip on his sword tightened.

"Hey, we have some sort of giant spider down here!" He shouted out to his friends, "It's big, weird, and white, with the creepiest bunch of eyes I've seen! Red! They're red just like Crimson's scales!"

Another loud crack graced his ears as the spider returned to attack him from the left. Arcturus still believed he had the advantage, yet somehow, the creature walked too straight. Too quickly.

It had regrown its legs, and now the vicious creature pressed on to finish what it started.

"Crap!" Arcturus raised his shield to block, but the wall of steel merely deflected the creature's attack so that the mandibles grasped around his armored leg. Thankfully, before the creature could slice his leg clean off, Arcturus stabbed downward with his sword into the creature's head. With another flash of white magic, the sword sunk right through the creature's head, causing it to flail and screech, but Arcturus held firm. The spider then collapsed, a corpse adding to the ground made of coins. Arcturus sighed when he withdrew his sword from the spider's head with a schlurp noise, flicking the ichor off the blade.

"Ever heard about a teleporting spider?" He asked, kicking the dead body over to get a good look at its underside. He looked to the legs next, and saw that there was no sign of the sword slice that had taken the creature's legs.

"Guess you creepy crawlies can regenerate quick enough to fly right back into the action, for all the help it'll do now. So long, spider." Arcturus said to himself as he started walking back towards his friends.

"Well, excitement's over, my friends. I killed the thing like a real hero! You should've seen how-"

"Arcturus, behind you!" Veledar suddenly roared from the hilltop of coins. The dragon then spread his wings wide and dived down the mountain of coin. Lyndis and Merlia could be seen gracefully rushing down the hill towards the stranded paladin as well.

"Guys, guys it's all fine! I told you, I had it handled!" Arcturus turned around to see not one, but seven of the large spiders. These ones looked to have thicker carapaces, green oozing mandibles, and those same horrible red eyes. He only managed a "Bloody hell" before the swarm of spiders rushed him.

Arcturus managed to block one as he heard a sizzling noise from his shield. Whatever was oozing from their pincers was definitely doing some foul things to the metal. With haste, Arcturus parried another set of mandibles, deflecting the attack just enough so it did not hit any of his vital areas. Whatever was in their ooze had no apparent effect on the sword he held, so he uttered a mental thanks to Bahamut as he fought to fend off the many legged monsters. He heard several more cracking noises. The spiders appeared all around him and forced the paladin to back up, duck, block, and parry everything sent at him. The spiders were certainly relentless, coming at him like a pack of rabid beasts, forcing Arcturus to focus everything he had into remaining on his feet. If he got knocked down again, chances are he would meet his end like one of the ancient kings: amidst piles of priceless treasure.

Through the wall of pincers and legs he finally saw an opening. He lashed out with his sword, quickly slicing into a spider's carapace. His sword exploded with magical energy upon contact. That particular spider let out a screech, jumping back, and with a crack, it disappeared back into thin air.

Arcturus mentally patted himself on the back for his achievement, but had little time to savor his small victory, as it seemed the beasts had tripled in number and now moved to surround him from all sides. He felt pincers latch onto his armored left shoulder from behind. One of the spiders got him. It tightened its pincers, ready to make the work for his friends easier. Luckily for Arcturus, the armor Matilda had made held strong even as he felt trickles of vile poison drip onto his exposed gambeson and start to melt the wool there.

Arcturus slashed out at the biting spider, but it let go and retreated, his sword only finding empty air. Another took advantage of his attack and caught his right arm. He felt the sharp pincer dig into his skin through the gambeson. Sharp pain took hold of his body...

Then he felt the fluid's hot bite. The same thing that devoured through his gambeson was now coursing under his skin, making him yell out in agony. He smashed that spider over the head with his shield, and with a crack Arcturus managed to dislodge the beast off him.

"Nraaah!" Arcturus fell backwards into the coins as his shield fell apart in his hands. The spider that poisoned him predictably disappeared with a crack. However, it seemed to hardly matter as the others closed in and tried to latch onto him just like the previous two did.

"I know you want me, bastards...but I got a dragon to return to!" Arcturus rolled out of a spider's reach and tried to use his strength to avoid getting skewered by their pinchers. He ignored the ever-growing pain in his right arm, and he was quite sure he would have to do his best to undo the damage right after he survived this horrific encounter. He moved around, jumped and rolled. On one such roll, a spider finally had him pinned to the ground.

"Naaaaah!" Arcturus screamed as he plunged his arm into the mouth of the beast. His sword met the spider's mandibles and held it there, struggling to keep the creature away as it pressed its bulk downwards onto him. His arm started to shudder, and for one moment Arcturus feared for his life. Thankfully, the other spiders seemed to avoid stepping too close, probably to let their web brother have its meal. A grim thought to be sure.

Suddenly the spider that had him so thoroughly pinned was ripped off him by a pair of white claws. The spider was tossed into the others, knocking the ones it hit like a bowling ball.

"Veledar!"

The dragon landed over him and let out an ear-splitting roar of battle.

"About time you climbed your way down from that mountain! I was beginning to think you love treasure more than me!"

"That armor you wear will surely prove a worthy addition to my own hoard."

"Not while I draw breath, you silly dragon." Arcturus accepted Veledar's paw, stood up, then resumed his battle stance beside the dragon.

Veledar whipped one aside with his tail while ripping into others with his claws. The one whipped by the tail found its end when Arcturus slashed at its underside with his sword. With the predictable white magic, he easily cleaved the little monstrosity in two. Veledar let out another roar before letting out a large breath of fire that swept over six of the spiders, setting them ablaze. They let out similar screeches of pain before disappearing with cracks.

"Show off!" Arcturus shouted out as he took advantage of another spider that was too focused on Veledar. His blade cleanly sliced the thing's head off, spraying him with its ichor.

"You best believe it!" Veledar replied with a grin as he continued ripping into the spiders. However, in spite of their progress, Arcturus could hear crack after crack of incoming reinforcements.

"I don't think they like us very much."

"You might be right about that. Quick now! Climb onto my back before I change my mind!" Veledar roared as he reared back to avoid the webbing being tossed at him by the literal army of spiders.

Arcturus could see Lyndis and Merlia were shouting at them to run as they climbed the hill.

"Hurry!" Hissed Veledar in anger. "I told you to get on!"

Quickly stowing his sword, Arcturus ran to Veledar and tried to get on him as if he was a horse. However, several spiders seemed to get what they were planning all along. Webbing seized Veledar on his two front paws, pinning him to the mountains of coin.

"Veledar!"

"I got this. Just gimme a..."

Several of the spiders soon found it much easier to fight the dragon as he struggled to pull himself free. "Grraaaaaawrrrr!" He roared in pain as several pinchers managed to latch onto unarmored spots of his body. "Insistent little buggers."

"Enough about that stupid plan!"

Arcturus leaped off his friend to defend him from the spiders. He drew their attention and made them pay if they tried to attack Veledar. The dragon had opened his maw and simply melted the webbing with his fire now that he had the spiders off him. Once free, the dragon spun around, his tail knocking the ones advancing on Arcturus away with a smack. It would have been almost humorous to see all the spiders collapse to the ground, belly up, with their legs kicking at the air if they were not in danger at the moment.

"Now quick!" Veledar shouted, lowering himself as to ease the human's mounting. Arcturus dashed to his friend and leaped onto his back, and with a great flap of wings Veledar lifted them both into the air. Arcturus hugged the dragon's neck for dear life as Veledar carried them both back to the top of the hill, leaving the army of spiders behind.

"See? I told you we can do it. A few icky spiders are nothing compared to me!" Veledar said after he landed softly with a bump, his soft paws touching the path. Arcturus thankfully leaped onto the ground. It was certainly not as bad as that dreadful moment when dragon had lifted him suddenly into the air. Arcturus imagined that, with a saddle, the ride would be even better. Or at least he would not be grasping the dragon as tightly as he had been doing so far.

"Why does yer gods damn mother have giant spiders in 'ere?!" Merlia shouted as she emerged onto the path from the hill. "It couldn'a be mimics, or rats, but gods damn spiders!" She continued, but Arcturus noticed she shivered at the thoughts of the spiders. He did not take Merlia to be one unnerved by this sort of creatures.

"I honestly don't know. She used to have a spell that would remove vermin such as that with a mere request." Veledar said calmly as the dragon moved his snout close to inspect Arcturus.

"See anything you like?" Arcturus said laughing, his heart still racing from the fight with the spiders.

"You're not injured, so yes." Veledar replied as he nuzzled along the human's armored body. "You know...for all my praises regarding this armor, I wouldn't imagine anyone else wearing it."

"So you do like me, you scaly bastard!" Arcturus stroke over the dragon's snout, who closed his eyes and hummed in delight.

"Just a bit. For saving my life."

"Twice now."

"Show-off."

The dragon continued to nuzzle until he found the paladin's right arm bleeding. "Is that-"

"Yeah." Arcturus said with a groan. "They got me. Give me a moment. Need to focus without your breath rolling over me like a hurricane."

"Sorry," the dragon backed off.

Arcturus used the same method he had done with Veledar last night and touched his injured arm. With a flash of light, he felt the wound close and the pain subside.

"Aaaah, much better. I don't know if you dragons pray...but make sure to thank Bahamut for her blessing every now and again."

"If that puts your mind at is, sure." The dragon said, then let out a short hiss.

"What's the matter?" Arcturus moved along his side.

"They got me in some places, but one really latched onto my tail... would you mind using some of those glowy powers on my tail?" Veledar asked, gesturing to his left flank, and then to his wiggling tail.

Arcturus moved to the flank of Veledar and touched the red dragon. From this close distance, he could make out several puncture marks beneath the dragon's scales. He focused on the healing energy once more and let it pour forth into the dragon.

"You know, it's possible your mother's defenses couldn't weed out the phase spiders." said Lyndis as she too now joined them on the path, "They make their home in the ethereal plane."

Veledar shifted slightly as the healing magic sealed his wounds. "That's better," The dragon hissed with relief. "Thank you, squire."

"With pleasure, my lord," Arcturus bowed with a smile on his face. "Anyone else in need of healing?" He asked, clasping his hands together.

"Please, I didna get anywhere near dose critters." Merlia replied, pulling out a flask and taking a swig from it. "Hate de damn tings, wit dere beedy little eyes an' hundreds o'legs!"

"Well at least you did not have to taste them." Veledar hacked in the air.

"Took two of my fire breaths just to get the taste out of my maw!"

"We should probably move along quickly. Phase spiders tend to be very territorial, and your recent actions down there haven't earned you any favor with their brood." Lyndis added, holding up a finger.

"THEY are territorial?" Veledar snarled, "This is my MOTHER's lair, you daft elf! Mark me, those VERMIN will be cast out as soon as we find her." Veledar turned back along the path and snorted angrily. Arcturus could make out little puffs of black smoke escape the dragon's nostrils. He did notice that Veledar had started walking faster than he had been doing previously. Clearly the dragon was growing more nervous than he was letting on.

They continued for several minutes, with the only sound coming from the carpet of coins upon which they were walking. Merlia finally broke out into a dwarvish drinking song to break the silence. Her singing voice cut right to Arcturus' core, like nails dragged slowly down a chalk board. He saw Veledar's wings twitch as if he wanted to fly away far as he could from the dwarf. Luckily, the vocal torture lasted only a minute as they came to a large clearing within the plains of unending coin.

One area was filled with blankets of every different color. Arcturus didn't doubt that they were most likely the finest from all the lands. Beside the dragon's bed was a bookcase at least twenty feet long and fifteen feet high supported by wooden beams to keep it upright. Along its shelves rested thick tomes that looked ancient. There were armor stands, weapons, and a large chandelier bathing everything around them in a bright light. It must have been connected to a ceiling, but Arcturus could not see where it began.

"Mother!" Veledar shouted out in joy, "Your son is here, and he brought guests!"

They waited a minute in silence before Veledar resumed talking again.

"Probably just out hunting." Veledar muttered to himself.

"For an entire day?" Arcturus raised an eyebrow. "We've been in her cave for quite a while."

"On a quest then!" Veledar snorted. "My mother's always busy with something. How else do you imagine she gathered all of this stuff? Not by sleeping on her hoard like the dragons from your childish human tales!"

From the ground suddenly rose the blue apparition of Auron.

"Oh look, it's Auron." Lyndis said casually to the dragon.

Auron coiled in on itself like a spring as it looked to all of them in turn.

"Greetings, Veledar. This one welcomes you to your hoard." Auron said in its monotone voice.

"Why did you not appear earlier?" Veledar snapped, "And did you know Mother had..." Veledar turned towards Lyndis. "What did you call those stupid things again?"

"Phase spiders," The elf said with conviction.

"Those." Veledar snorted with a flick of his tail.

Auron's ghostly form brightened a bit. "This one knew of the spider incursion, but was waiting on instruction to eliminate them. Why this one failed to appear earlier? It's because this one was instructed to meet you here, by your mother."

"Good. Whatever, let's just put the past behind us. Where is she anyway? We have come quite the distance to see her, and I bet she wouldn't believe this tale even if it comes from my own glorious maw." Veledar said, grinning with his teeth.

"Not here. This is what this protocol is about." Auron replied.

"Hmph," Veledar snorted in irritation as his tail twitched. "You're about as helpful as all these coins. When my mother returns, I will instruct her to bestow some much-needed enhancements upon you, Auron, because you lack tact. And manners. You're being rude to me right now."

"This one does not understand what rude is," Auron said blankly.

Arcturus thought back to the old woman's words back in Drakenburg, and an icy chill seemed to grip his heart.

"Ignore that. Let's focus on the real matter here. Surely you can tell me where has gone to, right?"

Auron went silent.

"Great. Auron, consider yourself promoted. You are now officially more annoying than all the nasty humans I met, put together. Honestly, this is why I despise this thing." Veledar turned to Arcturus and rolled his eyes. "He speaks with the voice of a silent lake and thinks with whatever boulder of a head he has in his...his..."

"Inanimate head?" Arcturus waved something around.

"Precisely!" Veledar nuzzled into the human's armored chest. "When my mother's back I will ask her to shape Auron in your image. Maybe then he'll learn to-"

"She is gone." The ghostly dragon suddenly said.

"Yeah, we know that, boulder-brained mist-head, but when is she coming back?" Veledar snarled. "When when when? Time isn't beyond your ability to understand, you blazing creation!"

"She is gone." Auron repeated, its voice still unchanged. "Your mother is not here because she is nowhere. This is your hoard now, Veledar."

Arcturus' heart sunk when his fears were confirmed. He could see Veledar's snout just stare at the ghostly dragon in disbelief. His snout wrinkled, eyes squinting in anger.

"Oh, that's rich. This is just exactly the amount of humor I need right now." Veledar turned back to the group. "My mother must've enhanced his sense of humor or-or instructed him to lie to me in case she's tackling an important mission. That's it. She doesn't want me or anyone to make themselves at home in her lair. I should know that better than anyone, for I would be annoyed too, were I in her place. Cleaning somebody else's mess is just...distasteful. Way beyond the patience of a dragon of my mother's ability. You all understand, right? A hoard such as this takes time, dedication, energy, ability, patience..." The dragon went over most of his mother's virtues.

"Veledar..." Arcturus began, only to be cut off by the dragon's fiery stare.

"Got a better explanation? Go on. Let's hear it!"

"Enhancements," Lyndis' voice carried through the room, silent, unsure.

"What about them?" Veledar turned his eyes to her.

"The food we ate, the table, chairs...why would she order Auron to keep guests away when she can clean everything with just a single thought?"

Veledar narrowed his eyes.

"Lass's righ," Merlia joined in, her head bowed, unable to even look at Veledar. "Somethin's feelin' wrong here."

"Shut up. Silence, all of you!" Veledar paced back to Auron. "Tell me again."

Auron did, and that only added kindling upon Veledar's blazing rage. "But that's preposterous, you stupid magical enchantment! My mother is the most amazing dragoness in all the land. Just look...look at all the treasure she's gathered. The friendships she forged, the people she saved, the...the son she raised," Veledar's voice started to break. "She can't be gone, because nothing can kill her, understand? She's too cunning for any human, dwarf, elf or otherwise to play their dirty tricks on her!" Veledar snorted, black smoke coming from his nostrils.

Arcturus watched Veledar fidget as he stretched his wings, then start to pace around as realization slowly seeped its way through his resilient scales. "No. No, she can't be gone. Can't be trapped. Can't be outsmarted, out geared, or anything of that sort." The dragon's eyes were looking to all of them, then out to the mounds of treasure.

"Veledar..." Lyndis said quietly to the dragon, her voice but a whisper.

Veledar seemed to ignore the fact that she had just called him by name as he thrashed his tail into the coins, scattering them every which way.

"Perhaps you would want to see the gifts she has left you?" Auron asked, only for Veledar to whip his tail through the ghostly dragon.

"Leave me!" Veledar roared to Auron, causing the dragon to flicker.

"As you wish, master." Auron vanished into thin air.

Arcturus could see the pain in his friend's eyes as he stood there, breathing heavily. The dragon seemed as frozen and stuck like all the objects around him.

"Veledar." He began to say, only for the dragon to cast him a look filled with anger.

"Leave me! All of you!" Veledar roared. "I am the master here now. Haven't you heard? I want you out this instant!"

He heard Lyndis and Merlia start to leave, but Arcturus held his ground. He saw Veledar's eyes stare at him as he just lay there, unmoving. He was almost unsure what the dragon would do. In his grief and anger, would he lash at him with words? Or with fangs?

"Come on, let's leave him alone if that's what he wants." Lyndis grabbed Arcturus' arm.

"Not yet," He whispered. Lyndis' concern was more than noticeable, but Arcturus remained steadfast in his decision. With a shrug, he brushed her hand away while he stared the dragon square in his blue eyes. What he saw there made him unable to leave. He saw the pain, the anger, the sadness swirling in those draconic eyes. How could he leave his friend now, when he was hurting the most?

"You go, I'll make sure he doesn't do anything stupid, like set fire to everything."

"Are you sure?" Lyndis was visibly concerned. She looked over to Veledar, who stood there, breathing in ragged breaths.

"His mother might be gone, but her hoard, her gifts, her memory...they will live on, same as my family did..."

"Shout if you need anything. No need to have you maimed even with these new powers of yours." Lyndis whispered as she patted Arcturus on the back. "Come on, Merlia, I think I saw a dwarven keg back a little ways. Let's go see what year it's from." Lyndis turned, grabbed Merlia, and walked back the way they had come.

Arcturus waited for a few minutes to make sure the two had left. Veledar still hadn't moved. He remained in the same place, his eyes locked on him with the same fury they had before. Arcturus started walking towards the furious dragon before him.

"I ordered you to leave twice already. Have your ears been affected by my roar? Or am I supposed to understand a paladin...no, a commander with years of experience, can't follow simple orders?"

"Veledar, I-"

"LEAVE!" Veledar roared, starting to circle the human like a predator might stalk its prey before striking.

Arcturus felt his heart quicken. In the back of his mind, he might have actually started to regret his decision to stay here with the angry dragon. However, with Veledar's next step, he saw his friend twitch, his blue eyes bearing the same pain as before. He recognized those eyes, for he saw them every morning he woke up in the mirror during the two years since his family suffered the same tragic, untimely end.

"I am not leaving you in this state, Veledar." He replied, gulping once as the dragon barred his teeth in a snarl. "Are you going to hurt me, Veledar? Your friend? The man who saved your life?" His eyes stayed locked on the dragon as he moved, never taking them off for a second.

"YOU SPEAK TO ME OF FRIENDSHIP? Veledar snapped his teeth, "WOULD A FRIEND BE SO DISRESPECTFUL AS TO STAY WHEN I DEMAND HIS INSTANT DEPARTURE?!" Veledar thrashed his tail and let smoke billow out of his nostrils, "I ENTRUSTED YOU MY NAME. I PROVIDED YOU WITH THE WARMTH AND PROTECTION OF MY BODY...and now you ignore the simplest request I've asked of you? HAVE YOU FORGOTTEN I AM A DRAGON, YOU TINY, FRAGILE HUMAN?" Veledar then roared and lashed out at Arcturus with his teeth.

Arcturus had to fight every nerve in his body that told him to run for his life. This sort of conviction surprised him even as he managed to thrust that feeling into the depths of his mind. For a crazy reason, he trusted the dragon more than he feared him.

Veledar stopped, his snout inches from Arcturus' nose.

"Even through this bravado and anger, you can't fool me, Veledar," Arcturus said, his voice full of sorrow. He placed his hand up onto Veledar's snout and caressed it softly. To his surprise, the dragon did not recoil from the touch. Veledar's eyes were still on him, however, and they had started to well up with large tears.

"If you truly wanted to be alone..." He gestured to Veledar's wings, "You would have flown away from us."

It was sudden, as Veledar moved in and grasped the human in a tight hug. Arcturus only let out a surprised yelp as the dragon's head wrapped around his back. He felt Veledar squeeze him tightly as he heard the dragon sob onto his shoulder. They remained like that for a while as Arcturus just hugged the dragon back and patted him reassuringly.

"Why did you not leave when I shouted at you?" Veledar asked, still not yielding his hug.

"When I looked at you, I did not see the large angry dragon that stood before me. I instead saw myself... I knew you wanted someone to stay here with you. Anyone to help you face the pain."

"She was my hero...my mother, I mean. She deserves to have her tale told and sung in taverns, not me. I'm not worthy of her hoard. I'm not even-"

"Shhhh," Arcturus caressed the dragon's neck calmly. "You are the most valiant dragon I know. Remember how you saved me from the gryphons?

How you fought the countless bandits in Drakensburg to protect your party? The same greatness that empowered your mother now shines in you, Veledar. And I am convinced that, in due time, you will create your own legend; a tale sung in taverns that would make your mother proud to call you her son."

He finally was released from the dragon's tight grip. Face to snout, they stared into each other's eyes for another two minutes before Arcturus reached up and wiped away the dragon's hot, crystalline tears.

Chapter 17: Memories

Veledar released Arcturus, reluctantly letting the human fall from his grasp. The dragon took a deep breath and stood on all fours to gaze out to the vast sea of coins before him, littered with treasures of all sorts. It was hard to believe that the glittering expanse, all the weapons, armor, and even the Drenedar carriage now belonged to him. In the back of his mind, a silent voice let him know that he no longer had to remain jealous.

Everything happened so quickly. *So soon...* Veledar wrinkled his muzzle as he paced around, letting his tail drag along the coins. He stopped to grab a clawful of metal disks, letting them fall through his digits like shiny pebbles.

"I am going to fly around and clear my head of the dark clouds that took possession of it." The red turned to the human who had yet to leave his side.

He had to admit to himself, standing up to an angry dragon was pretty brave of the human. To face him down when he was most likely so intimidating. Not many could stand their ground like Arcturus did when he neared with his teeth baring and snapping.

"Are you sure?' Arcturus asked, that same tone of pity still present in his voice.

"Quite so," Veledar sighed, "You needn't worry about me setting things on fire."

Veledar spread his wings wide and wiggled his tail in preparation for the take-off, then leaped from his position and took flight within the grand lair. He looked behind him after a few moments to see that Arcturus had started walking in the direction where Lyndis and Merlia had walked down before his outburst.

I should leave him alone for now. He returned his attention to the sea of gold laden with gems, then took a turn as his eyes fell upon a flag resting neatly on a wooden pole. His eyes narrowed as he remembered that flag and how he always hated it. The flag was a dark green with stitching outlining it. On the material rested a great lion holding a sword and shield. If only he could tear that beast from his mind...

Veledar sharpened his turn as he headed towards it. He remembered the day when that cursed memento arrived. He remembered it all so clearly.

His mother had come into the lair with the flag held in her mouth, spitting it out in disgust onto the floor. He had asked her why she had kept such a vile memento, the symbol of the hunters that had killed his brother.

"It is a reminder," She had said, "A trophy that reflects the justice I brought upon those who inflicted harm upon our family." She snarled, letting her teeth show and her muzzle wrinkle at the recent thought. Veledar had not questioned her after that, as she finally started to clean the blood dried on her claws. Human blood. Veledar could only imagine the ferocity that his mother had ripped into the humans that had torn her son from her side. She could have used her breath to freeze them in place, but she had taken a more intimate way of dispatching them.

"Are there any more?" He had asked her, his eyes at the time still tearing up over the loss of his beloved brother.

"No," She had replied sternly, "The ones responsible have been permanently eradicated from the face of this earth." She stopped her cleaning of her claws and gave him a hard look, "What if there were some left? What would you do?"

Veledar had no answer to give her as a wrymling. However, now being grown and flying towards the flag, he knew. Veledar knew his mother would feel deep shame. Still, in his heart, he had always known what needed to be done. With a simple motion of his jaws, Veledar opened his maw and unleashed his flames upon the flag. That grim reminder would not darken his lair any longer.

He landed to watch the flag burn slowly as the green turned to black and crumbled away to ash. His answer to his mother now was obvious. He would kill any human that sprouted from the legacy of those murderers. He would take from them, just like they stole from him. It did not bring him peace of mind that Arcturus, his mothers, or even the others would approve of his actions. He tried to hear the wisdom of the dragoness' voice, telling him that he should not base a whole on the actions of a few, but he could not hear it right now. She was gone, after all.

Veledar spread his wings again and took flight as the flag slowly vanished from his lair. He spotted the boat he had spoken of earlier with Lyndis, its mighty frame covered in coins, almost like it was going to sink. He landed by it, letting the leathery pads on his paws softly touch the ground. Veledar caressed the frame with one paw, remembering the times he would circle it as a wrymling and pretend he was taking the vessel as his own from pirates. He spied a spot on the underside he had scorched with his breath, claiming the vessel as his own. That's what he had told himself at the time, although he had never told his mother, of course. No need to tell her that the ship was his at the time.

Shaking his head out of the memory, Veledar bolted back into the sky of his lair. He remembered how he had been taught to fly very early in his life. His mother had carried him into the sky like any other time, but on that occasion, she had let go much to Veledar's terror. He remembered flapping his little wings desperately in a frenzied effort to stabilize himself as his mother followed down the entire time, with a look of concern on her kind face. However, he remembered the joy, the pride, and most of all, the warmth that was brought upon her snout as his wings caught the air to pull the small red dragon into a glide. Veledar had released a little roar of joy. His tiny victory. If he had to describe it now, it would of course be a mighty one, but he knew at the time some dragon lovers like Arcturus would call it cute.

Veledar flew over a large section of the lair that contained bookcases. Row after row of old tomes from every era were contained on those antique shelves. He remembered the late nights when he would read some of those stories. Some were good, like the stories of brave dragons, knights and other heroes that went on grand adventures. He chuckled as he remembered announcing to his sister that he himself was going to be an adventurer someday. That he would go on a grand quest just like those legendary dragons. Save fair maidens from distress, find glorious piles of abandoned treasure, and possibly save the day if required. He landed by his favorite bookcase that contained all the stories he had just thought about. Veledar looked to the aging spines of the plethora of books, still having a hard time to believe that now they were truly his. He sighed deeply as he sat down on his haunches among the books. He looked up and imagined his little brother leaping from bookcase to bookcase as he had done so many years ago. His heart began to ache as the memories flowed into his mind, accompanied by images of his mother.

I can't...can't think of them right now, Veledar pushed the thoughts down as he quickly walked out of the grand library and took flight once more.

His next pass along the lair had him pass over Lyndis and Merlia, who were in fact looking over kegs upon kegs of dwarven alcohol. They gave him a wave as he passed overhead. It occurred to him that they now had his name despite the thorough lack of conversation on that topic.

To flames with that mindless construct. I have to figure out what to do with Auron, now that he too belongs to me, he wrinkled his snout. Once again, there was yet another reason that he despised the thing. Well, it could not be helped now. He figured it was only a matter of time before the two females ended up weaseling his name out of him anyway, so he tilted his wing membranes and circled the two before landing beside them.

"Wat in da- make sure ye let us know when ye land, scale-burdened rock-headed dragon. Why, yer almost gave me a heart attack!" Merlia rasped with a hand on her chest.

"I am most sorry for that unpleasantness." Veledar replied, "but I just flew overhead and I figured your keen dwarvish eyes caught my dazzling scales."

"Not a chance, lad! For when ya were shoutin at Arcturus, we could hear ya across the damn place!"

"Oh. That. Well, about that incident..." Veledar trailed off, remembering the absolute fury he had felt. "I guess I should apologize for that as well, as undignified as it is for a dragon to admit his mistakes."

"I like it! Betta ast forgiveness den permission!" Merlia cheered at him.

Veledar managed a weak smile as he sat down on his haunches in front of the two women. He let his tail flick carelessly and tab behind him. "You know...there is something we need to talk about."

"We know," Merlia threw a glance at Lyndis who nodded at the same time as the dwarf with the same mischievous smile on her lips.

"Aye. T'was obvious from how fondly you grabbed each other."

"Sorry. What are we talking about?" Veledar cocked his head.

"Dat lone lover ye left behind! Dennae think we haven' noticed ye sneakin' glances an' talkin sweet words ta each other."

Veledar opened his mouth, only to close it in shock.

"Guilty as sin!" Lyndis pointed at his face. "You don't have to explain yourself when that face tells the whole story. C'mon. Spill it already. You have a thing for Arcturus."

"I..." Veledar took a quick breath. "I certainly do not!"

"Das' no problem, dragon. Tis your lair afta all. Ye can kick us out an warm up all dose bad memories with a bit o' huggin, a wee caress..." The dwarf started to stroke the air, chuckling in the most annoying of ways.

"Nothin' better than love to dampen the effects of tragedy," Lyndis raised her cup at Veledar. "To your new wedding. Mateship. Whatever you dragons call it."

Veledar's heart skipped a beat. His throat never felt so tight before. Was this how his countless victims felt when he teased the living flames out of them? He wanted to deny it with every ounce of his strength, yet he couldn't ignore the simple fact that the two women had a significant edge over him. Veledar had to do more than argue back. He had to turn the situation on its ass.

"I love Arcturus!" He declared, much to the glee of the women.

"Knew it!" Lyndis said.

"Aye. Saw right through ye devious scaly 'ead! Yer not as sharp as ye think, dragon."

"I love him in the same way you love each other," Veledar then added as the two exchanged a weird look. "As friends."

"Dats horse dung!"

"I'm not buying it either." Lyndis said, then took a quick gulp from her mug. "This is a cheap way to get out of that bind."

Veledar barred his teeth. "It's the truth."

"Aye. Like yer gropes an' kisses." Merlia said.

"How dare you accuse me of fraternizing with an important member of this party?" Veledar pointed over to the kegs of wine. "Clearly the wine numbs whatever remains of your wits, because there is no way a majestic dragon like me can be *in love* with a wingless, steel-wearing human that looks blatantly ridiculous in that thing he calls armor."

"Ah…" Merlia twiddled her fingers. "Now when ye put it dis way, I s'pose da dragon would have ta be really drunk to fall for a human."

"Or anything that doesn't have scales, wings, or even a tail," Lyndis said nonchalantly. "Your ego wouldn't let you."

"Exactly! So we should talk about real matters here instead of wild fabrications." Veledar said happily. Oh, how good it felt to take a proper breath. The tension just melted out of his body after the girls focused back on their thoughts and their drinks. Now he just had to turn the conversation elsewhere. "Hang on," He put up the best suspicious face he could form. "It occurred to me that, through an act of painful injustice, both of you came into the possession of my real name."

"Ah, that. Just so you know, I was prepared to keep calling you Crimson Sky" Lyndis said politely, "I did not get your name after all. Did you, Merlia?"

"Aye 'course I did lass! Dinnae hear dat blue basterd blurt it out like-" Merlia started, then stopped as her eyes went wide in realization, "Ahhhh of course, of course! I dinna hear a word of it."

Veledar grinned at the extent they were willing to go with this little self-inflicted lie. "I figured you would get my name out of me sooner or later, and even if you like to play games and pretend, we all know it won't be the same now with that piece of foreign knowledge lodged in your heads. I give you both permission to use it. Just don't roam, tossing it around everyone like that good for nothing Auron."

"Thank you, Veledar. You are most kind," Lyndis smiled, walking over and patting the dragon on his hide.

"Great, now I tink I might be getting' teary eyed." Merlia pulled out a cloth to wipe her eye.

"So where did Arcturus get off to? I thought I saw him heading to be with you two earlier?"

"Aye. We did see him for a moment, before he headed back to ya mom's...yer area of the cave." She pointed back towards the place where his mother used to rest.

Veledar turned his snout towards that particular place. It was a bit odd, that Arcturus would make that trip. He figured the human was checking on the girls before going back to exploring that area of the cave.

"Veledar?" Lyndis said, "You take as much time as you need, alright?"

He nodded before he saw himself in the air again. With his wings tucked to his sides, the red dragon swooped towards his mother's sleeping area, or more correctly, *his* sleeping area now. He frowned. Some things needed to invariably change. He figured he would just have to ask Auron, and the spectral dragon would change the location of all the bedding within the lair. He passed overhead, looking for Arcturus, but found no traces of the human.

I surely hope you haven't unearthed another weird creature, Arcturus. Veledar continued his search, flying towards a body of water within the mounds of coins. It looked like a mini lake within the place, with a fountain at its center shooting up water several feet in the air.

He landed at the water's edge and settled down on the cold ground. The dragon put his snout on his paws as he gave his tail a thump. More images sprang to mind. This time, he remembered how he had been taught how to swim near one of the lakes around his original home. He remembered splashing his mother with water and falling over, hissing with laughter. She returned the favor, of course, with a large wave of water that had left him drenched from snout to tail. He thought back on all the times that went so quickly past him, and how he would never see her again.

Mother...I am so sorry I'll never get to see, or play, or sleep under your wing ever again... The emotion was much stronger than Veledar anticipated. It felt like a knife jabbed into his heart as tears once again started welling up inside his blue eyes. His vision grew blurry as he imagined the conversations they would never have, the time they would never share, and how she would not see him in the splendorous glory of the present moment.

It's not fair! His tail lashed at the ground behind him. *How had she died? She had always seemed to have a plan, an item, a magic spell that had always seen her through the day.* Through the stories she had told to her hatchlings, Veledar and his sister learned of her adventurers and the struggles she had. It seemed so wrong for her to simply *not* be anymore. He wondered if she had simply found something that even a dragon could not overcome and died too quickly before she could escape. Perhaps she had tampered with a spell, and it had backfired, ending her that way. Not that the thought brought any relief. Veledar still felt anger rising in his chest as he thought on the last possibility; that somehow, his mother was hunted down by a band of dragon slayers and killed. After all, this is exactly what happened to him when Arcturus and his band of wretched knights ambushed him in his home.

Veledar breathed deep as he tried to calm himself. The method worked as he soon settled down from that thought.

The worse thing about the whole situation was that Avalina had no idea, or at least that's what he figured in the present moment; that his sister had no idea what had happened. He would have to find a way to locate her, or use a spell to tell her about their mother's death. He already recoiled from the thought of having that conversation. He would not enjoy watching his sister's snout fill with sadness as he shared the grim news. It was a shame that dragons were not mortals sometimes, as mortals could be brought back from death if you had the right magic, whereas a dragon, who was already a being of magic, could not be. He guessed it was a way of balancing things out. His kin had already been blessed with scales, claws, wings, breath attacks, magic, and nigh immortality. He figured that some God out there reckoned mortals had to have an advantage of their own.

"Veledar! Just the dragon I wanted to see. What have you been up for the last few hours?" came Arcturus' voice as he made his way over to the dragon. He had stripped his armor and was down to his black tunic, belt, sword, and scabbard.

How did the human find him? Did he have a third sense when the dragon was emotionally compromised? Veledar simply buried his head into his paws and closed his eyes. "Just been flying through my memories."

"Quite a place this is. Look there! It even has a mini lake!" Arcturus exclaimed. He opened his eyes as he heard the noise of something plunking into the water. Arcturus had his hand extended like he had thrown something into the water.

"Did you just throw one of my coins into the water?"

"Skipped it, actually," The human smiled. "And technically it's also your water."

Veledar had to give it to him, "Alright. You are free to continue to move my treasure if you wish. Not that it matters anyway." Veledar sighed.

"Auron, are you there?" Veledar asked aloud, and almost instantly the blue ghostly dragon emerged from the coin in front of him.

"Always at your service, master. What is it you need of me?" Auron asked just as Arcturus skipped another gold coin into the water.

What he needed? He of course needed plenty of things, especially after today. However, he decided to start with the damn spiders.

"I would like you to get rid of the phase spiders from my lair. I will not tolerate their presence any longer."

"As you wish, master. I will wipe out every trace of their existence."

"In the future, you do not need my permission anymore. Simply get rid of vermin whenever they sneak in." Veledar snorted. Why his mother had not conjured Auron to do that was beyond him, but at least the ghostly dragon listened.

"As you wish, master."

"You must like that. Having him call you master all the time," Arcturus said with a nervous grin.

He figured the human was doing what people would call testing the waters with some humor.

"It's not like anyone else is going to do it." Veledar held his head up high.

"Why would you want me to call you master?" Arcturus picked up another coin and skipped it once more onto the water.

"Would you?" Veledar grinned, scratching his head with one of this wing talons. "I suppose not. You humans do value your freedom, after all."

Arcturus was silent for a moment as he picked up another coin and moved it through his fingers.

"Auron, next up, I would like to know about our friends on the mountain."

"Master, I believe your friends are already here within your lair. Unless you mean the people and gryphons flying around the mountain?"

Veledar frowned. It seemed that Garroth had not given up the hunt, after all. Could the human even track them here? He wondered if the human thought him dead after the fall, or perhaps the knuckle-head figured the dragon lived and watched the skies for his eventual departure. Regardless, he hoped the illusions that hid the whole cave would hide them from the human's persistent gaze a awhile longer.

"Thanks for the information. I guess we have to lay low for another day at least." The dragon looked over to his human companion. "Your friend is very persistent. Eager to kill me and *save* you."

"That's friendship for you." Arcturus smiled.

"So you're saying you would go to those lengths for me? For anyone in our little band of adventurers?"

"Have I not already?"

Veledar snorted as he realized this was true of Arcturus. "Well, I suppose you have, after all that had happened."

The dragon flicked his tail for a few silent moments. "So, after our little mission to get my book back is completed, what will you do, my dear armored paladin of Bahamut?"

He watched the human put a hand to his chin as he thought about his question. "Now that certainly is a good question. Would you believe I have not thought about it yet?" Arcturus sat beside the dragon, still clutching his chin. "Maybe get far away from Entis. Leave all the war behind and go on another adventure.”

“Has the adventuring spirit grabbed you, Arcturus?” Veledar cocked his head to the side as he gave his tail another thump against the coins.

“I suppose it has! Certainly better than being a guard captain at the least.” He gestured to the mounds of treasure, “I can say for sure I never saw anything like this during my days on a Lumarian airship.”

“I suppose not,” Veledar chuckled, “It must seem pretty droll in comparison.”

“And there is no paperwork, no one harping you to keep everyone else in line. It’s... it’s... what’s the word I am looking for...”

“Freedom.” Veledar replied.

“That’s it.” The human smiled.

“Would you help me find out what happened to my mother?” Veledar asked suddenly, “You are good company, at least.”

If Arcturus was taken aback, he did not show it, and hardly skipped a beat to think about it. “Sounds like a noble cause.” Arcturus held up his hands as if reading a large sign. “Troubled dragon seeks aid from human paladin.” He stopped and gave the dragon a coy grin, “There would be of course fees to be paid in exchange for my service.”

“Fees? I thought we were friends, you sneaky kobold!” Laughed the dragon, realizing where this was going.

“Well, yes. In many ways, we are, but fees are fees, even between family. There’s one for endangerment, another for upkeep of the weapons and armor, and then I have to listen to Veledar boast every five minutes fee. That's the real expensive one.”

“It's going to cost me a fortune, isn't it?” Veledar wrapped a wing around the human as they looked to the fountain.

“It might cost you one or two of those.”

They sat in silence as they watched the water for quite some time. Truthfully, Veledar lost track of the time. Having Arcturus there with him was a soothing act in of itself. However, with the sound of his stomach grumbling, serenity gave way to other, more pressing concerns.

“Guess we should head back and get something to eat. The girls might get worried about where we are and figure you ate me.”

“Oh, certainly they know by now I don't eat mortals garbed in their silly dresses.”

“Garbed? What, are you going to tell me you tried eating a naked one?” Arcturus asked nervously.

“Well, only once, and it happened a loooong time ago.”

“Veledar! That’s not a viable excuse to eat people!”

“Oh, believe me, the world’s better off without this scoundrel in it. She made a whole village miserable before I put a swift end to her. Besides, I haven't eaten her whole," Veledar stuck his tongue out, "Too gamy. Honestly, I do not understand how some dragons in your stories developed a taste for something so...distasteful."

"Now by eatin an elf you mean like really eatin an elf." Merlia suddenly said as she emerged from a hill of coins. "Cause I have two pictures in me head, one more appeasin den de other."

"I assure you it was the food one, and not whatever strange things roam your inebriated head." Veledar responded, sticking his tongue out at Merlia.

Lyndis was next as she gave a chuckle at the dwarf's hearty joke. "So, if I understand this correctly, our next move is to hang low for the rest of the day?"

"How did you-" Arcturus began to ask, but Lyndis pointed to her ears. "Right."

Veledar explained of Garroth's inability to simply give up the chase when his quarry eluded him. He suggested to spend the day relaxing again, reading up on spells, meditating, and staying in good spirits. They would have to simply wait for an opening. More precisely, wait for Garroth to slip before they left the mountain. Veledar hated to admit it, but the superior speed of a gryphon in flight was a worrisome problem. If they saw him leave, Veledar and his party would not get far before the whole chase happened all over again.

They returned to the area where his bed now stood to spend the day as he suggested. Arcturus was passing time by doing his battle meditation nd trying to cast another spell and such, each time his face would look like a child in amazement of his deeds. He did not do anything too impressive on his own though, and, for both friendship and boasting reasons, Veledar tried to coach him on some spells like mirror image, fire bolt, and charm person. However, Arcturus could not perform the spells for some reason. Veledar snorted and simply wrote it off as human error. Lyndis pointed out that Veledar cast his spells through arcane magic, being a dragon and all. Paladins, on the other hand, cast magic through divine effort. She suggested that the lessons Veledar knew might not cross over into the paladin's repertoire of spells. For that, they would need to find another paladin, a book, or a divine spell caster that would help Arcturus focus on the proper way to cast his spells. Veledar and Arcturus were satisfied with this answer, as they wrapped up spell training for the day.

Merlia practiced with her bow by making makeshift targets to hit and placing them at further and further distances. She was a good shot for a dwarf. Veledar had to admit at least that of the lass. Before knowing her, he had always figured stocky people like dwarves would feel comfortable tossing axes or hammers when they didn't feel like beating or slicing people to death. He never heard any story of dwarves using bows or being rangers for that matter.

That night, Veledar dimmed the lights on the walls and set up a fire for warmth using the mental imaging spell that still remained active in the other section of the cave. They ate their food by the crackling fire, exchanging jokes and having a good time. Veledar had conjured up whatever his party asked for. Lyndis requested cooked fish with squash and green beans. Arcturus had asked for a steak, potatoes and broccoli, while Merlia just wanted lamb and mead. Veledar himself had some sheep, with the same sauce as he had the night before. After the meal he regaled them with stories of his mother's exploits, and it warmed his heart as they gasped in the right places, cheered or asked simple question like an excellent audience. Finally, he told them the other kind of tales he knew, about what his mother had told in regard to Bahamut's tears.

"Well, hopefully your mother is looking down on you right now, proud of the mighty dragon her son has become." Lyndis said with a smile.

"Aye, that I can agree on. De wey ya ripped up dose spiders, fed us an' joked an' told tales. Yer already a hero in me book!" Merlia burped, rubbing her stomach.

"Honestly, the only dragon I'd kiss instead of sticking him with the sharp end of my sword." Arcturus laughed, patting Veledar on his side.

"Wot?!" Merlia cocked her head.

"Knew it! I knew it!" Lyndis smiled and gestured at the two of them.

"What? It's just a harmless comparison!" Arcturus said, even as he moved to hide under Veledar's wings. "You believe me, right?"

"Yeah." The dragon nuzzled through his hair, then pointed his snout at the two laughing females. "Don't pay them too much attention. They're obviously drunk out of their minds."

"Oy! Come back 'ere! I 'ave a tale o' me own ta share!"

Veledar sat in silence as the others shared their own memorable events. He listened just as intently as they had to his stories, until the fire began to die down and yawns replaced the merry smiles.

They split off into beds conjured by Veledar, copies of the ones from the previous night. The red dragon curled himself up and hugged the stuffed dragon he created just for himself. It was an almost exact replica of the one that was stolen from his previous lair, although, as he laid there in his soft blankets, his bed still felt lacking. His eyes opened softly as he eyed Arcturus sitting on his own bed, pulling the covers over himself. That's what he was missing. He quietly climbed out of his own bed and padded over to Arcturus'.

"Mind if I?" He asked quietly to the human, who had been watching him slink over the entire time.

"Do you even have to ask? I'm standing in a bed conjured by you, in your own cave, stuffed with food you created," Arcturus chuckled. "The only thing remaining is to give me a set of clothes and ask me to call you master."

"Well then, my dear subject, would it please you to accompany your overlord to his bed?"

"As long as he doesn't eat me, sure." Arcturus kept on smiling through the affectionate nuzzles that assaulted his chest. "Alright, alright, you made your point, you scaly adorable thing."

"Thing?" Veledar narrowed his eyes.

"Don't be silly. You know what I meant."

"Maybe."

The dragon laid down and clasped the human within his claws. "Now you are my plaything, little human."

"Happy to oblige, when I'm getting all this warmth."

Veledar rumbled happily, nuzzled his human good night, then slowly lowered his wings over the bed. It was a nice feeling, to have the human's warm body pressed against his chest. Without a second thought, he disregarded the stuffed dragon. He thought he heard Arcturus sigh as he closed his eyes. Veledar listened to the human's heart beat steady until sweet sleep took him in its ethereal embrace.

Chapter 18: Dragon Rider

Arcturus woke up to the sound of Veledar's sneeze. The dragon held him firm as his body constricted. His eyes opened to find that he was still snug against the dragon's chest. To wake up, or enjoy the comfort of scales a bit longer? Arcturus smiled. He went to wiggle free, but it was simply so warm and comfortable to be tucked against that sea of warm scales that he shortly decided against it, going slack against the dragon and just enjoying the feeling of those big, protective paws.

"Did I wake you?" Veledar asked. Arcturus could feel the dragon's tail swishing gently.

"With your sneeze. Not with your claws, or with that fearsome elf-devouring mouth. With your sneeze, out of all things." The human chuckled at how ridiculous that sounded. "I contemplated leaving, even went for it actually, only that I found myself unable to free myself."

"I did not think I was holding you so tight." Veledar chuckled. The dragon slowly relinquished his grasp.

"Nah, wasn't your paws, you big winged lizard. It was just so comfortable and warm there, near your chest, that I had an impossible time crawling out into the cold." Arcturus stood up, stretching his hands to the ceiling with a yawn.

"Besides, you had to go and miss me," Arcturus smiled, "thought I was all done acting as a stuffed animal for you."

Veledar walked past him, the dragon's frilled tail tip touching his neck softly. "I found I needed some good company. My bed felt ever so lonely without you in it."

"Gods. You make it sound like we are lovers. You're lucky the girls aren't paying attention," Arcturus grinned, stretching to his side.

"Yes. Hardly so. Can you imagine something more ridiculous than that? Me, a dragon, reducing myself to the level of a mere human?"

"A paladin!" Arcturus pointed out with a finger. "And an attractive one at that."

"Sure, sure," Veledar snorted, then put a grin on his muzzle, "Although..."

"No. Let me. I have to admit one thing about this union. The warmth, your heart beat, I may be getting spoiled." Arcturus touched his hands to his boots. "I may never find sleeping in my own bed enjoyable, and it's all because of you. You are positively ruining my future here, dragon."

"One can only hope." Veledar snarked as he stretched his wings wide.

"You really mean that?"

"How good of a future can that be, without a dragon in it?"

Arcturus shoved the dragon playfully as Veledar summoned a table covered with breakfast. Arcturus managed to drink down a cup of coffee and a glass of water, then helped himself to some eggs and sausage before setting his utensils down with a burp. Lyndis and Merlia strolled over, finished with their morning preparations of magic. Lyndis once again covered Veledar's mouth before he could speak.

"Let me guess. Coffee?" The dragon smirked with a swish of his tail.

Lyndis nodded silently as she sipped from the coffee mug held in her hands.

Arcturus watched the dragon chat away, looking more like himself than he had the other day. Although this was a most welcome change, it still surprised him. It was a very hard day for the dragon, after all. To endure so much pain all of a sudden...the thought almost felt as dark as the night when Arcturus lost his own family.

"Auron!" Veledar said loudly, his voice filled with purpose. He walked through piles of coin, spreading them around with his claws. "You mentioned something about a treasure. Come on, come out wherever you are! I need to see the gifts you mentioned!"

Veledar stopped, then swirled his head towards the others. Arcturus saw a grin spread on the dragon's snout as their eyes met. "Now for the rest of you, I think I may have some items in this hoard that will be of use for our quest." The dragon then turned to Lyndis and held up a claw, "To borrow!"

Lyndis practically looked like she was jumping for joy.

"Now don't make me regret my on-the-wing decision. I'm still the master around here," Veledar added as he began to pace around, waiting for Auron to appear. Veledar called out again for Auron, irritation growing in his voice. However just as the rumbling of his annoyed growl left the red dragon's throat, Auron appeared before them in a crackle of azure light.

"Master wished to see this one?"

Veledar paused for a moment, "If you would retrieve my mother's..." Veledar seemed to choke on his next words, "Last gifts to me."

"As you wish, master," Auron vanished with a crack and a thin wisp of smoke.

"Are you sure you want to share your treasures, Veledar? I mean, I'm not one turn down a magical item when it is given willingly, but this is your hoard we're talking about!" Arcturus said, arms crossed.

"Which makes it mine to lend out as I see fit. Although I can see that you are as humble as ever, dearest Arcturus." Veledar started to circle the paladin with careful steps. "Have no worry for the sanctity of my hoard. I will get the magic items back, you see, so there is not really anything lost on my part." He snorted, "It's not like I am giving them to untrustworthy or incapable hands."

Veledar stopped dead in his tracks, giving Arcturus a look of pity, "Arcturus, you should act more like a dragon. Bahamut made you her champion. That is not just a title to boast with. You wield actual magic!" Veledar, with a wiggle of his tail, bounded behind a mound of coins, and started tossing items from around his body, causing them to rattle coins or occasionally clang. He tossed a goblet here, a jewel there, and the dragon moved several times while doing this.

"Are we sure he ain' been driven mad by all dis gold? Heard tales of cursed riches dat can make even dragons greedy beyond imaginin'," Merlia tilted her head to the side with a look of confusion on her brow.

"Yea, this is certainly new for him, but it makes sense if you think about it. He might actually be taking this more seriously than his other commitments." Lyndis said calmly opening her backpack. "He is on a quest to retrieve a lost family heirloom, and wants it to succeed for the sake of his whole family. Now that he has this wondrous hoard at his disposal, what stops him from using its resources to retrieve his item and more importantly, keep us alive to get to that point?"

"Aha!" Veledar shouted. He turned around to reveal something that looked like a simple gray cloak with a golden leaf clasp. With a flash of his wings and a bounded leap. Veledar landed next to Lyndis, who gave a surprised gasp. Veledar moved around her, holding up the cloak as if to fit it on her.

"This was one of my favorites as a wrymling." He gave a large tooth filled grin to them, "although I don't think it will fit me now. Not without a spell at least." Veledar turned around to look at himself, wiggling his tail back and forth.

"What's this dusty curtain?" Lyndis grabbed the cloak quickly from the dragon's grasp. "Is it for repelling fire spells? Shrinking? Flying?

Veledar went to speak, but she continued on with her barrage of questions.

"Or maybe it summons puppies? Does it make my skin like metal? Perhaps it can-"

Veledar put a claw over her mouth to silence her. "You are way too talkative and bad at guessing. You are a rogue, Lyndis."

"The technical term is adventurer."

"Precisely why I am giving you a cloak of invisibility." He chuckled, like a father to a very excited child. "You simply have to utter "Houpe" while holding the clasp. Then you will be invisible. Isn't that why I brought you into my party? To sneak around, steal things, bash people in the head when the need arises?"

"Actually, it was to make sure you two bonkheads aren't gracing the walls of a dungeon, yeah," Lyndis drawled. "So this invisibility spell of yours...how long does it last? It'd be far too good to sneak around indefinitely. Why, that'd make me a master rogue," Lyndis put a hand to her mouth. "I could even steal your hoard."

"No chance of that, missy," The dragon hissed at her. Lyndis spoke only in jest of course. "The enchantment on this cloak lasts for an hour or so, three times a day. It used to bug my siblings something awful, as I would use it to perform pranks on them," Veledar laughed and looked up as if he were looking at the scene playing out in front of him.

"Give it here." Lyndis hung the cloak on her shoulders before doing a quick twirl. She gave a large smile as she held the clasp and whispered "Houpe". Arcturus gasped as she vanished into thin air.

"Can you see me?" Lyndis asked, her voice filled with excitement. "I can't tell if I am invisible. How odd. This feels different than when I cast my own spell."

"Wouldn't be much of an invisibility cloak if we could see ya lass." Merlia laughed.

"Uh Veledar... how do I stop being invisible?"

"I forgot!" Veledar replied, tapping his claw to his snout. "You have to say the same word I believe, quite simple really." The dragon then bounded back towards his mounds of treasure. Lyndis said the same word over again and appeared before Arcturus.

"That was incredible! I just love magic items!" She exclaimed, her smile practically stretching ear to ear.

"Don't you already have the power to turn invisible?" Arcturus raised an eyebrow.

"Yea, but it feels nothing like this, and does not last nearly as long! Oh, imagine all the things I can pull with this. Nothing will stop LYNDIS, THE GREATEST ROGUE THE WORLD HAS EVER KNOWN!" She bellowed, holding her arms wide.

"Calm down, or we might think you're turning into Veledar over there." Arcturus laughed.

"How is that a bad thing?" Veledar replied, tossing a silver goblet over his shoulder.

"I tink we could only eva survive one of ya." Merlia chuckled, "Can ya imagin?"

"Well, there is only one of me, so tough luck finding a suitable impostor!" Veledar replied, no doubt his chest filling with pride like it usually did. "Now Merlia, what should your item be? An ever-filling flask of ale?"

"I wouldna mind that o' course, but how does that help ye quest?"

"Good point, good point. The quest comes first, always," Veledar rolled his eyes and went back to digging through the treasure. He searched through the piles of items, literally sticking his head in to look around as the rest of the dragon dragon wiggled his hind end back and forth. For a few minutes this process repeated in several spots as the others looked on in amazement. It finally stopped as Veledar had started to thrash his tail and bare his teeth.

"I found it!" He exclaimed, bounding back to them with an item held in his claws.

"What do ye have dere?" Merlia rubbed her two hands together expectantly.

"A magic version of that harmless stick-thrower you call a bow. Exciting, isn't it?" Veledar smiled as he forced the bow into Merlia's hands. "Take it! Tell me it isn't the finest bow you held in those pudgy dwarven hands!"

It looked about the same size of a normal longbow, but seemed to be made of near pristine white wood. Thin golden stripes spread from its golden middle all the way to its ends.

"It's called the Oath-bow."

"Thank ye," Merlia furrowed her eyebrows as she turned the bow around, "But how does it work, besides the obvious?"

"It's even more simple than that cloak over there. You see, all you have to do is focus on a person in front of you, and repeat the words. "Swift death to you who have wronged me." Veledar said the phrase slow, as Merlia started to practice saying it. "After the oath is spoken, the bow allows your arrows to seek your target easier, even being able to go around cover to hit them. Although mind this. When your bow is locked onto the target, you will find it harder to hit with every other weapon."

"Well dats goin to be a nasty surprise for me next foes. I bet I can hit plenty more knees wit dis!

"There should be an armory of minor magic weapons shortly over there," Veledar pointed over to a dune hundreds of feet away. "Just go pick out some more weapons you might be interested in."

The girls nodded in unison as they went to leave towards the indicated spot.

Veledar turned around towards Arcturus, his tail dragging along the ground. "Now for you Arcturus, besides the book I promised you, of course." Veledar started to circle the paladin once more. "What to do, what to do? This is more complicated than it looks like."

Arcturus held up a hand to tell him he had no need of anything.

All I need is you. As long as you stand by my side, I am the happiest paladin in Lumara.

That sounded so silly even inside his own head. No. He couldn't tell Veledar that. If the girls heard him, he'd have no respite from the myriad of those dragon-lover jokes.

"Veledar, really, I'm-" Although he did appreciate the offer, Veledar sensed this and cut him off before he could speak.

"Now don't turn this opportunity down so easily. It's not every day that a kind, striking dragon bestows such gifts to a... well...passable knight..."

Arcturus heard Lyndis and Merlia suddenly stop in their tracks as they stifled a fit of laughter between the two of them.

"What do you mean, passable?" Arcturus laughed, raising an eyebrow. "Should I also be alarmed that you are rating us on attractiveness?"

"Well by dragon standards anyway. I meant no offense to you, of course." Veledar continued without missing a beat, "See, your snout is too small, you have no scales to speak of, no wings, no claws, not even a tail to grab!"

"I don't see how that's fair. We're completely different species. You wouldn't rank a weasel lower than a bird, yes?"

"Your rules do not apply to dragons."

Merlia suddenly burst out laughing, her hands no longer holding it in. "Looks like dat dragon really fancies ya, Arcturus."

"Well I would not be laughing if I were you Merlia. After all, you are pretty low on dragon standards." Veledar smirked, sticking his tongue out at the ever-reddening dwarf.

"Is that so?" Merlia said slowly, her voice laced with anger, eyes squinted.

"Besides that, it's pretty bad of you to discriminate on sexual preference."

"I was makin a joke ya daft dragon, not discriminating!" Merlia held up a shaking fist.

"Careful there, Merlia, or you will stay that color of red for days. Although, if I think this through, this would improve your attractiveness on the dragon scale...." Veledar only reached the last word as Merlia ran after the dragon.

"That's it!" The dwarf yelled, "Get over here, ya great fire breathin git! I'll knock those words outta yer mouth with da very bow ye gave me!"

Veledar laughed as he bounded out of the reach of the furious female, "You're far too easy to rile, Merlia, I suggest seeing someone to work on all that anger."

They continued for a minute as Arcturus and Lyndis watched on in amusement. It was clear though the dragon was simply toying with the dwarf, as she never truly got close to catching him during the entire time she was chasing him around.

"Besides, what if I did find fancy the human? Would you suddenly turn against us?" Veledar turned as he leaped onto a tall mound of treasure.

"Yer twisten my words! I'd simply make fun of ya for a different reason. Now get down here so I can catch you!" Merlia shouted. "I swear one o' these days I will catch ya, and dere will not be a high enough mound o' treasure to keep me hands from ya tail!"

"That may be a while," Veledar replied, sticking his tongue out. "There is always a tree, building or rock to be get in your way, and I kind of trust those obstacles over your stubby dwarfish legs."

Merlia pulled out the bow, "Don't make me turn ya into a pin cushion, ye scaly git."

"Quick, Arcturus!" Veledar bounded to the paladin, then slunk behind him. "Save me, Paladin! Fulfill the sacred oath you swore to your master and protect me from the crazy dwarf!"

"Oh, I get it now, using human shields. Yer fightin dirty, dragon!" Merlia laughed, stowing the bow.

"Not in the way I expected, but true enough." The dragon nodded his horned head at Merlia first, then the rest of the party. "Now that excitement is over, Arcturus, you should follow me to your present. Although I warn you. The face you make might beat all the human standards for surprise. It is something special, after all."

Arcturus started to follow the dragon. He could feel the excitement building in his chest. How could it not, when Veledar practically radiated with joy?

"Oh, I will try to not die from praising this item too much." Arcturus smiled, patting Veledar on his flank.

"Careful dere, Arcturus. Dat dragon might want ta give ye a *special* present." Merlia laughed hard as she led Lyndis towards the armory. They only took several steps until both started giggling among themselves.

Veledar just snorted at them, stuck his tongue out, and returned his gaze to Arcturus. The paladin had to admit. That one was kind of funny, so he tried to hold in his laughter.

"Ignore them." Veledar waved a dismissive paw at the two females, "my gift is special of course, but it's not," The dragon then paused to lower his voice to a whisper, "You know, whatever that dwarf cooked inside her dirty mind."

Arcturus chuckled at Veledar's quick thinking. "Oh, I'd never dream you capable of something indecent. Why, your brilliance is an example to us all."

"Do you...mean that figuratively or-"

"Both." Arcturus rubbed his hand over the dragon's neck, making the scaly creature rumble with joy.

Veledar led him to what appeared to be a shrine nestled within the treasure. This time it was barrels and barrels that were labeled *finest silk of Rothdell*. On the pedestal of this shrine was an urn of blackened stone. Upon the urn was golden draconic writing if Arcturus had to guess by the harsh lines that looked as if they had been drawn by claw tip.

"It says, *here lies Carpenter the brave*," Veledar spoke softly as he slowly walked over towards the shrine. He moved his snout side to side, obviously looking for something.

"Why is this here in your mother's lair?"

"Mother liked this human at one point in her life. He was a dashing hero, judging by her words. If memory serves, he helped her so much during his rather short life that he earned a place of honor here in her lair, so that he could always be with her in a very sweet, dragon kind of way." Veledar replied quickly as he kept shifting furniture, coats, and other various treasures.

"Here we are. I figure he doesn't need this anymore. I also can't think of anyone else who would use them better." Veledar returned with a dusty brown book equipped with a fine leather binding in one claw. In the other claw he held a grey shield that appeared to be made from a large mirror. "Always liked this one," Veledar gestured to the shield with his snout.

"Only because it's a mirror," Arcturus chuckled, and reached out for the items. He grabbed the leather book first, finding the cover worn with age. He opened it up to see that the pages were filled with instructions in how to cast spells, their names, and draconic runes.

"Interesting." He carefully set the book down as he grabbed the shield. It was of course smooth, but it was also cold to the touch. He traced over with his finger several scratches along the otherwise pristine surface. This item must have been through many battles. The stories this shield could tell...

"What does it do?" He turned his head back to the dragon.

"Well, in addition to being tougher than a normal shield, I heard tales of how this shield could stop even the mightiest spell slung at Carpenter. Although, if I think about this right... this effect can only happen once or twice per day. I cannot remember which. Just be careful, as in, don't gamble your life on the off chance I might be wrong, alright?"

Arcturus nodded at the dragon's words. "This certainly is a most helpful item. I figure I should only rely on the one a day, and if trouble persists, I have my trusted scaly steed to rely on!"

"Be careful what you say. This steed can lick as well as he bites." The dragon mischievously flicked his tongue out to display the length of his 'weapon'.

"Come on now, Veledar. You don't want to get this ancient tome soaked, or worse, ripped apart." He placed the book softly on the shield. "Thank you.

I know these gifts mean a lot to you."

"Maybe enough to...kneel at my paws?" The dragon cocked his head with the same silly smile, only to grow serious when Arcturus actually crouched to touch his paws.

"H-hey, I didn't mean that literally!"

"I'm not gonna waste this chance to tickle something else than your wings!" Arcturus picked up his efforts until he found himself in another dragon hug as Veledar held him tight. He could tell from the dragon's shaky breath that this wasn't another playful hug. He wanted this. No...needed to hold someone he cared for in his paws, just like he did last night. For a moment Arcturus was unsure of what to do, so he returned the hug and patted the dragon gently on his scales.

"It's okay, Veledar, Everything's alright. Your wings and paws are safe from my hungry fingers," he said softly as he heard a sniff from the dragon.

"Hey!" Veledar suddenly said, turning his head around to look behind him.

The dragon had to let go of Arcturus so he could see Lyndis and Merlia had found their way over to hug the dragon from behind.

"Can't I go away without you two following me?" Veledar groaned, looking like he gave a halfhearted push for them to get off.

"Never!" Lyndis said back with a smile, "I guess you're stuck with this party of miscreants you assembled!"

Veledar turned back to Arcturus and shook his body hard enough to dislodge the two girls from his hide.

"Yer feelin mightily ornery today!" Merlia chuckled.

"Hey, leave him alone," Arcturus pointed a finger at her face. "He wanted to tell me something important."

"Oh," The two girls gasped at each other.

"Guess dey about to do it," Merlia chuckled, then quickly snuck behind a pile of treasure.

"Quick thinking there, partner," Veledar smiled and approached his head to nuzzle Arcturus, who smiled and scratched Veledar under his jaw in return.

"These jokes about us being lovers are starting to get old."

"Agreed. Ridiculous, how those two can't figure something better. Anyway, in regards to my gift, I figured you needed a shield after you broke the other one over the spider's face." Then Veledar gestured to Arcturus' tabard, "We should also focus on getting you a new frontal cape. I don't think brown is your color."

"It's called a tabard, you hundred years old sage. Honestly Veledar, I thought dragons were supposed to know everything!" Arcturus held up a finger towards the dragon.

"Call it whatever you want, but the truth is you need a new one. I'm thinking red, with a silver dragon on it." Veledar spread his wings to gesture the fact that said dragon had to be a sizable one.

"You're only saying that because you want the colors to match your scales, you tricky goblin," Arcturus laughed, picturing the red tabard in his mind. He had to admit though. The idea was not bad at all. He figured the red would look rather dashing with the silver.

"So?" Veledar replied, grinning wide, "red is a most attractive color."

"Is that so?" Arcturus replied, gently shoving the dragon. Did he just blush when Veledar had said that? He shook his head. Of course he didn't. He was a paladin with over ten years of fighting experience under his belt, fully in control of his emotions.

Suddenly, they both heard a crack from their left side.

"Excuse me," Auron suddenly said as he materialized from thin air. "This one has yet to present the master with the gifts left by his mother."

Arcturus watched Veledar's snout -previously filled with laughter and joy- suddenly scrunch into a pained expression. He saw Veledar give a gulp before he spoke, "Go ahead, Auron, I am strong enough to at least find this out, right? What is the gift?"

"Gifts," Auron corrected, holding up a ghostly claw. The ghostly dragon swirled in place to suddenly reveal, with a puff of smoke, a large looking leather harness with numerous pouches meant to stash various items. On top there was clearly a saddle meant for someone.

"Her riding harness," Veledar said softly, picking up the leather in his claws. Auron then clapped his paws together with a puff of blue magic before Veledar could react further. Arcturus watched things slightly shift as a transparent silver dragon stood before them all.

"Veledar," the dragon said, standing tall with the frills on her neck extended. "I have ordered Auron here to leave you my word on the day that you are fully grown, and I am no longer there with you."

The dragoness swished her tail like Veledar always did, "I have left my harness for you, along with Carpenter's old weapon. I know you spoke fondly about that one day when you would have the opportunity to become an adventuring dragon, so the harness will allow you to fulfill that purpose."

Her eyes seemed to look directly at Veledar, with a softness only a mother could show. "I know you will grow into a brave, strong dragon. One that will accomplish many great things."

"Really momma?" Came the voice of a little red dragon that bounded to the silver one and grabbed one of her legs.

"Of course," She smiled, nuzzling the little Veledar with her snout.

"But...why are you talking to Auron? Even he can't predict the future, right? Right?"

"Oh my gods you were so cute!" Lyndis exclaimed, looking at the tiny Veledar who was transfixed on his mother.

"Graaarrrr!" Veledar snapped, holding a claw to his muzzle. "Be silent please. My mother's still speaking!"

"I'm leaving a message for you to see when you are big and strong like I am now." She replied, continuing to nuzzle the wrymling.

"Bigger!" The small red dragon flared his wings proudly.

"Yes, yes. Much bigger," The silver dragoness gave him a fond lick under his jaw. "But even heroes have to start off somewhere, so you'd better listen to everything I have to teach!"

"Like this message?" The little dragon cocked his head.

"No, little one. This message is for later. Way, way later."

"Why would you do that? I'm here right now!" Little Veledar protested, sticking his tongue out at his mother.

"So that, when you become a mighty wyrm with a mountain of treasure, you will know how much your mother loved you. I will always be by your side, Veledar, and neither distance, age, nor time will change how much I love you, my dearest red hero," She swiped little Veledar off into one of her huge forepaws pressed the boisterous hatchling tightly against her chest, holding him there even as he started to squirm in her grasp.

"Not in front of future me!" little Veledar hissed, "You're embarrassing me, mother!"

Arcturus put a hand over his mouth, both amused and amazed. It was simply so adorable to see the grown dragon that stood next to him in the present so little, cute, and fragile, all at the same time.

"You're supposed to be napping with your brother and sister instead of complaining about my methods, you know."

"If I go take a nap, will you stop nuzzling me in front of future me? Heroes are supposed to be strong, and...and fearless! They fight evil on their own, or maybe with other adventurers, but not with their mothers!"

"Maybe you're right, my dear, wise Veledar," The silver dragon nuzzled little Veledar one more time, gave him a short lick along his neck, then relaxed her grip.

"Yuck. I'm all messy now! You better not let hero me see this!" Little Veledar quickly scampered away, disappearing from view.

The silver dragon seemed to follow the small red dragon with her gaze. "You were quite adorable then, my little Crimson, but don't you ever think that changed. Hero or not, you are still my son. Same as you were all those years ago." She then returned her gaze to the grown Veledar, holding claw and almost touching the real one's snout. If Arcturus did not know better, he would have sworn she could actually see her son right now. Veledar gave a loud sniff as tears started to stream down his muzzle.

"I know it might seem like an insurmountable obstacle right now, but I know you will muster the fortitude to come out the other side better and stronger. I am so proud of you, my son, and I love you with all my heart no matter where your wings carry you."

The image faded away, leaving them all victims to the sound of Veledar's heart-wrenching sobbing. His crimson snout was drenched in tears as he lowered it closer to the ground. Arcturus and the others moved in quick and embraced the depressed dragon.

"We're here for you, Veledar. All of us...including your mother." The paladin said.

Veledar buried his snout into Arcturus' chest as he continued to sob. The human stroked Veledar's head, letting him cry it out.

"Yer mother has been a mightily fine lass. May she soar wit da rest of her kin in da afterlife."

"I agree with Merlia," Lyndis muttered her own words after the dwarf. "She might be gone now, Veledar, but her love will always remain with you, same as this hoard. Doubt you can spend all of this in twenty dragon lifetimes. Who knows? You might have to get busy and make little dragons of your own!"

"Shut up, you silly thief," Veledar snorted, throwing a small smile in Lyndis' direction. "I've still got a few more tears to shed before I'm ready to laugh at your jokes."

"What's going on between the two of you doesn't really look like a-"

"Oy! Snap it shut before I snap it for ye!" Merlia hissed.

Veledar let the playful banter slide past his emotions and thoughts. He cried for a few more minutes, then, with a loud sniff, he wiped his snout clean of the translucent beads. With a thank you, the dragon gave them all a quick nuzzle with his wet snout. Veledar then grabbed the harness, and carefully attached it to himself. Arcturus saw that, at first, the dragon seemed to struggle with the larger size of the harness, but the longer he took in taking it on the easier it became, almost like the harness was enhanced with the ability to reshape itself according to the user's size. The dragon clasped the final belt before striking a pose for all of them. He held his snout up high, unfurled his wings, stood straight, and curled his tail slightly around his magnificent body.

"How do I look? Marvelous, I presume? Dashing? Breathtaking? Awe inspiring?" The dragon said each word with increasing pride, the smugness on his snout growing proportionally to the weight of the praise.

Arcturus had to admit. The dragon did look good with the harness on. The way it seemed to move with him gave the idea it was not that uncomfortable as he often heard it from the gryphons forced to wear such things. His eyes focused onto the saddle portion of the harness. He imagined himself on top of the red dragon as Veledar flew them both into the vast, blue expanse of the sky. Perhaps the dragon did look dashing. The human put his hand to his chin as the dragon waited for an answer, his eyes wide.

"Well, now you look like a proper adventurer." Lyndis smirked, "With all those pouches, I bet you can hold plenty of supplies."

"That's one way to put it, thank you very much. Guess I'll just be your winged, smelly horse instead of the hero that swoops in to save the day!" Veledar replied with a disappointing snout wrinkle as he ran a claw through the coins beneath his paws.

"So why put on the harness now if you're not looking to carry some things for us?" Arcturus asked with a meek smile on his face.

"That's a very good question, human. I am going to stretch these beautiful wings of mine, catch the wind, and let the cold air brush off some bothersome thoughts from my head." Veledar sighed, "Flying high in the sky always made me feel better even when I was a tiny, stupid hatchling."

"What about our friends outside huntin ya?" Merlia asked, already slinging her pack around her shoulders.

"If we see them, I'll head back to the cave. The only reason they got to us last time is that they followed us closely through the illusion. Figure they should be far enough away to confuse me for a bird or something."

"We?" Lyndis gasped, placing a hand over her mouth, "Who gets to fly with the magnificent Veledar?" Her eyes then fell to Arcturus knowingly. "Oh, who ever do we think it could possibly be? Tis a hard choice, is it not? Two sneaky maidens, one valiant man...it's almost like the tales say, yes?" She grinned.

Veledar faced the tunnel they came from. then curled his head around to look to Arcturus.

"Paladin of Bahamut. Would you like to accompany me into the skies?"

Arcturus did not even need to think about such request. His mind made the decision before the dragon could even finish his question. "I'll do it!" he exclaimed in excitement.

"It would be a delightful honor to carry your armored ass up there," Veledar finished. "Really?" The dragon asked, almost sounding as if he was surprised. However, it only lasted before a moment before the dragon charm once again took hold.

"Well I mean of course you would love to ride with me. My wings definitely beat those ugly sky ships your people use. Grah. Combustible wood everywhere mixed with the stench of metal and cheap alcohol...why, I'd pay somebody like my illustrious self to liberate me from that torture," Veledar grinned as he stretched his wings out slowly. "And Merlia. Could you turn Ulga into an eagle or something else that has the capability of flying?"

"Well I sappose I could try dat," Merlia replied, stroking her chin softly. "We gonna be flyin da rest o' de wey?"

"You mean Veledar will be flying us there?" Lyndis said suddenly, clasping her hands together loudly with a clap.

"Well, I figure it was about time I swallow my pride and got this journey over with as soon as possible."

"Finally," Lyndis grinned, "I was waiting for your scaly bottom to cave in."

"Don't tempt me to leave you behind, Lyndis. Treasure might look great, but it is a poor substitute for my enchanting company," Veledar growled with a chuckle.

Arcturus made his way back to his belongings. It was hard to avoid the temptation to rush packing his things with the dragon's wing beats always on his mind. He put on his gambeson, tabard, and every armor piece one by one. He lastly stowed his sword into its sheath, slung the mirror shield gifted to him by Veledar over his back, and took his place at the red dragon's side.

Lyndis pulled a map from her pack as she started walking with Merlia along the silver path back to the entrance. Everyone else followed in step beside her in silence. Arcturus stood on Veledar's left. With each step, he could feel his anticipation growing. After all, he had never been properly introduced to flying on a dragon's back. He had always been picked up like a scared stag in the dragon's claws, or had to hold on for dear life upon the creature's scaly back. This time, things were bound to be different. This time, he would fly properly upon the back of his dragon companion and friend.

Arcturus spent most of the time watching the dragon's movements, and hardly noticed when they had gotten back to the cave's entrance. Merlia pulled Ulga from her pocket, unrolled a mat, and keeled upon it gently. She closed her eyes and started chanting in dwarven quietly.

"Now don't get into trouble you two." Lyndis said, pointing a finger at Arcturus' breastplate. She then did the same with Veledar's scaled chest. 'We don't need any more company here so don't come along with any uninvited guests, friendly or not." She turned back to the map she had pulled out, her eyes scanning the parchment. "Still here? Fly, you two, so I can figure out the better route for us to take to Entis. Things are going to be a lot trickier with these thugs on our tails."

"Well you heard her." Veledar said, crouching slight with care, to allow Arcturus better access to get on the saddle. "Shall we?" The dragon swished his tail invitingly.

"Don't see why not." Arcturus climbed one foot over, just like he would on a horse, although the thought was quickly struck from his mind. He would never compare his friend to a horse outside of a joke, and he would probably get insulted at the very idea by his wife's memory, who'd certainly be able to make the difference between the monster that took her life and the friend Arcturus was about to ride upon.

The paladin tested his boot, pleased to find it was secure in the saddle. He found a cord latched on with a metal ring that he wrapped around his waist and secured it. He figured it was to help him stay on the dragon during turns and other maneuvers. Next thing he noticed was that the harness had no reins to speak of, which was right. It wasn't like he had to control Veledar like a steed. Despite that oddity with which Arcturus grew accustomed to from the hundreds of horses he'd mounted throughout his life, the saddle felt very much like a normal one.

"So where did you want to fly?" He asked, feeling the warm dragon flex his muscles with eager anticipation.

"I figured we should do a few loops around the mountain, coupled with some banks and turns so that you can get a feel of how my wings take the wind."

"Feel for you? That's what's this is about, eh?" He grinned. He suddenly realized that possibly the dwarf's humor was starting to rub on him. He just laughed it off, and witnessed the dragon giving him a quick smirk.

"You are not completely wrong there. If we are to be companions, we should get a feel for flying properly together. So that when we fight, we can do it together...as one." Veledar stretched his wings wide. Then, with a flick of his mighty tail, refolded them against his back.

Arcturus patted the dragon's scales, "Alright then, partner. I'm ready for whatever you want to throw at me."

"Are you completely sure that all your gear is stowed correctly?"

Arcturus saw that the dragon's eye had started to inspect him from head to boot. "Why are you asking?"

"Oh, I don't know. Just case I decide to do some maneuvers that might get this pristine armor of yours loose." The dragon said with a hint of innocence, although by the way his eye looked away, Arcturus figured the dragon had a trick or two up his scales, and honestly, he did not mind. In fact, he was a tad curious what Veledar had cooked up inside his scaly head. He looked to shield to find it latched on properly upon his back, his pouches too were all firmly closed, and then finally his sword neatly tucked in its sheath. The issue, as Veledar hinted earlier.

"Think I found the culprit," Arcturus tied the sword's hilt onto the scabbard by a thread. "All set now, Veledar. Ready for whatever you have planned."

"Excellent!" The dragon smiled, one that made the human a little flattered that he was bringing such joy to the dragon under him. Veledar walked along the tunnel that led them both out of the cave, then stretched his wings as he breathed in the cold air of the morning.

"Try not to fly too high. Might get a tad cold up there."

"Are you saying your shiny armor can't handle a bit of cold?" The dragon smirked.

"Oh, it certainly is capable of that. Can't say the same about the man who wears it.

"Good thing I'm warm then," Veledar's cocky smile grew wider. "Ready now? Or do I have to warm you up with my tongue?"

"I'm fine, I'm fine!" The human waved off the tongue poking out of Veledar's mouth. "Spread your wings and take us in the air before you get weirder ideas."

He felt Veledar suddenly bound forward, and with a great flap of his wings, the two of them ascended into the air. Arcturus watched with glee as the snowy ground they passed left them behind. Veledar kept climbing with every wing-beat, and Arcturus scanned the landscape below like a child who traveled by gryphon for the first time. In some ways, it was just like looking off the deck of an airship. He remembered doing this numerous times over his lifetime, but it felt different. This was more personal, more intimate, and it felt glorious. The constant rhythm of Veledar's wing-beats, even the cold wind blowing his face...it all felt different. Like he was safer than he'd ever been. Even the stomach lurching that usually accompanied their flights from before was not present. Perhaps he was destined to fly, after all.

"How is it going back there?" Veledar roared, his voice filled with happiness. The dragon then dipped to turn gracefully in the air.

Words failed Arcturus at first. He was simply too caught up in the sensation overload of the flight to focus on a proper reply. After all, he could never imagine such a sight from the ground. How the sun lit landscape could look any more beautiful than it did right now, when he rode upon the back of a real, friendly dragon? It certainly was not the first thing a normal dragon slayer would envision.

How can I ever go back to a normal life? Arcturus wondered as his hands tightened their grip on the leather collar wrapped around Veledar's neck.

There is nothing that can compare to this. Not even gryphon riding.

The human smiled when he imagined how Veledar would react when compared with a gryphon. Although he also realized perhaps he had waited a tad too long to reply to the dragon. He let the excitement out in a loud declaration of his feelings, "THIS IS AMAZING!" He shouted from atop his lungs and let that broad, honest smile wash across his bright face, without a hint of resistance or regret.

Veledar roared again in approval as they continued their turn in the sky. They ended it when Veledar tilted his wings back and spread them wide as he entered a steady glide. Arcturus closed his eyes and let the wind batter against his face. He took a deep breath from the crisp air as Veledar gave another flap of his mighty wings. Arcturus tried to picture himself as the dragon, flying right now in the sky. He did not know if it was his imagination at work, but he swore he could almost feel the wind that caressed Veledar's wings, kissing his many red scales.

The dragon spent the next few minutes in various banks or turns. Arcturus started to lean into them, slowly starting to predict how Veledar would turn by the strong muscles that moved beneath him. A dragon was not only wings, as many common people believed. Lots of muscles worked together to keep these magnificent creatures airborne. Truly, it was an honor to experience flying in such an intimate, indescribable way. Arcturus looked past the dragon as he finished yet another turn. A great forest spread across the land in the distance. Its green mass seemed to stretch on for miles upon miles, and he knew beyond the verdant expanse was the city of Entis. The forest of despair, some people used to call the amalgamation of trees, but Arcturus had never stepped foot in that forest, just as he had never heard of anyone going in it. Although the rumors whispered of monsters that lurked inside the shadows, ready to feast on the blood of foolish adventurers. Arcturus knew Lumara would've purged the forest of such threats decades ago.

"It's just tales meant to scare children." He brushed off the thought from his mind out loud.

"Did you just compare my flying to your stupid bedtime stories?"

Arcturus waved apologetically when the dragon turned his head to chill him in the saddle with one of his imposing azure eyes. "No, no. This forest that stretches ahead of us...heard some really interesting things about it."

The dragon checked it out for a few seconds, then blew a gust of black smoke. "It's just a bunch of trees. Now, are you ready for something a bit more advanced?" Veledar turned his head to look at the human. Arcturus could see in his eyes that the dragon was simply begging to show off for him. Distracted from his concerns about the weird forest, he found himself nodding to the dragon.

"You bet! Let's see what you can do, young hero!"

"That's the spirit! I knew I liked you!" Veledar cried, and with a mighty flap of his great wings, the eager dragon started to climb even higher into the sky. With each wing-beat Veledar continued his ascent, until Arcturus found it was starting to get harder to breathe. He was practically leaning forward to hug the dragon as the forces of the earth and sky pushed him against Veledar's back. Arcturus looked for a moment to the ground below, so far removed from his current position.

"Oh, sweet Gods," The human muttered and just hugged Veledar a tad harder. He had never been this high before, not even inside the protective wooden belly of an airship.

"Ready?" The dragon cried out.

"Always!" He found himself shouting back to him. Despite his slight fear, Arcturus trusted the dragon to see him through to the end of this magnificent journey, and pushed whatever slivers of fear that still existed within him down with the next flap of Veledar's wings.

"Hold on!"

Arcturus felt Veledar's wings slightly tilt, and the dragon had started flipping over backwards. Arcturus felt himself lift slightly in the harness. The world that was once below him was now above. He found himself cheering, his fear soon turning into excitement once more. Veledar then reoriented himself into a dive bomb. Arcturus could feel gravity pulling down as the wind whistled passed his cherry red ears. This was thrilling, exciting, making him forget that the ground was rushing towards him at a startling pace. Every nerve in his body told him that such a fall should be terrifying. However, his next cheer silenced those nerves once more. Veledar even joined in with an ear-splitting roar.

"Hold on again!" The dragon yelled, "It's not over yet!"

Veledar started spinning round and round. Arcturus could see that everything that was not Veledar or himself was a blur as he hung onto the dragon's frame. He gave a cheer as he clutched those crimson scales for dear life, until the dragon stopped, spread his wings and returned to a gentle glide.

Once again Arcturus found himself speechless. His smile was still on his face, and he imagined that it would be there for quite some time. That was probably the most fun he had had in quite some time.

"T-that was...Gods, I've never felt such intense feelings in my life!" He breathed aloud slowly. "Thank you Veledar....you can't imagine how grateful I am to taste the true freedom of the skies, just like a dragon."

"You're most welcome my metal-clad partner." Veledar replied, turning his head to look at him. "With the help of these great wings of mine, I shall set you free from the earthly bonds that kept you so horribly chained."

"Chained?" Arcturus raised a finger. "We had airships, you know. I could have always flown with a gryphon whose feathers keep warmer than your scales."

"True, but you said you never flew a gryphon," The dragon stuck out his tongue. "Besides, does one of those bloated airships even hold a candle to me? Can they spin or dive like we just did?"

The dragon gave him a coy smirk. He knew what Arcturus was going to say. How could he not? This was nothing like any other time he had gone flying. However, the dragon was waiting for his answer, wanting to hear him say it.

"No, nothing can quite compare to this kind of flying, Veledar. It was like seeing for the first time.... It was something beautiful, beyond what mere words can express."

"Well I have to say, Arcturus. In this light, you look rather good on my back. I think I might like you up there."

"Bah. Dragon compliments. Why do they have to feel so damn sweet?"

"Because I'm nothing but sweetness underneath these scales!"

"Yeah, I got that from our first encounter. Oh, and just so you know, I think you look good in any light." He laughed, rubbing his neck with his hand. He saw Veledar's eyes focus on him for a moment, as another grin found its way to his muzzle. Arcturus wondered what was going through the dragon's mind at that moment. Probably just loving the compliments.

"Oh, stop that flattering before you turn my wings pink."

"Really? You get that shy when somebody compliments you?"

"NO! Proud, magnificent, self-indulging at times, sure. But never embarrassed over a bit of praise!" Veledar turned his attention back to the mountains below. "However, I think we should go check in with our companions. See if they are ready for the journey. And Arcturus?"

"Yes?"

"I take it you would not say no to flying like this again?"

Arcturus did not even need time to think. "There is not a thing in the world that would stop me from flying with you again, Veledar." Arcturus held out his arms wide like they too were wings. "Arcturus and Crimson Sky, the greatest aerial warriors of all time!"

"I like it, although let's put my name first. I do not wish to confuse people about who is doing the real work here."

"Pffff. I don't think our adoring fans will mind how we put our names together."

"Adoring fans, you say?"

Both man and dragon gave a laugh in unison as Veledar descended towards the snowy entrance of the cave. Arcturus braced himself as Veledar landed on the ground. Although the sudden lurch of their landing never came, the dragon had been incredibly gentle as his leathery pads touched the ground. Arcturus undid all the straps as he dismounted the dragon, his boots landing in the snow. He saw that Lyndis came running over, flinging bits of snow around with each step of her boots.

"How was it? Were you afraid? Was he gentle? Tell me Arcturus! I need to know!" Lyndis spoke quickly, her voice almost running together with each question on her excited breath.

"It was great, no, he was when he needed to be." Arcturus chuckled at how fast he managed to answer all of those questions, "Don't worry though, we will head out soon enough, and you will see for yourself."

"You are volunteering me to carry the half elf?" Veledar asked, holding his snout up high.

"How can you deny her desire when she is in awe of your splendor, O' dear dragon? Can't you see she craves the touch of your scales, the sound of your wings taming the savage skies above, the marvelous sights only a dragon can see?" He figured any way to convince the dragon to let Lyndis fly with them as well would play the exact same tune as his vanity.

Veledar fidgeted for a moment, flicking his tail as he thought it over. With a final swish of his tail, and a roll of his eyes, Veledar replied, "Well, I suppose she can fly with us when you put it that way... After all, every group of adoring fans starts with one..."

"THANK YOU VELEDAR!" Lyndis cheered, running over to give his chest a big hug. The dragon simply returned it with one of his paws as he patted her back, "Yes, yes of course you're welcome. Just make sure to spread the word when this Entis business is all said and done, yes? Speak from the heart, and maybe add a thing or two about my scales. Humans love to praise them."

In spite of the vain tone he seemed to be giving, Arcturus knew the dragon was looking forward to it as well. He could just tell by the look Veledar had in his eyes.

"Now dear Lyndis, do you have the best path planned out? Entis is no mere village from what you all keep telling me." Veledar undid his hold, letting Lyndis go.

"Uh-huh," She replied, nodding and pulling out the map. Arcturus walked over just as she started pointing to it. "You see, it should be a straight shot right over this forest here. I also heard rumors that the Lumarians avoid this forest at all costs. Airships, caravans, patrols, anything you can think of. It's almost like the very source of plague dwells within that big wall of trees."

"And what is the plan when we arrive near the city?" Arcturus asked.

"Well, I figure Veledar there turns back to the size of a common drake, then I figure out a disguise for you. Merlia and I are lucky since no one knows who we are, so we can blend into the crowd as travelers. We walk in, find a way to get to the castle, and simply get the book back!"

"Oh great yer back!" Merlia shouted, leading a snowy eagle out of the cave. The eagle was large enough for someone to ride on it, but nowhere near the size of Veledar. Arcturus was thankful that the eagle was presented with the cave behind her. Otherwise he did not think he would be able to see her perfect white body and feathers. "Bout time ye get back. Ulga here was startin to get impatient!" The dwarf pulled out a brush and started to stroke the eagle's feathers. "Did ya at least have a good fly?"

"Yes Merlia, it was literally the best flight I ever had with him yet." Arcturus said cheerfully.

"Good, now we can be getting out of here and back to our adventurin'."

"Before we go, let me just present you with something I completely forgot about." Veledar said from behind Arcturus.

The paladin turned to see the dragon rifling through some of the pouches on his harness, until he procured a thin looking silver metallic rod. He gently handed it over to Arcturus, who grasped it softly into his hands. It was roughly eight inches long, and engraved of course with golden dragons.

"What is it? Some kind of scepter?" He asked, turning the rod over in his hands, then bringing it closer to his eyes.

"Be careful and look." Veledar replied, pointing to a small section at a gold dragon's eye. "Now press that button, and make sure you're not near anyone."

"What's it going to do? Shoot flames?" He chuckled.

"Just press it you stubborn human. The real fun is in discovering how how these things work!" Veledar playfully shoved him, then sat softly on his haunches several feet away.

"Well, here goes nothing," Arcturus pressed the dragon's eye firmly with his thumb. The rod expanded up to six feet, causing the paladin to jump back in surprise.

Veledar laughed, and Lyndis ran over with her eyes wide. From the tip of the rod came a blade that seemed to be made of fire.

"So, what did you and Merlia end up borrowing from my armory?" Veledar asked as Arcturus noticed the dragon's eyes were firmly locked on the blazing weapon he held.

"Oh, I grabbed a pair of somewhat ordinary magical rapiers you had in there." Lyndis held up a pair of ornate handled rapiers. Each one was black with silver lines running along the hilts. "Merlia over there picked up a chain shirt you had lying around in a pile of other armor. Once again, it had a minor magical aura which means it's more useful than it looks."

Arcturus watched the dragon take that bit of information down. He pictured he was making a note of it in his head. Then the dragon nodded, "Good, now we will be better prepared for whatever lays ahead."

Arcturus held the blade firmly in his hand. It was light, way lighter than he thought a weapon like this should have been. He swished it a few times, finding it put almost no strain on his arm when swung.

"Dats a fancy stick ye got dere." Merlia said, looking the weapon up and down. "Course, ye be findin me sticking to dis here bow o' course."

"Well, are you ready to go? Or shall we continue blabbering about weapons?" Veledar asked them as he spread his wings wide.

"Always ready ta go." Merlia responded, getting ready to mount Ulga.

"Yeah. Let's put our feet...err, wings to work already. We got lots of ground to cover today," said Lyndis.

Arcturus hit the button on the weapon, retracting it once more until it returned to its original size. He found a ring to hook it to on his belt for easy reach. With another crouch from Veledar, he slung himself on top of the dragon, once again feeling the same excitement building inside his chest.

"There's always this much anticipation to fly, Veledar?"

"Got a taste for it now?" Veledar smirked, "And yes, that's usually a good sign." The dragon turned his snout to Lyndis, who seemed to hesitate before mounting the dragon.

"Come on, I swear he's gentle." Arcturus extended a hand to the reluctant rogue. "There won't be any twists or sudden turns when I'm here."

"Oh Arcturus, don't coddle the girl. She might like surprises." Veledar wiggled his tail impatiently.

Lyndis grabbed the paladin's proffered hand firmly and pulled herself up until she was sitting behind him.

"Good Gods, Lyndis! Is it me or have you put on a bit of weight since we got here?" Veledar's limbs wobbled as soon as the rogue settled on his back. "I don't think I can carry you after the sumptuous meals I've served!" The red drake hissed.

Arcturus heard a smack as Lyndis struck the dragon with her first. Almost instantly the dragon regained his composure and showed no sign of struggling.

"I guess I really have lost my fine touch. Fine then. Let's do this flying thing again," The dragon grumbled, turning his snout to the sky. Arcturus felt him shift as his wings readied to flap. Behind him, the dragon's tail tip twitched with excitement.

Then Ulga suddenly shot past them into the sky.

"Hey, I was supposed to be the one in the lead!" Veledar moaned as he took off after the eagle and the dwarf mounted atop her back.

"Then ye gotta be fasta den dat!" Merlia shouted out over her shoulder. Arcturus saw her pat Ulga, though she leaned suspiciously close to the eagle's head, almost like she whispered something into the eagle's ear. If he knew any better, it was an encouragement for the eagle to fly even faster.

"Come on, Ulga! Make that scaly bastard eat yer feathers!"

"As if I'll ever allow that!" Veledar growled at the challenge.

Arcturus felt Lyndis hold his armor tight as Veledar sped up to gain on Ulga.

"Veledar. For Scales' sake, this doesn't have to be a race!" Arcturus shouted out, laughing as Veledar continued his pursuit.

"Oh, brighten up, you clanking bucket of metal! Our adventure has been lacking competitive spirit ever since I've stuffed you with meals in my mother's...in the gracious halls of my lair!" The dragon replied as they flew within feet of the dwarf. With a proud roar Veledar passed them before he turned back and stuck his tongue out at the dwarf.

* * * * * * * * * *

They all flew towards the capital with the darkened forest below them. The race they agreed to enjoy started to fade. Currently, the dragon and the eagle flew side by side over the tops of the clutter of oaks, pines and maples rushing past.. Arcturus shook his head, it seemed as if they were flying closer and closer to the sea of green below.

"Dis reminds me of them elven lands. Makes me wonder, what is da name o' da forest dere?" Merlia shouted.

"That would be the forest of despair!" Arcturus replied.

"Oh great. Dats a wonderful name for a forest. What's wrong wit you humans? Yer mommas read ya one ta many creepy stories?"

"She has a point, Arcturus." Veledar laughed, causing Arcturus to squint his eyes. He once again found himself watching Veledar as he flew high above the forest. The dragon slightly moved his wings, no doubt to stay with the air currents.

"So where did you guys end up flying to?" Lyndis asked in Arcturus' ear.

"Just gave the mountain a few loops. Veledar was just getting me used to the feel of his wings. It was way better than being picked up like prey for sure."

"He picked you up? You never told me that when you recounted your story!"

"He screamed like a banshee queen!" Veledar laughed, "No wonder he did not wish to tell you. It would tarnish his reputation as a brave paladin."

"Anyone would have screamed their guts when placed in that situation. We humans aren't made for such kind of thrills! Heights pose a serious danger you know." He shot back, pressing his finger on the dragon's back firmly. "Or if a certain dragon was going to drop him."

"I never planned on doing that, even if we were on much worse terms." Veledar snickered.

"Anyway," Arcturus continued, rolling his eyes. "He did a loop, then some rolls, and ended up with a nose dive towards the ground."

"Amazing!" said Lyndis in surprise. "Even the pegasai back home won't do a loop!"

"Wait, you have flown before?" Arcturus asked. He was almost sure that, judging by the excitement she had shown Veledar, that the elf never tasted the exhilarating freedom of the high skies. Perhaps it was Veledar's size that intimidated her.

"Aye!"

"I thought these pegasi were reserved for the royal knights of your country. Am I wrong?" He asked, certain he had read about that in reports from long ago. The sky knights were quite a force to deal with. They could get in really quick, hit their target, and extract before anyone knew what happened. Pegasi were even faster than gryphons, and it usually took some tricky maneuvering of forces in order to deal with them.

"That's a misconception. See, they are just knights, not just trained out by the royal guard." Lyndis replied, holding up her right finger as she talked. Sadly, Veledar, I think they might be faster than you."

"Most likely the only area in which they excel!" Veledar shot back with a growl. The dragon turned slightly right and started a decent down towards the forest. Arcturus started to wonder what Veledar could be doing. Did he want to skim the tree tops? He did not mention anything about wanting to rest his wings.

"Hey Veledar, why are you descending towards the forest? You can't be so tired that you want to rest now!" He stared as Veledar continued to descend without a word or snarky quip back.

"Is he alright?" Lyndis whispered into his ear. Arcturus could feel her hands tightening around his waist.

"Veledar!" Arcturus shouted out to the dragon, who was now practically touching the treetops as he flew.

"What's da matter wit da dragon?" Merlia shouted from above as Ulga brought her closer towards them.

"We don't know!" Lyndis shouted back, "Veledar just started heading towards the forest and won't answer us!"

Arcturus touched Veledar's neck scales with his gloved hand. He patted them gently, trying to ignore the trees that were almost hitting Veledar's limbs now.

"What is going on with you, buddy?" He whispered to himself. He then took a deep breath, "VELEDAR! Wake up from whatever the hell you're doing!"

The dragon shook his head with a savage swipe from left to right. He tilted his wings, and stopped in a hover above the trees. "Graaawwrrr!" He continued to shake his head as he let out growls of frustration. Arcturus thankfully managed to stay in the saddle, with Lyndis clutching him tightly from behind.

"What in the world just happened? Veledar. Lyndis. Are you alright?"

Arcturus didn't wait for an answer. Instead, he looked down at the forest and felt a pit grow in his stomach. Perhaps the rumors about this strange forest were true all along. There had to be some reason why everything from Lumara typically avoided this place.

"I'm alright, if you can call it that. Gods...I have a bad feeling about this." Lyndis said. Arcturus could feel her move one hand to what most likely was the hilt of her rapier. The man thought about doing the same, but he held his hand against the dragon's scales instead. He had to try and wake Veledar up from whatever ailed him. Perhaps he just needed to hear the voice of a friend.

"Veledar! Brightscales. Crimson head. Are you listening to me? No? Then focus on my voice. Listen to my voice Veledar. Focus."

Veledar shook his head for a final time as he let out a deep roar from his throat. He moved his head slowly to look around before turning around to look to Arcturus with one of his blue eyes.

"Arcturus. Lyndis. Where are we?" Veledar asked between steady beats of his wings.

"You tell us, dragon, because I certainly haven't used one of my charms to cloud your mind." Lyndis laughed nervously.

"I don't.... remember much," Veledar said, stumbling over his own words.

"Great. Just...this is a fantastic start to our journey. Is there anything you can remember? Any details on what caused you to bring us so close to these ugly trees?" Lyndis continued her questioning. Arcturus felt her hand move from her rapier back to his shoulder.

"I...I remember a voice calling my name from the forest below. Then everything started to get fuzzy and heavy, kind of like when you drink another barrel of ale after you had one too many. My next memory is you shouting my name." The dragon said.

"It sounds like ya fell fer de ole siren's song!" Merlia shouted from above.

"Strange, but believable, given the evidence. I might have to take your word for it. I have never met a siren." The dragon growled deep in his throat as he barred his teeth, "I think we should get as far away from this accursed place as we can. Right now!"

Veledar gave his wings a stronger beat that elevated them above the trees. That's when Arcturus saw something move towards them from beneath the forest's thick canopy. Dark green vines flew up to Veledar, easily wrapping around the dragon's limbs.

"What are these accursed things?" The dragon thrashed as he growled and snapped at the vines that seemed to grip tighter and tighter around his scales.

"I don't know, but I bet they've not just went through all the trouble of crawling up just to give us a welcoming hug!"

"Mraaaarrrr!" Arcturus felt the dragon jerk beneath him. Veledar pulled against constricting vines with a flurry of wing beats, and when that failed, the dragon pulled up a green serpent and brought his muzzle down to chew through a second, freeing his left paw.

"That's one way to say no to hugs," Arcturus pulled out the rod and activated it, letting it extend to its full length before his very eyes.

"Will you just stop joking about this and kill them?" Lyndis hissed from behind.

Like a valiant knight obeying the request of a maiden in need, Arcturus did a quick salute gesture, then swung the weightless flaming blade down to slice a cluster of vines off his friend's right paw.

"Look at them burn!" Veledar growled excitedly.

"Yeah! Stay off my dragon you nasty, jealous plants!" Arcturus too gave a cheer of victory as he slashed through yet another cluster, but it was short lived. From the severed vines, either cut by teeth or burned by sword, several more started to regrow. They sprang up with an inhuman force to start wrapping around the now roaring and snarling red dragon. One of the said vines wrapped around the dragon's neck and pulled hard. Hard enough to pull a fully grown, winged dragon down towards the tree tops that pointed their sharp tips right at his belly.

Arcturus sliced through the offending vine almost instantly. He wasn't about to give up his friend to whatever sorcery the forest produced. Veledar had moved his neck and grazed the fire blade on the pole. Thankfully, his mother thought of this scenario. Veledar, being a red dragon, was impervious to fire, magical or otherwise. Arcturus grinned, knowing he could actually slice his way wildly around Veledar and not physically hurt the dragon with the weapon. From behind, he heard Lyndis mutter all sorts of curses. Most of them ended with the word 'focken' with every breath as she too was no doubt working her rapiers against the vines that were now trying to wrap around her lithe body.

"Looks like ye need a bit o' help. Say hello ta ma big friend, ye crawly green snails!"

From the corner of his eye Arcturus saw that Merlia had pulled out the oath bow and was raining what arrows she could into the vines. However, despite their efforts to grant Veledar that one moment where he could lift himself about the trees, the vines held firm in their assault.

"Grawr, this is working about as well as a human trying to kill me with his fists!" The dragon snarled.

"Use a spell then!" Arcturus cried out.

"I've got something better. You might want to shield your eyes a bit, and maybe take a deep breath before the air gets foul!"

"Oh, for Bahamut's sake, dragon! This is not the time for fart jokes!"

Veledar threw a quick smile at Arcturus, breathed in deep, then unleashed a cone of fire down towards his own paws. The orange blaze touched the vines like a rain of pure sizzling destruction, turning their green forms black, drying out their wetness, and reducing the creepy things to ash.

"How is that for a joke?" The dragon licked his snout proudly.

"Great job!" Lyndis cried as the dragon got a few good wingbeats in to regain the altitude he had lost during the attack of the vines. Even so, Arcturus saw even more fly up towards the dragon, three times faster than before.

"More! There's more!"

"Oh, you gotta be focken kiddin'."

"Not exactly!" Arcturus grunted in response as he sliced his way through the vines with all the speed he could muster. The vines snapped in half, falling back to the forest like zombie vegetation, but the paladin's fury could not stop the wriggly monsters from wrapping around the dragon, and with a firm pull, dragging him down from the sky.

Arcturus was dragged along with Lyndis and Veledar through the canopy of the trees. Veledar struggled the entire time as his entire body tensed up to fight, but it was for naught. The vines simply had too well of a hold on the dragon. The paladin kept on slicing vines away from his friend, until Veledar was able to get another deep breath. Arcturus shielded his face as Veledar let loose a fiery inferno that washed over his underside. Arcturus could feel the heat rise from below as feet upon feet of vines were incinerated before the might of his dragon. With all this destruction raining down upon them, the vines finally let go of them, Veledar ruptured his way through the branches and fell to the forest floor below with a thud. Lyndis -luckily being the nimble one that she was- managed to jump off at nearly the last second and avoid harm.

Veledar groaned from the ground. "Why did I have to fall from the sky again?" The dragon then smacked the ground with his tail.

"Pulled, you mean. You did not fall out of your own volition," Arcturus corrected him as he felt his leg pinned beneath the dragon. He gave it a tug, but it would not budge. He hoped it was not broken.

"Thanks for the correction. I can die happy now that I have such a learned man by my side." Veledar rumbled as he got back onto all fours.

Arcturus sighed as felt his leg. Thankfully, it did not seem to be broken. "Well, knowledge doesn't do much good against whatever those were," he unlatched himself and dismounted the dragon.

"The forest has to earn its name from something."

Arcturus replied with a meek smile and dropped into a combat stance as he stowed the metal rod and drew his sword and shield. Veledar spread his wings wide, thrashed his tail against the ground, and barred his teeth. He heard Lyndis emerge to stand beside him, her rapier held aloft and her eyes alert.

Arcturus scanned the trees for any sign of movement, and he could see Lyndis and Veledar doing the same. Despite their waiting, there was no sign of the vines that had dragged them down into this forest. All that he could see were the numerous trees that seemed to litter the area. One oddity was that their current position had scarcer vegetation. It seemed the vines had picked this exact spot to fit them into. There were hardly any sounds from wildlife that Arcturus could hear, although he could easily blame that on Veledar's roars. With no threat presently attacking them, Arcturus breathed a sigh of relief. It seemed like whatever had caused this inopportune stop from their journey was granting them a reprieve.

"Someone has a funny way of inviting us to a stroll through the forest." Lyndis quipped as she stowed her rapier and began dusting off her leather armor. "They could have simply asked, or charm some plants to do that for them. I heard some mages in Rothdell keep singing sunflowers as pets."

Veledar just growled deep, hissed again, and thrashed his tail against the ground, causing a cloud of dirt to fly up around his body.

"Manticore's gnarly bottom. I'm grounded again!" The dragon roared, folding his wings up against himself. "Why do I always have to feel the dirt under my feet?"

There was a sudden rustling of trees that caused all of them to stop and focus on that one spot. Arcturus raised his sword, Veledar spread his wings wide, and Lyndis held up a cupped hand filled with an orb of fire.

"We might not have long before our host decides we need to keep moving." Lyndis said, lowering her cupped hand, the fire simply fading away from her relaxing fingers.

"Get off me ye dirty vines. Unless ya wanna hav some fun wit me! If dat's da case, tis best ta buy a girl dinner first!" Came the voice of Merlia from above. Arcturus could hear the dwarf continue to swear and yell as he pictured her slicing the things with her axes. When she came into view the vines let her drop from high above. Veledar leaped up and caught the dwarf.

"Got you!" Veledar smiled as he landed back on the ground and set the dwarf down gently.

"Well I sappose ye got yer uses." Merlia snarked, "Thank'ee laddie for da rescue. Ye might be my great hero today."

"Oh Merlia, don't you already know this? I am always great." Veledar shot back, swelling his chest up.

"So not ta sound impatient, but what we doin now dat dese vines dragged us down 'ere?" Merlia stowed her axes at her side in a single motion. Arcturus noted that she was missing arrows from her quiver, probably from all the shooting she did on the vines. "Cause it seems like dese vines be keen on keepin us down 'ere. Do we just wander about, whistlin a merry tune?"

"It's not like we haven't done that before." Veledar snarled, looking to the trees that had dragged him from the sky. Arcturus saw a hate flash through his eyes. The dragon really did not like having his freedom snatched away from him. The paladin stowed his sword as he too felt a tad of what Veledar was going through. They had just flown for real, only to be torn from the sky. When he found whatever person or thing that unleashed those rude vines upon his party, they would get a piece of his mind. He pictured Veledar spouting off threats, baring his teeth, snorting black smoke. He smiled at the thought.

"Besides, whoever wanted us down here clearly did not want me or the rest of you dead." Veledar continued, then stopped with a grin, "Although I am also inclined to chock it up to the fact that I am a dragon, and that's the only reason we survived. Can a gryphon breathe fire or endure the punishment of those stinky vines as long as I had? Not unless they grow scales on their entire body!"

"Yeah, yeah. Nothing new there," the human grumbled. "Dragon pride excluded, I think Veledar here has a point." Arcturus stowed his weapon back in its scabbard. "I think we just stay together, keep our eyes peeled, and try to figure out why we are here."

"See? Arcturus here gets it." replied Veledar, then rumbled with a deep growl in his throat, "and when we find whoever DARED to rip us from the sky, we are going to unleash the same retribution upon them in the form of words fitting their station!"

"So if they're a stone giant, you are going to praise them?" Arcturus chuckled.

"My bet is on a midget. Only they are cowardly enough to let magic do all their work." The dragon snorted.

Arcturus and Veledar looked through the trees to find what looked like a path winding its way through the forest. It was certainly large enough to fit them, even if they walked side by side, and any direction was good as any if they had no idea where to go. Arcturus started to walk, and Veledar joined him with a swish of his tail.

"Coming, ladies?" The dragon asked, curling his neck around to look at them.

"I most certainly am not going to stare at your butt all the way to Entis." Lyndis shrugged the offer down.

"Da elf speaks sense," Merlia agreed. "Ye gotta be on equal footing wit yer party if ye wanna be a good leader, dragon."

"I haven't actually told you to ogle my tail you know, but I understand if your eyes find it difficult to find anything more captivating amidst this...desolate landscape."

"You do have a nice tail." Arcturus commented with a whisper. "Just...don't let them hear that."

Veledar favored him with a quick smile. Arcturus thought to path that lay before them, and what new dangers were awaiting them in this forest. He thought to Veledar, walking ever so vigilantly alongside him, and why the king had wanted such a wonderful dragon dead. He hovered his hand over the hilt of his sword with each foot step that carried him along the winding path.

Whatever lays ahead, we will face it all together.

The girls soon caught up, and the group of four adventurers soon advanced into the eerie depths of the darkened forest.

<u>Epilogue</u>

Skywing walked along the smooth wooden deck of the mightiest ship in Lumara, the Indomitous. It was the same ship that the famous dragon slayer, Arcturus Lund, had set out on to hunt the red dragon that the gryphon found himself perusing as well. What started out as a simple mission of retrieving the red for the king had suddenly turned into a complicated ordeal. The gryphon gazed to the snow-covered mountaintops that were passing far below the ship's hull. They looked like a sea of vast white, with little rough brown rocks jutting out from the seamless blanket of snow. Skywing found himself puzzled by this discovery. When they had found out the dragon was not the flames, teeth, or rage that the paperwork had said he would be, nobody knew what to believe. And the paladin sent to find him? The reports claimed the dragon had killed the man in a fit of rage. That had proven to be false as well. After all, Skywing had seen the man with his own eyes.

He remembered bounding forth to strike at the man, furious that such a decorated hero would betray his oath to the king and let the beast free. However, when he had awoken from his blackout, Skywing found out that the beast had slain none of his wing-mates. Granted, there were wounds, bruises, and injured egos among the others of his flock, but each gryphon that he had brought into this hunt still drew breath. The only one that had died met his end at the ax of a dwarf, not the claws of the dragon. The snowy gryphon shook his head and closed his eyes as he let the cool mountain breeze ruffle his feathers. When he opened them, he found the cloudy sky was no less different, and his thoughts, no less confusing.

Was this red dragon even guilty of the crimes that had been listed on the paperwork? The ones that Garroth had kept reminding the crew during this hunt?

Truthfully, Skywing knew very little of the man that most were calling one of the best adventurers of the realm. Garroth seemed too ready to please for the gryphon's taste, his honor often swayed by the amount of coin dropped into his pouch. Skywing had heard the rumor that despite the dragon killing his friend, he had actually talked the king into paying him more money than was originally offered to do such a task. Skywing stuffed his angry screech in the back of his throat. If it were any of his gryphons that had been claimed by the dragon, he would have done the damn task for free, but then again, he wasn't the one leading this mission. With a soft clack of his beak that involuntarily ended with a chirp, Skywing resettled his wings against his back. This time, an irritated snort left his parted beak, his breath misting in the air.

He stood on the wooden deck for quite some time, watching the ship start to make its way towards the vast forest that Skywing had found his way in two years earlier. It even looked like they were actually heading towards the forest of despair; the forest that no soul was allowed to enter, above or below, without the permission of its green dragoness ruler. He stood transfixed, as the place filled with him with a cold sort of terror that grew worse the closer he approached. The red dragon had been nothing like that green monster. She had taken everyone in Skywing's party out with barely any effort, then made him feel like mere prey before her. A tiny thing that was meant to pay worship to her. She had even taken his wing-mates at that time from him. Two gryphons that had been loyal to him more than anyone else. Skywing scowled at the sky. They must have been either statues, or her reluctant slaves, or servants, whatever the dragoness preferred to call them.

"What's running underneath those feathers of yours?"

Garroth's voice pulled Skywing's anger-filled thoughts from the forest, and the gryphon spun around without a word, with his striped tail wagging behind him. "A past that's no longer relevant. Tell me. Are we going to the forest of despair?" He asked flatly.

"Straight to the point. That is what I like about you." Garroth chuckled. He strolled over to the gryphon with a smile on his face. "Yes, we are indeed going to venture into that horrid place, for that is where the dragon decided to flee to." The man gave a large sigh of relief as he placed his hands on the railing and gazed down to the vast patchwork quilt of green that was the forest.

"How are you certain he went there, human? He can be in a thousand of other places by now. Dragons might be slower than us, but they're not stupid. He will go into hiding first chance he gets," Skywing padded over to the human's side and tilted his head to the left.

"Well...let's just say I know things."

"Really?" Skywing clacked his beak. "What about the sting of my tail? Will you know that too, if I decide to whip some sense into your head?"

"Ah, there's hardly need for such barbaric methods when the ruler of this very forest graced us with this," Garroth pulled out a small, palm sized red orb from his pouch. It looked to be a perfectly smooth thing, with tiny clouds swirling around within its confines. "With a mere touch, this item can show me the closest red dragon for miles around." He chuckled, pointing to the forest with his other hand. "So unless there is a second red dragon that just happened to be in a place close to the snowy mountain where we lost our quarry, I believe it is safe to say the dragon we seek is hiding beneath those trees."

"That is sound reasoning human, except I can show you one error in your plan.”

“And what error is that, Skywing? I have a vast ship here.” Garroth turned to gesture to the wooden deck. “We have energy cannons that can blast a hole the size of your head through the dragon’s scales. We have hunters armed to the teeth with equipment, and on top of that, we also have your gryphons.” The human crossed his arms and gave the gryphon an amused smirk. “Surely that is enough to subdue one pesky dragon, yes? We already brought him down from the sky once when he bled all over that mountain, if it were not for that strong magic protecting him, we would have had him bound in chains and back in the belly of this vessel in no time!”

Skywing sighed and looked to the ignorant human with pity. “Sounds so easy when you put it that way, but you know what? You behave as if you own the land beneath you.” The gryphon held up his talon and cupped the air. “One does not simply venture into the forest of despair, not while the Emerald Lady rules over every leaf, every branch, every speck of dust that resides in that dark place.”

“Emerald Lady?” Garroth placed a hand to his chin, and rubbed his rough stubble. “Can’t say I ever heard of anyone going by this title. Is she nobility, by any chance?”

Skywing told the human everything he had known about that night, two years prior. He mentioned the vines, the dragoness that towered over them, and how in a matter of minutes she had brought down ten armored knights and three gryphons with merely vines. When he was finished, he was amazed by the human’s complete lack of concern.

“I will contact my king about this matter.” He said with a smile. “You can rest assured though, Skywing. With everything we have gathered, I am sure we can go in and snatch the red dragon. Heck, maybe we can even deal with that green pest you just described.”

He placed a hand onto Skywings shoulder and patted it softly. “Just you wait, alright? I will contact some people back in Entis. Call in some favors, as you will, and make sure what happened to you back then doesn’t repeat now in the present.” Garroth turned to the forest once more. “Don't worry, Arcturus. We shall have you freed from that red dragon's claws. Hold on just for a day or two, my friend. Garroth and his merry band of adventurers is coming to rescue you.”

“Don't forget the gryphons that yearn for a little payback.” Skywing chirped, thinking to his lost friends. “We will stand behind you all the way, Garroth, if you can pull the required strings.”

“Don't worry your beak with such details, gryphon. I will get a bloody army of mercs if I have to. Let’s see if that green lady of yours can pull the same cheap tricks on an entire army. In the end, she will bend the knee before us, just like everyone else."

Skywing had a moment of doubt cross his mind, but with the human's smile of confidence, as well as the sturdy ship beneath his paws, he felt like they could indeed succeed. With a final look to the forest, he steeled himself for what was to come. They would retrieve the dragon, save the paladin, possibly save his long-lost friends, and get rid of that green dragoness for good.

"She will know the same bitter taste I swallowed all those years back, and when her trees burn and the dragon lays defeated at our feet, stripped of both title and power, the world will call her lady no longer," Skywing replied with a confident grin.

The end of book one of

Scales and Honor

Some words of Gratitude

I sit here, dumbfounded at having something I've created come into being after all the hard work placed into it. I never would have thought that scribbling away at my papers several years ago would eventually lead me here, to my first published book. I think back to the years of role playing games and how they helped shape the world that you have begun to explore in this first book. How long nights with friends helped shape Arcturus and Veledar, through rolls of the dice.

Thanks cannot be given without note to my editor, who pushed and prodded to help get something out of me during this last year. Without his help, this wouldn book probably wouldn't now sit in your hands. I'd also like to pay thanks to a writer by the username of "Of the Wilds". He was the one whose writing showed me that dragons don't have to be the monsters that they are written out to be, that they can be caring and able to capture quite beautiful emotions. The other is an old movie that dealt with dragons and their hearts, which also helped cement the bond between dragon and knights within my own head.

I would also like to thank you for taking the time to purchase this first work of mine and invite my world into yours. I hope that you enjoyed your stint here in Sethera, and also the rest of the sequels that will be sure to follow.

As a parting gift, I it is my pleasure to offer you a bonus story called "One Good Deed" that you will find below. It tells the story of Arcturus when he was of the age of twelve, and how his past shaped the man he became. It might also include a dragon or two.

Sincerely,

Justin Lee

One Good deed

Arcturus held firm onto the wooden training sword he carried within his hands. The strong, athletic human boy of twelve stood tall, with a grin present on his fair face. Confidence sparkled in his bright green eyes. The golden rays of the sun above bathed his dark-green-shirt-clad chest in its warmth, as well as the rest of his form.

Arcturus stood opposite to two other children of roughly the same age and build as himself. One had long flowing blonde hair and bright icy blue eyes, while the other had olive skin with eyes of amber, and hair of mahogany. They too held training swords at the ready as they circled one another, their eyes looking for the first error to capitalize on. Arcturus already knew trouble was coming. He bravely stepped towards them, for he was trained by the best dragon hunter of them all. He was the son of Markis Lund.

His sword clashed with another as the enemy rose to block the upcoming strike. The rules were simple. Arcturus thought as such as he parried a child's swing, then back stepping and avoiding the other child that came at him. You get three strikes onto you and you're done. It did not matter where they were, nor how hard the blow hit. The only thing that mattered was the number. Three hits. That's all it took for one of the boys to step outside the dueling area.

Arcturus grinned as the first child took a swing, and he stepped under him, letting two hard thwacks of his wooden sword be the boy's reward. Right after his assault, Arcturus nimbly backed away with a laugh of victory. For you see, he had already bested this boy numerous times. That is why he currently had a partner, even if that partner was not doing him much good.

"Hey, watch it!" The blonde-haired boy yelled out, bumping into his useless partner.

"Watch yourself!" The boy sneered back, "He's fast."

Arcturus backed away, keeping his breath in check and his excitement from getting too high. He had not yet won, something his father had always warned him to be mindful of. Keep your eyes up and expect the unexpected.

"Arcturus!" Came the shout of a bearded man bearing the same eyes as him. They glared at him inquisitively, as they traced his body up and down. "Keep your form up and don't get cocky! Focus, remember? The concentration has to be as sure as your feet." The man thrust a finger at him. "Now, to add a slight twist to this challenge. If you fail to answer my questions correctly, I will count it as a hit against you! What say you?"

"Try your best, father!" Arcturus shouted as the two children advanced on him with grins of mischief. Clearly they were thinking they could get the best of him with this little change in plans. With a shrug, Arcturus met their attacks. He would just have to show them how wrong they were the hard way.

"Name the weak spots of a dragon!"

"That one's too easy!" Arcturus grunted as he shoved the olive-skinned boy back, only to strike the blonde haired one square in the chest during this moment of distraction. "Those are the eyes, the wings, the underside of the paws, the joints....and...Their genitals!" Arcturus flustered at that one, backing away from the other snickering children. "What? They have weaker scales there." Arcturus stuck his tongue out. "You would know if you read the books."

"Read books about their...regions?" The blonde-haired boy snickered, almost dropping his sword. "What sort of weirdo are you?"

"Right answer m'boy!" The man shouted. "He's right you know. Perceptive. More than I can say about the rest of you," he gestured towards the children, who no longer snickered once a respected Lund stared them down with the stern gaze of a hunter. "Good job, Arcturus." He turned his eyes upon his boy. "Good job. Now tell me, what kind of breath is typical for a brass dragon?" His father shouted out as Arcturus smacked the olive-skinned child, taking him out of the contest.

"Take that!" He cheered as the blonde-haired boy swung and struck him on the side. "Grahhh." Arcturus stumbled backwards as the other boy grinned at him.

"I'm waiting boy! Or do you want two strikes against you?" Came the demanding voice of his father. Clearly he did not care that he had just been struck so hard in the chest that even breathing came a little hard for him.

"F-fire!" Arcturus coughed, his eyes narrowing at the blonde child. If he was going to be swinging hard, he would not have to hold back now. "You asked for it now, blondie." Arcturus mumbled as he recomposed himself, holding his sword aloft to point the wooden tip at his annoying enemy.

"Good job! Keep it up Arcturus. Don't fall prey to distraction. Pain is your greatest enemy out there in the field. I've known slayers able to withstand wounds so horrifying they'd put a normal man on his ass. Now tell me, where do green dragons like to nest?"

"Forests, swamps, marshes!" Arcturus shouted, charging at the blonde-haired boy, blocking the child's strike, and then twisting his blade so that it struck the boy once on the underside of his leg. It hit just the right spot to make the boy fall backwards onto the dirt. Arcturus did not let up for an instant, as he easily avoided the boy's retaliation, and then struck him in his sword arm.

"And what do these dragons typically like to hoard?"

"Mortals!" Arcturus swung his sword hard enough that it sent the other boy's sword flying from his grasp to clatter on the dusty ground of the arena. Arcturus finished him off with a solid strike to the torso.

"Gah!" The boy exclaimed, falling back to clench at his chest. "That stings. you dolt!"

"Next time you'll know better than to swing with your entire might in a training match." Arcturus snapped as the boy rose up to glare at him with hateful eyes. Arcturus simply returned the stare as the clearly embarrassed boy walked out of the white fenced area. He headed back to a collection of pockmarked people in multicolored clothing, head down, like a defeated dog with its tail between the legs.

"Great answers, great fighting, great spirit! That was a splendid display of keen ability, m'boy!" His father cheered. The man quickly stepped into the ring, arms stretched wide. "You did your family proud, son."

Markis then turned towards the large collection of people "See there, Jenkins? Takes right after his old man!" His father placed a rough hand to his hair and ruffled it with a chuckle. "You're going to be the best dragon slayer this world will ever know. Just make sure you don't get lazy like the dragons you've learned about, eh? If they spent half as much time hunting us, well, we'd not be here today talking about a dragon's legendary laziness, would we now?"

"But not all of them sit in their nest." Arcturus peeped in.

"They do, boy. They do," Markis patted his son on the back. "There's a couple active ones who can't stay idle, but after you take your first one, you'll start to learn that dragons are just as capable of dying as we are. They just have a hard time learning that, so it is up to us to teach 'em a pair of wings and a few scales do not make them better than us."

Arcturus cringed. The thought of a life spent hunting the great winged beasts that roamed the country of Sethera did not fill him with the excitement one would expect. It was a darker feeling. Something that made his blood run cold every time his father ever mentioned it, especially when he looked so proud and happy with his boy's combat efficiency. Arcturus did not want to be a dragon slayer like the rest of his family, and he certainly did not want to spend his life hunting the creatures simply because he was told to. It was something his mother would have objected about, if she were still around, after all.

"Uh...Sure dad." He replied sheepishly at the man before him. Markis continued to grin.

"You know what? You did remarkably well in besting those two kids." Markis thumbed behind him. "I think I owe you a treat after that exquisite show of Lund swordsmanship."

A treat?

Arcturus' thoughts twisted to what ever his father could mean. *Did he bring chocolate? Perhaps my favorite paints? Is it a new horse? Possibly my own set of armor?*

"What do you mean, father?" Arcturus decided to seek a simpler answer to his dilemmas.

"Come here and I shall show you." The man grinned as he wrapped his strong arm around his son's shoulders.

"Come on, father. Don't keep me guessing. You look practically ready to burst with excitement as well!" Arcturus laughed as they strolled through the rows upon rows of brightly colored tents. The air was filled with the scents of hundreds of people massed together, mixed with sweat and the smell of cooking meats.

"Tis better if I showed you. Words cannot do justice to what I've prepared for you." His father held up a finger and pointed it skyward. "Trust me, Arcturus, you will be glad I did not spill the beans on this surprise." Markis chuckled. They passed a band of singing gryphons, who, by the sound of their slurred speech, had already gotten piss-ass drunk despite the sun being straight overhead.

Arcturus rolled his eyes at the three stumbling birds that nearly collapsed as the two Lunds, father and son, strolled on by. His eyes traced along the field, to a large green banner that was fluttering in the wind. One that had a golden lion holding a shield and sword. Arcturus knew this flag well, for it was the symbol of the Lunds, the greatest dragon hunters in all of Lumara. According to his father, of course.

The flag that bore his family crest was gathered with a collection of others. They were all different colors and symbols, each one belonging to a different family that came to this place to compete. Each one an opponent for Arcturus to best. For you see, this large collection of tents, this gathering of peoples from all over his nation was all about one thing to his family. It was a celebration of each family's strength, a chance for each bloodline to show off their latest offspring. There were humans, elves, dwarves, minotaurs. Heck. Arcturus thought he had even seen a gryphon bragging about his skills. It did not matter who you were, where you came from, when one single thing bound all these people together.

Each one of them was a dragon hunter.

Arcturus set his eyes on another collection of massed people that parted before his father's stern eyes like water. He thought he spotted his cousin Horace, a portly man who was a simple farmer, a man who had never harmed a dragon in all of his life. He was just one of the many that came to spectate these sorts of things, for it was not just for the dragon hunters themselves. It was something for all their clans to enjoy over song, drink, and cheers of happiness.

"This walk is starting to bore me. Tell me, where are you taking me, father?" He asked as it became apparent his father was leading him away from all the noise, the people, the drink, and the drunk gryphon that had just smacked a lady's ass, only to get a swift kick to the groin. Arcturus had stifled a laugh as the creature rolled around to the squawking laughter of his feathered friends.

"Be patient. What I prepared requires us to get away from all this commotion." His father waved around to the collected masses. "They did not want to disturb the gathering just yet." His father pointed to a larger tent apart from the rest. It was a dark brown thing, completely enclosed from all sides. It had one entrance, which was bound up tighter than a vice. "That is where we are headed."

Arcturus stared at the tent in wonder. As they strode across the brightly lit field of green, his heart started to beat faster with every careful stride. His thoughts danced around in his head at what could be kept waiting in that tent. He knew there would be challenges during the week for them to overcome. Each contestant would get to best a beast specifically collected and prepared for this moment. The moment that would test their skills to the limit. Although... what kind of beast would they hold out here, away from all the noise and the people? Would they not want to build anticipation? Get the crowd riled up for the games ahead? It seemed like something Arcturus would do, if he were in charge of these games.

"Wha-"

His father silenced his mouth with a palm. The strong man guided his son around the tent. "Shhh..." He held a finger to his mouth as their path carried them to the other side of the tent. His father gestured out with a wide sweep of his hand and said nothing, letting the sight before him speak for itself.

Arcturus felt his mouth drop at what his father had gestured to. Bound before them on massive wooden carts were the imposing bodies of dragons. They were bound with heavy brown leathers that seemed to be soaked in some sort of liquid, most likely a flame retardant. Their wings were bound tight against their mighty scaled bodies, and their limbs were shackled in irons. One was scaled in bright golden armor, with underscales of a soft brown. His wings were feathered and bore the color of fresh snow. The black horned male gazed out to the human with his emerald eyes. However, it was not this dragon that drew the boy's gaze, but the female that robbed his interest.

Her scales were a bright bronze that sparkled in the sun. Atop her back was a frill that extended down from her horned head, all the way to her tail. The base of the membrane was a dark navy, slowly fading until it turned into a light turquoise near the edges. She had talons and horns to match the color of charcoal black, and eyes like molten amber. Their carts were sitting still for the moment, each one of the carts still latched onto a team of large bay horses.

"D-Dragons?" Arcturus quickly snapped his attention away from the things he had only read about, and back to his father, who looked down to him with a stern face.

"Yes…Dragons. They were going to be used for the end of the tournament, but I figured we can extend their purpose to some other things, like an early preview for my worthy son." His father looked back to the bound creatures with a slight grin. "We helped bring in these vile creatures that were plaguing the countryside. It took some effort to overpower and subdue the beasts, but each one, as you can see, fell before our combined might."

"What did they do?" Arcturus asked, looking to the female that had locked her eyes onto him. They did not seem like the eyes that belonged to a monster. In fact, if Arcturus had to point to what they indeed looked like, he would describe them as rather kind, anxious, and full of fear. "What crimes did they commit, father?"

"Does it matter? They're here now, awaiting a most deserved end!"

He must have spoken louder than intended, for he quickly lowered the tone of his voice. "Theft of property, maiming of helpless farmers, burning of houses that still housed whole families. That bronze there has some heinous activities attached to her head, like the slaughter of hunters who wanted only to provide for their families, and the murder of some of our beloved lords. These beasts have no compassion for the other living beings they share the land with, and as such, they have to be punished. Oh yes, they all have to pay for their crimes."

Arcturus wrinkled his brow as his father continued to list crime after crime that the beasts had committed. He was unnaturally coherent, as if he had memorized the entire list. Arcturus even got bored of the humongous list of accusations. He even rolled his eyes as his father seemed to continue until he finally ran out of breath.

Arcturus focused on the beautiful dragons before him. Their strong looking scales, their smooth looking wing membranes. Arcturus twitched his hands as he wondered what one would even feel like to the touch. In fact… he had never actually touched a scale before. He laughed to himself. Here he was, son to the best dragon slayer in the land, and he had yet to touch a living dragon's scale or a wing membrane. He had only read about the mighty beasts in his books, and tested against the illusions his father had conjured with the help of spellcasters.

Arcturus wondered about the accusations. How could something so beautiful be as evil as the men said? He crossed his arms as the horses started to pull the dragons into the now opened tent, disappearing with a flapping of the fabric. He remembered the picture of the supposedly evil dragon, Radiant Flame, from his grand-father's dragonology books. The red dragon had tolled mortals and killed those who could not pay the fee to pass the bridge. After that, as a grisly sign of superiority, or perhaps a warning against the rest of the human kind, the dragon built a bridge from the very bones of the travelers that wandered too close. He always thought about how pretty her turquoise scales were, and her cerulean eyes that matched the color of the brightest sky. When he looked to them on the pages of that book, or when he went to his father's study, he found himself thinking that dragons could not all be evil. There had to be some good ones out there in the world, right? It just...had to be fair.

Arcturus let out a heavy sigh. These were questions his mother would have had. The mother that was no longer there, stolen away from the rearing of a horse, and the hard rock that connected with her neck in the most tragic accident Arcturus knew during his young life.

"Don't worry your mind about them, son." His father swung his arm around his shoulder again and started to lead Arcturus back towards the collection of people, tents, and ever-loud voices. "These wretched beasts are for the victors of this tournament. You can bet it will be your strong arm that gets the honor of delivering justice to these foul beasts. You are going to learn first-hand what it means to be the hand that delivers justice onto the world."

Arcturus felt his blood freeze once more at the thought of running a blade through a dragon's head. His hands quivered and his breath got short. In the blink of an eye, he felt sick to his stomach as he pictured their bleeding corpses, and blood dripping from his hands. He shook his head to force his mind towards something pleasant. The image of the dragonesses' bronze scales sparkling in the sunlight helped him more than he could ever admit to his father. Arcturus knew he had to sketch her. No. A mere sketch was improper for such a majestic creature. He had to paint her, and if he was able to, even speak with her.

* * * * * * * * * *

That night, Arcturus laid down on the bed of straw. It was not the most comfortable thing to be lying on, since they were away from home. It surely made him miss the oversized bed in his room, with the softest blankets he had ever known. The boy sighed at the pleasant memory as he gazed down to the book held within his hands. The soft glow of the mana lantern light was all that lit the tent serving as his room. Thankfully, he had gotten this one to himself, as his father had shared one with the gryphon nanny while they were here. He had rolled his eyes at her giggling laughter as she ruffled her earthen brown feathers, his father leading her away with a flick of her lion-like tail.

His eyes came across the picture of a bronze dragon drawn onto the pages. This one was a male. Arcturus could tell that by the way the horns were shaped. Sharper, more pronounced than the female's had been. He ran a finger along the old vellum, taking a deep breath and letting the pleasant smell linger his nostrils.

"What am I doing?" He tossed the book to the other side of his bed as he leaned back, his mind full of bronze scales. "Here I am... reading about the blasted dragon, when I could...

He shot up with a smile, practically tossing on his boots and belt as quickly as he could. He snatched a leather-bound pack and quickly stuffed some painting materials inside, including a vial of ink, some parchment, and his brushes.

"I'll just greet her...Ask her some questions maybe. Not like I'm breaking any of father's rules if I look at her from a safe distance."

Arcturus pulled a dark brown cloak around his shoulders. He smiled, pushing aside the curtain of his tent. He hesitated as he took his first few steps into the darkness. His father's cautious words rang in his mind.

"Always be able to protect yourself, my son. No matter how safe you think you are, it's always better to be cautious."

Those were words his father lived by, yet Arcturus did not think anything dangerous could happen. It wasn't like the dragon would wait for him to break free if it was able. Still, it always paid to be prepared. With a shrug of his shoulders, he quickly dashed back into the room, grabbed the dagger, and stashed it on his person before heading back towards the dragon's tent.

Arcturus looked over the sea of tents lit by the mana torches that were placed every ten feet along the rows upon rows of cloth. The only other light came from the sky, in the form of thousands of stars shining down on them from above. Arcturus wrinkled his brow. He remembered when friends had told him that the stars were all small portals to the realm of fire. He disliked this theory honestly, as it felt too mundane. Especially in a world where the impossible could be done by magic, like heal the sick. Legend said some people were able to even bring the dead back to life. Arcturus took a deep breath of the cool air, coughing on the scent of smoldering fires and horses.

Silent as a cat, the boy made his way towards the dragon. He made sure to ignore anyone walking around this hour by keeping his eyes low, and sticking close to the shadows of the night. There were typically only party-goers or drunks up at this late hour anyway. Even the tent Arcturus sought had no guard, although there was a chair planted there, supposedly to rest the absent sentry. Arcturus rolled his eyes. As ridiculous as that looked, he was nonetheless thankful the guard was out drinking, or as these celebrations often had it, passed out on the floor of some tent. The guard's absence saved

Arcturus the trouble of sneaking past a sentry, and he quickly slipped under the tent's door and into the wide, open area.

The tent was practically empty, except for the metal chains and piles of hay that littered the place. There were several mana lanterns that hardly did a thing to rid the tent of the darkness. However, that did not matter to Arcturus. He paid the surrounding tent little mind as his world narrowed onto the bronze dragon that was laying down in chains upon the layers of hay. He looked around quickly, not finding a scale or a hint of the whereabouts of the other one. He shrugged, figuring they must have hidden it in another tent. He felt his heart skip a beat as he crouched low to sneak over towards one of the stacks of hay for the sole purpose of getting a better look at the bound dragon. He peaked over the hay to see that the creature had leather belts wrapped tight around her neck. Arcturus remembered from his books this would prevent dragons from blowing their breath attacks. He wracked his mind for the information that told him bronze dragons could breathe bolts of lightning from their maws, then sighed in thanks for the belts. The last thing he needed was to be dancing around lightning bolts hurled by the annoyed dragon.

From the belts he looked to her forelimbs. Those too bound ever so tightly to her hind legs, with her tail having a belt wrapped around it, forcing her to curl it towards her bound limbs. Her chest was rising and falling in time with her breaths, and her eyes were shut. She appeared to be asleep.

Arcturus felt a small pang of guilt course through him as he looked to the dragoness, all defenseless, stripped of every sense of freedom. He thought she even looked kinda helpless, bound up like that. He wanted to take a step forward and introduce himself to the beautiful creature from his books.

But he quickly found he lacked the courage to do so, his legs refusing to budge no matter how much he tried to force them forward. "Come on…" He sighed softly to himself as he pulled his pack off his back and set it on the ground. "Fine…If you won't carry me over to the dragon so I don't have to shout…I will just draw her then." He spoke to himself, pulling out a piece of parchment, a bottle of black ink, and his feather quill.

He started to trace her form quickly with the quill, first doing the head, and then working his way to the rest of the body. His eyes would peer from the paper to the fine bronze scales on her body, though from this distance it was hard to determine any detail on her frame. How he wished to be closer and inspect her fine features. It would certainly help him get his picture right. He sighed as he finished making the latest stroke when he noticed something. He looked up to see that she had risen her head and was staring at him with her amber eyes.

"What are you doing over there, scribbling in the darkness?" She spoke sternly, her voice deeper and more booming than he thought it would be. However, it was just as surprising, causing him to jump back and fall into the hay.

"Woah....umppffhh..." He landed on his back, spitting out some hay as he laid sprawled on the ground.

"Is the hay giving you trouble, little human?" Her voice came moments later. It cracked slightly from the sternness she had shown. It occurred to Arcturus she may have been putting on an act for him.

"I-I-I...I'm fine. Isn't as hard as it looks, because it's hay, same as the one you sleep on, actually." He stammered slowly, dusting himself and sitting up, then turning to face the dragoness, who -despite what his father taught him about how all dragons were evil, had a silver tongue, and would eat him at a moment's notice- had kind eyes that stared to him as if a mother would a hurt child. He lowered his head as he remembered his own mother's eyes.

"Are you so sure about that?" She chuckled, "You are not supposed to say I three times...Unless I have been speaking the common tongue wrong all these years." She licked her nose with her long, dull pink tongue. "Did my speaking surprise you, hatchling? I had no intention of sending you sprawled onto the floor."

"N-No." The boy replied, looking to his picture that now had a large streak of ink down the middle. He scrunched up the side of his face at the ruined image.

"Why are you making such a weird face? The one where you are trying to fold your hide together?"

"Like this?" He made the scrunched-up face again, pointing to it with a finger.

"That's the one."

"I...well...I kinda ruined my picture when I fell." He sighed, glancing down to the drawing again.

"Picture? Is that what you were doing? Scratching away with that feather of yours?" She snorted in amusement. "You surprise me, perhaps even more than my voice surprised you. Can I see what you produced?"

Arcturus almost approached the dragoness when she had asked that all too inviting, dangerously suspicious question.

"I would want to...only that..." He looked to her many pristine teeth, only getting flashes of them when she talked. Despite her friendly demeanor, he knew the damage she could do with those. Even with a belt restricting her movement to mere inches, he could not help shake the feeling that she could reach out and grab hold of him with those deadly white daggers.

"You think I am going to bite you." She said flatly. The dragoness let out a small rumbling chuckle from the back of her throat. "That is most wise of you, young hatchling. it would be foolish to approach one such as myself without knowing me first." She snorted, letting out gusts of warm, humid air as she pointed with a claw to the ground. "You can stand fairly close without worrying about repercussions. Just hold out that bit of parchment for me. I shall see it fine even from a distance. Does that sound fine to you, hatchling?"

"Why do you keep calling me a hatchling? I am clearly a human." He took a few tentative steps towards her, his heart starting to beat faster as excitement built within his chest. He was *actually* getting closer to a dragon. One that didn't seem eager to hurt him, maim him, or kill him. Even so, he was reminded of his father's words to stay vigilant with every beat of his heart. After all, the dragoness could be lulling him into a false security.

"Hatchling, boy, child." She rolled her eyes. "All these things describe you in the same way, human. I just used the term I am most familiar with."

"Uh...yeah. Makes sense. Here. Take a look." He held out his parchment for the dragoness when he was close enough to her. He watched her eyes look right at the drawing, and waited with baited breath for her answer with his hand trembling slightly. "What do you think? Still pretty, even with that ugly smudge in the middle? I messed it up by falling down at such a bad time..." He trailed off, his face going a slight shade of crimson.

"It's wonderful, little human!" She smiled, eyes closing as she did so. "You really captured my likeness impressively well, although I think it would look even better in color."

"I do have paints that can do that." Arcturus excitedly thumbed back towards his pack. "I do like to do that as well. Painting I mean. It's even more fun than sketching." His mind drifted to a small cave near his home, where he had painted a rather large painting of the red dragon Radiant Flame. One that his father had not known he had done. No need for the man who hated dragons with a passion to know his son fancied painting them.

"Do you now?" She gave a slight croon as he watched her scales ripple and strain slightly against the leathers. Against his better judgement, Arcturus felt himself back away suddenly.

"Oh, don't worry your little snout, human." The dragoness groaned, looking back as much as her belt allowed. "I am thoroughly restrained...graaarrr...by your uncomfortably tight belts."

"Well... they are there to make sure you don't go killing everyone. Or using your lightning breath to do what your claws can't."

"Is that what you think I would do, if given the chance? You wound me, human." She gave a slight growl.

Arcturus stepped back further as she glared at him. "I..." Arcturus faltered for a moment. "Is that not why you are here? To be judged like a criminal? Did you not steal, kill, and hurt others?"

"I did none of these things, human!" The dragoness snorted almost angrily, then licked her nose. "Your brethren took me when I was going for my morning flight. They ambushed me like a pack of vicious monsters, tied me up, and dragged me here to be made an example of."

"T-they can't...be...monsters. I mean...no. We aren't like that. We punish evil dragons," He stopped his retreat as her eyes softened.

"Do you honestly believe that? Tell me, human...Are people that attack innocent creatures...bind them up...spout lies...and then kill them in front of an angry horde that demands blood the kind, gentle creatures you speak of? How is this justice? How are they not the monsters that should rightly scare you?"

Arcturus paused as he thought over her words. "Y-yes." He said after a pregnant pause. "You are...you aren't wrong. People like that are bad. Maybe even worse than some of the dragons I heard about."

"Indeed." She snorted, her mood instantly brightening. "The world is not a fair place, but let us cease this prattle about horrible deeds and monsters. It will only sour my attitude further. You mentioned you like to paint, little hatchling?" Her voice sounded sweet, as if it were a mother talking to her own child.

"Yes...Yes I did. Creating makes me feel much better than training, though father insists I should practice for...uhm, things. Stay in shape, I mean," Arcturus put a timely stop to his words to avoid upsetting the dragoness with further talk of dragon slaying. She seemed to understand him. Able to see past the hardened warrior he would become in a few years under his father's tutelage. She saw him. The real Arcturus Lund, not the offspring of dragon slayers.

"That is good. Becoming a master requires knowledge from all fields, including some that might be considered less important. Did you bring those painting things in your leather sack?" She gave him a tooth filled smile.

"You mean, my pack?" He asked, tilting his head to the side.

"Yes, that." She rolled her eyes. "Unless you brought two of them with you."

"I did. I mean I have one pack here, not two. Why would I need two?" He realized the female was joking, and, reddening once again like a ripe tomato, Arcturus looked back to the pack, then quickly back to her. "Why so interested in my crafts? Dragons can't paint."

"We can. Just not in the same way you do. Besides, I hardly think you look like an aspiring artist," Came her voice as he slowly made his way to his pack to retrieve all the tools he needed for the job at hand. It was when he grabbed it and turned around when did he truly take in her size. She must have been at least three times his height if she were able to stand up fully without the leather bindings holding her captive. Arcturus took a few more steps towards her. His eyes traced her entire body, from the tip of her snout to the end of her tail. He figured that she was at least seven times his length from head to foot, at least. He had not realized he was staring as he continued slowly towards her, because she chuckled at him.

"Admiring my splendor, little one?" She pulled against the straps gently. "I did not think my scales would have the same effect on a human as they do on other dragons. Ah yes, our species is very good at flaunting even the most basic of things."

"B-basic?" Arcturus stammered. How could she name such dazzling beauty *basic*?

"You think otherwise?" The female gave what Arcturus believed to be a snort right after he nodded. "I suppose you don't gawk at each other's hides. That's why you keep them hidden under these ridiculous crafts you call...cloth, was it?"

"Clothes," Arcturus said. "You were close."

She smiled again, her tail twitching slightly within her bonds. "I find the concept of adorning your body with the hide of prey and plants ridiculous. You understand that, right?"

"I suppose."

She must have noticed something in his eyes, for her lips moved to reveal her sharp, deadly, and at the same time, beautiful fangs. "Are you attracted by the way I look, little slayer?" She laughed deep in her throat. "That would certainly be amusing, considering our situation."

"I don't fancy dragons like that." Arcturus sat before her, cross-legged. He was at least three arm lengths away from her head when he opened his pack again and pulled out his painting supplies. He looked up to see her staring at him with her piercing, beautiful eyes. "I... just find your scales...beautiful...and... and striking, like the sun setting over endless fields of gold..." He stopped as he saw her grin at him from each edge of her snout.

"If you are trying to convince me you don't fancy dragons, you are doing a very poor job, little hatchling. To my ears, it sounds like you will have a dragon lover in your future." She chuckled again in the back of her throat, making her scales clink against one another."

"Ahaha, no, no," He laughed, dismissing her with a wave. "I already have a hard time with girls my age." He pulled out some brushes and set them beside the vellum he had procured. His thoughts went to all the time spent training, the hours and hours of reading, fencing, practicing. It felt like that was all he ever did. He never got a moment to himself to do anything he cared about. In fact, this was the most alone time he had gotten in the last few weeks. Inside, alone, with a beautiful living being that was seen by his family like any other dangerous animal. Arcturus wrinkled his brow as he pulled out a few pots of paints. "Seems like all I ever do is train, train, train. Going where? Doing what? I don't want to be miserable like my father. He hides it well, but I know he's not happy, and he pushes me so hard to follow in his footsteps. Like...he wants me to be...him."

"You sound like you're in a cage of your own." She gestured back to her straps. "Or wrapped in bindings, at the very least."

Arcturus chuckled. "Don't get me wrong, fair dragon. I do like the training. It keeps the mind fresh, and the body ready. I just wish...you know, that there was more to do besides swinging swords and learning how to...uhm...hurt dragons." Arcturus blurted those last two words out. He found it too difficult to lie when he stared right into her eyes. He wasn't proud of what his father wanted him to become, and, in many ways, Arcturus wanted the dragoness to understand that.

"Does that mean you look forward to slay a few dragons of your own?" She asked him with a slight raise in her voice.

"We don't train to just kill dragons. That's silly," He sighed as he grabbed a brush, dipped it into an open pot, and started with gentle strokes on the page. "We also train to kill monsters, undead, and anything else that would threaten a small village."

"How about your own kin? Do you train to kill other mortals as well?"

Arcturus stopped to think back to the many times his father had taught him how to wield a sword. How to analyze his opponent's movements. He remembered the weak spots his father taught him about, and how to easily strike and fell an opponent he was fighting. He had asked at the time what good it was, to learn how to kill other people when they were going to be fighting monsters and dragons. His father had only a single, obvious reply. It was dangerous times they lived in. Who knows what you would need to defend yourself from, when you land into the wrong place, at the wrong time?

"Yes, we did." He replied flatly, his blood turning to ice as he remembered his father talking in grisly detail of some of the numerous kills that he had gotten over the years. "But I do not fancy the killing part yet. Probably never will."

"Mmmmm?" Her eyes widened into amber slits. She looked surprised. Stunned, almost.

"I mean, I can kill a beast for food, like a deer or something of that sort. I can also defend myself...but to murder an intelligent creature in cold blood?" Arcturus shivered as he felt a cold tingle rush down his spine. "The mere thought chills me. I don't want to be a murderer for hire that is fueled only by the desire to get rich, or by hate for that matter."

"Those are strong words for a hatchling...What would you want to be, if given the opportunity?" She asked softly, in almost a whisper as she continued to stare at him.

"I prefer to be a knight." He thumbed his chest. "Protecting the innocent, helping others, defending those in need."

"You sound like a genuine paladin...Now hatchling." She cleared her throat with a snort. "What is your name? I would rather cease calling you that title, human, or little one. You have gained my interest, but perhaps you can earn even more than that by lending me your trust."

"My name?" He asked, sounding a bit more surprised than he should have. After all, she would be dead in a few days time, right? His mood darkened at the thought.

"Yes, your name. I assume you have one at this age."

"Ahem." He cleared his own throat in imitation of her, which got another mmmm along with a widening of her eyes. "Please call me... Arcturus Lund."

"Lund?" She wrinkled her snout at the mere mention of his last name. "You're *their* whelp?"

"Yes." He replied, cringing as she continued to glare at him. "I see you've already been introduced to that name by someone, or something..."

"Every dragon family that hasn't lived centuries inside their cave knows the Lunds." She growled slightly. "They have most likely claimed a life from every dragon family by now, at one point in your family history...So yes." She continued. "I know of the *Lunds*, and their legacy."

"Oh, I'm...sorry. I think. " There was a pregnant pause as he averted his gaze from hers. Arcturus focused back on the painting he was doing. He made sure to only take quick glances as he worked, finding it hard to look her in the eye. "What...excuse me. I shouldn't be so blunt as to demand. May I know what your name is?" He asked after a few minutes of passive silence.

"You may call me the Howling Tempest for now." She replied proudly.

"That's...a fancy name to have," He chuckled, dipping his paint again and returning to his work.

"What did you expect from a dragon, hatchling? The purry cat? The soft rabbit? Such names hardly befit a dragon."

"No, none of those." He looked up to her amused eyes. "But why Howling Tempest? I'm curious if you like storms or something like that, because I am a bit scared by them. Sometimes, I wonder if dragons even fly during a storm. Do they?"

"That, I'm afraid, is a tale for another time, little Arcturus. For now, all you need to know is what I've already told you."

"Fine." He sighed, shrugging his shoulders. "There!" He pulled the brush away, smiling at the fine work he had done. He was proud he was able to capture her radiance in a simple amount of time. Despite her talking and engaging him, he found it quite pleasurable to do.

"How did it turn out?" She asked with a pleased croon. It made him laugh to hear such a noise coming from quite a large dragon.

"You want to see it?"

"Why else would I suggest you paint it? Of course I want to see a picture of me!" She laughed. "Now show it to me! I wish to see!"

Arcturus turned the paper around and held it out proudly to her, just like he did with the drawing before. He saw her eyes squint this time as she stared onto the page.

"Bring it closer. I cannot make out the fine details from here...but it looks nice!" She smiled, closing her eyes as she did so. "Can you bring it closer so that I may gaze upon your fine work from a more proper distance?"

He stood up with a smile, finding that, despite the previous warnings of his thoughts, he was moving towards the dragoness, returning her good cheer. If she was trying to distract him and manipulate him through her mood and flattery, then it was definitely working. Forgetting his safety, he took one last step towards her, but his foot caught a loose chain. His leg snagged, and he fell forward, but when he held his hands out to catch himself, Arcturus did not hit ground. Instead, his little fingers found warm scales, and the dragon's snout, pressed against his chest.

She had caught him from falling with her head.

Terror gripped Arcturus' heart for a moment as he just realized she was right under him. And that if she wanted to, she could sink her bright teeth into him and end his life in a flicker of time.

So this is how it ends for me, huh? He thought as his breaths came quick, and his heart threatened to leap from his chest. He closed his eyes and waited for the end to come from the swift strike of the dragon's gaping jaws. However, after a minute of silence and frenzied breathing, he was still alive. There was no sudden jerk or a snarl. There was not even a growl of displeasure. The only thing that did grace him was a puff of warm air as she snorted into the vest he wore.

"As much as I enjoy your soft touch along my scales, little one, please remove yourself from my head. It is ill fitting of a dragon to be used as a mere resting place for your lazy body."

"Oh!" He pushed himself away from the dragoness as he resumed his sitting position before her. "I-I'm so sorry about that. Gods...I did not mean to...you know...."

He made sure that he was at least three arm's lengths away from her head. He stared into her eyes while she stared into his own. There was an awkward silence between them, as he could only hear his own breathing, and feel the rapid pounding of his heart. "You...you didn't bite me!" He exclaimed at last, louder than he meant to. He quickly covered his mouth with both hands in surprise. "Sorry. I didn't mean that either."

"No... No, I did not bite you." She replied quietly, then quickly snorted. "Why would I do something so...thoughtless? Senseless even!" She rolled her eyes. "One important thing you need to know about me, young one, is that I do not harm hatchlings with my talons nor teeth, no matter what species they belong to. That is simply beneath me. I am not the monster you Lunds painted me to be."

"Oh, that's...I'm relieved. In a weird way, I am happy to hear that." Arcturus placed a hand to his chest, his breaths calming him down with each exhale as he gazed at her. She held him within her stare, unblinking. "I-I would never harm a hatchling too. Goes without saying. I'm not like those monsters you talk about either." He said at last, causing her to smile for a moment.

"Then you might be different from the rest of your kin, even if you bear their name." Her eyes suddenly shot up over his head, Arcturus looked back too. He heard a rustling noise from behind him and the drunken burp that must have been the guard returning to his post. "I think you might want to spirit yourself away before you are caught, Arcturus."

Arcturus ducked low as he gathered his things, hoping that those flaps would not open. He had no idea what would happen if the guard were to return and catch him, but he was sure it was against the rules to talk to the dragon. After all, why else have a guard here in the middle of the night? Maybe it was to protect her from the others drunken people, in case they wanted to carve out a bit of personal vengeance from the female's scales.

"I am grateful for the talk we had, human." She suddenly spoke up, causing him to look to her once more. "You will return tomorrow, will you not?"

Arcturus tilted his head slightly to the side as he raised an eyebrow. Did she think she could predict his actions? That he was this easy to read, like an open book?

"What makes you think I will be back at all?" He lowered his voice to sound as though he did not care.

"Oh...well, a simple look reveals all the answers you need." She gave a rumbling noise in the back of her throat that sounded like a purr. "I saw the way you were transfixed by my scales, your hands, when you drew upon that paper of yours." She gave him a sweet smile and closed her eyes. "You will be back to talk to me...because you're...different." She ended the sentence with a soft snort, and a lick on her nose.

"Good night, Arcturus."

"Good night to you too, Howling Tempest." He waved to her, slipped under the tent as quickly as he could, and quietly made his way back to his own bed. He plopped onto his comfortable bedding with a sigh and tossed his pack onto the floor.

"What an encounter." He ran his hands through his hair with a smile. His heart was pounding as his thoughts went to what had transpired. He had talked to a dragon! An actual, living, breathing dragon! She had also been big and radiant, and much kinder than he could ever imagine of such a rugged beast. He sighed deeply as he sank down onto his bed. She had been a lot more different than what his father had kept on telling him. Once again, he found himself doubting his father's words.

"All dragons are evil, son. You must never trust the poison that comes out of their mouths, for even their words are a vile weapon. Allow your defenses to slip, and you're dead.

"Shut up," Arcturus sighed as he turned his face towards the window. This night was too beautiful to be spoiled by his father's hateful advice, so Arcturus looked at the stars until his mind became clear. Only then he allowed himself to fall into the realm of dreams, a realm where he could share the sky with his beloved dragons.

* * * * * * * * *

The next day was a blur for Arcturus as he went through the usual routine that preceded his combat training. Although it was true that the final test was still a few days away, his father had kept him training the entire time. There was the morning run of several miles, followed by pushups, sit-ups, squats. During these exercises, his father was shouting questions to him on a dragon's weak spots, along with various other inquiries about their lives, such as their eating habits. Arcturus got many of them right, and, as he began to get cocky, his father started asking him questions about other creatures like werewolves, vampires, and displacer beasts.

But as the day went on, it became harder for Arcturus to focus. His thoughts could simply not get away from the dragoness that was laying bound in a tent several hundred meters away. So, when his father and him split ways for lunch, Arcturus made sure to quickly gather something from his nanny. He asked her for two helpings of the pork that she had managed to cook up with her deft talons.

Her feathers ruffled as she had glared at him with her inquisitive eyes. "It's for a date!" She had laughed through a series of squawks and chirps. "I knew it! You finally took my offer to go date my niece! You really are doing yourself a favor." She gave a pleased chirp from her orange beak as she started to put the slabs of meat on his plate. "Gryphons are more fun, after all."

Arcturus rolled his eyes as the gryphon nanny gave him the requested food. She had always tried to set him up with her niece. The young lass had a fun attitude as bright as her snow-white feathers, and often spoke of interesting things that charmed Arcturus. Still, even with all those qualities, the gryphoness was not his type. Besides, he always was far too busy for pursuits of the heart anyway. "No... I'm just hungry is all...Growing boy and all that."

"Oh...sure, sure, my dear boy," She clacked her beak and handed him the plate. "Just don't get up to no good. Your father will have my head if he finds out you two got into any FUN activities." She gave him a wink along with a flick of her tail.

"You can certainly bet on nothing of that sort!" He protested as she just gave him a smirk like she knew something he didn't. Gryphons. They were always up to no good.

Not him though. Arcturus knew better than arguing. He quickly shoved a piece of bread into his mouth and left the cackling brown gryphon to her own devices. His steps carried him through the tournament grounds, past the people that frolicked around the sea of tents, past the stern-faced contestants, and across the brightly lit grass field. Soon enough, he had snuck around the tent he visited last night, and with a quick glance to confirm no one was looking, the boy slipped past the wall of cloth to greet his mysterious dragoness once again.

"Hello." She turned her head slightly towards him, seconds after he had emerged from under the flap. "I honestly did not expect you back so soon hatch- excuse me. Arcturus." She corrected herself with a smile. "What wind brings you back? The sun is still high. Is it not risky for you to be here in broad daylight?"

"This!" Arcturus blurted out as he held the plate out to proudly display the assortment of tasty meat he procured for her. "I know it's not the best food you can catch...but I figured they would not be feeding you anything." He scratched his head sheepishly while he waited for her response. The dragoness looked to him, as if in deep thought for the moment.

"Could you bring it closer?" She asked, to which he found himself complying, setting the plate down softly before her. She gave him a pleased croon before quickly snatching up the pork, and swallowing the pieces whole with a loud gulp. "Thank you.... that was most kind of you."

"You're welcome. It's the least I could do, heh." He turned to leave, quickly gathering the plate. He did not have long before his father once again would be looking for him to continue their grueling training.

"I'm sorry I have to leave so soon. Wish I could have talked to you more, but..."

"You must be going," The female's gaze drooped. "I understand, Arcturus. Do not feel sad. Even though it was short, your visit pleased me greatly, and not only because you brought me food."

"Really?" The boy's eyes lightened a little. "I'll return as soon as I can. Promise."

The way she spoke pinched his heart. Oh, how much he wanted to stay here and listen to one of her stories. To catch a glimpse on how life felt through the eyes of a dragon!

It'll just be a few hours. A few hours that felt like a drop of eternity for sure. Nevertheless, it was better than to risk an untimely discovery. Arcturus sighed as he went to leave the same way he had arrived, taking a quick peek back at the dragoness that was still looking at him. Her tail tip flicked ever so slightly, reminding Arcturus how a cat's tail might do the exact same thing.

"Fare you well, little Arcturus, and may the sun warm your path." She called after him as he slipped under the tent flap and quickly returned to the day's boring routine of training, with the thoughts of the dragoness swirling within his head.

His day was filled with sword training under the watchful eyes of his father, horseback riding, listing off weak spots of various monsters, and finally, techniques on how to kill a dragon swiftly. His little heart shriveled as his father listed off gruesome ways on how to stab a dragon right through the eye. With shaking hands, the young boy pictured himself with a cold, glimmering blade of sharpened steel in hand. He approached his quarry, pulled his arm back to gather momentum...

Then sunk the sharp tip into the beautiful eye of the dragoness that had been staring at him so kindly before. The voice that came out was not the calm soothing river that cascaded upon his ears the night before, but a wail, sharp as the knots that tightened into his gut. Arcturus closed his eyes. He didn't want to be here. To see *her*.

But after years of training, his father's voice had a way of slithering into the deepest crevices of his mind, filling his thoughts with vivid images of the techniques he imparted. Warm blood sprung forth like a river, washing over Arcturus like a tide, covering his body in a curtain of the sticky, warm, crimson goo.

"Imagining the glory of your first kill?"

The heavy hand that fell on his shoulder ripped Arcturus away from those dreadful images.

"You're shivering."

Arcturus froze. He dared not even look at his father, out of fear that somehow, his old man could read his very thoughts, so he kept his eyes on the ground and his lips tightly pursed, hoping that he would not be the death of the bronze female. Praying that the flashes of cruelty produced by his mind would not come to pass.

"It's alright, boy. There can be no strength without weakness."

Arcturus let out a short sigh once his father took his hand off. "I felt the same way when I was your age." He started to pace around with his arms crossed. "Afraid. Undecided. Wondering if my first dragon won't make a meal out of me instead. But here I am, standing in the same place as my father, teaching my own son the very things I've learned."

The man approached once again, this time ruffling through the boy's shaggy hair. "Worry not about the future, Arcturus. This weakness you feel will be forged into courage. The trembling in your arms will give way to strength! And when you are ready, know that I will look upon you with pride as you bring glory to our name."

Arcturus couldn't listen to another one of his father's words. There was no glory, only the sight of innocent blood being spilled for no reason. He ran to the shelves of books and buried his nose into a drawn-out lecture of dragon habitats as his father went on and on about how to kill the beasts. Arcturus did his best and managed to answer every question correctly, but during this time, he occupied his mind with more pleasant things. Things that did not have him killing such majestic creatures based on his family's history of hatred.

It was no surprise that when the sun sank below the horizon, and the moon started to bathe the countryside in its white light, that Arcturus quickly gathered his usual things and practically sprinted towards the tent of the bronze dragoness. With a quick, deep breath, he entered the tent to stand once more before the great bronze dragon. "Psssst....Howling Storm." He whispered harshly as he slunk his way through the dimly lit tent.

She turned her head slightly with a pleased trilling noise as her eyes locked onto him and narrowed into amber slits. "Welcome back, little hatchling."

"I thought you predicted my arrival?" He carefully made his way to her front, peaking his head up to make sure that indeed they were alone.

"I must confess that... I was not completely certain you would return." She licked her nose. "Although it is pleasant to know that my words proved true...So." She tilted head slightly to the side. "What wind brings you back? Do you wish to talk to the dragon you are supposed to hate? Or is it another reason that got you here?"

"I am not a hunter!" Arcturus snapped back rather harshly, pointing at her with a scowl. She had to understand he was not like his father, or the rest of the hunters.

The female didn't get angry. Instead, she just gave him a chuckle, her amused eyes sparkled with a set of feelings Arcturus could not fully understand. "You seem very sure of your words."

"That's...that's because I mean them, and I..." His words stopped coming as he thought back to the conversation they had the night before. How her words had proven so different than what he had come to expect.

"I don't want to harm dragons. Even thinking of that makes my stomach feel weird. Instead, I want to know more about dragons. About you."

He blushed and quickly looked down to avoid the female's eyes. "You think I'm weird."

"Not at all," said the dragoness. "I am a bit surprised by what I hear, considering you are a Lund, but I also realize that I cannot always see you through the eyes of my memories. You are not your name. That is what you try to convince me of, is it not?"

"Mhm." Arcturus quickly nodded. "So...you don't think I'm weird?"

She gave another chuckle. "Not at all. In fact, what I see here now is the same sweet boy that brought me a tasty treat this morning."

A rush of pride and excitement rushed through the boy's spine. Her warm words instilled him with the unrelenting urge to hug her, but she was still a dragon...and he, a feeble little boy. Arcturus settled for a meek smile instead of the hug and sat down before her, still outside her reach, but with a relaxed posture.

"What's on your mind, hatchling?"

"Nothing." Arcturus lied.

"Nothing, is it?" The female teased him with her wonderful voice. "Well then, *nothing,* one thing you need to know about dragons is that our eyes can not only pierce shadows, but lies as well."

Arcturus scrunched his face. She caught him. How, he could not tell, as the books mentioned nothing of a dragon's ability to divine lies. Sure, there were plenty of mentions on clever manipulation, yet in this case, he was the one doing the lying.

"Uhm...ok. I guess I...what I want is to..." He shook his head off the embarrassment that twisted his tongue. Do you think I could get a better look at your scales?" The confidence with which he spoke surprised him.

And by the look of it, surprised her as well.

"You may approach." The female smiled kindly.

Arcturus remained conflicted. Trust her? Or trust his father? Dragons were supposed to be dangerous monsters that lashed out at the world around them, harming any mortal they came in contact with. But when he fell on her last night, she had not attacked him. No slash of claws mauled his flesh, no teeth broke his bones. In the back of his mind, he felt a little more at ease, enough so that he pulled himself closer, so that she could reach him if she wanted to.

"I am curious about one thing. Why not look in a book to learn more about us?" She snorted, her eyes still giving him an amused look. "Your family is also renowned for its resources, and I am sure the answers you seek hide within the pages of a book."

Arcturus shook his head.

"No?" The female inquired. "Why not ask your father? He must have had a few close encounters with my kind during his life."

"I don't want to." Arcturus said sternly. "Please. Don't make me talk to him."

"Alright, little one. It is not my intention to put you in an uncomfortable position." She lowered her snout towards him, making his heart pound a bit faster. He fought the urge to run. She had not harmed him before, after all. "As for that closer look you speak of...I can always give you a better look if you undo some of these straps." She gestured back to the leather binding her. "They feel like rugged vines twisting and coiling around me. I'm not surprised if they peeled a few scales off."

"I know what you're doing." Arcturus scowled as she slowly turned her attention back to him.

"You're trying to play me. Trick me into freeing you!" He crossed his arms defiantly, like a knight standing in the face of danger. He was not Arcturus the child anymore, but Arcturus the dragon slayer. The boy who trained for years to resist a dragon's manipulation.

"Arcturus, I assure you that-"

"NO!" His frown deepened. "I won't be tricked into doing your bidding. You will have to find some other sucker."

"Sucker?" She laughed, "I begin to think you are, for assuming the worst. Have we not talked peacefully before? Have I harmed you in any way so far?"

Arcturus' conviction faltered a little. It wasn't fair to attack his feelings like that.

"I am only asking for this small favor so that I can offer exactly what you requested. Just release one limb at a time to get a good look at any part of me you wish. You would still get to gaze upon my scales up close, and I can stretch that limb. Then, after you are pleased, you can redo the binding, and undo another one. One by one, you can get a good look at all of me."

Her words were true. More than that, they made sense to him. After all, he yearned to see every part of her majestic body. He just wrinkled his face as she just smiled at him. It was like she knew what he was thinking. Aware that she was winning this little game with him.

"And the book thing? You can agree that you are certainly not a book written by mortals. You can give me deeper insight and knowledge that I would not be able to find there...as for my father..." His face darkened at the thought of the man that was so comfortable with killing that he could smile and joke about doing it. The man that despised dragons so much that he shut down any pleasant talk about them. They were always monsters, silver tongued devils, evil beings that were never supposed to be trusted or shown mercy. "I want to learn things unburdened by his hatred."

"Once again you speak strong words. Are you sure you are not a hatchling?" She gave a pleasured rumble from her throat. "Now...What was your first question? I do have one condition to mention."

"What is that?" He asked, raising an eyebrow. Despite being slightly against what the books had said about her kind, the dragoness still seemed to be planning something.

"For every question that you ask, I request you release a limb to inspect. It will pass the time and allow me to stretch. And besides." She snorted. "Maybe after a few questions and a thorough inspection of my scales, you will see that we are more than mere monsters to be hunted and killed. Do we have a deal?"

"We have a deal." He approached her further. "Uhm, so for the first question...I want to know...how does it feel like to fly with the sky beneath your wings?"

"Do you not know?" The dragoness seemed surprised. "I know you don't have wings, but surely you have been on a gryphon's back by now. I heard of no Lund, child or otherwise, to stay away from the grasp of the sky."

"No..." He fidgeted slightly. "I... I am afraid of heights. Never been on a gryphon or on the deck of an airship before." He looked away, his face reddening as he admitted that fact. He waited for a moment for her reply, then looked back when she cleared her throat. He turned to see she was gesturing to her right forelimb.

Mentally kicking himself, Arcturus approached her, placing his hands on the tight leather. He took a deep breath as he hesitated with the bindings. Was he really going to do this? Risk her getting loose to get some answers? He looked back to her kind eyes, and her soft smile that melted away his doubts. Of course, she could not escape, and she had been quite nice to him. Without another thought, Arcturus confidently undid the binding.

"Aahhhhh...That's better." She let out a small groan as she stretched the scaly appendage. "Thank you for trusting me, Arcturus. Here. Look as long as you wish." She replied, holding her limb out for him to see. The fine smooth scales shimmered in the mana lantern light as he reached out to touch it with his hand.

His breath quickened as he hesitated at first, hovering his fingers over the smooth armor. With a quick shake of his nerves, he ran his fingers along the warm scales. He could not believe what was happening as he traced them. Here he was, getting to touch the dragon without fear of getting hurt. He could feel her muscles tense and relax as she sighed from his touch. "How about that answer?"

"Hmmmmm...mind on task..." She chuckled. "The wind feels nice beneath my wings, dear little one. When I am up there, I feel as if I were more free than any creature that inhabits the world. To be up there along the white clouds is pure joy. I especially love the feeling of the sun bathing me in its warm rays. There is... hardly another way to describe it...it's pure bliss."

Arcturus closed his eyes as he continued to touch the dragoness. For a moment, he imagined himself as a dragon, with wings flapping high into the sky. His green eyes were full of joy as he let out his own roar of happiness. "That sounds delightful," He laughed as he made his way down to her paw. "Now tell me about-"

"That was not the deal, little human." She cut him off with a snort. "One limb for one question."

He retracted his hands, letting her place her limb back on the ground. "Okay." He grabbed the leather and rebound the limb. He was surprised when she did not resist and let him do so. "You... did not fight me."

"Why would I? I gave you my word that everything will go exactly as we agreed." She lowered her voice, taking a deep breath. "I do not lie to somebody I care about."

Arcturus looked back to her as the words lingered in his mind. They certainly sounded truthful, honest, and he felt that familiar feeling about his father's words spring forth. He followed her scales, down her belly, until he was near one of her larger hind paws. He undid the leather there to allow the female to stretch out her hind leg with a groan of relief.

"Are dragons afraid?"

"What kind of question is that, Arcturus? I am a living being blessed with intelligence...I have of course felt fear that has shook me to the very marrow of my bones. I have felt joy that has threatened to lift me into the sky aloft in its embrace. I have held love that has made my heart threaten to leap from my scaled chest." She suddenly stopped, as her mood darkened and her head drooped. "And I have also felt sadness that has stabbed my heart, and made me wish that I were dead." Arcturus watched the navy color of her frills turn a darker shade of blue, almost midnight black. It started out slow from her head frill and worked its way towards the tip of her tail.

"I..." Arcturus felt guilt strike him like a spear to the chest. He turned back to the dragoness. Her eyes were closed. For a moment, it looked like she had a tear trickling down from her eyes. That was ridiculous, right? Dragons could not possibly cry! However, with the lingering silence that engulfed the tent, he was not so certain anymore, as that tear dripped down her pebbly cheek and dripped onto the ground. "I'm sorry." He approached her snout without any thoughts for his safety, and wiped her tear away from her warm cheek. "What happened?"

"I..." She opened her eyes with a sniff, and Arcturus saw an honest look of pain within them. The look his father had the day his mother had died, the look he had seen in the mirror as well. "I lost a mate to hunters." She snarled, "hunters like your parents."

Arcturus took a step back as it felt like she had struck him with a dagger. "M-m-m...Mmmy..." He stuttered heavily as he remembered her kind brown eyes, her soft touch, and the voice that had brought comfort to him for seven years of his life. Despite her being gone for five years, he still felt like a frightened child when his thoughts wandered back to her. "M-My mother was not a hunter...she...she loved dragons." He felt his eyes start to mist up as he looked away from the dragon.

"Oh," He heard her voice, calm and gentle once again. "Are you crying, little one?"

"N-no." He wiped his eye with his sleeve. "M-men don't cry."

"That's stupid. You are not a man yet, little hatchling...Tell me please. What happened to your mother?"

"She...went on a riding trip with her horse. The horse got frightened and reared up. My mother fell from her saddle and hit her neck on the hard ground." Arcturus painfully gestured to his neck and made a cracking noise. "She died almost instantly." He wiped his eyes again, this time clearing away the crystalline tears that made his vision fuzzy. With a few deeper breaths and extra help from his sleeves, his eyes were dry again. He tried to focus on the dragoness in front of him instead of his missing mother.

"It's not wrong to cry." She said softly, sounding more like his mother with each word she spoke from her snout. "You don't have to hide your feelings from anyone. Especially me...I bet you miss her dearly."

"I do." He hung his head as he felt his heart wrestled away from his chest. "Even after five years, it isn't getting any easier. I miss her every day."

"Tell me about her." The bronze dragoness lowered her head towards him, slowly approaching him with those same kind and caring eyes. Arcturus found himself raising his hands and running them along her snout, with one hand on her nose.

Her scales were once again soft to the touch, and made him think of a warm blanket pressed against his skin. One that had been warmed by the afternoon sun. He told her through misted eyes about all the times he spent with his mother. He told her about the pleasant days, the great nights, and how he longed to hear her voice once more. When he finished, his throat was tight, sore, and his eyes were red from tears.

"She sounds like a very kind human. Please excuse my thoughtless words. I am truly sorry for judging such a fine human on a whim. I have allowed hatred to find its way back inside me, but that is wrong...so wrong. I know my mate would not approve of it. He...he would have..." She suddenly opened her maw quickly and gave him a gentle lick across his face with her large, slimy eel of a tongue.

Arcturus froze as the tongue retreated back into her maw, leaving him covered with a thin layer of clear saliva. His eyes widened in shock as he just stared at her for a few moments longer. She had just licked him. Right across his face! And he had done nothing to resist it. "W-Why did you do that?" He asked her quietly, looking up into her eyes once again.

"It's a comforting thing to do when someone is in pain." She replied quickly without skipping a beat. "That is something dragon mothers do to their offspring, to show them affection and help fight away the encroaching sadness that might lurk within their minds."

Arcturus wiped away the sticky liquid from his face, sticking his tongue out as it slowly dripped down his finger. He flicked it away without another thought. "It's gross."

"You're welcome." she snorted and narrowed her eyes.

He quickly snapped his mouth shut, as he realized that he might have hurt the dragoness. She was close, after all, close enough to bite him if she wanted to. "I-I didn't hate it though." He said, lowering his head. "It was warm, and it helped. Thank you very much."

"You are most welcome, my dear little human." She said soothingly. "Quickly, hide!" she then hissed, causing Arcturus to bolt towards the closest thing available, which was her. He crouched low behind her neck, finding himself pressed up against her scales. He lowered his head as he listened to the sounds of heavy footsteps moving within the tent.

"Anyone here?" Came the slurred voice of the midnight guard. "Cause ya ain' suppose ta be hya...its da rules!" Arcturus heard him burp, and suddenly take a large gulp from whatever he was drinking from.

The boy just stayed crouched low, trying to keep himself as tightly against her as he could. He covered his mouth as he felt his heart beat faster with each approaching foot step. He could feel the sensation of his heart being pulled in all directions at once. He dared not think what the guards would do if there were to find him here with the dragon. Would they disqualify him? The thought sent a shiver down his spine as he pictured his father's disappointed gaze, his wrinkled brow, and his stern words about failure.

"Coulda swore I 'eard someone talkin' wit ya." He heard the sound of a sloshing bottle as Howling Storm just snorted in disgust. He could feel her muscles tense up beneath her scales.

"There was no one in here except me, you sweaty pig. I suggest you go somewhere else before you fill up my tent with the fine scent of a distillery."

"Oy? What's tha? Ya haf da guts ta speak to me? Don't need a talkin' to from a fockin monster. Besides...who'd want to talk to somethin' like yaself?

Tis like...courtin' death or somethin." The man laughed, turned back around, and exited the tent as quickly as he had come. Arcturus emerged from the warm dragoness when he heard the sound of the flaps closing behind the man.

"That was close." She said, relief ever present in her voice as she looked to him.

"You can say that again." He wiped several beads of sweat from his brow, giving her a smile. "Thanks for acting as my hiding spot."

"Did not really have the choice, dear." She pulled against the leathers. "Not bound as I am, anyway. Arcturus, can I ask you a question?"

"Yes?" he found himself smiling as he placed a hand to her snout once again, running a hand gently up her warm cheek.

"We have grown...closer over the few times we spent together, and I am wondering if, perhaps, you can find it in your heart to free me from these shackles."

"I..I..." Arcturus stammered, feeling his chest tighten back up again. The dragoness spoke truly. They had grown closer, but to go against his father, his family, against everything he knew...it was too much, even for a friend.

"I can't," Arcturus pulled his hand away. "I'm sorry, but you are asking me the impossible."

"I understand. It was worth a try." She lowered her head, her eyes drooping. "I thought you would be able to help me."

"I want to, but..." She was a dragon sent here to be bound and killed. There had to be a reason for all of this. There had to be, unless his father was interested in killing innocent dragons for sport and glory. "I want to help you. I really do, but they'd start to suspect me, and they'll probably track you down and capture you again anyway." He finally admitted with a sigh.

"No matter then." She replied almost in a whisper. "I think you must go for the night. I wish to be alone with my thoughts for the time being."

"With who? Why?" he found himself asking as turned to sneak out of the tent.

"If you return tomorrow, I will tell you why."

Arcturus nodded as he snuck his way out of the tent, offering her a sweet goodbye. She just returned the sentiment with the same endearment she had shown before. Arcturus tried to fight the guilt building in his heart as he passed the plethora of tents, but it was of no use. He turned back to the tent to admire it flapping gently from the breeze in the air. He made a mental note to return tomorrow night. He had to know why she was here, and where her thoughts were keeping her.

* * * * * * * * *

"Welcome back, Arcturus," came Howling Storm's voice as he entered the tent the next night. The entire day had been a blur. Everything he had done was just a way to get back to the dragoness. The scaled creature that had him captivated with its magnificence, drawn in with her unnatural kindness.

"Hello." He said back quietly, looking around quickly and taking a seat cross-legged before her. "How was your day?"

"You ask as if I were not bound in these leather straps while I wait for my death." She glared at him, snorting a small plume of air out of her nostrils. "But to answer your question...Boring."

"Sorry. I could not sneak any food for you today. My father had his eyes on me like a watchful hawk." He looked down when she pulled against her bindings once more. "Can we go back to the conversation we had the last night? The one where I ask a question and I let you stretch a limb?"

"Once again, straight to the point." She sighed, lowering her head to the ground. "We may do that, but I have to change our little arrangement a little bit. Instead of being asked every time, I wish to ask you a few questions of my own."

"I...yes, that's doable," Arcturus nodded, "What do you want to know?"

"Arcturus...I want to know what you honestly think of dragons. I want to know what lurks within that part of your mind that is still unburdened by your father's judgment, your family's history, and most of all, their hatred. I want to know what the hatchling in front of me really thinks."

"That's...complicated. Need to think." He searched his mind for the right answer, finding it fairly easy. He remembered all the nights looking into his books, and every story where he wondered if his father was telling the truth. Every time he looked to Radiant Flame, or any other dragon, Arcturus wondered if there were more sides, more details to the story. "I don't honestly know, Howling Tempest. I want to know more about you...about all dragons. I want to learn so I can make my own decisions regarding them."

"Would you ever harm a hatchling that had done you no wrong? Even if their parents had done terrible things?"

"Never." Arcturus stuck his tongue out in disgust at the thought. "That would be horrible. Can you tell me what you were thinking about last night?" He moved closer to her as she rumbled in her throat, then took a deep breath that made her scales slightly clink.

"I can do that. Yes." She gestured back to her hind paws. "Although I wish to stretch my left leg if you would not mind. I think it has fallen asleep and that is driving me with a madness you would not even begin to understand."

Arcturus nodded and quickly undid the bindings on her leg, letting her stretch it before him with a groan.

"Mrawwhhhm...That is nice..." She closed her eyes and started to purr as she wiggled her leg slightly.

Arcturus ignored the cute noises she was making and touched the paw that moved towards him. It stopped wiggling as his soft hands caressed the digits there, running over the smooth scales and finding the hide beneath them. He laughed as she suddenly pulled away with a giggle. "Whoa....Didn't expect you to be so ticklish!" He gasped as she let loose another giggle as he followed her paw with his deft fingers.

"Grrrr...." She closed her snout, and continued to steadily pull from his grasp but, never getting away for more than a couple of moments. "As embarrassing as that is to admit, even dragons have their weak spots."

"Tickly dragon tickly dragon tickly dragon!" Arcturus giggled as he traced his fingers from the soft digits to the paw pads beneath them. He caressed the soft leathery hide with the palm of his hand, finding them rather warm and pleasing to the touch. It was hard to believe a creature like this would have such soft paws, especially when the rest of the foot was armored with heavy scales that could turn even metal blades with their strength.

"Ok, I'll slow down. Tell me about your thoughts." He continued to caress the soft toes, finding them captivating and soothing as his thoughts drifted to his mother.

"Well...this might not be what you expect." Her voice lowered as her laughter died and her mood darkened, almost like a shadow had wrapped itself around her heart. "I was thinking about the little hatchlings I left behind. They are small, vulnerable, just like you...waiting for their mother to come home and comfort them."

Arcturus' fingers froze on her paw. She was a mother? His heart began to feel heavy again as the guilt started to creep back in. Not just because it was his family that was keeping her here, but that she had a small family of her own. She had offspring that cared about her, that would miss her, that would...

Arcturus shook his head. His thoughts immediately flew back to his mother, particularly to how he had hurt so badly when she perished. How he still hurt after all this time. "I..." he coughed, the tightness in his chest getting heavier. "Sorry. Didn't know you had hatchlings."

"Oh yes." She snorted weakly. "They are a bundle of energy, and they make my heart crack and go as soft as your human skin. I cannot fathom what their life will become if they are forced to grow on their own...if they even manage that."

"No...they can't...die." Arcturus looked up to the female, trying hard to keep his tears where they belonged. "Can they?"

"They are still small, Arcturus," The dragoness' whisper seeped into his flesh. "Imagine you are left in the wilds to fend for yourself. How long would you survive?"

"I...don't want to think about that. Not if I can let you go back to them!" He found himself saying without another thought. He was surprised, covering his mouth instantly after the words flew from his mouth. He imagined his mother would have just been proud at his exclamation.

"You can do what?" She asked, as if she did not hear his words the first time.

He froze for a moment as she stared at him expectantly. Her breaths were the only sound he could hear as his heart rammed against his chest. He thought to his mother, who was surely watching him in this moment. He cleared his throat and found his bravery as he looked into that dragon's eyes. "I said I can free you.... on one condition."

"You but only have to name it, human. I imagine you want treasure or something of material value like most of your kind?" She rolled her eyes.

"No...I want to know if you did any of the crimes they accused you of. I want to know if you belong here, in these bindings."

"You want to know if I deserve to die over my actions." She chuckled. "I hunted in what one of your lords deemed his forest. I killed what he considered his deer, a big stag that I needed just for my hatchlings and myself. The coward must have hired your family to capture me, all in the name of one little beast I took for food. Are you happy now, little one?"

"Sorry. Didn't mean to sound mean."

"The fault is mine," The female spoke over him. "My hatchlings...I worry about them so much. If you'd only know how heavy my heart feels, maybe-"

"I will free you." Arcturus forced himself to smile. "A promise is a promise, yes?"

The dragoness closed her eyes.

Arcturus nodded. He felt his heart pound harder. With shaking hands, he undid one belt around her limbs. One by one the others followed, his quick fingers letting the leather plop onto the ground before he undid the bindings on her wings. His smile broadened as she stood up, easily towering over him.

"B-b-big." He stuttered as the female spread her beautiful wings. The dark navy of her membranes had shifted to a bright shade of pink that reminded Arcturus of the cherry blossoms that he heard about in Drenedar. "There you go, Howling Storm...Go home to your...."

His words were cut short as the dragoness suddenly wrapped her limb around him and charged through the tent. She bounded over the grass, stretching her wings wide and giving them a mighty flap that carried them both into the cold air of the night.

"Aaaahhhhhhhhh!" Arcturus screamed out, holding tight against her limbs as he felt his stomach lurch in his body. *This is how I die...Please....Not here. Not now. Not before I get to...*

He felt her tighten her grip on him, holding him firmly against her warm scaled chest. He felt sorry for himself as she carried him higher and higher into the dark, cloud filled sky. The chill of the biting wind made him shiver in her grasp. His heart sank as his father turned out to be right. Dragons were good-for-nothing, silver-tongued devils, and now he was going to die for being a gullible fool. If not from the fall, she was no doubt going to bring him somewhere and eat him. He cried out into the night air as loudly as he could, tears starting to trail over his flushed little cheeks.

"Cease your screaming, little human." She snarled out. "You sound like one of those banshee creatures that can kill with a shriek like yours. Stop it, unless you want me to cork your little snout."

"Eep!" Arcturus shut his mouth and hugged her fingers tighter. Fear wrapped his heart in its embrace as he continued to sob quietly into her scales. For he, Arcturus Lund, was going to die this evening at the claws of the dragoness that he had trusted. The one dragon he decided to help.

This is what your good deed gets you...Eaten by the dragon you tried to save.

It was almost ironic how right that sounded.

* * * * * * * * *

Arcturus shivered in the night. His breath, as well as his heart rate, slowed down during the cold flight. The dragoness had not looked to him once the entire time, her wings beating steadily against the air. It was their constant rhythm and her steady heartbeat that allowed him to shift his focus away from how high up they were right now. Not like he could turn around and look, for she clutched him so painfully close to her chest. He had stopped his sobbing a while back, trying to think about what needed to be done. He was trapped in a dragonesses' grip with little chance of escape. His mind went to his dagger as he wrinkled his brow. There was always the option of making a last stand, one final effort before he would be devoured alive.

His heart started beating faster when he felt her decent towards a rocky area located near the ocean, if the sound of the waves crashing against the stony shore was any indication. He closed his eyes and readied himself as he felt her back-wing and touch down with her hinds, her pads only making the softest of noises against the stone. Arcturus was let go softly, landing onto the stone, and falling backwards onto his read end. He was left staring up at the towering dragoness that had plucked him from the earth. The little boy immediately scrambled away from her as she refolded her wings against her back.

"Please don't try anything foolish. We are miles away from civilization, and I assure you, the best choice you can make is to stay here with me for the night." She quickly reached out to him with a paw like lighting. Arcturus made sure to turn, and in one swift motion, he yanked the dagger out of hiding and plunged the sharp tip into the soft underside of her paw.

"I will not be eaten without a fight!" He shouted out with false bravery as she reared back with a snarl.

"You call that an attack?" She lifted her lips to expose her teeth as she advanced on him. "I have felt thorns inflict more pain on my paws. What were you thinking, little Arcturus? What result did you hope for? Please, tell me. I am extremely intrigued to hear more about your escape plan." She snapped at him, causing Arcturus to yell out in fright.

"Stay away from me! I know what you plan. What you want to do. Dragons...You're all the same, and I stupidly fell in your trap!" He shivered, stuttering as she just glared at him. He looked past her, towards the rocky ground beneath her paws. She was blocking the only way out, and the way behind him led deeper into her cave. She had him trapped. She knew it, and he knew it as well. Arcturus narrowed his eyes and held the dagger out with both shaking hands.

"Oh, drop the act already." She smacked the dagger out of his hand with a swipe of her paw that made him stumble backwards, rubbing the reddened area. "You are not a warrior, Arcturus. Give up."

"P-please...you can't just...eat me..." He cried as she advanced and pushed him into her cave with her scaly tail. "I helped you! I let you go! Please, we're friends!"

"Will you ever stop talking? Consider yourself lucky that I bothered to bring you all the way here." She growled, guiding him with her tail whenever he slowed down or tried to shift directions. "You are mine now. I suggest you deal with your predicament in smarter ways than fighting like a drunkard or shouting like a little banshee."

How did I end up here? How? He found his eyes misting again as the female's tail smacked him roughly to force him into the dark confines of her cave. It was only like that for a short portion. A glow came from inside the cave, thanks to the glowing algae on the walls that painted the dark stone with a soft turquoise light. They did not stop as he felt another smack of her tail along with a growl that escaped her throat.

"Don't think about escaping." She pulled him again with her tail. "I have some dragons that are very eager to meet you, little hunter."

"For the thousandth time, I am not a hunter!" Arcturus stammered. "How many times do I have to say it? You're right! I'm not my father. I'm not a warrior!" He shouted out, causing her to turn to him with a great big snarl.

"That remains to be seen." She held her head up as they came to what looked like a large room of stone spikes jutting from the floor. On the opposite side of this open space was a rather soft looking nest laid out in a circular shape.

Arcturus' eyes widened at what lay inside the nest. Three little bronze scaled hatchlings, all huddled together, shivering and whispering to one another when they strolled over. He felt the female's tail leave him as she bound towards her little offspring.

"Momma!" They all cried in unison as she began to lick and nuzzle them with an affection Arcturus never witnessed before. The hatchlings bounded around her legs, grabbed at her scales with their tiny paws, all to get their share of attention. A bleak smile forced Arcturus' lips to move slightly. He was almost certain Howling Storm had forgotten about him completely now that she had been reunited with her children.

Maybe I can hide and avoid getting fed to her little monsters. Arcturus quickly bolted behind one of the stone spikes that grew from the ground, peeking out for a few moments as he watched the bronze mother continue to purr and pull her offspring close against her. She fell back with them clutched in her limbs, laughing as her wings hit the back of her nest. He could not make out what she was saying, as the only sounds escaping her maw were snarling, hissing, or growling noises. It could only be described as cute as she touched her hatchling's snouts, licked their cheeks and nuzzled their little bodies. She continued this up for several minutes before carefully picking them off her one by one and setting them on the cavern floor. It was when she shot her snout right in his direction that he noticed his hiding place had not been as useful as he imagined.

She advanced on him, looking like a great predatory cat as Arcturus scrambled backwards away from her. His heart threatened to burst out as she quickly closed the distance and cut off his escape with her lengthy tail.

"You will be staying for dinner, little human."

He gulped as he turned around to face the imposing dragoness. "Don't eat me!" He screamed out, tears filling his eyes as he begged for his life. "I'm sorry for stabbing you! I'm sorry for speaking bad things of dragons. Please, just don't eat me!"

"Grrrah! You are exasperating! I am not going to eat you." She snorted, "What I am going to do is hunt something that will fill my belly after the warm reception your family gave me." She thrust a talon right between his eyes. "You are to stay here with my hatchings. If I catch even a single scale of theirs out of place, I will start assuming things you don't even want me to think about. Then I will personally eat you, letting you experience digestion while still being alive. Do you understand?" She snarled loudly, snapping her jaws right in front of his face, causing the frightened boy to yelp.

"Y-yes!" He collapsed onto all fours as he hung his head. He only rose it when she had made her way out of the cavern and up the rocky path. Arcturus was left alone to look at three sets of green eyes staring at him from the nest.

Great...now I have them to deal with. Arcturus scrambled back towards his protective spikes as he saw three tails swish back and forth behind them. The little dragons started to whisper in those same growls and hisses to one another. He thought he saw them shiver, and crouch low to avoid his gaze, although he pushed that thought from his mind. What reason they had to be afraid of him? He was the one who had been captured by the deceitful dragoness. Probably find himself on the evening menu too, if she returned empty handed. He imagined himself as an appetizer, or possibly a snack after they feasted on whatever she brought back.

Arcturus waited among those cold stone spikes for countless minutes. Time seemed to freeze when he just continued to glare out in terror at the little hatchlings that looked back at him from the nest. He finally devolved into small whimpers as he hugged his knees and looked away. If only he had listened to his father, if only he was not stupid enough to fall for her lies. He might still be back in his tent, inside his warm bed, under the fluffy covers he looked forward to each night, instead of laying on a cold stone floor, about to be fed to a bunch of dragon hatchlings. Sure. She said she was not going to eat him, but she had already lied to him once. What difference did it make if she lied to him again? He shivered and hugged himself tighter when he heard the sounds of Howling Tempest's claws against the stone as she returned into the cavern.

Howling Tempest held onto the scruff of a large stag that hung limply from her jaws. Her bronze scales were painted in a thin layer of red that made Arcturus shiver at the thought of what she would do to him. Her eyes went to her hatchlings, and then straight to him. It felt like she was piercing into his soul with her fearsome eyes. Her stern gaze caused the little boy to crouch lower and hug the stone spike as the female made her way over to her offspring and set down the animal a few feet away from the nest. She spoke to the little dragons with the same hisses and growls, getting little pleased sounds back. Like little rumbling purrs or chirping noises the gryphons made in similar situations.

Arcturus' mouth dropped in horror as the female ripped into the stag, pulling it apart in one great tug, painting the stone beneath in dark crimson ooze. As if on cue, the little ones grabbed hold of sections of the stag with their little teeth and started to rip and tear just like their mother had done, chomping away happily as their little snouts started to resemble that of red dragons instead of bronze. '

Arcturus almost vomited as he continued to watch. The sounds of flesh ripping, snouts chewing, and the feasting lingered in his mind like a thick haze you couldn't get rid of. Despite how disgusted he was of what was ·

happening, he could not force himself to look away from them. To his surprise, something else happened in this feeding frenzy of blood. The dragoness was acting very loving to them. He saw her lick their snouts once or twice to make sure they were not splattered in the blood of the deceased stag. She also cut out sections with her onyx claws and handed them over to the hungry hatchlings. Arcturus was not familiar with sections of the animal, but it occurred to him she might have been offering them the best parts of the kill. The process continued until there was only a small section of the stag left. All three hatchlings purred with fulfillment. They pressed up against their mother, and Howling Storm licked each one in turn from snout to tail, until not a single drop of blood sullied their little scaled bodies.

"Are you ever going to come out from your hiding spot, fierce, brave Arcturus?" Howling Tempest looked up with a smile, licking her snout with what Arcturus painted as satisfaction. "You're not doing a good job at hiding, so I suggest you come over and grab this last piece of stag. For me, it is insignificant, but to you, this is very much life, unless you prefer to clutch your growling stomach throughout the night."

Did she want him to feed it to her little ones? He took a step out as she growled her instructions again.

Arcturus sheepishly walked over to the family of dragons. What choice did he have? She could just snatch him up whenever she wanted, and feed him to her hatchling with ease. Without a word he hung his head and sat down before them. "What is it you want me to do before you eat me?" He shut his eyes tight and fought off the sobs threatening to burst out of his throat.

"Eat you?" Her voice devolved into growling laughter. "It's the third time I have to explain that and you...Oh...I see what the problem is."

Arcturus opened his eyes to see that her snout was wrinkled up like she was going to sneeze.

"Ever since I snatched you from the bowels of that ugly cloth-home, you think I am still lying to you." She lowered her snout as the hatchlings dove under her. "I have a family like I said. My mate is not here for the reason I mentioned in our earlier conversation. To say I lied to you is an overstatement."

"A what?" Arcturus frowned. "You took me from my home!"

"Yes, for reasons you made me painfully aware of. If your hunters come looking for me, I can make a deal with them. Your life in exchange for the lives of my hatchlings."

"That's what I am? A pawn?"

"An insurance for a day that hopefully never comes. Now please, relax. I am not feeding you to my hatchlings, nor am I keeping you for myself." She gestured to the bloody mess of the stag. "I figured you were hungry, and since you were kind enough to feed me during my captivity, I thought it best to return the favor."

Feed him? He looked back to the stag, trying to not vomit as he looked to the ragged bits of flesh left still on the corpse. "I...that's not...I can't eat raw meat. It makes humans sick."

"Oh, that." She said flatly. "I forgot you mortals don't have strong stomachs in that regard." She reached down with a talon to cut out a section of the stag for him. She made several quick and precise cuts with her talons. Arcturus watched and imagined what those things could do to armor, or even her enemies if she wanted to really hurt someone. "Here," She held up another paw, and with a simple touch the meat started to change color from the dark red to a well-cooked brown. "Simple bit of magic, and you have yourself a cooked piece of stag that you can hopefully digest."

He felt his stomach rumble, as if wolves were ripping at his insides. When the dragoness lowered the meat, Arcturus grabbed hold of it with his hands, the juices leaking through his fingers. He wrinkled his brow at the thought of getting so dirty, but he was hungry, and the piece was not that hot to the touch. He took a bite as he saw her, along with the three sets of eyes, watch his feeding. It was not the tastiest meat, magic-cooked and without any sort of seasoning. However, he politely chewed, swallowed, and offered a pleasing sounding. "Mmmmm."

The dragoness gave him a pleased trilling noise as he continued to gobble up the meat she had provided, and when he was finished he set it aside with the stag, patting his belly as he did so. "That hit the spot. Thank you for being...well, like this, and sorry for my behavior. After you captured me, I jumped to the worst conclusions and eeeeeep!"

He was greeted by her slimy tongue in the most surprising and inappropriate of moments. The warm organ bathed him in dragon saliva in the same sloppy way it cleaned the hatchlings. "H-Hey!" He tried to protest, but she insisted. He tried to push her away at first, finding it disgusting and a bit weird for her to be doing it. But then it, occurred to him -as she continued his assault on him with her tongue- that she was licking him exactly like she had done with her little ones, so he stopped resisting and let her work. It was hard to describe what the tumultuous feelings that coursed through his body were as she licked across his brow, across his neck, and eventually all over his clothes. It felt like he was one of her offspring, and could feel the caring nature she held within her heart through each one of her tender licks. Arcturus found himself liking the sensation after the first few minutes of grooming. He even felt a pang of disappointment when she licked her nose and pulled away from him.

"There now. You are clean, just like the rest of my family."

Arcturus mumbled his gratitude when the shrilling voice of a hatchling startled him.

"Story, momma!" The little male jumped on her right forelimb, rustling his little frills that looked like his mother's, except he bore a dark red strike at the base.

"Yes! Tell us story!" Came the voice of another one, clearly a female, with a yellow stripe.

"Please?" The last one bounded over, another male with a blue stripe. He nudged and pushed the others out of the way as all three snouts looked to her expectantly.

"Story! Story! Story!" The three hatchlings chanted in unison. They tapped their tails against the stone, refolded their wings against their backs, and at times clacked their little charcoal talons together.

Arcturus felt a smile come to his face from that display. He let out a small gasp when, suddenly, a larger bronze tail pushed him to sit with the little bronze hatchlings. "Whoa…" He went to protest only to be silenced when she started speaking in a loud and booming voice.

"This is not a story per say, little ones, but a statement of facts." Howling Storm lowered her snout to each one of them in turn, including Arcturus. She lingered for a few moments on him, her eyes looking tired and pained as she began to speak. "We are leaving this home, these lands, and everything they offer behind." She rose her head to gaze out to the way that led outside. "I will take my clutch far from Lumara, away from the rule of a despot who kills dragons based on nothing but lies."

Arcturus was about to ask a question about this. His king, killing dragons based on lies? Was the man just like his father in that regard? Lumping the bad deeds of certain dragons in with the rest of their species? Before he spoke, however, Howling Storm carried on.

"Your king would end our lives based on numerous small offenses. Theft of animals, trespassing on his land." She snorted, "He spews such horrendous nonsense. As if all of us were the murdering monsters of old. As if all of us kidnap mortals, eat them, or destroy your villages. All we want is a patch of land to call our own, peace to raise our hatchlings, and freedom to soar along the sky. Surely that should not doom a whole species to death. Gryphons are not targeted for extermination as far as I know."

Arcturus said nothing as she continued telling her tale about the king's misdeeds towards her kind. Several more dragons that had been killed with nothing more than minor crimes, or some that had done nothing at all. It was a rather difficult thing for Arcturus to stomach on such a strange night, but with the conviction of her words and the honesty blazing in her eyes, Arcturus found himself believing every word that was coming out of her maw. He was even deeply saddened when he heard a story of hatchlings that were stoned to death by an angry mob of mortals, because they thought the little dragons were associated with a villainous monster that had lurked within their hills in ages past. He watched as her own hatchlings shivered at the story, quickly bounding under her wings. They even pressed themselves against her with little whining noises.

Arcturus felt his heart start to ache as she wrapped her wing around them, whispering soothing sounds to them, and nuzzling their little snouts. It made him long for his mother's touch, to hear her words once again grace his ears.

With her tale about the state of dragon kind finished, the bronze dragoness brought her little ones back into her nest, laying down and having them cuddle against her in one pile of striking bronze scales. She wrapped one wing around them and just looked up to Arcturus, then opened her other wing. Howling Tempest gestured to it with her snout. "Come and slumber with us. My wings and scales are warmer than the cold floor, and much more comfortable."

Arcturus looked to the dark stone, then back to the expectant female dragon that had fed him, shared tales, and licked him in the same affectionate way she treated her hatchlings. He shivered from the cold air of the night before scampering over to her. Once there, Arcturus lowered himself into her warm embrace. He felt her wrap a forelimb around him, followed by her wing. It was rather warm, pleasant, and the comfort of being protected by such a powerful creature made him want to sink further into her grasp. He closed his eyes, sighing at the pleasant heat exuded by her body and the pleasant comfort of her scales. Arcturus realized that with her breaths, and steady thumping of her heart, he felt at peace. With a final exhale, the young boy left his dreams take him away upon the ethereal winds of a realm where he too could soar upon the sky like a dragon.

* * * * * * * * *

Arcturus sat down on the grassy land that grew near the mouth of the cave's entrance. The sun hung in the air, sending its warm rays to bathe the human in its pleasing embrace. He took a deep breath, taking in the smell of the salty ocean. With a sigh, he gazed over the surrounding forest, with towering trees that bore the darkest bark and greens of every variety sprinkled in their leaves. Howling Tempest had allowed him to venture this far from her cave, yet he was still being forbidden to leave. Arcturus realized that despite her warmth, pleasing touch, and food, he was very much still her captive. He wondered how long it would take until someone from his clan came looking for him. How long until this place was swarming with dragon hunters of all kinds. How long until this family of dragons would lay dead around their own home.

His attention was drawn to a section of large rocks scattered around the grassy field. Like stone monoliths, they rose from the earth in a formation that reminded Arcturus' of teeth in a dragon's maw. The three hatchlings were climbing the tall stones, leaping from top to top with little growls as their talons dug into the stone each time they would catch hold of their destination. The activity repeated several times until the hatchling with the red striped talons did not find purchase. The hatchling kicked frantically for support, then fell with a yelp of surprise, landing right onto his wings. When the dragon stood up, he went to stretch his left wing, but suddenly stopped, let out a pained whimper, and tried to lick at the stiff pain that rendered his wing immobile.

The human hesitated for a moment as he watched the dragon try to move his wing several times, only for the hatchling to have the same heart-stinging reaction as before. With the latest bit of whining, Arcturus could no longer fight the impulse to help somebody in need. He ran a hand along the leather strap of his pack, and strode over to the little dragons, who separated themselves from their brother. He saw their eyes look to him with fear, as if he was going to kill them and turn them into belts or boots. Even the red striped one tried to get away, but Arcturus offered a soothing sound like their mother had done. This caused the hatchling to cease his struggles for just long enough for Arcturus to grab the limb that was troubling the dragon such.

He felt his way along the smooth scales, much softer than the female's. The hatchling's armor felt like leathery plates rather than solid material. With the next pass of his hand he saw the hatchling close his eyes and offer a whine. It did not appear that anything was broken. Arcturus's eyes traced along the limb as the little dragon tried to pull it away from him. It was then when he remembered having something similar when he was smaller.

"Your wing is dislocated." Arcturus said softly, patting the dragon's scales gently. "I can fix it...but it might hurt for a moment. Try to be strong, ok?"

The dragon nodded without a word, looking up to him with emerald eyes full of worry.

"Alright. Ready?" He asked, paying no mind to the other two snouts that descended on his hands, curious on what he was going to do. "One...two...three!" He shoved the wing joint back into the socket with a small yelp of pain from the red striped hatchling.

"There. The worst part is over." Arcturus retracted his hands and dusted them off, a smile coming to his face as the little dragon rose to all fours and started bounding around with a smile on his snout. He opened and closed his wings several times, letting out a little happy roar.

"My wing feels right again. You were right!" The hatchling cheered, stopping to stare at Arcturus, tail flicking eagerly behind him.

"Thank you!" The female hatchling nudged him with her snout, an act that caused him to push back against her, laughing.

"It was no problem, really. I could have been faster, but I had to feel my way around the wing to be sure, cause I just couldn't see....um...that bone that connects the wing to the back. It's called...uhhh, it's the...I forgot the name, but maybe you can help me? Uhhh..." Arcturus slapped his face with his palm. He wanted to feel heroic, yet instead, all he did was embarrass himself further. He gestured to the dragon he had helped, too shy to even ask the hatchling's name.

"I am Xervir!" The red striped hatchling proclaimed, slinking over and nudging the human, running his scales over his clothes. "Thanks again for the wing fix you did. It feels so much better now!" the hatchling looked over to his siblings, his eyes no longer filled with fear, or worry, but full of mischief. "Do you play games, human?"

"Arcturus." He laughed.

"What kind of game is Arcturus?" The yellow striped female asked, tilting her head to the side, and ruffling her wings. "Does it involve wings or tails?" She opened up her left wing and gestured to the soft membranes.

"No...that's my name." Arcturus chuckled, thumbing his chest.

"That can't be a name." The blue striped hatchling replied, licking his jaws like his mother did. "You look more like a Zenthyn." The dragon nodded. "Yup, most definitely a Zenthyn."

"I agree." Xervir laughed. "It suits you much better than this weird name you claim to have." The hatchling sat down onto is haunches, his snout tracing along Arcturus' clothes, until his gaze fell onto the pack that he had.

"I don't know about Zenthyn..." The yellow striped hatchling suddenly put both of her forelimbs up on the human as she moved her snout ever so close to his face. "I think.... he looks exactly like a....like...mmrrrrr." She gave a quick giggle before suddenly licking him across the face and scampering away. "I'd say an Ordis."

"Hey! That's not fair!" Arcturus wiped away the slimy strand of saliva.

"You have to be faster than that, Ordis!" The female leaped around happily.

"Ordis?" Xervir asked, turning to his sister and baring his teeth. "That is a stupid name for a healer!"

"It's better than spell-wrangling Zenthyn." She rolled her eyes and swished her tail, hitting the grass. "Right Arcturus? Ordis is a much better name, right? You don't look like a wizard at all."

Arcturus nodded with a laugh, causing the two male hatchlings to pout and glare at their sister, who was just smiling and puffing out her chest.

"See? The human prefers my name." She strode over to sit beside him, scooching close, and looking up to him. "Ordis here is on my team from now."

"Your team?" Arcturus chuckled nervously, concerned he had just entered a game he did not understand.

"Does he have any weaknesses?" Xervir asked, his snout getting close to sniff at his clothes. "Well...your scales are really soft...I bet you're ticklish like our wings!"

"Your wings are ticklish?" Arcturus laughed, causing Xervir's eyes to widen.

"N-no." The dragon backed away from him, folding his wings closer against his back. "Mrrr...no... of course not. Why would they be ticklish? Dragons can't be tickled." Xervir looked away as if he did not care. "That would just be silly...right?" The dragon snapped his gaze back towards him with a smile. "Get him! Let's find out human tickle spots!"

"Hey!" Arcturus managed to shout out before he was suddenly bombarded and tackled over by three eager hatchlings. He laughed as their little claws raked across his skin, one or two piercing into his skin by accident, but he paid it no mind, as Xervir found that, by licking the human's neck, Arcturus recoiled with laughter.

"His neck is ticklish!" The dragon proclaimed to the other two roaming snouts as Arcturus desperately tried to push them away.

"Stop it, you...little bundles of scales!" The human reached out with his fingers through the bouts of shrieking laughter coursing through his chest. The dragons did not relent for a moment, as one found the back of his leg made his entire body spasm and giggle without care. His eyes began to tear up as the dragons continued their tickling, until his fingers found Xervir's wing membranes. It was then when Arcturus wiggled his fingers. A wave of accomplishment surged through him as the dragon suddenly fell backwards with cackling laughter, causing the other two to suddenly stop.

"He's down! On him!" Arcturus gasped out, pointing to the fallen dragon, hoping his siblings would join in as he began to tickle the dragon on the ground. He was pleased when they both joined him with their snouts and claws as they ran them along Xervir's soft membranes. "Go go go! Show him no mercy! Give no pause to your assault!" Arcturus ordered with the gruff voice of an army commander, delighting in the dragon's whines, his cute small kicks, and his smile as he cackled into the morning air.

"Nooo! S-sssssstop! I'm not...you shouldn't-" He shouted out, his tail wiggling under the merciless assault. "Raawwwwwaaaaaahhhh I'm not the enemy!"

"WHAT IS THE MEANING OF THIS?" Came the loud booming voice of their mother. Arcturus and the others grew silent as they unwound themselves from one another once the dragoness strode over with powerful steps, her tail swishing back in forth, and her eyes full of anger. "What were you all doing together?"

"We were playing with Ordis here." Xervir rolled over on his belly, refolding his wings. "They all then ganged up on me to tickle my poor wings with-"

"WHY ARE YOU PLAYING WITH THE HUNTER?"

"Hunter? But I wasn't-"

"Shut your snout, human. I heard what you said about assault. You want to poison my hatchlings with the vile things you learned from your family?" She snapped her mouth at him, thrashing her tail, and growling from her throat. "I have you here in my clutches, under my roof. That does not give you the right to play with my hatchlings. I have not forgotten what your family had done, and still keeps on doing."

Arcturus looked to the others as Howling Storm continued to scold them, their little snouts drooping as her chastising words sank in through harsh growls.

Arcturus' eyes began to mist. Was this how his life was going to be from now? To be the puppet of this dragoness? Get shouted at? To be berated, snarled at? To be tossed in with his father's hatred? He could not help being who he was: a kind, cheerful boy who never dreamed of harming these hatchlings.

"I...I wasn't...trying to..." Arcturus turned his head back to the female to sniffle by himself. Tears began to stream down his face as he lowered himself to all fours and began to cry in earnest.

The female ceased her snarl, growls, and reprimands. Arcturus felt her snout press onto his back, and she let out a warm puff of air through his ruffling hair.

"What moves you to tears, little one? Was I too harsh?"

"It's..." Arcturus sniffled. "It's that...You welcomed me under your wing last night." He lifted his head, the tears still coming down his cheeks. "And now you snarl, hit, shout...We just played together, is all. I never tried to hurt them, or...or teach them bad stuff." He wiped his eye with a sleeve, sniffling. "Why can't I play with the hatchlings? I swear I don't want to hurt them! I thought...I thought we are friends. We were having so much fun together..."

"Yea!" Xervir went to speak.

Howling Storm silenced his little squeak with a pointy claw. Then, her eyes turned back to Arcturus. "Because, little human, we cannot ignore the truth. You belong to the Lu-" Her eyes then widened before him as she froze in place. The only movement she was making was her tail, wagging back and forth, and her chest rising and falling with her breaths. She then lowered her snout and averted her gaze. "By Bahamut's grace, I have been most unwise."

She turned away, her tail wrapping around the boy and pulling him towards her.

"Hatchlings...continue to play." She turned back to her offspring, offering them a warm smile. "I am sorry about my outburst. Continue to have fun together. I will return the human shortly...I just need to talk to him a bit."

Arcturus wondered what she wanted to talk to him about, but quickly scampered after her when the little dragons all nodded to her and resumed their wrestling match with one another. He followed Howling Tempest for a few more minutes, until she turned around, sat down on her haunches, and patted a spot on the ground by her tail.

"Sit here with me, Arcturus." She said softly. "Please." Her voice softened even more. Arcturus saw her eyes fill with the same fondness she had shown to her hatchlings. How could he resist? He took a seat within the curled confines of her tail, and she gently pulled him closer and brought her snout close to his face. "I am sorry for stealing you from your home against your will." She said after a long sigh. "I only wanted to make sure I could get my family away from danger without you raising the alarm."

"But I was the one who-"

She silenced him with a warm nuzzle along the side of his head. "You are a sweet boy, Arcturus, but I never fully trusted you. Your family name still blinded me from seeing the truth." She pulled away to show him her paw. There was still a dark red mark on the underside, where his dagger had found purchase. "Perhaps you would not have been so terrified to lash back at me if I unveiled my plan. I realize that was my first, and greatest mistake." She sighed again before returning her snout to his face. "Can you forgive me?"

"I'm sorry for stabbing you." He quickly replied, ignoring her question as his eyes returned to her paw. "I was so scared..."

"I know." She licked him across the face. "It was not your fault, and truthfully, I admired the courage you have shown. That, despite being placed in such a dire situation, you chose to fight your way out. You held your head high and stood your ground against me even if you had no hope of winning." She chuckled and nuzzled him gently with her snout. "It was a very dragon thing to do, little human."

Arcturus touched her enormous snout and held it close to his face when her words came to a stop. Then, he pressed his head gently against hers, sighing under her warm embrace, basking in the soothing air that rushed out of her flaring nostrils. "So, what happens now?" He asked softly, a sense of disappointment running through him when she rose her snout above him to look back to her hatchlings. They were still rolling in the grass with a series of growls when she called out in the same tongue.

The three hatchlings suddenly stopped and quickly scampered over with blinding speed, until they were right beside their mother's tail, paws pressed against the scales, and little snouts close to Arcturus, filled with smiles and grins.

"I think I would like you to meet my children." She smiled, "properly, this time."

"He already knows *my* name!" Xervir shouted, puffing out his chest and thrusting a wing talon in his direction. "He relocated my wing when it got hurt!"

"He did?" She smiled to the dragon. She flicked her playful tongue at him, causing Xervir to giggle out. "That is a most helpful human to have!"

"Uh-huh. He is a very good healer. Then we played wrestling, and I found out he's even more ticklish than us!" Xervir wrinkled his snout and glared at Arcturus. "And then he recruited Briva and Emmess against me."

Howling Tempest just chuckled, pointing to Xervir. "This little bundle of joy is Xervir." She then brought her snout over to the yellow striped hatchling, and licked along her spine, causing the little one to laugh in return. "And this one is named Emmess." The dragoness did the same thing to the navy striped hatchling, who turned to smack her snout playfully in an attempt to thwart of her assault of affectionate licks. "And lastly, this one is Briva."

"Hi...I am Arcturus, and I am not a game," He laughed, waving to the smiling hatchlings.

"So..." Xervir rose his head up to his mother, followed by the others joining beside him. "Can we play with him? Please?"

"Please, mother?" Emmess added, tapping her paw against her mother's scales. "We promise to not hurt him! Well..." She looked to the tiny scratches on his skin. "Besides scratches, but those were accidents! Honest!" Emmess' tail wagged like a blur behind her as she spoke.

Howling Tempest's grin only got bigger as her eyes went to Arcturus, then back to the hatchlings, who seemed to be bouncing on their paws as they waited her response. "He is all yours, little ones. Try to be gentle. He does not have the resilient scales we bear."

"Hey, that is not true. I have clothes and-and I'm more than capable of handling a couple of dragonlings!" Arcturus suddenly exclaimed.

"Oh really?" The dragoness inched her snout close to his confident face. "Guess we're about to see if you are indeed as strong as you say. Get him!"

The little dragons growled heartily at the challenge. They leaped on the human at the same time, once again tackling him with laughter and soft paws.

"Got you now, human!" Briva shouted out, giving a little growl in the back of his throat.

"Go for his tail, Ordis!" Emmess cackled as she fought Xervir away with her tickling talons. "That is his tickle spot!"

"On it!" Arcturus wrestled with the navy stiped hatchling, who now squirmed to get himself free when the human's deft fingers descended onto his tail.

"No! You won't get my tail, healer!" Briva kicked back with his hind leg, knocking Arcturus back onto his butt, allowing the hatchling to bound away with laughter. "You can't catch me, Ordis!"

How could he resist a challenge like that? Arcturus pulled himself free, letting Emmess keep Xervir pinned to the ground with her tickling attacks while Howling Tempest watched over them. The thought occurred to him, that she was watching over them all. Like...they were all one big family...and he was part of it.

Need to focus. No time for thinking! Arcturus shook his head and chased after the hatchling, who cackled and leaped around in glee.

Arcturus spent the rest of the day with the hatchlings as they practiced tag with one another, even if that game always ended with the hatchlings turning on him and tackling him once more to the ground with a series of cute dragon sounds. Next they explored the surrounding forests, although every so often, when they would look around, he would see Howling Tempest was always nearby like a ever watching sentinel. He smiled at her diligence each time, and went back to following the scampering little dragons through bushes, plants, flowers...He even joined them by rolling in a large field full of grass. They all ended that little play on their backs, looking into the sky. Arcturus pointed out clouds to them and asked the dragons what they saw. They all would reply with food, animals, or other dragons in flight. He was having so much fun with them he did not keep track of the time, and it felt like the day had passed in a blink of an eye. The sun was already sinking below the mountains in the distance, basking the land in the pleasant fiery caress of a gentle flame.

* * * * * * * * * *

Arcturus sat outside the cave's entrance, with all three hatchlings pressed up against him. He giggled as he put his arms around the scaly bunch. He figured that, if anyone were to come see him now, it would look like the dragons had adopted him right into their little clutch. Arcturus fought off another wrestling match that had started when Emmess had poked Bravis on his snout with her paw, laughing the entire time as he assisted his teammate in the affair. He thought back to his time with his own family, the grueling training, the demands of his overly exigent father, and the hatred he was trying to impart onto his son. With a sigh, Arcturus caressed the dragons as they all piled on top of him in a giant hug of affection. Their scales warmed him up to the very core of his being. How could his father be so wrong about such a magnificent species? Dragons were not all evil like he had said. Part of him wished to stay with this family forever, for how bad could it really be, to live among dragons?

He ate again alongside the small family when Howling Tempest brought back another meal for them to eat. She cut him off a section and used the same magic to cook the meat as her hatchlings worked away with little rips and tears. Arcturus diverted his eyes from the grisly work as he chomped away at his own morsel. When that was finished, another round of licks came from Howling Storm, to which Arcturus found himself laughing, not minding the shower of saliva in the slightest. His reaction even caused the dragoness to pull her snout away with a rumbling pleased noise from her throat.

"You seem to have adjusted quite well." She looked up fondly to her hatchlings that had started to yawn and cuddle against one another. "They seem to adore you. I wish their interactions with mortals were always this nice." She gave him one last lick before retreating to her nest. The dragoness nestled herself into the nest as the hatchlings bounded for her and wiggled under her wing.

"Come on, Ordis! Sleep here, where it's warm." Bravis squeaked, waving him over with a yawn.

Arcturus looked up to Howling Tempest's smile, then to the three hatchlings that looked at him with smiles and expectant eyes. How could he resist? He leaped into the collection of scales, and sighed with obvious fulfillment when they all squirmed and packed themselves around him tightly. He closed his eyes from the feeling of contentment he felt, and when Howling Tempest's wing wrapped around them all, he truly felt like he belonged here, as one of her clutch.

* * * * * * * * * *

"Come on, wake up."

Arcturus felt a warm snout press against his chest, his arms to raising to grab hold of warm scales. With his eyes still closed, the boy unleashed a satisfied sigh. He was still in the warm embrace of his new family. Nothing had changed.

It wasn't a dream.

Arcturus was so relaxed now that he almost felt like dreaming. The pleasant feeling of all the hatchlings still cuddled with him, the warmth from the dragoness they were snuggling against. He could not bring himself to move away from such serenity.

"You have to get up, Arcturus." The dragoness nosed him again, a tad more forceful than before. The last poke caused him to open his eyes as the three hatchlings scampered off him with little whimpers of dissatisfaction.

Arcturus rolled off the dragoness and stretched his limbs with a yawn. That had been one of the best sleeps of his life. Resting under a dragon's wing was surprisingly warmer than his bed, and even more comfortable. He found himself looking back to her stretching form, wishing to be back within her embrace. To be held so lovingly as he slept. It reminded him of his own mother, and for a short moment, Arcturus wondered what today held in store for him. Would they get a chance to explore the forest again? Would they fly with the mother in the sky? And more importantly, would she take him with her when she decided to leave this cave behind? His eyes widened when he realized he did not mind the last option at all.

I can live among dragons, Arcturus' fascination rose further the more he pondered on this. *I can fly with them, learn so much. And the best thing is, I never have to hold a sword in my life ever again!*

He could be a painter, selling off beautiful depictions of the dragons he would encounter along his journeys, at various markets, to people who found dragons equally captivating. Maybe even change a village's whole perceptions of dragons. How would his father feel then, when he, Arcturus Lund, would make the world love dragons instead?

The boy's little heart all but fluttered at the beautiful images his optimistic mind could conjure.

"You have to go home this morning." Howling Tempest said softly as she noticed his stare. "We are leaving, and you cannot stay with us."

Arcturus' dreams all came crashing down hearing those fateful words.

"Wh-what?" He blinked, unsure if he heard that correctly.

"I have to take you back to your real home, Arcturus. Please. Don't make this more difficult than it is. It's...hard for me to part ways so soon after..." She sighed and looked to the cavern walls.

"B-but, you can't do that!" Arcturus protested as his heart sank into a shadowy pit of disappointment. "I don't want to go back home! I have all the training, the testing, the expectations, and then there's my father. He wants to kill all of you!"

"Nonetheless, it is where you belong, little one." She lowered her snout, her eyes not daring to look him in the eye. "I want to keep you here, with us, but your family is big and powerful. They would send out scouts to track us down, then parties, whole squads of armed warriors...there would not be a single place in the world where they would not hunt us, and I don't wish to put my family in that kind of danger."

"But they won't find me! Can't you just take me with you and fly away?" He asked, tears starting to form in his eyes as the little hatchlings all gathered around him.

"Can't we keep him, Mother?" Xervir asked. "We will take good care of him!"

"Make sure he gets fed!" Bravis added with a smile.

"Ordis is not some pet to keep around." Emmess rolled her eyes, pressing herself up against Arcturus with a purr. "I'd like him as a brother. Who wants to adopt him?" She raised her paw, followed by the others doing the same thing with a bout of laughter.

"Please..." Arcturus whispered. "I don't want to be like my father. I don't want to be a... killer. I don't want to hurt dragons, least of all...murder them for no reason!" The tears stung his eyes now, rolling down his cheeks as he collapsed. The three hatchlings wrapped themselves around him as Howling Storm lowered her snout to him and gave him one long lick across his face. Arcturus sniffled, and with blurry eyes, saw that she too had tears in her eyes.

"I wish I could take you with us Arcturus. You are different from your kin, a child fair of heart, with a warm spirit unlike any other human I met. One that allowed you to cast off your father's words and free me. Thanks to you, I am not dead, and my family is reformed. I will always be grateful for your deeds." She gave him another lick across his cheek. "But I cannot take you, for your father would hunt us to the end of the earth, slaying us for taking his son away from him." She nuzzled him next, pressing her warm scales against him. "If you go back home, we have a chance.... I am sorry...know I truly wish to take you away from all the things that trouble you...and I would want to make you one of my own, but..." She pulled her head away, wiping the tears from her bronze cheeks. "The only thing I can give you now is my name. Rasionynth."

"Rays...ion..ynth." Arcturus stumbled with the words, trying several times but failing at each one. "What good is a name if I can't come with you guys? Can..." Arcturus wiped the tears from his eyes. "Can't I call you Howling Storm? It's the first name you gave me when...when we became friends."

"You may, little one. But I would keep saying my real one...practice makes perfect after all." She licked him one more time as he wiped away his tears. "Now come...I wish to show you something before we part ways." She rose up and guided all four of them to one of the cavern's walls.

Arcturus looked up to the grey stone, finding something that once again surprised him. Along the wall were pictures of all sorts, drawn, it seemed, with a claw of some kind. Most were at the same level of the hatchlings. These drawings were of things like trees, animals, the sun, the water, little stick figures for humans. He looked to the hatchlings that were on their haunches, tails wagging with big smiles as they admired their handiwork.

"Here." Rasionynth rose her claw and dragged it along the stone swiftly, drawing the shape for a human, and three little shapes for her wrymlings. He could tell by the little wings and smiles on their snouts. Lastly, she drew a bigger dragon around them all, with her tail curled around their playing form. "Now...no matter where we go...part of you will remain here, with us, in the same place we called home."

Arcturus approached the stone carefully, running a hand along the surface. The shapes were rudimentary, lacking the refinement he displayed with the brush, yet the gesture touched him deeply. Howling Storm drew art for him, same way he did for her shortly after they met. He felt more tears come to his eyes as the pain in his heart grew at such a touching gesture. "I...it's beautiful," Arcturus sniffled. "Please...take me with you. We can do so many things together! I can teach you how to draw with the brush, and-and color the sketches. It doesn't have to end like this. Please, I don't want to go back." He continued to look up to the dragoness, whose amber eyes started leaking honest tears.

"I know." She picked him up gently with her paws and pulled him against her warm, scaled chest. "And it kills me to let such a fine painter go." She wrapped her head around him, and pulled him tighter against her, as he felt her body began to shiver. They stayed like this for a moment before he was set down against the stone. "Well..." She looked up to the exit. "We should be off then. Get close enough to Drenedar before your family's scouts spot us."

Arcturus nodded. He had to be a man. If he truly cared about these dragons, he had to let them go.

Putting the stern look of a warrior, Arcturus went to follow her as she strode right past him with a swish of her tail, her onyx claws clicking on the stone with each step. He stopped after several steps, an idea forming to his mind as he remembered his pack. "Wait!" He shouted out, throwing his pack onto the ground.

"What is it?" Rasionynth turned around, tilting her head to the side.

"I know a way to keep you with me as well." He pulled out a small journal that he always kept in his pack. With a leather cover, and a belted binding, the book was as fine as it could get. He set it on the cavern floor and pulled out his vial of ink. "You just have to let me put ink on your paw, and you can press it against the pages here." He smiled to the hatchlings and gestured to the vellum.

"Mama, can we get our paws dirty for Ordis?" Emmess looked up to her, her eyes misting. "I want to play with him one last time, before..."

"You may." The dragoness nodded, causing all three of the hatchlings to cheer in joy.

One by one, Arcturus helped the hatchlings get their right front paws covered in the black ink, then letting them press it against the paper. They giggled about how cold the ink was, and it was amusing, how each dragon felt the need to press their nose against the vellum and sniff their handiwork. Arcturus finished off their art with a signing of their name right below the paw marks. When the task was finished, they all followed Rasionynth out of the cavern and into the morning light.

There was a slight fog in the air that made the surrounding countryside look lost in a sea of murky white. Arcturus took a deep breath of the crisp air, sighing in remembrance. His senses would soon be overfilled with horses, gryphons, and the smell of dragon hunters. He turned to the hatchlings, who bound to him and wrapped him up with their wings. Each one had tears in their emerald eyes as they wished him a hearty farewell.

"You will see us again at some point, right?" Bravis asked, his head drooping.

"Please mother, will he see us again?" Emmess looked up to her mother with expectant eyes. Her tail twitched slightly.

"I...do not know where out next home will be." Howling Storm sighed, "But I think Drenedar is a fine place to settle. I heard of a blue dragon that might help us find a place to settle. He goes by the title of Swirling Storm, if my memory serves."

Emmess looked back to Arcturus and licked him gently across his face. "You hear that, Ordis? Just look for this Swirling Storm one day." She nuzzled him with her snout. "Find him, and we can be a clutch again!"

"I will...one day..." Arcturus ruffled her frill with his hands, tears still pouring from his eyes as he wished them all goodbye. When Rasionynth picked him up and brought him into the sky, he never thought it would have been as hard as it was to say his farewells. He started to cry once more as he pressed his face against her scales, wishing to be held within her forelimbs forever, and never go back to the family of slayers that he was bound to.

* * * * * * * * *

Rasionynth settled him down within a mile of the fairgrounds. She made sure to keep low to the ground and hug the trees as she flew. When she said her goodbyes, she did so with tears, licks, nuzzles, and hugs. "Remember to keep your heart true, Arcturus." She licked him one more time across his face, like he was one of her hatchlings. "And if you want to be a knight, to protect instead of punishing... you go be a knight."

He nodded, caressing her scales one last time. "Good bye Ra...sionynth."

"May the summer winds lead you into a life of prosperity, Arcturus." Rasionynth spread her wings, and with a mighty flap, the majestic dragon was gone, her shining scales soon disappearing, leaving Arcturus alone near the edge of a vast forest. He looked around to see in the distance the large collection of multicolored tents, and the black smoke rising from the fires. He found his next few steps hard to make, like his legs were weighted down by stone to stop his advance. He glanced back, hoping to see that the dragoness had changed her mind. However, all he saw were trees. All he heard, silence.

"Be a man. I need to be a man." With a deep sigh, he picked up the pace

389

and made his way back to a family he no longer wanted.

Arcturus wandered into the collection of mortals. No one seemed to pay him any mind as he got lost in the sea of sounds, people, and smells. That was until he came across the familiar tent of his own kin, where he was assaulted by hugs, ruffled hair, and caring eyes.

"Where did ya venture to, lad?" Came the voice of one of his uncles, a farmer from the southern regions near Trost.

"Ye worried us half ta death, ye wee basterd!" Said one of his cousins, a gryphon rider from Whitedell to the east. She carried a concerned look in her radiant hazel eyes. "Found a lass an' spirited her away into the forest, eh? Needed a bit of lone time fer yerselves."

"I was...I was..." Arcturus tried, but he could not get out a word thanks to the storm of questions flung at him. Where he had gone, what he had gotten up to, if he had a fling with the gryphon nanny's niece. Even if he could do something that ridiculous, he could not tell them the truth. How could he, when it would put the dragoness at risk?

"Yes...Where did you get off to, son?" Came the demanding growl from his father, who pushed aside many of the Lund clan with a sneer on his face. "Where did you run off to? Is it true you went romancing some lass? How thoughtless is that? Did you not hear one of the dragons went missing? You could have been killed, boy!"

"Father...I..." His mind raced for an answer as he kicked himself mentally for not running over a comprehensible story. He figured he was just so distraught over not staying with the family of dragons, it had simply slipped from his mind. "I was hunting a boar in the woods!" He rubbed the back of his neck and gestured to his soiled clothes. "Damn thing sent me on a chase, and I got a little lost. Stupid, I know, but I wanted to prove I can be a warrior just like you, father."

"Awk, you poor thing. Are you hungry?" His nanny squawked as she pulled him right against her fur. "You must have been alone, cold, and oh, so, so hungry! I'll whip something up for you with a slice of a claw." She poked him in the stomach with her talon. "Can't have you hungry for the trials ahead, young man."

He looked up from the concerned gryphon to his father, whose stern eyes never shifted from him. For a moment, he was concerned what was running through his father's head.

Thankfully, the man did not yell, nor did he scream. Markis just gestured for him to follow. "Come. Don't make me ask a second time. We need to share words."

Arcturus gulped as he let go of his nanny in order to follow in the footsteps of his father, who strode away from their tents. He looked back briefly to see the rest of his clan dispersing and going back to the festivities around them. He picked up the pace and stepped in tandem with his father, who looked down to him with the same stern gaze, eyes filled with disappointment.

"A boar? Is that the best you could come up with, whelp?"

Arcturus froze. "F-father...I swear it's-"

"Don't patronize me, boy! I know it was you who freed the dragon." He growled as they came to a stop in a place far removed from anyone else. "What...on this fair earth... were you thinking?" Markis thundered as he slammed his palms together. "How many times have I told you of the destruction spread by their wretched kin? They're evil, vile, twisted monsters that wish only to see us killed to the last!"

"T-that is not true!" Arcturus shouted, clenching his left hand into a fist. "I got to see how dragons truly are. She was kind and caring and good!" Arcturus blurted out, his face stern, just like his father. There was no point to play the role of a coward any longer. He had to be a warrior. The same steel-hearted fighter that stabbed a full-grown dragon in the paw. After all, if his father divined the truth, he might as well go all out. "She was nothing like you said, and you are too blinded by what happened to your brother to see-"

Arcturus was thrown backwards as his father backhanded him to the ground. "Gah...". He picked himself up, glaring up the man who had raised him as he rubbed his warm cheek. "This just proves my point."

"Point? Point?!" Markis paced around. "You are my son, you daft child! How dare you disobey me like that?" His father picked him up by the scruff of his shirt. "How dare you accuse me, your own sire, of being infested with-with hatred to protect a beast?" The man spat that word as if it was poison. He led Arcturus to go continue his pacing, a look of disbelief present in his eyes. "I can't believe it. My son...my only son...my warrior would never betray his family for a dragon! I bet she enchanted you, boy." He pointed an accusatory finger at Arcturus' numb form. "Weaved some spell we could not block in time, or-or used her silver tongue to fill your young, gullible mind with a hoard of lies." He growled with clenched teeth.

"If that is true... why did she not end me, father? Remove the evidence, as it were?" Arcturus shot back. "Explain that to me. Try to think for one. Single. Moment."

"Easy." His father moved in again, taking his belt off as he did so. "After she fled our camp, she used you as a fockin' token. A distraction. Did not want me to go after her out of vengeance. Now she gets a chance to fly away, far enough where even our scouts can't find her. You denied us more then a dragon, boy. You stole our right to judge the beast for its crimes...and for that...you deserve to be punished.

Arcturus grimaced when his father struck him with his belt as hard as his arm could muster. The stinging lash made him gasp out and squeeze his eyes shut. "Gahh!" he could not help stifle the weakened cry when his father continued to hit him again and again and again, the firm leather connecting with various parts of his body.

"Dragons....*thwack*...Are....*thwack*...Evil....*thwack*.... I am doing this for your own good, boy!"

Markis lashed three more times. "Even if you hate me. Even if you curse me. You are still my Son! I know what's best for you!"

Each strike against his back was a strike right to Arcturus' heart. His gasps of pain filled the air as his father continued to lash him mercilessly, spouting off more lies about dragons. "Do you want to end up like my brother? That what you want? To get yourself killed?"

"Your...brother?" Arcturus gasped out, his brow sweating. He gave a weakened pull against his father, but still could not find the strength to liberate himself from all this torment. "You...never mentioned...that he..."

"He liked dragons, just like you, boy." His father narrowed his eyes. "But instead of returning the kindness shown to him, the beast my brother decided to call friend killed him where he stood! Was that a proper reward for a kind-hearted man? Hmm? I will make sure you never end up in that position."

Markis shoved Arcturus to the ground. "Lesson's over. Pick yourself up and get ready for the tournament ahead. You WILL do your best and beat the others, and when it's all said and done, we will drill into your head the evils of dragons until you forget all about this little slip in judgment. I will ensure you're never tempted by such evil ever again."

Arcturus groaned as he pulled himself to his feet once more, wincing in pain from the plethora of marks left on his back. He wanted to narrow his eyes and glare at his father. Tell him how futile this beating was.

But Arcturus stopped himself from doing something stupid. It would do him no good, to fight fire with fire. That would just give his father another reason to continue his beating with that awful belt. So Arcturus just nodded to the man, "I will do as you say." He hung his head, clenching his fist, then let his father grab him by the shoulder and lead him back to the others with a firm, painful hand on his shoulder.

"I'm doing this for your own good, son. One day, you will thank me for this, and you will teach your own son of the lesson I have imparted upon you this day. I love you Arcturus, and I won't let those beasts take you away from me. They've already taken far too much from our family. I will make them pay, understand? They will pay their due."

Arcturus kept his head bowed until he was finally let go to his tent. He rubbed his shoulders and winced as they ached. His thoughts drifted to pleasant warm scales, affectionate licks, and the sounds of the hatchlings.

With those thoughts he was able to push back the pain from his wounds as he collapsed on his bed. He knew it would be only a moment of rest, and a few bites of lunch, before his father came back for the usual training.

Arcturus wondered what he would be doing tomorrow at the tournament. He knew the top reward would be to slay the remaining dragon. That had to be it. But how could he slay the creature now? He just had the best day of his life with those dragons that were supposed to be his mortal enemies. What if this one was like the female he had set free?

Arcturus closed his eyes with a sigh as he thought to the gold dragon's scales. He made a vow internally to find the creature. He would free him, just like he had done with the female. He only opened his them when he detected the alluring scent of roasted lamb and when his gryphon nanny shortly called out to him.

"Arcturus! Come eat your lunch before it gets cold! Your father wants to go test shooting with you after!"

Arcturus sighed and strode outside to eat his meal. He sat down at a wooden table and wolfed down the roasted lamb, corn, and peppers that were mixed together on his plate. He sighed and savored the flavor. It was at least better than magically roasted stag. The spices made things so much better in his opinion. However, the relief did not last forever, and he soon found himself washing the meal down with a swig of water. He bowed to the gryph, who ruffled her feathers and offered him a kind smile. Arcturus straightened his back and made his way to the target range, where he knew his father would be waiting with his stern face and crossed arms.

* * * * * * * * *

Arcturus spent the rest of the day working with his father, trying his hand at an energy crossbow lent by the king. The weapon was usually something only reserved to those in the military. Arcturus liked the feel of it in his hands as he lined up his shots and easily blasted apart the targets that were brought before him. He rolled his eyes and groaned the entire time as his father continued to question him on dragon weak spots and how vile they were. With that done, he went into a drawn-out rant that included all of the horrible deeds they had done, most of which he'd witnessed with his own two eyes. Arcturus willed himself through by thinking of the dragoness and her hatchlings, so no matter what his father was throwing at him, it met a mind hardened by love and determination and protected by the pleasant memories of the dragoness Rasionynth.

That night, Arcturus quickly gathered his things around his room, ready to set out to find the other dragon. He just knew that all he needed to do was talk to the gold scaled beast. In his mind, the dragon would tell him a story about how he had been wronged by the hunters, and placed here to be killed unjustly. Surely that was the case.

Arcturus took a deep breath as he pictured the dragon flying away into the sky, roaring happily after being freed from his bonds. It brought a smile to his face when he went to open his tent, only to find a guard sitting on a chair, watching his flaps.

"Evening lad." The pockmarked guard in chainmail smiled, waving to him from his chair.

Arcturus quickly pulled his head inside, wrinkling his brow. His father must have placed that guard to make sure he never left his tent, knowing he would want to go find the other dragon. Damn it!

He went to the other parts of his "room" and peaked under each wall, only to find each one had a different guard placed in front of them. Double Damnation! He crossed his arms, as each of the sentries was positioned in just the right way that there would be no way around them, no way through without getting spotted.

Arcturus eventually collapsed onto his bed with a sigh, pulling his journal from his pack and opening it to the page with the paw prints. He looked to the ink, remembering how happy he had been that morning. How he wished he could have stayed with his better family. He eventually felt tiredness take him, and he closed his eyes when he could not fight off slumber any longer. He wiggled once in his bed, his dreams filled with dragons flying high in the bright sky.

* * * * * * * * *

Arcturus made sure to wake up early; early enough so that when he was peeking out from his tent, the guards that had been so vigilant a couple of hours ago were now fast asleep.

Perfect.

Arcturus slunk by one of them like a silent shadow. He made sure to change his clothes before heading out. The boy wrinkled his brow as he grabbed hold of the dark green tunic and the charcoal leggings he now wore. Arcturus shook his head and began his search, paying no mind to the sun that was just beginning to crest over the horizon. He checked the outskirts of the place, just like he did before introducing himself to the female bronze dragon, Rasionynth.

Only now, he was on the trail of a different dragon. Arcturus first went to her tent, thinking logically that the golden dragon's tent would be close to hers. It also had to be big enough to accommodate the size of such a looming creature. Arcturus scurried from tent to tent, quickly peaking under the cloth for any sign of the golden dragon. With each failed attempt, he would look up to the slowly rising sun and wonder how much longer he had before one of the guards would grab him from behind and shout all sorts of profanities in his ear.

I have to do this, Arcturus fought the pit in his stomach and pressed on. *I'm a man. And men aren't afraid.*

On the fifth such tent, he came face to face with a dark brown colored cloth. It was held down with many ropes, and bore a guard garbed in chain mail, just like it had been with Rasionynth's tent the nights prior. This man even bore a spear in his hands as he shifted his elven head from side to side. Arcturus realized someone must have told the men to be more vigilant after the first dragon went missing. He snuck past the man, going the long way around to the other side of the tent, where he lowered himself into a crouch and felt with his hands at the taught cloth. He hooked a hand on the underside of the material, then gave a great tug, but nothing happened. The tent fabric was being held down too tightly, and no matter how many tugs he gave, it would not budge.

No no no...come on. I can't just let him die, you stupid piece of cloth!

Simmering with apprehension and anger, Arcturus stood up and crossed his arms. He did not come this far to be stopped by this overly tight tent. He unsheathed his dagger, and like a hunter, plunged the sharp tip of the metal into the fabric. With several loud tearing noises, he cut a circle into the material and made his own entrance.

Arcturus bounded into the tent, his eyes adjusting to the dim light that illuminated the insides of the tent. He squinted and looked around the boxes, the hay, and what looked like torture equipment. The ground around the place seemed to have been ripped up with claws. Arcturus frowned as he realized that the knives, blades, and other such sharp objects had blood on them, most likely carved from the innocent dragon.

Don't worry, my friend. I will set you free from this unjust torture. Arcturus navigated through the maze of items, each drop of blood or torn ground slicing another painful gash into his soul. When he came to the golden dragon to see him bound and bleeding, his heart nearly cracked, for the beast that had looked so beautiful the day prior was now covered in thin red lines. Scales that had looked so majestic now bore cracks and dents, in some places looking like a spiky mess of twisted flesh. His feathered wings were bound just like the female's had been, and his limbs were chained together with a large lock in the middle that needed a key. *Oh no.* Unlike the female, there would be no undoing of straps or any way through them.

The golden dragon looked up to the boy with his worried, emerald eyes. His pained eyes filled Arcturus with so much guilt that it made him dizzy. They had done this. His clan, people he knew, had inflicted untold pain onto the dragon before him. A dragon that was most likely not at fault to deserve such unjust punishment. His mind went to the bronze female and her hatchlings, longing for their presence as he took a few tentative steps. The golden beast said not a word and simply watched him, most likely confused as to why this human was slowly approaching him.

"Hello." Arcturus spoke clearly, his voice soft and gentle. He even bowed slightly to the dragon, thinking it was the polite thing to do. He felt his heart quicken and beat with excitement as he neared the scaled creature.

"My greetings, little hunter." The dragon replied, his whiskers flicking as he rose his head slightly.

"I... I'm not one of them. Mhm. I'm not a hunter." Arcturus replied without skipping a beat. "I have actually come to free you."

"Really? What have I done, to deserve such stroke of fortune?" The gold dragon tilted his head as much as he could to the side. He did not stray his sight from the boy that continued his approach. "What compels you, young hatchling, to seek me out and lift my burdened heart with tales of freedom?"

"Uhm...well...there's this..." Arcturus gulped on his words as the golden dragon fidgeted slightly against the bindings. "Let's just say I have come to an important realization recently. I have seen...no. I've been proved that not all dragons are the shadowy evil monsters from my father's twisted tales."

"Mmm, intriguing words you bring to my ears. Perhaps this is the day when righteous justice finally dawns upon a land basked in darkness." The dragon gave a deep rumbling sound from his golden scaled neck akin to tumbling stones.

Arcturus cracked a meek smile at that. "Yes," He said as he was filled with the same exhilarating confidence he tasted when he freed Rasionynth. "I am just trying to do the right thing."

"Then by all means, little one." The gold dragon gestured to his bindings with a smile. "If you think you can free me from these shackles, go for it. I will make sure you are rewarded appropriately for your kindness."

"W-wait. Before I do it, may I know what your name is?" Arcturus made sure to stay away from the creature's head while he found his way around the metal bindings and the lock that fastened them together. His fingers traced along the cold smooth metal for a weakness. A few moments later he sighed with a frown as he realized they were fine craft. Probably the finest he had ever seen. The same kind his father would use if it were up to him, and in this case, it probably was.

"You may have my title, savior of dragons. Please refer to me as the Shining Sun." The dragon swelled his chest out proudly, his scales clinking together. Shining Sun then let out a pleased sound like a purr that made Arcturus giggle. Did all dragons make such cute noises? Arcturus could easily compare them to oversized cats after he lived among a real dragon family for two blissful days.

"That's a pretty name to have. Hold on a bit. I have to see...what I can do to..." Arcturus continued to examine the lock. He had practiced picking them from a young age, it was yet another skill his father had drilled into him. However, with each passing second, it was becoming clearer that he would not be able to undo this lock without the blasted key. His only hope was to pickpocket it from the guard outside, if in fact he was the one who possessed the key to the lock and not a fake.

He was about to tell the dragon this when he heard the voice of the last person he wanted to hear. The voice of the only man that could make his blood run cold.

"Arcturus! Where in the blazes are you?" Came the loud booming voice of his father from the entrance of the tent. His face was contorted into a snarl and was the brightest red known to mankind. The fuming man stomped his way across the tent as Arcturus froze up. "What?! What in damnation's name did I tell you!?" Markis barked through his teeth. Within two stomping steps he was upon the boy, roughly pulling Arcturus away from the dragon, who looked away and snorted his disapproval.

"F-father, I-" Arcturus could barely find the words to defend himself. What he was doing was much too obvious to explain. There would be no lie that could get him out of this. He had done this knowing the risks.

"Father, you are wrong! They are not all evil! If you'd just let me prove this to you, please! He's a living being, and if you'd talk to him just for a moment-"

"Silence, you gnat!" Markis slapped his son across the face. "You dare to tell your father what to do?"

"Please..." Arcturus winced. "If you...if you'd just treat that dragon like a fellow human..."

"He's not a human boy. That there, is a beast!"

Arcturus refused to back down. He spouted more of his young wisdom, but every word, every plea fell on deaf ears as he was tossed to the ground by his father, who stared down on him with the hungry, evil stare of one of the dragons that he hunted with such passion.

"We will drive this poison out of you, Arcturus." Markis grabbed some rope and bound them around his boy's smaller hands. "I will make sure you don't end up like my brother, even if you kick and scream the entire time. I will not let the dragons take what I have from me, Arcturus. They might have my brother, but they won't rip my only son away from me!"

"Please...if I mean anything to you, just...just listen to my words." His voice cracked as his father finished his bindings around a wooden pole that was thrust into the earth. "Dragons are not inherently evil. In many ways, they're just like us, with families and-and loved ones. They only want to live, father!"

"That's a load of hog shit." Markis thundered as he shoved a finger between Arcturus' eyes. "What does a boy know of war, eh? What do you know of loss? The dragons use you as their plaything because you're too fockin' stupid to see the truth!"

"Please..." Arcturus winced. "If I mean something to you...if you ever loved me... just listen to my words. Mother...you know mother wouldn't have wanted this. You know this, father. You know it!"

His eyes began to mist as his father backed away, disappearing for a moment, only to return a few moments later with a cat o' nine tails. Arcturus' eyes widened at the thin ropes held tightly in his father's white-knuckled hand.

"N-no. No father, please, don't torture me!" Arcturus cried out in desperation. "Think of mother. What she'd say if she was here right now?" He desperately called out as his father grabbed his shirt and raised it to expose his back. He then held the device back, ready to strike.

"She would smile at me." The man's gruff breath fell over Arcturus' back. "She'd approve of anything I'd do to save your life, boy. Now let's set you free of the poisonous words the beast injected inside your head."

His father lashed out with the device.

Arcturus winced and cried out as the tails of the device struck his skin. The vigorous lash made his whole body tremble as he fought to stand up.

Then another came. And another. The whip crackled upon his back like the forks of lightning that split the sky apart during a storm. Arcturus' vision blurred as his father continued his incessant whipping, each stroke bringing a fresh wave of pain that made the young boy scream his guts out. However, despite his screams, despite his words, his father continued with the flogging.

Arcturus' thoughts struggled to become coherent words through the nightmare he was living. Each time he got several words out of his shaking mouth, they were cast from his mind by the forceful arm of his father. He was left gasping after the twentieth such whip, the feeling of warm blood dripping down his ragged skin strangely soothing.

"Now boy...tell me again about the wretched dragoness you foolishly spirited from the grasp of deserved punishment. What happened? And what do you think of her? I want to hear it all, down to the last word, until I am sure her poison leaves your body." His father said, his voice laced with hatred.

"Mghh...nrrrhhh." Arcturus knew what his father wanted him to say. He wanted to hear the same lies that came from his own vile mouth on the subject. He wanted to hear about the dragon's evil, and how she had manipulated an innocent boy in freeing her. He wanted to hear that his son, the soon to be great dragon hunter, had not been swayed by the beast. "She was...a monster." Arcturus whispered, his hollow eyes staring into the ground. A bead of saliva made its way down his lower lip, trickling onto the ground beneath.

"When her words failed to succeed...she enchanted me with magic. Twisted my mind. Made me... think of dragons as if they are my brothers."

"Correct. Correct!" Markis beamed with evil satisfaction. "I've seen the effects of such spells before, and you are describing it perfectly m'boy. More. Tell me more, son. What did she do next? Tell me how you freed her."

"I...I just did." Arcturus said with the same helpless, confused voice.

"No. They can twist the mind. The mind, son. Your head." His father tapped at his own skull. "But they can't control your body. So tell me again. How did your hands find their way to her bindings?"

"Her claws..." Arcturus gestured towards the golden dragon's sharp talons. "She threatened me with evisceration. Told me that...she'll skin me like a deer and hang my pelt in her cave. I was afraid. Had no choice. She told me of all the gruesome spells she could cast on me if I didn't obey."

"Wretched creature." His father spat on the ground and stroke his chin to vent out some of the anger that made his temples tighten. "To threaten my son like that. My son!"

"If I wasn't a Lund, she would have killed me where I stood!" Arcturus cried out. The words that flowed from his mouth made him hate himself with each passing moment. Lying was always distasteful for him, but he just wanted the pain to stop.

"You...you're lying to me, aren't you?" His father grabbed the boy by his chin and sneered into his face. "I can see it in your eyes, boy. You're only forming words to appease me, but you don't truly believe them, because your head's still with them! With those blasted, deceitful, worthless creatures that took so much from our family!"

"Father, that's-I'm saying the truth. I can't lie to you. Come on. Did...did I ever lie to you?"

"Yes, son. You did. And not just once. Aaahhh, no matter." The man sighed, pulling back the cat o nine tails again. "We can keep this up all morning, until your eyes speak the same truth as your words. If I ever catch that dragoness...oh, my young, stupid boy...you can bet she will be getting more than she ever bargained for. This flail, see this?" He flaunted the blood-dripping tool before Arcturus' frozen face. "I'm going to craft a flail ten times the size with teeth sharper than any dragon's, so I can rip the scales from her body, like this!"

"No, father pleeeaaasse! AAAHHHHHHHH!" Arcturus screamed out to the heavens as the coldness of the whips once again kissed his bleeding back. He collapsed onto the ground, a squirming mess of hisses, groans, and endless pain. He cried out to any god that would listen, but no matter what deity he called on, the man above him silenced his desperate pleas with rivers of pain. It continued for so many strikes that Arcturus completely lost count. He only remembered standing slowly up, wincing at all the pain he had endured. His hands shook as his father undid the bindings and thrust a red potion into his hands.

"Drink it down to the last drop. We need you at top performance for the events we have prepared today."

"I..." Arcturus could not find the strength to resist his father and just took a long swig from the horrible tasting liquid. He could not find the taste, but it reminded him of curdled milk, and he forced himself to swallow the entire potion if only to rid himself of the infernal pain. He finished with a gasp, and a wipe of his mouth, finding his strength starting to return. The lingering pain from his wounds soon started to fade away as the magic potion swirled through his body like Rasionynth's comforting licks.

"Perhaps not now...but I hope that, one day, you'll come to understand that what I've done is for your own good." His father spoke almost the same words that he had used when he had whipped him the other day. Arcturus just looked to his father and nodded, internally hating the man that was staring back at him expectantly.

"I understand." He lied again, handing Markis back the empty bottle. Arcturus looked around to see the dragon was now missing from his resting place. However, the metal bindings were still lying on the ground, including the lock that had stopped him. They must have traded those bindings for something that could be more easily moved. Someone had obviously come to retrieve the beast while he was being tortured by his father.

Arcturus narrowed his eyes when he was led out into the light of the day. The sun hung midway towards the center of the sky, among a vast, vibrant blue expanse that knew no clouds on such a fine day. The warm rays bathed the entire collection of tents in a warm glow as tournament goers walked through the boisterous crowd, chatting away about the upcoming events.

Today came the day of the festivities, at last. The noise of the crowd was almost deafening, and Arcturus was led right through the thickest crowd. The folks parted before him and his father like water, signifying the respect they had for the name Lund. Arcturus lowered his head and looked to his boots as he heard a mention of his name in passing. It seemed like an eternity before he was tossed back into his old 'room', ordered to get ready.

"The games will be starting any moment now, son." His father crossed his arms and waited for him outside. "You will do your best. I know it. Then, after you defeat the rest of those buffoons, you will stand proudly at my side. We'll face the beast together, but it'll be your hand that gets to finish off that spawn of filth for good."

Arcturus scowled as he gathered his things. He strapped on a darkened, worn leather vest that bore the symbol of his family stitched into the hide. He ran a hand along the surface, disgusted by how it looked, and how it made him feel sick to his stomach. Arcturus imagined a dragon would look way better on his chest.

The thought flew from his mind when he grabbed his steel sword, thrusting it into his leather scabbard, then tying it with a belt around his waist. With that done, Arcturus closed his eyes and took a deep breath as he tied a dark green cloak around his neck. He would win this little talent of contest, and he would stand at his father's side, just not for the reason the old man expected. In spite of his words, Arcturus still had a mind of his own. When he was supposed to kill the beast, he would set the dragon free, to prove his father, the Lunds, and all of the attendants how wrong they were. He would let everyone see with their own eyes that not all dragons were monsters.

And then, Arcturus, savior of dragons, would stand proudly up there, a satisfied smile on his face and a final look of defiance thrown in the way of his stupefied father. Arcturus opened his eyes and nodded to himself, rather liking the mental image of that. Without another word or thought, he strode out into the sun and took his place at his father's side.

* * * * * * * * *

Arcturus took to the center of the arena surrounded by cheering people. He was lined up with many other young aspiring dragon hunters from all around the kingdom. Their own faces were full of good cheer and expectation, and were thrilled when the dwarven announcer had proclaimed the winner would indeed be the one finish off the golden dragon. Arcturus watched as they had wheeled out the dragon on a cart, bound in leather. The crowd had gasped at first, then suddenly roared their approval at the excitement that was going to soon follow.

He just gripped the hilt of his sword until his knuckles went white. *Make sure to watch me, father...I will win...and then the dragon will be out of your torturous hands for good.*

The tournament started with a target practice of any weapon the combatants chose. Arcturus went with a hand-sized energy crossbow like the one his father had him practice with. He lined up his shots carefully, and nearly got bullseyes the entire time, only getting outperformed by an elven child with a bow and arrow. They next moved onto beasts. This involved setting each hunter against a magical beast the trappers had captured for the purpose of this contest. Arcturus was set against a pair of blink wolves. These brown canines could teleport short distances as they hunted their prey.

Arcturus made short work of them, easily side stepping or avoiding their attacks. He met their throats with his metal blade, wincing as their blood stained the green grass. When the last wolf had fallen back with a whimpered cry Arcturus, offered a short prayer for the creature that was being used in such a gruesome way. He finished it off with closed eyes, ending the thing's pain once and for all. With the deed done, he cleaned his sword and ignored the praises being thrown about in his name. Even the cheering from the crowd fell deaf to his ears.

The day continued with numerous challenges. Some were mental ones, others involved testing the weak spots of creatures. There were also more physical ones in nature, like the beast contest. In each one, Arcturus was one of the best contestants, once again only being followed by that elven lad that had bested him in the target practice portion of the contest. The last challenge presented before them was a tie breaker, to decide which one of them would be able to slay the beast. The elven warrior, or the human hunter? The crowd went into another screaming frenzy when Arcturus held up the training sword they provided him for the upcoming duel. There was no need for the contestants to maim themselves, after all.

He took a deep breath and focused on the golden scaled dragon that needed him right now. He could not afford to lose to this elf. A child that was most likely three times his age. If he did, that dragon was going to end up with a slit throat, or a sword straight to the eye. "For Howling Storm," Arcturus mumbled under his breath as he bounded at the elf with his sword held high.

The elf side stepped his attack easily, striking at him in a horizontal fashion.

Arcturus crouched, the sword passing over his head by mere inches as he brought his own sword up, striking the elf right in the chest. He backed away with a smile as they separated and started to circle one another. Arcturus held his sword out as the elf narrowed his eyes and did the same.

They then met again and again. Wood on wood clacked out, only to be drowned by the cheers around them. Arcturus grit his teeth as they went at it like a blur, trying to find a weak point in the elf's defense.

With a pinch of luck, Arcturus found it. He took a step back as the elf swung down at him. The wooden blade missed his torso, and Arcturus struck him twice with his own sword. Once on the shoulder, followed by a quick strike to his left leg.

"ARCTURUS IS THE WINNER!" came the shout of the dwarf announcer, adding to the screams of the excited crowd. A few men strode over, grabbed Arcturus' wrist, and rose his hand up for all to see.

I did it! Arcturus smiled to himself. *Just like I knew I was going to!*

He glanced back to the bound golden dragon, his heart not letting up for one single moment. Arcturus did not pay any mind to any of the words the dwarf was speaking until he mentioned finishing off the bound dragon in the company of his father. Arcturus was given back his steel sword and was led over to the golden creature as the whole crowd grew silent.

Arcturus looked to his father, who wore a grin from ear to ear. He could see pride swell in his eyes as he looked back to his son. It made Arcturus almost happy to see that look on his father's face, but he frowned when he realized it was only because the man thought he was going to follow in his footsteps and murder the dragon that was displayed before the cheerful crowd.

You're about to be proven so wrong, father. Arcturus returned his father's grin as he was brought before the beast. He unsheathed his sword with a hiss, the sun shining brightly off its metal surface. He took several deep breaths as his hands shook at what he was about to do. He saw the golden dragon look away and close his eyes, clearly resigning himself to his fate. *Don't worry, Shining Sun. This human hatchling is going to save you, and you can fly away and live your dragon life in peace. Have mates, hatchlings, do whatever you wish.*

He twirled the sword in his hand as his father started his speech.

"Dear warriors, beloved clansmen, families, and friends. We thank you all for participating in these glorious events. It truly is a chance to show off the best and brightest among us while we hone ourselves for the battle ahead."

Markis then clenched his fist. "For we must all remain at our best to fight against the looming threat of dragon kind. For years, we have tried to teach them a simple lesson. Tell them that we humans only want to live in peace. But such savage beasts know not the sweet embrace of calmness. They thirst for blood. Our blood! The same blood that courses through the veins of our children, who now have the distinct honor of carrying forth the flame of our unyielding justice. Behold, Arcturus! Winner of today's tournament, and soon to be slayer of dragons!"

Markis smiled as the crowd erupted into frantic cheers.

"See? They love you," the man whispered and gestured to his boy with a wave of his hand to address the crowd once more. "There is a time in every child's life when the boy must become a man. Today, it is my honor to see my son take the first powerful steps into a much larger, and far more dangerous, world. By finishing off the vile gold dragon we have dragged before you, Arcturus is going to prove that he is indeed ready to carry the mantle of a true Hunter. Turn your eyes upon his wretched prey. Behold, Inferno's Bite!"

Markis all but had to point at the captured dragon, and the crowd started to boo, throw insults, vegetables, and whatever objects they had on hand at the helpless dragon.

"Your feelings stir within my chest as well!" Markis thundered, "for the horrible creature that now stains the grounds of our tournament with his festering presence laid waste to an entire village. A village full of good people, same as you. Why? Because the honest, kind hearted people refused to fall into his schemes."

Markis took a deep breath, then pressed on. "They fought against the beast's greed, paying no gold for misplaced protection, because they put their trust in their rightful king -our king- to protect them, as he promised to us all. Sadly, it had not been so. After the dragon dispatched the scant number of guards that gave their lives in defense of their village, this terrible monster killed every last woman and child, then burned the whole village to the ground, bathing its accursed deeds in the same wretched flames it draws its name from!"

The whole crowd gasped, while others called for the beast's quick death.

"I know, fair people. Believe me, I know what must be done. There's only one thing a rampaging monster deserves." Markis pointed to the dragon once again. "That is why we have the beast here, right now. Displayed before your very eyes, to be made an example of by none other than the winner of the tournament. My son!"

His father turned to him with a smile. "Please finish off the beast, just like I have taught you." He pointed to his eye and gave Arcturus a wink, a signal he wanted Arcturus to plunge his blade right into the gold dragon's eyes, delivering his steel blade right into the beast's brain and finishing it off for good.

This was it. This was the moment of truth. Arcturus felt sweat come to his hands as he raised his sword. He took an anxious breath from his lungs to steel his nerves. *Am I really going to do it? Defy my father and all the young hunters right in front of their parents?* His thoughts flew to his mother, and her own love of dragons. She was a gentle creature. As good and kind as Howling Storm. He remembered falling asleep under the bronze dragoness' wings, with her three hatchlings pressed against him. *Yes...I am going to do it...I am going to become a knight. Be an example to the others. Teach them that hatred is not the only way to peace.*

"No, father." Arcturus said with a resolute voice. "It is you who is the monster, for condemning an innocent creature to its death."

The man's eyes widened with shock. A wave of power surged through Arcturus. Moving his eyes towards the dragon, he slashed down rapidly into the leather bindings, easily cutting them in two with the razor-sharp sword. "THESE DRAGONS ARE NOT EVIL!" He slashed again, and again, until Shining Sun's bindings were reduced to tatters.

"Arcturus! What are you doing, my son?!" Markis Lund snarled as the crowd gasped in horror at the newly freed creature. The golden dragon shook his head and stood proudly onto all fours, spreading his majestic feathered wings for all to see.

"I am doing the world a good thing this day!" Arcturus turned back to the crowd with a large grin. "We need to move away from old concepts. We need to understand that dragons are just like us!" Arcturus winked back at his father and sheathed his sword. "No matter what words you sneak into my ear, no matter how much you whip me..." He gestured to the dragon as people began to scream. "I will prove you that dragons are not the monsters that-"

His words were cut short as the golden dragon opened his maw to unleash a large golden ball of fire that flew straight towards the crowd. To everyone's horror, the flaming meteor collided with the stands and exploded with a bright flash of white light. It sent splintering wood in all directions, bodies flying, and horrible screams cried out into the air as the same people that cheered moments ago were now melting before the very eyes of the boy who freed Shining Sun.

"N-no...this...this can't be hap...happening..." Arcturus felt his whole body go numb as the golden dragon took flight and fired another ball of fire into the crowd, claiming more lives with his engulfing flames. Thick smoke started to billow up from the stands as Arcturus fell to his knees in horror. What had he done? His eyes looked to the bodies, broken, unmoving, scattered in the crowd, and he clutched at his heart when he spotted the burned, tattered colors of his own clan. People that left the comfort of their homes and came to the tournament to watch the new generation train over a laugh and good food. People that had never hurt or even dreamed of inflicting pain upon a dragon in all their lives. Friends, relatives, acquaintances, now dead because of a stupid boy and his naïve actions.

"The debt is paid," Shining Sun landed near Arcturus. "Run now. Find your bronze female."

"Wh-" Arcturus choked, his chest so tight he could barely speak. He knew? How in the blazes could this monster know of Rasionynth? How could he even speak of her after he unleashed such destruction upon innocent people?

"The drunk told them everything." The golden dragon growled back at the stunned Arcturus. "He knows, boy. Your father heard every word you spoke to her. He's been testing you from the beginning!"

"Shut your blasted lying mouth!" Markis shouted with the same spiteful voice he used during the flogging. "I'll carve your blackened heart out, hear me? I'll rend the limbs from your pitiful body and thrash your mangled scales beneath my boots!"

"Rrrraaaaahhh!" The dragon quickly looked at the several men that started to surround him. He swiped the first attacking force with his tail, buying himself a small reprieve to look at the stunned winner of the tournament. "What are you doing, you stupid boy? Fly away from this wretched place. Free yourself from their shackles before it's too late."

Run where? Arcturus was more confused than ever, head feeling on the verge of bursting from the sudden turn of events.

The dragon snarled as he forced back another group of attackers. He threw several looks at the boy's petrified body, and when Arcturus failed to move, the beast gave a mighty shake of his head and flapped his mighty wings, beating hard against the air, lifting himself higher above the stands. It looked like the dragon was going to get away, as it roared into the afternoon sky. His tail flicked behind him as the sun shinned off his scales, almost mocking the human that had let him go. How in this world could something so beautiful cause so much destruction and death? How?

"Fire the blasted cannons already!"

Arcturus was brought back to reality by the forceful sound of his father's voice. Like a light in a vast sea of darkness, it broke through the screams of terror. It made Arcturus look up to the dragon once more, who was almost gone now, probably smirking to itself. That's when he saw a group of nets fly towards the dragon at a speed he thought impossible. They collided with the golden dragon, wrapping themselves around his scaled body, binding his wings in such ways that rendered him unable to keep himself in the air.

The dragon hissed and fell from the sky like a stone. Arcturus could not see where he had landed, but he could hear his pained roars as hunters undoubtedly converged upon on him with poisoned weapons, wicked blades, and righteous hearts.

"Come this way." His father grabbed him roughly by the scruff of his neck, easily dragging the boy across the field. "You have embarrassed our family in a way I never thought possible." He hissed, his words filled with hatred. "That you have defied me so crudely.... despite your punishments...speaks louder than any lie! Look what you have done, you dumb child!" He gestured out to the charred stands, covered in the corpses of spectators and clansmen alike. "Look at how many died for your little show of defiance!"

Arcturus could not look away. Not when his eyes began to mist. He did not mean for this to happen. He had not meant to trade so many lives just to prove a point. "I...nghh, I'm...I can't..." He stammered, words failing him as his father violently pulled him again by his neck.

"We will work on this every day, if needs be. No son of mine will be led astray by the vile lies of the dragons. I want you to remember this day, Arcturus." His father brought him to the golden dragon that was now being bound once again, his pained hisses and snarls of protest useless against the army of hunters. The creature was flailing, but it was no use. The many gryphons and other mortals had it completely pinned, Arcturus' eyes were drawn to the numerous arrows that had been plunged into its hide, no doubt covered in dragon bane poison.

"Like what you see? You should. Here. Have a closer look." Markis roughly shoved his son towards the dragon as the hunters finished binding its snout to the ground.

Arcturus felt so small and alone when the other hunters looked to him. He could see their accusing eyes judging him for what he had done, so full of hatred. He truly felt like he did not belong among these men. These...strangers. He wanted to run away, like the dragon said, never look back and forget this entire thing ever happened.

"Blame nobody but the monster standing before you. My son, though addled in other ways, has done no evil, for he was enchanted by the beast's foul magic!" His father spoke loudly and clearly for the crowd. "I should have seen the signs, and that is my failure. We all know the magics these things can conjure to twist the minds of untrained boys. But we have snapped him out of it." Markis snapped his penetrating gaze towards Arcturus in a snarl. "Isn't that right, boy?"

Arcturus nodded through tears. What else was he supposed to do?

"Now, we shall have my son take his share of rightful vengeance by finishing off the beast that had enchanted him so! The beast that settled itself free with the arm of my son, and loosened its destruction on the innocents of the crowd!" Markis grabbed Arcturus by the shoulder and brought him to the beast's head. "Now, you are going to cut into every weak spot the dragon has, and only when I give the order, you will kill him. Do you understand, boy?"

"B-but..." Arcturus stammered, tears coming to his eyes, rolling down his cheeks as he looked to the dragon that had killed so many.

It's my fault. All of it.

"You will do this, Arcturus...or so help me, I will have your clothes used to hunt down that dragoness that you so vehemently defend. Her scent is still in there, and you know how good our gryphons are at tracking their quarry. Why, you grew up amongst them."

"Y-You wouldn't!" Arcturus gasped, his heart cracking as his father's face refused to falter. He knew that the man had meant what he had said with every fiber of his being.

"Do not think me the fool for not standing up to my own words. I am not weak, even if you'd like me to be. Now face your prey, hunter." He turned Arcturus' head roughly towards the dragon. "Finish off the beast here, extract vengeance for all those who have fallen, and I promise to you that we will not pursue the bronze female. This dragoness of yours will be given a day to flee from my hunters. If she seeks peace, like you said, she'll leave our lands. But should I hear even a single report of a bronze scaled terror inflicting pain upon another one of us ever again...there will be no forgiveness for her actions."

Arcturus nodded as his father pulled away, and once again, unsheathed his steel sword with a hiss. He held it out in front of him as tears continued down his face. Despite the death the creature had caused, Arcturus still felt guilty for what he was about to do. Maybe if he was not bound the entire time, the gold dragon would not have felt the need to strike out in revenge.

"Now Arcturus! Show us the work of my craft! Show us all the weak spots of this dragon!"

Arcturus hesitated as he stared into the dragon's clear eyes. There was no hint of malice there. No monstrous intentions that made his hairs stand on end. His mind jumped back to what the dragon said to him after he blew up the stands. Of how the drunk guard was not what he appeared. He was playing a role. The role of a spy hired by his father for a much grander test than what Arcturus had been led to believe.

He tried to...help me... Arcturus' blood chilled at the gruesome realization that the convenient meetings with Rasionynth had been nothing more than a ploy orchestrated by his father. The simplest, surest way to test the strength of his son's conviction was not to order him to kill a dragon. No. What his father wanted was for Arcturus to take upon the mantle of a slayer himself. To want to kill the captive dragons with his own hands, on his own volition.

But something went wrong. Nobody could expect -not even Arcturus- that human and dragon could find common ground. The unlikely friendship that grew between them threw a wrench in his father's plans...That's why he had been so driven, so angry.

He feared that he started to lose control of the same son he tried to groom into a slayer.

Arcturus looked at the sword he held in his shaking hand, then back at the dragon whose eyes had not moved in the past few seconds. There was something strange swirling deep within his eyes. Sadness that he would not be able to take upon the skies again. Regret that his life had to end here.

And shame that his actions condemned a young, kind-hearted, dragon-loving boy to a fate almost as bad as death.

You wanted to... free me... Arcturus' chest tightened when the dragon moved his eyes to the sides, where a thick pair of leather straps bound his limbs, then back at him. *I'm as much of a prisoner as you are...*

The dragon's lips twitched briefly. He could not speak or form any other sounds other than a whine, followed by the closing of his eyes. He had made peace with his sins, his past, his failures, as well as the inability to prevent this very moment.

A man must be strong, even when his heart feels on the verge of crumbling, Arcturus formed a steel-like grip around the handle of his sword and sniffled hard, forcing himself not to cry.

"Have you not heard me the first time, boy? I told you to show us the weak spots of his beast! Proceed. NOW!"

Arcturus shot his father with a piercing glare. "I heard you...father..." Arcturus' voice cracked as he plunged his sword expertly into every area that had been drilled into his mind during his father's obsessive lessons. He started with the wings, easily slicing into the unarmored feathers, draping a curtain of blood over the dragon's shivering joints. He coated their white plumage with a sick layer of crimson as he worked relentlessly on a creature that had not coaxed a single whimper. Each cut from his blade was like a dagger strike to his armored soul as he danced around the dragon like a storm of steel and destruction.

He rammed his blade against the base of the wing's muscular joint, and hit, and hacked, until the whole wing toppled over the ground in a gushing spray of broken bones and spurting blood. The dragon shivered from every corner of his body. Only now, Arcturus realized that the broken whimpers were not his own sniffling, but the dragon's cries, his eyelids jerking over his tear-flooded, half-closed eyes.

"Next one, son. Strike him when he's weak!"

Arcturus ducked under the two men that lifted the dragon's numb leg and dug his blade deep into the creature's pink, fleshy, unprotected genital slit. His sword sunk through the flesh far easier than expected, and Arcturus had to wrench himself back to avoid sinking his entire arm into the dragon's soft insides.

"There we go!" He heard his father cheer as a pair of hands pushed him back to his feet. "Do you hear that, people? The beast is poised on wetting itself!"

The dragon stared at him with pained, flooded eyes. Thick strands of saliva poured down his jaw, and bubbles of froth gathered at the edges of his trembling mouth.

Arcturus stared back, feeling...nothing. His nerves went completely numb, making him immune to the sharp scent of blood and the pained noises that assaulted his ears. It was easier to perform when he distanced himself from his actions. This was not Arcturus the protector, savior of dragons, but the dark image of his father's perfect future. A trained slayer that performed his duty with utmost efficiency. Oh, how proud Markis must have been now, to see his own heated vengeance passed down to his son. He was not one to care about pain and suffering, as long as it accomplished his goals. Why, he was the same man who used a good dragon and her hatchlings in order to cement his son's transformation into a killer.

"Good, Arcturus, good! A fine display you've put up, but you have not yet finished your training. The wings and the genital slit are obvious targets, but some of the weaker spots are hidden from your eyes."

With a snap of his fingers, Markis had two of his hunters unwrap the dragon's snout. They grabbed onto the dragon's upper jaw, then pushed, and pushed, until they spread the dragon's jaws wide enough apart to reveal two sacks small sacks at the base of the creature's tongue.

"The fire glands," Arcturus said with a flat, emotionless voice.

"The very root of destruction. Pluck them out, son. Show this beast what happens when a dragon plays with fire."

Arcturus stared at the dragon's fire glands. The things that helped him kill so many of his kin. With a swift strike, he plunged his blade into the dragon's neck and slashed wildly from side to side until the things came off, forcing the dragon to literally choke on his own blood.

Arcturus backed off from the creature's sickly coughs. This time, when he carved his way into the dragon's flesh, he actually felt a small bit of pride. Like he was getting vengeance for the dead that had been piled up on the stands. The people that had only come to cheer him on.

"Fine job, m'boy." Markis patted his son proudly on the back. "The dragon is starting to fade, like all things born of darkness. Kill him. Kill him now."

Arcturus retrieved his sword and lowered his head, pushing the pleased thoughts from his mind. Now came the last moment. The last thing that his father wanted of him.

Arcturus carried his limbs to the front of the dragon. He pulled his sword back and stared into the beast's emerald eyes with an iciness uncharacteristic of a boy his age. The dragon just glared at him, with no regret for its actions. No remorse for the scores of mortals that now lay dead because of its fire, because in his mind, fulfilling a debt was more important than human lives.

A small part of Arcturus felt bad for the dragon. The dragon used wrong methods to accomplish something he considered good, but that little bit was insignificant compared to the shock of seeing his clan mates perish. Arcturus could not forgive, nor forget the screams, the pain, and all that suffering. He plunged his sword as hard as he could into the beast's eye, carrying himself right to the hilt of the sword and right into the dragon's brain, coating his arms and hands with a warm spray of fresh, red blood.

"There we go!" His father pronounced loudly, pride latching on every one of his words. "The beast is brought to deserved end, and justice is finally served by none other than my son! Who else is better fit to extract retribution than the very boy they used to inflict their hate upon us, eh? Arcturus!"

Markis shouted, and the crowd cheered with him.

"Arcturus! Arcturus! Arcturus!"

The man clasped his hand around Arcturus' shoulder so hard it made him wince. "You've done well, but don't ever think I'll forget about your treachery. Clean your sword now, and smile for these people. You killed the damn beast. Might as well pretend you enjoyed it if you have any respect for the dead."

The world faded away as Arcturus cleaned his blade and sheathed his sword. His nerves were numb, his feelings, shot. He heard fragments of what his father said; whispers lost among the pained whimpers of the dying beast. Part of him still lingered deep beneath the numbness. A fragment of the protector he wanted to become, not the killer he now was.

Arcturus forced his numb mind back to the dragoness he had saved. He ignored the cheers of victory from the hunters, fools who still believed he was free from the dragons that had enchanted his mind.

As he walked back to his tent accompanied by his father, Arcturus looked up into the sky, wishing he was flying high and free as the golden dragon wanted him to, for all his father had done was cement his feelings on the subject. He was not going to be like that man, cruel and horrible. He was going to be a knight one day, protector of the innocent, defender of the weak.

"I...I'm sorry," He closed his eyes and began to cry once he found himself alone in his tent. Warm, honest tears once again returned to his eyes as the pained cries of Shining Sun echoed in his head. "I had no choice. You knew that. I had no choice..."

Arcturus jerked when a dragon's roar echoed in the distance. He looked through the flaps of his tent, past the sea of tents and the trees, wondering if what he heard was real, or if it was nothing more than a manifestation of his own, broken feelings.

The End